Firefly Summer

Books by Maeve Binchy

Firefly Summer

Maeve Binchy

A DELL BOOK

Published by
Dell Publishing
a division of
Bantam Doubleday Dell Publishing Group, Inc.
1540 Broadway
New York, New York 10036

This work was first published in Great Britain in 1987 by Century
Hutchinson Ltd.

ISBN: 0-7394-0612-4

Reprinted by arrangement with Delacorte Press

Printed in the United States of America

I want to thank all my friends for their support and encouragement, particularly Rosie Cheetham and Chris Green.

And to Gordon Snell, who has made my life so good and so happy, I would like to dedicate *Firefly Summer* with all my gratitude and all my love.

London and Dublin, Summer 1987

PART ONE

Chapter I

The sun came in at a slant and hit all the rings and marks on the bar counter. Kate Ryan managed to take a cloth to them at the same time as she was kicking off her house shoes and pulling on her wellington boots. She tucked her handbag under the counter and in almost the same movement opened the kitchen door to make sure that Eddie and Declan weren't torturing the new girl. The new girl had red eyes and a sad face and was missing her farm home. She might run back to it if Eddie and Declan were at their worst. But mercifully the appeal of the tortoise was still very strong even after three weeks. They lay on their stomachs and fed it stalks of cabbage, screaming with delight when it accepted them.

"John," she shouted, "will you come down to the bar, I have to go across the river and see what's keeping the twins. They have to be polished and smartened up for the concert and there isn't a sign of them."

John Ryan groaned. His train of thought was gone again. He had thought he would manage an hour or two on his own, struggling with his poetry. "Give me a minute," he called, hoping to catch the idea before it was gone.

"No, they'll be late as it is. Listen, bring your paper and pencil down, there's likely to be no one in, but there has to be someone behind the counter."

The door banged behind her and John Ryan saw, through the bedroom window, his wife run across the small footbridge opposite the pub. She climbed over the gate like a girl instead of a woman in her thirties. She looked altogether like a girl in her summer dress and her boots as she ran lightly across to the ruined house, Fernscourt, to find the twins.

He sighed and went down to the pub. He knew there were poet publicans, he knew there were men who wrote the poetry of angels in the middle of the stinking trenches of war. But he wasn't like that.

John Ryan moved slowly, a big man with a beer belly that had grown on him sneakily during the years standing behind a bar, jowls that had become flabby at the same trade. His wedding picture showed a different person, a thinner more eager-looking figure, yet the boyish looks hadn't completely gone. He had a head of sandy brown hair only flecked with grey and big eyebrows that never managed to look ferocious even when he willed them to, like at closing time or when he was trying to deal with some outrage that the children were reported to have committed.

Kate had hardly changed at all since their wedding day, he often said, which pleased her, but she said it was just a bit of old soft-soaping to get out of having to stand at the bar. It was true, though; he looked at the girl with the long, curly dark hair tied back in a cream ribbon that matched her cream dress and coat. She looked very smart on that wet day in Dublin, he could hardly believe she was going to come and live with him in Mountfern. Kate hadn't developed a pot belly from serving drinks to others, as she often told him sharply. She said that there was no law saying you must have a drink with everyone who offered you one or pull a half pint for yourself to correspond with every half-dozen pints you pulled for others.

But then it was different for women.

John was the youngest of the seven Ryan children and the indulged pet of a mother who had been amazed and delighted at his arrival when she had been sure that her family was complete. He had been overfed and given fizzy drinks with sweet cake as long as he could remember. As a lad the running and leaping and cycling miles to a dance had kept him trimmer. Now, between sessions of writing his poetry and serving in his bar, it was a sedentary life.

He didn't know if he wanted it for his sons; he had such hopes for them—that they might see the world a bit, study maybe and go on for the university. That had been beyond the dreams of his parents' generation. Their main concern had been to see their children well settled into emigration; the church had helped of course, educating two nuns and two priests out of the Ryan family. John didn't see any vocation among his own offspring. Michael was dreamy and thoughtful: maybe a hermit? Or Dara a resourceful Reverend Mother somewhere? Eddie was a practical child, possibly a missionary brother teaching pagan tribes to build huts and dig canals. Declan the baby. Maybe they could make a curate out of him near home where they could keep an eye on him.

This was all nonsense, of course. None of them would end up within an ass's roar of a religious life. Still, John Ryan never saw the future standing surrounded by three sons and possibly his daughter all in the trade.

There would never be enough business, for one thing. Like many Irish towns Mountfern had the appearance of having far too many pubs already. If you went down the main street, Bridge Street, there were no less than three public houses. Foley's at the top of the town, but that was hardly a pub at all these days, just a counter really and a few friends of old Matt Foley drinking at night, they'd hardly know how to serve a real customer. Then there was Conway's which was more a grocery but it had the bar at the back. Conway's had a clientele of secret drinkers, people who didn't admit to any kind of drinking, who were always going out for a packet of cornflakes or a pound of flour and would toss back a brandy for their health. Often too, it had a funeral business since old Barry Conway was the undertaker as well. It seemed only right to come back to his place to drink when someone had been buried up on the hill. And Dunne's was always on the verge of closing. Paddy Dunne never knew whether to reorder supplies; he always said that it would hardly be worth it since any day now he'd be going to join his brother who ran a pub in Liverpool. But then either there would be a downturn in the fortunes of the Liverpool pub or an upswing in the drinking patterns of Mountfern. There was an unsettled air about his place and constant speculation about how much he would get if he were to sell his license.

John Ryan's pub had its rivals then, three of them in a small place like Mountfern. Yet he had all the business that came from the River Road side of the place. He had the farmers on this side of the town. It was a bigger and better bar than any of the other three, it had not

only more space but it had more stock. And there were many who
liked the walk out along the river bank.

John Ryan knew that he was a man who had been given a great
deal by fate. Nobody had gathered *him* up to swoop him off to a
religious order when he was a young impressionable boy. Neither had
he been sponsored out to a life of hard graft in America like two of
his elder brothers. By all their standards he had a life of ease and
peace where he should well have been able to run his business and
write his poetry.

But he was a man who did one thing at a time, almost
overmethodically, too predictable sometimes for his wife who felt
that people should be able to fire on several cylinders at the same
time.

John wanted time to write or time to serve drink, he couldn't
switch from one mode to another like lightning. Like Kate. He
couldn't switch toward the children like she could as well. Either
they were good or they weren't. He wasn't able to see the swift
changes of mood like Kate was. He would not be cross and then smile
minutes later. If he was cross he was very cross indeed. It was rare but
it was all-embracing when it happened. One of Daddy's great angers
was remembered long, whereas Mammy had a dozen quick and easily
forgotten angers in a week.

John sighed again at his wife's swiftness and the annoyance at
having to leave his work, his real work, just at that time. He knew
that in this pub fate had handed him something that many a man in
Ireland would envy mightily. It didn't bring in enough money for
them to employ another pair of hands, but it wasn't so slack that a
man could sit at the counter and write undisturbed. John Ryan
hadn't brought his paper and pencils with him, any more than his
thoughts. If customers saw you with paper and pencil they thought
you were doing the accounts and making a small fortune. Anyway,
what would have been the point? There was Jack Coyne from the
garage who had just sold a heap of rusty metal to some unsuspecting
farmer and they were in to seal the bargain with a pint.

Jack Coyne had a face like a ferret and two sharp eyes looking
around him for a bargain or a business deal. He was a small wiry man
equally at home underneath a car, covered in grease and shouting out
about the extent of the repairs, or in a suit showing off his newly
acquired vehicles which was what he called his second-hand stock.
Everything about him seemed to be moving, he never stood still;
even now at the bar he was shifting, moving from foot to foot.

"Great day, John," said Jack Coyne.

"It's been a great day all the time," said John, preparing to pull the pints.

"Bad for the crops," the farmer said.

"When were you lot ever pleased with the weather?" Jack Coyne laughed, the happy sound of a man who could sell second-hand cars no matter what the weather did.

The children of Mountfern had a place to play like no other children in the land. It was Fernscourt, the ruined house on the bank of the River Fern. It had been burned down one day forty years ago in 1922 during the Troubles. The Fern family had not been there on the day of the fire, they had been gone for many months before.

The children often asked their grandfathers about the fire but found a strange lapse of memory. The passions that had run so high in those years had settled down as time went by. The Ferns and all they symbolized had been forgotten. Their house stood as a beautiful ruin, where once it had stood as a beautiful big empty shell anyway. Now as a place to spend the long summer days it was quite simply perfect.

The orchards that the Ferns had asked their gardeners to plant all those years ago still grew wild and plentiful. The apple trees didn't know that the Ferns had gone. Their old gnarled branches bent to the ground, sometimes making even more places for the children to play.

There was thick trailing ivy everywhere over the walls that remained of the house. The outhouses which had once been the stableyard had survived better than the main house. Here there were still rooms with roofs to run through, here there were limestone arches and well-made stone walls. In the days when Fernscourt had been built people saw the stables as being very important; guests would expect them to be of the same high standard as the rest of the house.

As Kate Ryan marched through the laurels that grew wild now on each side of the path up from the river she could hear the cries and the laughter. She thought back on her own childhood in a small silent house in Dublin, her mother always an invalid. She had not had brothers and sisters to play with; friends were frowned on and kept well away from the home.

These children had a wild, free life by comparison.

Fernscourt belonged to the group that were here today. Those who were the right age for it. It had always been like that. You were too

young if you were Eddie and Declan's age, you were hunted away and
sent about your business, which was anywhere but here. Then the
older boys and girls went to the bridge and showed off to each other.
Where boys dived from the ledge to oohs and ahhs, where girls were
sometimes pushed in horseplay and had to climb up the bank with
wet dresses clinging.

But if you were in Fernscourt, no other world existed. It had been
a fine summer and as soon as any work that had to be done in the
various homes in Mountfern was finished they gathered, coming in
dribs and drabs across the fields, up the River Road and across the
footbridge in front of Ryan's, or some of them braving the brambles
and briars on the towpath at the other side of the river, a disused way
that saw no traffic these days.

Fernscourt belonged to all the children but it was Dara and Michael's special home. The twins had their own place, a pretend-
house. They played there even when none of the others came up to
join them. They had an old table and two broken stools from the bar.
There was cutlery too, a twisted fork and a rusty knife, and some
chipped plates. These were for private feasts. Ever since they had
been old enough to go across to Fernscourt alone the twins had said
that this is where they would live when they were grown up.

It would be nice and near home, they said reassuringly, but it
would be theirs. They would buy the whole place and have a boat and
go everywhere by river instead of by road.

It would be their palace, their castle, their home.

It was because they lived so close to the place, because they could
see it from their windows over the pub, and they could go there every
day winter and summer, that they felt it was their own.

But of course they didn't want to own it exclusively. Fernscourt
was also for everyone, particularly during the long summer holidays
when no day was long enough for the games they all played there.

There was no form to the games, but the huge mossy stones, the
crumbling walls, the great fronts of ivy hanging down like curtains,
and the window and doorway gaps in half-standing walls meant there
were plenty of places to climb, to perch, to jump, to sit and giggle.

The girls had made a makeshift home in the old clock tower which
still stood in the stableyard, though the clock and dome were long
gone. The boys would use the long shallow steps that were now
almost indistinguishable as steps, so overgrown with weeds and moss
had they become, and arrange a jumping competition that was a
cross between a longjump and a chicken run. They would all gather

to see who could jump down the greatest number of steps; it was the sissy who would opt out of the jump that seemed likely to break a limb.

Yet they had ways out of being a softy. It was always time to go home or to milk the cows or to go for a swim. The boys of Mountfern had no death wish as they played in their own magnificent ruined house.

Kate saw that some of the children were already heading for home where they would be ill-received because of the need to smarten up for the concert. She saw Tommy Leonard racing down to the towpath—it would be a bit quicker that way for him. Leonard's paper shop was near the big bridge, he would do the distance faster than by crossing over to the River Road where there was a proper surface to walk on. At Tommy's age children didn't mind having half their clothes and even bits of their arms torn and scratched by the thorny branches, Kate thought in wonder. Little Maggie Daly, who was Dara's great friend, was heading toward the laurels and Kate.

"Just running, Mrs. Ryan," Maggie said, knowing well that the twins' mother was not coming to pay a social call. "I think Dara and Michael are just finishing up now."

"I'm sure they are." Kate was grim. Maggie Daly had big anxious eyes; she always looked startled by the most ordinary things. She was terrified of Leopold, the pub's big harmless dog. When poor Leopold stretched his misshapen body in the sun, little Maggie Daly would look at him fearfully as if he were about to go for her throat.

And Maggie's older sister Kitty, who was nearly grown up enough for the crowd on the bridge, was sauntering down the laurel path too. Kitty was too mature to scuttle; she was being bored this summer, bored by Fernscourt and the games they played, bored by having to go home and dress up for the concert. Bored by being neither one thing nor the other. Neither a real person of fifteen who could have a smart red bathing costume and be able to sit on the raft having a crowd laughing and admiring; too old to find fun every day climbing up to an old room in a ruined clock tower, or squeezing through the chinks in the mossy walls. Kitty Daly sighed heavily as she passed Kate Ryan.

"I suppose you're coming to beat their heads in," she said as if this was the usual practice of elderly parents when they arrived in Fernscourt.

"Not at all," Kate said brightly, "I came to wonder was there

anything they'd like, afternoon tea on a tray maybe, I'd be delighted
to . . . my beloved twins . . ."

Kitty moved on hastily.

Dara and Michael had taken after their mother. No sandy brows
like John Ryan—those only seemed to come out in Eddie. They were
thin and wiry too, but of course their father had been as a boy. But
Kate realized that in their strong dark good looks they didn't have the
Ryan laugh lines either, the face that always seemed to smile even
when nobody was watching. All the Ryans looked like that—even the
disapproving old mother-in-law who hadn't thought Kate a suitable
wife for her favorite son, she had had a face that seemed to smile.
Dara and Michael often looked solemn, their eyes big, dark, and too
concentrated. Like her own. Whenever Kate saw a photograph of
herself she would scream and say she looked like the hag of Bearra or
an avenging angel. She always seemed to be burning with intensity
rather than smiling at the camera.

Nobody else noticed it at all.

And everyone always said the twins were a handsome pair, particularly in the summertime when, tanned and eager in their shorts and
colored shirts, they roamed the countryside far and wide and explored
every corner of Mountfern and its environs.

Kate wondered briskly how they would accept the blame today.
They should have been home a good half hour ago to get smartened
up for the school concert. She was annoyed but she would try not to
show it, otherwise they would be mutinous about the washing and
brushing and maybe less sure in their party pieces. Dara had a poem
in Irish to recite and Michael with the boys from the brothers would
be singing Moore's melodies.

Young Miss Lynch up at the school had been so enthusiastic and
given so much of her free time to organizing it that everyone in
Mountfern had been drawn into the whole thing unwillingly. Normally the convent and the brothers had few joint undertakings but
old Canon Moran thought it seemed a much better notion to have
one concert rather than two, and everyone agreed with him, so Nora
Lynch had won the day; it was being held in the church hall and all
participants had to be there in their finery at five o'clock. The concert began at six o'clock sharp and promised to be finished by eight.

Kate was nearly at the house now. In the old days it must have
been an impressive place: three stories tall but with high, high ceil-
ings, big rooms, and tall windows. The Fern family who had lived
here, different generations of them for over a century, surely loved

this home. Kate wondered if any of them had ever paused in their gracious way of life to imagine that one day it would be a ruin played in by all the children of the village who would never have gotten inside the walls except to carry scuttles of coal or great jugs of water in the old days.

The children had all scattered. Only her own two were inside. What could they be doing that made them stay when all the others had gone? A wave of annoyance came over Kate at their disregard for any kind of order in life. She pushed through the hanging wall of ivy and saw them: sitting on a great fallen pillar and looking ahead of them through the gaps in the wall.

They looked at something in the distance with a caution that was more like fear than anything else.

Below them two men with instruments mounted on tripods peered and wrote notes in their pads. Then they would replace the tripods and start again.

Kate came up behind the twins.

"What are they?" Michael asked in a whisper.

"They're called theodolites," Kate said. "I know that word, it's always very useful in crosswords."

"What do they do?" Dara wanted to know.

"It's a sort of survey, you know, getting levels. I'm not totally sure, to be honest."

"They shouldn't be here, the theodalists," Michael said, face red with upset. "Tell them it's private land. Go on Mam, tell them to go away."

"No, the things are called theodolites, not the people. The men are surveyors, I suppose. Anyway it isn't private land. If it was we couldn't be here."

"Could you ask them . . . like will they be coming back again or is it only today that they're doing their photographing or whatever? You could ask them, Mam," Dara pleaded. "You're good at asking people awkward things. Please."

"I have one awkward thing to ask at the moment and it's this: Why, when I gave you my good alarm clock and the strictest instructions to be back home at four o'clock, why is it half-past four and we're all here? That's the awkward question I'm asking today, and I want an answer to it."

The twins seemed not to hear the rising impatience in her tone; they barely heeded her.

"We didn't really play at all, we've been wondering what . . ." Dara said.

"And hoping that they'd go away . . ." Michael finished for her. They often finished each other's sentences.

"And not understanding it one bit . . ."

"And not liking it one bit . . ."

Kate took them by the shoulders and marched them back for the alarm clock and their uneaten lunches, then headed for the foot-bridge. There seemed to be a commotion on the other side. Eddie and Declan were lying on the edge of the water trying to reach something that was floating downstream on a piece of plywood.

Carrie, the new maid, was standing twisting her hands helplessly as the boys screamed, and Kate realized that Maurice the tortoise was heading off into the unknown.

"Get the garden rake, and the big broom," she shouted. Michael and Dara raced across to find them, delighted to be released from the pinching grip and abuse. Eddie, who was eight, was scarlet with the knowledge that he would get the blame; Declan was only six and the baby—he got off with everything.

Kate maneuvered the tortoise ashore and with a face like thunder brought it back to its original home in the mudroom. Watched by the four children and the terrified Carrie, she dried the animal with a clean towel and put it in a bed of hay. With a voice that was going to take no argument, she said that she would very much like to see Carrie at the kitchen sink washing the faces and hands of Eddie and Declan. She would like to see Michael and Dara in the bathroom and emerging in five minutes with necks, ears and knees all shining. She mentioned knees, ears and necks only because *particular* attention would be paid to those parts, but the rest was to be spotless too. A great deal of heavy scrubbing took place, and after inspection Dara and Michael were allowed to head off toward the hall. An unusually silent Eddie and Declan sat waiting sentence from their mother. They didn't know whether they were going to be barred from the concert . . . which mightn't be a bad thing. Or if there might be a slapping of the legs administered. The slapping wasn't too likely; if it was coming at all it would have been done at the time.

They were unprepared for the severity of it.

"That is no longer your tortoise, Edward and Declan. That is now my tortoise. Do you understand?"

Things were bad when Eddie was called Edward.

"But do you mean . . ."

"Yes, he's mine now. And I can do what I like with him. I can bring him back to the pet shop where I so stupidly bought him, thinking you were the kind of children who could love a pet. Or I could eat him. I could ask Carrie to serve him for lunch tomorrow."

They were aghast.

"Well, why not?" she continued airily. "You tried to drown Maurice, why don't I try to roast him? It's a hard old life being a tortoise."

Eddie's eyes filled with tears. "Ma, we weren't trying to drown him. It was to see if he could swim, and when he didn't seem to be managing it too well we got him a raft, then it floated off."

"Thank you, Edward. You are telling me it was just a careless accident, is that it?"

"Well, yes?" Eddie thought salvation lay this way but he wasn't totally sure.

"Right, well now that he's mine other careless accidents could happen. I could let him fall into the oven or something. Still, that is none of your business now. You are forbidden to go near him in the mudroom or near the stove or wherever else he happens to be."

Declan let out a roar. "Mammy, you wouldn't burn Maurice. Please don't burn my tortoise."

"It's mine," Kate said.

"You're not allowed to kill things," Eddie raged. "I'll tell the guards. I'll tell Sergeant Sheehan."

"Certainly do, and I'll tell him about the drowning."

There was a silence.

"Don't be stupid," Kate said. "I'm not going to hurt Maurice, but he *is* mine, you know, so you can't play with him anymore. And no ice creams in Daly's tonight after the concert."

It was bad but it was better than what might have been. They accepted it.

"Come on, Carrie," Kate said, suddenly pitying the seventeen-year-old spending her first Saturday night away from home. "Tidy up your hair a bit and we're off."

"Am I to come with you?" Carrie's face lit up.

"Of course you are. Did you think we'd leave you here on your own?" Kate had only just thought of it, looking at the stricken face of the girl as she had listened to the possible future of the tortoise.

"You're a real gentleman, Mam," said Carrie, and ran to put on a clean blouse and fix two new barrettes in her hair.

* * *

Canon Moran was small and fussy, a kind man with pale blue eyes that didn't see very far or very much. He believed that basically most people were very good. This made him a nice change from many other parish priests in the country who believed that most people were intrinsically evil. The word went around for young curates that Mountfern would be a great posting altogether. And the young priest Father Hogan knew he was indeed a lucky man. Once Canon Moran had a nice big chair for the concert and a little footstool because he sometimes got a cramp, then he would be happy. He would clap every item enthusiastically, he would praise all the brothers and the nuns by name, he would know that old Mr. Slattery the solicitor had made a contribution so that they could have proper curtains instead of the desperate old screens they used to make do with before. The canon would thank him briefly because that was all the Slatterys would need, but he would dwell longer on the generosity of Daly's Dairy in providing the cakes for the tea at eight o'clock, and the excellence of the programs printed free thanks to Leonard's the stationers. The canon began confessions on a Saturday at five, and he would make sure that they were all well completed in time for the concert. Father Hogan knew that Canon Moran believed a kind word of encouragement and a pious hope that things would be better soon helped a lot of his parishioners. And they felt sure, because of his pale dreamy blue eyes, that he was also somehow deaf and wouldn't recognize the voices that whispered their sins.

Father Hogan thought Mountfern was a warm, kind place to live, and though it didn't perhaps offer as much of a challenge as he had dreamed about in the seminary, he followed his canon's belief that there were souls to be saved everywhere, and that running a concert for the people of this place might have equal value in the great scheme of things to working in the missions or running a boys' club for delinquents in a tough city parish.

Miss Lynch was more or less walking out with young Mr. Slattery so he had to come to the concert as moral support. He sat beside Kate Ryan and the two chastened small boys, and the girl with reddened eyes called Carrie.

"And how does the master of your house escape this great cultural event?" Fergus Slattery asked with envy.

"Someone has to run the bar. I know it looks as if half the county is here, but you'd be surprised how many men find the excuse for a drink when their children are up here on the stage," Kate said.

"Well for him, then." Fergus was genuinely admiring. "I can't say that I have to work on a Saturday evening, they don't think solicitors work at all, but my office is too near. I'd actually have to be in the window in my shirt sleeves before they'd believe me."

Fergus grinned boyishly. He was very like a tall gangly boy, Kate thought, though he must be in his mid or late twenties now. She had always thought of him as a kind of irrepressible student home for the holidays. Even though he ran his father's office almost entirely on his own now, it was hard for her to think of him as a grown-up. Maybe it was because he looked untidy; his hair was sort of jutting out at an angle no matter whether he had been to the barber or not. His shirts were perfectly and lovingly ironed by the Slatterys' faithful house-keeper, Miss Purcell, yet the collars sometimes stood at an angle away from his neck. Kate wouldn't be at all surprised if he bought the wrong size or had the button in the wrong place. He had dark eyes and if he had held himself differently and worn long smooth dark coats he might have been thought very handsome and elegant indeed.

But part of his charm was that he would never be elegant; he was totally unaware of his tall, dark and almost handsome looks, and that he had caused many a flutter and several specific hopes around Mountfern.

"You mean you wouldn't want to come—what with that Nora Lynch killing herself to impress you?" Kate was disbelieving.

"Impress *me!*"

"Of course. Why else would that young girl kill herself and show herself to be part of a small backwater like this unless it was to prove to you that she could fit in and be part of it?"

"But why would she prove that to me?"

"Aren't you and she going out?" Kate wondered about men a lot. They couldn't all be as dim as they often seemed.

"Yes, sure, we go out to the pictures and we go to a dance, but there's nothing in it." Fergus looked baffled and honest.

"What do you mean there's nothing in it, aren't you a right beast to be leading her on and then tell me there's nothing in it? You know, the older I get the more I believe the nuns were right; men are basically wild animals at heart."

"But there *is* nothing in it," Fergus pleaded. "I mean we don't love each other or anything, or have the same plans or the same hopes. Nothing's been said or agreed. Truly."

"I believe you." Kate was cynical. "O Lord, protect me or mine from ever falling for a lawyer. You'll have yourself covered from every angle."

"But she doesn't think . . ." Fergus began, but at that moment Nora Lynch, resplendent in a new hair do from the Rosemarie salon, in a new yellow dress short enough to be fashionable but not so short as to cause adverse comment from the canon, the nuns and the brothers, appeared on stage. She said she hoped everyone would enjoy this show, the first combined effort; she thanked the canon, the brothers, the convent and the sponsors, the children and the parents, and knew that everyone would have a wonderful evening. She said that as an outsider she felt very privileged to be allowed to get involved in something as much a part of the community as this was. But then in many ways she felt that she had always been part of this place and always would.

"How old are you, Fergus Slattery?" Kate whispered suddenly.

"I'm twenty-seven," he replied, confused.

"Twenty-seven years in the world and you try to tell me that young woman has no hopes of you. May God forgive you, I mean it, Fergus, may he forgive you and send you some kind of sense."

"Thanks, Kate," said Fergus, not knowing whether he was being attacked or pitied, and not liking it whichever it was.

Dara Ryan felt as if she had swallowed an ice cream whole; her stomach was cold and heavy and she wondered if she might be sick.

"I'll never be able to say it," she told Maggie Daly.

Maggie believed Dara could do anything. "You're great, Dara, you never minded saying it at school in front of everyone there."

"That's different." Dara hopped around on one leg and looked through the door that they were meant to keep firmly closed, to see how big the audience was.

"Lord, it's full of people," she said theatrically.

"They'll love it." Maggie was loyal.

Dara would have fought with her shadow at this stage. "No, they'll hate it, it's in Irish, they won't understand a word of it."

"But it will *sound* terrific."

"Why don't I just go and make sounds then, nice sounds, or better still take up a gong and just bang it for three minutes and bow to the applause?"

Maggie giggled. Things were all right once Dara started making up outlandish things.

Maggie was not doing any solo piece. She was in the girls' choir which would sing Gounod's "Ave Maria," and later on come back and sing "I think that I shall never see, a poem lovely as a tree." But Dara would stand in front of the whole of Mountfern and recite "Cill Cais" which Miss Lynch had told them was a lament for an old house, a ruin like Fernscourt, except that it had been a different kind of household who had lived there, an Old Catholic family who used to have mass said in the stately home and everyone would come from far and near to attend it.

"Dara, you're on."

Crossing her fingers and giving Dara a squeeze for luck, Maggie Daly stood and watched her friend walk up on the stage.

Miss Lynch, knowing very well that hardly anyone would get even the vaguest glimmer of what the poem was about without some kind of translation, said that of course everyone knew the story of "Cill Cais," and told it without appearing to. The audience, flattered to be thought of as people who would know this, nodded at each other sagely and waited for the young Ryan girl to tell it to them again in Irish. Dara's voice sounded confident and she fixed her eyes on the back of the hall as Miss Lynch had told her to do. There was a storm of clapping and people told each other that she made a very good fist of it, then she was off and it was time for the choir from the brothers.

Brother Keane had chosen three of Moore's finest Irish melodies. He announced that the boys would sing them in the same magnificent spirit that Thomas Moore had brought to bear when he was writing them. Brother Keane had calculated without the enormously humorous content that the songs seemed to hold for his choir of twelve-year-olds, depleted as it was by six whose voices chose the time of the concert to break.

"Silent, O Moyle, be the roar of thy water,
Break not, ye breezes, your chain of repose."

Brother Keane loved this above all other of Moore's melodies. He could see none of the allusions to breaking wind, pulling chains and passing water that the entire group in front of him seemed to see written in letters of fire on their song sheets. He glared at them ferociously as with the most enormous difficulty the forty boys tried to stifle their mirth, and led them into the next song called, unhappily, "The Meeting of the Waters." The entire choir seemed to choke with the daring double entendre of the name and Brother Keane resolved to deal with them very sternly in a less public place.

The admission price had included tea, sandwiches and cakes. The sandwiches had been supervised by Mrs. Whelan who ran the Post Office and was generally accepted to be the nicest person in Mountfern. A small wiry woman with a skin that seemed to have been tanned by whatever sun shone intermittently in the Irish midlands or beaten by the winds that blew more regularly from one coast across to the other, Sheila Whelan had three cameo brooches she had bought from a tinker: a pink one, a green one and a beige. She wore them at the neck of her white blouses and had done for as long as anyone could remember. She owned about three skirts which she must have worn forever and a series of soft knitted cardigans which she must have made herself. Usually she was knitting for someone else, for the new babies that were arriving with great regularity around Mountfern, or shawls for the old, even school jumpers for the children who might need them. She always managed to have an extra bit of wool which she said it would be a pity to waste. She had a kind, dreamy face and far-away pale blue eyes that were never known to concentrate inquisitively on anything that might not bear too much scrutiny.

She seemed to have no interest in the private lives of the rest of the parish: she never appeared to notice, let alone comment on the emigrants' remittances that came home or didn't come home; nor did she seem to notice the disability pensions for people who were perfectly well, or the dole for those who were obviously working. She was able to discuss the most direct questioning about the whereabouts of Mr. Whelan with calm and even with interest, but without ever revealing that he had left her for a married woman in Dublin, and that the two of them now had four children. If anyone asked whether he was coming back, Mrs. Whelan was always able to get into the same interrogative mood and say it was very hard to know, wasn't it? She found that some things were almost impossible to work out, weren't they? And somehow the questioner found himself or herself enmeshed in the Meaning of Life instead of the specific whereabouts of Mrs. Whelan's husband.

She was the kind of woman you'd go to if you had committed a murder, Fergus Slattery had always said. And oddly, there was one killing near Mountfern. A farmer's son had attacked his father in a drunken fight and killed him. It was to the post office, not the presbytery or the Garda station that he had come, carrying the murder weapon, a pitchfork.

Mrs. Whelan had involved the presbytery and the Garda station, but gently and in her own time. Nobody had thought it even remotely unusual that the demented man had come to Mrs. Whelan nor had she made anything of the incident; she said she supposed he was on his way to the canon and her light had been on.

Nobody knew, either, that it was Mrs. Whelan who had encouraged the sandwich makers to cut the crusts off and to do just one plate each. That way she was sure of getting what everyone had promised, though it meant much more work for her. Fergus knew, because Miss Purcell had been fussing about whether to have chicken salad or egg and mayonnaise in her offering and this had meant at least three calls to Mrs. Whelan for discussion.

"You are the only sensible woman in this town, Mrs. Whelan," he began.

"What can I do for you, Fergus?" she asked simply.

"You mean I wouldn't say it unless I wanted something?"

"Not at all." But she waited.

"Is my name up with Nora Lynch?" he asked.

"Why do you ask?" she said.

"Because Kate Ryan, a woman I like and respect, told me it was, and as true as the day is long I didn't mean it to be."

"Well if there's any misunderstanding I'm sure you'll sort it out."

"But *is* there any misunderstanding, Mrs. Whelan? That's what I'm asking you. I don't want to go sorting things out if there's nothing to sort out."

"Ah, nobody tells me anything, Fergus."

"But I'm only asking you about *me*, not about other people."

"As I said, I've not got an idea in the wide world, but I know if you think that there's some confusion you'd be the man to clear it up. One way or another."

"By saying something out straight, you mean? Like 'I don't want to marry you'?"

Mrs. Whelan's eyes were shuttered. Open but closed at the same time. They told him he had gone too far in his revelations. That she expected a solicitor to be even more discreet than a postmistress.

"Other people go to you with their business, Fergus, you're as much in demand now as your father, and that's your job after all. If there's a need for the right words you'll find them."

"You'd have been great as a prisoner of war, Mrs. Whelan," said Fergus. "The secrets would have been safe with you all right."

Fergus and Nora went for a drive after the concert. The last thank yous and congratulations had been said; people walked home in the sunny early summer evening. The older children had gone to sit on the bridge. The cinema had a special late start, so many of them headed to the pictures. Fergus had the car out ready and waiting. Nora Lynch came running over to join him.

Small and slightly plump, she had the perfect skin and apple cheeks of a picture poster. Her fair hair was curled carefully, and she wore a little lipstick but not enough to do any damage.

"I thought we might go up on the hill," he said as Nora put on her white jacket with the little yellow trim which matched her dress so well.

"The hill?" She was surprised.

"It's a nice quiet place to talk, and I have something I want to say to you."

Nora's eyes lit up with pleasure and her face was pink. "I'd love that," she said in a sort of husky way, not in her usual voice at all.

With a sickening lurch of his stomach Fergus realized that this pleasant, empty-headed, chirruping little teacher whom he had kissed a dozen times thought that he was about to propose marriage to her.

Slowly he started the car and headed for the hills.

Chapter II

Ryan's Licensed Premises, like any other pub in Ireland in 1962, had a steady clientele that would never desert it. There never seemed to be any need to do renovations to attract new trade. The trade was there, like it had been in John's father's time; the people who lived on that side of Mountfern found it handy to call in rather than walk all the way down to the center. Ryan's had the great advantage, some thought, of being on the outskirts. The whole place didn't see you going in and coming out as they would if you visited Foley's, Conway's or Dunne's.

When John's father was alive the place still sold groceries but though the big old chest of tea drawers still stood there they held no stock now. There was a little huckster's shop run by Loretto Quinn, whose husband had been killed in a terrible accident. It wouldn't have been right for the Ryans to take the bread from her mouth even if they wanted to get back into the grocery business. And anyway most people liked going into Mountfern proper and walking along Bridge Street to see what was going on. Ryan's was a bit out of the way in terms of doing your weekly shopping.

John Ryan was glad that Kate agreed with him on this. For a Dublin woman she had adapted extraordinarily well to Mountfern; she knew better than he did all that went on, who was speaking and who not. It was Kate who helped the children with their homework, found and trained the girls from the country who would leave for brighter lights and noisier towns once they knew the way to run a house. Kate served behind the bar as if she had been born to do it. She knew when to join in the conversation and when to stay far from it.

She polished glasses and cleaned the big ashtrays with Gold Flake printed around the rim. She loved the words Whiskey Bonder on the sign over the door, even though it wasn't true anymore. John's father, like many a publican, used to buy whiskey in a cask from the distiller, lodge it in a bonded warehouse and pay the excise duty when he took it from the warehouse for bottling and sale. In those days the name James Ryan was on the bottle, but nowadays distillers discouraged such fancy and old-fashioned notions. They preferred to sell whiskey already bottled. But Kate would still polish the sign lovingly, getting up on a ladder early in the morning with a soapy cloth, a wet cloth and a dry cloth.

She was the same behind the bar, she shined the bar decorations as if they were precious ornaments. A lot of pubs had the mock Staffordshire figures of a hurler and a footballer standing on a plinth, dressed in the colors of the particular county. Underneath it said, "On all grounds, Players Please." Kate had explained the puns to the twins as John had marveled. He had looked at the thing a thousand times and never even noticed the words and what they meant. Fine that for a man who thought himself a poet.

And Kate had been great about that too. She never came up with any talk about what did a fat, country pub owner think he was doing rambling away in verse. Far from it, she would sit at his knee and ask him to read what he had written. Sometimes her head rested on his lap, and she would sigh in appreciation or else she might question it and ask what image was in his mind. She had long dark curly hair and very dark brown eyes, almost black. She never grudged the time he spent up in their bedroom trying to write—and trying it often was. She minded the bar happily, only suggesting that John should be there at set times like for the lunchtime trade and for the time when they had the half-past-six news on Radio Eireann, and the customers would expect the man of the house to be present to serve their pints and comment on the day's events.

John Ryan was not a great man for formal prayers. Mass time was spent as near the back of the church as possible; in summertime right out in the open air and in thoughts not connected with the actual liturgy taking place. But he did offer prayers of thanks to somewhere, that he had met Kate. He could so easily have not met her. Suppose Jack Coyne's had not been closed that time when she came in with the puncture, suppose the puncture had happened eleven miles on down the road—they'd have gone to the big town instead. Suppose she had been traveling with a girl who could mend a puncture instead of that giggling friend of hers, who could hardly ride a bike.

All these things were too much to think about. Like the really black bit after John had seized his chance and arranged to meet Kate again and again, and his mother had said that he was to bring no flighty Dublin girl into this pub, the business belonged to the whole family. John had nearly upped and off at that stage, but Kate had begged him to be understanding. What did the poor old mother mean except that she was afraid of losing him like she had lost her husband and all the rest of her family, two sons priests and far away, two daughters nuns and even farther away in Australia, and the other two sons in America without a notion of coming back.

Kate said he should be patient, sit it out. Old Mrs. Ryan would come around in time: in the meantime Kate would learn the bar trade in Dublin. And learn it she did, dropping her good salary as a secretary in a firm of solicitors and becoming a maid of all work in a small hotel so that she could become accustomed to working the bar.

By the time Mrs. Ryan had mellowed, Kate knew all she would need to know about serving a ball of malt, a half one, a black and tan, and a half. She knew when a customer had too much and when to cash a check or start a tab. They had been married quietly. It was 1948, there wasn't much money about and not many relations either. John's mother was there, face sour, clothes black, but at least she was there.

Kate had no family at all. Her mother had died after a life of martyrdom and self-pity. Her father had married again and believed that his new wife had been slighted by everyone, so went nowhere. No amount of persuasion would make them come to her wedding, so Kate O'Connell stood with four friends including Lucy, the girl who couldn't mend punctures either, and married John Francis Ryan, sandy-haired, plump poet who had to run his family pub to please his mother and then to continue running it after his mother's time to keep his wife and four children.

Kate told him that she thanked God for him too. Yes, seriously, when she prayed at night as she always did on her knees for three or four minutes no matter how great his need and desire for her.

"You can say your prayers afterwards," he used to beg.

"Not at all, I'll fall asleep in your arms afterwards," she would reply.

But she assured him she thanked God for his honesty and his kindness and the marvelous way he had of looking at things, and for the four marvelous children. She, who had nobody for so long, had everybody who mattered now. Outsiders said they were well matched but they had no idea how well.

Nobody watching the quick Kate and the slower John as they smiled at each other across their busy public house would know how much they needed each other and relied one on the other for the qualities that they each lacked. Probably the men might have thought that the youngest of old Ryan's sons did well for himself getting this handsome city girl to liven up his business. Possibly the women in Mountfern might have said that Kate O'Connell, who came in one day on a bicycle and seemed to have no people to speak of, fell on her feet marrying into Ryan's pub. But this was to miss the point.

Kate, uncertain of herself in so many ways, unsure that she had a place anywhere, was more aware than anyone would suspect of how she had found a home and a base and an anchor in the reliable John Ryan. She knew he would never change and cease to love her, as her father had. She knew she didn't have to act out a role to please and entertain him as she had done to everyone else in the world since she was fourteen. She had got by through being brisk—and sometimes she knew that she was too brisk, she left the children bewildered and bothered, and only John could make the world seem sensible to them again.

Kate marveled at the time and patience John had with their children, how he could sit for what seemed like forever on the bank of the river with them, making them as still as he was himself to lure the fish out of the water. Only the other day he had them all—even Declan, who never stopped moving around—transfixed over the workings of the old clock which he had taken to bits and put back together. He told them stories of the Fern family who lived over the river, tales of long ago, since John Ryan never knew the house when it stood. The twins would listen forever to how the provisions might come up the river by boat.

"How would they get them up to the house?" Dara had asked and her father had led the children out to the footbridge and they had all stood speculating what way the great boxes would have been carried up to the mansion. All this when he should have been seeing to the barrels and getting the pub ready for opening.

But Kate loved him for it, and sometimes she wanted to go over and put her arms around his neck and kiss him full on the lips to tell him how much she loved him and how good he was. Not only to his children and to her, but to the old farmer who would tell the same story twice a day. John could nod and polish a glass and hear it again and again. Kate sometimes got a lump in her throat as she watched his patience and his respect for people, for all kinds of people.

She felt a tenderness and love for him that was just as strong as any love you saw in the pictures where she sometimes went on a little outing with Sheila Whelan as a treat. But she didn't show that love too openly. Mountfern wasn't a place where endearments were used openly. There were no darlings or loves or dears used in Ryan's pub. They accused each other good-humoredly of all kinds of failings. . . .

"My wife would spend the takings of the year if you didn't watch her . . . all women are exactly the same."

"John, would you ask Mrs. Connolly there would she like a drop more lemonade in her port? A man wouldn't notice your drink, Mrs. Connolly. If it wasn't a pint or a glass of whiskey he wouldn't know how to handle it."

But together, alone together, they knew they had something that a lot of people didn't have. That their own parents certainly didn't come anywhere near having. And they determined on the day that the twins were born that no child of this new family would grow up in a house of uncertainty and loneliness like the young John and the young Kate in the dark days. Money was not important to either of them but recently they had realized that four children did not live off the air and neither were shoes, schoolbags, dentists' bills, notebooks, winter coats, more shoes, text books, to be found growing in the rushes along the river bank.

One of the reasons they had gotten the young country girl to come in was because Kate was going to get a job. She had discussed it with Fergus Slattery last night after the concert and he had said there was no reason she couldn't start right away. With office experience in Dublin, with day-to-day experience of balancing the books in a business, she would be perfectly qualified to help in the solicitor's office. Kate Ryan was known not to be a teller of other people's business. This was most important of all.

She was looking forward to the whole business of going out to work. The children did not share her enthusiasm.

"Does this mean we're poor?" Dara wanted to know.

"Of course, we're not poor," Kate snapped. It was hard enough to find something that would look smart for going out to an office from all her shabby clothes in the bedroom cupboard without having to answer questions like this.

"Well why are you going out to work for a living then?"

"In order to keep you and your brothers in leather shoes which you will kick to bits, to buy nice schoolbags that you'll lose and a few things like that." Kate looked without any pleasure at what she had always thought of as a smart green two-piece and which now turned out to be a crumpled, faded rag.

"Will we have to sell the pub?" Michael was behind her, always the more anxious of the two. His eyes seemed troubled.

"Lord, not at all, what has the pair of you so worried?" Kate softened her tone.

"You look very upset, you keep frowning," Michael said.

"Oh that's only because my clothes look like a lot of jumble."

The other two children had come to join in. It wasn't usual to find a council of war upstairs on a summer evening; Eddie and Declan had come to investigate.

"Are you afraid of looking like Miss Barry?" Eddie asked. Kate looked at him. Miss Barry was the elderly alcoholic who lived in the presbytery and passed by the dignified title of Priest's Housekeeper. In fact she was there because of the goodness of the canon, who couldn't bear to turn her out on the roads. For long periods of time Miss Barry didn't touch a drop and was a sober if rather erratic worker, cooking and cleaning for the two priests. When she did go on a tear it was an almighty one. At no stage did she ever look like anyone Kate would wish to be compared to.

"Thank you, Edward," she said.

"What have I said?" Eddie wailed.

The twins felt the conversation was degenerating, as it usually did when Eddie came into it.

"We'll be off now." Dara was lofty.

"We'll leave Eddie with you, Mam," Michael said. He could see an awful clinging look in Eddie's face that meant he wanted to come with them.

"The last thing I want is any of you with me." Kate rummaged deeper. She had to have something that looked like what a person wore in an office.

"It's a free country," Eddie said, his face red with fury. "I can go anywhere I like in Mountfern, anywhere. You can't stop me."

"It shouldn't be a free country," Dara said, "not if it means Eddie's free to go wherever he likes."

"Go away from me," Kate cried. "And Declan, if you set one foot outside this door you are not going to like what happens to you."

"Why isn't it a free country for me?" Declan asked. Not very hopefully.

"Because you're the baby," Dara said.

"Not that so much. It's because you're six. Six-year-olds, in places with rivers in them, stay at home at night." Kate smiled at his round cross face.

"Will we have another baby?" he suggested.

"We will not, thank you," Kate said firmly.

Dara and Michael giggled at this, and Eddie was put out because he felt there was something else he was being kept out of.

"What am I going to do? It's ages before it gets dark," Declan complained.

Kate was going to give in over the tortoise and let him have visiting rights to the mudroom where the tortoise was going to live under her sole control. But it was too soon, they wouldn't realize the seriousness of the near drowning if she weakened so quickly.

"Why don't you go and teach Leopold some tricks?" she suggested, not very hopefully. You couldn't teach Leopold any tricks. He had joined the household when he was found with a broken leg and a poor bark by Jack Coyne in the back of a truck, and when nobody had claimed him, the Ryans saved him from being put in a sack by Jack Coyne and meeting a watery death.

Leopold's bark had never improved significantly, he did have a plaintive yowl, but Jaffa, the huge orange cat who had a purr like thunder, would have been a greater source of alarm to any burglar than the lame and silent Leopold. But there weren't burglaries or crimes like that in Mountfern. Sergeant Sheehan was always proud to say that people in his place didn't have to lock their doors at night.

Leopold was more of an indulgence than a watchdog.

"Teach him some tricks?" Declan was astounded.

"You couldn't even teach Leopold to walk straight, Mam." This was undeniable.

"You could exercise Jaffa in the garden," she offered.

"We don't have a garden."

"We do. I call it a garden, you call it a yard. Go on, Jaffa would love a bit of exercise."

"Will I make her do handstands?" Declan was interested now. Kate realized this had been a wrong road to travel down. She would never find anything to wear, she would spend the rest of the evening wondering if the big orange cat's back would be broken.

"Sit in the garden until it's dark . . . tell Jaffa to come toward you and then go to the other end of the garden and ask her to come back," she told Declan.

"That's a very dull thing to do. There's no point in spending the evening doing that," Declan complained.

"You'll find as you grow older there's a lot of things you'll spend morning, noon and night doing that there's no point in," Kate said, holding a blue houndstooth skirt up to the light. It looked so respectable there must be a reason why it was not to the fore in her meager selection.

"When I'm old I'll have a great time," Declan said wistfully. "I'll have bags of potato chips for every meal and I'll stay out all night until even eleven o'clock if I feel like it."

His small round face looked sadly out the window at Dara and Michael racing off down River Road, and at Eddie, hands in pockets, striding across the footbridge.

Kate Ryan had discovered the fatal flaw, a broken zipper and a triangular rip where she had caught it on a door handle.

"Maybe half-past eleven," Declan said, looking at her sideways to show that he was a person of no half measures when it came to long-term plans for the future.

It was a bright warm evening. Eddie looked at the men with the clipboards and instruments.

"What are you doing?" he asked them.

"A survey."

"What's that?"

"Making a measurement of the land."

"Why haven't you got a ruler, then?"

They looked at each other. Eddie was small and sandy and tousled-looking. He was like a caricature of a Troublesome Boy.

"We managed without one," one of the men said.

"Is it a game, like guessing the weight of a cake?"

"A bit more scientific I hope."

"Who wants to know how wide it is?"

"The fellow who's going to buy it."

"There's someone going to live in there?" Eddie looked up at the ruined Fernscourt in amazement.

"That would appear to be what it's about all right."

"God, isn't he lucky," Eddie said with feeling. "I'd love to live in a place like that with no roof, and no floors and no wiping your feet."

Dara and Michael went first to Loretto Quinn's for sweets. Mam had always said to give Loretto the turn, toffees were the same price there as everywhere, but Loretto would appreciate it.

The twins thought they must be her only customers for Scots Clan. The jar showed no signs of any other takers. She weighed out the two ounces and gave them an apple each free.

"We couldn't," Dara said. A polite and meaningless protest since Michael had already sunk his teeth in his.

"Ah go on, don't I get them for nothing," Loretto said.

This was not strictly true; she got them from an old man, Papers Flynn, a tramp of sorts who had encircled Mountfern all his life. He lived by picking fruit from low-hanging boughs or feeling gently into the soft nesting places that contrary hens used to find for themselves far from their rightful quarters. Sometimes he offered these as gifts to shopkeepers, who gave him a cheese sandwich or a mug of tea in return.

"Fierce activity across the river: fellows with cameras on long stilts," Loretto said conversationally.

She liked the twins, full of chat without being cheeky. Their young brother Eddie was a different kettle of fish.

"They're theologists," Dara said confidently.

"Or something a bit like that." Michael was a stickler for getting things right.

"Maybe they're going to make a film." Loretto was hopeful. "Like *Quiet Man* all over again, wouldn't it be great?"

Dara didn't smile. "I think it's something to do with changing it all over there, someone buying it and making it different."

"We'll let you know if we find out anything," Michael said.

Loretto stood at the doorway of her shabby little shop and watched the twins as they headed for the bridge and the heart of Mountfern.

People used to say that if you bent your head to light a cigarette on the main road you'd miss the two signs to Mountfern and that even if you did see one of the signs and drive off the road through the semi-circle that led down Bridge Street to the River Fern and then back up River Road to the main road again you would wonder what kind of a place it was that you had been through.

One street, Bridge Street, more or less petered out at the bridge where the church was. The road got narrow across the bridge, and went off meandering to the various townlands and small farms. Bridge Street looked well when the sun shone on the different pastel colors of the houses and shops that fronted right onto the road. Some of them were whitewashed still like Judy Byrne's house and Conway's, the place that was both undertaker and pub. Others were pink like Leonard's the stationers and paper shop, like Meagher's the small jewelry shop where watches and clocks were mended and gifts were displayed in boxes with cellophane fronts. Daly's Dairy was a very bright lime green. Mrs. Daly had been very pleased with the color, and was flattered when Fergus Slattery said they would all have to wear sunglasses now to cope with the sudden brightness that radiated from its walls.

There were some houses that didn't have coats of paint on them. Like old Mr. Slattery's tall house with the steps going up to it, which was covered with ivy. And the Garda barracks was just stone, as was the presbytery. The Classic Cinema had once been a smart beige color but it had gotten very shabby-looking, with paint peeling off. Mr. Williams, who was the rector-in-charge of the small Protestant church, had a cottage that was all covered with climbing roses—his wife spent from dawn to dusk gardening. To the outsider Mountfern looked a slow sleepy place, badly planned, straggling toward a river, but not having any real purpose.

It had been an estate village, of course, a collection of small holdings which all depended on the big house. The days of a community depending on one family seat for livelihood and living quarters were long gone. But Mountfern had not died with the house.

The farmers would always need somewhere to send their children to school, and shops where their wives could sell vegetables, eggs and poultry, where they could buy the essentials without having to travel to the big town, sixteen miles down the main road.

The visitor might have thought Mountfern a backwater but there were few visitors to have such thoughts. It hadn't anything to offer to the sightseer; you had to have some reason to come to Mountfern, otherwise you would think it was a place where nothing happened at all.

Dara and Michael Ryan never thought of Mountfern like that. It was the center of their world and always had been. They hardly ever left it except to go to the town maybe four times a year. They had been to Dublin of course, with the school on educational tours, and once with Dad and Mam when they were very young and there had been an excursion to see Santa Claus in the various Dublin shops. Eddie always resented hearing about this excursion and wanted to know why it hadn't been repeated for the rest of the family.

"Because Santa Claus would vomit if he saw you," Dara had explained.

This evening, however, they had forgotten what a thorn in the flesh their younger brother Eddie was. They were setting out with a purpose. To find out what was happening to Fernscourt. They had seen the men with the measuring instruments but had not wanted to ask them straight out—it was almost too direct. They felt without actually saying it to each other that they would find out what was the collective view first. Then armed with this knowledge they would face the people that Loretto thought were making a version of *The Quiet Man* (a tamer version, the scenery in this part of the Irish midlands wasn't spectacular and there were very few Maureen O'Haras around the place).

They passed Coyne's Motor Works before they got to the bridge. Jack was working as he always seemed to be, day and night, a cigarette hanging out of his mouth.

The twins had heard their father say that it was the mercy of God that Jack Coyne hadn't set himself alight with all the petrol and oil around the place, and that one day he could well blow the whole of Mountfern sky high with his dangerous practices. Dara and Michael didn't like Mr. Coyne much, he always looked as if he were about to have a fight with someone. He was old of course, nearly as old as Mam and Dad, small and pointed looking. He wasn't married, and he always said that a man who voluntarily took on a wife to nag the life out of him, and spend all he earned, was a man on whom no sympathy should be wasted. Dara had once said to him that if everyone had felt the way he did, the world would have come to an end long ago. Jack Coyne said that everyone might have been better off if it had, and let Dara remember that when she grew up and her head got full of nonsense about love and the like.

"Good evening Mr. Coyne." It didn't matter that he might be an old grouch, they still had to be polite and salute him.

"Out gallivanting," he said disapprovingly. "Still I hear that they've big plans for Fernscourt. That'll put a halt to your gallop, the lot of you."

"What plans?" The twins ignored the gratuitous offense; they had never done anything to irritate Jack Coyne.

To his own immense annoyance Jack Coyne didn't know what plans were afoot. Those fellows doing a survey had been far from forthcoming. But he had his own views.

"A big religious house I hear, so that's the end of all the trick-playing by the children of this parish, I'm glad to say. You'll have to start to do a day's work for a change and be like we were at your age."

"Is it brothers or nuns would you say?"

"That would be telling," said Jack Coyne, who didn't know.

"Isn't he a pig?" Dara said cheerfully when they had left him. "A small dark offensive-looking pig."

"Imagine him young," Michael said, as they passed the bag of toffees between them. It was a feat of imagination too difficult for either of them.

"An offensive piglet," Michael said, and they were in a fit of giggles by the time they reached the bridge and turned left up the main street.

There would be no place for Dara and Michael on the bridge, even Kitty Daly was a bit too young for the small group that met there in the evenings. They saw fellows sitting up on the stone parapet clowning, and a group of girls laughing. There was Teresa Meagher whose mother and father were always fighting. If you went past Meagher's any night when the shop was closed you always heard voices raised. Teresa was going to get a job in Dublin it was always being said, but then her parents would cry and cling on to her so she had to relent and stay. Nobody on the bridge was courting. If you were courting you were down the river bank, or in Coyne's wood, or at the pictures.

Devotions were over and Father Hogan was closing up the church. He waved at Michael.

"Any hope you'd be able to sing *Panis Angelicus*?" he said without much confidence.

"No Father, sorry Father, I haven't a note in my head," Michael said.

"Come on out of that, you were in the choir at the concert. Why don't you . . ."

"No Father, I can't sing, and anyway you'd never know what might happen to my voice." Michael had been dying for his voice to

break like Tommy Leonard's had. Every morning he tried it out and
was disappointed that it still sounded the same.

Dara was no help. "You should hear him singing from the bathroom, Father, he'd have the tears in your eyes."

"I'll kill you," Michael said.

"Well I'm certainly not going to beg and cajole you." Father Hogan was huffy now. "I didn't think a Catholic boy would have to be
flattered and pleaded with to sing in the House of God."

Dara realized she had gone too far.

"I was only saying that to tease him, Father. Really and truly he'd
be no good, he'd embarrass you, it's like an old tin can. I know he
would sing if he could, but he's just in the choir to make up the
numbers for Brother Keane, to sort of fill the stage up a bit."

Father Hogan said that was all right then.

"Now." Dara was triumphant. "Didn't I rescue you?"

"You needn't have gone on so much." Michael hadn't enjoyed
being described as an old tin can that would embarrass you. There
were times when Dara felt the need to give far too many explanations. They had reached Tommy Leonard's house. The stationery
shop was closed for business so the twins knocked at the door beside
the shop. Tommy was there to greet them, his finger on his lips.
Behind him a voice called.

"Where are you going, Thomas?"

"Just out for a bit of a walk."

"All right, but be back at nine o'clock, and no giggling and playing
with all that crowd of hooligans."

"Right oh." Tommy was good-natured. It was easier not to bring
the whole thing down around your ears with a catechism of questions. That was Tommy Leonard's view. Just say yes and no, don't get
involved in long explanations. Michael thought he was dead right; if
he had desperate parents like Tommy's he would be exactly the same.
Dara thought that this was entirely the wrong way to handle things,
and if she were Tommy she would make it all clear from the word go,
instead of giving in to all the cracked notions. That only made them
come up with more cracked notions still.

Maggie Daly said they were to wait until she showed Dara the
gorgeous yellow dress that had arrived in the parcel from America.
There were often parcels from America for all of them. Not as many
as years back, when Mountfern was poorer maybe, and American
uncles and aunts more generous, or postage cheaper. An American
parcel was a rarity nowadays. Mrs. Daly probably would say nothing

about it and its contents, but Maggie was so excited by the yellow net that she couldn't wait to show it off.

The bad thing was that Kitty was in the bedroom.

Kitty yawned when Dara came in. "Going to try on the yellow are you?"

"Well look at it anyway," Dara said. Kitty was a pain.

"Not at all, you're coming to try it on. Half of Mountfern will pass through here trying it on, I can see that. The room will be full of people in vests and knickers bursting into the yellow dress."

"Are you going to wear it?" Dara asked Maggie, deliberately ignoring the elder girl.

"I don't think so." Maggie was pleased to be consulted.

"You see it's a bit low-necked, and it's a bit big, I'm kind of lost in it. And it's so gorgeous it would be a pity to cut it down for me. Wasting so much material, you see." Her face showed her longing for the yellow satin with an overskirt of yellow net, and with yellow embroidery and sequins on the bodice. It was like something you'd see in the pictures; it was far too old for them in one way, and yet it was a girlish-looking dress with big puff sleeves. Dara was dying to put it on but she wouldn't give Kitty the satisfaction of watching her.

"You wouldn't have to get much taken out of it, Maggie, wouldn't Miss Hayes do a great job on it?" Miss Hayes did some dressmaking in Mountfern but had never been let loose on exotic fabric like this, to their knowledge.

Kitty was lying on her bed reading the life story of Helen Shapiro who had managed to escape from childhood by having a voice that took her into the hit parade. She'd never have escaped if she had been born in Mountfern, Kitty Daly thought darkly.

"It would look ridiculous on Maggie, no matter what Miss Hayes did to it. That's a dress that needs a chest. Maggie hasn't got a chest to put into it."

"None of us has a chest to put into it yet," Dara cried with spirit. "While we're waiting we could put a rolled-up pair of socks. Like you often do, Kitty Daly."

"You told her!" Kitty's face was dark red with rage, and she looked menacingly at Maggie.

"I didn't know!" Maggie was transparently honest and terrified.

"Come on, Maggie, let's leave Kitty the room to herself, we're only in the way." Dara felt it was time to escape. They hung up the yellow dress carefully and pulled back the transparent plastic cover that came with it. It was the most beautiful thing they had ever seen.

They envied the cousin of the Dalys somewhere in America who had
worn it to her Junior Prom. Whatever a Junior Prom might be.

They were going to the Protestant graveyard at the top of the
town. Nobody would disturb them there. Mr. Williams the vicar had
realized that the children didn't tear around playing hide and seek
among the headstones, there was no disrespect to the graves of the
various members of the Fern family and the rest of the small Protestant community hereabouts.

It was a peaceful place for the children to come and talk. Mr. and
Mrs. Williams had no children of their own, they were indulgent
with the children of others.

Up Bridge Street the little band walked slowly. They looked wistfully at the Classic which was showing *The Glass Mountain*. Imagine
having the money and freedom just to drop in to the pictures whenever you wanted to.

"We'll be able to do that when we're old," Dara said.

Tommy Leonard didn't think so; he thought being old was going
to be more of the same.

They looked into Conway's grocery and pub. At the back, hidden
away, they saw the feet of three drinkers in the discreet bar area.
They often had a game guessing whose feet they were.

They never tried to play this game in any other pub since anyone
who drank in Foley's or Dunne's, or indeed in Ryan's itself, did so
openly. It was only in Conway's that they pretended not to be there.

Beyond Conway's was Dr. White's and they called there for Liam
and Jacinta. That was it for tonight; some of the other children they
played with lived out in the countryside, and others weren't allowed
out to wander in the evenings. There were some boys who were up at
the brothers' in the football field and there were some girls who had
to help in their houses, or who had been bad and therefore denied
the night's outing.

The six went to the graveyard and sat on a tombstone which they
particularly liked.

It was the memorial for a William James Fern who had died in
1881 at Majuba Hill in the Transvaal, aged eighteen. It was during
the Boer War they knew that, and he had been fighting for the
British against the Dutch in South Africa.

"It was a long way to go," Maggie Daly often said.

"I suppose he wanted to get away." Tommy Leonard could understand it only too well.

Dara had never understood it.

"What did he want to go off and fight in other people's wars for? If he was a Mountfern man then, why wasn't he here having a great time? And if he was eighteen he could have done what he liked. Think of it, he could have gone to the Classic every night." She looked at their faces. "That is if the Classic was there in the 1880s, which I don't think it was."

But tonight they didn't talk long about the dead William James who fell at Majuba Hill. Tonight they talked about what was going to happen to William James's old home. What was happening in Fernscourt.

They were not alone, this little group, in their speculations. If they could have seen into every house down Bridge Street and along River Road they would have come across conversations on the same theme.

Over in Foley's Bar at the top of the town old Matt Foley and his friends said that there was oil sighted there. Some fellow had pulled a pike from the fern and his gills were full of oil. So the drilling would start any day now.

Next door to Foley's, in her neat little house, Judy Byrne the physiotherapist sat with Marian Johnson whose family owned the Grange, a country house which took guests of a superior type and even arranged hunting for them. They were women of around the same age, one side or the other of forty, not married and not likely to find any husbands at this stage of their lives in this part of the country. Neither ever admitted that to the other.

They had heard that Fernscourt was going to be an agricultural college, which would be very good news indeed as it would mean lectures and all kinds of talent not seen in these parts before. While saying that the people would probably be quite unspeakable they were having a small sherry to celebrate.

Seamus Sheehan in the Garda barracks was taking a lot of abuse from his wife. Why had he heard nothing about Fernscourt? Everyone else in the place had some view on what was happening. There was no point in being married to the sergeant if he was the one man in the whole country who seemed to be too remote as to inquire what was going on in his own back yard.

Next to the barracks Jimbo Doyle lived with his mother. Jimbo's mother had heard that the new place had been bought by an order of contemplative nuns. They would have a grille on the window and pull it back so that one nun, the Reverend Mother, would be able to address the outside world. When it was necessary, which would not be often.

Jimbo's mother told him that they would need a reliable man around the place, and that he should get in quick before someone else did.

Jimbo, whose idea of opportunities in life did not include being a reliable handyman to an order of contemplative nuns, asked what his mother expected him to do. Write to the pope, or just the bishop saying he was the man? His mother said he should be glad that someone in the family was looking to the practical side of things instead of singing raucous songs and laughing loud laughs.

In Paddy Dunne's pub all talk of emigration to Liverpool to the brother's pub had stopped. This was now the hub of the universe. Paddy Dunne had it from one of the traveling salesmen who came in trying to get him to take biscuits. Biscuits in a pub! Anyway this man knew all about Fernscourt: it was an agricultural research place. Foreigners were going to come and test soil and plants and the place was going to be a boom town as a result of it. The smart man would expand now or expand a little and then sell when prices were going up. It provided hours of speculation.

Sheila Whelan sat in the comfortable sitting room behind the post office and listened to a concert on Radio Eireann. She loved all that Strauss music and it didn't sweep her into a world of people waltzing in Vienna; instead it reminded her for some reason of the first time she had come to Mountfern with Joe Whelan. He had taken her to Coyne's wood which was full of bluebells. Literally carpeted with them. They had picked armfuls of them and Joe had told her that he loved music and that he would take her to concerts. He told her lots of things. Sheila lay back in her chair, tired. She knew a bit more about Fernscourt than the others because the telegrams all came through her post office. But she didn't know it all. She sighed and wondered what the changes would mean.

Across the road in the Whites', the doctor was telling his wife all the theories he had heard. It was mainly nuns, he reported, but there was a considerable weight of opinion behind a college, and a strong vocal minority thought it was going to be a development of twelve luxury bungalows each with a quarter acre of garden and a river view.

"What would be the best?" Mrs. White wondered.

"It depends where you stand." Dr. White was philosophical. "If Jacinta were going to join the Poor Clares or whatever, it would be nice to have her down the road; on the other hand if she were to land a millionaire let's hope she might buy one of the new bungalows."

"It's going to make everyone look out for themselves," said Mrs. White suddenly, as if the thought had just hit her.

Close to Dr. White's house, in Conway's, Miss Barry was having a small port for her stomach. She sat fearfully on a high stool. The Conways wished she would buy a bottle of port and take it home with her, she made everyone uneasy by looking around nervously and protesting that she had a cramp which meant that her body was crying out to be warmed.

Miss Barry had heard that there was definitely oil in the ground, that a research organization was going to come and test it, but they were going to install an order of silent enclosed nuns there as a disguise to keep people away—three theories rolled comfortably into one. She found a ready and unexpected audience in Conway's. They looked at her as if there might be some truth in it; they had all heard elements of this story and this explanation would at last tie it all together.

In the Classic Cinema twenty-three people sat and watched the romantic tale of *The Glass Mountain* unfold itself on the screen, while Declan Morrissey who ran the place sat in the projection room and read an article he had cut out of a Sunday newspaper. Are the days of the cinema numbered? He wondered should he get out now or wait and see if these daft rumors about half the civil service being transplanted from Dublin to the midlands were true. Wouldn't it be a very stupid thing to sell the Classic just as the horde of possible cinema viewers were about to arrive?

In Meagher's, the watch-menders and small jewelers, Teresa's parents fought on bitterly. Mrs. Meagher said it didn't matter if the Prince of Wales had left and that Mrs. Simpson was coming to live in Mountfern and give parties, life still wouldn't be any way good for her. It had been a vale of tears since she had married Mr. Meagher.

Mr. Meagher tired suddenly of the arguments; he had a pain in his chest and down his arm. He said he would call a halt to the fight and go to bed. He might feel better in the morning. He said that his wife was probably right. Life was a vale of tears and perhaps he had contributed to it. In the morning he would try to consider what could be done about it.

Next morning Teresa Meagher was sent running for Dr. White but it was too late. Mr. Meagher had not recovered from his heart attack. Dr. White knew that he was dead but still arranged for him to be taken to the hospital in the town. It would be less distressing for the family. That's what a lot of his work was about. Minimizing the distress. There was little he could have done to prevent Frank Meagher's heart attack. The man ate like a fat man in a circus, smoked four packets of cigarettes a day and existed on a level of tension that should have finished him off years ago. Dr. White left Mrs. Meagher weeping to the canon, whose faded blue eyes clouded further with the memory of the happy family life the two Meaghers had led, and before long Mrs. Meagher began to believe it herself.

The news of Frank Meagher's death did not take long to travel around Mountfern. In Leonard's stationers, Tommy's mother and father discreetly moved the Deepest Sympathy cards to the front of the stand. They hunted in the drawers for the black-edged Mass cards and flowery Spiritual Bouquet cards as well. People would want to pay their respects.

In Conway's they realized that a coffin would be needed. Discreetly they set about getting one ready. Frank Meagher was a big man. It would be a big coffin. His wife would be as guilty as hell about the life she had led him, it could be an expensive one. But they probably didn't have much insurance, maybe standard was the right thing to suggest.

At seven o'clock mass that morning he was prayed for. The religious bent their heads. Miss Purcell, Miss Hayes and Jimbo Doyle's mother exchanged glances. They could have said a lot about the Meaghers, but they would say no more now, not after a bereavement like this.

Miss Purcell looked after the Slattery household with an unsmiling face and unstinting effort. Old Mr. Slattery's clothes were clean, ironed and mended, his shoes were polished and his newspaper laid in front of his well-served breakfast at eight-thirty every morning. Miss Purcell would already have been to seven o'clock mass, she was a daily communicant; she would have collected fresh milk at Daly's and the newspaper at Leonard's. His son Fergus was equally well looked after. His shirts were ironed for him, and left hanging on the big heavy wardrobe in his room. Miss Purcell always took the one he was going to wear next day to give it a little warm in the hot press. She had a horror of the damp.

Fergus had a series of sleeveless vee-necked knitted pullovers, almost all of them in a grey to blue shade. In the long evenings when others went out looking for diversion Miss Purcell knitted fresh supplies and darned the existing force. Though old-fashioned and obviously home-made, they gave him an even more boyish charm than he had already. Many a girl's heart turned over to see him sitting at his desk in his shirt sleeves with the light on of an evening, reading through papers with hair tousled and glasses often pushed back into his thick dark hair.

If someone had offered Fergus a thousand pounds to strike attitudes or adopt a pose he wouldn't have been able to do it. Like his father he was a pleasure to work for, Miss Purcell told her few cronies, a courteous and considerate man, always opening doors, carrying buckets of coal for her, and saying how much he liked whatever she put on the table. It would be hard to find his equal in three counties or more. Miss Purcell never understood any of his jokes but Fergus seemed to be very witty and make clients laugh. Often when they were leaving she heard them say that he was too human to be a lawyer. She had been worried about this and made two novenas that he should become less human in case he endangered the practice. Sometimes Fergus cleaned his own shoes—he didn't think it was right to let a woman polish the black laced shoes that had been on his feet all day—but Miss Purcell didn't like any changes in routine. She sniffed disapprovingly at his efforts and said she would prefer if he wouldn't disgrace her in the town by going about with such ill-kept feet.

It was said that Canon Moran had often looked with envy at the Slatterys and wished they would give him their housekeeper. The purse-faced Miss Purcell who kept such a good house would be indeed a delight compared to poor Miss Barry, but she had been there so long and had no other home to go to, so in Christian kindness Canon Moran couldn't, and made no efforts to replace her.

Miss Purcell was tall, thin and had a small face with two deceptively cheery-looking spots of red on her cheeks. These were not jolly ruddy cheeks, they were in fact two spots of color whose redness increased according to how disapproving she was. At breakfast that morning they were very red indeed: a sure sign that something was about to blow up. Father and son avoided recognizing this for as long as they could.

"Do you want a bit of the *Independent?*" Fergus's father offered him the middle pages.

"I wish we'd get the *Times*, it's a better paper altogether," Fergus said. They were both avoiding the eye of Miss Purcell who stood ready to sound off.

"Well it is and it isn't, but nobody dies in the *Irish Times*. You don't get the list of deaths in it like the *Independent*. A country solicitor needs to know who has died."

"Couldn't we go into Leonard's and sort of race down the deaths without buying the paper at all?" Fergus suggested.

"Fine thing that would be to do in a small town, depriving the Leonards of their income. Couldn't the whole town do that? Couldn't they come in here and look at our law books? Where's the sense in that?" Mr. Slattery rattled his half of the paper in annoyance.

Miss Purcell cleared her throat.

"Miss Ryan is here. A bit early I said to her but she seemed to think that you expected her before nine."

"Is that Marian Ryan come to make her will again?" Old Mr. Slattery looked over his glasses.

"No, it's Kate, Kate Ryan from the pub up the River Road," said Fergus. "Isn't it, Miss Purcell?"

"Oh yes, Mr. Fergus, that's the Mrs. Ryan it is, all right. And if I might say . . ."

"Yes, Miss Purcell?" Fergus decided to take it manfully, whatever it was.

"Mrs. Ryan arrived five minutes ago with the information that she is going to be working here."

"That's right," Fergus said cheerfully. "She's going to start this morning. Well she's nice and punctual, that makes a change from the rest of Mountfern."

"I can't recall any occasion anything was late in this house . . ." Miss Purcell began to bristle.

"Oh not you, Miss Purcell, for heaven's sake, everyone else."

"And what work will Kate Ryan from the pub be doing here, and why wasn't I consulted?" The spots on the cheeks were dangerously red now. Even old Mr. Slattery had put down his paper and was looking anxiously like an old bird from one to the other.

"Well, lots of things, I hope." Fergus was still bewildered by this storm, and the sudden dropping of the Mrs. Ryan, and changing it to Kate from the pub.

"In nineteen years working in this house I have never had such treatment." Miss Purcell looked ten feet tall; she had drawn herself up into a long thin stick quivering with rage. "If my work was not to your satisfaction, the very least I would have expected was to be told. Instead of allowing me to be humiliated by seeing that Kate Ryan from the pub, come along with her apron and things in a basket prepared to do my work for me."

The eyes were very bright. Old Mr. Slattery's glasses had fallen off his nose with shock.

Fergus was on his feet. "Miss Purcell, Miss Purcell! What an idea, what a thought that we would dream of improving on your house-work! Don't you keep the best house in the town? Aren't we the envy of the whole of Mountfern, including I might say the canon himself? You can't have thought for a moment that we'd as much as contemplate getting anyone else, let alone doing it without telling you. . . ."

"But Kate from the pub out there with her basket?"

"I don't know what she has in the basket but Mrs. Ryan is going to work in the office. She was trained in a solicitor's office in Dublin, you know. She'll be doing the files and typing letters."

"Oh," Miss Purcell had to spend a moment doing some social adjustment.

"So you see you were quite wrong to think we have anything except the highest regard for you, isn't that right, Dad?"

"Heavens yes. Oh Miss Purcell, the house would fall down without you," said Mr. Slattery anxiously.

"But that would mean Kate . . . that Mrs. Ryan and her family would know all your business, confidential business of the town." Miss Purcell wasn't going to give in.

"We wouldn't take her on if we didn't know she could be trusted. It's not easy to find the kind of discretion and loyalty that you have, Miss Purcell. You are, as my father has said, the mainstay of this house, but we think we have found someone who will be able to keep our business private, as you do. It's very good of you to be worried about it."

There was no more to be said. Miss Purcell had to go back to the hall where she had left Kate standing, and usher her into the office, asking the while whether she took sugar in her tea and if she would like a plain biscuit, a sweet biscuit or a slice of home-made currant bread. Kate wisely chose the home-made bread and disclosed four pints of raspberries which she had brought as a gift because she had heard it said that Miss Purcell made the best jam in the county. The pink 'spots began to lose their ferocity and the "Mrs. Ryan" was pronounced without the sarcastic overtones. Kate was in, she was starting a new career. There was hardly any trade in the pub in the mornings, and John was in agreement with her that the few pounds the Slatterys paid would be helpful. Young Declan was off at school, so they were all out of the house, and Carrie knew how to put a lunch on the table at the stroke of one. It would be nice to be behind a typewriter again for a change rather than behind a bar. Mr. Slattery was such a gentleman, a real old-fashioned man who was spending more and more time fishing; and Fergus was the best company in the world, self-mocking and droll, full of compassion for some of the people who came to see him, slow to send a bill where it would be a hardship to pay it, but also quick with his tongue to abuse anyone who wanted to work a fiddle or hide an income.

Fergus had told her that it wasn't a big practice and that normally he was well able to deal with the clerical side. He could type like the wind with two fingers and he had a fairly reasonable filing system but he wanted his father to take more time off; now people really did trust him with their affairs rather than thinking of him as a boy in short trousers. So Kate would be a godsend. And indeed she was. It took her about three days to see that his reasonable filing system was hopeless, and to set up a better one.

"Come here till I show you what we do with these papers now," she ordered him.

"No, no, that's your work, that's what we pay you inordinate sums of money for, so that I don't have to look at things like that."

"Wrong," Kate cried. "You have to understand it, otherwise it's useless to any of us. You won't know where to put back a letter, find a counsel's brief, where the deeds are, anything. Suppose I get flu or you sack me, or you're working late at night. Come on now, it will only take ten minutes a day."

"Do you run the pub like this too?" Fergus asked.

"Of course not, but I do the accounts, and I've insisted that John does them with me otherwise he'd have to leave them till the wife gets back and it would just double the work."

"I'm surprised the place isn't a gold mine with your organizational skills."

"Come out our way one evening and have a pint in it and you'll see what a gold mine it is. Would I be in here setting up filing systems for beautiful idle professional men too lazy to look at them if it was a gold mine? Now suppose you had this query from the town agent's clerk about the fee in that workman's compensation case which was appealed, where would you look first?"

"In the bad old days I'd look on the table at the window."

"But in the good days that have now come?"

"I've forgotten, young Mrs. Ryan, show me, show me."

"Oh thank God I'm happily married. You'd break my heart."

"You're sure you're happily married?"

"Very sure. And isn't it time you had a romance yourself? Now that Nora Lynch has gone off to fresh fields and better chances we hear nothing about your activities."

"Listen to me, after that business with Nora I'm afraid to lay my hand or eye on anyone. There's no activities to hear about. It was all a terrible misunderstanding."

"You lost us a fine schoolteacher over it all. My Dara loved her. She hates the new woman, about a hundred she says, and a habit of hitting them accidentally on the knuckles with a ruler."

"Poor Dara, maybe I should have given Miss Lynch an engagement ring to keep her in the town, and keep all the little girls like Dara happy."

"I don't think anything's going to make my Dara happy for a long time, but no stories about children. This workman was called Burke, Fergus, in the name of God where are you going to look for this file?"

"Under the Bs, Miss?"

"We have a child prodigy," said Kate Ryan and went back to her typewriter.

"What are you doing, Daddy?" John jumped guiltily at Dara's voice.

What he should have been doing was writing. This was the time that Kate stood minding the bar, tired already from her morning in the office. But there was just so long you could look at blank paper without it beginning to drive you mad. John Ryan had nothing to say and no way of saying it. He had come out to what Kate called the garden and everyone else called the yard to do a little experiment. Ryan's licensed premises was flush on the road. Its front door opened straight onto River Road. It would have been unheard of to have a pub with a garden in front. The supplies came to the back yard and the barrels took up most of it . . . a place of half-used outhouses and sheds. That was where the back door of the house was, that was the only way the children were ever allowed to enter their home. But beside the house there was what they called the side yard. Here the hens wandered, and Jaffa sat like a buddha in calm control, purring and lazily washing her big orange face. Leopold didn't sit much in the yard, there wasn't an audience sufficiently sympathetic to his whimperings and cringings. He liked to cower in the pub. Maurice was still in the mudroom after the ugly river-bank incident. John had devised a marvelous way to avoid working on his poems: he was going to build a large hen coop, a wired-off area for the hens to live in, so that they could scratch and wander but be away from the few pathetic attempts that Kate had started in the line of making a real garden. Once the hens were corraled life would be easier. But John Ryan had wanted to do it quietly and undisturbed by his family. He didn't want to admit, even to himself, that he was shirking his writing work, and playing hooky. Dara stood with a mutinous look on her face. Her eyes were dark and cross under her fringe of black hair . . . her hands thrust into the pockets of her shorts.

"Are you changing things, is that it?" she said in the tones of someone looking for a fight and determined to find one.

"I have a bit of a plan. I was working it out, that's all," her father said, looking guilty and shifty.

"I bet it's something new and desperate," Dara said.

"It was just a plan to gather the hens all together in a run, that's all it was," John said mildly.

"They're perfectly all right the way they are, they don't want to be gathered, they don't want to be changed, they love things just as they are." Her eyes were suspiciously bright as if she could start to cry any minute. Dara had never expressed any view about the hens up to this. The hens were like the river bank and the crates in the yard, they were just part of the background.

John Ryan sat back on his haunches and put an arm around his daughter's knees. "Come here and give your old father a hug."

"There's no point in hugs," Dara said.

"Right." He stood up. "I know exactly. It's the same with me. I don't feel like writing now so I came down to play with the chickens."

Dara couldn't help laughing at the thought of her father playing with chickens. She managed a snort but John Ryan wisely didn't build on it. He knew she was upset and it would all come out. He supposed it was a row with Kate. But he was wrong.

"Daddy, are we poor?"

"No we're not poor. You know that."

"But we're not rich are we?"

"You don't have to be one or the other, you can be in between, like most of us are around here."

"Will we ever be rich?"

"We'll be all right. What's this worry about money?"

"We're going to need it to buy our house." Her face was very determined.

"But we have our house, silly old thing, this is our house," he indicated the pub and the whitewashed walls of the house with a wave of his hand.

"Not here, our house across in Fernscourt. You know where they have the bulldozers. They're clearing it for someone to live there, some American, he'll live there unless we can buy it."

"Now, now, Dara," John began soothingly.

But she was on her feet full of anger and wouldn't be soothed.

"It's our house, Michael's and mine, and everyone's."

John sighed.

"Will you come for a bit of a walk with me?"

"I don't feel like a walk."

"I don't feel like a walk with such a disagreeable weasel as you, but it might help."

"Where will we go?"

"We could go to Fernscourt."

"All right then."

Kate Ryan was in the bar talking to Jimbo Doyle and Jack Coyne, who were not her idea of the best of company, when she saw through the window the two figures crossing the footbridge. Her husband who was meant to be working on his poetry and her daughter who had been like a bag of hedgehogs all week. Her knuckles ached to rap on the window, but she wouldn't give that sharp-faced Jack Coyne the satisfaction of seeing her act the bossy wife.

Kate had always spoken impetuously, and not long ago in confession had told Canon Moran that she was quick-tempered. Canon Moran had suggested that she think of Our Lord's Blessed Mother whenever she was tempted to say something sharp. She should think what Our Lady might have said. She needn't actually say what Our Lady would have said, but thinking it might delay the caustic response or the hurtful crack.

Looking at the man and girl hand in hand walking across the footbridge Kate Ryan thought that the Mother of God might have blessed them and wished them well and happiness and thanked God for her good fortune. Right, Kate Ryan would think similar noble thoughts. She turned around and faced Jack Coyne and Jimbo Doyle with what she thought was a saintly smile.

"Jesus, Kate, have you a toothache?" asked Jimbo Doyle in alarm.

* * *

"And Michael and I planned to live here when we grew up. Everyone knew that we'd get a proper roof made over this bit, and probably build windows and a door." Dara was pointing out the extent of the house.

"But it was only a dream." John was gentle.

"No it wasn't."

"Yes, of course it was . . . and is. Like going to see the man in the moon. Do you remember when you were very young we used to take you out to have a look at the man in the moon before you went to bed? Now you don't think it's a man up there, you're quite happy to look at the moon for itself, as something beautiful lighting up the sky over Mountfern."

"Yes but . . ."

"And when you were very young altogether you and Michael used to be staring up the chimney in the kitchen, didn't you, at Christmas time, the way Declan did last Christmas? You thought that if the chimney was too old and too awkward you wouldn't get any presents. But they came all the same, didn't they, and you don't mind now where they come from?"

"That's not the same . . ."

"I know it's not the same . . . but I was just saying that the way we look at things changes as life goes on, it couldn't always stay the same, otherwise we'd all be still living in caves with clubs or if we didn't grow up in some kind of way wouldn't we all be in nappies waddling around the place in playpens . . ."

"You don't understand . . ." she wailed.

"I don't understand completely, but I understand a bit. Don't I?" She looked up at him, her face softening.

"I know, Dara, it'll always be here in some way for you, not the same way, remember the man in the moon. The moon didn't go, and it still looks beautiful, doesn't it, when you can see all the cattle over on the hills, and the spire of the church and the woods and . . . and Fernscourt . . ."

"Will it be the same when this awful man comes, him with all his American money?"

"He's not going to be awful. He has children, we hear, you'll love them as sure as anything."

"I won't, I won't."

"Well you'll meet them anyway, and you *might* like them. Would that be reasonable?"

"And we'd never be able to afford to buy it ourselves."

"No, that isn't a thing you should think about, that's not a possible thing, that's like imagining a square circle, or imagining that Jaffa grew a long neck like a giraffe in the picture books. Cats don't grow long necks, this isn't a *real* home for you and Michael, it was a home for last summer and before that."

"And now?" Her lip had stopped trembling.

"It's still special but it isn't anything you start getting all het up about and start saving your pocket money to buy. That's like the days when you used to want to know if the man in the moon had to wash his neck."

"Will you explain that to Michael, Daddy? I'm not great at explaining."

"I'm not great at it either."

"Well, you're better than me," Dara said in the matter-of-fact voice which meant that he had sorted this one out anyway.

John Ryan hadn't written a poem or built a hen run, but he had convinced his angry little daughter that the world wasn't going to come to an end. Now all he had to do was to get into the house without his wife knowing he had played hooky from his poetry writing.

It was a busy night in the bar, they had hardly time for a word of any kind let alone the attack that John feared was brewing. Kate moved so quickly around the place, she had glasses swept up, and washed or refilled quicker than he would have decided whether to move the glass in the first place. Yet she didn't give the customers the impression that they were being rushed, only that there was an urgency in getting their pint in front of them.

Kate had decided to say nothing until everyone was gone, then she was going to force her voice to stay low, not to get high and excited, and she would not allow herself to speak too quickly until it became a gabble. She was going to point out—in tones that no one could find offense in—that she got up every morning and saw the children off to school, then she went and did what amounted to a day's work in an office, and not that she was complaining but she spent the afternoon listening to almighty bores rambling out of them instead of getting on with her own work of which she had plenty, but she had stood in the bar to let her husband work . . . She would keep her voice very calm as she told him how she would like to take a cleaver to him and split him in two.

Her humor was not helped by the behavior of Eddie and Declan who had come into the pub, despite all the strictures against this, to know could they take possession of the tortoise again. They had burst into the pub, mouths stained with the jam which Carrie had been making a very poor fist of setting. They looked like the children of tinkers both of them in the most torn clothes that they could have found. In front of the drinking population of Mountfern—who probably had looked at her askance because she was an outsider from the first day and had now committed the crime of going outside the family home to work—she had been guilty of the worst sin of all . . . neglecting her children. And had John supported her, had he removed them with an authoritative wave and a thunderous warning? He had *like hell*!

John Ryan had put an arm around the shoulder of each small furious son and he chose with a slow deliberation for each of them a chocolate biscuit from the shelf behind the bar and he had walked them out as if they had been honored guests instead of his own children who had broken his own most strict rule of coming into the family pub.

But Kate would not let her tone betray her rage, otherwise he would just walk away from it saying that the last thing on earth he wanted was a fight. It was infuriating. The only way she could convince him of how badly he was behaving was to speak in a reasonable tone as if she were the most contented woman on earth.

For a wild moment she wondered how the Mother of God would have coped, and then realized that Mary wouldn't have had nearly as many problems in Nazareth. There was never any mention of her running Joseph's carpentry business almost single-handedly and doing another job for a local lawyer as well. Kate's resentment knew no bounds.

The last straggler finally went home. The glasses were washed, the windows opened to air the place, two clean dishcloths lay out to dry on the counter. Kate felt sweaty and weary, not in the mood to list her wrongs.

Her husband smiled at her across the counter. "May I pour you a port wine?" he asked.

"Oh Jesus, Mary and Joseph isn't that all I'd need tomorrow, a roaring port hangover."

"Just one glass each, we'll bring it out to the side garden and I'll tell you my plans for it."

She bit her lip. He was like a big child.

"Well?" He had the glass and the port bottle ready.

She was too tired.

"Hold on till I rinse this blouse out," she said, and took off the blue and white cotton blouse that was sticking to her back. Standing in her slip top and dark blue skirt, she looked flushed and very beautiful, John thought. He touched her neck where the long dark curly hair was loosely tied with a narrow blue ribbon.

"That's lovely for them to see that kind of carry on if they pass the window," she said shaking his hand away.

"Well you're the one who's half-dressed, I'm quite respectable," he laughed.

The blouse was left to hang on the back of a chair, it would be dry in the morning. Kate gave herself a quick sluice with the water in the sink that was meant to wash only glasses.

"If we're going to go to the side garden, let's go then," she said more ungraciously than she felt; she was glad at any rate that he was calling it a garden rather than a yard. That was an advance.

The moonlight made it look a great deal better than it seemed by day. Jaffa sat still as a statue on the wall. Leopold was dreaming of beatings and his hard life. He gave a gentle whimper now and then in his sleep. From the hen house there was a soft cluck.

John folded a sack and left it on an upturned barrel. "I was to ask you about the tortoise."

"No, no." Her eyes flashed with rage. "It's not fair, John, really it isn't. You're always the lovey dovey one, ask poor old Daddy, he's so soft, he'd melt as soon as he looks at you. Mammy's the nagging old shrew . . . It's not fair to let them grow up thinking that."

"They do not think that."

"They do, and they will more if you say they can have the tortoise back. Do you think I want the smelly old thing in the mudroom looking at me like something out of one of those horror pictures they have in the picture house? I've wished a hundred times it would die one day and we could have a funeral and it would all be over, and all the fighting."

"They live for years, you know, you're on a loser there," he grinned.

She wouldn't give in. "No, they can't have it back, they broke all the rules coming into the pub like pictures of children you'd see when they're collecting for charity. They're worse than Leopold, they pretend they never got a meal or a bath in their lives."

Kate Ryan was very aggrieved.

"Did I ever try to countermand any of your decisions?" John asked.

"No, but you try to get around me. We've got to be consistent, John, otherwise how do they know where they are?"

"I couldn't agree more."

"But?"

"But nothing. I couldn't agree more."

"So what about the bloody tortoise? What were you going to suggest?"

"Come here, I want to show you something . . ." He took her by the hand and pointed out where they should build a long hen run, with netting over it. The hens would have freedom, but within frontiers. The rest was going to be a garden. He showed where they could have a rockery. And how they would build a raised flower bed maybe and she could grow the flowers she had always said she would like.

"You should have been writing your poetry."

"It's not like making things in a factory, Kate, you can't sit down in front of a conveyor belt and turn out bits of writing and in the end a poem emerges." He spoke quietly and with dignity.

"I know, I know." She was contrite.

"So when it didn't seem to come, I thought I'd do something for you and plan you a garden."

"That's lovely."

"I'll have a word with Jimbo Doyle and he could do a couple of days and build up a few beds. Now wouldn't that be nice?"

"It would." She was touched, she couldn't deliver her attack now. It would be ingratitude, flying in the face of God, to attack a husband who was so kind.

"I was over in Fernscourt today, there's heaps of stones lying around the place. We could get some nice big rocks, Jimbo could wheel them across the footbridge."

"I don't suppose they belong to anyone." Kate didn't want her voice to sound grudging . . . "That would be grand," she added.

"And this thing about the tortoise, I wouldn't countermand your orders. God, what would be the point? What I was wondering was now that the hens have a place of their own someone will have to feed them properly you know, mix up the scraps with the bran . . ."

"Yes."

"So suppose we made those two scallywaggers do that? They'd be well able for it, and they'd give the hens a feed twice a day . . . and to encourage them maybe they could have some kind of access to that tortoise, maybe take him out of your way in the mudroom, not have him looking up at you like a prehistoric monster. What do you think?"

Kate tried to hide her smile. Unsuccessfully.

"What do I think?" she said, laughing in spite of herself. "I think I might be persuaded . . . but . . ."

"But it would have to come from you. If you think it would be a good idea, then you should suggest it." He was adamant about this.

"I suppose you sorted Dara out too," Kate said gently and with admiration. "They should have you up on the platform in Geneva sorting things out for everyone."

"Ah, the poor child was very upset, it's giving up a bit of fairyland. None of us like doing that."

"People like you didn't have to, it's still all there in your heads," Kate said, but she said it with a hint of envy in her voice, and she kissed his lips softly so that he tasted the port wine.

Chapter III

That night Michael sat on the landing window seat and looked across at Fernscourt in the moonlight.

The curtains of ivy waved over the hummocks of moss. It was easier than ever to see the ruins since some of the big straggly trees and bushes had been cut down.

Eddie and Declan were long asleep in their bunk beds. Michael had been reading with a torch, but his mind had strayed from the knight who had rescued the Lady Araminta with the golden tresses. He wanted to look at real life, which was Fernscourt. For a long time he looked at the shadows over the moon and the patterns they made on the soft green banks up from the river toward the house.

Then he saw a figure moving in the moonlight. Nobody *ever* walked there at night. Michael knelt up and opened the window to have a better view. It was a man, an old man even older than Daddy. He was wandering around with his hands in his pockets looking up at the walls. Sometimes he touched the moss, sometimes he pushed aside the ivy. Michael was kneeling on the window seat now, peering and straining to see as the figure disappeared and emerged again behind the ruined walls. He felt a hand on his shoulder, and there was his father in his pajamas.

"Dad, I think he's come. I think he's here."

"Who?"

"The American. I think that's him in our house." The boy's face was white even on the shadowy landing with moonlight coming in irregular darts through the window.

John Ryan looked out and saw a figure walking around touching walls and almost patting the bits of building that still stood. John felt he was spying somehow. The man was as if naked over there, in that he didn't know he was being observed.

Michael was wriggling off the seat. "I'll have to wake Dara," he said, his face working anxiously.

"Wait, Michael."

"But it's our house, he's here, he came after all. People said he might not be going to live here. But look at him, he *is* going to live in it, isn't he? Isn't he?"

John sat down on the window seat, and lifted his feet a little off the cold linoleum floor covering. "Michael, don't wake the child up."

"She's not a child, she's twenty minutes older than I am."

"That's true. She's not a child any more than you are."

Michael's face was troubled. "She'll need to know, Dad."

"Nobody needs to know."

"It's partly her house."

"It's *his* house Michael." John indicated the man across the river.

"I know, I know." The boy's thin shoulders were raised, tense. He was troubled and unsure what to do.

"Give me something to put my feet on so they're not like two big blocks of ice when I get back into the bed with your mother."

Michael rooted around under the comics and books that were on the window seat and found a raggedy cushion.

"Will this do?"

"That's fine, thank you son."

Some of the quivering tension had left the boy. He sat down, still looking out of the window, but prepared to talk rather than wake his sister and the whole house in his grief.

"Do you know, when I was a lad your age we used to go over there and play too. Your Uncle Barry, now, he was a great climber, there was nothing he couldn't get right up on, and there were more bits of wall then than now."

Michael was interested.

"And then your Aunt Nuala; my heavens wouldn't those little Australian boys and girls be surprised to know that their Mother

Superior used to climb trees like a boy? She used to tie her skirts up around her waist and climb with Barry."

"What did you do, Daddy?"

"Sure I was only like poor Eddie, looking at them," John sighed. "They usually wanted me to go away, if I remember rightly."

Michael took this as a criticism of the twins' own attitude to their younger brother.

"I'm sure you were fine when you were young, Dad. But God, you couldn't have Eddie hanging around with you, I mean really and truly."

"Oh I know that, I'm not disputing it, Eddie would have your heart scalded. But I was only talking about the old days across there . . . and the kind of things we used to do . . ."

He talked on gently, his voice low enough that it wouldn't wake Kate and have her storming out onto the landing. Yet raised enough for Michael to think it was a normal conversation and that these were normal times.

John dug deep into his memory of games played, and accidents averted, of guards on bicycles, of two young bullocks that ran wild, away from someone's secure field up the hill. He talked until he saw the lids begin to droop on his son's thin white face, and knew that sleep was going to come at last, that Michael wouldn't wake Dara and sit all night watching in helpless despair as this stranger walked through what they still wanted to think their home.

That night old Mr. Slattery couldn't sleep and he came down to get himself some warm milk. He dozed off at the kitchen table as the milk boiled and didn't smell the burning until Fergus appeared, wild-eyed with shock.

"Don't put me away, don't put me in the county home," wept the old man. "I'll take milk to bed in a flask. I'll never try to boil it again. Please."

Fergus had been filling the blackened saucepan with water and opening the windows.

"Are you going mad altogether, Father? Would I put you in the county home? Would I?"

"If I were mad altogether you'd have to," Mr. Slattery said reasonably.

"Yes, but you're not, and even if you were I don't think I would."

"Why not? It would be the right thing to do, we've often advised clients ourselves."

Maeve Binchy

"You're not a client. You're my father."

"You've got to get on with your own life."

"But I *do* get on with my own life, for God's sake. I was out getting on with it this evening and I'd only just gotten to bed. That's why it was my nose that caught the milk, not Miss Purcell's."

"I'm a burden, I don't do much work in the office."

"You're not a burden, we don't *have* much work in the office."

"I've let the place run down, why else didn't we get the business for Fernscourt?"

"Oh is *that* what's worrying you? I'll tell you why. Your man O'Neill is in business in a big way over there, really big, owns at least half a dozen restaurants or bars or whatever they are. He has other business too, he pays accountants and lawyers big fees. Now he's opening here, the big lawyers look up a map . . . Ireland they say, Ireland, where's that? Then they find it. What's the capital they say, what's the capital? Then someone tells them and they get Dublin solicitors. That's all."

"You make it sound so simple. I suppose it will be good when he arrives, this American. He's given work in the place already."

"Here's some fresh milk." Fergus had boiled another saucepan. "We'll tell Miss Purcell that I was drunk and burned the arse out of the saucepan. The American? It has to be good for the place. I suppose the poor devil will be full of nonsense and trying to hunt and shoot and fish. We'll have great sport with him. Imagine worrying about the American! It'll be the best sport we ever had. I can't wait for him to arrive."

That night Sergeant Sheehan found somebody lying in a very awkward position, legs splayed, head lolling, and stretched right across the footbridge at the end of the town. Sergeant Sheehan was a thick-set man who used to be a great hurler in his day, a man with ferocious eyebrows which made him look very frightening when he had to. But he was running to fat now, with slow and undemanding life in a country town. He felt his uniform was constantly tight around his neck, and rolls of fat gathered when he buttoned his top collar.

He loosened the collar now by opening several buttons, and looked at the sleeping woman. It was Miss Barry, the canon's housekeeper. A fine place for her to have passed out and to be snoring at 1 A.M. Sergeant Sheehan went back to the station to think the matter over, having tidied her legs into a more respectable position. He wasn't quite sure what his next move would be. To wake the canon with such bad news would be unwise. To allow Miss Barry to be found by someone else, asleep and obviously the worse for wear, would hardly be wise either. To wake Miss Barry might be the least wise course of all. What a pity Mrs. Whelan wasn't around. He walked up Bridge Street. There was still a light on.

He tapped gently. She came to the door fully dressed.

"Do you ever sleep, Sheila?" he asked, full of relief to see her.

"Not so much these days. Telegrams come in at funny times too. They don't know what time we wake or sleep," she said.

He told her; she pondered. She decided it was best left; even another three or four hours would mean she had slept the worst off. Had she anything to support her head? No, but the sergeant would arrange it.

"I get up early," Mrs. Whelan said. "I could throw some water over her at around six, and then we could pretend she had been out early to pick mushrooms for His Reverence's breakfast and fallen into the river."

This way face was saved. He couldn't thank her enough. Mrs. Whelan said they would speak no more of it; she was flattered to be asked for her advice. She would sleep now for a couple of hours.

It was years since Patrick O'Neill had stayed up all night. He tried to think back. In the 1930s during the Depression often, very often, hardly a week went by when nights were not spent hauling boxes and crates, doing favors here, moving goods that had to be out of warehouses there. Counting, taking note, proving himself reliable. Telling Italians and fellows with long Polish names that they could always rely on Patrick O'Neill. He used to say his own name with pride to these men, roll it around as if it were an incantation. He spoke of himself in the third person to these business associates in the early days: "Patrick O'Neill won't let you down. You can always rely on Patrick O'Neill."

They could rely on him and his truck at first, and then on his fleet of truck drivers who didn't ask questions but just shifted what had to be shifted.

And then Patrick O'Neill's name was over neighborhood bars. He was one of the first to welcome the end of Prohibition, just as he had enjoyed the income and lifestyle which Prohibition had created for him, and those Italians and Poles who had given him early jobs were not forgotten. When life became less risky Patrick O'Neill invited them and their wives to his bar-restaurants and treated them with respect. Flowers for the wives, discreet smiles when they brought girlfriends instead. They appreciated it; they sent him custom. But it had meant a lot of staying up all night. There had been the night when he had gone through the books over and over again. It was dawn when he had to admit that it was a fellow Irishman who had been cheating him. He called to Tom Brady's house at seven, shirt open and eyes red.

Tom Brady realized what had happened and tried to run.

"Mrs. Brady," Patrick O'Neill had said quietly, "take the children out, maybe for the day. To family perhaps? Don't let them come back before nightfall. Oh and move any really good ornaments and pieces from your front parlor."

"This isn't a movie, Patrick," Tom started to bluster.

"Sure it isn't, otherwise you'd be dead on your floor for what you've done to me."

Tom Brady's wife gasped.

"Take the children," Tom had said, "and do what he says. He's not going to kill me."

Patrick beat him with a violence he didn't even know he possessed. With every blow he grunted and spat out more rage. *This* was for the false smiles and the drinks after a day spent cheating. *This* was for letting Patrick fire an innocent Italian two months back. *This* was for the sleazy shabby way the goods were stolen, taking them out in trash cans and coming back later to root among the garbage and remove the good bottles of liquor. *This* was for taking a bonus last Christmas, and *this*, the hardest blow of all, had been for being an Irishman and doing it all to another Irishman. He had been up all that night all right. And on the night he had met Kathleen.

He had never intended to marry, or fall in love. There wouldn't be time. Work was scarce first and then it was too plentiful, and then came responsibility and long hours. There wouldn't be time for a wife and family. But Kathleen had looked so lovely and she was so lively then, eyes dancing, long fair hair swept up into a top knot of some sort. She had been so excited about his bars and restaurants, and so enthusiastic. She said over and over that America was so alive and so full of hope she pitied anyone who lived anywhere else.

"Except Ireland, of course," Patrick had said.

"Particularly Ireland." She had tossed her curls.

It was the one thing they differed on. Huge in ways, and yet it never mattered all that much, because he knew that when he was ready to go back—"to go back" was how he put it, though he himself had never seen Ireland—Kathleen would come too. He wasn't to know that as her health deteriorated she would become less and less interested in any scheme, be it in New York or in Ireland. Kathleen, who used to sit on the tables in a new bar holding swaths of material up to the light at the window to see which would make the classiest curtains, lost her involvement in anything except the big white house in New Jersey, and in the latter years even that couldn't hold her frail attention.

He hadn't spent any night awake over Kathleen's illness; there was not one night when he knew she wouldn't get better. He was never given any bad diagnosis, or expectation or time when her illness would run its course. Possibly, the last time he had stayed up all night without going to bed or lying down was the night Kerry was born. In 1947. The child had been born at home and the doctors told Patrick it was going to be long and hard, even though Kathleen was still young and strong in those days. He had spent all night pacing, trying to read, doing anything to distract himself from the cries upstairs. It had been a clear bright dawn when he held his son in his arms and rocked him. Kerry's tiny, scrunched-up face was so touching, Patrick had swallowed hard and swore that no harm would come to this boy, and that he would go back and walk in his rightful place in Ireland with head held high.

As he clutched the little bundle to him he felt tears in his eyes and wondered how his own father, Michael O'Neill—amiable, drunken, good-for-nothing Michael O'Neill—felt when he had held Patrick in his arms. Did he not wish too that he could take his son back to Mountfern? No, Patrick's father must have felt no such thing. At the age of twenty Michael O'Neill, his parents, brothers and sisters, had left Mountfern because there was no work and his father had been thrown out on the road. He never went back, nor had he ever thought it possible. He had sung songs about Ireland, and told tales, and filled young Patrick with a hatred of this Fern family whom he had never met.

Patrick was eight when he heard that the Ferns' house had been burned down. The news came by letter. It was too late to be any good to any of the O'Neills then. There was no O'Neill around to watch the flames lick through the windows of this house, the house which had held the family and brought them down.

Patrick O'Neill touched the moss-covered stones almost religiously; he leaned against the ivy-covered walls and walked by the moonlight into a room which still had its walls. To his surprise there were orange boxes as furniture, and toy tea-sets. Some local children had obviously been playing there. He smiled at the jam jars full of wild flowers. He wondered who the children were. Certainly they wouldn't have been allowed in the door during the Ferns' time. He would love to see their faces when they heard his plans for the old ruin.

Mrs. Whelan was the first to see him. She had just delivered a dripping Miss Barry back to the presbytery while Father Hogan and Canon Moran clucked sympathetically at the mishap that caused their housekeeper to fall into the river. Mrs. Whelan had even provided some mushrooms as a kind of proof that the bewildered woman had been on an errand for her employers. Just as she was walking back to her post office, she saw a man in a crumpled suit, tie loosened, walk up Bridge Street toward a hired car. It could be no one else.

Patrick O'Neill stood handsome and pale in his unaccustomed dark suit. Big and broad-shouldered with a head of dark brown curly hair, he was a man who normally wore tan or beige jackets. Few people in the States ever remembered seeing him in dark colors. Even if there had been a formal occasion he had worn a green tuxedo in deference to his national origins.

His enemies in business had often said that he had the thickset looks of an Irish paddy who should still be shoveling dirt. This pleased Patrick rather than otherwise; he said he was glad to wear the signs of his forefathers so openly, and to be living proof that they had to work hard and that they survived. But he didn't have the pugilistic face of a man who would like to have a fight, he had no boxer's scowl, nor the low forehead of a man who found it hard to cope with whatever life dealt him. His face was broad and open, his eyes blue and twinkling. From his eyes lines came out like a star, meaning that they often looked as if he was smiling even when he was far from it.

He was more attractive and younger than Sheila had expected. But then, what should she have expected, just seeing telegrams and telex messages pile up for him? He looked as if he could do with a welcome.

She crossed the street. "And you're very welcome to these parts, Mr. O'Neill," she said warmly.

Patrick looked at her gratefully. "How did you know it was me, did you know my people?"

"Who else would it be, Mr. O'Neill? And I have a foot of telegrams and messages for you up at the post office. Would you like a cup of tea and I'll give them to you?"

"Now that's what I call efficiency." He threw back his head and laughed.

Mrs. Whelan led him through the post office to her room behind. She put him sitting down beside a pile of communications and put on the kettle. She said no more till she placed a cup of tea beside each of them, and some buttered soda bread. Yes, a very handsome man, she thought, he was going to cause a bit of a stir. Mrs. Whelan smiled to herself, thinking of all the excitement there would be.

Patrick read the telegrams from Gerry Power, the man who had replaced Tom Brady as his second in command all those years ago. He read the telegrams from Rachel too quickly, and put them into a different pocket. He felt the heat coming back into his body with the strong tea and the thick buttered bread. She was a gracious woman, this Mrs. Whelan. No curiosity about him, no need to talk and chatter like so many women, telling you their business and wanting to know yours. If they were all going to be like this in Mountfern, he had made the best move in his life.

Despite the hard, silent disapproving face of Gerry Power.

Despite the hurt, bewildered eyes of Rachel Fine.

Despite the confused chirrupings of little Grace.

And the stern scornful look of Kerry, the tall golden-haired son. The boy he had promised to take back home. The boy who said so little to him these days that Patrick had no idea what he was thinking about, at all.

Fergus wondered what it would be like to be a solicitor in a big place where you had no idea what the day would bring. In other places he supposed he could stand on his own doorstep and stretch without four passers-by asking him had he a bad back like his father, and sending messages in to Miss Purcell or advising him on the rather glum-looking window boxes. Still he wouldn't change it. And he could escape and get on with his life a bit, as he had told his father last night, if he went twenty-five miles to a dance organized by a rugby club. There were grand girls there who wouldn't expect to be taken to Meagher's jewelry shop next morning if a kiss and a cuddle had been part of the night's entertainment.

He saw Kate Ryan walking up River Road and turning into Bridge Street. She waved.

"Are you out with your stopwatch in case I'm a second late?"

"Just waiting for the bells to ring for mass. If there had been one peal you'd have been fired. No, I was having a good stretch actually."

"Don't you look like a young Greek god. Did you have a good time in Ballykane last night?"

His arms dropped to his sides mid-stretch. "How did you know where I was . . . ?"

"I was there myself dancing away beside you. You never saw me?"

"No you weren't, don't be ridiculous, who said it to you?"

"Jack Coyne. Some fellow couldn't start his car and rang Jack at all hours in the morning to go and pick him up."

"God, you can't do much in this place, can you? And there was I thinking it wasn't such a bad place. No surprises."

"It isn't a bad place. Do you want surprises?"

They were walking companionably in to start the day's work as the church bells began to peal at ten to nine to let the devout know it was time to put on the hats and pick up the missals for daily mass. The early devout would already have attended seven o'clock mass, said this morning by a perplexed Father Hogan, whose mind was as much on the dripping and drunken housekeeper as it was on the liturgy.

"No I don't want surprises," Fergus said. "In the last few hours I've found my father nearly burning the house down, and now you tell me Jack Coyne has the entire details of my little escapade last night."

Kate was at her desk opening mail. It was a job they did together since the invention of the filing system. Kate wanted to check that the young master knew not only where to find everything but where to file it as well. She had arranged a bowl of flowers, a blotter and pens on his famous table by the window where every document used to end up in the old days.

"I think I'll lay off surprises for a while," Fergus said, throwing a heap of papers on the floor beside him out of habit, and picking them up sheepishly to place them in the pending tray on the desk.

"You know they say they come in threes," said Kate absently, as she began to read a letter which had been delivered by hand. It was a request from Patrick J. O'Neill that Slattery and Slattery should act for him in his application to build a hotel and apply for a pub license as well. He thought that since he was going to live in the area he would very much like the local man to act on his behalf.

"God Almighty, he's going to build a hotel," Kate said, standing up.

Fergus had come to read the letter over her shoulder. "I won't act for him—he can find his own attorney and counsellors and whatever they call them over there," he said after a long silence.

She looked at him blankly. "Why won't you act for him?"

"Because if his application is granted and he gets his license, then he'll open a pub . . ."

"You have to take his business . . ." Kate was pale.

"I do not have to take his business, thank you. I can accept or refuse any work I like. I am not going to accept anything which is going to take the bread and butter out of your mouth." He looked angry and upset as he stood beside her and she found herself weeping on his shoulder. "Do you want to go home, and tell John?"

"No, not yet." Kate shook her head and sat down purposefully at her desk. "Not for a while. If our bread and butter's going to disappear in the pub I'd better make sure I don't lose the job in the office as well." She gave a smile to show that the emotional bit was over.

"You'd never lose a job here," Fergus said gently. "I just wish it paid better. Maybe you should tell John now, before someone else does."

"Nobody else will. It's silly but last night he was saying, when we were sitting out in the side garden bit . . . he was saying that nothing bad was ever going to happen to us. Maybe this isn't very bad. I want to have a think before I tell him. That's all." There were no words to say. It was about as bad as it could be. Fergus didn't say anything. He took off his glasses and polished them. He saw Kate looking at him gratefully.

"All right. All right, I know I have a weak face without them, I'm putting them back on. Let's open more mail, shall we? Who knows what other little surprises may be lurking in these nice brown envelopes?"

Patrick O'Neill drove to the Grange, some three miles from Mountfern. It was a big, gracious house that had always been in the Johnson family. It had known good days and bad, and just now was going through a fairly prosperous phase. Marian Johnson had discovered that there was a business in offering riding holidays. City people and English visitors liked to come and stay in the vaguely country house atmosphere. The Johnsons always left a decanter of sherry out instead of charging people by the glass, it gave them the feeling that they were guests on a country weekend. Last summer Marian had quite a few Americans, who usually came in groups. This big, handsome O'Neill man was different.

He said he would like to ride, but since he had not sat on a horse's back for years he wondered if it was foolish to begin again at the age of forty-eight.

Marian Johnson aged thirty-nine looked into his blue eyes with the crinkly laugh lines coming away from them at the sides. No, she thought that was the perfect age to start again. She would take him riding herself.

Marian was fair-haired, but no one would ever have called her a blonde; her hair was wispy and flyaway, and no style ever seemed to tame it. She had a big soft bosom and often wore twinsets, mauves or pale green light jumpers with a matching cardigan. She looked her best when her hair was tidied into a net and under a bowler hat, and her soft drooping bosom gathered into the mannish coat of the hunt. The Johnsons were people who considered themselves of importance in the neighborhood; normally Marian would never have shown the slightest interest in any American visitor. A man passing through, a man with no family, no background or stake in the area. Marian would have little time to waste. Yet there was something about Patrick O'Neill that attracted her.

"Does your wife like the idea of riding?" Marian asked.

"My wife passed away this year," Patrick said.

"Oh, I am most awfully sorry."

"She had been in poor health for a long time," murmured Patrick.

Marian said no more; she arranged for the horses and assured Patrick that there would be no broken bones.

Companionably they walked the horses over to a stile where she advised Patrick to mount his animal.

"Go on," she laughed. "It's more dignified than all this getting a leg up by putting your foot in someone's hand. It's like stepping on."

"It's too easy," Patrick complained. "I don't mind the undignified way."

Astride their horses, they rode down the quiet lane with the fuchsia-filled hedges. Marian pointed out landmarks, towers on small hills and when they came to the corner she said, "And that's Fernscourt . . . they say it's going to be . . ."

"I bought it. It's mine," he said quickly.

"Of *course,* they said you'd be here soon. How stupid of me not to recognize it must have been you, I thought you were another tourist.

Well, well, what a beautiful place you've got for yourself, Mr. O'Neill, and will you be making a home of it, or what?"

"I'm going to be the opposition, Miss Johnson," he said simply. "I'm going to build a hotel. I don't know whether we will be exactly in competition or not; I feel sure that we will be going for different markets. But what I was hoping was that we might be able to cooperate . . . If you wanted to expand your riding school say, and incorporate some of the guests from Fernscourt . . . ?" He looked at her openly and eagerly.

It was very honest of him to come right out and say it straight, she thought. Another man might have sniffed around her hotel to steal a few ideas before declaring his hand.

"Do you know anything about the hotel business?" she asked.

"I have one small motel in New Jersey. I bought it really for tax purposes, so I'm not what you'd call experienced. But I have bars and restaurants, so I guess you could say I know something about what the public wants. Only the New York public mind you, but New York is pretty cosmopolitan, and it might be a good sample of what all kinds of people want." He wasn't only after the American package-tour business, he explained, he wanted local people to feel involved. It was to be their place too. Too long the walls of Fernscourt had kept them out. For nearly a hundred and fifty years the real Irish people of the parish had been refused access to places that rightly belonged to them. That wouldn't be the way anymore.

"I don't think people were refused access," Marian said. "It's been a ruin for years. It belonged to the Land Commission, didn't it? We used to go there on picnics when I was a girl."

"No, I mean before that, when the Ferns were there, barring everyone from their door."

Marian was cheerfully vague about that side of things. "Did they? How stupid of them. They were gone long before my time, of course, but I think my father remembers them. He used to play bridge with someone called Fern. But it mightn't have been them, the people from the house. It could have been a cousin or something."

Patrick was slightly irritated by this affectionate view. He thought that perhaps Marian had been overprotected and didn't really know the story of the big house. After all, the Johnsons were Catholics, Patrick had seen the Infant of Prague in the hall and there was a picture of Our Lady of Perpetual Succor in the bedroom where he had laid his case. Suddenly the tiredness of last night began to reach him. His eyes felt heavy.

"Do you think it's a possibility . . . our getting together over some aspects of the tourist trade?" he asked Marian.

"I see unlimited possibilities," said Marian, running her tongue lightly across her lower lip and thinking that life was looking up.

Chapter IV

Now that he was here they all claimed to have been the first to meet him and the one who knew him best. Those who had been telling stories only hours ago about the certainty of the nuns or the agricultural research institute were now eager to tell how they had known all along that it was going to be a hotel. The possibilities of a big tourist undertaking were legion. Patrick O'Neill was said to have told people that this was going to be his home, and his home would be open three hundred and sixty-five days a year, no closing down in the winter leaving the boys and girls to find some other jobs for the long harsh wet months from September to Easter.

Judy Byrne was peeved to note that he had been spotted riding horses with Marian Johnson in the morning light. That was fast moving of a spectacular nature. Kate Ryan had heard that he was seen in Conway's and Dunne's, and she was sure he must have been in Foley's too. Rita Walsh, who ran the Rosemarie hair salon, had seen what she thought must have been him in the moonlight over at the ruin. Hard to see at that distance but he had looked a fine cut of a man.

Tommy Leonard's mother said that Tommy was under no circumstances to be seen running wild with that gang of young criminals he called his friends. This was a chance sent from heaven for him to better himself. Maybe his whole future could be assured if he were seen by the new owner of Fernscourt to be a sensible boy. Tommy wondered how could it sort out his future if he turned his back on his friends? But Mrs. Leonard said there were a million ways if Tommy would put his mind to it. That hotel was going to need a shop on the very premises to sell things to its visitors who mightn't want to walk the whole way to Mountfern. What more sensible than to offer the concession to the local existing stationers and booksellers? Tommy must be ready to seize the chance.

"But I'm only twelve," Tommy wailed. "How could I seize a shop in a hotel?" He saw his whole youth and adolescence trickling away standing behind counters of one sort or another.

"By the time that hotel is up and ready to have a shop you'll be well old enough to work in it," his mother said firmly.

Maggie Daly's mother couldn't understand how it was that they hadn't seen him. He was meant to have been in Sheila Whelan's, and in all three pubs on Bridge Street; he had been seen standing looking at the Stations of the Cross in the church, but Canon Moran hadn't focused on him properly and didn't want to interrupt a man at prayer, so he was no use as an informant.

Then he had been observed driving up past Coyne's wood. Could he have been going to the convent maybe? The whole thing might still have something to do with an order of cloistered nuns. The only people who knew for sure were Sheila Whelan, because he had been in the post office for an age, but of course it was hopeless trying to get anything out of Sheila. And Marian Johnson, she didn't talk to everyone easily in Mountfern, so there would be no news from that quarter.

Jack Coyne was very anxious for a description of the American who had bought Fernscourt and was going to turn it into a hotel. Very anxious indeed. Yesterday he had gotten a call from the railway station in the big town: an American wanting to hire a car. Jack had driven in to him.

"Why did a well-heeled person like yourself not hire a car from Avis or Hertz?" Jack inquired.

"Always believe in supporting the local industry," the Yank had said.

"Here for the fishing?"

"Yup," the man said.

Jack Coyne had too much on his mind to make conversation with a taciturn foreign visitor whom he would never see again. He charged the American two and a half times the normal price and gave him a poor rate for his dollar. Jack was ashen-faced trying to get a proper account of the Patrick O'Neill who had bought Fernscourt. He had an uneasy feeling that he might have cheated the man who was going to live across the river from him. The man who could have brought him the kind of wealth he never dreamed of.

Miss Barry was quite unaware that she had met Mr. O'Neill. She had been struggling under the weight of two heavy shopping bags when a man stopped to give her a lift. She had climbed clumsily into the car, opening the window with that native cunning she had when she smelled of drink. Fresh air was an ally, closed spaces were a giveaway. She told this man about the saintly Canon Moran, the angelic young Father Hogan and even sang a few bars of a song.

"Tell me does your poor wife take a drink?" she asked him suddenly. She got the reply that the late Mrs. O'Neill had not in fact been partial to liquor.

"Best way to be," Miss Barry said approvingly. "She'll live to be a hundred, God spare her."

She rattled her plastic bags which contained bottles and smiled at him beatifically.

But none of this remained in any part of her consciousness.

Patrick had indeed gone to the convent when he had been sighted driving toward Coyne's wood. He left the car at Coyne's garage and walked up the shabby ill-kept avenue to the school. Sister Laura greeted him, a small shrew-like woman, eyes dark and bright in her round face, like two currants in a bun. She saw within minutes why he was there. He was trying to work out whether this country school would in any way approach his hopes and plans for his only daughter's education.

Sister Laura was a sensible woman. She knew that it would be counterproductive to encourage this American to believe that hers was the finest educational establishment in Ireland. She spoke praisingly of the Sacred Heart Convent, the Loretto nuns, the Holy Child Order, the FCJ (Faithful Companions of Jesus), all of them excellent sisters running very highly thought of boarding schools for girls. But that was just the point. They would be boarding schools. And if Mr. O'Neill wanted his child with him, then this was the only game in town.

She didn't put it as racily as that, but Patrick realized that if she had known the phrase she would have.

She listed the disadvantages. Grace would be much more sophisticated than the simple girls who came from smallholdings over the fields to this school each day. Grace would have to learn Irish: it was compulsory in schools, and they wouldn't have any facility for her to study something else at the time Irish-language lessons were taking place. It would be fairly rough and ready; sports would not be as she had known them in the United States, the girls played camogie, a form of hockey. Sister Laura said it was the female equivalent of hurling for boys.

But on the plus side Grace would grow up with the children among whom her father intended her to live. She would be at his side, she would make friends of all kinds, which was essential if a family were to live in a small community. She would avoid the princess-in-the-castle role. Patrick had looked with dismay at the shabby building, and particularly what Sister Laura described with pride as the new extension: classrooms thrown together, without thought or design. The finish was shoddy, obviously a local builder doing it for half nothing and knowing that the nuns weren't going to complain. The library where the small nun lingered so lovingly was a big barren room lined with jerry-built shelves. Soon to contain a couple of hundred books, most of them the lives of the saints. But the nun was right, he could see all this. He knew that he would send his child to the convent. What Grace Mary O'Neill might lose on polish and a broader approach to education, she would surely gain in a sense of belonging. And that was what this journey was all about.

Sister Laura had pursed her lips over the thought of Mr. O'Neill's son being educated in Mountfern. Of course the brothers were the best in the world. But . . .

And of course one had to take into consideration that a boy, a young man would have to be prepared to make his way in the world. Especially a young man who would inherit a huge property. So, she didn't actually say that he should forget the brothers, nor was there a mention of any inadequacies. But there was a veiled hint that only a madman might entrust the son and heir to Brother Keane and his colleagues in the big red-brick school behind the church. Mention was made of Jesuits, of Benedictines and of Holy Ghost Fathers. All known to Mr. O'Neill, certainly, in the United States, she was sure, and all running exceptionally good boys' boarding schools in Ireland, for the sons of gentlemen and people who were going to get on in life. After all, with a boy it was much more important. And with a boy there wouldn't be the same sense of loss seeing the child go to boarding school.

For courtesy and diplomacy Patrick O'Neill called on Brother Keane too. He went with no sense of apology. Instead he asked the man for advice. He had to send his son as a boarder. He would be most grateful if Brother Keane could mark his card. Would he favor the Jesuits in County Kildare, the Benedictines in Limerick, the Holy Ghost or Vincentians in Dublin?

Brother Keane had never been so flattered in his life. He gave great care to his deliberations and between them the two men came up with the ideal school for Kerry O'Neill.

Patrick O'Neill felt that slowly things were placing themselves together.

He was back in Mountfern, the sale of the land was going through. He had been assured there would be no problems with the licenses. The grants toward building a hotel would be even greater than he had thought. The people were friendly from what he could judge; usual sprinkling of rogues and drunks but basically a solid place. The place his people had come from. He let his mind rest lightly on the images of his children. Grace with the beautiful curls and dimples, Grace almost twelve now, the prettiest girl in her year, the apple of his eye. And Kerry. Handsome distant Kerry. Fifteen and as tall as Patrick. No paddy features in Kerry, his face was chiseled and had classic good looks. Even as a small child.

What would his two striking children make of Mountfern? They had never really believed that he would change their lives so totally. Part of them thought it was a huge adventure, another—perhaps the greater—part would find it a wrench to leave their surroundings, their friends, the memory of the way things had always been when their mother was alive. Patrick squared his shoulders. There was to be no wallowing in the past. This had been his dream, to take his family back to the place they had come from.

This town would be their home now. It had its shortcomings. He was not so blinded with the yearning to return that he couldn't see that. The untidiness of it irritated him. An Irish village, his Irish village shouldn't have yards full of rusting, broken machinery, there should be bright paint on all the doors. There should be a fountain or something at the end of Bridge Street instead of just letting it peter out and wind away.

He had called into the local public houses, each one in turn. None of them would be any opposition to him, of course, but even more importantly he didn't think his hotel would be a threat to any of them. Dunne's looked as if it were about to do a moonlight flit,

Conway's had three serious drinkers sitting on high stools behind its grocery. You'd need radar to find out that there was a bar there at all. And in Foley's he had the distinct impression he had wandered into a private house. Matt Foley had eyed him beadily but the chat died down while he was there. No, there was only that place with the nice old sign, Ryan's, which was right opposite his new estate. He would need to handle them with tact. If anyone was going to lose by his plans for Fernscourt it would be this little place. While still incognito he had inquired about the family. He heard that the mother went out to work, a rare thing in Irish country towns, and that the business was steady. The rest of the brothers and sisters who had owned the place had all emigrated, so John Ryan had only his own family to support out of it.

Patrick had looked at it often when he had been visiting the site. He had even looked at it by moonlight last night when he was walking around his land. It had been very still with everyone asleep, and nobody knowing that he watched it from across the river.

He walked from the brothers past the church and along in front of the bridge, and looked up Bridge Street. It could be a fine town. He would make so many changes here, give people a bit of pride in their surroundings again. He would walk to Fernscourt now. This was not New York, home of the automobile, this was his place, to walk around, to stop and talk, or just to watch the river if he wanted to. Past Jack Coyne's, past a shabby little store with the name Quinn in faded lettering, then across a rickety footbridge. He would walk his land before going to introduce himself to the Ryans in that attractive little shebeen.

He heard the sound of children's voices as he walked through the laurel bushes on the path from the footbridge to the house.

Then he saw them.

A boy and girl obviously twins, dark-eyed, dark-haired and moving in exactly the same way, gestures and smiles utterly identical.

Patrick looked at them fondly.

"Hey, is it moving day?" he asked good-naturedly.

They hadn't seen him arrive. They looked at him, startled. There was no doubt in their eyes. They knew who he was, the man who had come to take away their place for playing in.

He knew he would have to walk warily. His smile was broad but it got nothing in response.

"You're packing up. Is that right?"

The dark-eyed twins talked to him alternately, one beginning a sentence and the other finishing it, as if they had always done this.

"People always come here . . ." the girl said defensively.

"Always as far as *anyone* can remember," supported the boy.

"So it's not as if it was trespassing . . ."

"Or being on private property . . ."

Patrick gave a big infectious laugh.

"But I know that, I *know*. I saw your home last night, it was mighty impressive. I came up to see the place by moonlight. Have you lot ever been here in the moonlight?" They shook their heads.

"It's very strange. It has a life of its own, all the shadows seem to mean something. You'd really like it." He spoke as if he were their own age, suggesting they do something as out of their world as going off on midnight treks across the river. Mammy and Daddy would kill them.

"Come some evening with me, I'll square it with your folks, and I'll go off for a walk by myself and leave you in your . . . in your house?" He sought for the right word to describe the dismantled room.

"It's not going to be knocked down, is it?"

He answered the girl indirectly. "Changed a bit," he said. "You know, roofs and good firm walls."

"You mean it *is* to be knocked down."

He decided not to talk baby talk to the girl with the big dark eyes under her bangs of black hair.

"That's it, knocked down to be rebuilt. They tell me a lot of these old walls are dangerous, you could tip them over with your little finger. Not the things to build on, unfortunately."

She nodded silently. The boy nodded too. It was as though they had both accepted what he said in exactly the same way and were thinking about it.

"Still, it won't be for a while. No need to move all your things." He indicated with his head their box of possessions.

"If it's coming down anyway . . ." Michael began.

"There's really not any point . . ." Dara took up.

"In leaving things here . . ."

"That'll have to come out anyway."

"Sure, everyone's got to do what they've got to do. All I'm saying is that there's no great rush. It will be weeks before anyone gets as far as this room. What do you call it, by the way?" He smiled at them, looking from one to the other. They were not to be won over.

"What do you call what?" the girl asked.

"This . . . this room . . . do you have a special name for it or anything?"

"No. No special name," she said.

"It used to be the morning room," the boy said. The first offer.

"Not by us. We didn't call it the morning room. Or any name." The dark girl was giving nothing away.

"I guess it was the morning room because it got the morning sun. It faces east, southeast. That's right, would you say?"

But the boy felt he had been too friendly, and his sister was suggesting they leave.

"We've really got to go now."

"Come back again, anytime; you're welcome here always," he said. Somehow he knew it was the wrong thing to have said.

"Well, like you always were. When a place is special you don't need anyone to welcome you to it. That's right, isn't it?"

They nodded at him, shoulders slightly less tense, their stance not so hostile.

"So we have to be off," the boy said, picking up one side of the box that contained their life in this room.

"So goodbye," said the girl, picking up the other side. They walked away from him, two little figures probably the same age as his Grace. Reasonably well cared for, grubby knees and dirty hands from playing . . . or indeed packing all their house things—they must have been covered in clay and dust. He watched them through the open walls of the house. They headed not for the town and the big bridge across into Bridge Street itself, but they went the other way toward River Road. Going to cross that little footbridge . . . maybe they belonged to that crook Jack Coyne?

Patrick was glad he hadn't asked them if they were twins. It was obvious they were and yet people always had a habit of asking the obvious. He found it very irritating even when it was well meant, like when people said to him "You're an American!" with an air of discovery. They were fine kids, a little prickly, especially the girl. He'd catch up with them again, give them some job maybe, make them a few pounds. Or maybe they might resent that. He'd see. And when Grace came over, she'd charm them to bits anyway.

Now to see the Ryans in the poky little pub and then back to the dark room with the heavy mahogany furniture which had been in the Johnson family for generations, and the picture of Our Lady of Perpetual Succor which had helped them through some of the bad times. And a long, long sleep.

Kate had come back early. Fergus was right. She couldn't really concentrate and John would have to be told before anyone else came with the news.

The angelus was ringing as she walked down River Road. She looked across the banks and tried to imagine what it would be like with a huge hotel, a car park, with signs for a pub, with music maybe . . . Americans did things in style. She called into Loretto Quinn's little shop for a bag of sugar and a dozen candles. She always tried to give Loretto the turn; the small white face behind the counter moved Kate to pity. Loretto and Barney Quinn had saved and saved for a business, any business. They had done any work to get the deposit on the tumbledown place. They could be seen night and day working to make it right. They knew they were no competition to the shops on Bridge Street, so Barney Quinn had bought a van in which to do deliveries.

A week after the van was delivered, Barney threw it into reverse and went into the river. It happened so quickly that Loretto never even knew. She was still out in the back filling bags of potatoes when the alarm was raised and she realized half the town was outside her front door with ropes and pulleys trying to get her husband, dead now in his van, out of the River Fern. There had never been any color or much life in her face after that. The child she had been expecting was stillborn, and she kept the shabby little shop as a memory of her young husband and in honor of the way things might have been.

Jack Coyne had been helpful about the unpaid-for van and the insurance and everything. People had been kind at the time. Not everyone continued to be helpful like Mrs. Ryan. Loretto knew it would be very easy for her to get things cheaper in Bridge Street where she went to work, or to get them delivered, but nearly every day she called in for something. Today she was early.

"You're not taken sick coming home early?" she asked, concerned.

"Ah, not at all Loretto, nothing would make me feel badly, thank God. No, it's light there this morning and I thought I'd come on back to John to give him a hand. Not that there's likely to be any custom much for another hour."

"Will the place across make any difference to you? Jack Coyne was in earlier. He wondered would it take any of your custom. I said it would be a different class of person entirely . . . ."

"Thanks, Loretto." Kate should have left earlier. John Ryan must know by now that his livelihood was threatened and that the days of Ryan's, Whiskey Bonder, were numbered.

John was sitting on a high stool reading the paper. He put down the newspaper automatically as the door opened.

"That's never the time!" he said, amazed, looking up at the old clock and back at his watch trying to work it out.

"No. I came home a bit early." Kate put down her parcels and sat up as if she were a customer.

"Couldn't wait for a ball of malt?" he teased her.

"John."

"What is it?" His face showed that he knew something was wrong. "Are you all right, do you feel all right?"

"I'm fine." Suddenly she was weary; she knew it would be an uphill struggle trying to make him realize how serious things were going to be.

"What *is* it then?"

"Did you hear what's happening to Fernscourt? They're going to make it into a hotel, have a bar. Americans are going to stay there, and there'll be a bar the size of a football field. He's put in for planning permission."

"I heard that it was going to be a hotel all right. Tommy was round with the mineral water deliveries. Oh, he left the invoice there on the shelf, by the way, it's behind the—"

"Will you stop bleating on about invoices? It's mighty few of those we'll be seeing in the future. Did you hear what I said?"

"I heard you, Kate. There's no need to shout like a fishwife."

"Like a what?"

"A fishwife, look at you; you have your hands on your hips even. Stop being so impatient, and let's discuss this thing properly."

"I'm the one who ran the whole way back from Fergus as soon as I heard about it. Don't you think I want to discuss it properly?"

"Yes, Kate. But not in public. Not in the middle of the bar."

Kate looked around at the empty room.

"God Almighty, have you lost your mind? Who's here except Leopold, are you afraid the dog's going to start gossiping about us and our business around town?"

"Don't let's start something that we'll have to cut off as soon as someone comes in that door."

"All right, all right." She made a gesture with her hands as if calming things down. "Very well, but in the meantime do you mind if we talk about what's going to become of us, or would you rather read me Curly Wee out of the paper, or have a discussion about the weather?"

"We can't know what to think, until we know what's going to happen. How many times do I tell you not to go off at half cock about every single thing? We'll hear in good time what he's going to do. It might be the making of us for all we know. A whole lot of new people coming to the place, a lot of business we never had before. How many times have we wished that we were a tourist area where the people came on holidays? Now we will be, if what Tommy said is true."

"The making of us; the making of us. How could it be anything except the end of us? For as many times as we said we'd like tourists, haven't we been thanking the stars that they're all so dozy in there in Foley's and Conway's and half packed to leave in Dunne's? We never had any competition, and even then we barely make a living. How can you be so blind?"

A flash of annoyance crossed John's big, good-natured face.

"Listen to me, I know you work hard, I know you put in all the hours that God gives you making a life for us, but answer me this, why am I being blind? What should I have done? Should I have bought the place myself? Or killed the fellow who did? Come on now, tell me. I'm standing here minding what I agree is at the moment a very slow business, some would say non-existent . . . and hoping that there's going to be some kind of good spin-off instead of doom and disaster for us, and you come rushing in the door shouting at me like a tinker's woman and saying I'm blind. That's a lot of help, Kate, thank you very much."

Before she could reply the door opened and in came Marian Johnson, face flushed and wispy hair blowing all directions. Rita Walsh of the Rosemarie hair salon said that she had often known people with two crowns in their head of hair, but Marian Johnson had three. The woman couldn't be blamed for looking like a refined haystack. Marian was anxious to know if John Ryan could oblige her with a bottle of Jack Daniel's.

John Ryan couldn't. He had Scotch all right, but nothing else except Irish whiskey. They might have it in the town, he supposed.

"Very fancy tastes you're getting above at the Grange," he said companionably. He couldn't have said anything more welcome. Marian was dying to release the news. It was for the American, the man who was going to buy Fernscourt, or who had bought it in fact, but was going to open a hotel there. She went on and on, words falling over each other in excitement. There were going to be fishermen, not people like from here, not just the visitors from England who stayed in guest houses, but rich Americans with their own rods going to come and fish the Fern for pike and rudd, for bream and perch. And there were going to be Americans who would want to ride horses, they would even come in winter so they could hunt. They'd be here the whole year round. She was unaware of the silence that she spoke to. But eventually even Marian ran out of wind.

"Isn't it great?" she said, looking from one to the other.

"I'd have thought you'd be very put out. Isn't that all your kind of business that he's going to be taking?" Kate said, avoiding the look of caution that her husband was trying to beam at her.

Marian tossed her head. "Heavens no, isn't it all to the good, isn't it going to build the whole thing up for all of us? They're going to want horses. Apparently I'll be expanding all that side of our business. It's going to change the whole place." Marian hugged herself almost girlishly at the thought of it.

"That's what I'm afraid of," Kate said. "That it's going to change the whole place."

"Oh, Kate Ryan, you're as young as I am," tinkled Marian, who was most definitely the older of the two. "Don't be an old stick-in-the-mud. It's going to transform your lives. Think of all the people that'll come tripping across that footbridge there to have a drink in your place. It will be just what you need."

John seized her words as if they were a lifeline. "That's just what I was saying to Kate when you came in the door. It could be the making of us. It could be the bit of luck we were always hoping for." His face was bright with enthusiasm.

Kate watched, wordless, as her husband and Marian Johnson made plans for the future. They never talked about all the people who would like to go and have a drink in the big hotel, who would trip across the footbridge in the other direction. She looked at John and tried to work out whether he really believed this optimistic line of chat, or if he was only trying to buoy up the Ryan family. She decided that he really believed it; he wanted so much for things to turn out well that he refused to look at any other possibility. She felt a mixture of annoyance that he should be so naïve, and a protective, almost maternal anxiety because she had this cold fear that things were indeed going to change, and that something very bad was about to happen.

The twins crept in through the back door. They were filthy and carrying a big battered box between them. They looked like small dark criminals. They both put their fingers on their lips, warning Carrie not to cry out.

"Oh God, you'll get killed," Carrie said, half pleased and half worried on their behalf. They'd been up to no good whatever they'd been doing.

"We'll be clean by the time Mammy gets back," Michael said to reassure her.

"She's back already," Carrie cried triumphantly. "She'll take you apart so she will."

Carrie, who greatly feared Mrs. Ryan's hurricane-like visits to the kitchen, and her great ability to see things that were not done right, was always guiltily pleased when the wrath fell elsewhere. Carrie had long straight hair that fell into her frightened eyes—except when she saw Mrs. Ryan looking, then she took a barrette from her apron pocket. She was a mousy little thing who could look very nice when she tidied herself up. Mrs. Ryan was always finding a blouse or a brooch or some little thing for her. Carrie only wore this finery on her day off when she walked four miles back to the farm from which she had been glad to escape.

She was fine unless she was fussed, and this was fussing her, the twins having skipped school and dragging this big box guiltily upstairs. Nobody ever came to Carrie's kitchen during the mornings except young Declan. And now here were Dara and Michael home, way in advance. And the mistress was home early too. Really it was very troublesome. Carrie always arranged to have the kitchen looking well when Mrs. Ryan came back at one o'clock; the pots were washed and put away. Now it looked a mess, and she was bound to be criticized. She sighed heavily and started to clear up the things that were most likely to offend.

Gently Michael and Dara eased themselves into the bathroom to shake out their crumpled school clothes and wipe off most of the grime. *What* was Mammy doing home so early, on this of all days? They had banked on at least an hour to get themselves to rights. This was the very first time they had ever played hooky from school. Dara had told Sister Laura that she had a pain in her tummy, and Michael had told Brother Kevin that he had eaten too many potato chips. Sister Laura had been understanding in case it might be Dara's first period, Brother Kevin had been dismissive and said what could you expect of a boy brought up in a pub but to eat like a pig all the rubbish in packets that was put in front of him? But it was too dangerous for them to go to school that day. If the man had been wandering around Fernscourt in the middle of the night they had to go and take their things away. Somehow they both knew that at the same time and realized it had to be done. They never dreamed they'd meet the man himself.

The Ryans never ate lunch together as a family since John was always in the bar. And the first rule of the house was that the children never appeared in the bar at all. John said that most of his customers came there to escape from households of screaming children racing around the place, and they mustn't be allowed to see a hint of the same thing in Ryan's. So Dara and Michael would have had no idea who was in the bar as they sat down to lunch.

Eddie and Declan had come in at the normal time.

"You were quick," Eddie said to Michael. Normally they all raced together from the brothers, beyond the bridge down River Road. Dara's convent was up the other way, past the Rosemarie hair salon and Jack Coyne's. Nobody could tell whether or not she had come home. It was only Michael who might have been missed.

"Yes, we got out a bit early." Michael looked from under his lashes to see if Mammy had made anything of this exchange, but her mind seemed to be miles away. She hadn't even noticed how crushed their clothes were from being bundled in a bag.

The twins hadn't decided what to do for the afternoon. They would have to walk toward school of course, and then they could meet somewhere else. Eddie and Declan had no afternoon school so there would be no need for Michael to go all the way to the brothers. There were a host of possibilities. But before any were settled, the door of the pub opened and Daddy came through.

"Kate, Kate, come out and meet Mr. O'Neill who's bought Fernscourt. He's called to pay his respects. And bring the children too, he says he'd like to meet them."

Leopold, who was the most antisocial dog in the world, decided for once that he was included in the invitation too. Looking exactly like an advertisement from a Cruelty to Animals brochure, he walked ahead of them, sidling and cringing as if expecting a blow at every turn.

Kate smoothed her skirt and shepherded the children in front of her. There was time only to wipe the excess of food from Declan's mouth; to pause and titivate them would have been a weakness with the door open and the great O'Neill waiting for them. Declan and

Eddie hung back and had to be pushed forward. Dara and Michael were equally unwilling. In fact they both looked as if they had been caught out in some crime. Kate supposed they felt awkward meeting the man whose arrival they had hated so much. She didn't realize how deadly accurate her first thought was. They had been caught out. He was going to say he had met them this very morning. They would be discovered.

Kate was surprised at his looks. Like a handsome Irishman on a fair day with a drove of young bullocks to sell. Not like an American tycoon. He had a tweed jacket in a pepper and salt color. It was very well cut. It would suit John, she thought, hide some of his stomach. This man was big, with bright blue eyes and a million laugh lines. His big hand was stretched to her.

"Mrs. Kathleen Ryan. My own wife, the Lord have mercy on her, was Kathleen too. I'm glad to know you."

He *seemed* glad to know her.

She had never gotten such a shock in her life.

All morning she had been thinking of him as the enemy, and here he was standing in their own pub, all smiles. No man could do that if he was going to take all your business. Even in America, where you had to be shrewd and tough to get on, they wouldn't do that. There were half a dozen customers all eager and interested to see the introductions. They, too, would be introduced, they knew. But first the children.

"These are the twins, Dara and Michael, and here's Eddie. Take your arm from over your face, Eddie and Declan. Declan, come out from behind me."

He repeated their names slowly. *That's* why Americans were so good at remembering people. They didn't just say how do you do, or hello. They actually repeated the name.

"Dara . . . there's a name. Is it short for something?"

"It means oak tree. You know Kildare. That's Cill Dara, the churchyard of the oak tree."

"Oak tree . . . Isn't that something? And Michael. That's the archangel, I guess?"

"And my grandfather," Michael said more prosaically.

"And you'll come back and spend more mornings in Fernscourt, I hope," he said.

The twins were glum. Here it was. The discovery.

"They will on their holidays, if they aren't in the way," Kate said, filling the silence. "But these days it's all schoolwork, I'm afraid. No idle mornings playing in Fernscourt until they get their holidays."

Dara closed her eyes.

Michael looked at him in desperation.

"Sure," said Patrick O'Neill. "Sure, I know that, but after school or at weekends or any time. The place is always there and I'm sure you must love it, what with living so near and everything." He wasn't going to say anything.

They looked at him in amazement.

John and Kate Ryan also exchanged glances of relief. Whatever else was going to happen, at least this big man understood somehow that the place was important to the twins. What a relief that they would not be getting into trouble over trespass or being a nuisance. The man in full view of the whole bar had literally invited the children to continue playing in the house.

"That's very kind of Mr. O'Neill; thank him, children," Kate said.

"Thank you," said Dara.

"Very much," finished Michael.

It was time for them to go back to school. They were hurried out back through the house again. The children had never been known to go out on to River Road through the pub entrance. Kate went silent behind the bar and helped to serve. Nobody would move until the introductions had been properly made. Jimbo Doyle, the man who did a bit of everything in Mountfern, was particularly pleased. If he could be present as a friend of the establishment it might mean work on the new place across the river. He was a big fair man with hair like straw and a healthy red face. He often wore a check shirt and looked about to break into a square dance at any moment.

Charlie, who worked in Daly's, would be sure to be a frequent visitor there anyway, with milk and cream. Unless, of course, the man was going to have his own cow, his own dairy. Maybe Charlie could ask him now.

Patrick O'Neill was open with all of them. He wasn't at all sure if they would have their own cows. Someday possibly. But not for a good bit. He'd be needing all the milk, butter and cream that Daly's Dairy would provide. Charlie felt very important to be the bearer of this news and specially so when Mr. O'Neill remembered his name.

"See you again then, Charlie," and a cheerful wave as he was leaving to ride down River Road and back to Bridge Street to Mrs. Daly with the good tidings.

Jimbo Doyle's red face was positively scarlet after the encounter.

Mr. O'Neill said that the work on the site was all in the hands of an overseer, a Brian Doyle who came from the big town sixteen miles away. Possibly Jimbo and Brian were related? It could be, couldn't it? Jimbo shook his head ruefully. Ah no, there were lots of Doyles and if this man was a building contractor and in a big way over in the town then it wasn't likely that he would be any family to Jimbo. But still, maybe it was an omen. If the man's name was Doyle, he might find it hard to refuse another Doyle.

"He won't refuse you, Jim," Patrick O'Neill said. "I'll tell him I met you and that your work has been highly spoken of."

Kate polished glasses with a snow-white cloth and watched the big, handsome American speaking easily with them all. One by one they left, secure in the knowledge that they would be remembered, and somehow warmed by his interest. Kate felt admiring and then a little fearful. It wasn't that she feared he would forget these men in their working clothes, with their humble hopes. No, she was afraid more that he *would* remember them. And this all meant that he was very determined to come back to some kind of roots. Roots which he was finding it increasingly hard to establish, as he'd just told them in the bar. Nobody, not even the older men, could remember any O'Neills around the place, not living on the demesne in Fernscourt anyway. There were O'Neills up the other side of the town, the far end of Bridge Street. But Patrick's kith nobody could recall. "It was all a long time ago," they said, as if to forgive themselves and each other.

Yet the man who had come back to build here remembered it all. As if he had been present.

Kate made the glasses shine as she puzzled over it. A man like that must have another wife in mind, someone in America, an Irish-American widow perhaps. Would she be coming over too? He must be worth a fortune. Look at what he must have paid out already for site investigation, and that was before he started work on the house. He must be very determined to make this a success. And if he did, what would happen to them?

They were alone in the bar now, the three of them. Patrick had let them buy him a drink to welcome him to these parts; now they let him buy one for them. Kate's small port felt as if it were choking her, but she drank it and smiled at the handsome man with the open face, the open shirt and the well-cut tweed jacket.

"To the dream." He raised his glass. "John, Kate . . . I want you to be part of the dream as well. I want us all to share in it."

"Well sure, we'll be glad to share anything there is to share," John said, a bit at a loss.

"I'll drink to the dream," Kate said. "And to your happiness and success across the river. You won't find it too tame for you after New York?"

"All my life I wanted to come back here," he said simply. "In the middle of big deals and buying more neighborhood bars I always said to myself . . . Patrick, this is one step nearer coming home."

"Imagine that, and you weren't born and brought up here at all." John shook his head in wonderment.

Kate hoped her voice didn't sound tinny. "And what exactly do you plan, or have you worked it out yet?"

She tried to listen to the words as they came out, and wondered, did they betray her anxiety. If they had, the big man didn't seem to notice. He leaned over the bar eagerly, and like a boy told his plans. The house was going to rise again, like it had been before. There were old pictures and drawings, and he had people working on those country homes built all over the land in the 1780s; it would all be in keeping and in the right period. It was going to be a hotel for the kind of Irish-American who wanted to feel welcome, and as if he had come home. Limo services would be arranged to take them to their own part of the country so that they could find their own roots. There would be fishing and horse riding, and in the correct seasons there would be shooting and hunting. Very few of the Irish who had emigrated to America had any of the gentlemanly sports like these in their background. They had gone to the States because other gentlemen, gentlemen of a different race and religion, had ousted them from their homes. It would be a real homecoming in every sense of the word for any American of Irish stock.

And there would be names on the rooms instead of numbers. Like the O'Brien room, or the Lynch room, or the Kennedy room, or whatever. Kate listened to the list and gave her little oohs and aahs to coincide with the genuine ones of her husband. Her lower lip was almost flattened with the effort of staying calm until he came to the bit about the bar.

Oh, there would be a cocktail lounge certainly, for pre-dinner drinks where orders could be taken before guests went into the dining room. And then there would be the Thatch Bar. A thatched cottage on the grounds in what Patrick thought must be the exact spot his own ancestors lived before they were thrown out on the road. There was a lot of talk about ancestors being forced to workhouses before

Kate could get him silkily back to the Thatch Bar. A real traditional Irish Bar, with fiddlers playing and every night some little entertainment, like Irish dancing or a singer, or some old storyteller telling a tale.

And there would be ordinary prices in it too, not fancy ones. Patrick O'Neill wanted his own to come to his bar, not just the gentry. The pint would cost the same in the Thatch Bar as it would anywhere else. It would attract the local people in and the visitors would really and genuinely get to know them.

Kate looked at the boyish face in astonishment. What kind of a mind did you need to get on in America if this was the proof of it sitting opposite her? What did he *mean*, he didn't want just the gentry? What gentry would go to a flash place like this anyway? Could he see the Walters, or the Harrises, or the Johnsons from the Grange even, spending an evening in the Thatch Bar? The man must be mad. But what was he thinking about, telling them these plans? He must know that he would ruin their trade if this all came to pass. He must know they would try to oppose his license on the ground that the area was well covered with licensed premises already. What was he talking about, telling them that he wanted to share a dream with them?

Kate looked at John for some support, and found that she couldn't read his face. It was just as it had been when he was talking to Marian Johnson earlier on, smiling and thoughtful. Was he really taken in by all this patter, or had his heart missed a beat when he heard of the Thatch Bar and all the dangers it looked like bringing on top of them? She could find no words to speak; everything she wanted to say would sound harsh and hysterical. She wanted to take this O'Neill man by the lapels and look straight into his smiling blue eyes. Burrow into them until she could see the truth. She would like to beg him not to ruin their business. She wanted to tell him that, as he had so much money, and so many chances, could he not just have Fernscourt as a home, to entertain his American friends. Surely he didn't *need* a bar business there. Then that mood vanished, and she wanted to tell him there would be no further pretense at amicable conversation. She and her husband would oppose his getting a license, and they would raise everyone in the neighborhood to support them in their case.

But Kate Ryan knew with heavy heart that she could do nothing of the sort. Had she not seen the gratified delight already on everyone's face? There would be a very slender army to raise against Patrick O'Neill.

John was asking all kinds of questions, idiotic questions, Kate thought, as if he were delighted to see such opposition arriving on his doorstep.

Would the guests go around in buses? What part of America would they come from mainly?

Kate could have killed him for his eager interest in the unimportant side of things. What did it matter if these visitors traveled by bus or by wheelbarrow? Who could care less if they came from one part of America or another? They didn't know *any* parts of America, for God's sake. And yet little by little John was learning more about the whole undertaking across the river than anyone else would have learned from this clever American. There could be a purpose to his questions. She looked hard at John, fighting the lump in her throat which made her want to burst into tears. He looked so good and patient; he had worked for so many years at a job that he would never have chosen. It would be cruel to see it swept away by this successful man who could have had power and riches anywhere else on the earth.

Kate knew she should join in the conversation. She had been conspicuously silent. In fact she saw John glance at her, his face still cheerful and his smile all-embracing.

"Well I can't tell you, Patrick, what an excitement all this will be." He looked at his wife as if he were leaving the way open for her to add her words of delight and welcome. Kate was still too full to trust herself to conversation.

"The excitement is mainly mine," Patrick said. "If you knew how many times I dreamed of this, and often I had to say it aloud to myself, you know like a chant or a prayer. It will happen; it will happen." He looked at them both with an engaging smile.

"Now I almost have to tell myself it *has* happened, it *has* happened." He looked so boyish and delighted it was hard not to like him.

Kate decided to speak. "And how would we come into all this? How can we . . . um . . . help you in it all?" she asked. Her voice was definitely faltering and she wasn't far from tears.

"But that's what good neighbors will always do," he cried triumphantly. "I'll get my guests to come to you, send them over to you before lunch or in the early afternoon . . . when maybe you could do with an injection." He looked around the empty bar and left a short significant pause. "I guess this would be a good time to send a group over for an Irish coffee or something. And you can tell your regulars when there's entertainment on in the Thatch that they might like to come and see. Or better, any of them who are talented, if they want to come and perform. Play for people. It's their place now." He smiled from one to another.

"I guess you know that it's a principle of business that one successful establishment leads to another. Business grows out of custom to an area. Mark my words, there's going to be new places starting up out on River Road before we know it. By the end of the sixties they'll be asking where Bridge Street is . . . they'll all think that River Road is the center of the universe, and the Ryans and O'Neills will have been here from the outset."

John was smiling back at him. Was John Ryan under the net? Had the web of companionship and complicity caught him? Kate realized that there were going to be very few people who would not be caught in that net. Even her own Dara and Michael, who had vowed never to speak to the new owner of Fernscourt, were flashing him grateful smiles and friendly glances when he said that they could continue playing there.

So far only Fergus Slattery had managed to remain aloof, and he hadn't met the American yet; perhaps he would be bowled over like the others had been. Kate smiled on, though she felt there was a distant ache in her face. If John could smile so could she. Anyway there was nothing to be gained by showing her hand now. She must remember that if she came straight out with all her worries and hostilities, it would do nothing but harm. Living all these years with the solid John Ryan had taught her that much anyway.

So she accepted with a dimpling smile when the laughing American begged to be allowed to buy them one more drink so that they could toast the success of River Road and especially those who were in at the very start.

Fergus Slattery heard that the American was doing the rounds. He didn't want to be in. His father had gone fishing; he put a closed sign on the door and headed out.

"Where will I say you've gone?" Miss Purcell asked, not because she thought anyone would call, but because she wanted to know what was taking him away from his business in the middle of the afternoon.

"Go out on the doorstep every hour and say to the crowds that

Sergeant Sheehan and I have raised a posse of men and we've gone out to see if we can bring in any poachers. Dead or alive. That should satisfy them," he said.

"You have a very strange way of going on, Master Fergus. It's not every woman that could stay in this house and put up with it."

"Haven't we always said you are a woman in a million, a woman different to all others?" Fergus said, and he was gone before she could put another question to him.

He took the car not because he had any idea where he was going, but at least in the car he wouldn't have to answer half a dozen questions about where he was going in the middle of the afternoon. He waved and nodded as he drove up Bridge Street to the main road. He saw the signpost to Dublin and parked for a while. Suppose he was in Dublin, he wouldn't be even slightly affected by a licensing application. He would do it; there was no chance that he would know the people it would hurt, there was no way in Dublin that he might already feel slighted by this applicant. Without meeting Patrick O'Neill, Fergus was somehow prejudiced against him. He had heard about the way he had bought the fishing rights and it was perfectly legal, the way he had organized the searches on the land, and dealt with the Land Commission, was all above board. If in the future he was seen to have had drinks with this politician and with that local councillor, nobody was going to cast an aspersion. This was how things were done. The planning permissions and the license would go through and he would build his monstrosity. After a few years it might be a white elephant and it could be written off as a tax loss. Patrick O'Neill was of the breed who would start again. Somewhere else, different scheme.

Fergus was old-fashioned, he wanted things to remain the same. The same kind of quiet practice, the same kind of food. He didn't like moving on, cutting losses. He didn't at all like the notion of a stage-Irish bar across the Fern, and taking all the trade from Kate Ryan. It took a lot to upset that woman, and today she had left early, saying truthfully that she couldn't concentrate. Perhaps he would call in and see had they any news. A half of Guinness would go down very well on a warm summer afternoon.

He decided to leave the car parked where it was near the main road to the big town in one direction and Dublin in the other. He could walk down that lane which came out through Jack Coyne's wood, right onto River Road, not far from Ryan's. He whistled as he walked. Partly from the sheer freedom of being out among the trees, and partly because he wanted to cheer himself up over this Yank business. The rhododendrons were out in a great purple show, and darker red ones too. In other countries, Fergus thought, this place would be a public park with manicured grass and seats and litter bins. As he was debating to himself whether this would be good or bad he came across four frightened dark eyes.

Kate Ryan's twins Dara and Michael who were quite obviously meant to be at school, and had no business, any more than himself, wandering the woods on a working afternoon.

"You see, Mr. Slattery . . ."

"We didn't exactly say at home . . ."

"Just we weren't going back to school . . ."

"If you see what I mean . . ."

Fergus pretended neither to hear nor see them. He began to talk to himself.

"Ho hum, what a lovely thing it is to walk in a wood, and see nobody at all. That's what I like best: a walk where you don't see another human being. That's the kind of thing that does me good when I'm on my way to Ryan's Bar to have a drink. A walk where I don't meet another sinner."

He began whistling.

Dara and Michael looked at each other in amazement.

"Grown-ups are extraordinary," said Michael.

"They seem to be improving all the time."

That was twice in one day they had been rescued. Dara wondered if it would be possible to leave school entirely. There seemed to be a great conspiracy working for them at the moment.

Patrick O'Neill declined the invitation of Marian Johnson to dine with her that night. He pleaded great fatigue, and said he would be no company. A glass of milk and a sandwich and bed in the elegant room were what he wanted. He noticed the disappointment on Marian's face and the fact that she had had her hair fixed since they had been out riding; maybe she had gone to a beauty parlor specially.

"You look very nice," he said tiredly.

Marian's face lit up. That was compliment enough.

He said that if she were free he would love another ride on that nice mild-mannered horse tomorrow. That brought on further smiles. He could go to bed now without being thought boorish.

He wished there were phones in the bedrooms. He wanted to call Grace back home. It would be great to dial direct and hear the reassurance of Bella and Andy that Grace was at home. It was eight-thirty here in Mountfern: it would be three-thirty in New Jersey, just the time that Andy was driving Grace up the avenue. Patrick's sister, a fussy woman called Philomena, was in residence as chaperon. Kerry was away at school. Rachel was in her apartment. He really should call her. But not from the hall of the Grange. Not with Marian Johnson listening to every word. There were obviously some calls which were going to be made through that pleasant woman who ran the post office, who had made tea for him this morning. Was it only *this* morning? Lord, why had he stayed up all night in Fernscourt? His bones ached with tiredness.

He took a hot bath and felt much better. Better still after the milk and sandwiches. He lay on his bed and looked out at the green fields leading off to clumps of trees. Behind those trees was the winding River Fern, and his own place. It had been some day. Still he had done almost everything he set out to do. The lawyer chap hadn't been in, which was rather lackadaisical. Even in a sleepy hollow like this, someone should have been looking after the shop. And Kate Ryan hadn't been convinced. She was the only real opposition—not that she had said it, of course. That made her smart. A handsome woman too, probably the brains of that business. The dreamy pleasant husband was not a man with much drive. Bright smart children too. Lucky he had been able to get them on his side by shielding them. Little rascals, skipping school.

Canon Moran had been so helpful about looking up records, and the young curate had promised to inquire about burial grounds and possible tombstones. Strangely, that old wino bag lady he had picked up in the car was their housekeeper. She looked extremely ropy today, as if she had just had another night on the tiles.

And the Dalys had been magnificent, and the Leonards, and Jack Coyne—knowing now too late that he had blown it by overcharging Patrick for the car—said that he hoped they would be able to talk man to man about business one day. Patrick had smiled and said of course, but he and Jack Coyne knew that not one cent's worth of business was ever going to cross the River Fern from Fernscourt to Coyne's Garage. He talked to Sergeant Sheehan casually, to Dr. White who happened to be in Daly's, to assorted others whose names would come back to him when he was less tired. He had an excellent memory and never had to write down the names of the people he met through work. To some people today might seem like a leisure day, wandering around talking to folk. But to Patrick O'Neill it was work. His life's work. And really and truly it had gone very well today. It wouldn't take long to convince that fine tall Kate Ryan that he didn't mean her and hers any harm. It was true he did not. And it was always a bit easier convincing people if the thing was actually true.

Rachel Fine applied her throat cream exactly as the label had advised with short upward strokes. She then applied her eye cream in the recommended manner with a feather-light fingertip so as not to damage the delicate tissue around the eye. She sat in her cotton nightdress looking without pleasure at the reflection that stared from the mirror. She looked like any sad Jewish mamma left on her own this night. There must be a thousand of them in this area alone. But she hadn't even the satisfaction of being a mamma. And her husband, Herbert had been in California for eight years. She and he had ended their relationship long before hers with Patrick had begun. Herbert had given her the apartment and a car. The divorce had been genuinely amicable. They sent each other postcards even; they remained casual friends, bewildered that they had ever thought they knew each other well enough to marry and to remain married for so long.

But however lonely, Rachel would not telephone Herbert for company. And she had very few friends left. When you devote your life to a man, his business, and his limited free time as Rachel had done, it didn't leave much time for friends. She still had work to do for O'Neill Enterprises even while he was in Ireland, but she did it in a mechanical way. When there was no Patrick to discuss her ideas with the fire went out of them.

Sure she was a designer. Sure, sure, everyone realized that she was worth her salary, her ideas had been praised in the newspapers and magazines, and her style had lifted the O'Neill chain way out of the commonplace. Rachel had never wanted to see her own name over the smart corner-bistro-type restaurants, it was quite satisfying enough to know that her choosing of colors and fabrics, her layout and her selection of decor, waitresses' uniforms and lighting techniques contributed to the O'Neill empire. When Patrick had eight pub-restaurants and the motel in New Jersey he said he had enough. He bought no more until this huge bottomless pit that was Fernscourt, bleeding away his profits in a way that nobody would believe.

Gerry Power, Patrick's second in command, knew this. He was tight-lipped and disapproving, but not even to Rachel, whose position he knew very well, would he hint that he took anything less than delight in all of Patrick's schemes.

Rachel looked again at the telephone. It was ten P.M. here. It was three o'clock tomorrow morning in that godforsaken place. Perhaps he would call tomorrow. Perhaps he might even call at his lunchtime, which would be getting up time here. Yes, surely that's what he would do.

Rachel laid a towel over her pillowcase. The only advantage of not having your man living with you all the time was that you could do your beauty routines adequately. On the nights when Patrick stayed, there was a satin nightgown, not a cheap cotton one, there was no throat cream or eye cream. There were certainly no exercises.

But what was Patrick's great phrase? "It's always either a feast or a famine." Rachel Fine sighed deeply. It had been a famine for her for a very long time, and the worst bit was that she could see long lean years of famine still ahead.

Mrs. Whelan understood without being told and without the need for comment that Patrick would need to make calls in privacy. She settled him next day in her own sitting room, two closed doors away from anyone who might be standing in the post office with their ears flapping.

She gave him a table for his papers and said she would add up the charges each time and he could pay at the end. Another cup of strong tea, a cushion to cure his saddle sores.

"You're a wonderful woman. Did the late Mr. Whelan appreciate you?"

"He's not late, he just went off," she said simply.

Patrick knew how hard it was for a woman in a small community to admit something like this, she would say it to him once because her common sense would tell her that he would hear it elsewhere, then it would never be mentioned again. He too would acknowledge it once and then forget it.

"A foolish man. Did he find the happiness he thought he was going to find? Most people who run away don't."

She thought about it.

"At first he did, I'd say. But times aren't great now, I hear. When I do hear, which isn't often." That meant the subject was closed. "I'd better leave you and start to get through to the operator for you."

Patrick hadn't been thinking of phoning Kerry in his big school. But why not? They would certainly get him to the phone. As he settled himself into the chair and cushions provided by Sheila Whelan, Patrick realized that in ways she was a little like Rachel. She knew how to make a man feel welcome and comfortable and important. How strange that Rachel was sitting alone in Brooklyn just as Sheila lived alone in Mountfern. Did it prove that it was a bad thing to make a man comfortable?

Patrick had never been able to understand people who could use the telephone for long chatty conversations. For too many years now he had used it for work to be able to think of it as a way of talking unselfconsciously. Grace could talk for hours on the telephone to friends whom she had just left at school. People told Patrick that it was the same with their daughters, and indeed their wives.

He put the first call through to Gerry Power. At least Gerry felt the same way about telephones. A necessary but unappealing part of business life. He wouldn't complain that Patrick was not being sufficiently warm or forthcoming over three thousand miles on a piece of machinery.

Gerry Power wasted no time congratulating him or expressing any surprise. If Mr. O'Neill had said he was going to go and throw away his fortune on this heap of old stones, then this is what he was going to do. He listened to instructions, and nodded and grunted. At the end of the catalogue he read them back. Patrick smiled; he could almost see Gerry Power in his shirt sleeves, writing with a stubby pencil.

"And that's three air tickets you want. Three not four?"

"You're very numerate Gerry, three. One each for Kerry, Grace and me."

"Just checking." Gerry Power was in no way put out. He hated grey areas and wanted to make sure that his boss hadn't expected him to book a seat for Mrs. Fine, without asking him directly to do so.

Grace was always excited to hear from him. When was he arriving? Good, good. And how long was he staying home? Only a few days, but that was awful! He had been gone so long. He was *what?* Was this true? He was really and truly going to take Kerry and Grace with him to Ireland? And she could go to school there? Grace's voice disappeared into squeaks of excitement.

Patrick spoke to his sister Philomena. She shared neither Grace's excitement nor Patrick's enthusiasm. She listened to the facts in a disapproving silence. Yes she would have clothes organized; and she would explain to the nuns here that Grace would not return in the fall.

"Well, what do you think of my getting back to the old country in the end?" Patrick hated having to ask her, despised himself for fishing for the praise and congratulation that he felt were his due.

He was getting none of them from Philomena anyway.

"You've always done whatever you wanted to do, Patrick, and to be fair, the rest of us have done well out of your endeavors. But it is quite beyond us to know why you want to go and undo the work of the very people who got us here. Our grandfather as sure as hell didn't come over here on the deck of a ship so that his grandson and his great-grandchildren should end up going back to the godforsaken bog that he left behind him. But it was never any use talking to you and it won't be any use now."

They got Kerry out of class to talk to him. It was the first time he had ever called his son at school; he could not credit the time it took to find the boy. Kerry could not believe that his father had called just for a conversation. Especially as he learned, he would see his father within a few days.

"I wanted to share the good news with you." Patrick felt a trace of tears come into his voice, and fought it desperately. Kerry hated emotion. More than once he had accused his father of being what he called Italian. In flatter tones than he intended, he told his son that the dream was now a reality. He said that the land had been bought, the plans were underway. And that he had heard of a good school where Kerry would start in the fall. There was a silence at the other end of the telephone which chilled him.

In business Patrick had never pleaded on the telephone, and he knew it was pathetic to ask if someone was still there when there was a silence. Sitting in Sheila Whelan's floral armchair, he steeled himself and waited. But Kerry waited longer.

Eventually Patrick spoke. "So we'll talk about all that when I see you. Right?"

"What do we talk about?"

"About how great it will all be. So many people have something that they always want to do, all their lives they talk about it and so often it never happens. Your mother and I talked about this for so long . . ."

This time Kerry spoke. "Mother never talked about it to me," he said.

"But you know it was what she wanted?"

"Maybe."

With difficulty Patrick controlled himself. His hands were shaking when he put down the telephone. He had one more call to make, and he needed something stronger than tea to steady him for this one.

Sheila Whelan wouldn't hear of his going to buy a brandy. She would slip into Conway's for it. No point in his getting a reputation in the first couple of days. She was back in minutes and the half bottle of brandy, glass and jug of water were beside his elbow on a round tray advertising Craven A cigarettes. Patrick O'Neill took a long swallow and made a person to person call to Mrs. Rachel Fine.

Afterwards he walked out into Bridge Street; he looked down to the river as his grandfather must have done, and up the town. It would all have changed so much since those days. There would have been no calling the States. And no calling home once he had arrived on the other side of the world. Patrick crossed the street, nodding at Mr. Conway, the man who unbelievably ran twin trades of publican and mortician without anyone thinking it was slightly odd. He waved at the two young White children going into their house and he gave a glance to see what ancient movie the Classic was offering tonight.

His grandfather would have had no contact at all with the family. Going to America was like going to the next world. No wonder the Irish held American wakes for the man who was leaving for America and would be out of touch with his kith and kin from now on. Maybe it might have been sensible, Patrick thought gloomily. His sister, his son, his manager and Rachel Fine had hardly been overjoyed to hear from him.

"He's only staying a few more days," John said. "He was in here earlier with some plans, showing me an artist's impression. You never saw the like of it."

"No permission or no license granted yet," Kate remarked coolly.

"A formality," Fergus Slattery said. Fergus had called again. It was a restful place, Ryan's. You could read your paper, or you could join in the chat. It made a nice stretch to his legs after his supper. And anyway he felt an overwhelming loyalty to the shabby little place.

"You shouldn't have refused good money," John Ryan said in a low voice so that the others wouldn't hear. "Kate told me you won't handle his business in case it might be in conflict with us . . . No, no . . . let me finish. Fergus, you're a decent man as your father before you is, but there's no conflict. There's nothing but coopera-tion with that man. The best man you could meet; he'll put new life in the place."

"I did meet him," Fergus said.

"Well. Didn't you like him?"

"Of course I liked him," Fergus growled. "You couldn't not like him. I told him that I'd feel it more sensible not to get involved in his application just in case there was the unlikely event of one of my fellow parishioners wanting to get involved on the other side."

"And what did he say?" John and Kate were both eager. This was new; this had happened this afternoon.

"Oh he was charm itself. Said he quite understood, said it was very ethical of me, showed I was a man with a community spirit, hoped he'd be able to prove that he felt the same community spirit himself."

"That's just it."

"I know, John. I'm not disputing it. I'm just saying that he's a mixture, we're always one thing or the other here; he's more than one thing."

"How do you mean?"

"Well at the same time he was telling me how much he wanted to feel part of the place and a member of the local community, he also made sure I realized that he had extinguished a license. Ahearne's pub, way beyond. Now that's sharp legal talk for an innocent Yank who's building his own place. He not only knows that you have to buy up and extinguish one pub license before you get another, but he's done it. That's a bit quick for me."

John Ryan smiled as he polished the bar counter. "Well by God you're a very impatient young fellow, Fergus, for all your great education and studies at the universities."

"Stop making fun of me. Wouldn't I need to be impatient with all that's going on around here?"

"No," said John slowly. "That's the last thing you'd need to be. There's all the time in the world. Look at all that could happen before any of this comes into being."

"What do you mean?"

"Your father would understand better than you. He has a feeling for the river, and how things go on and on. That river was there just the way it is now when your man's grandfather left Mountfern, and it will be here forever."

"John, you sound like some old soothsayer, will you stop it?" Kate laughed at him good-naturedly.

"No, I mean it. Patrick O'Neill has great plans like fireworks but they may never materialize."

"He's hardly bought Ahearne's license just for fun," Fergus said.

"No, but look at what could happen. I remember that place that was going to be built about ten miles out on the Galway road. *That* never materialized, did it?"

"They ran out of money," Fergus said.

"Exactly," said John.

"But that fellow O'Neill has a fortune."

"So had the other crowd. Or maybe he'd lose interest, or something else would distract him, or it wouldn't turn out right for him."

"But aren't you only helping him to install himself instead of praying that it will turn out wrong for him?" Kate was mystified.

"None of us would pray that things would turn out wrong for people, Kate, that would be only asking for trouble to come on ourselves. All I mean is that there's no point in getting hot and bothered until things do happen."

"That's not the American way," Fergus said, doing a poor imitation of Patrick's accent. "That's not your up-and-attem-boy."

"That's not my way," John said quietly.

"We're two of a kind then, John. Give me another pint, if you will. I can't see myself practicing law for ten minutes in New York without having a very bad nervous breakdown."

Kate smiled at them affectionately as they toasted each other on the notion of savoring life, rather than racing through it. She would prefer to race a bit faster herself, but not as fast nor in the same direction as the smiling American, who had seemed to read her mistrust of him and smile yet more warmly on the two occasions in two days that she had met him. She was glad he was going back soon.

A few nights later Dara crept from her room to the window just at the very moment Michael left his bed. They were never surprised that their timing was so exact, they took it for granted that they would turn up at the same time. In Fernscourt they could see him walking, touching this wall and that.

"If he loves it so much why is he tearing it down?" Dara asked yet again.

"Well he keeps saying he tried to think of ways of keeping the old ruin like it was," Michael said, always his defender.

"He didn't try very hard. He's so rich, all he has to do is to say let it stay and it stays," Dara grumbled. "Look, he's leaving now. I wonder where did he park his car?"

"He leaves it up a bit when he comes at night, so as not to wake people when he leaves. Look, look he's coming over the bridge."

They watched as Patrick O'Neill paused on the little footbridge opposite their pub and stared across at Fernscourt in the same way that they had done so often, a hand on each railing of the narrow bridge.

"He's saying goodbye before he goes home," Michael breathed.

"Will you ever realize that to him this is his home?" said Dara.

The moonlight wasn't bright enough for them to see the tears on Patrick's face as he said goodbye to Fernscourt.

Chapter V

It took a little time to get things organized, but compared to the speed that most people would have moved at, Patrick was a human tornado. The finances had been organized already. The big white house in New Jersey, the symbol of his success, would be put on the market. Not at once, because that way he would have to take any price from any bidder. But it would be rented for a year first.

Bella and Andy, the couple who had looked after him, had to be paid off, thanked, found new positions. Aunts and cousins had to be placated and reassured that it wasn't the act of a madman. He saw to passports, visas for the children, had endless discussions with numerous priests and nuns in the two schools, all of whom were sorry to see Mr. O'Neill, the number one benefactor, disappear off to Ireland with his two handsome children.

There were never quite enough hours in the day for all the form-filling, document-signing, telephoning, crating, packing, sorting, and deciding what had to be done.

But in a far swifter time than anyone would have believed possible, Patrick had everything done. He was ready to come home to Ireland.

Patrick was so proud of his children when they stepped from the plane at Shannon Airport that he wanted to cry aloud to anyone who would listen that these two shining golden people belonged to him. Even after the night flight when others were blinking sleepily into the dawn, Kerry and Grace O'Neill looked untouched and stared around them with interest at the land that was going to be their home.

Patrick had noticed the looks of admiration that the brother and sister had gotten from onlookers both in Idlewild Airport, New York, and here in Shannon. They had clean-cut looks and they both seemed in such high good humor. They had always gotten along well together, no rivalry, no resentment ever. They had spent long hours together during their mother's illness, and since he had been away from home before, after and even during that time, they had been thrown together a lot. They always enjoyed each other's company. In the plane they had chattered together happily. He had never been close with Philomena or Catherine or Maureen like that. Nor with his brothers. There had been too much hardship in their family. The fight to exist had taken all their time. Friendship was a luxury they didn't have when they were growing up.

He had hired a car from one of the big companies that had a desk at Shannon Airport. Jack Coyne had had only one chance. One chance to be in car rental in a bigger way than he had ever dreamed, but he had lost it forever. To have cheated Patrick O'Neill was the most foolish act of his life.

"Come on, kids," Patrick called as he held the door of the car open. "Come on, climb in, I'm going to take you home." Their faces showed the excitement they felt.

Patrick looked at them with a lump in his throat. They were extraordinarily beautiful, he thought, both of them. It was not just the pride of a father who has worked his guts out so that his children would have everything he never had. Surely he was being objective as he looked at them standing close together in the early morning sun.

Grace had a head of hair that looked like an advertisement for a shampoo, her curls seemed to be shiny and bouncy and there was no way they could be kept down. Two minutes after she came from her shower, or even running out of the waves when they went to the ocean, it was the same. She had big blue eyes and a dimpled smile. Her father called her his little princess, and her brother had called her a baby doll. Her mother said she was like an angel in human form.

It was just as well for Grace O'Neill that she went to a school where the nuns did not believe in praising the girls and that she had an aunt who regarded all good looks as a personal calling from the devil leading to sin and possibly damnation.

Grace was a cheerful child, not nearly as spoiled as she could have been, the idolized baby in that big house. She had realized early in life that you got your way much more easily by smiling and thanking rather than sulking and crying. Nobody told her this; she had always known, or else she had seen it work with her brother and picked it up from him. It was unusually nice to be the center of attention, with people admiring and patting her on the head.

Kerry O'Neill was tall and blond; he looked like a Swede, not as if he came from Irish stock. His hair curled softly around his neck; on another boy it could have looked sissy, but not on Kerry. His skin was always lightly tanned, summer or winter. His eyes were a bright and unsettling blue. They were rarely still, but moved here and there almost as if they were looking for something. It didn't matter, though, because they looked back at whoever he was talking to often enough to show he hadn't lost interest. You got the notion that Kerry's restless eyes moved even when he was asleep.

His smile was wide and all-embracing. Nobody could smile like Kerry; all those white teeth seemed to crack his face in half. The smile never got to his eyes but that's because his eyes moved very fast. They hadn't time to smile. Grace had once seen a picture of the Blue Grotto in Capri, and said that it reminded her of nothing as much as Kerry's eyes.

Kerry never said much, but people didn't realize this. They usually thought he was very interesting because he agreed with them or listened or seemed to be taking part in conversations all the time. It was only with Mother that Kerry had talked a lot. When he came back from school he would sit and talk for ages in Mother's room. Mother had been in bed for so long it was hard to remember when she had been up and around.

They drove across the countryside in the early morning sunshine, pointing things out to each other. Patrick told them that this was a city, Limerick, and that Nenagh was a big town. City? Big town? They couldn't believe it. It was like seeing one of those model villages he had taken them to once, where ordinary mortals seemed like giants.

"We don't go on too much about how much bigger things are back in the States," he began carefully.

"Of course not," Kerry said. "They'd think we were boasting about home."

"And it would be bad-mannered," Grace agreed.

They couldn't believe when they saw signs for Killarney. Please could they go there. It was in the wrong direction, their father said. People in Mountfern thought Killarney was the other end of the country nearly, but one day he'd take them there. And there were signs to Galway. Yes, he had seen Galway Bay on his last visit. Then the roads became narrower, they left the main routes and headed into the midlands. Soon the signs for the town came up. "Not far now," Patrick said. His heart was beating faster at the thought of taking these golden children to the spot they had come from. Back to their home.

They wanted to know why were there no signs for Mountfern.

"It's too small for a road sign. It's only when you're on the road going past it that there are directions. It's only a little place." He hoped he had explained this sufficiently to them.

"It's only little now," Kerry said. "One day everyone will know it."

Patrick flashed him a grateful look and then said no more. They came to the first of the two signs saying Mountfern half a mile.

"Hey, have you passed it?" Kerry called out.

Patrick explained that this was one way which brought you along River Road, he wanted to come in by Bridge Street so that they could get an impression of the place.

"Will they have a band on Main Street?" Grace giggled.

"Nothing would surprise me," Patrick said as they came to the turn and approached the place that had always been a name on his father's birth certificate.

Everyone knew they were coming. From their garden the vicar and Mrs. Williams waved at the car.

Judy Byrne was parking her small car outside her house; she peered out of the window to get a good look at the handsome American and his family.

Mrs. Sheehan was looking out of the top window of the barracks. There were two or three people standing outside Conway's, who held their hands to their eyes to shield them from the light and get a good view. It was too early even by Conway's peculiar opening hours to have gathered drinkers; these must be people talking on their way back from mass.

Patrick explained that some people in the parish went to mass every day.

"Do we have to?" Grace asked anxiously.

"No way." Her father patted her reassuringly.

Daly's was opening for business, so was Leonard's. Sheila Whelan's blinds were up long ago, but normally it was a sleepy, slow-moving place.

On the bridge a group of children had gathered; they bent forward to glimpse the passengers in the car, then they hung back again, lacking in confidence. It annoyed Patrick to see the Irish children so uncertain when his own two were so sure, so easy.

Quickly he turned the wheel and maneuvered them into River Road. Loretto Quinn waved enthusiastically from the shop, young Father Hogan striding along in his soutane waved his breviary cheerfully. Then they were passing Ryan's licensed premises.

"Is that a real place where they sell liquor?" Grace asked.

"Yes, why?" Her father was interested.

"It looks like a kind of toy shop, you know, in a board game. It just needs a thatched roof and it's a typical Irish cottage."

"Ah, we'll be having the thatched cottage bit ourselves," Patrick said.

"Why are we stopping?" Kerry asked.

"Let's get out for a moment." Patrick held the doors of the car open for them.

They scampered out, stretching their legs after the drive. With an arm around each shoulder he walked them to the footbridge and pointed out the ruins of Fernscourt.

"That will be our home," he said. He was glad that they were looking at the old house which stood magical in the morning mists and sunshine, its ivy walls and odd shapes looking more picturesque than anything Hollywood could have dreamed up as a beautiful ruined castle. He was glad that they couldn't see the tears in his eyes. The effect couldn't have been more satisfying. His son and daughter looked in amazement at the sight in front of them.

Across the river from the little wooden bridge where they stood was a great path of laurel bushes. On either side cattle grazed among old rocks and boulders, some covered with moss. The ruins of a great house stood open to the skies. Ivy tumbled from the highest walls, and old portals stood open: doorways leading nowhere except into further open-roofed space. There were gorse bushes and heather dotted around the place, splashes of bright yellow and deep purple.

"You're going to build all this up, make it like it was?" Kerry was unbelieving.

He had seen the artist's impressions certainly, but nothing had prepared him for seeing the place as it was . . . a magnificent ruin.

"That's what we're going to do," Patrick said proudly.

"It's going to look like a castle," Grace breathed.

"That's the idea," Patrick said.

"And how much land, Father?" Kerry was shielding his eyes with his hand and looking around the landscape of a dozen different shades of green.

"Not as much as I'd have liked. You see a lot of people were granted their land back, you know they were tenants but they were able to buy it outright, so naturally that's theirs now and they don't want to sell. It was only the house and the immediate surrounds we got from the Land Commission. I got a couple of acres from fellows who were anxious to sell . . . but you see the problem . . ." He was about to explain, but Kerry saw it too.

"You don't want to be seen to be buying up the land, taking it away from the peasants again, in case you are seen to be the bad guy wearing the black shirt, instead of the good cowboy."

"Right son, got it in one." Patrick was pleased mainly that Kerry was so interested.

"And will this all be gardens . . . ?" Grace gave a sweep of her hand.

"Yes, coming down to the river . . . there's going to be a dock for boats there, and footpaths."

"And where will the entrance be?" Kerry looked left and right.

"Funny, that's one thing still in dispute. The original one went off that way. There's a big overgrown path, that's the way vehicles will be coming on site. I'll take you around and show you. The Dublin architects want to keep it that way. They say it follows the original plan, even though nothing else will be like the original. The American architects say it would be better to open up that overgrown path over there and have the entrance coming from the town, from the big bridge."

Kerry said nothing for a while, just looked at each side and then straight ahead.

"Why couldn't it be here?" he asked.

"Here?"

"Yes. Just here, where we are. This is the best view you'll get of the place with the river in front, and you say it's going to be facing the river, so why not here?"

"But there isn't room. People would have to get out of their cars and coaches and haul all their bags way up there. It's only a foot-bridge, Kerry."

"No, make it into a proper bridge and have that part of the drive. Hey, why *don't* you do that? It would be very impressive."

His handsome face lit up thinking of it.

"It's a great idea but there isn't room. Look how sharp the turning would be. The buses would back into the unfortunate pub, go through the front window."

"Knock it down," Kerry said simply.

"I can't knock it down."

"You're going to knock Fernscourt down," Kerry said, indicating the ruins.

"Yes, but it's falling down and anyway it's mine."

"That pub's practically falling down, and you could buy it, then it would be yours to do what you wanted with it."

It was so simple when you were fifteen.

"Where would they go? Kerry, suppose we were to do it, where would the family who live there go?"

"If they're publicans then they could work for us, just moving across the river from their home, *and* they'd have a nice lump sum."

"I'll think about it," Patrick said. "But as I was going to suggest we have a drink there now, maybe we should sit on this possibility for a while, don't you think? No point in alarming people or telling them too much."

"You're so right," Kerry said. "Then they'd know we're interested and they'd raise the price to the roof and stick, knowing they had us over a barrel."

Patrick looked at his son with a mixture of dismay and pride. It wasn't hard to know where he had gotten his business sense. But did it always have to be as cold as that? Transplanting a family who had hopes and dreams of their own. He looked back at his site. The boy was quite right, the only possible place to have an entrance was here at this little footbridge. A big wide entrance with lanterns maybe, and should there be old gates or not? It was something he would discuss with Rachel when she arrived. Later on.

Kate and John had seen them coming and she had run in to change her blouse. She put on her best one, the one with the high neck, and fixed on the cameo brooch. This way she felt she looked more like the lady of the house than someone helping behind the bar. She dusted on a little face powder and added a dab of lipstick.

Carrie saw them as she was slipping out to give the hens a cake of bread that she had burned. The poor hens weren't at all particular, but Mrs. Ryan was. Very recently she had been rather sharp with Carrie about the late hours spent with Jimbo Doyle and had reminded her tartly that she was responsible for Carrie's welfare while she lived in the house. When she heard the voices and recognized Mr. O'Neill's, her heart skipped a beat. Jimbo had taken a four-day job helping a roofer in the big town. Mr. O'Neill thought he was working for him. Oh God, there would be trouble in store.

Eddie and Declan saw them coming and sighed. It meant they would have to wash their faces; they went glumly to the kitchen and took up the facecloths like robots. They had the worst grime removed by the time their mother arrived to do the very same thing for them.

The twins saw them coming and stopped dead in what they were doing, which was playing chess on the landing window seat. Never in their lives had they seen anyone like Mr. O'Neill's family as they stood in the sun on the footbridge pointing and waving and making a sort of diagram with their hands.

Dara looked at the face of the young man in the grey sweater and white flannels. His head was thrown back and he was laughing. He was the most magnificent boy she had ever seen in her life. And this wasn't in a magazine, or at the cinema. This was here on their own bridge in Mountfern. She was about to say to Michael that he was gorgeous, but she saw her brother staring at the blonde girl. She wore a short tartan pleated skirt and a lemon-colored sweater. Her curls had a tartan ribbon in them, holding them up in what wasn't really a pony tail because it wasn't all tied in but could have been one if she had managed to squeeze in the curls. Michael was looking at her as if he had been blind from birth and had suddenly been given his sight.

Judy Byrne was furious when she realized that she had not been quick enough. Mr. O'Neill had asked her about what he called her fine cottage. Had she thought of letting it and moving to some smaller place even temporarily? Judy had not seen the drift of his conversation. She had been anxious to make it clear to this handsome and charming American, the first serious bachelor to come their way for a long time, that her roots were firmly planted in Mountfern, that she was a woman of this place who would not be moved.

In fact the little house would have been ideal for the O'Neills. Every time Judy thought of it she raged again at her own blindness. It would have been central; it was just the right size. He would have paid most generously anything she had asked. But the real benefit would have been that Patrick O'Neill and his children would have been living there in her house. There were a million places Judy could have gone for the months that were involved. Sheila Whelan had a spare room. Poor Mrs. Meagher of the jewelry shop was thinking of letting a room. Oh why had she been so foolish as not to see that of course the man would want a place to live while he was building his hotel? She would have had every right to call, to be a family friend. What more natural than that she should return to her own house from time to time?

Judy worked three afternoons in the physiotherapy department of the hospital in the town. But there was plenty of work for her in Mountfern and around. She had come home when her mother was bedridden, and even after her mother's death she saw no reason to leave the small quiet country practice. Dr. White made sure she had plenty of work. He always said that she was indispensable with patients who were recovering from a stroke or who had broken an arm or a leg. It was a satisfying life in many ways. But she was lonely, and there were so few chances to meet anyone at all suitable in these parts, at her age. And now that she had met one, and he had been very charming, she had sent him right into the arms of that foolish Marian Johnson.

Marian Johnson had nearly died of delight when she realized why Patrick O'Neill was asking about the gate lodge. In the beginning she had been about to apologize for the place, saying that it was so run down there was hardly anything that could be done with it. In fact it was a perfectly serviceable house where Joe Whelan's people had once lived. That was long ago; they used to open the gates and take the messages, and lived rent free for years, but the family had all scattered. Even before Joe Whelan hightailed it for Dublin after some peroxide blonde, he had been living in Bridge Street with Sheila in the post office.

There had been vaguely unsatisfactory people in it since then, but the Johnsons had never stirred themselves to arrange a better let. Suddenly she saw unlimited possibilities.

"I was hoping to do it up so that people, nice people, could live there. I can't think who would like it, though." She smiled an arch smile, but let it fade suddenly when she got the feeling that Patrick might have seen through it. He spoke quite directly.

"I had been thinking of asking you about it myself. I was wondering, though, if it might be a little too far from town."

"Not at all," Marian cried. "Don't you have a car? Won't the girl have a bicycle, and won't the boy be off with the Jesuits or the Benedictines or wherever?"

Patrick had smiled.

"If you're sure it won't be too much trouble?" he said.

Marian Johnson said it would be no trouble at all. It would be a pleasure for her.

And indeed it was. Jimbo Doyle was in and instructions were given in crisp barks by Marian. No expense was spared, chimneys were swept, baskets of logs were cut, the best bedding from the Grange Hotel was brought to the Lodge. Some of the antiques that Patrick had admired in the house were also given a new home. Windows were stripped clean of the overhanging ivy; the little garden was dug, a space cleared for Patrick's car, and he was assured that all would be ready when he came back from America with his children. He would also need someone to look after them.

This, Marian found a bit of a quandary. No young skit of a girl would be any use, it had to be someone responsible. A local widow, perhaps, Patrick had suggested, someone who might be glad of the chance to live with a family for some months. Marian thought deeply. Not Mrs. Meagher in the jeweler's. She was too recently widowed to think of making any plans, Marian said. She was also a handsome if neurotic red-haired woman who would most certainly cause trouble of some kind. Not poor Loretto Quinn with her little huckster's shop on River Road. She could hardly cope with her own establishment. Certainly not Mrs. Rita Walsh of the Rosemarie hair salon, whose reputation was widely known.

Marian decided to consult Sheila Whelan, who of course knew exactly the person. Miss Hayes. She was sixty if she was a day; she was efficient. She could cook, she could mend, and she would stand no nonsense if the children were troublesome.

Miss Hayes was an inspired idea. Marian Johnson took all the praise and the thanks.

"And what shall I call you, Miss Hayes?" Patrick said to her on the first evening.

"Miss Hayes would do very well," she said.

"It's just that everyone is so friendly around here. I didn't want to do the wrong thing."

"Oh I'm sure you would never do that, Mr. O'Neill."

"I hope the children will settle in well here." Patrick was not a man who was ever at a loss for a word, but Miss Hayes was proving that his charm was not as irresistible as he had hoped.

"I'm sure they will, Mr. O'Neill. It would be strange children that wouldn't love a house like this, a room each, their own wireless and a bathroom for themselves and no one else." Miss Hayes shook her head in awe of the second bathroom.

Grace and Kerry giggled behind Miss Hayes's back after their first evening meal. But not too loudly; she had an air of authority about her, and also she had just fixed them a truly great meal.

Grace fell asleep almost at once. The door of her room was open and Patrick went in to kiss her forehead with the curls damp from her bath. She looked babyish, younger than her twelve years as she lay asleep there. He stood and looked at her for a long, long moment.

Kerry was not sleepy, he said.

"Do you want to drive over with me and walk in Fernscourt by night?" he asked.

Kerry shrugged. It was as if he had gone back to his old self—the Kerry who had nothing much to say to his father.

"Not really," he said.

"Sure." Patrick was easy. He wouldn't rush the boy. "Go in your own time; see it your own way."

"Yes, that's what I'll do, Father," Kerry had said. His face, in spite of his golden tan and his piercing blue eyes, looked curiously empty.

They were the talk of the town. Tommy Leonard said that he had asked Kerry how old he was. He had asked him straight out.

"You spoke to him?" Maggie Daly was over-excited by it all.

"Yeah, that's the way people ask questions," Tommy said. "With speech. Words and all."

"What did he say?" Michael rescued poor Maggie.

"Didn't you ask him yourself? Wasn't he inside in your place for ages?" Tommy Leonard was jealous of the time that the two star-like Americans had spent in Ryan's.

"I couldn't ask much. Mam asked us to show them the animals. God, imagine asking *anyone* to look at our animals let alone people like that."

Tommy Leonard was mollified. He was actually in the poor position of not knowing *what* age Kerry O'Neill actually was. He had asked, it was true, but Kerry had just smiled at him knowingly and asked him to guess.

Tommy Leonard had guessed fifteen, and Kerry had just smiled again. As an encounter it hadn't pleased Tommy, he got no glory in recalling it.

"Wasn't she beautiful?" Maggie said, in what was almost a whisper.

"She was more than beautiful," Dara said firmly. "She had classic good looks."

Dara didn't know exactly what that meant, but she had heard it said once about some actress. It seemed the highest praise there could be to have good looks that were classic. It gave them a virtue somehow, took them out of the ordinary variety.

"Imagine, she's going to be at school like the rest of us." Maggie could hardly take it in.

"I'm sure she'll hate it." Dara was sympathetic to Grace and outraged that school wouldn't live up to her hopes.

"Everyone hates school," said Jacinta White, who hadn't met Grace and Kerry personally. She had only waved to them as they passed in the car with Mr. O'Neill. Jacinta and her brother Liam were peeved not to have met the new arrivals; it left them at a disadvantage somehow.

They had planned to go fishing that day; often the six of them waded up the river with their simple fishing rods. They had all been catching fish for as long as they could remember, and they used to laugh at the fishermen who came from Dublin and far-off places with all their expensive tackle. Young Mr. Slattery had once told them that the whole principle of fishing for thousands of years had been some sort of an old hook, some sort of an old stick and a length of thread to connect the two. Only fancy folk who wouldn't know a pike from a perch, or either of them from a brown trout, went to all this ungodly fuss about rods and tackle. Sometimes young Mr. Slattery came and sat with them and told them things about the river. He always sounded as if he were making some kind of joke about it, or as if he didn't really believe what he was saying himself. He said that the Fern wasn't cold enough or fast enough for game fish. You wouldn't find any salmon leaping around it or refined sort of trout. These were classier fish that needed a load of oxygen. The Fern was a coarse fish for a coarser fisherman. It was low in oxygen, and full of slow ponderous fish like the tench that could live with no oxygen at all. Like the people of Mountfern themselves. Young Mr. Slattery puzzled the children, he was neither one thing nor the other.

Today, somehow, the fishing had lost its appeal. And they didn't play in Fernscourt anymore. It was not the same now that they knew the bulldozers were coming to take it down. They were all restless and unsettled. They wanted Grace O'Neill and her big brother Kerry to be there again. Like they had been yesterday. But nobody said it. Jacinta White said it in a sort of way.

"Will we go up to the lodge and ask them if they want to come fishing?" she suggested.

They all looked at each other doubtfully.

The mood was against it. Grace and Kerry O'Neill were the kind of people who made the running. You didn't go knocking on their door. They came to join you when they were ready.

Jack Coyne made one attempt to regain the lost business. He called to the lodge formally. He was met by Miss Hayes, a quiet woman who did dressmaking and who lived in a couple of rooms in Bridge Street.

"What has you ending up here?" he asked ungraciously.

"Did you wish to see Mr. O'Neill?"

"Yes, I wished that, please." He was mocking her now.

"Would you like to come into the sitting room? The family are at breakfast at the moment."

"Who's that, Miss Hayes?" Patrick's voice called out good-naturedly.

"It's Mr. Coyne, a car dealer." Miss Hayes was disapproving.

"Oh, Mr. Coyne, I had the pleasure of doing business with you once. Do come in and join us for coffee. Another cup if you'd be so kind please, Miss Hayes?"

Jack Coyne was distinctly wrong-footed now. He came into a sunny alcove where two smartly dressed children were having breakfast, at a table by a big window. The children stood up politely at his approach. Jack Coyne wished he had dressed more smartly for the occasion. He had thought he would find them unpacking and confused.

"I didn't want to disturb you but I was going to inquire if you wanted a car." Jack decided to come straight to the point. He nodded at the two children who sat down again, realizing that there would be no further greeting. Patrick made a great play out of pouring the coffee and was extremely anxious that Jack Coyne had the right amount of sugar and cream. Then he turned his blue eyes and his crinkly smile directly on Jack.

"A car?" he said, interested and amused, as if he had been offered a flying saucer.

"Yes, you won't want to be hiring that car-rental job outside for any longer than you have to."

"No indeed." Patrick still looked amused.

"And since I'm the local man, a businessman too, in my own small way, I thought I'd put it on the line for you, Mr. O'Neill, ask you to come down to Coyne's Motor Works and tell me what you had in mind, and I could go and look for it for you."

Patrick looked at him blankly. As if he didn't understand. "You mean *you* would go and get *me* a car from a third party? Is this what you are proposing?"

"Yes, well that's what getting a car for someone is." Jack was confused now.

"But why would you do that, Mr. Coyne?"

"Why? Well so that you would get a good deal, a proper car from someone you could trust."

"Who would that be, this person I could trust?" Patrick's eyes were innocent and blue.

Jack Coyne shuffled and stumbled over his words. "Like I'm here, I'd know the people, I'd be in the way of knowing who would give you a fair price and who would . . . well . . . who would be the kind of fellow who would see you coming as it were."

Patrick looked at him directly. "I'd have to avoid those, wouldn't you say?"

"You would too, and sometimes it's hard to tell one from another; the man who would look to your interests and serve you well, and the man who would just try to make a quick few quid out of you."

"Yes." Patrick was grave.

"And we're all in business, as I say, Mr. O'Neill, and there are those of us who might make a quick few quid always from passing trade as it were, people who had more money than sense, but when it comes down to a good working relationship . . ."

Patrick O'Neill beamed all over his face.

"I think that's very neighborly of you, Mr. Coyne, and I will take your point about the kind of sharks who would fleece the passing trade for a few quick bucks . . . It's that kind of thing that can destroy a place. One visitor leaving with one story like that could kill tourism stone dead. I agree with you so much. So thanks again for marking my card. I'll be on the look out."

Jack Coyne heard the goodbye in the tone. He stood up.

"So you might call in to Coyne's Motor Works?"

"I'll sure as anything see you around these parts, Mr. Coyne."

In the hall Jack Coyne got the feeling that the wordless Miss Hayes had heard everything, and realized he was getting the bum's rush.

"Haven't you a good enough living below in the town making clothes for people without cleaning up after this lot?" he said to her.

"Like yourself, Jack Coyne, I'm always willing to see a business opportunity," she said with a smile.

Olive Hayes had no relations left except a sister who was a nun in New Zealand. She had always dreamed of going out to spend a winter in the South Island. If she worked for Mr. O'Neill, if she let her little place behind Meagher's jewelry to this building fellow who needed a place in Mountfern, if she continued her making of curtains and any other dressmaking she could manage, then she would have the fare in a year.

Mr. O'Neill thought he would be out of the lodge and into his new castle in a year but he didn't understand about the way things were done here. It would be several years. And in that time Olive Hayes could gather a small fortune, enough to take her to New Zealand, and to give her sister's order a financial contribution which would make her a welcome visitor for as long as she wanted to stay. Indeed she thought sometimes that if the weather was as good as her sister wrote it was, and if she liked it there, she might stay altogether. But these were only half-formed plans. And nobody except Sheila Whelan in the post office had any inkling of them. She hadn't told that bossy Marian Johnson who hired her, and she certainly wouldn't tell that crook Jack Coyne. She closed the door after him and went to refill the coffee pot.

The girl was a lovely little thing; the boy looked as if he could be a great deal of trouble.

Judy Byrne called the Grange. She said it was about old Mr. Johnson's arthritis.

"You said yourself there was nothing more you could do for him," Marian said.

"Yes, I know, but in this fine weather he should be feeling a lot better. I was wondering did he want to go over the exercises I tried with him before."

"He said they weren't worth a curse. You can neither lead him nor drive him. It's always been the same."

"Oh I don't know, sometimes the right word at the right time . . . I have to be over that way, will I call in and have a chat with him?"

"No point, Judy, he's gone fishing."

"Well tell him to take care of himself and not to get damp out on that river bank."

"You're very nice to be so concerned," Marian said.

"Not at all. How are things?"

"Things are frightfully busy, what with the lodge and everything . . ."

"Oh, are you getting involved there? I thought they wanted to be left on their own."

"I wouldn't dream of interfering, but there are some things of course that simply have to be done, and poor Miss Hayes is splendid but she does have her limitations." Marian gave a little tinkle.

Judy Byrne banged down the receiver and told herself aloud yet again that she was possibly the most stupid woman on earth. It would serve her right if she were to be invited by that Marian Johnson, whose face was like a meringue, to the wedding of the century at the Grange, with a honeymoon to be spent across the river in the elegant Fernscourt, new home of the bride and groom.

The children of Mountfern could talk of nothing but the O'Neills but they didn't know how or when they would meet them again. It was solved on the day that Grace was driven by her father to Fernscourt. And left there.

Patrick was engrossed in conversations with surveyors and engineers. Grace wandered around touching the long strands of ivy and holding them up so that they trailed in different directions.

With solemn dark eyes Dara and Michael watched her. After an eternity, Dara made the first move.

"We'll ask her would she like an ice cream in Daly's," she said firmly.

"We don't have enough money," Michael protested.

"We have enough for two."

"But we'd have to buy three."

"You can suddenly decide at the last minute you don't want one."

"All right."

They walked hesitantly up to Grace, who was standing on tiptoe to examine what she thought might be a bird's nesting place.

"Would you like to come for an ice cream or something?" Michael asked gruffly.

Grace's face broke into a dazzling smile. "Can I?" she asked.

Michael was wordless again.

Dara took over. "We'd love you to come down to Daly's, and show you the rest of the town."

"I was longing to see everything, but I didn't want to . . ." Grace looked doubtful. "You're all friends already, I didn't want to get in the way."

"Nonsense." Dara was brisk. "You're just as much entitled to have an ice cream and walk around Mountfern as anyone else."

She linked Grace O'Neill's arm and walked purposefully across the footbridge. Michael followed happily, and Patrick O'Neill watched from a distance with a pleased smile.

Eddie Ryan was escorted home to the family business by an irate Declan Morrissey, the manager of the Classic Cinema. Eddie had drawn mustaches on Audrey Hepburn, and on Doris Day. He had drawn them not with a pencil, nor even a ballpoint pen, but with creosote which could not be removed and which meant that no new poster could be affixed on top of the mutilated ones. Declan Morrissey said he did not want the child to be disemboweled but as near to it as could be done within the law.

"You are a thorn in my flesh," Kate Ryan told her son as she marched him upstairs to where John was working with papers and notebooks scattered around him.

"John, I know that Wordsworth and the lads never had this kind of distraction, but I'm going to have to interrupt you and ask you to beat Eddie within an inch of his life."

"What has he done now?" John was weary.

"According to Declan Morrissey, he has defaced the Classic Cinema in a manner from which it will never recover."

"Didn't Declan do that himself with his rows of colored lights around it?"

"*John!*"

"I know, that has nothing to do with it. Right, Eddie, before I take my belt to you . . ."

"Ah no, Dad, please no."

"Before I take the belt, have you *any* reason or explanation? I am a reasonable man. I will listen."

There was silence.

"Pure badness, I'm afraid," Kate said.

"There's nothing else to do. If there was anything at all to do I'd do it, but there isn't." Eddie looked very sad.

Kate and John looked at each other, weakening momentarily.

"But the others don't put creosote on Morrissey's walls," Kate said.

"And have us heart-broken every day of our lives," John said.

"They've got a life of their own," Eddie said. "A life with people in it."

For some reason that he never understood the strap was not raised.

He was ordered to go and apologize to Mr. Morrissey, to take a scrubbing brush and Vim and do his best. To tell Mr. Morrissey that his parents would pay Jimbo Doyle to have a go at it if all else failed.

"A life of their own with people in it," Kate said wonderingly to John. "Imagine, that's all he wants, poor little clown."

"I suppose it's what everyone wants," John said and went back to his writing, delighted that he didn't have to beat his small and very difficult son.

Nineteen sixty-two was the summer of the bicycle.

Mr. O'Neill had done an extraordinary deal in the big town. It all happened the time he went to buy a car. Apparently he got friendly with the man who sold it to him, and had gone to have a drink with him. The man's brother had been trying to emigrate to America, but he had no one to stand for him at the other side, no one to give him a job and to be responsible for him. This was a great pity because the poor fellow had just been crossed in love. A woman he had his eye on for many years had upped and married another man entirely. So the brother had only one hope and that was to start a new life in the New World. He wasn't a man who was afraid of hard work.

It all evolved in the conversation that Mr. O'Neill could get his manager back in the States, a Mr. Gerry Power, to sponsor him in, and the thing was arranged in a matter of days. All the man had to do now was to have his medical and get his visa. Nobody could believe the speed at which it was done. How could this benefactor be thanked? Mr. O'Neill had seen a load of old bicycles. What about a job lot of those at a knockdown price. A price? Not at all, they were a gift. Thirty-odd bicycles were delivered to Jack Coyne's for nothing.

Jack was to test the brakes and do any re-fitting that was necessary. The bikes were available for all who wanted them. Dara and Michael cycled around in circles on theirs; they were the first to get them. The Whites had bikes already, and so had Tommy Leonard, but Maggie didn't, so a small one was found for her. Grace and Kerry had theirs and there had been some cans of paint thrown in with the deal. The bicycles were all the colors of the rainbow.

Jack Coyne scratched his head many times as children came to choose their free bicycles and to paint them on his premises. He had a suspicion that Patrick O'Neill had in fact pulled a fast one on him. The man had not bought his car through Jack, that was all right, that was his privilege to go where he wanted to. But this business of unloading all these broken bicycles on him. In theory it looked as if Coyne's were being given the turn. But in fact it was different. There was no money anyway in fiddly jobs like that, and then added to it was the problem that Jack would have to charge half nothing to Patrick O'Neill anyway to try to show that he had mended his wicked ways. And half the kids in the town painting their bicycles on the premises.

He felt sure that Patrick O'Neill wasn't so stupid as to think that this was doing him a favor.

"Who can have bikes? Is it only people of eleven?" Patrick looked down at the small furious boy with hair sticking out in all directions.

"Who are you?" he asked.

"That doesn't matter," the child said. "I just wanted to know if it was worthwhile or if I'd be belted out of there." He jerked his head at Jack Coyne's.

"What do people say?"

"Mr. Coyne says he can't get them out of his sight quick enough. Father Hogan said we should give them to those in need first."

"But aren't we all in need?" Patrick asked him.

"That's what I said, but you couldn't argue with a priest."

"I know it." Patrick was sympathetic.

The small boy wasn't prepared to let the conversation wander into philosophical waters.

"So what are the rules, Mr. O'Neill?"

Patrick liked him, he was a little toughie.

"You know my name, why can't I know yours?"

"Because then you'd say there were too many bicycles gone to our family because of the twins," Eddie said.

"Oh it's young Mr. Ryan, I see."

"Well it's no use now." Eddie's hands were deep in his pockets.

"Are you able to ride a bike?"

"Everyone is." Eddie was scornful.

"No they're not. Come on, pick one out. If you can ride it straight up and down here for me without wobbling, you can have it."

Eddie was back like a flash with a bike and a following of half a dozen children.

Patrick watched him attempt a few false starts and then get going. He came back triumphantly.

"Well?" he cried.

"No," Patrick said.

"What do you mean no. I stayed on, didn't I?"

"Yes, but you rode on the wrong side of the road, you young fool. You'd have been killed if anyone was coming toward you."

"You didn't *say* you were counting things like that."

"Sorry, friend. Try again next week, same time, same place, new test."

Eddie grinned back at him. This was the kind of deal he understood.

Grace O'Neill said she thought that Mountfern was the most beautiful place she had ever been. She said that they were all so lucky to have grown up here, it was like a magic place. The children preened themselves when they heard this. Grace didn't boast about all the places she had been. She didn't say that New York was better than Mountfern, and she had been to all kinds of things and places they had only seen in the films. She had been up the Empire State Building, and on Broadway. She had been up the Statue of Liberty and she had been across the Brooklyn Bridge. But this was only revealed when they questioned her. Normally she said little about what had been her home up to now. Her chat was all of the future. They knew that her mother had died. They asked her was it awful. Grace said that the worst part had been knowing somehow for ages that she was never going to be really well. They had stopped making plans for the things they would do when mother got cured. She didn't know when it began but that was the worst part. The time she had died was hard to remember, there were so many people coming in and out of the house.

She had looked so sad when she talked about that, they changed the subject. Maggie Daly had asked could they see some of her American clothes and all the girls had gotten on their bicycles and cycled off to the lodge just like that. Of course Tommy Leonard and Michael Ryan and Liam White were far too grown up and male to want to do anything stupid like cycling nearly three miles to see clothes. But they felt a bit empty sitting there by the river when all the girls had gone. It wasn't that they would have gone if they had been asked. But they would like to have been asked. They would have preferred if the girls hadn't gone at all.

Kerry didn't come and join in the games. He was far too old for them. He was nearly old enough to be on the bridge with the fellows and girls who were almost grown up. But he didn't hang around there either.

Grace said he cycled a lot on his own; he had found some ruined abbey he liked. And he used to read too, and he was catching up on some work he had to do before he went to his boarding school, and he had some Latin lessons from Mr. Williams the vicar, who had said that life was very droll when you had the Protestant parson teaching the Roman Catholics Latin, even though it was never used in Mr. Williams's church and nothing else was used in Canon Moran's establishment down the road.

"O'Neill's children seem to have taken over the place like the Lords of the Soil," Fergus said to Kate.

"I'm quick to find fault, quicker than you are, and I can't see anything against them," Kate said.

"Oh, cocky little pair of swaggerers," Fergus grunted. "Sailing around on their bicycles as if they owned the place. Which they do of course. Own the place."

"Ah, come on, Fergus, at least half the place is on wheels now, that can't be bad."

"That's what the people of Hamelin said to each other about the Pied Piper. At least they're all dancing, that can't be bad."

"God, Fergus, nothing would please you about that unfortunate family. Seriously, the children smile and they're being patronizing, they don't smile and they're being standoffish. What could they do to please you?"

"Go back to America," he said.

"You're worse than Eddie when you have that puss on you. What have you so much against them?"

Kate was bright and fresh-looking in a pink blouse and a red pinafore dress. She had bought the blouse in a sale and the pinafore dress was something she had worn years ago, before Declan was born. With a smart black belt to take the maternity look off it she felt as smart as paint. Fergus looked at her, a long admiring look.

"The main thing I have against them is that they are going to take your business away."

"Oh Fergus." She was touched to the heart.

"Don't 'Oh Fergus' me, go on being nice to them, silly little over-dressed vipers in your bosom." He blew his nose loudly. "Just wait until those children have taken away your children's inheritance. See how you'll feel then."

Kate was totally at a loss.

"It's not the children's fault," she began.

He put away his handkerchief. "You're quite right. They make me feel old and grubby and silly. Your children make me feel . . . I don't know, splendid, fascinating."

"Which is what you are," Kate said, and then went back to work.

Chapter VI

Everyone asked Miss Hayes what they were like at home, the Americans. Was there a ton of money spent in the place? What did they talk about? Olive Hayes was never sufficiently forthcoming. They were very nice people, she reported, thoughtful and considerate. She had never worked in a house before, it was all a very new experience for her. People thought Miss Hayes was a poor informant. Soon they didn't bother to ask her anymore. She was a woman with no stories to tell.

Olive Hayes was a woman saving her fare to New Zealand. She was going to keep her position in this small comfortable house with the American family. There would be no tales about the arrogant resentful Kerry, the impatient father who could find nothing to say to his son, but who idolized his beautiful daughter. Nor would Miss Hayes talk about Grace outside the house even though there was nothing but good to report. She was a delightful child, anxious to help, willing to learn. She made her bed and kept her room in perfect order. She always asked permission if she were to invite the other children into the house. She had a ready smile and she soldiered on bravely to keep the peace between her father and brother. Miss Hayes had never felt any yearning to marry and rear a family. But sometimes when she looked at Grace O'Neill in the kitchen, helping her to wipe dishes and tumbling out stories of how the day had been spent, she sighed and a soft look came to her long angular features. It would have been good to have had a daughter like Grace O'Neill.

Kitty Daly had thought that the summer would never end, long endless boring summers with that crowd on the bridge being so dismissive and all Maggie's friends being so loud and awful. But it all changed when Kerry O'Neill came to town. He came into Daly's Dairy from time to time. Kitty hated working in the shop during the summer and was normally so sulky and unhelpful that her parents thought it was counter-productive to have her behind the counter. They had a girl from out the country, and Charlie who hauled and dragged things in and out and did deliveries.

Kerry held out his hand the first time he called.

"Hi, I'm Kerry O'Neill," he had said, as if Kitty didn't know. As if everyone for miles around didn't know.

She shook his hand and mumbled.

"What's your name?" he asked, as if he had expected her to give it.

"Kitty. Kitty Daly."

"Oh this is your place?" He looked around the clean bright shop in admiration. Its cakes and bread in one section, milk, butter and bacon at another counter and the main body of groceries all together behind the main counter.

"Yes, it is." Kitty wished she could think of something else to say, but she couldn't. She gave a big shrug to let this gorgeous fellow know that she thought it was all terrible. So that he wouldn't think of her as a poor country hick. But he didn't seem to think it was dreadful.

"It's a very handsome store," he said. "You must like working in it, you must feel proud of it."

Kitty was about to change her stance completely and express great pride in the dairy.

But her mother spoke first. "Oh there'd be white blackbirds before Miss Kitty here would do a hand's turn in the shop."

A dark red stain came into Kitty's face, but Kerry seemed to understand at once.

"I'm just the same," he said, looking straight at her, though he spoke lightly. "I'm very interested in my father's hotel but he thinks I'm only fooling around. It's not just, is it?"

"No it isn't." Kitty Daly was hoarse with excitement as the bright blue eyes of Kerry O'Neill rested on her for a little longer. Then he had bought a bar of chocolate and was gone. She watched him walk easily down Bridge Street and go into Leonard's. She resisted the urge to run after him and talk more. She would see him again. He was here forever. And he liked her. He had made it obvious. Kitty saw her mother looking at her and immediately put on a face.

"I suppose you'll go getting notions about him now, that's the next cross we'll have to bear," Mrs. Daly said in tones of great weariness.

"It's a pity that older people have such sad, sick minds," said Kitty, and resolved to be very nice to Mrs. Walsh from the Rosemarie hair salon in case there was a chance she might give her a cheap hair-do.

Grace O'Neill said that she would love to catch a fish. A real fish herself, and then she would cook it and eat it. Nobody she ever knew before had done anything like this. She made life seem much more exciting than it was for the children of Mountfern. She loved everything. She thought it was wonderful that they had a river all for them, not in a park or anything, but in their own town. And she thought it was great to know everyone's names. Grace made a point of saying, "Good morning Mrs. Williams; Hi, Mr. Slattery; Good day Father Hogan." She said that in the United States you never met anyone you knew or who knew you. Reluctantly the others agreed that it was all right. Before Grace's arrival they had always thought it tiresome to be under the ever-watchful eyes of the whole town no matter what you did or where you were going. It was hard to see it as a positive asset.

But fishing. That was something the girls hadn't been involved in.

"You won't like it, the fish look terrible when you do get them out of the water," said Maggie Daly.

"They have all blood by the side of their mouths," Jacinta White said.

"And their eyes look terrified," said Maggie, maybe with fellow feeling. Her own eyes often looked big and frightened.

"And they wriggle and twitch and you'd be dying to throw them back in," Jacinta said.

"Except that the poor mouth is torn off them." Maggie was perplexed by the enormity of the decision. "So you wouldn't know what would be for the best, to kill them quickly and get it over with or let them back with half their jaw gone."

Dara hadn't joined in, which was unusual.

Then she spoke.

"I think that's a lot of sentimental rubbish. If Grace says she would like to fish then we should. After all we've lived beside the river for all our lives and we've never objected before . . ."

Grace flashed her a grateful and admiring look.

"But we never did it ourselves . . ." Maggie began.

"Because we've no guts," Dara said firmly, and with that female fishing was on. They were going to get rods and hooks. Michael was terrific, he'd show them.

"Michael won't want us hanging around with them," Jacinta said.

"I'm sure he won't mind showing us how it's done," Grace said, with a sunny confident smile.

Michael didn't mind showing Grace how it was done, and he was pleased that his twin had suddenly developed an interest in fishing. Tommy Leonard was helpful too, and Liam White. They bent over hooks and bait. Maggie Daly forced herself to look into jars of maggots, even though it made her stomach heave. Michael explained that you had to just nick the edge of the maggot with the hook so that the maggot still wriggled about in the water and the fish would believe it was a live grub and snap at it. There was other bait too: bread made into a paste, or bits of crust. Maggie wondered could they stick to this, but Michael and Tommy and Liam said you had to use maggots and worms as well.

Jacinta said she felt sick watching the hook going through the worm. But Grace and Dara looked on steadfastly. Taking a deep breath, Maggie looked on too and said nothing about the nausea rising in her, together with the feeling that this was all a silly phase. They would get over it soon, and go back to being as they were. She hoped Grace would like looking at the tombstones in the Protestant graveyard, but it was probably wiser not to suggest it too soon.

Grace wanted to know could she try out some of the rods which Michael said they had back at the pub. It was nearly teatime. There was indecision. Suddenly the twins looked at each other in the way they often did, as an idea seemed to come to them at exactly the same time.

"We'll ask can you come to tea," Dara said.

"Just what I was thinking."

"Oh no," Grace protested.

"Yes, then we can look at the rods."

Grace was firm. "Miss Hayes will have my tea ready. No, I can't call her, that would be very high-handed. But maybe I could ask Father if I can cycle back again tonight."

That was agreed, and they scattered to go back to their houses as the six o'clock bell pealing out the angelus was heard all over Mountfern.

Maggie walked along River Road with her hands in her pockets. Dara hadn't asked her to come back after tea. Michael hadn't been keen to show her any rods. Tommy Leonard and the Whites were chatting on cheerfully. They didn't notice that Maggie hung behind and was very quiet.

But next day Maggie was called by her mother.

"Come down quickly, Maggie, your friend is here."

Something about the way she said friend was unusual. Usually Mrs. Daly said that Jacinta or Dara was there, in a way that you knew she was casting her eyes up to heaven. Maggie ran down the stairs of Daly's and into the shop.

There was Grace, full of chat to everyone, asking questions about what kind of pastry this was on the cream cakes, and what kind of filling was in the eclairs.

"Would you like to taste one?" Mrs. Daly asked her.

"Heavens no, thank you Mrs. Daly, thank you so much; I was only interested, that's all. I ask too many questions, I'm afraid."

"Nice to see someone awake and not half dozy all the time." Maggie's father was full of approval.

Maggie stood there, feeling very shabby in her beige shirt and brown shorts. Grace was in a yellow and white dress with a big white collar, she had little yellow shoes. She must have a dozen pairs of shoes, Maggie thought enviously, always something to go with her outfit.

Grace took her arm. "Is it all right if we go off now?" she asked to nobody in particular but to everybody at the same time. Grace forced other people to be charming too. Mrs. Daly was nodding and smiling, Mr. Daly was wishing them good weather, Charlie looked up from the boxes he was collecting, to grin at them.

Out on Bridge Street Grace looked at Maggie anxiously. "It was all right to come, wasn't it? I wanted you to show me the tombstones you were talking about."

"Yes, but . . . ?" Maggie was bewildered. Surely Grace wouldn't want to go off with her, with just Maggie when there was so much else to do, so many other people to meet and such an amount of revolting wriggling maggots to be threaded onto those hooks.

But apparently that was what Grace did want.

"Please, Maggie," she said. "I'd love to see the names and the things people said."

Maggie was still hesitant.

"The fishing . . ." she began.

"Oh we can join them later, I met Liam on my way here. I said we'd be along in about an hour or more."

"What did he say?"

"He said 'fine' or something." Grace was unconcerned.

She left her bicycle parked at the back of Daly's, and arm in arm, they went up Bridge Street to the top of the town. Grace peeped into the Garda barracks just to see what it looked like, she said.

Sergeant Sheehan told her to come in and have a look around.

"Do you have prison cells here?" Grace asked with interest.

"Not here, child." He looked at her affectionately.

Seamus Sheehan had only sons; this was a beautiful sunny girl. The little one of the Dalys seemed dazzled by her almost.

"What do you do with criminals?"

"They go to jail in the big town. I've a room back there with a big padlock on it if you'd like to be kept in detention."

Grace giggled. "No, I was only getting to know the place."

"Quite right too." Sergeant Sheehan seemed much more cheerful today, Maggie thought, like her father was, and her mother, and like Miss Byrne the physiotherapist who made it her business to come over and ask Grace how they were settling into the lodge, and hoping it wasn't too damp for them.

Grace was fascinated with the graves and the tombstones. She said she would bring a notebook the next time so that she could write them all down.

"We won't be buried here, of course," Grace said conversationally.

"No, we'll be in the Catholic graveyard. Well *we* will, anyway," Maggie explained. "If you stay then I suppose you will too."

"Of course we'll stay, why would we not stay?" Grace sat on the edge of an old untended grave. "Hey, we should do something for this poor James Edward Gray, nobody's weeded around him for years. Of course, we're going to stay."

Maggie was helping to remove some of the bigger dandelions from James Edward Gray's resting place.

"People were wondering would you not find it all too dull for you here," she said in a small voice.

"Heavens no, it's fantastic. You want us to stay, Maggie? You don't want us to go away, do you?" Grace's beautiful face was troubled. She looked really anxious.

Maggie couldn't remember why she had felt so upset yesterday evening as she had walked home along by the Fern, and how she had wished that the O'Neills had never come here.

She looked at the worried blue eyes of Grace O'Neill, and with a great big smile that went all over her face, Maggie Daly said, "Of course we don't want you to go away; it's great that you're here." And she meant it.

She meant it not just at that moment but for a long time. Like when they joined the fishing party which was waiting for them at the footbridge.

"Sorry," Grace said casually, "I dragged Maggie off to show me the graves. You're right, they're fabulous. We're going to try and smarten up James Edward Gray a bit."

"Where's he? In the corner near the wall is it?" Dara asked.

Maggie breathed a sigh of relief. Dara wasn't a bit annoyed that Maggie had taken Grace away. People like Dara didn't get annoyed, Maggie told herself. Only mean-spirited people like herself got jealous and possessive and annoyed. Grace was telling Michael that on consideration she wondered could he bait their lines with those lumps of bread they had been talking about yesterday; she said she thought it would be easier to learn on bait made from crusts and then she could progress to maggots later.

Dara was disappointed. She had a jar of maggots ready for threading onto hooks. But Michael said Grace was right, better get used to this kind first, because it was always easier to hand.

Grace flashed Maggie Daly a smile. Things were much easier than they seemed, the smile said.

Kitty Daly thought that Mrs. Ryan wasn't bad for a grown-up; at least she wasn't a religious maniac like her own mother was. She was a woman you could talk to a bit.

"Do you think I could work for a bit in the bar, Mrs. Ryan?"

"No, Kitty, I'm sorry."

"Why not?"

"You're too young. That's one reason. We don't need anyone. That's another."

"I'm almost fifteen. That's not young."

"I know it's not." Kate sighed. All this terrible sulking and mulish behavior probably lay ahead with her own Dara. "But it is too young for bar work. I suppose this is a silly question, but why couldn't you work in your own shop?"

She took one look at Kitty's face and decided that it was a silly question. The girl looked distressed.

"Did you want the money for something in particular?"

"Yes."

"Well, maybe you could try to see if there is any other way of getting what you want. Like if it's clothes, could you make them?"

"It's hair, Mrs. Ryan."

"Hair?" Kitty had the Daly curls, frizz really. There was nothing startlingly bad about the child's hair. It was clean and neat, and a brownish reddish color.

"Yes, a good cut would make all the difference, and no matter what else Mrs. Walsh is she does know how to cut hair."

Kate let the comment pass. No point in drawing an argument on herself with this difficult girl.

"Could you do a deal with her? Sweep up the hair from the floor, make people cups of tea, put the towels out to dry for two weeks, say, and then she might give you a haircut free?"

Kitty considered it without much pleasure.

"It wouldn't be much fun."

"No, but if she agreed it would get you the haircut."

"Two weeks is an awfully long time."

"True. I suppose you'd have to work out whether it's worth it or not."

Kitty thought a bit. Mrs. Ryan was a lot better than most people's mothers. She didn't say things like, your hair was fine the way it was, or, at your age I didn't have the chance to go to hairdressers. She put her mind to the question properly.

"Yes, well I'll give it a go," she said ungraciously.

"Kitty."

"Yes, Mrs. Ryan?"

"Do you want a hint?"

"All right."

"If I were you, I'd tell Mrs. Walsh how much you admire her own hair, and the way she cuts other people's, and you were wondering if you could make her a proposition. I'd be over-polite if I were you, because Mrs. Walsh is a very busy person with a lot on her mind, and

she'd be quick to dismiss an idea unless it was put to her nicely."
Kate Ryan saw the defensive look on Kitty's face, and hastened to
say, "I mean, Kitty, I couldn't care less if you shaved your head bald
and painted the Irish flag on it. I think your hair is fine as it is, but I
know what you mean about a good cut giving it a better shape. So
you can take my hint if you like, or ignore it if you like. Now I must
get along with my work."

Kitty thanked her, less grumpily than she had been going to. And
in fact it was a good idea. She would ask Mrs. Walsh straight away.
Imagine Mrs. Walsh going to bed with men for money. It was unbe-
lievable, but that is what she did. Everyone knew, but no one talked
about it much. Imagine men paying to go to bed with anyone as old
as Mrs. Walsh.

Kerry O'Neill had no great hopes about his new school. He had
gone there with his father for an unsatisfactory visit, and Father
Minehan had marked out a certain amount of work that would have
to be done. He had agreed that since Kerry was fifteen it would not
be practical for him to learn the Irish language at this stage, but he
would be expected to master enough of it to get the general sense of
things Irish.

He was a forbidding-looking man, white, ascetic, with a nervous
smile. He had managed to suggest more than once to Kerry's father
that the school, which was a very illustrious one, had fallen on hard
times due to a massive and expensive rebuilding program. There was
a building fund that would cripple the community eventually; they
couldn't raise the fees yet again this year, so they often had to rely on
the generosity of those parents who were lucky enough to be financially secure to help in some of the extreme times of need.

Kerry had been quiet and respectful through most of the interview.
At an early stage in the proceedings he realized that Father Minehan
didn't respond to charm. He walked admiringly around the old buildings and asked bright questions about the original building and the
time that the order had first set it up.

"It's only been here a hundred years. It's not one of our older
foundations," Father Minehan had said a little testily.

"Don't forget, I'm from the United States. That seems very old to
me," Kerry said with a smile.

Father Minehan softened then. Kerry had said the right thing.

Coming home in the car his father looked at Kerry.

"You handled that one well, son. Our sort of cleric, wasn't he?"

Kerry didn't join in what he considered his father's all-men-to-gether mode. "I think he was all right, he has a job to do."

Patrick was annoyed. "What do you mean, he has a job to do?"

"Well, just that. He has to keep me in my place, arrogant young American know-it-all, trample me down a bit. He has to try to fleece you for his building fund. Irish-American: more money than sense, get him to sign a check."

Patrick gave a genuine shout of laughter.

"It didn't take you long to sum him up. Still, it's got a great reputation. It's one of the finest schools in Ireland."

Kerry turned away to look out of the window; he knew what his father would say next, and he knew the tone he would say it in. Patrick was about to say that he got the poorest of educations in grade school and had to go back when he was twenty to learn more than reading and writing. He often said this. But he never got the response he was hoping for. Kerry O'Neill never once said that it certainly hadn't made any difference, as Father had done so well. He never said anything at all.

Grace, on the other hand, was looking forward to starting school. It was different for her, she told Kerry, she knew all her friends already, she would be in the same class as Dara and Maggie and Jacinta. They had told her all about the worst things, and how to get around Sister Laura. Grace was going to have to learn Irish, and Sister Laura had suggested she become familiar with the alphabet and a small amount of vocabulary before term began.

The others had been very helpful, although the boys had taught her a really rude phrase which she might easily have said unless Dara had told her what it meant. She had gotten her navy uniform in the big town, and even the plain skirt and jumper and the pale blue shirt which looked so dull and drained the color out of the other girls, could not take from Grace O'Neill's healthy good looks. She bought a navy hair ribbon and tied up her golden curls.

She paraded with her school bag for her brother.

"How do I look?"

"Great." His mind was elsewhere.

"Thanks a lot."

"No, seriously, you do look great. You look older than you are."

"Older in this?" Grace was disbelieving.

"Yes, you look much more grown up than all the other puddings here. Don't let these fellows make any more rude remarks. You hear?"

"Oh Kerry, it wasn't fellows telling rude remarks. It was Tommy and Liam and . . ."

"Just not anymore."

Grace wished now she hadn't told him. He didn't understand how funny it had been.

"Sure, sure," she said to placate him.

"You've no mother, Grace, and Father lives in his own world. Somebody has to look after you. That's why I sound like an old bear, an old hen . . . whichever it is that does the clucking and fussing."

"I think it's a hen," she laughed, and ran toward him to give him a hug. "It's hens that fuss. It's the bears that hug. You're very good to me, Kerry."

The door opened and Patrick came in.

"Is that your new uniform? You look fantastic; a real scholar," he said admiringly.

Grace still had her arms around her brother's waist.

"Kerry's been setting me right, and giving me all kinds of good advice about going to school."

Patrick looked pleased. He often wondered what the children talked about when they were on their own. They seemed quite content.

"I just thought someone should mark her card," Kerry said with a note of insolence that Grace noticed too. She looked up at him anxiously, and let her arms drop.

"Good." Patrick was easy and relaxed. "I'm glad you're doing it. I'm afraid that I have too much faith in you pair; I think you were born knowing everything, being able to do everything. I don't mark your cards enough, I suppose."

"That's a good complaint to have, Father." Grace was hasty in her attempts to avert this scene, whatever it was.

She spoke quickly. "I hear so many people complaining about their parents who tell them this and order them to do that. You just stay as you are. Tommy Leonard says his father is at him night and day."

"Not enough to get him to keep a clean tongue in his head," Kerry said.

Suddenly Grace felt weary. "Look, fight if you want to, I'm not going to keep chatting. I think I'll go to bed."

The light had gone from her face. Both her father and brother looked stricken.

"I wasn't fighting, Gracie, really," Kerry said.

"Listen to me, honey, I couldn't fight with anyone, not tonight, now that I see you all dressed up to go to your Irish convent school. My heart is so full, Grace. I wish, I wish so much . . ."

They knew what he wished. They knew that Father wished their mother were alive. But he didn't say it. He just said that he wished things were different.

Grace had met most of the girls who would be in her class and who lived in Mountfern. But there were quite a few from out in the country. When they saw the newcomer they were dazzled. At first they giggled a bit at the beautiful girl with the golden curls tumbling down from a topknot tied with a shiny navy ribbon. And they nudged each other at her American accent.

Sister Laura made a small speech of welcome at assembly and said that she knew the girls of Mountfern convent would be, as they always were, welcoming to a stranger in their midst and help her to feel at home. Dara whispered to Grace that this was all nonsense. There never had been a stranger in their midst before. Grace was the first one. Maggie saw Grace and Dara laughing together at assembly, and tried to stop this feeling that she was being left out of things.

Sister Laura was speaking about the school year that lay ahead. She had every hope that 1962–1963 would be a year that they would all remember for the amount of hard work they put into their studies. Even those who had no formal examinations this year would, it was hoped, show a diligence that would long be remembered in the establishing of the convent in Mountfern as a legend in the houses of the order. Sister Laura said that sister houses had been achieving a reputation for scholarship which had so far evaded Mountfern. Let 1962–1963 be the year that all changed, the year they emptied their minds of silliness and let the sun of learning shine in.

They stood there in the navy uniforms. Kitty Daly splendid with the new hairstyle which had caused Kerry O'Neill to say "You look nice. Did you change something about yourself?" and sang the hymn to Our Lady to mark the beginning of the new term. Kitty had put all silliness out of her mind and was concentrating heavily on the information that Kerry did not go to his boarding school for another week. Grace would be out of the way at school. If Kitty were to feign a terrible sickness and go home, they would never suspect her of malingering, not on the very first day of term. Then she could walk up as far as the Grange, and if that old bag Miss Hayes didn't get suspicious, she should surely find a chance to run into Kerry. Sister Laura was right, start the year as you mean to go on.

Dara sang lustily as well. It had been a great summer holiday after all, in spite of all the changes at Fernscourt. She and Michael had said last night, as they sat on the window seat, that they wished they had somewhere to go, some special place still like that room they had in Fernscourt that was theirs. But wasn't it funny that none of them ever wanted to go back and play in the ruins now? They had only been once with Grace and it was like going back somewhere that belonged to another part of their life. Mr. O'Neill had urged them to continue playing there, but things had changed, there were bicycles for one thing, and the fishing for another. And it was great to have someone as lively as Grace around. Maggie was a great friend, but she was very mousy, and always afraid of what would happen, and of someone objecting or getting annoyed. Grace hadn't a fear in the world. She was magnificent.

Sister Laura sang to Our Lady, Queen of the Angels and Star of the Sea, and wondered why she felt Grace O'Neill was unsuitably dressed for school. The child wore her navy school uniform; she had no hint of make-up. She did not have pierced ears and great loops of earrings. She had no bosom apparent beneath her navy jumper. She was singing the hymn as assiduously as the others. What was it about her that made her seem not a twelve-year-old, but something much more precocious? Sister Laura liked to consider herself a fair woman. She hoped that she was not taking an unreasonable dislike to the child just because she had a beautiful face, tanned skin and golden hair.

Jacinta White nudged Maggie Daly to ask her why she wasn't singing.

"Sorry," whispered Maggie, and joined in the hymn.

Jacinta was relieved. She thought Maggie's face looked very worried, as if she had something that was upsetting her. But of course Maggie often looked like that.

Fergus Slattery called to the Grange to see old Mr. Johnson about a sale. It appeared that Patrick O'Neill had made an offer, a most generous offer for a small paddock owned by the Johnsons, and the right of way to bring horses to and fro from this field from the main road across the Johnsons' land.

"I can't see a thing wrong with it myself, but the American said to be sure, and do it through a solicitor, so here we are, Fergus. I'm sorry for bringing you all the way up here, I thought maybe your father might come, and we'd have a bit of a chat."

"He has a cold on his chest, and Miss Purcell won't let him out of the house. He says he's going to look for a writ of habeas corpus if she keeps him there much longer." Fergus spoke absent-mindedly. He was looking at the papers. "What does this fellow want the land for up here?"

"I can't tell you, that's for certain. Marian says he's doing it out of the generosity of his heart, because he knows we're a bit strapped for cash. We wanted to get a bit of a paint job done but it costs the earth these days."

"Is that field useful to you?"

"Not at all, it's only a nuisance to us. The hedges and walls are all broken, anyway, but it says somewhere there, doesn't it, that he's going to build them up?"

Fergus had been reading this. "Yes, he can build walls and low constructions for the maintenance of cattle, livestock or horses. I suppose that's what he wants, to set up a rival stables, take the one bit of business you have left."

"I don't think so." Mr. Johnson was mild. "He's signed an agreement with us about using our horses, paying a retainer even, in case he doesn't have sufficient guests for them. He's going to be the making of us, Fergus. Paying a great big rent for that falling-down Gate Lodge, too, and a year in advance because we had to do a bit of smartening it up."

"Smartening it up! From what I hear, you practically built a new house," Fergus snapped.

"What have you against him, boy?"

"It's a good question, Mr. Johnson, and a timely one. I'll look at this document now, and stop all this sounding off."

Fergus read the totally straightforward deed of sale drafted by a perfectly honest solicitor. Reluctantly he agreed that if Mr. Johnson wanted to sell, then there was nothing here that was out of the way, and that the price offered was well higher than the normal rate per acre hereabouts.

As a last, and almost petty gesture, Fergus asked whether Mr. Johnson could see *any* reason, apart from the goodness of Patrick O'Neill's heart and his wish to give them decorating money, why a businessman should suddenly make an offer for that particular field.

Mr. Johnson's mild old eyes looked surprised.

"Well of course there's a reason, Fergus. He needs a place where he can keep horses himself. And suppose he and Marian fall out, suppose Marian sets her cap at him too obviously and he isn't willing, well he'd need to have a fall-back position if he's offering his guests riding lessons, pony trekking, hunting and all. It's to cover himself."

Fergus was astonished at such clarity of vision.

"And does Marian see it like this?" he gasped.

"Now, now, now Fergus, do women ever see things the way they are? Have you known a woman who could see further than romance and yards of veil and wedding days? Let them go on like that, it doesn't do anyone any harm."

Fergus felt a chill. It was like playing God with people's future, he thought, as he arranged the signature of the deed of sale.

Olive Hayes wrote a long letter to her sister in New Zealand every month. She kept a carbon copy of it, and knew her sister probably did the same. They could refer back easily to small incidents that each had described over the years and they never forgot anything, no matter how trivial. Miss Hayes knew of the health of the elderly Reverend Mother who was always expected to die and then rallied, just when a successor had been more or less agreed for the community. Over on the other side of the earth in a convent on a cliff in South Island, Sister Bernadette knew about the O'Neill family, and how little Grace continued sunnily her life in Mountfern. Grace had even asked Miss Hayes if she would like to come to the sale of work up at the convent which was usually for the children's parents.

"You helped me make all the jam and cakes. You're more entitled than anyone," Grace had said.

Miss Hayes had been very pleased, but she wondered was she stepping out of place.

"Perhaps Miss Johnson?" she had said tentatively.

"Ugh, ugh, no thank you very much," Grace had giggled. "We don't want to be giving her ideas, Miss Hayes."

Olive had found that very endearing. She told her sister that Patrick O'Neill had gone to the States again. He traveled the whole way there as easily as some people took a train from the big town to Dublin. Miss Hayes felt that he had waited until Kerry was safely installed at his boarding school before he went. It was no trouble to look after Grace, but Kerry might have been a handful.

Miss Hayes looked back at the carbons of her previous letters and noticed with satisfaction that she had made this very same pronouncement in July when the O'Neills had arrived. Now, five letters later, she was interested to know that she had been right.

Kate Ryan decorated the Slatterys' office with holly at Christmas time. She thought how strangely unfestive it all was compared to everywhere else in Mountfern. The church had its huge crib and in the window of the presbytery there was a Christmas candle and another smaller crib, lovingly tended by Miss Barry who hadn't touched a drop since the summer.

Leonard's stationery and paper shop was all done up with the paper chains and streamers it sold. Mrs. Meagher was still in mourning for her husband, but she had sprigs of tinsel and glitter around the Christmas-wrapped brooches and earrings in the window of the shop. The cinema had two large Christmas trees with lights that flashed on and off. Declan Morrissey said it gave him a headache to look at them, and every single year he managed to fuse the lights in the cinema when he was putting up these ridiculous Christmas decorations. Daly's Dairy had very smart plaited rings of ivy and holly twisted around each other and tied with a red ribbon. They had been made by Kitty apparently, who was a changed girl according to all accounts, and had seen how to do this home-made decoration in one of those American magazines she was always reading.

In the post office there were some colored paper chains, a big silver banner saying Peace on Earth, and a collection box discreetly placed in case anyone might interpret the season of good will as a time to give a few pennies toward gifts for a children's orphanage. Dunne's pub had a big plastic Santa Claus in the window. There was hardly any point in their putting up any further decoration since they were yet again on the verge of packing up and going to Liverpool. Jimbo Doyle had put a Christmas tree for his mother in the window of their small house, and had agreed after much nagging to get proper fairy lights that worked. His mother had said that she was sick of hearing all the work Jimbo was doing in other people's houses while their own looked like a very good imitation of a rubbish heap.

In the Garda barracks, Seamus Sheehan looked in some doubt at the decorations Mary had bought on her last visit to Dublin. He wondered whether they were appropriate to the walls of a Garda Siochana station. Arty-looking cut-out robins and reindeer with little holes where you inserted mistletoe or holly. But Mrs. Sheehan had been adamant. She had read about them in a magazine which said that all the best people in Dublin had these in their homes now, and she wanted to drag a bit of style into Mountfern no matter how much they all resisted it.

Judy Byrne had planted two neat window boxes of her small house with holly bushes and miniature Christmas trees. They looked very festive and elegant at the same time, people told her. Patrick O'Neill had made a point of coming in to congratulate her on them. He had stayed for a drink at Judy's insistence because of the season. She ran next door to Foley's with a tray and came back with a large whiskey for Patrick and a small sherry for herself.

She told Patrick that she didn't keep drink in the house. She thought it was a pity for single ladies to start opening the bottle at a regular hour each evening. Single women had to be so careful. Not that she was saying a word against Marian Johnson of course, and in a hotel poor Marian had to be sociable. Still it *was* a danger, and it could run away with you all too easily.

Across the road Mr. and Mrs. Williams had their house neatly draped in holly and ivy. The Protestant church had been decorated by their few parishioners. Dr. White and his wife had threatened to have no decorations this year if this ridiculous row about mistletoe wasn't solved. Jacinta wanted a big bunch of it on the door just as you came in; Liam wanted none of it in or near the house. Never had a battle been fought so long and bitterly. Tommy Leonard said it was better than being at the pictures listening to the two of them. Dr. White decided eventually that a small discreet sprig of mistletoe be placed over the kitchen door, that it should not be publicly referred to, and that if this row began again, both Jacinta and Liam would remember Christmas 1962 as the year they not only had no decorations but no presents and no turkey either.

Miss Purcell wasn't best pleased when she saw Kate Ryan on a chair with a sprig of holly and a pack of thumb tacks.

"It was never the way here; Mr. Slattery never requested it," said Miss Purcell, lips in a hard line and the two red spots coming up magnificently on her cheeks.

"I know, Miss Purcell." Kate was falsely apologetic. "It's quite ridiculous really, but the children went up to Coyne's wood and they picked lovely bits full of berries, so I thought the least I could do . . . you know Mr. Slattery wouldn't want to offend . . . and in the spirit of Christmas . . ."

She finished no sentence and did not explain that she had asked Michael and Dara to collect a big box and deliver it to the office for

her. A Christmas card from Fergus's sister Rosemary in England and
then old Mr. Slattery, Fergus and Miss Purcell in paper hats sitting
around a small turkey dinner. It didn't seem nearly celebratory
enough for someone as warm and funny as Fergus.

He was pleased and surprised. He had been at the district court in
the town, his father had gone to talk to an old crony on the grounds
of a will that might be changed, but really in the knowledge that a
bottle would be opened. Fergus looked at the holly with pleasure.

"We never had that; it's lovely," he said simply.

"Not even when your mother was alive?"

"Not really. She was never strong, you know. She didn't have all
that energy like you have."

To herself Kate thought that it didn't really take much energy to
stick a few bits of holly on a wall behind pictures, or around a doorway for a man and a boy. But she said nothing. She didn't mention
that Grace O'Neill had said the very same thing; her mother had
been unwell always. They didn't have Christmas decorations, it
would have been tiring for her.

"I got you a present, Kate," Fergus said. "You're a hard person to
buy for; you have everything."

"I felt the same about you." She produced a big wrapped parcel.

"Isn't that great, to be the two people who have everything,"
Fergus said, and waited for her to open hers first. It was a day excursion ticket to Dublin, two gift vouchers—one for Switzer's and one
for Brown Thomas—and a note saying: "On presentation of this
paper to her employer, Mrs. Kate Ryan will be granted one day's
leave from her lawful employment during the working week."

Kate stared at it in delight.

"I thought you could go to the January sales, and those vouchers
are to make sure you go to Grafton Street and see nice things. You're
not to be buying up household goods in Clery's, mind." He spoke
gruffly to hide his pleasure in her delight.

"I'll enjoy every minute of the day." She hugged him. "Fergus, you
are a darling. Thank you very much."

"Well now, let's see what you gave me." He opened the box. It was
a beautiful edition of *Moore's Melodies* with huge over-flowery illus-
trations by Daniel Maclise.

"I remembered you said you like Thomas Moore—that day at the
concert, when Michael's class was murdering some of the melodies. I
thought you'd like this." She beamed at him and saw to her conster-
nation that his eyes were far too bright. She spoke quickly until he

had recovered a calm voice himself. "I got it inside in the town. You know, Gorman's bookshop, I asked them to look out for an old edition and they came up with this. John and I have been looking at it ourselves. I hope you like it."

Fergus had recovered his voice.

"I love it. Miss Purcell and my father won't know what's ahead of them this Christmas day. They're going to get a blast of the lot here . . . I might come over to your place and sing them through for you as well."

Kate said that was a promise and she was holding him to it. At some stage over Christmas Fergus Slattery was to walk up River Road with his Moore book in a plastic bag in case it rained on it, and he would sing the entire repertoire for whoever was in Ryan's Licensed Premises.

"That should empty the place for you and lose you your trade before O'Neill takes it away," Fergus said.

"Now Fergus, it's Christmas time. Stop talking about him. And wasn't John Ryan right, as he is in so many things? For all his great chat and plans there isn't a sod turned on that site yet. It's going to take longer than he thinks to get his hotel going in a place that moves as slowly as Mountfern."

Kerry came home from school on a day when Patrick had to be in Dublin for further talks with the Tourist Board. The train would need to be met. Marian Johnson was only too happy to oblige. She had heard that Patrick was trying to arrange that Brian Doyle the builder see to it, and Brian had replied with spirit that he was a building contractor, not a chauffeur. He would be quite happy to do anyone a favor, but would not be asked to do a driving job as if it were part of his terms in getting the Fernscourt contract.

Patrick had admired this viewpoint and apologized. Many another man would have had less pride and courage than Brian Doyle, and would not have jeopardized their chance of the biggest building job in these parts in years. But Brian was not one to sit back and allow anyone to assume he was what he was not. He did himself more good by his truculent attitude with Patrick than he ever knew.

Marian was pleased too, although she thought Brian Doyle was insane. She stood on the platform raking the crowd of passengers who got off, looking for Kerry.

He seemed to have gotten taller or thinner somehow at school. Very handsome in his school blazer, and carrying his sports bag as

well as his suitcase. He smiled pleasantly at Marian, and looked
around for Grace.

"She's busy decorating the lodge for Christmas," said Marian, who
had told the child there was no room in the car. "She'll see you back
at home. Your father has to be in Dublin. He said to tell you he's very
sorry."

"I'm sure he is," Kerry was polite and cold.

"So I thought we might have a little lunch, you and I in the hotel
. . . to get to know each other." She twinkled at him, but Kerry
didn't twinkle back.

"We do know each other don't we . . . ?" he said, bewildered.
"You're Miss Johnson . . . from the Grange."

"Marian," she said.

"Yes, well."

It was most unsatisfactory. Marian had wanted to lean her elbows
on the table of the Grand or the Central and have a lunch with this
handsome blond son of Patrick's. Now it was all falling to pieces.

Kerry looked at her carefully and long. It was as if he were deciding
what to do. And then it was as if he had decided to turn on the
electric light of his charm.

"Well Marian . . . if you're sure I may call you that, I'd love to
have lunch with you even though we do know each other already.
That would be very nice."

They went to the Central. Marian waved at the people she knew
whose heads went close together to discuss what she could possibly be
doing with this teenage boy. They had tomato soup, boiled bacon
and cabbage followed by apple pie and ice cream. Kerry told her little
about school, less about his father and nothing about their life as it
used to be in America. However he did learn about what had been
going on in Mountfern, and that Grace seemed to love her school,
had plenty of nice little girls as friends. Grace and his father had
been taking riding lessons and both were progressing very well. There
had been endless delays about clearing the title for the final land
purchase in Fernscourt.

Marian prattled on in what she had hoped would be their lunch of
getting to know each other, and she managed to present herself to
Kerry as three different ages during the space of half an hour. She
was getting younger as the lunch continued. She said that she was
quite demented trying to get the O'Neills to give up this ridiculous
idea of having Christmas lunch on their own, as a family. They
should join her and her father, and there would be four other guests,

charming people whom they would like, one of them was actually the Honorable and was terribly natural and unassuming, as if she were like everyone else.

On the journey back Marian had the vague feeling that she had gotten to know Kerry O'Neill not at all, but he had gotten to know almost all there was to be known about her.

"I'll call in later when your father gets back from Dublin," she said as she dropped him at the lodge and he was thanking her courteously.

"Why will you do that?" He was perfectly polite.

"Well. Gosh. Well, to see if he got back all right and to tell him that I met you safely."

Kerry looked at her, a clear unflinching look.

"Or maybe I'll drop in tomorrow . . . or sometime," Marian said foolishly.

She saw Grace racing out of the lodge to throw her arms around Kerry.

"Where *were* you? Miss Johnson said I couldn't come. I've been looking out for you for ages. Come in and tell me all about it, I've been dying for you to get here . . ."

The door of the lodge closed behind them. Marian saw the long stern face of Olive Hayes who was washing up at the kitchen sink. Marian told herself, as she had done many times before, that she mustn't rush it. Patrick O'Neill was a man not long a widower, a busy man with a million things on his mind. He had a tight self-sufficient little family. It would be foolish to try to break into it until they were ready.

That was the silly mistake Judy Byrne was making all the time, with her little invitations to a drink, and then fluttering in and out of Foley's instead of realizing that any man likes a woman with a good Waterford glass decanter on the sideboard.

They had a tradition in Mountfern that there was only one mass on Christmas Day. It meant that one priest was then free to go around and take holy communion to the people who weren't able to leave home. The mass was at nine o'clock. And the whole parish was there.

Judy Byrne wore a mantilla to communion, which looked very well on her. Miss Purcell, who really would have preferred a seven-thirty mass but would never criticize the clergy, wore a nice blue scarf that Kate Ryan had knitted for her, because she knew Miss Purcell had a blue coat.

Sheila Whelan had had a tiring night: young Teresa Meagher had had yet another row with her mother and wanted to leave home. There were no buses on Christmas Eve. Sheila had spent a great deal of time making cups of hot chocolate and taking further bars of Kit Kat out of the shelves. She cajoled and soothed. She told Teresa that if somebody left home at Christmas it had a terrible effect because it didn't just destroy *that* Christmas, but every other Christmas afterwards for both sides. She knew this, she told Teresa, very very well. She didn't go into details about how Joe Whelan had left her at Christmas, and how the big row over the road many years ago with Rosemary Slattery had been at Christmastime also. There was something about the season and all its expectations. Sheila talked long and gently about Teresa's mother feeling sad and lonely this Christmas, the first since her husband died; she must be given some little extra understanding; no of course, not over things that were totally unfair, but just an overall understanding.

Eventually the troubled child went to sleep on the sofa. Sheila put a rug over her, and a cushion under her head. Then she crossed the road and heard the whole story again from Teresa's mother, the insolence, the selfishness . . . Again she tried to talk of a daughter who had lost her father, and eventually Mrs. Meagher's red puffy eyes began to close, so Sheila left her.

She had urged them for form's sake to dress properly and go to mass as if nothing had happened. They were all going to Christmas lunch with the Whites. Judy Byrne was going too. Sheila would have preferred to have spent the day stock-taking, or sitting and listening to Radio Eireann. They had lovely programs on Christmas Day for people at home. It would be a real treat not to have to leave the house at all.

Patrick O'Neill walked his son and daughter up the church for their first Christmas Day in Mountfern. They had given Miss Hayes a lift from the lodge, but she didn't sit with them. She said she had friends to meet, and Christmas greetings to exchange. Everyone looked at the trio. Patrick in his camel-haired overcoat, stocky and handsome, smiling at this one, at that. Kerry taller definitely, he must have grown another two inches during his first term at boarding school. He wore a belted tweed coat, the kind many a youth of his age might wear, but it looked impossibly stylish because of the way the collar was turned up. Grace had a new outfit brought back from New York. It was a soft pale pink, a dusty pink coat with big velvet cuffs and collar in a darker pink. She had a velvet beret, a sort of tam o'shanter perched on top of all those golden curls as well. People turned to each other to smile at the beautiful child. Grace saw Dara and Michael and gave a little wave; they both stared at her open-mouthed.

Her father must have given this to her this morning already. She hadn't mentioned it yesterday. Maggie Daly sat in her brown coat which used to belong to Kitty. She felt like a colorless blob. Canon Moran was blessing everyone and wishing that the spirit of the Holy Child be with them now and always, and all Maggie Daly could think of was her own awful coat. No wonder Our Lord wasn't kinder to her, if she couldn't even drag her mind to think of him on his birthday of all days. Maggie gloomily accepted that she didn't deserve golden hair and a pink coat, or to be Dara Ryan's best friend.

The children all went for a walk in Coyne's wood on Christmas afternoon. It was a lovely clear, crisp day, and they wrapped up well and set out.

Kerry O'Neill came too. He told them about his school and spoke as if he were exactly the same age as everyone else, instead of being fifteen. Grace hung on to his arm a lot, and encouraged him to tell more tales, like the night the boy in the dormitory was listening to a transistor radio on an earphone and forgot where he was, and kept singing along with the Beatles. Yeah, Yeah, Yeah . . . and all the time Father Minehan was standing at the end of the bed watching him.

Kerry O'Neill remembered everyone's names. He was interested in everything they did. Tommy Leonard did one of his great imitations of Miss Barry the priest's housekeeper when she was on a tear. Michael explained to Kerry the best parts of the river, and told him a great hint about always noting a place where the cattle went to drink from. The cows stirred up mud, and also disturbed the water plants as they came to drink, so this meant fish would find it a good area for feeding, and you should position yourself about ten or twenty yards downstream and wait for them there. Kerry took all this in gravely and agreed with Jacinta White that Christmas wasn't Christmas without mistletoe, and at the same time agreed with her brother Liam that too much palaver could go on about it, just let it be there was the best solution. He asked Maggie Daly if all their family had that nice auburn hair. Did her sisters who were away nursing in Wales have it too? And Maggie pinked up happily and said that nobody had ever called it auburn before. Kerry said he heard that Dara was a demon fisherwoman, great at threading the maggots on the hooks and had caught a huge pike that struggled and fought. He said he thought Mountfern was the greatest place in the world, and as dark fell and they all went back to their homes, there wasn't one of the children who had come to Coyne's wood that would have remembered the day six months ago when they thought it was the end of the world because somebody had bought Fernscourt.

PART TWO

Chapter VII

Old Mr. Slattery died in the spring. He died exactly as he would have liked, sitting on his fishing stool and leaning back against a tree. Many people must have passed him by that afternoon thinking he was asleep. Miss Purcell's back was like a ramrod at the funeral mass. Her little wine-colored hat was replaced by a precisely similar one in black, and her disapproving face was set in harder lines than ever.

Fergus had felt achingly sorry for her.

She had mothered and bossed and bullied the old man for years. In return she had received a courteous fearful attention from him. What would she find as a replacement? He was very swift to tell her that he wanted no change in the situation.

"Oh indeed, and then when you up and marry, Master Fergus, when I'm an old woman, what will happen to me then?"

"I don't think I'll up and marry, I'm nearly thirty, and anyway if I do, won't she be a lucky woman to get the both of us?" He didn't say that Miss Purcell was an old woman already.

Fergus had one sister, Rosemary, married and living in Manchester. She came home for the funeral but she and he were like strangers. Rosemary was ten years older, she had been headstrong, he believed, and impatient. There had been rows, he remembered, when he was only six or seven and then she had left home. It had been made up of course but only in a fashion. Not properly. Letters at Christmas and cards on birthdays. No visits, no phone calls. There had been no rows with her little brother, but somehow Fergus hadn't expected his sister to come home. She came without her husband James, and without her sons. There was little mention of her family during the preparations for the funeral. She wore smart black and smoked the moment they were outside the church. Miss Purcell, who had been with the family at the time she left, hated her and barely disguised it.

"Back for the money," she hissed at Fergus, who only laughed. There was very little money, he had read his father's will. A legacy for Miss Purcell, a couple of hundred pounds to the church for masses, a small insurance policy whose small proceeds went to his grandsons in Manchester. There was nothing for the long-gone Rosemary. She would know that too. The business and the house were for Fergus. There was a touching personal note of gratitude that the young man had come back to Mountfern to keep the business going. Fergus had blinked a bit over that, he hadn't known how much his father had appreciated it. Rosemary sat and drank a whiskey with him; the conversation was brittle. He had the feeling that this was the last time he would ever see her, and he was determined for both their sakes that he would be pleasant and allow no recriminations to come into the conversation.

"Does it seem strange to be back home again?" he asked her.

She shrugged. "It's not home to me, never was really."

He hid his irritation. "I know. I forget. Well, people were glad to see you again."

"Did you think so? I think most of them had forgotten I ever existed. Real country bumpkins most of them."

"I suppose they must seem that way to you."

"And to you?"

"Oh I'm jes' an ole country bumpkin myself . . . like to sit in me ole rockin' chair and talk about the times gone by." He smiled at her, expecting some kind of an answering laugh.

Rosemary frowned at him. "You're turning into an old man, Fergus. It's a fact. You walk in small steps as if you were wearing slippers, and a sweater . . ."

Fergus felt the smile die on his face. He had been playacting to entertain her.

"Good Lord, I must watch that," he said, deliberately taking giant steps across the room. "Is that any better?" He took her glass to refill it and strode across the room as if he were playing grandmother's footsteps. This time it worked. She laughed at him affectionately.

"You're much too smart for here, Fergus. This is a dead-end town. Quit while you can, get to Dublin, even if you haven't the guts to sell up entirely. Drop it before it's too late and you turn into a vegetable or an alcoholic, or both."

He didn't comment on the fact that it was she who had had three whiskies while he had not finished his first.

"And what would I do that would be so exciting in . . . say Manchester?" he asked, hoping he kept the sarcasm out of his voice.

"You'd meet real people, not just the butcher, the baker, the candlestick maker. You'd find someone for yourself, instead of having to be like a eunuch here."

"Is that what they say I am?" He was very angry indeed. But there must be no more screaming matches with Rosemary in this house. History must not repeat itself.

"It's what I can see you are," she said, her eyes too bright, her hair slipping from the coil at the back of her neck. "What else could you be in a place like this, making sheep's eyes at that woman from the pub who does your typing? And never doing a thing about it."

"Sorry, Rosemary, hold on a minute, I've got to get us more water," he said.

He went into the kitchen and filled the jug, which he gripped with both hands to the sink until his knuckles were thin and white. How *dare* she speak of Kate like that? He would like to have hit her across the side of her silly drunken head. But it was a matter of hours. They would talk for another short while, then tomorrow she would have breakfast and he would drive her to the train in the big town. He would offer her something from the house as a souvenir. He had been going to suggest an old Victorian sewing box that had belonged to their mother. But, God damn it, no. It was too good for her, and Rosemary didn't look like anyone who would ever sew. Just keep the peace for a few more hours. That wasn't a weak thing to do, surely; it was a strong thing. He came back in smiling.

"Sorry, I was waiting for it to run cold. Where were we? I was making sheep's eyes at Kate Ryan. Who would I be making sheep's eyes at in Manchester?"

"I didn't say you were to come to Manchester." She sounded sulky now.

"But I will someday, surely. Not to work but to visit. I'd love to see my nephews. They must have nearly left school by now. Tell me about them."

He settled himself in his chair, his smile of interest and concern masking his rage.

"They've left," she said gruffly.

"Surely not? Hugh can only be barely sixteen?"

"Headstrong, impatient, won't wait, won't get an education." She looked into the fire.

"And what does James say about it?"

"He's hardly ever there to say anything. He's not around much." Rosemary still looked into the fire.

Fergus poured them both a last drink, and moved to less troubled waters. He suggested that Rosemary take a silver cigarette box back with her as a memento. Awkwardly she accepted it, and before she went to bed she gave him what passed for a kiss on the cheek. A sort of lunge.

"You're not the worst, Fergus, even though you're a bit of an eejit," she said, and her tones were those of love and praise, inasmuch as she could give either.

He lay awake for a long time and wondered about sheep's eyes. What way did one sheep look at another that the world regarded as foolish?

Eddie Ryan asked Mr. Williams the vicar if he could become a Protestant and be accepted into the Church of Ireland faith. Mr. Williams listened to him gravely and said it was a very big step and perhaps he should think more about it, maybe even discuss it with his priest or his parents. Mr. Williams was a kind man; never for a moment did he betray his knowledge of Eddie's latest deed, which involved breaking the little shutter in the confessional, something that had never been done since the church was built and had hardly ever been done in Christendom according to Canon Moran and Father Hogan. Eddie explained that the church was empty at the time, and he wondered what it felt like to sit where the priest did, pushing the shutters back and forth to listen to the penitents. He got a bit excited and kept whizzing them to see which one would close quickest, and that was when one came away from its moorings entirely.

Jimbo Doyle had to be summoned, and it was all very serious and high level. Canon Moran said he couldn't believe that the child would say the church was empty. Wasn't our Blessed Lord in the church in the tabernacle, watching Eddie Ryan desecrate church property and disassemble the place where the holy sacrament of penance took place?

Father Hogan kept saying, "What Cromwell left undone Eddie Ryan will finish," and pretending to panic when he saw him coming near the church.

It would be easier for him to be a Protestant.

"I have thought about it," he assured Mr. Williams. "I'm dead certain. Would I need an admission card to start coming here on Sunday?"

"Of course not, Eddie, but . . ."

"And if there's any questions, trouble like, you'll tell them I asked to join. That it's all above board. If they come hounding me?"

"Who would come hounding you, Eddie?"

"Almost everyone in the place, Mr. Williams, you wouldn't credit it. My mother said if she set eyes on me again today she wouldn't be responsible for what she'd do. Sergeant Sheehan said he has a room in the barracks with a lock on it and he's thinking of putting my name on it because it's where I'll end up. I couldn't tell you what the priests are like, because we're all meant to be . . . whatever it's called these days, you know loving all other religions . . . so it wouldn't do you any good to know what they're like down at the presbytery just now."

"Life can be very difficult." Mr. Williams was trying hard not to smile.

"You wouldn't know the half of it up here, with no flock so to speak of, and pots of money."

The impoverished Mr. Williams listened to this wryly.

"I don't have all that much, Eddie."

"I bet you have four pounds though," Eddie said.

"Well, I do, but I need it. I can't give it to you, no matter how great your need."

"No, my need isn't great. If I join your church I won't have to pay it."

"How, exactly?"

"I can say I'm a different faith, a different crowd altogether. I can't be responsible for some sum of money they say I owe in the last faith. For repairs. I'd never make four pounds. Never."

Mr. Williams was very kind. He could see that Eddie Ryan was not trying to put a touch on him; the sum was too huge to be possible even for the wildly optimistic.

"Why don't you weed a few graves for me, Eddie, tidy up the

graveyard. I could pay you say, five shillings. If you did a good job, then after several five-shilling days you could return to your old faith and pay your debts, and everyone would be happier."

"I thought you were supposed to be looking for converts, and snatching people away from the true faith."

"Oh no, we don't do much snatching here, more patting people down; that's what it seems to be about these days. Will I give you a sack for the grass and the weeds?"

Dara and Grace were in the graveyard looking after James Edward Gray. They had brought cowslips and primroses and had made an unsuccessful attempt to remove some of the moss and lichen from his stone with Vim. It had looked much better before their efforts, they realized. Maggie had been a bit funny about James Edward Gray, claiming that she found him and *she* was the one to look after him. Grace and Dara had agreed and gone to look for someone else who was pretty neglected. But Maggie had come after them in tears and said they could have James Edward Gray and keep him, she didn't care. Then she had stormed off home. She had been a bit like that lately, maybe it was trouble at home.

Maggie's elder sister Kitty was a bit bossy, and she had two sisters who were nursing in Wales. They could have lost their religion or not written home, or something. Mrs. Daly was an awful one for doing the right thing and the trimmings on the Dalys' rosary at night were as long as the rosary itself. Maggie must be getting some kind of trouble from her mother. That could be the only explanation of why she was so touchy these days.

Tommy Leonard came to collect Michael.

"There's no fish. What's the point?" Michael said.

"There's often no fish. As far as I'm concerned there's nearly always no fish. What are you after, some kind of record catch?"

Tommy was indignant. He had spent half an hour explaining to his father why a boy of thirteen should be allowed to go and fish with his friend, and now Michael didn't want to come.

"It's pointless, can't see any reason to drag all that stuff miles up the bank and miles back," Michael said.

"Lovely! When did this happen, this road to Damascus? Just when I was assuring my father that there was no better, healthier way of spending the afternoon."

"I don't know," Michael said.

"Listen Michael, you are a pain, and a big pain. What *is* it? Why was fishing what we did yesterday, and suddenly today it's what we don't do? I don't mind, I just want to know."

Michael punched Tommy to show that there was no personal ill-will involved.

"You know the way it is sometimes. There seems no point in anything. Anything at all," Michael said.

"Do I know how it is? Of course I know how it is. I feel that way most of the time. But why today? Now I'll have to go on my own or go back to the shop and say to my father he was right, I am a selfish pleasure-seeking lout . . ."

"Oh all right, I'll come with you."

"What about Dara and Grace and the others? Where are they? Did they all give up fishing too, suddenly? Did everybody except me?" Tommy wondered.

"Oh, who knows where they are? The Whites have gone to Dublin with their mother for the day; Dara and Grace are giggling some-where, you can be sure of that."

"Where's Maggie?"

"I don't know. I think she's as angry with all this giggling as we are. Come on then Tommy, if we're going to spend the day getting pneumonia for no fish, let's go and catch it."

"The sun is shining, you clown," Tommy said.

The sun had come out and Miss Hayes was planting some pansies that Kate Ryan had given her. Mrs. Ryan was very good about all kinds of flowers and Miss Hayes had heard some disparaging remarks that Judy Byrne had made about the appearance of the gate lodge of the Grange. Miss Hayes was feeling personally slighted. She had called at Ryan's merely for advice. Mrs. Ryan had given her the pansies and gotten her a lift back too from a passing customer. It was too far to walk in the sun, she had said.

Olive Hayes watered them well in, just as she had been advised. She would make a macaroni and cheese for the tea, that little Ryan girl was coming this evening. She and Grace O'Neill were very thick with each other. They never stopped talking and laughing. It would do your heart good to see them.

Grace and Dara left the graveyard hastily when they saw Eddie being instructed in the details of grave-tending.

"It's more than flesh and blood could bear, we'll have to leave," Dara said as soon as she saw her small brother.

"He's not that bad," Grace laughed.

"You don't know how bad he is, he'll probably dig up half the bodies in the graveyard. We're well out of it before he gets at it."

They scrambled to the wall where they had left their bicycles.

"We'll walk home through Coyne's wood. That way we won't get drawn into the fishing," Dara said.

"Yes, sure. Or else we could just say that we're not going fishing today." Everything was simple to Grace.

They wheeled their bikes through the woods which looked beautiful in the Easter sunshine. They heard pigeons and cuckoos, and small rabbits ran across their path as they walked.

"It's like fairyland here," Grace said happily.

"Is your father glad he came?" Dara asked.

"Oh yes, of course he is. Why?"

"He was in our pub the other night. I thought he looked kind of tired and upset."

"He gets upset over Kerry. Remember at Christmas I was telling you; and there's been something on his mind at the moment. I don't know what it is, he won't tell me. That means it's either about Kerry or about women."

"Women?" Dara's eyes were round.

"Yes, women falling in love with him. You know, I told you yucky Marian Johnson has."

"Oh yes, but you wouldn't mind that," Dara dismissed Marian.

"And I think Miss Byrne, you know, the chiropractor."

"Physio."

"Yes, whatever. And there's this woman in America." Grace looked troubled.

"Lord he *does* collect them," Dara said in mystification.

"I know, he's very old and everything, but he's very nice," Grace said defensively. "And rich of course," she added, in order to be strictly fair.

"Who's the woman in America?"

"A Mrs. Fine."

"Do you think it's serious? Isn't she married to someone else, if she's a missus?"

"No, he's dead or separated. There's no Mister Fine around."

"Do you like her?"

"She's OK. I don't want Father to marry anyone else. That's all."

"I know, but maybe he's not going to. Wouldn't she be here or he be over there if they were getting married? After all they're pretty old. They wouldn't want to be wasting time."

"He calls her a lot. He called her twice on Christmas Day."

"Oh that means nothing. Mrs. Whelan says people are always telephoning each other on Christmas Day and putting the heart across everyone else."

"I don't know." Grace was doubtful. "I had this friend in the States, Brigid Anne Moriarty. Well, she told me that her mother said Father was going to marry again, that everybody knew it, that he had a lady friend he worked with, and that they were going to get married quietly in New York."

"How did Brigid Anne know all this, and you and Kerry didn't?"

"Who would tell us? Anyway I told Kerry this on the day of mother's funeral."

"You mean Brigid Anne knew your father had a lady friend *before* your mother died?" Dara's face was horrified.

"But you see it wasn't true; obviously it wasn't. It was only a tale people told because Father was so well known among all these people, and because Mother was an invalid for so long."

Grace looked wretched as she went over this. Impulsively Dara threw her arm around her friend's shoulder.

"Don't worry about it, Grace, *please*. It's not happened. It's not going to happen. We can head off the awful Marians and awful Judys, and Mrs. Fine can't be any threat, otherwise she'd be here."

"Yes, I'm sure that's right."

"So why are you still sad?"

"Because I'm thinking about the day of the funeral and how upset Kerry was when I told him about what people were saying. But you're right. It's not going to happen: I won't think about it anymore."

They came out of the wood and cycled to the lodge. Miss Hayes said that Mr. O'Neill had been on the telephone to say he would not be back for tea. He had gone to Kerry's school. The boys had spent some of the Easter holidays there to take part in the Easter vigil and church services. They were meant to be getting holidays in a week. But Kerry was coming back tonight.

All through their macaroni and cheese they chattered excitedly about Kerry coming home. They cleared the table and washed the dishes with Miss Hayes. Dara marveled at the peace and quiet in this house, no Carrie clattering pans in the kitchen, no bar on the other side of the green door, no Leopold howling, no Declan complaining that he was going to be the baby in this family until he was an old-age-pensioner, no Eddie bringing some new doom and destruction down on them. No bustle. It must be lonely for Grace sometimes too, of course, so far from everyone.

They sat in Grace's room, and Dara tried on all her clothes. The shoes were a little too small, which was a pity since Grace had so many she could have given Dara any amount without missing them.

"Does your father ever fight with Michael?" Grace asked.

"No, no he doesn't."

Grace sighed heavily. "No, I think it's just my father and Kerry. It's something in them that doesn't mix."

"Of course Daddy gets very irate with Eddie, almost every day of our lives," Dara offered, in the hope of reassuring her friend.

"Eddie's different, as you said yourself."

"Yes," Dara agreed. "Eddie's very different, nobody could mix with him."

Dara cycled home and saw a man slipping into the Rosemarie hair salon, having looked up and down River Road nervously first. Could the unlikely rumor they had heard at school *possibly* be true? She must tell Grace tomorrow morning. She hoped Grace wouldn't be lonely as she waited for Kerry and her father to come home.

Grace wished she had never told Kerry about that stupid thing that Brigid Anne had said, about the gossip that Father had some other lady in mind to marry. Obviously it hadn't been true. It was nearly two years since Mother had died, and Father had no intention of marrying again. Father Devine had introduced him to several likely people, awful women from the parish, widows and terrible people. But Father used to laugh about them with her so Grace had no worries.

Kerry had a picture of Mother in his billfold, and also in the plastic folder at the back of his assignment book. Grace had seen him taking it out to look at it one day when he thought nobody was watching. And the picture of Mother that stood on the piano . . . Kerry was always adjusting it and making sure it stood right where it was best lit.

There was a portrait of Mother hanging in the hall. Mother had never liked it, she thought it made her look as if she had been dressed up to play the part of a fine lady. Father had laughed and told her that she *was* a fine lady. Kerry didn't like that picture, he never stopped to look at it. Once Grace asked him why he didn't like it, and he had said that Father had only dressed Mother up in jewelry and silks and paid a society painter to do the portrait, to show what a big man *he* was. It had nothing to do with Mother herself.

Kerry had said that when things were his to do what he liked with, he would take the picture outside and burn it. Then Mother would know how well he had understood her. Kerry said some very odd things from time to time.

Grace wished she knew why her father had driven all the way up to his school to collect him. Perhaps it was a sign that Father was going to be warmer to Kerry, but somehow she didn't think so.

Father Minehan was a fussy man. Anything that could be said directly and simply, he managed to dress up and obscure. Patrick had been fifteen minutes in the dean's study and still didn't know why he was being asked to take Kerry away. That very day.

"So, when all aspects are considered, and taking everything into account, very often, the greater good is achieved by the simpler option," Father Minehan said.

Patrick looked at the priest with disgust. His blue eyes were hard and unsmiling.

"Briefly, what did he do?" he asked again, but his tone was more curt.

"There are so many explanations and ways of looking at what we do and why we do it . . ." Father Minehan was beginning again.

"In two or three sentences, Father." Patrick had never been so ill-mannered to a man of the cloth. His old training made him feel a thrill of wrongdoing because he was interrupting a priest with a bark of command.

"If it were as easy as that . . ."

"It is as easy as that. I have driven for two hours to a school where I thought you were educating my son, a school to which I have given generous contributions I may add, and I hear, or think I hear that you want him to leave. Now. Why?"

Father Minehan was at a loss to answer a question so directly put. He remained silent.

"Come on, Father, I can't stay all week playing guessing games. What did he do?"

"Let's take it slowly, Mr. O'Neill."

"Let's take it at a nice brisk pace, Father Minehan. Did he bugger one of the other boys?"

"Mr. O'Neill, *please*!"

Now, for the first time, the priest was shaken into a direct response.

"He's a fifteen-year-old boy, Father, almost sixteen. Eventually, I suppose, if I ask enough questions we might get an answer. Was he drunk? Did he hit one of the masters? Did he miss mass? What in God's name prompted all these letters and phone calls that the FBI couldn't work out?"

"I'm trying to explain."

"God damn it, you are not trying to explain. Did he screw one of the maids? Did he deny the infallibility of the pope? If I drive here and take him away with me leaving behind buildings I'm goddamn paying to erect, I would like to know why."

"He took a great deal of money."

Patrick felt an ice-cold pool in the base of his stomach.

"That's not possible."

"I assure you . . ."

"How much?"

"Two hundred pounds."

"Have you any proof of this?"

"Oh yes."

"Perhaps you would be good enough to let me have it."

"Do you want your son here?"

"Not immediately. Let me hear it from you first, then we'll ask Kerry his side of things. Right?"

The old Patrick had returned on the outside. A brisk smile, the kind he used in his business deals . . . a charm not fulsome, just there. He composed his face to listen.

It was a tale of a charity football match in aid of deprived children. Patrick held his mask face with difficulty. The priest was so unctuous. He spoke of deprived children as if they were another species of life. The rugby match had attracted a lot of attention. People came from all over to attend it. There were three Irish internationals playing on each side. It wasn't often that you saw such talent gathered on one afternoon on the playing fields of an Irish school. The entrance fee had been two shillings.

The boys in the school all attended, of course, people from the neighborhood and rugby fans from all over Ireland, as well as some people from the newspapers. Father Minehan's voice lowered again, in case someone from the newspaper might be in the room with them. It was all highly unfortunate. Over fourteen hundred people

attended the match, many of them being men of property and generosity who gave much more than the two-shilling entrance fee.

Over two hundred pounds had been collected at the small tables
placed near the school gate. It was taken into the school in leather
bags, each with the amount it contained neatly written on a label
attached to it. The money was in Father Bursar's office ready to be
checked into a bank account next day. It disappeared. There was a
search. The search revealed among other things that some of the
senior boys were not in their dormitory; they came in later over the
wall. They were met by a reception committee.

Kerry O'Neill had an envelope with fifty-seven pounds of the collection still in his pocket.

"Balls," snapped Patrick. "Nobody could spend all that in a night.
What did he do? Buy a couple of properties down town?"

"He has not said what he did with it," Father Minehan said simply.

"But he hasn't said he took it, surely?"

"He cannot say otherwise. He is not a fool."

Again Patrick felt ice water moving in his stomach.

Kerry had packed. They had told him that morning that he was to
have everything ready; he would be leaving with his father. When he
came to the dean's study he had his fawn overcoat thrown casually
over his shoulders.

Patrick was annoyed by this, and by seeing the boy's luggage outside the door. It was showing they were beaten before they began.

"Can you throw any light on this, Kerry?" He was firm, not accusa-
tory, but wasting no time in pleas or expostulations.

"I'm sorry you had to drive up here, Father." Kerry was perfectly
calm.

"Tell us what you have to tell." Patrick didn't look at Father
Minehan, who stood there in classic thoughtful pose with one arm
across his waist, supporting the elbow of the other arm. A hand with
long white fingers spread discreetly over his face.

"I'm afraid there's nothing to tell, Father."

"You deny you took this money."

"No, I can't deny that, I'm very sorry."

"You don't mean you took it?"

"Yes, I did."

There wasn't a sound from the priest.

"In the name of God why did you do that? I could have given you money. I give you a bloody allowance every month, for Christ's sake."

Kerry stood still; regret was the only emotion Patrick could see on his face. Mild regret. No shame, no sorrow.

"So what did you want it for?"

An inclination of the head toward the priest, that was all.

"Could you leave us alone, Father Minehan?"

"No, Mr. O'Neill, this is my study. I do not choose to leave it."

Patrick made a decision.

"Yes, that's your privilege. Now you asked me to take my son away. I shall do that. Thank you for the part your community has played in his education so far."

Father Minehan had been prepared for a day of recriminations and explanations, and bringing in bigger guns like the Father Superior. He couldn't believe it was over already.

"Well, I have to say . . ." he began.

"I hope you have to say very little. We will not discuss any fees that might be owing by me to you, since I think we will agree that donations already given would make the pursual of those fees a grotesque impertinence on your part . . ."

"I assure you that . . ."

"I accept all your assurances. If I am owed any balance why not add that to the already significant sum I have given to the college? And I expect full and favorable reports and references on my son's progress and achievements in this school. I have fulfilled to the letter your request to me, once I understood it. I am taking him away with me in the next five minutes. Within the next five days I expect a detailed report which I can give to the principal of the next college he will attend. *And*, Father Minehan, I shall expect the most glowing of verbal references, should any school call you to inquire about Kerry."

"Well, there will have to be—"

"You are quite right, there *will* have to be arrangements made to that effect immediately, otherwise, I will create such a stink and a scandal that the smell will remain over these college walls for three generations to come. I will talk of the blackmail in order to get subscriptions, the extortion of further money from the children by making them pay to see rugby matches in your own premises. I will speak to the newspapers about the lax security and discipline that allows children in your care to scale walls and disappear in the evenings." He lowered his voice suddenly. "But all this would be very unpleasant and I am sure quite unnecessary."

He walked with Kerry from the school to his car. He looked at the creeper on the walls and remembered the day he had driven here to start Kerry off as a pupil.

Kerry sat in silence as they drove.

Patrick waited five minutes for an apology, an explanation.

He looked at his son's arrogant profile; he remembered his dead wife's hopes. He drew into a petrol station. Beyond the pumps where there was some waste ground.

He got out and with deliberate steps went around to Kerry's side of the car and opened the door. Kerry got out, a look of polite mystification on his face. Patrick hit him.

As Kerry reeled from the blow, Patrick hit him again on the jaw and rained blows into his body. Winded, Kerry made no real effort to defend himself, except to cry out . . .

"You big ape, you bog man . . . you're nothing but a bloody Irish bog man; that's why you wanted to come back to the bogs, you never left them."

Patrick had stopped punching anyway. He indicated a gents' toilet. "Be back here in five minutes. We're going home," he said, and he got into his car, wearily watching Kerry stagger away, bruised and bloodstained, to try and repair the damage to his face and clothes.

❄ Chapter VIII ❄

They knew that something had happened in the O'Neill family. And whatever it was, Grace was not going to talk about it.

Tommy Leonard thought that it was because Mr. O'Neill was being bad-tempered. He had heard stories of him shouting at people about delays and messing and inefficiency. And to Tommy Leonard all fathers were bad-tempered, because his own was a demon altogether.

Jacinta and Liam White thought that it might have something to do with someone being sick. Their father had been called up to the lodge one evening. So maybe it was an illness. Dr. White wouldn't tell them; he never talked about his patients. But if it was something simple like measles or mumps he would have said, so it could be a fatal disease.

Maggie Daly had heard that they were going away, people had said that Mr. O'Neill was so fed up with not getting the hotel built straight away he was going to pull out and forget the whole thing. Maggie half hoped they would, but in another way she wanted them to stay. She didn't hate Grace; she wanted to be her friend. The best that could possibly happen was that Grace would want the three of them—Dara, Maggie and her—to be friends, to be a proper gang with nobody left out.

Kitty Daly kept asking Maggie why Grace didn't come to play anymore, and whether Kerry had come back from boarding school. She was not at all satisfied when her little sister didn't seem to know.

Dara knew that Kerry had come back from school because she had been there the evening that Mr. O'Neill had gone to collect him. But the next day she had a telephone call from Grace asking her not to say anything to anyone about anything.

"What do you mean?" Dara was totally confused. "If someone says hello, am I not to say hello back?"

"This is serious," Grace said.

"I know it is. I'm serious too. Why can't you *tell* me what I'm not to say anything about? Why aren't you here anyway?"

"Is anyone listening to you?"

"No, I mean Dad's in the pub. Mam's at work, Carrie's in the kitchen, Michael's in the yard, Eddie is probably eavesdropping somewhere. What *is* it?"

"There's been a bad row, and I can't come out for a few days. Not till we're back at school, we might even be going away."

"Where, where are you going?"

"I don't know, *please* Dara, don't tell anyone what I told you."

"You didn't tell me anything. I don't understand any of this."

"About my father and Kerry not getting on. You know?"

"Oh that. No, I won't tell anyone. I wouldn't have anyway."

"And could you try to take the drama out of it all?"

"I didn't know it was a drama . . ."

"I've got to go now." Grace hung up.

They didn't see Grace until the first day of term, a whole week. She looked very pale.

Jacinta was triumphant. "I told you it was a disease," she said proudly. "It could be TB."

"Why don't you ask her?" Maggie said.

"You don't ask people who are riddled with TB if they're riddled with it; you pretend everything is normal," Jacinta, the doctor's daughter, replied.

Maggie noticed that Dara wasn't racing up to Grace as usual. Dara was on her own.

Good, Maggie thought. Now she knows how it feels to be left out of things.

But if anyone looked left out of things it was Grace. She was like someone recovering from a bad bout of flu.

Even Sister Laura warmed to the girl.

"Did you get any time to do those Irish lessons I set you?" she asked, in a kinder tone than she usually used when checking on homework.

"Yes, Sister, I have them here." The girl produced pages of sentences:

"I am going to town. Was he going to the town? We were not going to the town." All neatly written in the slopy writing and purple ink that the nun objected to, and was annoyed with herself for the unreasonable objection.

"That's very good," she said, impressed. "You must have spent a lot of time working."

"I spent all last week. I sat in my room all day, Sister." She looked downcast.

"Well, you're an example to them all, I must say. How is your brother getting on at his school, tell me?"

It was a courtesy, a little personal remark to show that Sister Laura cared about Grace and her family. The girl's face flushed a bit.

"He liked it very much, but the place was a bit damp so they decided because he has a weak chest . . . they thought . . . they said it would be better if he went to another school. Which isn't damp. More modern. So he's going there."

"Very wise, you can't be too careful with chests," Sister Laura said.

It was an odd thing to move the boy at the beginning of the summer term, very upsetting to child and school to have changes in the middle of the academic year. And surely the place couldn't be all that damp in the summer.

Still it was no business of hers. Sister Laura put her mind to the business of keeping the children's minds on school when everything outside was tempting them out of the classroom and on to the river bank, into the woods and over the springy green fields around Mountfern.

Patrick and Kerry sat at the breakfast table in the lodge. Miss Hayes left the refilled coffee pot on the table and explained that she was about to cycle into Mountfern for the messages. She wished Kerry good luck at his new school and said she hoped it wouldn't be damp like the last place. There was nothing as bad as a chill that settled on the chest. And she was gone.

She knew of course that there had been hell to pay between father and son.

Mr. O'Neill had said to her on that evening when he came back with the boy, looking as if he'd been in a fight with a crowd of thugs, that there were a few things the family wanted to discuss in confidence and they would probably go away for some days to do so in privacy. Olive Hayes had given it a little thought and said that it would be much better if *she* were to go away and let them have the house on their own. She had stocked up the larder and gone to a cousin in Galway without either giving or getting any further explanations. She knew that she had done the right thing; Mr. O'Neill had gripped her hand firmly when she returned and said that they had been greatly blessed to have found someone like her. He had also added that there would always be a place and role for her when the new hotel was built. *If* it was *ever* built. Life was full of obstacles, he had said with his engaging smile.

And so now she left them alone once more so that the father and son could say goodbye in whatever way they wanted to without having to lower their voices for fear of her overhearing them.

In fact they sat in silence for some minutes after they heard her bicycle creak out through the big iron gates of the Grange.

"I've done a lot of thinking, Kerry."

Kerry looked at him politely.

"We seem to have discovered that it wasn't for drugs, or for alcohol. It was not for anyone else . . . you do not appear to have made any friends. It was hardly for a woman, and at your age you are unlikely to have done anything for which you could be blackmailed. There was no race meeting where you could have lost it, and you aren't known in the bookies near the school, so it couldn't have been that. If you bought anything with it then that item was not delivered. You will not tell me and I have not been able to find out."

Kerry said nothing.

"Is that a summary of what has happened?"

"Yes, you left out a bit here and there." Kerry rubbed his bruised jaw.

"I wish that I hadn't beaten you. I've said that."

"I don't mind. It makes us quits."

"It *does* not make us quits. In no way does it make us anything like quits."

Patrick stood up and walked toward the window.

"It leaves me knowing that I can't control my temper; that's a weak position to be in. I am also left with the knowledge that you stole an enormous sum of money for a purpose which you cannot or will not explain, which leaves me in an even weaker position. How am I to continue in this way of life that I am trying to build for us if I cannot trust you? You may take money from Miss Hayes's purse; you may reach over the counter in Daly's and put your hand in the till. I may have to drive to this new school and hear a similar story.

"All that's happened to you is that you got beaten. Your life goes on exactly the same—new school, clean slate, reputation totally unsullied even to your little sister."

Kerry remained very still.

"In five minutes Marian is coming to drive you into the town, and you are getting the train to a school I have not seen. The principal has had a lying letter from that death's head Minehan. I've seen a copy of it. He will *not* have gone behind my back, so you start here with nothing on your record. This is your last chance, Kerry, your only chance."

"Yes, Father."

"No, I mean it. We've done a cosmetic job on it; we've papered it over. The last school was damp, you had a wheeze in your chest, medical advice . . . even Grace more or less believes it now. You've been given a new start. I'd like to embrace you and come with you to the school, and tell this new head priest, whoever he is, that I'm proud of my son and I want him to do well, like I did last time, but I don't have the stomach for it. So Marian is taking you to the train. And we agreed that in front of anyone around here we act as normal, as if we were the best of friends."

"Sure."

They heard the wheels of Marian's car.

"And maybe we can be the best of friends again someday."

"I hope so, Father."

He looked so handsome and straightforward standing there. Patrick really did believe that it was going to be all right. He had gripped Kerry's hand and put his other hand on the boy's shoulder when Marian came in.

"Yoo hoo! I'm not too early am I? I always think it's best to leave plenty of time, that way nobody's rushing too much." She glanced eagerly, like a bright fluffy bird, from one to the other. Patrick felt a sense of shame at using her like this. She was an honorable if boring and fussy woman. It was not fair to keep involving her like this when he had no intention of involving her more permanently. Marian would be useless in a crisis. She was perfect for domestic trivia. But she would have no idea what to do in any important area of life. Unlike Rachel Fine.

Patrick had telephoned her immediately after he had gotten his son cleaned up, seen by the doctor, and sedated. After he had reassured Grace with bland words, he had asked Rachel what to do. Rachel said that since he hadn't beaten it out of the boy, he was unlikely to discover it by any further force. She said that if she might draw on a metaphor taken from her own trade, the design and decor business . . . he should paper over the cracks. Pretend that everything underneath was as elegant as the surface, and make sure he created a believable surface. He had waited long enough to get back to his roots and realize his dream. Surely he wasn't going to let it all disintegrate into a public dog fight that would entertain the locals and people for miles around. Dignity had to be kept, position maintained. Give Kerry one more chance.

For a week Patrick had worked on her advice; it seemed the natural thing to do. He had almost forgotten how practical Rachel was, and how well she knew the right thing for him.

He wished Rachel were here in Mountfern.

He wished he had encouraged her to come with him.

After the first day of term Grace seemed to be all right again. Not as cheerful as last term but still more like her old self.

"Do you mind if we don't talk about it?" she asked Dara.

"That's all right." Dara was a bit huffy.

"It would be the same if there was a problem in your family, you wouldn't want to tell an outsider . . ."

Dara agreed grudgingly.

Maggie was much more understanding.

"I'm sorry I've been a bit . . . I don't know . . . recently, Maggie. I was just worried about something. Do you know the way it is?"

Maggie knew. She said so clearly. Grace was pleased.

Arm in arm with Maggie she went off to the graveyard, and they finished the tomb of James Edward Gray to everyone's satisfaction.

Mr. Williams said it was wonderful to see young people be so helpful. Not far away Eddie Ryan gloomily chopped nettles and gathered up sacks of grass and groundsel and dandelions. Grace discovered that Maggie took the same-size shoes and said she must come along to the lodge some evening and see if she wanted any that were there. Maggie never asked Grace what it was she had worried about. From time to time she wondered but still didn't ask.

Dara made a few pronouncements that if you were a true friend you could tell *everything* and any holding back meant that it wasn't friendship at all. But Dara bore her no ill-will, and organized Irish classes for Grace which worked so well that soon Grace O'Neill was getting better marks in class than the rest of them. Maggie's wish had come true, they were a gang, with Jacinta on the fringes of it.

They were all very disappointed when the summer holidays were approaching and Grace announced out of the blue that she was going to go on a trip with her father and brother. It was meant to be a familiarization tour of Ireland, she confided, but really it was a spying mission. They were going to spend a night in lots of different hotels and see what they were doing right or doing wrong. They would get ideas for their own hotel. A friend of Grace's father, who used to work with him back in the States, had suggested this would be a good thing to do. They were off as soon as term ended, just after Kerry came back from his boarding school.

Kerry had liked his new school very well, he said. No, he didn't want to ask anyone back during the holiday; it wasn't a place like that. You got to know everyone a bit, rather than a few people a lot. He was very enthusiastic about the voyage of inspection.

Once more Patrick O'Neill marveled at the wisdom of Rachel Fine. Even at three thousand miles she seemed to know what was best both for him and his troubled son. He would call her and say that she must come to Ireland this summer. After all, if John Fitzgerald Kennedy, the President of the United States, was coming to Ireland, why shouldn't Rachel Fine do the same?

It wasn't only the O'Neills who went away. Suddenly their whole gang started to disintegrate. The twins looked at each other in dismay.

Tommy Leonard was told that he was a grown man now, thirteen and a half going on fourteen, no less. He could stand in the paper shop this summer and work to build up the business that was going to be his one day. And he would like it. There would be a smile on his face, and none of his scruffy friends trick-acting in and out of the shop.

The Whites were sent to Irish College. Their father said it was pointless half learning a language, and they were both packed off to learn Irish dancing, to a place where they fined you if you were heard to speak in English and the man who ran it, An Fear Mor, was a person of great power and authority.

Maggie Daly had to work in Daly's Dairy, just like Tommy had to be in Leonard's. They both envied Dara and Michael for living in a business that didn't allow them to be behind a counter.

The twins were on their own again. They never actually admitted that they had grown apart in the last year or so. But they knew it. They missed golden-haired Grace with her plans and her excitement; they missed Tommy with his good humor, and the two Whites who argued with each other about everything and had outlandish views on almost every subject. They missed Maggie, who never dreamed anything up, but who always, after a little hanging back, would join in whatever they suggested.

The only problem was getting rid of Eddie.

Eddie wrongly thought that because Dara and Michael were now without their usual group, they would be delighted to have his company. More than once he got ready to go out with them and was bitterly disappointed when he was not allowed to go.

"I'd be better than no one," he said.

"No you wouldn't," Dara replied.

"You'd be much worse than no one, actually," Michael said.

"Why can't I come?"

"Because you're not our generation. You're a different generation to us. We are going to be thirteen in September, teenagers. You are only a very juvenile person."

"How will I ever grow up, unless I am with older people?"

Eddie was stung by the lack of avenues.

"Listen Eddie, enough is enough; it doesn't matter if you ever grow up, it couldn't matter less. You begin all nice and please this and please that, but by the time we'd have gone twenty paces with you, there'd be some row."

"No Dara, there wouldn't."

"Look at the past," Michael said mildly. "It's always happened."

"Now we must be off." And they were gone. Eddie kicked the stones around the back yard in disappointment.

"I can find you plenty to do if you like," Kate said. "And stop kicking. You're taking the top off your new shoes."

"They're not new," Eddie said mulishly. "Nothing is new, they're only Michael's shoes."

"And we'd like to have them for your brother Declan too, please, so kindly stop kicking with them or you'll have them taken away for the day, and you won't go far in your bare feet."

John had watched sympathetically. He waited till Kate had gone, and then called Eddie into the bar.

"Come here, I want to show you something."

"I don't want to do any work," Eddie said.

"Not at all, why should you, haven't you done the crates?"

"Yes."

"Well come on then. I'll show you something funny."

This was better than anything that had been offered so far. Eddie went suspiciously into the bar, his hair standing up in spikes that no amount of combing, brushing or even dampening would ever change. His father had an old, faded chocolate box out on the counter. Eddie scrambled onto a high stool to see.

"Look at this, Eddie, come on, it's funny."

"What is it? It's only an old picture."

"It's me years ago."

"Why are you wearing women's knickers?"

"Those aren't knickers; that was trousers."

"Go on."

"Yes, that was the day your Auntie Nuala went to Australia with the nuns, there was a picture taken here outside the door. That's your Aunt Nuala all dressed in black."

"She's very young-looking to be a nun."

"Ah she was too; they gave them a school education you see, and then in turn she became a nun and educated children out there."

"It seems daft to me," said Eddie, who was not a great scholar.

"There's a bit of daftness in it, certainly," his father agreed. "Wouldn't she be better up with Sister Laura in her own home town? Still, what I was going to tell you was this: look at my feet."

"You've no shoes on."

"Didn't I kick the front of my shoes out just like you were . . . No, no, not giving out to you. Shoes are your mother's province. I wanted to tell you the whole front came away, and I couldn't go with them all to see her off in the town. That was the last I ever saw of her, that day in 1930. Imagine. And I was so put out that I didn't get the trip to the town, I went for a walk up to Coyne's wood, and in my poor bare feet I spent the whole day building myself a house in a tree. I was covered in scratches and cuts, and when they all came back sobbing and crying from seeing Nuala off, they nearly murdered me, but the house was there. It's still there. I went past it the other day."

"It couldn't be."

"It is, bits of it, thirty-three years in the wood where it's very hard to find. Anyone could have a house that's easy to find. I thought having a secret one was better."

"You never told anyone?"

"No, not until now."

Eddie believed his father absolutely, but he was suspicious.

"So why are you telling me?"

"I've been having all kinds of old rheumatic aches; I don't think I'll climb into it again. I thought you might go and keep an eye on it for me."

"How would I find it?"

"Good question. When you go into Coyne's wood from this side, you go up the path; you know, the one that has all the rowan trees."

"The red ones, is it?"

"Yes, the mountain ash trees. Anyway where they end you go in to the right, you'll have to bend down a bit and then it's in there. You'll find it. Maybe you could even build it up a bit."

Eddie was looking enthusiastic at last. "It'd be better than having a place of my own," he said eventually.

"Much better."

"You won't tell Dara and Michael, and have them spoiling it? They'd come and take it over and turn me out of it."

"Not at all. Not a word."

"Right." Eddie gave a last look at the box of photographs. "Were we desperately poor in those days that they couldn't get you a new pair of shoes?"

"We'd be hard pushed to get *you* a new pair of shoes these days, so will you wear your old ones when you go up to Coyne's wood?" his father said. "And for the love of God, will you make sure you've done your jobs before you go."

They all had chores to do each day before they were free to play. Michael had to polish the brass and shine up the counter in the pub. The ashtrays would have been emptied, and the glasses washed the night before, but he had to air the place and see that there were no grease stains or dust where the customers would sit.

Dara had to feed the hens, now moved to the backyard, as their coop had become very smelly and messy in the side garden and completely spoiled the classy look of the place.

The hens clucked enthusiastically over household scraps mixed with bran. She also collected the eggs they laid in their nesting boxes;

she gave Jaffa her breakfast; took Leopold for a run up as far as the Rosemarie hair salon and back; and inspected the whereabouts of Maurice the tortoise, in case he had got stuck under a stone, or in case Eddie and Declan had broken their vow and started to play with him again.

Of all these jobs, Dara hated most being seen out with Leopold. Whenever another human being approached, Leopold would cower and shiver and whine piteously, rolling his eyes as if expecting a further beating. Never had a dog been lavished with such love, never did a dog give the impression of being whipped by his masters to within an inch of his life every evening.

In the Rosemarie hair salon, Rita Walsh, who sometimes had an overnight guest leaving in the morning, didn't like the regular appearance of the Ryan girl with that awful dog racing up to her doorstep and turning around again every morning.

"Why don't you take him down toward the bridge?"

"I'm too ashamed to be seen with him, Mrs. Walsh," Dara said truthfully. "Up this way I don't ever meet anyone except you, or maybe Mr. Coyne, so I don't have to explain."

The child probably never noticed anyone leaving at an early hour. That was a relief.

Eddie and Declan had to stack boxes neatly for the distributors and collectors who picked them up when they brought new supplies. All four young Ryans had to bring in vegetables from the back field: potatoes that had to be washed at the yard sink, cabbages or cauliflowers, carrots or turnips. Then they were free for the day, lunch at one sharp.

Patrick wanted a history of Fernscourt written, and who better to ask, he had said, than the local scribe literally on the very doorstep. Of course there were people in Dublin who would do it, and do a professional job on it. Later indeed some aspects of their expertise might be used in editing and layout and even some of their hints in how to express parts of it. But there could be nobody who would do the job with such local knowledge and in such personal terms as John Ryan.

"You're never going to do it for him?" Kate was astounded.

"Why on earth not? It's a job, a writing job, there'll be something at the end of it, not just a few pages of a child's notebook scribbled on. That's what *you've* always looked for, something to show for it."

"But not this. Not glorifying him and what he's doing."

"It's not glorifying, and he's doing it whether I write the history of

Fernscourt or some Ph.D. up in Dublin writes it. It's a professional job, there's a fee, whoever does it."

"I don't know." Kate was troubled.

"Well I do. My only problem is, will I do it right? Maybe he has too much faith in me; I could have sold myself too well."

Kate changed immediately.

"I don't know what you're talking about. Won't you do it as well as anyone? Better, because you're from these parts. You're the obvious one to do it."

John smiled quietly. The battle had been won. First it meant he had to do a lot of reading and research. His head was ever now in books about Georgian houses, antiquarian journals and the records of archaeological and historical societies. He became a familiar figure in the library in the big town where he went once a week, and they bent the rules in order to let him take some of the reference books back to his pub. It was different when a man was writing a book. He wasn't an ordinary borrower.

He discovered that Fernscourt was only one of many houses built at the time and all over the country. That year 1780 seemed to have been a great year altogether. He told that to Brian Doyle one day, and Brian said that it was always a feast or a famine in the building trade. You either sat on your backside for three years eating crusts or you had them screaming at you to dig the foundations for almighty jobs in three counties. It was interesting to know that the lads in 1780 had the same kind of aggravation.

Of course it was the time when Grattan's Parliament was sitting; it was the eighteen years when there was an Irish Parliament in College Green in Dublin, before it was snuffed out and the Act of Union was passed. Those parliamentarians needed big houses all over the place. But the Ferns didn't sit in Parliament, they were farmers with estates in the north of England. They had bought the land here in the 1770s for one of their sons. The house itself had been built in the same style as many others.

John Ryan was affronted to read in one journal that Fernscourt was considered a minor and rather inferior example of the art. He had shown it to Kate in disbelief.

"The wise man would forget that piece of information," Kate advised. "Patrick O'Neill is not paying for any reference to minor and inferior houses: you should pretend you didn't uncover that particular bit of lore."

"I'm meant to be doing serious research." John's face was very red.

"Of course, and you are, but that's only one person's opinion. You don't have to give some crackpot's view, do you? I mean if I met someone up in Bridge Street who said that you were no good to man or beast would I believe them?"

"What?"

"Of course I wouldn't anymore than you have to believe that fellow. Just get on to the facts, the things that can't be challenged, how many windows there were, what kind of people worked on it. Oh, Fergus said to tell you that he'll help you get documents from the land registry if you want; he says that once you translate legal documents into English instead of fusty old law you get great information out of them. I don't agree with him myself, typing them as I do all day. But Fergus would understand anything you put in front of him. He could make sense of the Dead Sea Scrolls at a glance."

"He's got a very quick mind, Fergus," said John admiringly. "You must find it a great change working with him." He smiled quietly.

Kate thought for a moment.

"Yes, he is great to work for. He's a real schoolboy though, a tall thin overgrown schoolboy, he's not a fellow you'd fall in love with like you are."

"Okay, that's all right, then," John Ryan said in mock relief.

It was a great relief to get rid of Eddie. The twins knew they were harsh to him, but Eddie wasn't like other people. He didn't understand hints. You had to be fairly brutal. They didn't have any money for ice cream, so there was no point in going to Daly's. It would only embarrass Maggie and make Mrs. Daly cast her eyes up to heaven and mouth silent prayers. Mrs. Daly's mouth was moving the whole time. Maggie said she got through dozens of memorares that she was saying for special intentions, while she was serving in the shop.

The twins knew that they mustn't be seen in Leonard's unless they were buying the paper or getting a writing pad. Grown-ups were allowed to leaf through the magazines, but there was no similar facility for children with the comics. And Tommy would hate them there.

There weren't many people on the bridge. Those who were there had organized a jumping competition. Usually you jumped from the big rock at the side. But today they were raising it and making it higher in stages. First by an old box, then by a stone on top of the box. Then by a plank on top of the stone. Dara and Michael watched for a bit. It was mainly boys that were jumping, shivering in their underpants. But there were a few girls too. Teresa Meagher in a black bathing costume much admired by all, and laughing overexcitedly as she jumped with the best.

The twins tired of it after a while. They walked across the bridge away from the town and back down the river bank on the other side. This was the road which would soon change. Instead of being a path with reeds on one side and a hedge on the other, it would be a road to the huge hotel. They didn't talk about things like that; it had been long accepted. The hedge was full of fuchsia growing wild as anything. Mam had told them that in city places this was a very rare flower, and people paid big sums of money to buy little bushes of it to put in their gardens; sometimes it didn't even grow properly. Dara stopped beside a huge tree of it.

"Isn't it like something in the South Sea Island picture book?" she said.

"Here, I'll climb it and be like a native," Michael said, leaving their picnic bag on the path.

As he went to the back of the tree to find a good starting-off place, he gave a great shout.

"Dara, look, careful, careful you don't fall."

In front of them, totally hidden by the trees and bushes, was an opening. A cave, or better still, a tunnel. They couldn't believe it. They had found their new home at last. They hardly dared go in beyond the entrance in case it was already somebody else's home. Those colorful tinkers who came by once a year and annoyed everyone old, by stealing chickens and leaving all their mess and rubbish behind them. They might be in there. Mad Marty who disappeared for months on end and then turned up again, wilder than ever. It could be his home. It was too good a place to be nobody's.

"Helloo . . ." they called as they went around the corner. It was pitch dark.

They paused and shouted again.

"Do you mind if we come in?" Dara called.

"Just for a moment," Michael added.

There was no reply. Surely if anyone was there they would have said *something*.

The twins looked at each other in delight and pealed with laughter at their over-caution and politeness.

"There's nobody here at all," Dara said.

Michael ran to Mrs. Quinn's for candles; he was back in no time and they went in together. They each held two of the half dozen candles that Loretto Quinn had parted with so willingly, as well as a box of matches. It wasn't like a cave or a tunnel in books or comics. There were no dripping rocks, just earth and stone, and it was quite high. Even grown-ups could have walked without bending.

The twins stepped forward, each with a tight feeling of anxiety about what might be ahead.

"It doesn't smell like coffins or anything," Michael said.

"We don't know what coffins smell like."

"No," Michael agreed. "But it doesn't smell frightening."

Dara wanted to show she hadn't been superior. "It doesn't look as if it's going to fall and block our way back, either," she said, more to reassure herself than her brother.

"No indeed, it's very sound."

"And it might be coming out somewhere soon?" Dara's voice was thin.

"Bound to, we must be up at the house now."

And then, around the next turn, they saw the urns and the long shallow steps at the back of Fernscourt. They saw them through the branches of thorns and brambles. Beyond those were huge big beds of nettles. That's why they had never seen the opening. Who would want to wade through feet of nettles, big high stinging ones, when there were so many other things to explore?

They realized it couldn't belong to them if they told anybody. So they told nobody at all.

But they thought about it all the time, and they brought back their belongings, slowly and little by little, so as not to create any suspicion. The old orange box, the tableware, the so-called curtains and rugs, the broken cutlery. Once more it was home. This time by candle-light. When they were older and could do what they liked they would ask Brian Doyle, if he wasn't dead, if they could make a skylight in the tunnel, because sometimes it was a bit hot and dark, and they would have liked the sunlight.

The roof looked sound enough. Surely Brian Doyle and his workers would be able to put in a window for them. There was a scaffolding: a very rough and ready kind of arrangement of wooden poles and boards keeping the ceiling up. It looked very firm and steady. The twins tested it gingerly, and then more firmly. It was rock solid. They wondered who had built it and why it was there. But they were afraid to ask anyone about it now in case it might all be taken away.

At home they tried to find out what an underground tunnel might be doing in these parts.

"Would there have been other ways into big houses in the old days?" Michael asked one suppertime. Dara frowned. It was too obvious.

Their mother had noticed nothing out of the ordinary.

"Like back doors, do you mean?" she asked absently. "Carrie, don't leave the saucepan on the table, there's a good girl. It just means it harder for you washing the cloth." Mammy was very good at scolding to Carrie; it didn't seem like scolding at all.

"I don't know. I suppose there were, and in those kinds of places people probably didn't bring in a ton and a half of mud with them. Eddie, do you have to bring half of Coyne's wood home with you every day?"

Mam ˜obviously didn't have any idea of a tunnel. But then she hadn't been brought up here. Maybe Dad knew. Dad had been here forever.

But they'd have to be even more careful approaching him.

"You're very interested in old houses, aren't you, Dad?" Dara had a prissy kind of face on, not her normal look at all.

"Well, I suppose I am a bit," John Ryan agreed.

"Would you remember what Fernscourt looked like before it was burned down?"

"No, child, I wouldn't. I was only two when it was burned. Tommy Leonard's father would remember, and Maggie Daly's dad, but don't go asking them too much about it. They were there at the burning of it. In those days it seemed the right way to go. My own father stood looking at the flames from our front doorstep. He said to me often. But there's pictures of it of course, you'd be able to see what it was like in those."

"Yes well, but . . ." Dara didn't want to be sidetracked by old pictures and the possibility of a history lesson.

"Would they have had secret rooms in it do you think? You wouldn't be able to see those in photographs."

"I don't *think* so. Why, did you think they might?"

Michael came in hastily. "We were just wondering, you know, taking an interest in everything around us, like you're always saying to do."

"Oh that's great," John said approvingly. "Yes, I love to see you doing that."

"So we take an interest in all kinds of things you see," Dara added. "Like, would they have had tunnels out of a house like Fernscourt, you know, underground tunnels?"

"All tunnels are underground," Michael said quickly, not to put her down, but to warn her not to be too explicit.

If John saw the way the wind was blowing he gave no sign.

"I never heard of any underground tunnels around here," he said absently, brushing the earth and dust off the thin shoulders of his son. "But as I say, the place was well gone by the time I was old enough to play in it, so there could have been. I'm sure it would be quite possible to find one if you looked hard enough."

He caught the look of alarm, and went on. "But it would be so well covered over, that sort of thing, that I don't think anyone would ever find the entrance."

There was a hint of relief in their faces.

"What would they have been for, if there were tunnels? That is from houses like Fernscourt, say?"

"Do you mean, say, possibly going from the house to the river? That is if there was a river?"

They nodded eagerly.

John Ryan paused; they waited for an explanation. He seemed to know the kind of thing they were talking about, but then his face became puzzled again.

"It's very hard to say. It would have been exciting, whatever the reason was. Of course if you found one of those things you'd have to be very careful. I mean a person would have to take great care that the roof wouldn't fall in, or that it wasn't all crumbling before they went and explored it."

"Oh there's no danger, it's quite safe," said Michael. "I mean I'd say they'd be quite safe."

"No parts where it's supported with props or anything?"

The twins looked at each other. *How* could he know?

"Like scaffolding," their father said helpfully.

"Well . . ."

"Um . . ."

"That'd be the bit to stay well away from if you ever found one," John Ryan said firmly. "It's like in old mines; those would be the parts where it would all cave in."

"I suppose you could test it by pushing and pulling at bits near the entrance if you ever found one," he went on.

They went away in case they let anything slip.

"He said it would have to be an exciting reason for it," Michael said.

"We knew that," Dara said. "But what could it have been?"

It provided hours of happy speculation for them.

Dara decided it was built by a young Miss Fern to meet her lover in a boat.

Michael decided it was built by a cousin of the Ferns who had an intent of storming Fernscourt one night and claiming it as his own. But they told no one. Without actual lies they managed to suggest they spent the time hanging around the bridge in the town. Kate was glad to think that they were making other friends.

"Am I beautiful, Carrie?" Dara asked. She was sitting on Carrie's bed, watching the preparations for the day off.

"I don't know." Carrie giggled at the question, but mainly concentrated on her own appearance in the speckled mirror over the dressing table. The table was covered with powder and hairpins and nearly finished pots of make-up that had been cast-offs of other people.

"I think I might be beautiful, if only I had curly hair," Dara persisted.

"You might be." Carrie was doubtful. "Isn't it sickening that we don't have curly hair. Your Mam has a rake of it, and she doesn't need it at all."

"Why doesn't she need it?"

"Well she's old and she's got her fellow. It's the likes of yourself and myself that need curls." Carrie looked at her reflection without pleasure.

"Why do you want to get all dressed up just for going home?" Dara asked with interest.

Carrie looked at her suspiciously. "Well, why do *you* want to be beautiful?" she countered.

"I want to be beautiful so that Kerry O'Neill will admire me," Dara said simply.

Carrie looked at her and softened. "You're grand as you are," she said. "And listen, I'll tell you a secret; I'm not going home to my people at all today, I'm going on an outing, with a fellow. With Jimbo Doyle."

"Not Jimbo Doyle," Dara screeched.

"Why not? He's very nice, Jimbo is, and he said he'd take me for a walk up to Coyne's wood on my day off." Carrie looked annoyed now, and a little uncertain.

Dara bit her lip. She had offended Carrie greatly, she must make it up somehow.

"I know he's nice, and he's a great singer. I heard him singing

"The Yellow Rose of Texas" when he was building the rock garden. You could ask him to sing to you up in Coyne's wood."

"Yes, I suppose I could." Carrie was doubtful. She felt that Jimbo Doyle hadn't planned on an afternoon of singing among the quiet trees and on the springy moss of Coyne's wood.

They held their resolve to tell no one about the tunnel. No one at all.

"Not even Grace?" Michael said.

Dara paused. She thought about it.

"Not even Grace," she said.

"If we told Grace, we'd have to tell Maggie and Tommy and everyone else," Michael said.

"Yes." Dara frowned. "And that would change it. Do you think we're being a bit childish about all this?"

"Not at all," Michael reassured her. "I think we're doing the right thing."

They grinned at each other. The twins were back where they had always been. Best friends against the world.

There was a postcard from Grace from Donegal where the waves were huge and they had been swimming. They were having a great time, she said, and whenever she thought they were coming back to Mountfern, Father thought of somewhere else to visit. But they would be home soon; she missed everybody and longed to see them again. She sent cards to Tommy and Maggie too, and sent her love to Jacinta and Liam but didn't dare to write to them in case they would be punished for having communications in English rather than Irish.

Ryan's pub filled up with all the men who were working on the site. Every lunchtime there was a good crowd around the bar. Kate found herself rushing back from Slattery's office and straight in behind the bar. Sometimes she looked at John with a smile of triumph. At least some of their fears about the new hotel were proving groundless. There was a bit of business coming their way. For the moment anyway.

Judy Byrne ran into Marian Johnson in Meagher's jewelers. Mrs. Meagher had to send out the repairs and she was most apologetic that the clock wasn't ready.

"I did want it for the lodge by the time they came back," Marian was saying.

"Oh, when will that be?" Judy Byrne had come in to buy a brooch for her niece's birthday. She was looking without much pleasure at Mrs. Meagher's selection.

"Hard to say. Any day now, I imagine," Marian said airily.

"He doesn't keep in touch, then?"

Marian was furious.

"Heavens, Judy, it's their house to come and go as they please. I'm not a boarding house landlady type, you know, Judy. They've just rented our gate lodge, that's all."

"So he doesn't write. Well, I expect we'll know they're back when we see them." Judy thanked Mrs. Meagher for letting her see the brooches and said she would think about them and come back later.

Sheila Whelan knew exactly where the O'Neills were, and when they would be back. She had telegrams from America and messages that didn't go through to Brian Doyle the builder. Patrick rang her every second day.

Brian Doyle had the demolition men ready; he was surprised that O'Neill said they could go ahead and make the arrangements to take down the walls without him. He thought the man would have been on the crane that swung the great ball himself.

Brian Doyle didn't know that Patrick O'Neill and Rachel Fine had discussed this lengthily on the phone. They agreed that it would be wiser for him to stay away from the tearing down. Be there for the building up, not the pulling down.

Chapter IX

Patrick O'Neill had discovered that few Irish hotels stayed open in the winter time. Very few of them. They said that nobody would come to Ireland in the bad weather, and it cost a fortune heating a place up and paying staff all through the lean months when there would be no business.

Patrick thought that this was short-sighted. Nobody ever came to Ireland for the weather anyway. When you thought of sunshine, you didn't immediately think of Ireland. It was the people who brought visitors to Ireland, the people and the scenery and the activities. Those things were there in the winter too, and cheaper to get to.

Charter flights in winter from the United States would be very reasonably priced. But there was no point in telling that to these hotel owners. They saw their season as beginning in May and ending in September. Some of the more adventurous opened as early as the Easter weekend.

Patrick O'Neill sighed at the waste of it all. But then he sighed a lot these days. It had been much harder than he would have believed possible to get this far in his attempts to rebuild Fernscourt. It had been a year since he had bought the place. Twelve months of delays and impediments, and only now was he able to get the ruins knocked down so that the building proper could begin.

It was the biggest test of Patrick O'Neill's character that he had ever known. A vein began to jut out on his forehead with anger and frustration. He found himself standing up, sitting down, taking long deep breaths in the middle of ruinously expensive transatlantic phone calls.

Twice he decided to abandon it, but slept on the decision, and the following morning decided that he would go ahead. Three times he was on the point of firing Brian Doyle and shouting that any builder in the goddamn Western world would be on his knees for a lifetime, begging for such a job. Three times he restrained himself. He did bawl out an architect, a mild man who said that it was always the same with Americans. They came over here like God Almighty and expected the people to change their ways for them. Patrick didn't see himself in that role; he liked to think of the O'Neills as the sons of the soil coming back, not the overlords giving orders. He apologized to the architect, who told him not to think of it again. Everyone knew that the pressure in New York drove most people mad most of the time.

He had been back to America twice. At the end of that time not one stone had been laid on another. But he kept his smile.

And he convinced the conservationists that he wasn't destroying anything valuable. That had been a stroke of luck, sighing over it in Ryan's pub one day, and then John Ryan discovering a quote from some archaeological journal to back up his claim that the house was of minor importance architecturally.

He found himself telling genial lies in two continents. Standing on the bridge with Fergus Slattery: Was he disappointed at the length of time things took? No, no, this was the pace, this was the way it had to be done. He would not have the town typecast him as a rushing, bustling Yank. And then back in the other home, in his New York headquarters talking to Gerry Power: Sure, sure, things didn't get done at the same speed. They hadn't the technology; no of course he didn't have second thoughts. No, he wasn't mad at them.

And to Rachel Fine, sipping a brandy in her red-gold apartment, which always looked so soft and restful compared with the rest of New York, he told more truth than to anyone. He told her that at times he thought he would blow up into a million pieces with frustration over it all. He could see now why his countrymen back home had achieved nothing, *nothing*. No wonder their economy was so pathetic, so shabby. He knew now why they stood toothless and laughing with their hats on back to front, because they had never bloody learned to work. They knew nothing of the actual ache that work brings, and they didn't want to know it. No goal was high enough to force them to do more than the very minimum. He could rail like this to Rachel because he knew she would never agree with him. She would smooth his forehead and tell him that Irish people rose in every walk of life . . . they had their own country . . . well almost . . . Look at her people, the Latvians . . . they had let the Soviets take over and Latvia would never rise again. All the Latvian Jews who could escape had come to America, but there would be no going back and building castles there nowadays.

Rachel would encourage him softly, remind him of all he had achieved so far, tell him that no other grandson of a cottage dweller had gone back to buy the big house and make it into a great business that would employ his own far and wide. He liked to hear that; it gave some reason to all the work and the endless delays and complications. One evening he asked Rachel why she encouraged him. She had been against it at the start, and wanted him to make his life in New York.

"Only a very foolish woman wouldn't encourage a dream. What would you be if your dream were to be taken away, or people talked you out of it? You would lose your fire and enthusiasm. You would only be a shell."

He held her closely to him. She was a wonderful woman. What a shame, what a bloody great shame that she was who she was, a divorced Jewess. Even if everyone else would let him, he could never marry her. It just wasn't possible.

But the day came, and the machinery moved in, huge cranes and a great ball that swung backward and forward, and the stone walls of Fernscourt came down. Rachel Fine had advised at long distance that the stones should be kept to form any walls or rock gardens. There must be a place to store them and surely big stones dating from the days when America was still a fledgling must be attractive and beautiful in themselves. Brian Doyle had said it was a cracked idea, but then he had been hoping to use the stones himself in other building work if they had been thrown out, so he secretly admired the Yank with the big notions and the belief that everything could be done in five minutes.

Grace linked arms with Kerry happily as they walked in the Irish countryside. This was the first real holiday they had taken together.

She chattered on about the convent in Mountfern and told him tales of the girls and the tricks they played on the nuns. She begged him for stories of his school. Did he like being away at boarding school? Was he lonely? Was he glad it was holidays now? Grace wanted Kerry to be glad about everything. Like she was.

"It's a shame we can't be there," Grace said for the tenth time, as the O'Neills walked along a cliff path in Donegal. "I'd love to see it."

"Yes." Patrick was absent-minded. He looked out at the ocean. Had his father seen these hills when he was leaving Ireland, or were they too far north? He could never discover whether it had been from Galway or way down in Cork from the harbor at Cobh that those earlier O'Neills had taken a ship for the United States. None of the family knew or ever wanted to find out. John Ryan said it might have been Galway. It would have been a likelier place to have started from rather than all the way down in Cobh. Ships used to go from Galway all the time in those long-ago days.

"It wouldn't take us all that long to go back. Why didn't we leave last night?" Grace was insistent.

"Oh, I don't know, Gracie. We'll see it in a few days when we get back there. Aren't you having a good time?"

"Oh yes, but . . ." It was such a big thing, why were they missing it? She wished he would explain.

"Father doesn't want us to be there for the demolition, it would be better not to associate ourselves with destroying . . . with knocking down what's there." Kerry spoke without blame or praise, just as if he were giving directions from a map.

Patrick looked at him sharply. "Hey, what makes you say that?" He half laughed.

"Well it's true, isn't it? That's the way I'd feel."

"Yes, it *is* true in a way." Patrick was very surprised.

"We're the good guys, the ones who ride into town when all the shooting's over. Right?"

"Right in a sort of a way."

"I think it's ridiculous," Grace argued. "Everyone's delighted we're building a new hotel; they love us for being there. Why all this running away and hiding for the best bit, the big machine going boom boom? I'd *love* to see that."

"So would I," Patrick said simply.

He was going to call Brian Doyle and find out how it all went. He wished that Brian had the gift of explaining things in style, with some description, a little color. Doyle would be likely to tell him about the overtime, the breakages, the need to revise this figure and that, and leave out completely any of the symbolism about the old order changing.

"I wonder what they're doing at this very moment?" he said as he led his son and daughter down a sandy path onto a magnificent beach and they ran along beside the waves like any ordinary family.

Not like a man who watched his son nervously, wondering what could have made the boy step so out of character and remain so adamant about not discussing it again. Not like a man who had arranged the demolition of a huge house and planned to build his own monument on the spot where his father and grandfather had been turned out onto the roads.

Half the town came by and watched the demolition machinery getting into action. The best view was from Ryan's pub on River Road and many of them watched with a glass in their hands.

Jack Coyne stood with a look of false cheer. He cursed that day long back when he had shortchanged Patrick O'Neill. The man had always been perfectly courteous to him since, but not one bit of business had he thrown his way. Jack Coyne's small pointed face glanced from one to another. Everyone else had benefited from the Yank. Look at the trade that John Ryan had, and it was the same in the town; there wasn't a business that hadn't been promised or already received some profit. Why on that day of all bloody days in the world had he taken the quiet American for a fool who didn't understand the rate he would get for a dollar? Why had he not seen that those blue eyes were the sharp eyes of a businessman?

Jack Coyne stood, hands in pockets, looking across the river at all the machinery which could all have been hired through him. Coyne's could have gotten the demolition people in and taken a legitimate ten per cent. He shook his head and told himself that in this life you never knew. You never bloody knew.

"Big day this," Jack Leonard said to no one in particular.

"Nearly as big as the day we burned it down," said Tom Daly, and there was an uneasy laugh. Nobody talked much about those times now, the days and nights when big houses all over the country were burned as a symbol of all they represented.

It was forty-one years since Tom Daly, Jack Leonard and a dozen more had joined hastily organized groups from the big town to go out on their mission. Old Mr. Leonard and old Mr. Daly were so respectable now, such pillars of Mountfern with their dairy and their newsagent businesses, it was quite impossible to imagine them as twenty-year-old firebrands. It was a different time, a different culture. Neither Tom Daly nor Jack Leonard had a good word to say for those young fellows who had been going up north on the border campaign blowing up electrical installations, taking pot shots at sentry posts and considering themselves national heroes. No, the 1920s had been a proper war.

John and Kate pulled pints, filled small glasses of whiskey, and even dragged a few chairs out into the sunshine. Leopold stood shivering with terror at the noise across the river and recoiled from every attempt to stroke or reassure him.

"You're such a kind woman, Kate, why don't you have that animal put to sleep?" Fergus asked as Leopold turned two anguished eyes on him and bayed to the skies.

"That animal is healthier than most people here, and much better looked after," snapped Kate. "I can't bear people who make superficial judgments about things they know nothing about."

"Don't bite the nose off the man," John laughed. "Leopold's a great actor, Fergus, he plays to the gallery. He goes and lies outside Reidy's the butchers every day after he's had a good meal here and they give him a bone, every single day. And he howls at Loretto Quinn until she gives him half a pound of biscuits. Wherever the unfortunate cat sits he goes and wails at it, until Jaffa has to get up and let him sit there."

"He's just making up for having had a desperate childhood," Dara said. She was nearly thirteen now, tall and strong. Her thick dark hair went in slightly underneath as a result of heavy hair-grip work at night. She would have loved a perm in the Rosemarie salon, and Mrs. Walsh said she would do a light natural perm, but Dara's mother wouldn't hear of it. A perm at twelve? Who would permit such extravagance? It was all very well for her mother, who had curly hair anyway, to speak like that. Dara was full of resentment. To make matters worse Michael, who didn't need curls, had a great sort of wavy fit in his hair. *And* he had longer eyelashes. Much. It was so unfair, like almost everything.

"Tell me about Leopold's childhood." Fergus liked the leggy girl who was so like her mother in looks, and in that independent streak.

"He was found in one of Jack Coyne's trucks."

"That's a poor start," agreed Fergus.

"And someone had squeezed his throat, and hurt his hind leg," Michael finished for her.

Fergus often thought they could make a good double act on stage.

"And for ages after we got his poor back leg mended, he used to hold it out to people to shake hands with them," Dara said.

"Oh all right, you've convinced me, he had a rotten childhood, puppydom wasn't the best time of his life. Let him live, let him grow older and madder like the rest of us."

The twins giggled.

"I thought you two would be very upset to see it all come down." He indicated across the river.

"No, one time maybe . . ." Michael said.

"But not now, not now . . ."

"Not now that we're more grown up . . ."

"And have our own life. It used to be a bit of pretend life there, you see."

"Oh well, it's different now that you've grown up. I see what you mean." He could have been laughing at them, but they didn't think so. "And have you found somewhere else to live when you grow old, really old like me? Now that you won't be living across there?"

"We have our plans . . ." said Dara.

"Nothing definite of course . . ."

"That could be spelled out . . ."

Fergus hastened to agree. "No, no, much better not. Spell out as little as possible, I always say."

"There is one thing, Mr. Slattery . . ." Dara said.

"Yes . . ."

"It's sort of advice we might need . . ."

Michael flashed her a warning look.

"No, it's all right, I'm only going to speak sort of generally."

"Best way to start," Fergus agreed encouragingly.

"Yes, well, it's like this. Does every bit of land have to be owned by someone?"

"I beg your pardon?" They had never taught him how to answer questions like this when he was up in Dublin at the Incorporated Law Society.

"I mean, is the whole of Ireland all divided up and parceled up? You own your house, we own this place, Mr. O'Neill owns Fernscourt now. Are there bits nobody owns?"

"That's a bit difficult to answer in general terms. There *are* bits, I suppose, that nobody really owns, like say the Curragh. You know, in Kildare. If you have land near it you can graze your sheep there, and it's the same with some bogs. A lot of people can cut turf there without actually owning it. Is that what you mean?"

"Not quite. You know, would all fields and ditches and boreens be owned by some one person? You couldn't say suddenly, I own this ditch because I found it."

Fergus scratched his head.

"But you couldn't really *find* a ditch, could you? It would be there all the time. You couldn't look at it one day and claim it?"

"But suppose you couldn't see it?" Dara persisted.

Michael didn't want her to say any more.

"God, Dara, you have me foxed," Fergus said. "But as your mother will tell you, I'm no good at all as a solicitor. I ask stupid questions like how in the name of the Lord could you try to own something you can't see? I only irritate clients. I'll be struck off the rolls any day and be left wandering around with straws in my hair."

Dara looked alarmed. "No, please, it's our fault. You see, it's that we have to ask these questions so that you won't actually know what we're talking about . . . No, shut up, Michael. It's all *right*. Mr. Slattery's not going to tell anyone, he's like Canon Moran."

"The image of him," Fergus said ruefully.

"No, you can't tell people's business, like he can't tell their sins," Dara insisted.

"That's a fact. They'd strike me off the rolls."

"Would they hit you?" Michael asked interested.

"I think it might mean rolls, like the rolls at school. You know, for roll call," Dara said helpfully. "But anyway, it won't happen, because you won't tell anybody what we've been discussing."

"I most certainly will not," he said solemnly, not that he had any idea of what they *had* been discussing.

"Wouldn't you think Patrick would have been here to see his day of triumph?" John Ryan said as a great cheer went up when the last bit of wall fell down.

Kate neatly scooped the froth off the top of five pints of stout with a wooden spatula.

"He knows all about it, you can be sure. He'll be on the phone to Brian Doyle in ten minutes' time."

"I was sure he'd have been here. He hates that house and all it stood for. He doesn't want me to say a good word about the Ferns, he hates the bit about them being fairly decent in the Famine. He would be delighted to see the stones going down."

"No, Patrick O'Neill is more interested in what's going up there instead," Kate said, putting the pints on a tray and coming around the counter to take them outside. "He's forward-looking like all the Americans."

"Would we have been better if we had gone to America, do you think?" John asked, half seriously.

"I don't know, maybe now isn't the time to debate it." Kate laughed good-naturedly as she swept out with the tray of pints to the people outside.

Rita Walsh wondered if the arrival of the hotel might mean that there would be a proper living out of hairdressing after all. It would make a nice change. She had heard a great deal about the plans for Fernscourt from Marian Johnson who now had her hair done regularly and had even sought advice about skin creams and manicures. Rita thought it unlikely that a man like Patrick O'Neill would think seriously about Marian Johnson, whose dry scalp and flyaway hair were getting so much attention these days. Yet it was hard to know. A man like that might be keen to ally himself with old money, and the quality. The Johnsons knew everyone in the hunting set.

Rita surveyed her little salon without much pleasure. American women or rich Dublin women might not find it to their liking, but it would be madness to spend good money on new equipment. Rita had a fair bit saved for the days when she would no longer be able to stand on her feet and give perms. And indeed earn money from a position that didn't at all involve standing on her feet. Both of these sources would end eventually. She kept all her savings in Sheila Whelan's discreet post office. There was no bank in Mountfern and Sheila often acted as an unofficial adviser on people's finances.

Rita decided to be swayed by the advice of the postmistress. Sheila was not one to inquire why the earnings were large sometimes, and irregular. She would answer only the questions that were asked, never raising any others.

Sheila Whelan said that her advice would be to hold on a while until the building of the hotel got under way, then when it really did look as if Fernscourt were rising from the ground and about to bring new life into the town, that was the time to buy new hairdressing equipment. And chairs and anything else that would make the Rosemarie hair salon attractive to visitors. There was no sense of irony in any of this, no hint of what might be the present attractions of the establishment. Just wait until the hotel got under way, then everyone could make their plans.

In Rachel Fine's New York apartment the small travel clock on the table beside her bed said that it was six-thirty in the morning. In Mountfern it would be lunchtime and the ruins might well be down by now. Rachel had not slept well. All night she had dreamed that there had been some terrible incident at this demolition ceremony.

That a body had risen from the ruins calling out, "I am the spirit who will not be mocked . . . you shall not build here in peace."

She had gotten up twice in the night and sat beside the window, looking out on the moonlit city to reassure herself that everything was normal. She wished this part was all over. Perhaps when this part was finished, then things might go well. He might send for her and she would come to Ireland and make herself part of the place, so that he would never send her away.

Patrick found the afternoon went very slowly. He didn't want to call until he was absolutely certain that it had actually happened. Later that evening he would talk to the States, tell Gerry Power that it had been done, and tell Rachel. Already it was a picture in his mind . . .

He could imagine it. Even before he called Brian Doyle, he could see knots of children coming onto the bank to watch. He hadn't realized that the rest of the town would come too and that they would drink pints in John and Kate Ryan's during the day, and cheer when the walls fell. He made Brian tell him every detail. At first Doyle thought he wanted proof that the job had been done properly, and had been full of huffing and shrugging, but when he realized that the man only wanted a description of the day, he became most lyrical.

Patrick couldn't believe it when he heard that the people had cheered the walls coming down.

"What did they say . . . did they call for three cheers or what?"

"Well, it was just a big cheer went up," Brian said.

"Like what? Did they say 'Hurrah,' or 'More, more,' or what?"

Brian was beginning to wish he had never mentioned the cheer. "You know, a big shout. No words, just a shout."

"There *have* to be words in a shout."

"No there don't, Mr. O'Neill. It was like, let me say a great *Waaah!* Now do you know what I mean?"

Patrick said he did. He was very pleased.

"Do you know they gave a great cheer when the last walls of Fernscourt went down?" he said when he called Gerry Power.

"Is that a fact?" Gerry was a man who was quite happy to go back to Ireland sometime in the future for St. Patrick's Day and maybe ten days there. He thought Patrick was insane to plow all his fortune into this venture.

"I wonder why they cheered," Patrick said.

"So shocked to see a proper day's work done for once, they couldn't help cheering, I guess," said Gerry.

He told Rachel that evening. "A big cheer, Brian Doyle said. Like a great *Waaahh!* sound. Oh God, I *wish* I had been there. I would have given anything to be there, to have heard it."

"I think you were quite right not to go," Rachel said. "Your instinct is always right for that sort of thing. Don't associate yourself with the knocking down, only with the building up. You've always done it here."

Rachel knew why they had let out a cheer. It was something to do, something to see on a dull morning in a one-horse town. It all meant a bit of work here and there and the promise of more work for the people who stood around, apparently, if the story was to be believed, with great double glasses of beer in their hands in the middle of the morning. No wonder they cheered.

"They cheered because the dream is coming true," she said. "Because the old house is gone and the new life is about to start."

The site had been excavated, the foundations were ready to start. Brian Doyle had already had four major rows with the architects. The Irish architects had refused to work with the American architects unless guarantees were received that there would be no more last minute interference. The Irish Tourist Board had revised its grant, the situation on charter groups was still not clear from Aer Lingus. Two farmers whose land had not been bought up by Patrick O'Neill tried to get Fergus Slattery to claim they had been victimized. Two small tenant farmers, who had willingly sold him half an acre each a year ago, now felt they hadn't gotten enough for it, and wanted

Fergus to represent them. Fergus refused to have anything to do with any of them.

"Greed. That's what this man has brought to Mountfern, inordinate greed. Those men never thought of profits on their miserable bits of land before, they were bloody glad to have it."

"I don't think you can go around preaching to them like that, Fergus," Kate Ryan said disapprovingly. "You should shrug and say that it's a pity but there isn't really a case. Pretend to be on their side, be clever."

"Like Hereford bullock O'Neill," Fergus growled.

Kate laughed. "He *has* got curls but that's no nickname for him. Yes, like him. He's great at being tactful. That's what's got him so far, I suppose."

"Or telling downright lies," Fergus said.

"He hasn't really, has he? I know you don't trust him, and neither do I. I don't trust him because I think he knows he'll ruin us if his business ever gets off the ground. I don't know why you care about him."

"Because he's hurting you . . . all of you," Fergus said.

Kate looked up, startled, and Fergus remembered his sister's drunken slurred accusation . . . he was good for nothing except making sheep's eyes at the local publican's wife. Was that so?

No, in truth, hand on heart, it wasn't just Kate, it was the whole household. That stupid dog with the terrified eyes trying to shake hands with you by raising its twisted back paw. That John Ryan scribbling his poetry in a child's exercise book and thinking that Patrick O'Neill was a great fellow. Those two small lads with a face on each of them that spelled out devilment. Those dark handsome twins, entirely self-contained, speaking half a sentence each, suntanned and energetic as wild monkeys; he used to see them scrambling in those brambled hills on the other side of the Fern . . . There was something about the whole family that touched him in a way it was hard to understand. Truthfully, it was not the handsome mother with her quick wit. No, eunuch or no eunuch, he was making no sheep's eyes at her.

Fergus made a series of promises to himself there and then. He resolved that he would go off for a long weekend to a seaside town and have a sexual adventure of great passion with a young attractive woman. That he would close the office when President Kennedy arrived and drive as many of the Ryans as wanted to come with him to Dublin to see the parade. He would speak in less eccentric tones to local farmers who were, after all, only anxious to get a bit of whatever was going. And lastly, he would watch Patrick O'Neill like a hawk. Never in his life had he known a feeling so strong and convincing as this one. That O'Neill and his family were going to destroy the Ryans.

The O'Neills were back. Everyone knew it half an hour after they had driven down Bridge Street. Judy Byrne knew because she was polishing her brass. She hated being caught doing anything so domestic. She preferred Patrick to think of her as a woman in an important medical role.

Sheila knew because she heard someone in the post office calling out that their car was parking. Sheila gathered her telegrams and messages quietly, and put them in a big anonymous-looking envelope to have them ready.

Maggie Daly knew and was delighted.

Grace and Kerry came into the shop. They were buying cream cakes and bacon and eggs for their tea. Miss Hayes hadn't expected them, so they were getting supplies. Maggie's smile nearly split her face in half when Grace raced over to hug her. Kitty, who was filling the shelves in a very bad humor, was equally delighted when Kerry came over to her without any prompting at all.

"Hi," he said, "did you miss me?"

"Were you away?" Kitty asked with spirit.

Kerry liked it. He had his elbow leaning on the shelf.

"Yes, we *were,* and I bet you knew it," he said.

"Sorry." Kitty was triumphant now. "I don't really keep up with all the comings and goings of people I hardly know. I'm much too busy."

"Then I'll have to get to know you better, so that you *will* notice when I'm not around," Kerry said, with a smile that would melt all the ice in the deep freeze.

Tommy Leonard knew they were back because he saw their car, and his father said he hoped there would be no racing out on the road and abandoning his post. Tommy fumed behind the counter, but the O'Neills came in to buy papers and postcards. They were going to send a card to all the hotels where they had stayed, to say thank you. To show them what Mountfern looked like. In a few years they would all know only too well where it was and what it looked like.

Kerry asked Tommy about the fishing, and wondered had they been swimming in the river. He said that, after all the beaches they had seen around the country, he was dying to go for a swim.

"Not until after the shop closes," Tommy's father said firmly.

Tommy wished his father wouldn't. Not in front of Kerry O'Neill, who was a grown person, and who seemed to be treating Tommy as equally grown.

"Workers of the world," Kerry said sympathetically.

"We close at six," Tommy said rapidly. "It would be lovely then."

"Tea at six," said Mr. Leonard.

"Seven then?" Kerry suggested.

"Right oh." Tommy was thrilled.

"At the bridge?"

"It's a bit crowded and noisy there." What Tommy meant was that he and his friends were considered too young for the gang on the bridge.

"The footbridge, then?"

"That's it." Tommy started patting the papers and magazines, proudly happy.

"See you then, Tommy."

Grace looked gorgeous. Very suntanned, in a blue and white striped dress.

"See you, Grace," Tommy beamed.

"My God, when I think of the time you children have today," said Tommy's father, a sour displeasure coming over his face.

The twins didn't know they were home because the twins were in the tunnel. Kate Ryan said they were out. She didn't know where. Hadn't they been down on the bridge? No? Well, they'd be back for their tea at six. Had Kerry and Grace enjoyed the tour? Were they impressed with Ireland? What did they think of the land over the river there without the ruins? It took a bit of getting used to. Wasn't it a pity they had missed it all? Kate chattered on cheerfully to the two blond children who stood in the crowded bar as easily and confidently as they stood in any other place in Mountfern. Their father was getting a drink for a group that was busy describing in detail the moment when the old ivy-covered masonry toppled down.

The twins would be very sorry to miss Grace. No, she had no idea where they were; they always came back at teatime covered in dust and dirt. Like they did every day.

Going swimming at seven o'clock, yes that was a great idea. Not right in front of the pub, if they didn't mind. People liked the idea of a quiet stroll down River Road in the evenings, not to get into the middle of a screaming mob of children splashing. A bit further along. No, not exactly opposite the Rosemarie hair salon either, that mightn't be such a great idea; just on the bend. Sure, she would send any stragglers up that way, and tell Dara and Michael.

"Aren't you marvelous the way you can talk and work, Mrs. Ryan," Grace said admiringly. Kate was pleased.

"Ah, it's a knack, like riding a bicycle. You find yourself pulling pints and washing glasses almost automatically. I don't even notice myself doing it, like those people who can knit and look at television. You'll find it yourself if you work in the bar over beyond. Or will you work in the hotel, do you think?"

"I don't know, Mrs. Ryan. Isn't that funny? We never seem to talk about what it's going to be like when it's a working hotel. Just getting it built seems to be as far as we go."

She smiled almost apologetically, and Kate realized, with a sudden stab, the power of such beauty. A man would do anything for a face like Grace O'Neill's, anything to keep those blue eyes laughing and happy.

Patrick asked the children to telephone Miss Hayes and let her know they were on their way. Brian Doyle had a litany of complaints that had to be heard. Jimbo Doyle had backed a lorry-load of tree branches into the presbytery and broken the front windows, and had to spend two days replacing them with new glass.

Father Hogan had been very droll about it, and said that the canon and himself had been very relieved that it was only Jimbo and a lorry-load of timber. They had been afraid it was something serious like Eddie Ryan about to dismantle the place on them.

Teresa Meagher had hitch-hiked to Dublin and sent a message through the post office that she was never going to come back to Mountfern as long as she lived. Mrs. Meagher was going to sell the jeweler's. Brian Doyle wondered did Mr. O'Neill want to buy it.

"What do I want with a souvenir shop like that?"

"It might be useful as property on Bridge Street. She'd be glad of a few thousand now; you'll always need an office or some kind of base in the town." Brian was a businessman.

"That's the kind of thing I'd expect from Jack Coyne, not from you, Doyle. I have no intention of buying a woman's only property when she's in a state of distress. What will she feel in six months? Conned and resentful."

"You're a smart man, all right," Brian said grudgingly.

Papers Flynn was at the back door asking to speak to the lady of the house; he had some lovely little bantam eggs for her.

Declan asked, could he bring a ladder around to the front of the house. Eddie was stuck in the chimney.

"Mother of God! What is Eddie doing in the chimney? Is he all right?" Kate was very alarmed.

"He's all right, it's just that he can't get out."

"Which chimney did he go up?" Kate's eyes were wild.

"He didn't go up any. He went down one."

"He *couldn't* have! He wouldn't fit."

"Only his arm," Declan said.

"Oh God, *what* are we going to do with him?" She ran out and was relieved to see Eddie perfectly safe but with his arm wedged in a chimney pot.

"Don't move," she shouted up at him. "I'll send someone up to you, though by rights I should leave you there for the night."

"I'll explain it all when I get down."

"Indeed you will," said Kate.

She turned to Declan. "I don't suppose you could throw any light on what possessed him to start climbing into the chimney, could you?"

"It was going to be his new career, I think." Declan sounded doubtful.

"Terrific," Kate said. She went back into the pub and looked around to see who might go and rescue him. Who would be the best person to disturb? Her eye lit on the tall figure of Kerry. She explained the problem and told him where the ladder was kept. Kerry said he had always fancied himself as a knight doing brave deeds for beautiful ladies.

Even though she thought it was far too flowery, it pleased Kate.

"It's all great fun," Grace said wistfully. "It's so quiet at home. It's like a three-ring circus here."

"You can say that again," said Kate resignedly.

Eddie's sweeping brush had fallen down the chimney. He had bent down to try to retrieve it, and in the effort his foot had slipped. He was well and truly stuck now, no way of getting his footing on the slippery roof from which three slates had already been dislodged and many more were beginning to shift.

Kerry climbed up easily and, watched by an admiring Grace and an anxious Declan, walked lithely over to the struggling boy.

"Relax friend, Superman is here," said Kerry.

"This is not as easy as it looks," Eddie said firmly.

"It doesn't even *look* easy," Kerry said. "It looks very dangerous indeed."

That was the right thing to say. Eddie didn't have to worry about his dignity anymore.

Kerry maneuvered Eddie's feet onto a sure base, then he was able to withdraw his arm from the chimney himself.

"Something very wrong with the flue," he said.

"You could be right," Kerry said.

"Should have a cowl, in my view."

"Very possibly."

Kerry had no idea what the child was talking about; possibly he was even mentally deficient. He always looked fairly sinister, and was reported to be in constant trouble.

"I'll be off now," Eddie said, sliding down the roof. "It was handy you happened to be passing."

"Yes, one of those coincidences."

Eddie slid to the drainpipes and nipped down the ladder, which he was about to take with him.

"Leave the ladder, you bonehead," Kerry shouted.

"I need it for my trade," Eddie shouted back. Then thought better of it. "But I don't mind leaving it here for a bit."

Shamefacedly he went around the side of the bar and in the back door. Nothing, not even his rescue from the jaws of death in the chimney, would excuse his walking through the pub during opening hours.

"Were you frightened, Eddie?" Declan asked.

"Oh shut up, Declan, you're a stupid pudding," Eddie said ungratefully to the agent of his rescue.

Kerry sat on the roof of Ryan's and looked over the river at the site where the new hotel would rise. How much better it would be to approach it from here, turn the footbridge into a magnificent wide bridge with big lanterns on each end. On the other side of the river he saw Dara and Michael walking along the towpath.

They were startled to see him sitting on their roof. When they got near enough to shout, they saw Grace. She ran across the footbridge to meet them, and they all stood in a little semi-circle looking up at him.

"What can you be doing up there?" Dara called.

"If I told you, you'd never believe it, so let's say I came early for Christmas," Kerry laughed.

He looked so handsome up there with the sun shining on his hair, a white open-necked shirt and a dark suntan. Dara shielded her eyes as if she were looking at an angel.

"Will we all go up there?" she asked.

"I don't mind, but your folks might object," Kerry called.

"It's six o'clock," Michael said. "Time for tea, anyway."

"Typical male, thinking of what to eat," Dara said scornfully.

She ran to the ladder and climbed easily up. Kerry reached his hand down from the rooftop to haul her up over the slates. He made room beside himself.

"It's *great* up here," Dara said excitedly. "Look at all you can see." River Road below them wound slowly to the bridge. They could see the cars inside Coyne's Motor Works. Usually you only saw the outer walls. They saw all the empty boxes and crates in the back of Loretto Quinn's, and further over they could see into the small back gardens of Mr. Slattery's house and of the other houses in his terrace, the back of the Classic Cinema and as far up Bridge Street as into Dr. White's. Companionably they pointed out places to each other. Behind them Coyne's wood stretched away up toward the Grange and down the river to the other side they could see the banks getting greener and more country-like as they were further from Mountfern and leading on toward the ruined abbey. From here Dara could see very clearly the big bushes of thorn and bramble that hid the entrance to their tunnel at the Fernscourt end. The fairy fort had remained untouched. Her eyes followed what must be the path of the tunnel—a slow incline, easy for rolling barrels or shifting crates or whatever they used to do in years gone by.

She felt Kerry looking at her and following her glance.

"Where do you go during the day?" he asked.

She wondered if he was psychic.

"Here and there, different places," she shrugged. A bit too casually, maybe.

His arm was touching hers as they sat side by side. He picked up her hand.

"Well, wherever you go, you sure get scratched," he said, looking at a great scrape from a coarse blackberry bush at the mouth of their tunnel.

"It's nothing." She was about to take her hand away.

His fingers traced the length of the scratch from the inside of her wrist up her arm.

"Looks painful," he said sympathetically.

"No, no it's okay." She found her voice was suddenly hoarse.

"You should take more care," he said.

"Why?" Her voice was quiet. He was still holding her arm and lightly tracing the long red mark.

"We're all going swimming later. You don't want to have cuts like this that will sting when we go swimming."

She looked up at him in alarm. His words were innocent, casual. She felt suddenly that he was saying something else.

It was like a lot of little electric shocks prickling all over her.

Chapter X

Kerry came home for a long half term.

Without the others knowing exactly why, this seemed to change things for everybody. Having him join in made things different, more grown up somehow.

Sometimes Kerry came along when they went swimming up at the bend of the river. And sometimes he didn't. They never knew if he was going to be there or not. Grace never knew either.

Sometimes he would cycle along with her, other days he would head off in a different direction. Or he would lie in his room and read.

Kerry got on much better with Father these days, Grace thought. There had never been anything like those awful days at Easter when she had to go to her room and work all day on those Irish exercises, while her father and brother had this war that involved Kerry refusing to explain something, and Father alternately wheedling or shouting threats.

Grace didn't believe that Kerry had left his first boarding school because the walls were damp. But Father had said he would greatly appreciate it if Grace did not interfere and ask questions. Kerry had only shrugged when she asked him. They had both said she should put it out of her mind, and that was what Grace had tried to do.

Sometimes it was easier than others. When the three of them were running along the beach up in Donegal and laughing. Then it was easy. Sometimes when they were there in the lodge, all three of them, Father's eyes would leave his papers and look at Kerry long and thoughtfully. Then Grace knew that whatever it was had not been forgotten.

She loved it when Kerry joined them. She was so proud of him, and he was such fun to be with. It was Kerry who said that it had to be simple to make a raft. After all, people had been doing it to explore the world or escape from desert islands for years now. It had to be only a matter of binding bits of wood all the same length together, didn't it? Suddenly they were all looking for wood—Tommy Leonard in the back of his shop, Maggie trying to break up the packing cases behind the dairy, or beg bits of wood off Charlie, who worked there. Michael found old poles in a shed in the back yard. Liam White sent a postcard from the Irish College which he said was diabolical, with awful girls giggling and terrible dances that four-year-olds would be ashamed to do at night, and nobody being able to speak any longer in any language. He had been driven mad with jealousy by Grace's letter telling him about the raft.

"You wrote to Liam?" Michael asked.

"Sure," Grace said. "Didn't you?"

Michael felt mean, somehow, that he hadn't. Grace was so nice to everyone. First she had made certain that it wouldn't cause dreadful punishments for Liam to get a letter in a language like English, and then she sat down and wrote. Michael wished he was away somewhere so that Grace would write to him. He could imagine her going in to Mrs. Whelan to get a stamp and licking it carefully to put on the envelope. He could imagine her sitting at the desk in the sitting room of the lodge, looking out the window and thinking of more things to say.

The raft looked great and Kerry had been quite right, of course it floated. They wondered why they had never made one before.

"I hope it's not dangerous," Kate said when she heard about it. "Kerry's much older than you lot. Make sure you don't do anything foolish."

The twins were annoyed. It was like a criticism of Kerry. And some days when they expected him, he never turned up.

On Wednesdays it was early-closing day, and so Tommy and Maggie could escape from their shops. Kitty came along too, unexpectedly. She was much more pleasant than usual, and admired the raft greatly.

"Can it go on long journeys?" she asked.

"Yes, to the sea, if you like," Kerry offered.

Dara didn't like Kitty coming along, with her waist and her chest. She looked around for support but didn't get any. Maggie was Kitty's sister after all; she had to be nice to her, and Grace was literally nice to everyone. Nobody seemed to be shooing Kitty away.

"I expect you could take the raft all the way down to the old abbey, if you wanted to," Kitty said.

Kerry was interested in the abbey; it didn't sound too bad, but there'd be a lot of paddling the raft, coming back upstream from that far. Wouldn't it be easier by bicycle?

"Much," Kitty said, and they exchanged a long look.

That had been a lovely day. Kitty had drifted off and Dara was glad she hadn't sulked over her having joined them. In a way it was a compliment, older people wanting to be with them.

They climbed on and off the raft all day. Tommy had said it was a great pity that they couldn't get empty barrels, or oil drums, then it would float magnificently. But who would give them anything like that?

"They'd have them in Coyne's Motor Works," Kerry said.

"Mr. Coyne wouldn't give you the time of day," Michael said.

"I'll ask him nicely." And Kerry had raced down to Jack Coyne's yard.

Jack Coyne thought there might be a belated chance to get back in O'Neill's good graces if he were nice to the lad. He carried up two empty oil drums and even gave them a couple of lengths of rope.

It bobbed up and down like a dream then, and they all jumped on and off it. Dara's long hair got into her eyes, she envied Grace's springy curls which seemed to dry in seconds. Even Maggie's frizz looked great when it was wet. Only drippy, dopey Dara looked awful. She sniffed and pulled at the damp, straight locks in disappointment.

"Here, I know, we'll gather it up with a rubber band," Kerry said.

"It would look worse than ever then." Dara hated him looking at her, suddenly. She felt cold and ugly in her navy swim suit and all this lank wet hair. But Kerry was full of practical ideas. Just as he had insisted it was easy to make the raft, he knew what to do with Dara's hair. Unselfconsciously he got his own comb and combed the long wet strands. It felt lovely sitting there on a tree trunk while he combed. She never wanted him to stop. The others were maneuvering a complicated way of climbing on to the raft straight from the bank; nobody noticed Kerry combing Dara's hair.

He went to where his trousers were folded on the bank and found a rubber band; he tied the wet hair neatly into a pony tail, having pulled out the dark fringe first.

"Now," he said triumphantly, "now that's better. It won't get in your eyes. And it looks great too. Truly grown up."

Dara saw the admiration in his eyes and she yearned for a mirror, but of course there wasn't one.

"Look in the river," he said, reading her thoughts.

She looked and she could see the reflection of the clouds racing across the sky and she could see herself. A bit stern, she thought, and severe. But she saw the reflection of Kerry behind her and he was smiling.

"Thanks," said Dara in a shaky voice. "I think it's much better like that. Tidier, you know."

"And prettier, you know." He smiled.

Dara felt an ugly red flush like a rash starting on her neck and going down her chest. She was terrified he would notice.

"Race you into the river," she said suddenly.

He had dropped the comb and was there before her. A clean dive far out into the center of the river. Dara flopped in at the edge and swam out toward the raft.

"Your hair is smashing like that," Maggie said admiringly.

"Kerry always says that Dara looks like Pharaoh's daughter," Grace said.

"Is that good or bad?" Dara had seen a picture of Pharaoh's daughter in a book of stories from the Bible; she looked terrific.

"Oh good, of course," Grace said.

"But old, definitely ancient," Tommy added.

"Not in *her* time, she wasn't, Tommy." Michael was defensive.

Kerry was sitting on the raft.

"Don't forget what she found down by the river, Dara, a baby in a basket. I don't think they'd believe you here in Mountfern if you came home with that story."

"I don't know. Canon Moran might, he'd believe anything."

"He's about the only one who would," Maggie said seriously. "I think we'd better look away from the weeds and the rushes in case we find anything like that. It would only lead to endless trouble."

They all laughed at Maggie; Grace put her arm around her, and Kerry said that she was magnificent. Maggie was never so pleased in her life, and quite glad that Kitty had gone away. She would have felt foolish being the center of all this praise and laughter in front of Kitty.

Her mother thought her hair looked better like that, which gave Dara grave doubts about it.

"It would look great if I had pierced ears," she said without very much hope.

"Out of the question," Kate said.

"I *knew* you'd say that, no debate, no discussion, just out of the question. It's always the same."

"No, it's not. I'm a magnificent mother," Kate said.

"Huh."

"I was just telling Fergus the other day how good I was. How I didn't murder you and Grace when you wrote Maurice's name on his shell with nail polish."

"We took it off with polish remover," Dara protested.

"But it might have hurt him."

"It's a *shell*, Mammy. Next you'll be saying it hurts the potatoes to dig them up, or the cabbages, and we'll all die off like flies because you'll be afraid of hurting things."

"I am endlessly patient. Fergus agreed."

"He must be bored to death, listening to you telling this litany of how great you are." Dara was full of scorn.

"No, he was fascinated. And so was Grace when I was telling her about what it was like when I was young. She thought it was very interesting. Not like you, my Dara, who would run a mile rather than hear my views on anything."

Kate spoke lightly, but Dara felt that her mother was being serious.

And it was true, Grace *did* love to hear tales of the old days. She wasn't just pretending in order to be polite, she would sit and ask all kinds of questions. She told Dara and Michael that their parents were far nicer than anyone else's, which was true, but it was nice to be told. Dara wondered what Grace would do if she wanted to have pierced ears. She would ask nicely and she would get what she wanted. That's what happened every time.

"Do you know, Mammy I was just sitting here thinking."

"And what were you thinking, Dara?" Kate looked at her and smiled. "You know, pet, you really do look very nice with your hair pulled away from your face like that. I think you've inherited my excellent bone structure, instead of the puddingy, sandy looks of the Ryans."

"I was just thinking that a fine-looking woman like yourself would want to be proud of her only daughter. Glad that her one girl would be a credit to her, with a smart appearance . . . and possibly to complete the look, pierced ears."

"No, Dara."

"Why?"

"Because you'd look like a gypsy, like a tramp. *No.*"

Dara looked crestfallen. She could read the tones, and this was a very definite no.

"Listen, I know it's not the same thing, but I'll get you a nice ribbon for your pony tail, you know the way Grace wears those ribbons."

"Oh Mam, Grace could wear anything in her hair and it would look great. I'd look like a jack-in-the-box with ribbon."

"You've no idea how lovely you are," said her mother. "And we will discuss your ears when you're sixteen. Not a day before then, not an hour."

"That's over three years. I can't believe it's going to be as long as that," wailed Dara. "I'll be so old then, nobody will want to look at my ears, or any part of me."

"Yes, well that's possible, but just to get value out of these days when everyone *is* looking at you, I'll get a ribbon. Would you like a striped ribbon or spots?"

Dara spent a long time curling her pony tail with pipe cleaners. It looked great next morning, tied up with an old blue ribbon she had found in Carrie's room.

Dara was first at the raft, but Kerry O'Neill didn't turn up. Dara thought the day was very long. No Maggie, no Tommy, no Whites, and mainly no Kerry. Three times Dara asked Grace where he might be. Three times Grace shrugged; you knew what Kerry was like. He turned up or he didn't.

Grace and Michael lay on the raft for ages, just talking. Dara felt very discontented, and dangled her feet in the water from the bank as she looked back up at Coyne's wood in case she would see Kerry O'Neill approaching on his bicycle.

The twins sat on the window seat and looked at the moon shining on the river.

"Can we take Grace to the tunnel, do you think?" Michael asked.

"We *said* it was going to be ours," Dara complained.

"Yes, well it is, of course."

"So why take Grace?"

"She's your best friend."

"I know. That's not the point; we'd have to take Maggie and Tommy. It would stop being special."

"We wouldn't, we could have it as a secret, the three of us."

"You can't keep secrets in threes."

"How do we know? I bet you and Grace have secrets. Things you don't tell me."

"So, if we do, what is the point?"

"The point is that if you do, then it means she *is* able to keep a secret. It would be great to bring Grace to the tunnel."

"No," said Dara.

"Okay."

"What do you mean, okay?"

"Just that. If you say no, then we don't. If you'd wanted someone to come and I'd said no it would be the same."

"No sulks, Michael?"

"No sulks, Dara."

Fergus Slattery left his invitation to Dublin too late. The O'Neills had gotten in before him. Just two hours before him. He called formally to the pub and told John that he was going to hire a station wagon to take the Ryan family to Dublin to see President Kennedy. He had friends with a solicitor's office on the very route of the cavalcade and they could sit at the window there above the crowd and see the whole thing.

John's good-natured face had a look of sorrow to refuse such generosity. But hadn't Patrick O'Neill been in that very morning with a similar suggestion? Imagine the Ryans being asked twice in the one day to go to see the President of America! Patrick was taking his own big car, Marian Johnson was taking her station wagon, and between them they were inviting the Ryans—John had decided to close the pub—and Sheila Whelan, whose nephew was going to be at the post office to deal with emergencies.

"Well, well, that's a pity," Fergus said between clenched teeth. "And what a chance to pass up. A seat on the very route itself."

But it appeared that Patrick had some American friends with three hotel rooms overlooking the route so they would miss nothing.

Fergus had a whiskey, which burned his throat. Would he even bother to go now? The whole outing had gone as sour on him as the drink. He could hardly swallow. And to think that O'Neill had the decency to ask Sheila Whelan. That was something Fergus should have thought of himself, but hadn't. Why did the man make all the right moves, *and* make them first?

Fergus walked back down River Road and back home.

"Miss Purcell," he shouted. "Miss Purcell, would you like to go to Dublin next week and see John Fitzgerald Kennedy with me?"

"Are you drunk, Mr. Fergus?"

"No, Miss Purcell, I am sober. I am, however, inviting you to watch the President of the United States visit Ireland."

"There's no need to shout, Mr. Fergus. I'll think about it." Miss Purcell was flustered—the red spots were beginning to burn brightly, like bicycle tail-lamps.

"Good, while you think about it I am going across the road to invite Father Hogan if he'd like to come too. I think the canon's a bit too frail for the journey, and anyway some cleric had better mind the shop in case there's a call for spiritual assistance."

"You're inviting Father Hogan?" Miss Purcell was now in seventh heaven. To travel to and from Dublin with the curate!

"Yes, I hope he'll have the graciousness to say thank you Fergus, I'd love to come, rather than deciding he's going to *think* about it."

"I'd love to come, Mr. Fergus, thank you very much," said Miss Purcell. "You see, I didn't really believe it was true. I didn't want to say yes too quickly."

Fergus found a strange stinging behind his eyes, and wondered was he going soft in the head, or had the whiskey in Ryan's been drugged.

Dara dreamed that Kerry could drive and that he had invited her to go to Dublin in his car, and it had broken down, and they had to stay in a wood. They built two beds out of bracken and moss and slept beside each other holding hands.

None of them would ever forget the day that John Fitzgerald Kennedy came to Ireland. He was so boyish and young, they all said. Imagine him having that huge responsibility, and being in charge of half the earth, in a manner of speaking.

Fergus met Jimbo Doyle, who said that a van had been arranged on loan from Jack Coyne for a few pals, and he was taking Carrie out of Ryan's with him. He told Fergus that he had asked her only just in time, because there was a question of Mr. O'Neill himself including her in his party as part of the household.

"Would you believe that?" Jimbo said wonderingly. "And Carrie just a maid in the house."

"She's not just a maid, she's your girlfriend. Hasn't she as much right to go and see Kennedy as anyone?" Fergus snapped.

"I know she's my girlfriend, Mr. Slattery, but she *is* the maid in their house too. I mean, that's her job." Jimbo spoke in some bewilderment.

"I'm sorry. I'm an ignorant lout."

"You are not," Jimbo said. "You're one of the most educated men for miles around these parts."

The solicitor who had invited Fergus to bring some friends with him may have been startled at the young priest and the elderly housekeeper. But then he was a city man to begin with; he probably expected country people to be eccentric.

The crowds were shouting and cheering long before the cavalcade even came in view. Two newspaper photographers perched from nearby windows and they could even see a television camera team on the corner. Father Hogan and Miss Purcell waved the Irish and American flags they had been given, and as he saw their great excitement and pleasure, a lump came in Fergus's throat, and he made himself a promise that he would try to be less selfish. All right, so he didn't walk over people like that O'Neill did, but on the other hand he didn't have the same genuine feeling for what would make people happy. Once or twice he had wondered how the Ryans were faring in the unfamiliar posh hotel. But soon the momentum had gathered and taken over, and like everyone else he was leaning out of the window waving, certain that there was a special wave and smile up at them.

Marian talked a lot about the trip to Dublin. She told everyone in the Rosemarie hair salon that Patrick O'Neill was a simply superb host.

"Has he done much entertaining in that cottage of yours?" Judy Byrne asked as she waited, thumbing through Rita Walsh's rather old magazines.

"No, they keep very much to themselves in the lodge, just family, you know." Marian sounded much more knowing than she was. She could not believe it possible that a family could live in her grounds and she would know so little of their everyday life. They were perfectly pleasant, if mildly startled when she came to call; they refused all offers of hospitality that she and her father showered on them. Marian had heard that a woman was coming across from New York, a Mrs. Fine. There had already been two phone calls to the Grange for her. It was a mystery. Patrick had made no booking; usually he was assiduous about booking well in advance and paying a full rate.

Who was Mrs. Fine?

She longed to ask if anyone in the salon knew, but she hated to reveal her hand.

She would call at Ryan's perhaps, and inquire there.

Marian didn't even need to do that. She met Grace and Dara as soon as she left Rita Walsh's door.

"Your hair looks lovely." Grace was always so enthusiastic, so willing to praise.

"Thank you, dear. Grace, who is Mrs. Fine?"

"I don't know what you mean."

"I mean is she somebody who is a family friend?"

"No, she's not a family friend."

"Is she coming over here to Ireland?"

"Not that I know of, Miss Johnson."

"It's just that there have been two calls for her, and I hadn't heard anything. Your father is usually so good about booking people in; I was wondering whether it had slipped his mind . . ."

"No, it wouldn't have slipped his mind. She can't be intended to stay in the Grange. They must have gotten it wrong back in the States."

"So who *is* she then, dear?"

"A sort of designer, I think; someone rather old who works with Father."

"And she and Mr. Fine aren't friends of yours back home?"

"No, I think it's all a work thing."

"I see." Marian was satisfied.

Grace linked arms with Dara on the way toward their raft on the bend of the river.

"I'll tell you something, because I tell you all my secrets."

"You don't have to." Dara still felt guilty about the tunnel.

"Well, I will. The woman that Marian's rabbiting on about, she's the woman I was telling you about. The one that was meant to be interested in Father. You know, the things people said."

"Oh heavens." Dara was worried for her friend.

"No, it couldn't be anything. I know that now. Father isn't interested in women and all that sort of thing. It's too late, and he's only interested in being part of things here."

"Well, that's all right then." Dara was relieved that there were no more storm clouds on the horizon.

"Kerry, Mrs. Fine's coming."

"She's not. He wouldn't dare."

"I thought I'd tell you now, so that you wouldn't make a scene."

"He can't mean to bring her *here*." Kerry looked around the lodge in dismay.

"No, not here, I mean to Mountfern."

"Is she staying in the Grange?"

"No, or Marian knows nothing about it, if she is."

"It's revolting." Kerry was walking around, agitated.

"Please don't make a scene. We've been over this a hundred times. We've said it *can't* be true. Not all this time, not at their age."

"Look at what we hear about the people going to the Rosemarie hair salon, they must be about a hundred."

"But not Father!"

"Why not? He's just the same."

"I'll ask him if you like. Let me ask him." Grace was anxious to avoid what would happen if Kerry asked.

"No, don't ask him. Don't sink to asking him. If she comes to this place then he'll have to explain her, let him explain her himself without us asking." Kerry's lip was curled in disapproval.

Papers Flynn called to Dr. White's office as if he were the most regular visitor there, coming for prescriptions and patent medicines. Mrs. White was surprised to see him at the office door; his usual approach was to the kitchen door in search of cardboard, when he would not be averse to a cup of tea.

Then she saw he had a gigantic bump on his forehead and a cut all around it.

"Oh Papers, have you been in the wars?" she asked, concerned for the gentle old man whose wits were long gone.

"I don't know what happened, Mam, but I was sitting there minding my own business in the dump near the brothers' school and I saw Miss Barry from the presbytery, who often gives me a cup of tea. Anyway she threw this bag of bottles in, and she didn't look at all to see if there was anyone there, and it's opened my head. I can't imagine what came into her."

Mrs. White sighed. It was about time for one of Miss Barry's batters. But really and truly she was getting quite dangerous, if she had nearly laid out Papers. Still she could hardly be faulted for thinking that a rubbish dump might be free of people sitting on the debris having their tea. Mountfern was a very mad place, Mrs. White often told her husband, on the frequent occasions when she was trying to encourage him to find a practice somewhere with a bit more life in it.

Jimbo Doyle put his head around the door of Leonard's paper shop.

"Tommy, do us a favor."

"What is it, Jimbo?" Tommy looked around to see if his father was watching. His father had accused Jimbo of reading every paper in the shop and buying none of them; it had been highly embarrassing.

"Look up the paper and tell me what's on in the Slieve Sunset tonight."

"What's on there? Is it turned into a cinema?"

"No, smartie, they have different kinds of talent contests. I wanted to know about the Country and Western one. If it's tonight I might have a go, get Carrie out there, have a real night."

"I'll look it up for you." Tommy was good-natured. It wouldn't cross his mind that Jimbo should be buying a paper.

"Ah there you are, Jimbo," his father cried suddenly. "Come to mend your ways and buy a paper at last, have you?"

Jimbo was very hard to insult.

"Not a chance of it Mr. Leonard, just called in to say hallo to your fine son here. We were having a bit of a chat about matters musical."

Tommy loved this; his eye had been racing down the advertisements in the local paper and found the appropriate listing.

"Yes, Dad, Jimbo and I were just talking about these talent contests. There's a very interesting one on tonight out in the Slieve Sunset, tonight at eight o'clock sharp, it says Jimbo, and it's Special Nashville Nite, spelled n-i-t-e, with fun for one 'n' all."

"Isn't it terrible to think that it was for the likes of this the republic was born," Mr. Leonard sighed. "For people who spell night, N-I-T-E. For half-wits who name their hotels half in one language and half in another and who encourage louts to get notions, togging themselves up in fancy dress as cowboys."

Jimbo thought Mr. Leonard must be talking about some loutish element which he imagined patronized the Slieve Sunset.

"No, it's a very nice crowd you'd get out there," he explained. "They have all kinds of restrictions, and there's no bad language of any kind allowed near the tables. The bar is different, but once you get near the tables where the ladies sit, it's out you go if a curse word is heard. You'd be impressed by it, Mr. Leonard, I tell you."

"I would," said Jack Leonard. "Oh I know I would."

"I'm taking Grace into town, she wants to get a couple of things to wear. Would you like to come for the trip?" Marian asked Kerry.

She loved this motherly role with Grace and thought she could extend it to the whole family.

"No thank you, Miss Johnson, I'm off to go bicycling."

"Will you be back for lunch? Did you tell Miss Hayes?" Grace asked him.

"Oh, I've explained to her, I'll be gone all day. I'm going to look at that ruined abbey down the river. She's making me some sandwiches."

Grace knew that Kitty Daly was taking a picnic off on her bike too that day. She knew also that Kerry was keeping well out of Father's way. He was very annoyed to hear that Mrs. Fine might be coming to Mountfern.

Rachel Fine looked at the Slieve Sunset hotel in disbelief. It was quite bad enough of Patrick to say they couldn't stay in the same hotel for discretion . . . but to put her up in this dump was inexcusable. The Grange was a country house, covered in virginia creeper, the Grange had horses in stables. It had a decanter of sherry to which the guests helped themselves before dinner. It had a lady with a plummy voice called Marian Johnson who was the daughter of the house and who ran the place very well. So what was Rachel doing in this fleapit? It was such a low-grade motel, it was definitely an insult.

She pulled off her long cream gloves and sat on the bed to inspect the room. There was no chair to sit on. Hideous drapes in huge sunbursts clashing with a carpet of equally hideous, but non-toning, shades. The light switch was not even beside the bed. There was no bathroom, you could share a tub or shower room with Lord knew how many people. A handbasin with a dripping faucet, a small uneven-looking wardrobe as an excuse for a closet. Four rattling wire coat hangers inside.

Rachel's head was aching. She had flown from New York to Shannon. She had rented a car on Patrick's suggestion. He had been hard to pin down on the telephone, but it was something to do with wanting her to see a bit of the country. Big clown. She could still see the countryside if he had come to meet her.

And what was all this need for discretion, here of all places? Here nobody knew them. It could be like that one week they had spent in Mexico where they could check into any hotel as man and wife, where they could hold hands at dinner. Who in Ireland would know or care that they stayed in the same hotel? Why, there was even his daughter as chaperon.

Tired and angry, Rachel began to unpack. She smoothed out her best silk suit; she had expected to hang it over a tub of steaming, scented water when she arrived, but *that* was not on. She looked at her face in the mirror. She looked every day of forty-eight and a few more days as well. She could *kill* him. But she wouldn't. She hadn't waited this long, and put up with so much already, to blow the whole thing in a dump in a one-horse town in a second-rate country.

Patrick was locked in a never-ending argument with architects and structural engineers all morning. He had said goodbye to Kerry the previous night, glad that the boy would be gone before Rachel arrived. He hadn't even said anything about her coming. With Grace there was no problem; the child had no idea of any relationship, and anyway she was so taken up with the Ryan twins she had no time for anyone else.

It was a warm day and the architects were being excessively stubborn; the whole planning could be negated even at this stage, they insisted, if he wouldn't tell them where he had finally decided to place the entrance.

"I'll tell you any goddamn place to get the show on the road, but we can change it again later, that's the deal," Patrick said.

That was not the deal, apparently. It was very wearing. Brian Doyle had been no help either.

"There's only two places you can put the entrance, in the name of God, Mr. O'Neill," he shouted, exasperated. "Where it is, where it was always meant to be. Or where the Yank architects say, which is along that sort of overgrown towpath, which will cost you another thousand pounds just to cut back the brambles. All you've got to say is one or the other."

None of them had seen what his son had seen, that the best and indeed the only place to have an imposing entrance, was from the small piece of ground where Ryan's Licensed Premises stood at this very moment.

Patrick decided to end the meeting. Kerry had left. Rachel was arriving. Marian was billing and cooing about dinner for the two of them that evening, when he most certainly would not be free. But most important of all, he realized, he had to talk to the Ryans. He had always despised other businessmen who pussyfooted about. He was going to ask those people straight away if there was any chance that they would consider selling. It was tempting to let other people do the dirty work, ask the questions that were almost impossible to ask. But Patrick O'Neill knew that in almost every aspect of life, if you want to do something it's best to do it yourself. If he did it quickly he might even have the conversation finished one way or another before lunch. Then he'd hightail it up to the Slieve Sunset and pray that Rachel wasn't spitting blood once she had seen the style he had relegated her to for her visit.

Miss Purcell had been in a very good humor since the trip to Dublin. She had been treated as the highest in the land with a window seat at which the young president looked up and waved directly. There had been tea and sandwiches, and Father Hogan had been a delightful companion for the day. Mr. Fergus was so odd of course, and put people off by his funny manner, but there was no doubt he had a heart of gold. She had ironed his shirts lovingly for him; she hoped he would look very well in this nice hotel he was going to, and people would admire him. She hoped he would meet a nice class of person, and have a good social life. He refused to play bridge, and he was on his own far too much. Miss Purcell didn't really want to see a wife for Mr. Fergus—that would mean too many changes—but she would like him to have more people of his own class and education to talk to in the evenings. He had taken to long walks, and heavy pints in Ryan's Licensed Premises with farm laborers.

She was glad of the thought of two weeks on her own. She could spring clean the house properly. It would be very quiet, of course, without Mr. Fergus and Kate Ryan and the clients trooping in and out. But the Lord knew the man was entitled to his two weeks off, and she went out on the doorstep to examine the skies, hoping for good weather for the young master on his holidays.

At that very moment a small car drew up and a very well-dressed woman jumped out.

"Pardon me, but seeing that you live here, can I ask you where I should go to find Mr. Patrick O'Neill who is doing major building works in these parts?"

Miss Purcell was delighted, an American lady just arrived in town. What a chance to meet her at once, just because she had gone to look at the weather.

"Of course I can tell you," she said. "You turn right at the big bridge you see here before you, then go along River Road. Park your car outside the public house called Ryan's and cross a footbridge. It's a bit of a walk but that's the site."

"That's where the old Fernscourt was . . ." the American lady said.

"The very place," Miss Purcell said. "Mr. O'Neill's building a fine new hotel there, they tell me."

"So I walk over the footbridge and it's a fair way?" The woman looked down at her very elegant high-heeled shoes. "Well, I guess I'm going to have to get used to different ways."

Miss Purcell was bursting with assistance.

"Seeing you have the car with you, you could always go back the way you came up to the main road, along a bit and then you'd see a rough sort of entrance, and a narrow path where there are lorries and tractors and the like. They have all kinds of signs telling people to beware of this and beware of that, so you should blow your horn at them all the time to let them know you're coming."

The woman thanked her. "No, I'll risk the little walk. And if I can't make it the whole way, I'll just holler."

Miss Purcell looked after her with interest. Now, who could she be? She looked a bit . . . overdressed, a bit foreign to be any kind of lady friend. Maybe someone he had met on an aeroplane or somesuch. Time would tell. They'd soon know.

Fergus Slattery had been out in the country making a will for a dying farmer. It was the last thing he had to do before he went back to pack. The old man clutched at him and thanked him for his patience.

"But then you wouldn't be your father's son if you were any other way," he wheezed.

"Was my father patient?" Fergus had worked beside the older man for years and realized that he was certainly well read and certainly slow.

"He had all the time in the world for you. It's the hallmark of the busy man; they never look rushed."

That was true of Patrick O'Neill, Fergus thought ruefully; he seemed to have time for chats and pints and strolls along the river bank. He had time to come and talk to the angling club and show them new flies he had brought from somewhere on his travels, chatting in a leisurely way, while all the time there were huge deals being done in New York to move money here and there, to finance even huger investments for his Fernscourt project. Already the walls were in evidence—only feet above the ground, but within a few months of leveling of the ruin the new order was beginning to appear.

Fergus shook himself back into the present.

"Well, I do have all the time in the world, so now if there's any little thing here that isn't clear to you, I can read it over again with you, Danny."

"No, it seems fair enough, fair enough."

"And sure, you've all the time in the world yourself, if you want to change anything," Fergus lied into the man's eyes. "When I come back from my holidays you can ask me to come up here again, if you've anything you want to add or take away."

"When you come back from your holidays, boy, I'll be in the churchyard, and we both know that. I'll tell your father that you're doing a good job."

"If you see him, will you ask him to send me a message about what in God's name he did with the papers in the Scanlan case? They're irretrievably lost and I have someone on to me about them every month."

The old man laughed, the thought of death pushed further away.

Fergus felt better himself. He thought he might call into Ryan's for a lunchtime pint. Since he had closed his own office he was childishly light-hearted; he felt his holiday had begun. He said goodbye to the old man he would never see again, and drove off toward Ryan's.

That funny thin woman with the dutch-doll coloring hadn't lied, Rachel thought, when she saw what a fair step it was to walk toward the busy site. She looked again at her shoes and said this was madness. Even squinting into the sunlight she couldn't see Patrick among the bulldozers and the men going in and out of a prefab hut which must be the site office.

She stood for a while looking at the scene which was the heart's desire of the man she loved. It was as incomprehensible to her, now that she was four hundred yards from it, as when she had been three thousand miles away from it. Perhaps she had been foolish to come here on her own. Maybe she should have waited. But that hotel was beginning to make her flesh crawl. She had lain without closing her eyes on that uncomfortable bed in the garish room. Sleep would not come. But it had benefited her nothing to come this far. Unless, of course, he was in the habit of calling at this public house for his lunch. She went up to the front door and into Ryan's.

She had assumed it would be a simple place; it certainly didn't look much from the outside but at least they had the good sense not to change the front and destroy the whole feel of the place like so many others, notably the dreaded Slieve Sunset, had done. She had thought it might be dark, and there might be men who would resent a woman calling in for a morning drink.

What she had not expected was a totally empty saloon with a husband and wife embracing each other behind the bar. The woman was dark-haired and good-looking, with tears running down her face. The man was sandy and plump, and looked as if someone had just told him that he had won the Irish Sweepstake.

But it was far better than that. John Ryan was holding the *Irish Press* newspaper of that day, in which his first poem had been published.

It was a poem called "Sleep in Peace," and it was telling the Fern family to sleep peacefully in their graves because the old order had changed. They must rest on and never come back because everything was so changed that they wouldn't be able to walk as Lords of the Soil, as they once had. It was both gentle and savage. John had written it to put in the book that he was doing for Patrick, then his confidence had failed and he thought that perhaps Patrick wouldn't like it. Kate had urged him to show it to someone who might know. She had typed it out and posted it to the *Irish Press*, which sometimes published poetry.

There it was, in black and white in the paper. He had only turned to the page five minutes before, and had come in shouting and roaring like a bull from the garden. Leopold, genuinely frightened for once, was whimpering under a table.

Rachel Fine had never seen such intense excitement and pleasure.

She felt utterly out of place, as if she had intruded into a marriage bed.

"I guess I'm a little early for bar hours," she said.

They disentangled themselves and Kate wiped her eyes.

"You must excuse us, Ma'am," said John. "But you arrived at a big moment for us. Can we ask you to share it . . . whatever you like to drink. Anything at all. This is a big celebration."

Kate was composed. "My husband has just had his first literary work published. Here it is in the newspaper. We're so pleased. It's been *so* long."

"And Kate never lost faith in me; she never thought for a minute that I wouldn't succeed." The man's face gave off rays like the sun.

Rachel looked politely at the paper. "Oh, it's about the Ferns," she cried.

"They used to own that house . . . well the house that *was* over there." John was so excited he could hardly talk.

"John, give the lady the promised drink and give me one too," Kate said.

Rachel looked from one to other. "I'm useless; I'm an orange-juice lady. I have no business being in a bar at all. I'm sorry not to be more festive on your great occasion."

"I'm often an orange-juice lady myself," Kate confided. "But I daren't say it in a public house. It's bad for business. You are most welcome to a nice glass of Club Orange if you're sure that's what you'd like."

John was staring at the paper as if it might vanish before his eyes.

"I'm Rachel Fine," Rachel said, stretching out her hand. "I work for Patrick O'Neill, I'm his designer and adviser."

Kate thrilled with sudden recognition. My God, he's got a fancy woman, she said to herself as she shook hands with the well-groomed woman and poured her a Club Orange to celebrate the success of the poem.

Rachel suggested that John go and buy up several copies of the paper, which he thought was a great idea. If Leonard's didn't have any more copies left, they could telephone somebody in the big town to keep some copies, or even the paper itself. They could get them copied too on a photocopier. He would inquire about that too when he was in Bridge Street.

"Don't be gone all day," Kate said. "There's bound to be a bit of a crowd in at lunchtime."

"I'll be back. Won't I want to show them?" Like an excited child he headed off down River Road. Kate knew he would stop first to tell Loretto Quinn, and could see her clapping her hands with pleasure for him.

"You must think we're quite mad," Kate said to Rachel. "Any other day of the year, you'd come in here and find us the most quiet respectable pub in the country. In fact I'd be up in the solicitor's office where I work in the mornings. But today is such a red-letter day, you have no idea, you really don't."

"I do, I can see only too clearly how pleased you are for him," Rachel said.

It wasn't the words, which were ordinary enough, but it was the way she said them that made Kate more expansive than usual. Normally she never told anyone what she felt about John.

"You see I wouldn't mind if he never wrote a poem that was published. I wouldn't want any fame or money or anything for me or for us out of his writing. But it's him. Often he says he's only a fool to be scribbling and writing, and maybe he's half-cracked to have such notions. Now he'll never think that again. His dream is official, as it were." She gave a little laugh at this definition of John's dream.

"That's a wonderful way of putting it," Rachel said. "His dream is official. Like Patrick's dream. I suppose now that he sees brick going on brick, he knows it's official." The two women looked across the river at the huge building site up the slope.

In a gentle voice Kate said, "Patrick will be over shortly, he nearly always comes in at lunchtime."

In a couple of sentences they had exchanged a great deal of information. And without saying very much at all they knew they were going to be great friends.

It was indeed busy at lunchtime as Kate had predicted, and with all kinds of unexpected people. Miss Barry had decided to begin what looked like a spectacular breakout by sitting on a bar stool and ordering a brandy and port. She had rarely been seen in a public house before; all her drinking had been done from surreptitious paper bags bought in off-sales in the big town.

Kate managed to get her out by saying that they had neither brandy nor port for sale in the pub, but if Miss Barry liked, she could give her a half bottle of each in a private transaction since she was sure that Miss Barry wanted them for medicinal purposes at home. This brought Miss Barry to her limited senses and she slipped away with two small brown-paper parcels toward a three-day binge and a spectacular hangover.

Fergus Slattery came in to say goodbye and said the place was like Portsmouth on pay night, with all the activity. When Kate told him about the poem, his pleasure was so genuine it touched her heart. He went straight to John and congratulated him loudly. He promised to tell everyone at the hotel he was going to that he knew the poet himself, and John Ryan's ears pinked up with the pleasure of it all.

Jimbo Doyle, who wouldn't have read a poem in a million years normally, said that all the children above with the brothers and the nuns should be made to learn it off by heart, and that it should be recited at the next concert.

In the middle of it all Patrick O'Neill came in. He didn't see Rachel, now on her third orange juice and happily settled in. He looked preoccupied and somehow annoyed to see so many people.

"Any chance of a word with yourself and John today?" he asked.

"Fire ahead," Kate said. "I may have to interrupt you, John's buying drinks for everybody, he had a poem published."

"That's good," Patrick said mechanically. "It's just that . . ."

"Oh Patrick," Kate's face was stricken. "Don't say, 'That's good,' it's much more than good. For God's sake the man has had his first poem published and you just say 'That's good.' It's magnificent, that's what it is." Her eyes had begun to blaze at the inadequacy of his remark.

Patrick realized he had been crass. "I'm sorry, I had something on my mind . . . I beg your pardon . . . where is he . . . must tell him how pleased I am."

"That's more like it."

"I am sorry, I know it sounds mean-spirited of me, I genuinely am pleased, it's just that there's something I'm anxious about . . ."

"Oh, she's here . . ." Kate cried triumphantly. "I'm sorry, I should have said it before . . . she's over there in the back rooms. Rachel, Rachel, Patrick's here."

Patrick's face was in a tight line where his mouth had been. How had it happened that Kate Ryan seemed to have guessed immediately that Rachel was more than a member of his staff, and why did she feel able to call this fact out familiarly across the pub?

He had been mad to let Rachel come here in the first place. He saw her then, surrounded by local people and laughing. But she looked wrong, she could never be part of this place. He must make that clear soon. Sweet Lord, how had it all turned into this, making things clear to people, speaking his mind?

Rachel looked up and waved at him nice and casually, as she would have done back home.

"Well Mr. O'Neill, I made it to Ireland. Isn't it a great place?" she said, and his heart softened toward her again.

Things were getting very complicated indeed.

By three o'clock the bar was empty. John and Kate were exhausted. The glasses were washed; two clean cloths, washed through after the polishing, lay across the beer and stout pumps. The place was ready for any afternoon visitor who might stray in, and for the teatime trade.

"God, if we were to have a crowd like that again we'd have to hire a young lad," John said.

"There speaks the man with the second income," Kate teased.

"Wasn't it great when Patrick read it out?" John said.

Kate had thought Patrick's mind was miles away but she didn't say that.

"I'm very, very proud of you," she said.

"Would we risk it and go up to bed for a while?" he said.

"Are you mad?"

"Ah go on, we could ask Carrie to step in here."

"And what would she think?"

"Does it matter what she thinks?"

"Don't be ridiculous, John, the children could come home."

The twins had gone for a picnic with Grace, Eddie was out with his gang of toughs, Declan could be anywhere.

"Let them, the door would be locked."

"We'll lock it tonight instead," she said.

"And what am I going to do here, mad with desire for you?"

"Why don't you look through your other poems, the ones we liked, and you could maybe give me some of them. I'll type them and you can always say I have had work published already, I enclose an example . . ."

"But there's only one example . . ."

"You don't have to tell them that," Kate said.

"God, you're a fox, Kate. Between yourself and Patrick O'Neill you could rule the world. There's a pair of you in it."

"I hope not," Kate said, shivering slightly.

"And what are you going to do if you're not going to fulfil your marital duties?" John asked sulkily.

"I'm going to have a little walk. I'm restless and over-excited . . . but *no* I do *not* see a way to cure all that. I'm not going to let us become the talk of the neighborhood by abandoning our pub and going off to bed in the middle of the afternoon." She skipped out of his way and took her cardigan off the back of a chair.

"Go on, John, get your poems down, truly now . . . I love the one about the nun looking into the river, the nun with the very sad face."

She walked out and stretched in the sunshine. She had said the truth, she *was* restless and over-excited. She was happy for John in a way she had never expected to be, but everywhere around her, like a big black cloud, she felt a sense of danger. Even when Patrick had said he wanted to talk to them she had thought it was going to be something bad, and was glad that the crowds and the circumstances had meant he couldn't bring up whatever it was. It was like a reprieve.

She felt there was something odd about Kerry. It wasn't that he never smiled—his face was one big smile, for God's sake, with those perfect white teeth. And he couldn't be more polite. It wasn't anything to do with Grace. The twins seemed to love her, and she was a warm little thing, all smiles too.

She really couldn't say that the work on Fernscourt had harmed their business. When else had they been full on a Tuesday at lunchtime? And perhaps these people would keep coming back even when the building works were over. So why then was she restless? Was it the holidays and knowing that young Fergus was off to find himself a woman? Surely not. She *wanted* Fergus to find himself a woman.

She crossed the footbridge and looked up at the site. Patrick would not be there now, he had told Rachel that he would drive out to the Slieve Sunset with her and see if they could make any improvements. Kate wondered why on earth she hadn't been allowed to go to the Grange and then remembered that Grace was at the lodge and might suspect something. Could that be it?

It would be very hard to be in love with Patrick O'Neill, hard to come first in his life. There would always be business, or the children, or travel or long-distance telephone calls. Kate sighed thinking of it all, and wished Rachel Fine luck in her uphill struggle. She remembered how warm and nice Patrick had been that day last week when they had gone to see President Kennedy arrive in Dublin. He had been so anxious to please them all with drinks and sandwiches in the big Dublin hotel. He had hardly ever stopped smiling and laughing. It would be easy to fall in love with him. She walked up the slope that the twins used to think of as their own private path at one time, now more open and exposed with a lot of the brambles and briars cut away. She hadn't been in to look at the site since the foundations were dug and already the walls were showing, so that you could see the shape it would be.

Kate felt she must know what it was going to be like, no point in being like an ostrich anymore. She was going to go right up there and look, and ask Brian Doyle which room was which, and talk about it to Patrick O'Neill, and ask Rachel Fine what kind of colors it was going to be. She quickened her step and threw back her head with confidence. *There's a time for everything, she thought. I wasn't ready to know about it before, but I'm ready now.*

She saw Brian Doyle waving at her frantically as she approached the site. He had both hands in the air and was shouting something. But she hadn't heard what it was by the time she felt the terrifying sharp pain. It was so sudden and worse than anything she had ever known, like the terror in a dream or a nightmare. And it only lasted seconds, because that was all it took for Kate Ryan to be hit sideways by the huge bulldozer, flung up in the air and crashed to the ground. It only took a few seconds to break her spine.

John knew only when the third person rushing away from the site to get help refused to look him in the eye and tell him what had happened. Roaring like a bull, he ran across the footbridge and had to be held back from the scene by three men. White-faced Brian Doyle begged him not to go near her.

"Jesus, the only thing we *do* know, John, is not to move her. For God's sake believe that. Stand back from her, don't touch her. You could make it worse."

John sat down like a child and put his big face into his hands. Strong men who had known him and had drunk pints in his pub for twenty years couldn't find the words or the gestures to touch him. They stood awkwardly around, eyes averted from the crumpled body on the ground.

Patrick O'Neill knew when there was a great hammering on the door of Rachel Fine's room in the Slieve Sunset hotel.

"No, of course Mr. O'Neill is not here," Rachel called through the door. "What on earth makes you think he is?"

"Sorry ma'am," the young girl called. "We've had a message from Brian Doyle, he said he's trying everywhere in the country to find Mr. O'Neill, there's been a terrible accident . . . a terrible accident and Mr. O'Neill's got to come at once."

Patrick was out of bed and had pulled his trousers on.

"What kind of an accident?" He shouted through the door.

"On the site of the new hotel in Mountfern."

"What happened?" Patrick had opened the door now; Rachel was cowering behind it. Patrick had pulled his shirt on at the same electrifying speed.

"Someone's been killed, I think. Some woman."

"A woman, killed on the site?" Patrick's shoes were on and he had picked up his car keys.

"Did he say what woman? What was a woman doing there? Did he say how it happened?"

"No, he said if we found you to get you over there as quick as possible."

Patrick was down the corridor by this stage and the girl was round-eyed at the thought of the American millionaire who was building the big hotel five miles away being in bed in the middle of the afternoon with a strange American woman and not being a bit ashamed of it. Weren't things going to liven up a bit here when the Yanks started coming over in force?

Mrs. Whelan in the post office knew fairly early on because Dr. White stopped his car outside her door and ran in to collect her.

"Put some kind of sign on the door, do anything but come with me, Sheila. They're going to need someone sensible at the pub to look after them."

She didn't question whether she was the right person or not, she just closed the door behind her and stepped quietly into his car.

"Have you told the canon?"

"Someone has. Father Hogan will be there in a minute, he's got his own car."

"Do you know is she bad?" Mrs. Whelan's voice was calm.

"No, all I know is that they've had the sense not to move her. I've got the ambulance coming anyway. I didn't wait to see her, we can always send it back if it's not needed." His face was set hard as he headed for the accident.

* * *

The twins were the last to know. They had been in their tunnel all afternoon. Grace had gone to the big town with Marian Johnson to get some more summer clothes. The invitation had not included Dara and Michael, pleasant but scruffy children from that pub. Anyway Marian wanted to get to know Grace, make an ally of her.

So for the first time in days they had a chance to play again in their home. They had been happy to note from the Fernscourt end of the tunnel that there seemed to be no intention of clearing the undergrowth and bramble which disguised the tunnel's mouth. The new gardens would end well over two hundred yards further on. The string had already been stretched over the part where the high hedges were going to be planted and the stone walls were to be built.

All they had to worry about now was whether the entrance would be down by the towpath.

They had torches with batteries, and an old bicycle lamp up high on a ledge. They had rescued a torn tablecloth that Mammy had said was beyond mending. There were two boxes filled with hay which were sofas and would double up as beds when they came to live here permanently. The day's play had seemed long for the first time. The kind of games they used to invent in the ruins seemed suddenly rather childish. But neither wanted to admit it to the other. Nor even to admit it in the heart. If the game was over, what was there?

In the hot tunnel, which for the first time seemed a bit close and smelly today, they played and hoped it was soon going to be evening.

They came out and pulled across the fuchsia bush as they always had done. Not twenty yards down the towpath they heard the people calling them. There must have been a search party out for them.

It was Loretto Quinn who saw them from across the river. She waved and shouted. "Where on earth have you been?" she cried.

Dara and Michael looked at each other in dismay.

"Nowhere."

"Just playing."

But by this time the children from the bridge had come toward them in a group, and then suddenly hung back as if not wanting to be the first to say the words.

"You've got to go home now," Tommy Leonard said eventually. "They've been looking for you for hours."

"We've only been just around . . ."

"Just around here and there . . ."

Tommy's face was serious. "Something very bad's happened."

The other children held back.

Loretto Quinn was there by now, she was kneeling down on the ground in front of them to be nearer to their height, but that made her much too low and then they had to bend to hear what she was saying.

"You have to be as brave as two little lions now. Do you hear me? They all need you to be brave."

"What happened?" They spoke together, faces calm, timing precise.

"Your Mammy got hit by a machine up in the site, she hurt herself very badly. They've taken her to the hospital in an ambulance."

The children crowded closer to hear. Now that someone else was telling the twins, now that a grown-up had taken the burden off them, they wanted to be part of it.

"Is she dead?" Dara asked.

"No, she's not dead," said Loretto Quinn.

"Is she going to die?" Michael asked, equally calmly.

Loretto remembered the people who had given her false hope and told her that her Barney might recover when they took his lifeless body from the River Fern all those years ago. They had meant well, but they had been no help.

"They think she might die, yes," she said. The group of children drew back suddenly and Loretto held the twins in her arms and supported them from the towpath, across the bridge in the eyes of dozens of people, and back to the pub.

Mrs. Whelan took them into the kitchen. "Your daddy's in hospital now. Do you think your place is in there with him, or is it here with me looking after the children?"

Eddie and Declan's faces were swollen from crying. They sat in unaccustomed stillness on kitchen chairs while Carrie made bread at Mrs. Whelan's suggestion.

Dara thought for a minute. "I suppose she'd want us to keep an eye on Dad in case he'd get too upset at the hospital."

"Right," said Mrs. Whelan and she sent someone in the bar for Jack Coyne who would drive them into the town.

PART THREE

Chapter XI

The church was crowded at eleven o'clock mass on Sunday. The two priests, who were faced with getting their own lunch due to the non appearance of Miss Barry, had answered many requests to say masses for Mrs. Ryan. Young Father Hogan became impatient when a poor old tramp called Papers Flynn came with half a crown to have a mass said for the poor woman in the pub.

"No need to give an offering, Papers," Father Hogan had said gruffly. "We'll be saying mass for her anyway."

"I want my mass said for her," Papers insisted. She had been very good to him always, he said, given him a yellow blanket to wrap around him under all the newspapers he normally wore when sleeping in a ditch. She had never given him a lecture about sleeping out. It was as if she understood somehow.

The young American girl had come with five dollars.

"I guess this might not be the way to do it, but when my Mother was alive she used to give an offering for a mass. Could you write Mrs. Ryan's name in your book, Father? And could you say a mass for her?"

Tramps and children. Father Hogan had never thought it was going to be like this. Tramps, children, drunken housekeepers, kind if doddering parish priests. And trying to explain why it was God's will that a young woman, mother of a family, should be struck by a huge bulldozer as she walked unheeding on a summer's day. They never told you in the seminary that it was going to be like this. But maybe, of course, they didn't know.

It was Canon Moran who would say eleven o'clock mass; Father Hogan would go and struggle with the range. He sighed as he folded his own vestments from the earlier mass in the vestry and watched Canon Moran take tottering steps out toward the altar. He had arranged sensible altar boys like Tommy Leonard and Liam White. With the canon you couldn't have any possible troublemakers.

The canon turned to face the congregation and in his thin reedy voice he said, "Your prayers are asked for the happy death or speedy recovery of Katherine Mary Ryan of River Road."

Fergus put a finger in his collar to loosen it. He wondered what he was doing sitting here listening to this mumbo jumbo. Happy death! Should it not be speedy death rather than lying there paralyzed, in traction, so heavily sedated because of the pain that she didn't even know her own family or where she was? What did this old fool mean? Praying for happy deaths and speedy recoveries, that's what you said about old people lingering on and on, it was a way of announcing to the parish that old Jimmy this or Michael that was on the way out. Like the old fellow he had made the will for a few days back. It wasn't for Kate Ryan, a young woman. A young woman who had been killed—or almost killed—by a machine on that man's land.

Fergus felt himself getting a hot flush of anger and loosened his collar and tie still further.

He thanked God for the wisdom of Sheila Whelan who had phoned him the night it had happened. She had simply said that she knew he would want to know, rather than come back a week or two later from his holiday and find out what had happened in his absence.

Miss Purcell had sniffed, of course, and said that Mrs. Whelan had a deal of impertinence interrupting the man on his holiday. But Miss Purcell knew nothing, and Sheila Whelan knew everything. She knew that he would have come back from the ends of the earth.

Loretto Quinn was not following the mass; she was saying the thirty days' prayer. She had promised Our Lady that she would start the prayer immediately. She knew that Our Lady would realize how important Kate Ryan was to her family, and spare her. She prayed determinedly, trying to mean the words, and never once thinking that Our Lady might also have known how important Barney Quinn had been.

Sheila Whelan wasn't following the mass either. She was trying to work out a plan in her head. The Ryans hadn't thought a day ahead of the day they were living. Someone had to think for them. They couldn't live on the way they were. They needed a woman in the house, someone who could serve in the bar, someone who could keep an eye on the children, and see to it that Carrie did what she was meant to do. She had a cousin.

She wondered would it work. The cousin had been disappointed. A man had given her an engagement ring and there were plans for the wedding. Mary Donnelly had given up her fine job teaching and drew out her savings to put a deposit on a house. The man had disappeared, with the savings.

In fact Sheila Whelan was the only member of the family to know anything. Mary Donnelly felt that Sheila, having been abandoned by her own husband, might understand. She had told her everything only six weeks ago.

Mrs. Whelan decided to ring her and suggest it anyway. No harm could come from suggesting something and for poor Mary, bruised and betrayed, anything would be better than staying where she was and enduring the pitying glances of friends and relations.

John Ryan was not at mass, he was at his wife's bedside. Kate's face was very white, her breathing was troubled and she gave little snores and half-choking sounds. Kate had never snored although she claimed that John would raise the roof unless she nudged him and pinched him to change his position in bed.

There was a tube attached to her arm and another to her bladder. She didn't look like Kate, she looked like a picture of Kate that had been given to medical students to experiment on.

Once or twice she seemed to know him.

"John," she said once.

"I'm here, love."

"I'm sorry, John."

Then nothing more for a long time.

"The children?" she asked quite clearly.

"Fine, not a worry about them, in great form."

"Who . . . who?"

"Carrie's coping very well, Loretto's in and out, Sheila Whelan came in all three days. We're fine, they're fine."

"Three days?" She seemed mystified.

"Since it happened," John said.

"My God, three days."

"Don't think about it, you're getting better, they say you're on the mend." His face was red with exertion.

Kate had slipped away into unconsciousness again.

Dara had washed Eddie's neck and Declan's ears before they went to mass. She had refused their protestations.

"Mammy says she could plant rows of potatoes in your neck, Eddie. Stand still and let me scrub it."

"Put some soap and water on the facecloth," roared Eddie.

"There's plenty on it. It's just that you're so filthy."

Declan stood waiting for his turn. "Maybe I'd do my own ears to save you the trouble," he offered.

"No," Dara said. "I'll do them."

Michael sat saying nothing. Carrie had come back from early mass and was standing unhappily wondering about the lunch.

"Are you clean, Michael?" Dara asked.

He shrugged.

"Ah, come on, Michael, it's the only thing we can do for Mammy, not to be like tinkers. That's what she'd say."

"We don't know what she'd say." He was mutinous.

"What do you mean?"

"You have half of Mountfern saying 'Your mother would say this,' and the other half saying 'She'd say that' . . . When will she be able to say something for herself, not have us all listening to other people saying it for her?"

"When she *is* able to say something I'm sure she'd prefer you to stop moping and *do* something."

"All right." Michael went at Declan's ears with such savagery that the boy roared for mercy.

"Isn't it disgusting to think that our mother has to look at such awful things as necks and ears," Michael said.

"I bet yours were just as bad and maybe still are, for all we know."

"Stay *still*, Declan. It hurts less if you don't move, you clown."

Michael thought he'd like to skip mass; he felt sure that God would understand that he could pray better for Mam if he were to walk up the bank a bit. He remembered a great day he had walked off for miles up the Fern and met old Mr. Slattery who was deep in conversation with a Dutchman. The Dutchman was telling him all the names they would call the fish if they were in Holland. A perch was a *baars,* and a pike was a *snoek.* Old Mr. Slattery had been delighted with that word and had said that if ever Michael went to foreign places like Amsterdam or The Hague he could talk about *snoek* with the best of them.

Michael had often thought that he and Dara might take trips to foreign parts when they lived in Fernscourt. They would travel once or twice a year. How stupid and babyish they had been. He should have known that good things never happened really. Everyone said that Mam was going to get better, and they said she'd be running in the door again like she always did in no time. But Michael didn't believe it. People were saying it the way they said that it was going to be a great summer or that they were going to beat Offaly in the match. Just a hope. Not something real. Michael wished he could tell God about this on the river bank, and explain without being all mopey and dismal-sounding that it couldn't help anyone to keep Mam sick in hospital, but it would help everyone to make her better. He was sure that God would listen better on the banks of the Fern than in the church with everyone coughing and fidgeting. But there was no way you could explain that to anyone.

Only a madman or a heretic would suggest not going to mass on a Sunday when his mother was lying with a broken back.

Mrs. Daly caught sight of Maggie leaving the house. "Where are you going, Maggie? It's too early for mass."

"I was going down to collect Dara and Michael to walk them to the church," Maggie said.

"Don't be going in there on top of them all, they'll have the house filled with people."

"No, their Dad's gone into the town, they'll have nobody," Maggie said.

"You can see them in the church. Don't be dragging up there and living in their pockets at a time like this."

"But isn't this the time they *would* like people around?" Maggie asked simply.

"Stop contradicting me at every hand's turn. Comb that mop of hair of yours, will you, Maggie, and wait till the bell rings before going to mass."

Mrs. Daly's mouth was in a thin disapproving line.

* * *

In the lodge Olive Hayes was sitting at the kitchen table writing a long letter to Sister Bernadette on the other side of the world. Miss Hayes had put a breakfast on the table but none of the O'Neills had been able to eat. There had been yet another row between Mr. O'Neill and his son. And Grace had wanted to go and stay in the Ryans' pub after the terrible accident. But her father had said no. You could have cut the atmosphere at breakfast with a knife. As Olive Hayes wrote page after page she paused now and then to think how true it was that riches did not automatically bring happiness. This very morning she had seen the O'Neills sit white-faced around their table leaving the scrambled eggs, crispy bacon and home-made bread untouched. She had seen Marian Johnson go by in a ridiculous hat that must have cost a fortune and looked like a bird's nest. Marian's face was tense and anxious.

And now Mr. O'Neill and his daughter had driven off to eleven o'clock mass but Kerry had not gone with them. He had gone to his room. That meant he would miss mass entirely this Sunday. Olive Hayes wrote on in wonder to her sister about how changed the world had become. Could either of them ever imagine a situation where a boy of sixteen would refuse to go to mass on a Sunday because of some row with his father? It was outside their comprehension.

Tommy Leonard came up River Road and called to collect the Ryans for mass.

"I thought I'd walk with you," he said to Dara. "It's the only thing I can think of that might help."

Dara was grateful.

"And Dara, I did something else. I went up to Miss Byrne and asked her did backs ever mend, and she was full of information. She said that after a bit when they know how bad the injuries are they will decide on what program to follow. It's programs, you see, one kind for one kind of a back one kind for another. She said they do marvelous things now."

Tommy's face shone with the good news. Dara managed a watery smile.

Michael looked very white, Tommy thought, as if he had been sick.

"I'd say you could have a dispensation not to go to mass," Tommy said after some reflection.

"Did you get that straight from the pope?" Michael asked with a sort of a grin.

Tommy was pleased. At least he had made both of them smile a bit. They walked down River Road, the four Ryan children and Tommy.

"Will I have to walk ahead of you or behind you?" Eddie asked.

"Of course not," Dara said.

"You're all right with us," said Michael.

Eddie's face registered great alarm. Things must be worse than he thought if he was allowed to walk with the twins and Tommy Leonard. Mam must be in a very bad way altogether.

Kitty Daly wheeled her bicycle out quietly.

If anyone asked her why she needed a bike to go the few yards to mass she would say that she was going out to her best friend's house afterward. This was a girl who lived on a farm three miles out beyond the bridge.

But nobody asked her, so Kitty looked up and down Bridge Street and set off at a great pace toward Coyne's wood. While the mass bell was ringing over Mountfern she pedaled on and got to the old stile at the same time as Kerry O'Neill.

Hand in hand they walked through the paths that had hardly changed since their grandparents and great-grandparents had been young and had visited Coyne's wood all those years ago.

Patrick O'Neill could have done without this parade. But he knew that not to have come to mass would have caused more comment still. His face was grim as he walked into the church. A year ago he would have known nobody here, now there wasn't a face that he didn't recognize nor a person who didn't know him.

He knelt beside Grace and wondered to himself how the church had survived so long with ineffectual old men like Canon Moran in charge of parishes. Possibly because there were no thrusting young men anxious to topple them as there were in ordinary business.

Or if the thrusting young men *did* feel like that then they were not in the right calling. Thrusting young men reminded him of his son, and the great wave of annoyance came over him again. As it had when he had spoken to Kerry and told him about the accident.

"We're insured aren't we?" Kerry had said.

Patrick had remained silent.

"Well we are, Father, hey?" Kerry's voice had sounded impatient.

"Yes we're insured," Patrick had said.

"And Father, the whole place is hung with notices. Christ, they can't even expect *our* insurance to pay."

Patrick hadn't trusted himself to speak. He realized that if Kerry O'Neill reacted this way he had inherited it from his father.

Patrick saw Fergus Slattery loosening his collar and tie and looking around him a bit wildly. He wondered was the lawyer coming adrift in some way. There had been that very unpleasant and unexpected scene in the hospital where Fergus had shouted at him, not caring who heard.

"Don't think you can buy your way out of this, O'Neill, as you bought everything else."

The man had been almost deranged.

Patrick had put out a hand to calm him and Fergus had flung it away.

"Your tactics won't work with me, O'Neill, you can't glad-hand me like you do everyone in the county. Kate Ryan was injured—possibly fatally injured—on your premises by a machine in your ownership by a man in your employ. Making a few grand gestures about American surgeons, friends of yours no doubt who'll say that her spine was broken always . . . that's not going to change the mind of the courts of law."

"Ah Fergus, will you stop and think? Who's talking about courts of law? We're talking about making Kate better."

"*I'm* talking about courts of law, district courts, circuit courts, the High Court, the Supreme Court. Don't worry, O'Neill, this time you're not getting away with it. This time you won't smile your way out of ruining people's lives."

They had calmed him, other people had. Patrick had walked away knowing that his presence was inflaming Fergus Slattery more every second.

Patrick wondered if Slattery was sweet on Mrs. Ryan. There was something very passionate and personal in the way he talked. But he realized that in fact it didn't matter whether Fergus Slattery was in love with Kate Ryan or not, what mattered was that he held Patrick totally responsible for the accident. And so might a lot of other people.

Marian Johnson was at eleven o'clock mass. She had tried on her three hats and examined herself with distaste in all of them. They were aging, every single one of them. She looked like a middle-aged frump.

But then she didn't want to wear a headscarf. People like Marian Johnson always wore hats, it said something about who you were to wear a hat at mass.

She had driven quickly to the church and looked in the mirror of her car without pleasure. She saw Patrick and Grace, and thank heavens there was no sign of that foreign-looking American woman who had arrived a few days ago. She had heard some very unsettling stories about Patrick being discovered in the same room as this Mrs. Fine when they were searching for him after the accident.

But that couldn't be so. Anyway she would be here at mass with him if she were a close friend of any kind.

She had hardly spoken to Patrick since Kate Ryan's accident. He was so preoccupied and either on the phone to America or over in the hospital as if it were his fault.

Heavens, everyone was saying that he hadn't a thing to blame himself for. It wasn't his fault if that woman didn't know what dangers and hazards there were there. Living right across the river from them. It was terrible for her of course, and all those children.

Marian's eye fell on them in a row: the solemn dark-eyed twins who were such friends of Grace O'Neill, and two scruffy little boys with spiky hair.

She heard Canon Moran's reed-thin voice pipe on about happy death or speedy recovery. The man must be getting senile. How could you recover from a broken spine speedily, for heaven's sake? Then she saw Dara taking the smaller scruffy boy by the hand and leading him out of the church.

With his other hand rolled into a fist and stuck into his eye, the child was roaring.

"He said happy death, Mammy's not going to have a happy death; they said she was all right. They *said* she was all right."

Kate struggled during the night. She was very agitated and wouldn't be comforted.

"Shush shush now. I'm here, there's nothing to worry about," the night nurse soothed.

"There's everything to worry about." Kate was suddenly clear and rational. "I can't stay here, I have to go home. They'll never manage."

"Of course they'll manage, they're managing fine, isn't that what your husband has been saying to you every day for a week?"

"A *week?* I don't believe it."

"Don't think about it now, try to rest."

"It can't be a week," Kate Ryan said, and her over-bright eyes closed heavily as she went back to something that was neither sleep nor complete unconsciousness. She had been there for a time that she couldn't work out. Every time things cleared people told her some different time scale.

Her breathing was heavy and jerky.

The night nurse took her pulse and marveled at the resilience of the human body. To be able to survive those injuries. To be able to lie still while people worked out just how bad those injuries were.

They were managing in a sort of a way. Often it was the well-meant curiosity and concern that was the hardest to take. People came with stories of bone setters who had made the crippled walk, with details of saints who had interceded with God in startling ways and with herbal cures which had been known in these parts for years and never once known to fail.

People came with kind worried faces saying that Kate should be kept still for six months or that she should be on her feet now before the paralysis had time to set in, or that she should have hot seaweed baths.

The support of a small community had its good side and its wearying side. Nobody could be offended, nobody could be ignored. And it didn't have the advantage of taking their minds off things. Everyone was talking about the same thing. How to get Kate Ryan cured and back in their midst.

Jack Coyne was the last person John wanted to see come into the pub.

"It's all right, don't stand up. I'm not here socializing."

"Sorry, Jack, what can I get you? It *is* a public house; I have to try and keep things normal for everyone's sake."

"No you don't, things are *not* normal. You've contacted a solicitor, I suppose."

"Ah Jack, stop will you . . ."

"Someone has to keep you straight, John. You'll need a big firm of solicitors, Fergus will be the first to tell you that. Don't just go to someone in the town, go right to Dublin. You'll have to in the end."

"It's doctors she needs and a run of luck, not lawyers for Christ's sake."

"She's the businesswoman in this family, she'd be the first to agree with me."

"Please, Jack. I know you mean well. You're not helping."

"I can give you the name of a big firm. I let one of the partners have a car last year, he came down here fishing. Jesus Mary and Joseph, John, O'Neill has to be stopped. He has to be stopped, I tell you, and you'll need the big guns on him. He can't come in here to this parish throwing his weight around, favoring one, ignoring another and in the end getting Kate into this terrible mess."

"It's not the time . . . I beg you."

"If you don't act now it'll be too late, he'll outfox you. There's a lot of people in this place standing up for you, John, don't let them down."

"Mr. Ryan?"

"What is it, Carrie?"

"Mr. Ryan, Jimbo asked me to find out kind of if you were going to be taking Mr. O'Neill to the law for all that's happened to Mrs. Ryan."

"And what on earth business is it of Jimbo's, can I ask?"

"I know, Mr. Ryan. I didn't want to ask you at all, but he said a lot of the fellows who work for Mr. O'Neill were wondering and that I was in a grand position to know, working here and all."

She looked wretched, her long lank hair falling into her eyes. John knew that if Kate were standing here she would hand Carrie a hair clip so that she wouldn't blind herself.

He looked at her helplessly without saying anything.

"I'm very sorry, Mr. Ryan." Her face was scarlet. "It's just that he said it would be easy, but I didn't know what else to do but ask. There'd be no point in my listening at doors."

"No point, Carrie." He was weary. "Tell Jimbo that you think suing Patrick O'Neill is the last thing on my mind. There's no plans to stop him in his building, their jobs will be all right. That's what it's about."

"I suppose it is," Carrie said miserably.

"Was that Miss Johnson from the Grange leaving in such a hurry?" Mrs. Daly from the Dairy wanted to know.

"It was indeed." Rita Walsh tossed her head. She had just had words with Marian Johnson. Unpleasant words. Rita had said like any human would have said that it was a tragedy about Kate Ryan, wasn't it appalling to think she had been so badly injured only yards from her own home, in a place that used to be green fields and wild brambles.

Marian Johnson had taken this as some kind of criticism of Patrick O'Neill; she had answered hotly that the Ryan woman should have been able to read the dozen notices around the building site.

It had all been very unfortunate; the hair-do had not been a success. Every attempt to organize a parting in Marian's many-crowned head had been interrupted by further defense of the American. Rita had been foolish enough to pass some remark about Patrick being well able to look after himself and if he wasn't, hadn't he that foreign-looking woman, the one he had installed over in the Slieve Sunset, to look after him? This had caused an unexpected reaction, and Marian had left before her hair was finished.

"It's pathetic at her age," Mrs. Daly said disapprovingly. "She's well into her forties, what does she think is going to happen? A big white wedding up in the church with Canon Moran blessing the happy couple? She should have sense."

Mrs. Leonard from the stationer's was coming out from under one of the big heavy chrome hairdryers. She didn't want to miss anything that was going on.

"I was in Conway's this morning—you know, the shop part, not the pub of course." She gave a tinkle of a laugh. "They were saying in there that they hoped there'd be no bad feeling over this. An act of God is all it was."

"Well yes," Rita said unthinkingly. "But an act of God that happened because of that man's machinery and bulldozers. If he hadn't come back and filled the place up with things you'd never expect in the heart of the country . . ."

She felt Mrs. Daly's shoulders tense slightly under the pink cotton cape. She knew that for a second time that morning she was going to find herself in disagreement with a client.

"That's all very well, Rita," Mrs. Daly said, "but it doesn't do to forget what benefits that man is bringing to this place. It would be a pity if people were to go around saying things carelessly that might drive him out of it. He's in a terrible way, I hear, near to tears over the whole thing, and he's like a child about Mountfern and wanting to be part of it. The smallest thing could blow him away from here like a puff of wind. We'll have to watch what we say."

Rita looked in the mirror and her eyes met Mrs. Daly's eyes, small and round like Mrs. Daly's face, satisfied with life the way it now was since the American had come to breathe hope into the town and to give Daly's Dairy the chance of supplying a large hotel.

"I know what you mean," Rita Walsh said. "It doesn't do to give the wrong impression."

"Exactly." Mrs. Daly wriggled her plump little shoulders and waited for Rita's expert fingers to arrange the finger wave to the best advantage on her forehead.

Dr. White came into the post office with relief. Here at least nobody would expect him to know the ins and outs of Kate Ryan's injuries, the likely chance of her ever being able to walk again.

The door to the back room was open and the doctor saw the big stocky figure of the American at the telephone.

"Well, Sheila," Dr. White said mildly, "I didn't know this was going on. Is it a serious romance or are you just setting up an opposition to the Rosemarie hair salon?"

"Ah, leave poor Rita alone." Sheila Whelan didn't bother denying the reputation of Mrs. Walsh's establishment. Neither did she offer any explanation for the presence of Patrick O'Neill in her sitting room, but she had quietly closed the through door with her foot.

"Can I get you stamps, or are you eligible for the old-age pension suddenly?" she asked.

"God, I feel I could do with the pension. Be like old man Slattery used to be, take my little stool and bag and spend my days eyeball to eyeball with lovely eight-pound—ten-pound, even—pike. Dangle a few little herrings in front of them, that's what a man should do with his days on this earth."

"Never saw the sense of it myself," Sheila Whelan said. "Taking one kind of fish to attract another kind of fish, and not even eating the ones you take out of the river. Still."

"That's it. Still, let people do what they want to. I came in for one thing and one thing only, to avoid running into the canon. I saw him coming up the road, and I fled in here. I can't take another dose of the Lord's will, and the goodness of Our Blessed Lady."

Sheila Whelan smiled. "Come on out of that, you're a very saintly man."

"Yes I am, but it's not the kind of saintly that sees the hand of God and his mother in paralyzing Kate Ryan all in the cause of building a flashy hotel."

"She'd have been paralyzed whether the hotel was going to be flashy or whether they were building a library for cloistered nuns over there."

"You always stand up for him." Dr. White jerked his head toward the door.

"No, that's not so. I don't always stand up for him or always stand up for anyone, but Lord God it's not his fault, is it?"

"I suppose like the rest of the town you're terrified he'll go, and take his money with him."

Sheila was mild. "What do I see of his money? I'm hardly making a fortune from his being here. A lot more work, and certainly revenue for the Department of Posts and Telegraphs. I'm hardly benefiting myself."

"Of course not." Dr. White was ashamed.

"I know what you mean though, Martin. And it's very hard to look at it. The way people look out for themselves. But it's not a thriving place, this. I suppose you'd have to expect it."

"You're too tolerant."

"I'm not. I can't sleep at night thinking of Kate Ryan's injuries, but that doesn't mean I blame that poor man in there. He can't even make a call without a circle of people around him waiting to hear what he's at."

"And hasn't he a phone above in the lodge?"

"A lot of these are calls to the States, it's easier on him to be here. I've shown him how to get through."

"Oh well, that's all right. Business as usual then, or maybe he's onto some smart lawyers over there, fellows that will come over here and say he isn't even in the remotest way responsible for what happened."

"That is very unjust and very unlike you, Martin White."

The doctor looked at her, startled. Perhaps he had gone too far. He waited to see if she would explain why it was so unfair. But Sheila Whelan said nothing. It wasn't up to her to explain that Patrick O'Neill was on the phone to America trying to get a particular specialist to come over from America and examine Kate Ryan.

He had been on the telephone all day trying to get the right people. His phone bill would be staggering.

Patrick said he didn't care how offended anyone was, he was flying the specialist from New York and he would be here on Monday. No, he didn't care whose toes were being stepped on, in a case of life or death, in a case of paralysis he would presume that medical men and women would be large enough and sufficiently generous-spirited to realize that the patient came first. No aspersions were being cast, no offense should be taken.

He knew that the New York man would probably confirm everything that was being done here, so where was the harm, where was the insult?

The hospital, which had been horrified to hear of outsiders, succumbed as Patrick had known they would.

He couldn't bear to think they might bungle it, move her when she shouldn't be moved, or leave her in a country hospital when she should be at the remedial center in Dublin. Only when he heard an independent and expert view from a man he had chosen and paid would Patrick believe that everything possible was being done.

The whole thing had an air of unreality to it. He thanked God that he hadn't broached the matter of the entrance to them; if he had spoken of it then he would always have felt sure that Kate's accident was in some way connected.

One night John found the twins asleep on the window seat.

Before he woke them he made three mugs of hot chocolate, and they drank them together as the summer moon shone down on the river and the building site.

"You're very good the way you manage, but you'll have to get some proper sleep, not with crooked necks and cramps here on the window." His voice was gentle.

"Everything's different," Michael said.

"I know, son."

There was a long silence.

"Do you think . . ." Dara began.

"I don't know. I hope so, but I really don't know."

A little later he took their empty mugs and left them on the chest of drawers under the Sacred Heart lamp and saw the twins off to bed.

Dara had wanted to have Grace O'Neill to stay. She said it would be lovely to have someone to talk to at night.

John Ryan had hated saying no, but he felt it would be wrong in some way. He felt that until things were sorted out, O'Neill's child shouldn't really sleep under their roof.

Chapter XII

Kate stirred in the hospital.

"Mrs. Ryan, you're fine. Fine. Don't move too much."

"Nurse, is my husband here?"

"He's been here all morning, he stepped out for a smoke. Will I get him?"

"No, send him home."

"He doesn't want to go home, he wants to be here with you."

"He has no business wanting that, he's got a business to run. How will he keep it if he's here?"

Kate was fretful and worried. Sometimes it was clear to her that she had cracked her spine and broken several vertebrae, sometimes nothing was clear. There were bits when she wanted to cry and cry it all out of her and then she knew she would feel fine, she could get off this ridiculous table she was on and tear out these tubes and go home. There were other bits when she thought she would never move again. It wasn't clear to her what happened.

Sometimes she would ask. But she would drift off before the explanation.

John had peeped through the circle of glass in the door and seen that Kate was awake. He had stubbed out his cigarette and come in eagerly.

"What time is it?" she asked.

"It's midday, love, I just heard the angelus."

"Then what are you doing here?"

"What?"

"The pub opens in half an hour, John, who's going to open it?"

"Not today, love, they all know I'm here with you."

"They won't know that till they get to the door and find the place closed. John, have sense. Please. Please don't leave me to make all the decisions, even though I'm lying here with a broken back. For God's sake do something on your own initiative. Just once."

The nurse had called for assistance and the houseman came in. Kate was thrashing around and the injection was swift in coming.

John stood rooted to the spot.

Kate's face was calm again as if in a normal peaceful sleep.

"I don't know what to do," he said to the young nurse pitifully.

"I think you should go home, Mr. Ryan, she's had a very strong sedative now, she won't be able to talk for a while."

"But what would I do at home?"

"I don't know, maybe you could open the pub as she said."

John Ryan turned and went out with a heavy tread.

Sitting outside in a hired car was Paudie Doyle, the younger brother of Brian. He was eighteen and had a drivers license. Patrick O'Neill had hired him with the car and said that he was to drive the Ryan family backward and forward from the hospital to Mountfern —a hundred times a day if needs be. And to be there always at their beck and call.

He was a kind young fellow and he couldn't bear to see the look of pain on John's face.

"In about twenty-five minutes the pubs will be open, or maybe you might know someone who'd open early for you. Would that be nice? A drop of brandy maybe?"

"Thanks, Paudie. Drive me home to my own place like a good lad. I've got to open up, got a business to run, you know."

"Of course you do, I thought you'd have someone else doing that. They would you know, people are very willing to do anything to help. You know they are."

"I know," said John dully. "I just don't seem to be able to think of anything they could do."

Kate had been right of course, there were plenty of people anxious to know how she was and to give the Ryans their custom.

Grace wanted to know was it all right if she stayed to lunch.

"Certainly." John was pleased that the twins would have company. He sent her on into the kitchen behind and concentrated on serving. Patrick sat on a stool and asked about everything, and when Fergus came in, he sat on the stool beside the American.

"And what did the injection do, did she go out at once or did it take time?" Patrick asked.

"Why don't you ask him to put a bulletin up on the door as they do in Buckingham Palace?" Fergus asked suddenly.

Patrick looked at him, startled.

"There are fourteen people in this public house needing pints, half ones, glasses of whiskey, bottles of minerals opened for them. Would you not have the common sense to let the man get on with it instead of interrogating him about every twist and turn of his unfortunate wife."

"Fergus." John was shocked.

"I mean it, John, you get on with serving while you still have a pub to serve in." Fergus had a voice very near tears.

"He's right, of course." Patrick stood up. "I'll call back to ask about Kate when you're not busy, John." In four steps he was out the door.

John Ryan was very upset.

"Ah, Fergus, what did you have to go and do that for? Now I'll have to go after him. He's been so good to us, Fergus, you have no idea. He has cars for us everywhere, we'd never be able to get in and out to the hospital, and he's paying for a specialist to come from America, someone who actually treated the Kennedys coming the whole way to look at Kate. What did you have to go and insult him for? He was only being interested and asking."

"*I'm* interested but I want you to keep your business," Fergus hissed, indicating a small group at the other end of the counter needing refills. "And I could drive you in to see Kate, I could give you my car, for God's sake. He's not the only one who wants to help."

"But that's it. He *does* want to help. Don't be on at him like you were up in the hospital. It only makes things harder." John was still looking at the door wondering if he should run after Patrick.

"No, you're right." And Fergus swung off the stool to stride out also—leaving John Ryan without two customers he realized as he walked sadly along River Road and saw the figure of Patrick O'Neill walking sadly among the machinery and small walls of his building site on the other side of the river.

* * *

Kerry O'Neill had bought a get-well card in Leonard's. He had chosen it carefully. Not a funny one, and not a mournful one either, full of flowers and verses about Good Friendship and Health.

Tommy Leonard thought that Kerry was very considerate to put so much thought into it. A lot of people just bought the first thing or the cheapest thing they saw.

Kerry's father didn't share this view. He thought Kerry was cold and distant about the accident, he felt there was something a little calculating about finding a meaningless printed card and signing it ". . . from all your friends in Mountfern, and Kerry O'Neill." But then very little that Kerry did or said pleased Patrick these days. The boy seemed to be entirely wrapped up in himself. There was no room for anyone else in his life.

The chicken was boiled a long time now. Carrie looked at it anxiously—it was beginning to break up in the pot. Usually the mistress came out and made a white sauce at this stage; she used to come like a whirlwind into the kitchen. Up to the stove and pound pound pound in a small saucepan, flinging in the milk, the butter and the flour at random, it seemed. The instructions were given to Carrie like a series of short and rapid machine guns being fired. Kate Ryan used to speak firmly but kindly:

"Potatoes drained and into the dish, now. Thanks, Carrie, and plates warming, there's a good girl. Thanks, Carrie. Pass me the carving knife and fork. Right, call Michael, it's his turn to serve today." It used to go like clockwork. But today nothing was right. Carrie didn't have enough hands. The children were all sitting inside like lords and ladies waiting to be served, the master was in the pub where it seemed half the parish had come up to drink like pigs at a trough.

Carrie was flustered and confused. When she put the chicken down it started to go cold out of the pot so she put it back in again while she got out the potatoes, then the chicken seemed to have broken into fragments with all the shifting it about.

Since the mistress wasn't here to criticize her, she thought she'd risk taking the potatoes to the table in the big black pot. She ran with it because it was so heavy. She hadn't known that the young O'Neill child was sitting at the table inside. She began to run out again but the pot slipped. She banged it on the table and there was a noise, a sizzling noise. The pot had burned a huge weal into the table.

Carrie looked at it, her face as aghast as the five children's faces that looked first at the burning table and then at her.

She couldn't bear it anymore. There was nobody to advise her. Carrie ran from the room in tears.

John heard a commotion and excused himself from the bar.

In the breakfast room the children were trying to scrape the burn marks from the table. They looked up guiltily.

"Well God, that's a nice way to behave," he said, looking from one to another to see who was the culprit.

"Nobody here was responsible, Mr. Ryan." The clear voice of the little American Grace was coupled with a dimpling smile.

She was like a little blonde angel interceding for frailer folk. But he knew without her having to tell tales that poor Carrie had done it again.

In the kitchen things were worse than he had expected. The chicken looked more like chicken soup than any kind of boiled fowl. The cabbage was overcooked and smelling badly in its saucepan. A pot of something else that might have been a milk pudding had burned dry. Wearily he took the burning saucepan from the stove and looked glumly at the scene.

There was no sign of Carrie but he thought he saw a figure in the back yard near the old pump, sobbing into her apron.

Dara was beside him. "Try to pick the best bits out of the chicken, Dara, and give everybody two potatoes. Leave the table, we'll see to it later."

"What about the cabbage?"

"Give it to the hens when it cools down."

"And the rest of the chicken, all these stringy bits?"

"It would hardly be tactful to give that to the hens, if you see what I mean."

Dara giggled. "You're very funny, Daddy," she said approvingly.

"Wouldn't I need to be?" said John Ryan.

"It's all hopeless, Father," Grace said. "There's this maid and she brought the pot of potatoes to the table and burned the table top and then she ran out and cried, and it's all just hopeless."

"What do they need?" Patrick asked.

Grace was thoughtful. "I think they just need proper help, you know, someone efficient like Miss Hayes."

"Yes, yes."

"Well, will you get them someone?"

"I think not, Grace. I think we might do more harm than good. We wouldn't know who to send in, we could pick the wrong person."

"Marian should know, she runs a hotel."

"I don't want to get Marian involved."

"She has a crush on you," Grace said.

"Don't be silly."

"You know it too. Don't you like her?"

"She's fine, but don't give me this silly talk about crushes. That's teenage stuff, not old men and old ladies."

"So we won't get them a maid? The Ryans I mean."

"No, there are times when I think you have to stand back a bit."

Grace said she wanted to help. Please, she didn't *mind* things being untidy, or whatever they were trying to keep from her because she was a guest. Couldn't she just join in like the family?

Michael and Dara found things for her to do. She took Leopold for his walk, she picked vegetables, she brought the washing in from the line.

She encouraged them to go out to play. They hadn't been allowed to visit their mother in the intensive-care ward but Grace said she was sure Mrs. Ryan wouldn't want them sitting around the house being gloomy. She'd want to think of them swimming and doing normal things. Little by little they agreed, but there was always such confusion at home it was easier not to go out at all.

"I never knew running a house was like this," Dara wailed.

"I don't know what anyone gets married for," Michael said with feeling.

"But it needn't be like this, I suppose." Grace meant if you had enough money to pay someone to do it properly.

Like Miss Hayes was being paid to keep things right in the lodge. There was always bread in the bread bin, cake in the cake tin. There were clean towels and sheets. Why were things so confused in the Ryans' household?

"We used to think that we'd live in Fernscourt once," Michael said unexpectedly. "Dara and I had a section of it all planned. And we'd have no proper mealtimes or bedtimes, or sheets or cleaning shoes . . . I think it would have worked."

He sounded very wistful.

Grace patted his hand. "It's terrible for you being the eldest," she said.

"Yes, well, joint eldest," Michael said, struggling to be fair.

"But it's harder on boys, I remember—" She stopped suddenly.

"What?" The twins spoke together.

"Nothing."

"Go on, Grace, what do you remember?" Dara was insistent.

"I don't want to remember it, I can't remember it."

"Please, Grace." Michael had a better way with him, obviously.

"Okay, the reason I didn't want to finish it was because . . . well, I remember when my mother was ill, Kerry said it was harder being a boy because you wanted to cry just as much as a girl wanted to cry but the world didn't let you cry, you had to pretend somehow that it didn't matter so much to you. Kerry said that was the hardest bit because he couldn't show Mother how much he loved her by crying with her."

The twins were silent.

Grace looked apologetic. "So now, so you see why I didn't want to finish it, I didn't want to talk about my mother who *did* die in the same breath as talking about your mother who is *not* going to die. Do you see?"

Dara gave her a great hug and Michael squeezed her hand.

Grace lost her troubled look and smiled with them both. "Let's finish these goddamned apples and then we'll go for a swim."

They peeled and cored the apples in the gloomy knowledge that somehow Carrie would make a brown unappetizing mess from all their hard work.

Mrs. Whelan was quiet and to the point, it would be doing everyone a great favor if John could see his way to providing a busy life and home for her cousin Mary Donnelly. There was no need to go into details but the girl had a bit of a crisis in her private life and the last thing she needed was to be left alone brooding. She was extremely capable, she would not want a large salary—just a change for the few weeks, months, whatever it was until Kate was home.

John was never so relieved. He had been shattered by the events of the day: Kate wrestling with her pain and shouting at him that he couldn't take the initiative, ever; Fergus and Patrick almost coming to blows and then both walking out of the pub; Carrie having retired to bed in hysterics and the kitchen looking as if a bomb had hit it. Opening time in another half an hour. He was never so relieved as to hear of this efficient Mary Donnelly who could come on the bus in two days if called for. Where would she sleep?

Mrs. Whelan had thought of that too. There was an outhouse at the back and it didn't need a great deal of work. They could get a couple of men off the site to fix it up, run an electric wire through it, a coat of paint.

There would be plenty of beds up in the Grange and Marian Johnson had offered any kind of help, a small second-hand bed would be great.

John didn't know if he could accept all this. Sheila was adamant that he should.

"When something awful happens people feel helpless, the one thing they want to do is to be of assistance. Let them help, John, it will make them feel much better if nothing else."

John held her hand gratefully. Only this morning he had been thinking, when young Paudie Doyle had said that people wanted to help, that he didn't know what to ask them. And now Mrs. Whelan was making it possible.

Once she got the green light from John, Sheila went to Brian Doyle.

"You said you wondered what you could do," she began.

And it was done in a trice. Men and materials were arranged. The old outhouse was stripped of its rubble, broken wood and boxes were carted away. Other things which most certainly were rubbish but should not be thrown out without reference to Kate were transferred into an even older outhouse which was around at one side of the pub. They were stacked neatly there waiting the verdict of the mistress on her return.

The whitewash on the walls was done three times to make sure it looked presentable.

The new house became the focal point for all the children.

Jacinta and Liam White were back from their Irish College, even more at loggerheads with each other than usual and according to themselves still unable to speak a word of Irish.

Liam said that Jacinta had been tiresome and in love with the boy who taught dancing. Jacinta said that Liam had been embarrassing and was caught smoking first and then caught being sick later as a result of the earlier smoking. They told the twins that their father had said Mrs. Ryan was most definitely not going to die, but he said that nobody knew when she'd be home. They had asked him would it be days or months or years and he still couldn't say.

"I suppose it must be months anyway; this is why we're doing the place up," Dara said gloomily.

Maggie Daly wanted a more cheerful view. "Listen, it could be tomorrow for all we know, but she'll still need someone to help her. Didn't you say yourself it's non stop?"

Dara brightened. "That's what it is, non stop. As soon as one meal's finished and washed up it's time for the next. People eat far too much, you know."

Maggie burst out laughing.

Brian Doyle who had come to supervise, gave them a shout. "If you two girls have come to be entertained by all this and to giggle would you think of putting on a kettle and getting some tea for these men here? All right?"

This reduced Maggie and Dara to further hysterics.

"Non stop, a woman's work, non bloody stop," Dara said as they headed for the kitchen.

"Dara, you'd better mind your language, your mother'd make a swipe at you if she heard you saying bloody," said Carrie, shocked.

Dara paused a moment thinking how great it would be to have Mam running around the place like she used to and able to make a swipe at anyone instead of lying on her back in the hospital.

Grace told Marian Johnson about the new room and she sent down a bed from the Grange. Fergus Slattery brought a wardrobe he said he didn't need. He drove it up in his car and carried it in himself. Maggie's mother sent Charlie with a small table, a blue cloth and a statue of Our Lady with a little blue glass that held a night light which you could put in front of the statue. The Leonards sent a rug for the floor and a brand-new unopened pad of writing paper and envelopes, in case the new lady wanted to write home. Loretto Quinn gave a chair. The Williamses said they had a roll of linoleum which they had bought by mistake and the shop wouldn't take it back; they had been hoping to hear of a place that might need it.

John looked in from time to time and said that as far as he could see it was better by far than any other room in Ryan's Licensed Premises and private house.

When Mary Donnelly got off the bus on Tuesday her new home was ready for her.

She was given a short briefing by Mrs. Whelan in the post office and then she walked purposefully down River Road carrying her small grip bag. She had left her big case with Sheila Whelan so that the family would not realize how long she was coming to stay.

She knew the most important place to head for, and went straight to the kitchen.

"I'm Mary," she said to Carrie. "It must have been an awful shock for you and nobody telling you what's expected and what's not."

Carrie looked at her gratefully. "That's just it, Miss," she said. "If only I knew what they all want . . ."

"We'll have to sort it out," Mary Donnelly said, hanging up her coat on the back of the door.

"Why didn't you come to me, Sheila? I'd have gotten a better job done, anything you wanted," Patrick said.

"I thought it was better not to deal with you directly." Her voice was bland.

"Whyever not?" But he knew. He knew exactly why.

"Better let others do it, I thought."

"I feel responsible, yes, that Kate hurt herself on my property, but I don't feel guilty about it, for Christ's sake."

"Of course not."

"And everyone else must feel the same. They do, don't they?"

"Not really. People take sides easily in a thing like this. For one reason or another."

"I thought it was that crackpot attorney that was the only one, and that he was upset because he's got the hots for her."

"Really!"

"No, sorry, I shouldn't have said that, but you know . . ."

"I don't know, and you should not have said it, and it is *not* true."

"Sheila, don't turn against me, you were the first person who welcomed me to this place, don't turn on me."

She patted his hand. "Don't be so dramatic," she said. "I'm just marking your card a little like I did at the start, and you were glad then. Maybe I've stepped over the limit."

"Do they really think it's my fault?"

"Some of them do."

"But it's so unfair," he cried out.

"Who said life was fair?"

He remembered her own personal circumstances and nodded in silence.

"You see . . ." she began.

"Yes?"

"You see, logical or illogical, this is what they think. If you had never come here, there would have been no machines and no bull-dozer on that site. None of this would ever have happened."

"If I hadn't come here, everything would have been all right?" he asked quietly.

"Well, for the Ryans it would," Sheila said simply.

Dr. White didn't like the American. It had nothing to do with his importing a Yank specialist. That rather pleased White because it got up the noses of the hospital consultants, always an arrogant bunch.

But the American felt that money or business was the universal answer.

Once he had commented that Dr. White's practice would expand considerably when the hotel was built.

"I hope that your guests will have scant need of my professional services. It would spoil their holidays," Dr. White had said politely.

"Yes, but when they do get a bellyache they'll be people of sub-stance, you can charge them properly."

"I'll charge them what I charge everyone, I won't fleece sick peo-ple just because they happen to be rich and American," Dr. White had said haughtily.

He knew Patrick called him a stuffed shirt.

The doctor was surprised to see him calling at the office.

"Can you give me something to make me sleep, knock me out for eight hours at a time?" Patrick asked.

"No. Not just like that I can't."

"What do you want, my life story?"

"Why didn't you ask that Yank doctor who treated the entire Kennedy family? He could have given you something."

"Goddammit man, he's an orthopedic surgeon." Patrick's annoy-ance was so great that Dr. White smiled, and the American smiled too.

"Sorry, I'm very edgy, a proof of lack of sleep."

"Tension, I suppose. Strain. Do you have a prescription already?"

"Never needed them in my life, thought they were the tool of a weak man. But if you're lame you use a walking stick. I guess I'm lame as regards sleep."

"Fine, whatever you say."

"You'll give them to me?"

"Mr. O'Neill, you are a grown-up man, you could buy and sell everyone in this town and probably will. Who am I to deny you a prescription for two weeks of non-addictive sleeping pills?"

"What do you mean, buy and sell?"

"It's an expression, Mr. O'Neill. If you meet a bright child, you say, 'That boy would buy and sell you.' It's a term of high praise."

"Why are you mocking me, Doctor?"

"I beg you not to think that. Will two weeks be sufficient? One a night, warm milk. Keep warm, don't try to go to sleep. It will come, I assure you, with these."

He signed his name with a flourish and handed Patrick the small piece of paper.

"Do you think I'm responsible for Kate Ryan's accident?"

"No, of course not."

"You don't?"

"No, how could you be? Weren't you miles away, they say, at the time?"

"But morally responsible?"

"I suppose we could argue that since no man is an island, we are all involved in everyone's life and death and success or injury. No more than that."

"I'm so sorry it happened, if you knew."

"I know. Most people do know. Aren't you moving heaven and earth to get her better?" The doctor's voice sounded kind.

"But she's not going to get better, that's what they say."

"They say it will be long."

"They say she'll never walk again. Your doctors say that, my doctor says that."

"They say long useful life."

"In a fucking wheelchair."

"Alive not dead."

"It's like talking to the priests talking to you, Dr. White."

"I hope you use better language talking to the priests."

"I hope so, I'm sure I forget sometimes."

"Listen, it was great that your man from Cape Cod or wherever said they were doing things right in the hospital. Now everyone's happy."

"Up to a point," Patrick said.

"Sure, I know, but if you see as much difficult birth, hard life and rotten death as I do you'd realize that a wheelchair isn't the end of the world."

"No," said Patrick. "It's not. Thank you, Doctor. Your bill?"

"Forget it."

"I can't do that."

"I don't see why not. I only wrote my name."

"It has a price, your years of training, remember?"

"No, it has no price if I wish it to have none. Believe me, there are things without a price on them."

"And you believe me too, Dr. White." Patrick's eyes blazed with anger. "I know there are things that have no price. If I was out for a return on my money do you think I would be building this folly here? That's what my manager back in the States calls it, O'Neill's Folly. There's no price on this that anyone could recognize. It's an act of love. Of faith. It's not the act of a businessman who wants to make a quick buck, or indeed any bucks for a very long time."

Dr. White shook his head sadly and said nothing.

"Well, go on, say it whatever it is?"

"But of *course* there's a price. The price is your wish to be home, and to be a person of importance in these parts where your grandfather came from, not just one of a few million Irish in America. That's what you want—isn't it?—much more than money. I was just saying there are some people who want nothing or very little."

"Like the Ryans," Patrick said sadly. "They wanted very little indeed, and look at what they have now."

"It will be better for you now that you've got someone to look after things," Grace said.

"She looks a bit fierce," Dara complained.

"It doesn't matter, she's going to run things, that's what it's about."

Grace was always so sunny. Dara wondered did she ever have great times of doubt and worry? Was it only Dara? Maybe if you were as beautiful as Grace was, there was no need to worry about things. Everyone loved you.

"Are things okay at your home now? You remember you asked me not to talk about that row ages ago between your father and Kerry, so I didn't, I didn't even think about it until now . . ."

Grace was full of understanding. "I know you didn't tell anyone. You're a great friend."

They were sitting in Dara's bedroom. Grace got up to walk about; she seemed restless.

"No, things are not great at home. But I don't know whether that's because of Kerry and Father, or because of Father being so worried about everything, your mother and all that."

She looked terribly young somehow. Those curls could make her look like a toddler sometimes, otherwise they made her like a film star.

"Do they fight?"

"No, that's just it, they hardly talk at all. They sort of talk through me, if I weren't there I think not a word would be said."

"It's hard to believe that with Kerry, he's so nice and such fun."

Dara was wistful for those care:ree days which seemed so long ago now. Kerry was one of the few people within miles who had not come to the pub to say how sorry he was, but perhaps he had not been able to think of anything to say.

"He's definitely no fun with Father," Grace said. Then she deliberately forced herself into a good humor again. "But I think it will all blow over, you know, this Mrs. Fine. I think Kerry was very uptight that she came to Ireland. You know, in case she and Father . . . Well, I told you."

"Yes, but it's not true, is it?"

"No, not true at all." Grace was her sunny self again. "No, she's staying miles away and she doesn't see Father at all, it was all a false alarm. Kerry must realize that now, and things will be back to normal again."

Maggie Daly wished that her mother wouldn't see things in such black and white ways. Her mother had this fear now that if everyone made too much of Mrs. Ryan's accident it would look as if they were criticizing all the progress Mr. O'Neill brought to Mountfern. This was the biggest and best thing that had ever happened to their town and they must be sure that no foolish sentimentality was allowed to intrude.

Whenever Maggie said she was going up to Ryan's, her mother said that she should watch her step and not make herself into a camp follower on one side or the other. Yet when Grace asked Maggie to come to the lodge Mrs. Daly was delighted. She spent ages hunting for a nice white collar to sew on Maggie's dress and gave her a cream cake free to present to Miss Hayes with her compliments.

Mrs. Daly had not said anything about it being camp following to go to tea at the lodge.

Judy Byrne was delighted to see Patrick O'Neill at her door.

"This is a professional call, and I must ask you to keep it very much to yourself," he said.

"Certainly." Judy's eyes sparkled with interest and anticipation.

"We don't have the same medical schemes in the States as here. Can you tell me how you work? Are you attached to the hospital?"

"Only in a part-time capacity. Sometimes I do a day here and there when some of their staff are away. And I cover for people's holidays."

"But mainly you are in private practice, is that it?"

"Yes." Judy wondered where this was leading.

"But you don't have a clinic, an office here. Is your work mainly done at people's homes?"

"I do go to people's homes, or I can go to Dr. White's office if I am needed. If it's a matter of teaching people exercises or movements they can come here." She looked defensively around her small sitting room with its desk and her shelf of text books. She didn't like him dismissing it so casually.

"And who pays you?"

"I beg your pardon?"

Judy's eyes were round in disbelief.

"I am sorry. I did say it was a business call. I must learn to speak less crassly." The famous O'Neill smile was there now. Lines radiating out from his eyes, head on one side, half contrite, half mischievous. It was the little-boy look that Patrick O'Neill had been wearing for so many years he did not even realize when it was on his face. Not until he saw Judy smiling back. Then he pressed on.

"You see, I'm just a poor hick from the States, I don't understand the way things work here. The hospital is free . . . for one thing. I didn't know that."

"Well, the county hospital is free if you go through the dispensary doctor, certainly," Judy said. "If you are a person of means then of course you would go to the nuns in the nursing home, or perhaps to one of the private rooms that the consultants have for their patients in the hospital." She thought she was explaining what he wanted to know clearly but she couldn't see the drift of his conversation.

"Yes, I see that now." Patrick had endless patience.

He knew the system now. Kate was in intensive care, when she left it she would go to a ward. Unless he got her a private room. This he had arranged to do. But she would also need physiotherapy both in the hospital and when she returned home. This was the knotty problem he had come to discuss with Judy and had wrongly thought that it could be done crisply and quickly if he designated it a business call. He must learn—he would learn eventually—that in Mountfern the dividing line between business and socializing was a minefield.

"And in your own case?" he tried delicately. "Are you reimbursed by hospital, patient, or is there someone else like the doctor that one goes through?"

He thought that if he said "reimbursed" she might find it less offensive than using the word "paid."

Finally, like drawing teeth, Patrick O'Neill extracted the information he needed.

Judy Byrne was indeed a private physiotherapist. She did not make what anyone could call a living wage by her work. She had come back to live in Mountfern when her mother was elderly. Her mother had died leaving her this small attractive house, a car and a small undisclosed sum of money in the bank.

It was possible for Judy Byrne to live comfortably on the fairly limited amount of work that came her way through Dr. White, through part-time work in the hospital, and anything else that consultants recommended her for.

She was fully qualified; she would be ideally placed to give Kate Ryan the physiotherapy she would need. Her rates were, to Patrick, very reasonable, and he thought that others would think so too. But he reminded himself yet again how different were his circumstances from anyone else's in Mountfern.

If he were to book Judy Byrne to come three times a week to Kate Ryan on her return, surely it would suit everyone? Kate, Judy and himself. But perhaps it would humiliate everyone and be the worst thing to do.

"You're doing very well, Mrs. Ryan," the nurse said.

"Did they tell you it was going to be like this?" Kate asked wearily.

"Like what, Mrs. Ryan?"

"Like wiping bottoms and pulling soiled sheets out from under people?" Kate said.

"That's only a small part of it, the main part of it is people getting better."

"It's not much better if I can't decide when to go to the lavatory. It's not better if I'm going to relieve myself over anyone and everyone who comes near me."

"Tut tut, it's not like that."

"It *is* like that, Nurse, for God's sake, that's the second time this morning. If I had ten seconds' warning I'd shout for you, but it just comes out."

"It doesn't matter to anyone but you."

"I hope it will *always* matter to me; I don't want to get to a stage where I expect people to wipe up after me."

"I've told you it won't always be like this."

"But when? When will it get better? Last week you said it would be better this week. The week before you said it would be better last week."

"If you knew how well you're doing, Mrs. Ryan, you'd be pleased instead of worrying about things that honestly don't worry us. You'd be rejoicing like we are that you've made so much progress."

"That's a load of nonsense and you know it, Nurse."

"Now Mrs. Ryan, please."

"What's your name, Nurse?"

"Geraldine."

"Right, Geraldine, and you call me Kate. We're obviously going to be together for years and years, let's not have any formalities."

"It's not going to be years and years, Mrs. . . . er, Kate."

"Will I be home by Christmas? Answer me that."

"I can't. I don't know."

"It's only July and you don't know if I'll be home by Christmas. Oh God, oh God, what am I going to do?" Kate began a low moan.

"I only said I don't know. I'm only a nurse, I'm not a doctor or a surgeon."

"Stop apologizing for yourself. What do you mean *only* a nurse?" Geraldine grinned.

"Stop laughing at me," Kate snapped.

"You're marvelous, no wonder they're all mad about you back there in Mountfern," the girl said.

"They're not mad about me, they've forgotten me."

"Well they don't sound as if they have, we get a ton of requests from people wanting to see you, but we say only the family."

"Requests. Who in the name of God would want to come and see someone who might have diarrhea all over the bed in front of them?"

"There's a Mr. Slattery telephones two or three times a day, a Mr. O'Neill telephones every day over and over, and others—Coynes, Walshes, Quinns, Dalys—and there's a foreign woman called twice to see you, she was the one who left the plant."

"I don't know anyone foreign, she can't have been for me."

"Mrs. Fine."

"No."

"Well I'll check again, she thinks she knows you—small dark American but foreign at the same time."

Something stirred. But the events of the day she had met Rachel Fine were still blurred. It was the day John had his poem published, so he had told her. And the day that Patrick O'Neill had come into the bar urgently saying he wanted a consultation with the pair of them. John had told her that too but she couldn't remember it. Was there a Mrs. Fine? It seemed familiar and the memory was good rather than bad.

"If she comes back I'll see that Mrs. Fine," Kate said.

"And what about these other men—the Slattery man and the O'Neill man?"

"No. Not yet. I'd cry with one and I might fight with the other."

"Right. That's understood. Now."

"Oh God," Kate said. "I know what 'Now' means."

Now meant more of the same. The endless round. Changing her position in the bed every four hours to avoid the bed sores that she felt sure were going to come anyway, so great was the pressure where she touched the bedclothes under her. Now meant the physiotherapy. So far she only had to lie there but they told her that soon she would be taking part herself and strengthening her own muscles.

There were the hopeless attempts to make her control her bladder and her bowels. It was useless trying to go at certain times, the body didn't work like that. It betrayed you. There was the painful business of putting in the catheter and taking it out. Lord, had she ever valued the whole business of being able to run into a bathroom and close the door behind you with no agony and pulling of flesh?

Had she ever given one minute of thought or sympathy to all the people she heard having records played for them on Hospital Requests? People having catheters and bedsores and drips all the time. Did they ever learn to accept it as normal? Would Kate ever learn?

Chapter XIII

On the day that Mary Donnelly arrived in Ryan's, Leopold got ready
to give her one of his traditional welcomes. He cowered against the
wall shivering from his large misshapen head to his long awkward-
looking tail. Then he rolled his eyes, flinched and gave a whimper of
terror.

"Oh for goodness sake dog, will you stop that?" Mary Donnelly
said to him firmly.

Leopold looked at her doubtfully. Usually he got a different reaction: people said, "Poor dog," "Nice dog," or "What has him so
frightened?" There was nothing of this in the new woman's tone.

"I saw you, dog, not half an hour ago up in the main street of this
town and you had a bone the size of a hurling stick."

Leopold hung his head as if he had been discovered.

"Now I'm not against that, it's good that a butcher gives a bone to
a dog instead of burning it, but all I want is you to quit putting on
the poor mouth, there's no call for that."

The children stood open-mouthed as Leopold almost nodded in
agreement.

"We'll get on fine once we realize that there is no point in either
of us feeling sorry for ourselves," she said.

Her eyes moved around the watching group.

"What is this fine animal called?" she asked.

Eddie was the only one with enough breath to deliver the dog's name.

Mary pronounced it several times, rolling it around to see if she liked it. She decided she did.

"Leopold," she said loudly. Just hearing his name was usually enough to set Leopold baying to the moon as if he were being tortured. He began, but stopped in mid yowl.

Mary smiled. "That's better," she said. "Any other animals?"

"Jaffa and Maurice," said Eddie, an unaccustomed spokesman for the family.

"Can I see them?"

Gravely she inspected Maurice in the mudroom and Jaffa on the wall.

On her first day she toured the house, asking the role of this and that.

Everywhere she nodded with instant understanding and convinced them that she knew the place had been run magnificently before the accident. This way they didn't feel they had to keep explaining or apologizing.

When the pub closed the first night she asked John to give her a quick instruction in her pub duties.

"It's not a thing that can be done quickly," John smiled. "A pint must be poured lovingly, slowly. No, a lot of bar work is the complete reverse of speed."

"You may or may not be right," Mary said, "and in the matter of the slowly poured pint, I have to believe you because there can be no other reason why men would sit in a bar and wait interminable lengths for froth to settle. But there are other aspects of the pub business which must be swift. Can you explain the measures to me, and what people call them, naggins and noggins and jorums and the like."

"There'd be a month of explaining in that," John said.

He saw a frown of impatience cross her face. "But we can make a start on it anyway," he added hastily.

Mary Donnelly seemed to settle in immediately. She introduced herself to the local women Loretto and Rita Walsh as the cousin of Mrs. Whelan who had come to help out until Mrs. Ryan was home. Nobody felt threatened by her. She was a small woman in her thirties, with curly brown hair and freckles. She might have been attractive with a little effort, but she wore brown jumpers and skirts and brown laced shoes. Around her neck she wore a gold chain with a cross on it, and she never put on any make-up.

Because she had been a teacher she was able to make everyone listen to her without even raising her voice. The house became much more quiet with Mary Donnelly's arrival. If anyone shrieked for each other as they had been accustomed to do she would walk purposefully over to them and say, "I wonder why you had to raise your voice like that?" It was very effective.

Because she had been a teacher she knew exactly what they should all be doing at school, and prepared a small amount of holiday work for them. This was badly received, and the children appealed to their father for a judgment against it. However, Mary had presented her case so well that they found him firmly on her side.

"She says it's only a matter of half an hour a day. It will keep you well up with your books, she'll correct it like a teacher above in the school. It'll distract you a bit in the mornings not to be thinking about your mother, and best of all your mother will be delighted with you for it."

Mary Donnelly gave most of her attention to Dara. "You'll need it in this world," she said gloomily.

"Why will I need it more than anyone else?" Dara was alarmed.

"What life is there for a woman unless she equips herself and trains herself and gets on? Women have to fight in this world. Better believe it and know it now, and don't let any soft soap about love and marriage get into your soul and start to rot it."

It seemed a bit far fetched as a reason for doing fractions and parsing sentences.

At the start she hadn't wanted Mary Donnelly at all. They could manage, she had said, she was nearly thirteen. It was grown up. In some countries you could be married at that age. But everyone had insisted and it was true that Mary did make things easier.

After the homework, she gave them their jobs like Mam used to. The hen feeding, the box stacking and the pub sweeping went on, and she was just as adamant as Mam was about being home in time for lunch. Then there was the journey in to see Mam in the hospital and the instructions to bring all the news and information. And there were books provided for them to read as they sat in the waiting room while Dad was in with Mam alone.

Mary served the bar for the afternoon. She fixed all the clients with a baleful glare, filled their pints and gave their change, but would be drawn into no conversation. If any of them dared to pass her a compliment she would say that she had no time for fancy talk, which came cheaply to an Irishman. She would ask them cuttingly if they gave such praise to their wives and indeed if they ever favored their wives with an invitation out to share a drink with them. No. No indeed. And they really thought the wives would not want to join them? How very interesting. How fascinating a mind which thought that a wife *liked* being at home sweeping floors, cleaning boots, minding children, cooking, serving and washing up meals. How hysterically funny to think that men assumed women *liked* that sort of thing.

The men in Ryan's took no more notice of her than they did of Leopold cringing and whining by the wall. Mary Donnelly was obviously cracked in the head over some imagined slight or wrong that some man must have done to her in the past. But she poured a pint properly and she was a great help to poor John Ryan and his family in their time of need.

At night Mary Donnelly helped in the bar by washing glasses, joining not at all in the conversation. John gave up trying to make her feel part of the place. Without being actually rude she made it clear that she thought his clientele were the scum of humanity. She would withdraw to the kitchen and tell Carrie that she was setting up a store of trouble by painting and preening herself for the weekly dance, or else attempt to teach Declan and Eddie to darn.

"Why are you teaching the little fellows?" Carrie asked, mystified.

"Because there might be some hope for these as the young men of the next decade if we teach them to be normal and share in women's work," Mary said.

Eddie was quite good at darning as it happened and said he regarded it as a puzzle where you had to fit all the pieces in. He threatened to knock Declan's head off his neck if he ever told anyone at the brothers that they were being taught darning at home.

Mary had no time for Michael. At first Michael was very pleased about this. He considered himself well off to be away from this bossy woman. But as the days went by and she had become part of their lives it was somewhat galling to be dismissed so summarily. He was never asked to clear or serve as he used to do, his role as a shoe polisher was laughed out of the way. Mary said she would prefer to be in charge of the shoes herself so that she would know for certain that they would be done. She didn't like leaving things to a young man to do.

She said the words "young man" as others might say "village drunk" or "known criminal". Sometimes Michael felt that there was no need for him in the home—everyone else had their little jobs to do, only he stood there useless and idle.

He offered to help Dara and Carrie clean some candlesticks. They seemed to be enjoying the Brasso, it got all over their hands and they were laughing companionably. But Mary Donnelly refused him. She was courteous but firm. Thank you, but she would really prefer the job to be done properly without any trick-acting or distraction.

Moodily Michael left the kitchen. Kicking a stone all around the back yard, he was spotted by his father.

"Would you have a moment, son?"

Michael was pleased. His father had a great box of papers out on the table in the breakfast room. Since the accident he hadn't opened any of the research he was meant to be doing on the book for Mr. O'Neill.

"Michael, I have to do something about this, even if it's only tidy it up and let Patrick give it to someone else to finish. He must have his book, that's only fair."

"I suppose he'd wait a bit, with everything." Michael sounded very down.

"Oh of course he'd wait, but that's not the point. I must leave it in some kind of state that another writer—well, that a real writer—could see what I've done. Could you help me here for a minute?"

"What am I to do?"

"Suppose I were to fill this folder with what has already been written . . . not very much of it, I'm afraid. Then this one for under way, and that one we could call 'still to look at.' "

Michael separated the three piles on the table and his father called out which category the pages and the scribbled notes were to go to. In spite of his low form Michael became interested.

"Look at those drawings. Is *that* what it looked like?"

"No, that was a much grander house. It's in the style, though, so we could point out the feature that would have been the same."

"Is that what his hotel is going to look like?"

"No, no, it's going to have the middle bit the same. He's building up the old house more or less like it would have been, then there's going to be a wing back on each side from the main house, that's where the bedrooms will be."

"I wish he hadn't come here."

"Michael."

"I know. I'm sorry. It's so hard, you see."

"Ah, don't I know myself," John sighed. "Look, that's an old engraving of what the river used to look like years and years ago." He was deliberately changing the subject, trying to steer them both away from the fruitless wishing for the impossible. "Isn't it extraordinary to think that's the same river, that's our Fern, all those years ago. Lord, George the third was still the king of England then. Do you know anything about him?"

"Was he the one who was always half cracked, in and out of mental homes most of the time?" Michael asked.

"I don't think there was a question of mental homes, but he was certainly wandering in mind. Not that the Ferns of Fernscourt probably ever knew anything about that, they'd have been snug there in their grand house and no news of the royal goings-on would get to them for months and by that time it would all be changed . . ."

Michael wasn't listening to him . . . he was looking at one of the line engravings that had come from an old journal.

His father followed his gaze. It was a drawing that showed a barge delivering goods to what looked like a flat landing place behind which there was the mouth of a cave.

It was just like their tunnel even though it was a picture of some other county entirely. Michael studied it intensely, turning it around and drinking in every detail. He raked through the text to see if there was any mention of it.

John Ryan broke in on his thoughts. "Oh, I see you're getting interested in it now! That's the whole problem I find, anyway. You start reading little bits and they make you interested and you read more little bits and you travel far from what you were meant to be writing in the first place. What's that you're looking at?"

His voice was deliberately casual—he had seen the boy find a prosaic explanation for the magic tunnel.

Michael's face was red and white alternately.

"Nothing. I mean it's not anything."

"Oh, that's one of those ways they had of getting deliveries up to the grand houses without offending the eyes of the quality. You know, like a tradesman's entrance." John was light but not dismissive.

"Oh, is that all they are?" The disappointment was huge.

"Well, that's one use for them of course, those kind of tunnels, but like anything they could have a million other uses."

"Like what?"

"Well, like whatever was needed, I mean a tunnel's a tunnel isn't it? It could be used for anything—smuggling, for lovers' meeting, for secret societies, kidnappings, escapes . . . Come on, Michael, it doesn't matter what it was built for, it's what happens to it that's important."

The boy was greatly cheered. "Do you think there might be one across there?" He nodded toward the river.

"There might well be." John was mild. "Kind of thing that could be left unearthed for years and years. Even with all the big hotel coming."

"I don't mind helping you whenever you need a bit of a hand," Michael offered. "I have a bit of time on my hands these days, Mary doesn't think I can do anything."

"Ah, be tolerant of her, will you, she has a mad figario in her head about men, that's all."

"But it's very unfair. I'd do as much as anyone to make things a bit better, or keep things going . . ." His lip trembled.

"Listen to me, Michael, I'll tell you a secret. Not for anyone else— is that all right?"

"Dara?"

"Yes, if you tell it properly, but not to be talked about outside of you two. Poor Mary was all ready to get married, she had saved all her money and given up her job, she was making her wedding dress, even sewing things on it so as to look lovely on the day—"

"Mary Donnelly married? Looking lovely on her wedding day, you must be joking." Michael interrupted.

"No, shush or I won't finish it."

"All right . . ."

"So anyway this fellow was a rat, he didn't love Mary Donnelly at all, he only loved her money, and she had given him everything she saved for to put a deposit on a house . . ."

"And he ran off with it?" Michael's eyes were bright and he was rushing ahead in the story.

"It's easy known you're so young you can see anything in it except black treachery. Think of it, every week—or every month I suppose, teachers get paid by the month—she put so much away for the great day, and this boyo took the lot . . ." John Ryan's kind face was misty at the thought of it.

"Yeah, well it wasn't fair."

"It was worse than just taking her money, you see, he took everything else, he took away any pride she had, and made a fool of her in
front of everyone in her place . . . Like she'd always be remembering how she had talked of her plans, saying we're doing this and we're
doing that, and all the time he had no plans for anything except to
separate her from her bit of money."

"Maybe he didn't always intend to steal her money, he could have
loved her and then went off her," Michael said as if it were only too
possible to go off Mary Donnelly.

"I don't know whether that would be better for her to believe or
worse." John spoke thoughtfully.

"Anyway she's sure taking it out on the rest of us," Michael grumbled.

"But big strong men like yourself and myself can cope with it
surely?"

"We've a lot to cope with these days."

"Indeed we have, son." The sigh was very deep.

"Dad? I don't ask you this in front of people, but . . ."

"Ask away."

"Will Mam ever be able to walk again? Nobody ever says."

"That's the problem, they don't ever say. Not to me either."

"But what do you *think*, Dad?"

"I think there's a possibility that she may not. And that it's going
to be very hard for her, Michael. The hardest thing in the world."

Fergus invited Mary Donnelly to the pictures.

"Why?" she asked him.

The real reason was because Fergus, hearing how good she was in
the Ryan household, feared that Mary Donnelly might leave unless
some little diversion was planned for her.

He could hardly say that.

"Because I like you and would like to get to know you more," he
said.

"How would you get to know me at the pictures?" she asked.

Fergus felt sorry he had started on this course.

"Well it's a way to go out, isn't it? Perhaps you would prefer just to
go for a drive if you don't like the cinema."

"I never said I didn't like the cinema. I just wondered what way
two people would get to know each other if they sat in silence watching a film."

"I suppose it would be a matter of talking about it afterward," Fergus said desperately.

Mary thought about this.

"Usually it's a matter of taking liberties during the film, that's what I've noticed," she said.

Fergus had never gotten such a shock in his life.

"I assure you nothing would be further from my mind," he began, horrified. "I am a solicitor, a grown man."

"What a pompous thing to say, Mr. Slattery, as if desire were confined only to the lower orders. It is there in men of every class and breeding."

"Yes, well," Fergus said, totally at a loss. "If there's ever anything."

"I doubt if there will be, but thank you for raising the matter," Mary said.

"How in the name of God do you get on with that one?" Fergus asked John when they had some privacy.

"She's a godsend, that's what she is. It's the one thing that keeps Kate anyway calm in there, the thought that we've got a cousin of Mrs. Whelan looking after us. It's the next best thing to having Sheila."

"But Sheila's normal, John, she's not a nutcase like this one."

"Ah, she has her ways like everyone has their ways. She's a bit off men, that's all."

"That's a bit steep, to be off half the human race, and isn't she living in a family of four men and a girl, for God's sake?"

"I think she prays for us." John was tolerant.

"I'm surprised she hasn't taken a pike to you, and the day might well come when she does." Fergus was still smarting.

"She's certainly taking no chances, she got Jimbo to fit a lock to her door. I suppose she was afraid I'd lose the run of myself and come in and savage her."

"Do you tell that to Kate?" Fergus asked wistfully.

"I do, she doesn't believe me."

"I'd love to go and see her," Fergus said.

"She'll tell you when. You know Kate, she's very proud. She hates people seeing her the way she is, with all the tubes and the bags."

"As if I'd mind."

"She minds."

"Tell her . . . well, just tell her."

"Sure, Fergus, I'll tell her."

* * *

Dara and Michael had finished their work. Mary had made them sandwiches and a flask of soup. They weren't normally given a flask. This was an honor.

"I understand that you can go off on your own."

It had been cleared with their father. The twins nodded. They were nervous. This was their first day going back to the tunnel since the day of the accident. They were almost afraid it would be bad luck to go back there again. They might come out and find the whole of Mountfern waiting to tell them more bad news.

Without saying it they both remembered that it hadn't even been much fun in the tunnel that day, even before they learned of Mam's accident.

They had almost forgotten how much earth and rubble there was around the place and how dirty it made everything. Still, in the new system that Mary Donnelly had set up they all had to steep their own clothes in a big zinc bath of detergent. Twice a week all the shorts and shirts and underwear and pajamas went in. That way extra grime wasn't really noticed.

They pushed forward and there it was, with the tables and chairs they had been arranging at the very time that Mam was having her accident overhead. It was strange and almost frightening to think about.

They went around the tunnel as they had often done before, stroking its sides and marveling at how well made it was and how long it had lasted.

"They must have been desperate in those days to keep their groceries hidden from the public if they went to all this trouble to hide them, building a whole tunnel just so the neighbors wouldn't see," Dara said in wonder.

"They didn't *have* neighbors." Michael was more authoritative. "It was so that they wouldn't have to look at them themselves."

"What was so bad about groceries?"

"I don't think it was just a few brown-paper bags like we'd get in Loretto Quinn's, it was barrels and boxes."

"Well that's even more posh, they must have been half cracked, the Ferns," Dara said.

"Apparently it's all over the country, I read it in all that research Daddy's doing. Mr. O'Neill says that the book will be on display at the hotel with Dad's name on it."

"Do you think the hotel will ever get built?" Dara asked suddenly.

"I don't know, I suppose it will. Why?"

"It doesn't seem real anymore."

"Nothing does."

The twins sat there for a long moment. Neither wanted to say anything falsely cheering.

As usual they spoke at the same time when they did speak.

"Do you think Lourdes would work . . ." Dara began.

"I wonder if there really are miracles . . ." Michael began.

They burst out laughing.

"Maybe our minds got divided," Dara said. "We didn't get a full one each but between us we have a fantastic Super mind."

"Which is why we can only work out things when there are the two of us," Michael agreed.

"So what do we think about Lourdes?" Dara said.

"There must have been some miracles there, some of them have to be real." Michael's face was full of hope.

"Yes, Sister Laura said that if it was all a fraud the enemies of the Church would have found it out." Dara was eager also.

"So maybe if we could get her there. It could work, couldn't it?"

"And it would be better than just sitting around waiting."

Dara and Michael were much revived. It was like old times, having some kind of project. Something important to do.

The twins didn't know that the village of Mountfern was already planning to send Kate to Lourdes. Money had been collected, people had been in touch with the travel agencies in Dublin and had received details from the Joe Walsh Travel Agency and the Michael Walsh Travel Agency.

The collection had begun. Sheila Whelan was approached to put the money in the post office. She thought it should be a proper fund administered through a solicitor's office.

At first Fergus didn't want anything to do with it. It was grotesque to build up people's hopes, Kate's hopes too. Why let simple people believe that there was a way that a place would mend a broken spine? Perhaps John Ryan would feel patronized, he might not like the idea that the people of Mountfern should pay for his wife to go to Lourdes instead of waiting for him to send her himself.

"If you don't start it for us then as sure as anything Patrick O'Neill will organize it," Sheila said.

"I'll open a bank deposit account tomorrow," said Fergus.

"Father, did you know that there's a collection being organized to take Dara and Michael's mother to Lourdes?" Grace asked.

"Yes, people are very generous, they're digging very deep in their pockets."

"Who's organizing it?" Kerry asked.

"I don't know, I don't think anyone is. You can give your money at the church to either of the priests, or at the post office or to Mr. Slattery, you know—the lawyer."

"Slattery. That figures," Kerry said.

"Why?" Grace asked.

Kerry smiled knowingly. His hair was longer than he usually wore it, it clustered around his neck. His father thought it made him look like a girl. Kerry said that there wasn't a barber within miles and that he might be misjudged if he went to the Rosemarie hair salon. He was tanned and relaxed looking, like a boy who had been on a holiday in a resort, Patrick thought with some annoyance. He had seen the young Ryan boy and Tommy Leonard today; both of them looked peaked and as if they had not seen a ray of sun all year.

"Well, your sister asked you a question. Why does it figure that Slattery is taking up the money? Sure he is. He's a lawyer, as Grace said."

"And he's the leader of the other side."

"Yes, but when the time comes for litigation the Ryans will have other lawyers."

"I mean the other side here in Mountfern. He's the head of the pack that wants to run us out of town. So naturally he collects money to send the injured Mrs. Ryan to Lourdes."

"He doesn't want to run us out of town. Does he?" Grace looked alarmed.

"Of course not, your brother is playing games."

"Not so, Father. He hardly welcomed us here with open arms, did he? And now we are blacker still, one of the great and good has been injured on our property. Of course he wants us out, like a lot of them do."

"Where do you get these kinds of ideas?" Patrick's tone sounded a lot milder than he felt.

"Because I'm not stupid." It was very arrogant the way Kerry said it. The direct implication was that Patrick was stupid. Very.

"Neither am I, Kerry. I'm not at all stupid no matter what you might believe."

Kerry shrugged as if it were a matter of indifference to him what his father thought or was.

"I do know all about the collection, Grace." His remarks were now addressed to his daughter. Patrick didn't trust himself to speak to Kerry.

"I think it's a great idea. I don't believe it will cure her but they do say, and I've heard all kinds of people say this, even people who would scorn the whole idea of miracles . . . They say that nobody ever comes back from Lourdes the worse for having been there, they all come back better in some way. Happier, more resigned, feeling that compared to what they saw there then they aren't too badly off."

Kerry smiled. "That's well put," he said admiringly. "Send people off there so they see what terrible things other people have, they come home resigned . . . I never heard that line."

Patrick ignored him. "I could have given Kate Ryan a check to take her to Lourdes, Gracie, but I didn't, I felt it had to come from her own people here. Not from us."

"Like Mary Donnelly?"

"Exactly. So of course I've contributed to the fund, but nothing excessive."

"You know, I misjudged you, Father." Kerry seemed genuinely admiring now. But with Kerry it was often hard to know.

There was no time to discuss it. A shadow passed the window.

"Oh Jesus," Patrick said, "it's Marian."

Marian was full of chat. She had come to invite them all to be her guests at an upcoming angling festival.

Patrick would simply love it, she said, it was tailor-made for him, he would get the entire atmosphere of one of these occasions at first hand, he would know how to describe it to those Americans who were keen fishermen. There would be an excellent buffet lunch in a tent to which they would be invited.

It would be frightfully boring for the young people of course, lots of standing around talking and drinking. But possibly they would love it too. Or it might even be that they would prefer to be with their own friends that day. They must do whichever they pleased, come with her to the lake or stay here in Mountfern and have a great time. Their decision entirely.

Covering the snuffles and giggles of his children, Patrick said graciously and firmly that he would let her know tomorrow. He hadn't yet been able to work out their plans next week.

Patrick thought that it was no mean achievement that he had

managed to conduct the entire conversation extremely courteously but without allowing Marian to sit down. In what was after all her own house.

Brian Doyle telephoned Patrick to say that it was probably unimportant but there was some paint daubed on the wooden fences around some of the digging on the site. They'd have it removed but he thought Patrick should know.

"What does it say?"

"It says Yanks Go Home, but I wouldn't take a blind bit of notice of that," said Brian Doyle.

Marian Johnson was extremely put out when her offer to show Patrick the lake and introduce him to the people who ran angling in the country was so suddenly and almost curtly refused.

Patrick had been apologetic but had given no real explanation. Marian had the bad luck to run into Jack Coyne who had said that it was devoutly to be hoped that Patrick O'Neill hadn't any plans to build a monstrosity like the Slieve Sunset, because that was the place he was seen hurrying in and out of at all hours of the day and night, and that he was there at this moment with that foreign-looking woman, the one with the beautiful hair.

Marian Johnson patted her own sparse hair, newly arranged in the Rosemarie hair salon for an outing which was not now going to take place.

It was impossible to make sense of Patrick O'Neill. He had spent his entire life getting ready to come home, to mix with the best in the land. She had been ready to introduce him to people from Prosperous and Belturbet, from Boyle and Ballinasloe. She knew the families who owned the fishing rights from Lough Ree to Lough Allen, from the Erne to the Lee. She had already made sure he had met the Master socially so that he would not be considered an outsider when it came to foxhunting. And what was the thanks she got, his sneaking away to see that woman in the Slieve Sunset. But there couldn't be anything in it. Not after all his hopes of coming home and being Irish, properly Irish. He could never get involved with a foreign woman, not at this stage.

Kate didn't remember meeting Rachel Fine before. She was dark and exotic-looking, with a beautiful suit that must have cost a fortune. She wore a scarf in such an elegant way too. Usually you only saw people in photographs wearing scarves like that; when they moved it would go into a rag.

She came toward the bed. "Your husband says you have a very sketchy memory of the day."

"Very." Kate felt at a loss with this elegant woman.

"Perhaps that's good, it means you won't remember too much about the shock and the pain."

"No, I can't remember that at all. I can only remember waking up here and someone telling me it was three days before." Kate's face closed up in pain at the memory.

"I believe there are some wonderful surgeons here, Patrick tells me that his hotshot from New York was highly impressed."

Patrick. She called him Patrick. Nobody else who worked with him did. It was coming back to her. John had told her that Rachel Fine was some kind of decorator or designer, she had been staying out in the Slieve Sunset, and then she went on a tour to see about ordering Irish fabrics and things. John had been very vague.

"You're very good to come and see me. Especially as I've been a bit like a madam and saying I didn't want people to come."

"No way should you have people gaping at you if you don't feel like it."

Rachel was gentle and easy, she was no effort to talk to. She explained that she had brought glossy magazines, the kind of thing you wouldn't dream of buying for yourself or reading when you were well. Kate, who had read nothing in the weeks she lay here, was pleased. Those magazines she could just about manage, she felt.

"Why *did* you come?" she asked suddenly.

"Because . . . when I had just arrived in Mountfern you made me welcome. I was sitting in that pub waiting for Patrick to come in, I was anxious and tense and you were kind to me. I liked you."

It was a flowery speech. Kate paused for a moment. Then it came back to her the way it had before. She was Patrick O'Neill's woman!

Perhaps the woman saw the recognition in her eyes. Anyway she went on to speak of it.

"I thought you were someone I could talk to. I can't tell you how distressed I was. How unreal it seemed when you were so lively and laughing . . ." Her eyes filled with tears.

Something in Kate responded to her warmly. Here was someone who was not afraid to say it was a bloody tragedy. For the first time since it happened, she looked into the face of another human being who was prepared to admit that Kate was very very unlucky, someone to be pitied rather than jollied along. It was a huge relief.

"Thank you," Kate began, and found to her horror that she was beginning to sob. "Thank you. I *was* lively and laughing, wasn't I? I wasn't always like this. I *was* able to run and move and grab things up rather than lie here while people rub oil and powder on me like a giant baby. I used to decide what to do and where to go myself. I did, I did."

"Yes, that's the way you were." She was matter of fact.

Kate waited for the cheery sentence saying that she'd be like that again someday. But it didn't come.

"It's so unfair," Rachel said instead. "I'd be able to cope with life if it wasn't so terribly unjust. All you were doing is looking. Standing looking and thinking about what the place was going to be like, and you end up with your back broken, lying here."

Such warmth and sympathy meant that Kate didn't have to put on any act in return, she didn't have to bite her lip and be stoic like she did for John, nor pretend a jolly getting-better-every-day role as she did with the children.

She cried and cried and Rachel held her face to her and didn't mind about the tears all over her good suit, and didn't call the nurse. After a while the crying stopped as unexpectedly as it had begun. Kate looked tired.

"Can I come and see you again?" Rachel asked.

"Please. Please."

Patrick wasn't pleased.

"Why didn't you tell me you were going to see her?"

"I don't have to tell you everything."

"It was sneaky and underhanded."

"I honestly think you can't be well to say something like that. What on earth could be underhanded about going to see someone in the hospital?"

"You didn't ask me if you should go."

"I am not your servant, nor your ten-year-old child. You have told me often enough that you want us to lead separate lives here. I am trying to do that, and now that doesn't seem to please you either." Rachel's eyes flashed in an unaccustomed display of anger.

"No, but you wouldn't have mentioned it, I would never have known if Grace hadn't told me."

"Grace. Yes."

"Oh, don't take that tone, Grace was full of how much Mrs. Ryan loved you and how nice you were, she got it all from the twins. She told me in innocence, not tattling as you are trying to imply."

"This conversation is getting nowhere. Shall we talk about something else? Work perhaps. I have some samples to discuss with you for wall hangings."

"To hell with wall hangings . . . What did she say?"

"Kate Ryan? Not much really. She cried a lot. But that was between us." Rachel stood up and walked restlessly around the plastic and formica lobby of Slieve Sunset. Since the incident of their discovery in Rachel's bedroom on the day of the accident Patrick had been most anxious that all meetings should take place in the public eye and that they be known as colleagues.

"It's just that it wouldn't be a good idea to say anything," Patrick began. He looked troubled and not like his usual decisive self.

"Say anything?" Rachel was nonplussed.

"Yeah, well I know this sounds a bit odd, but the lawyers said not to say anything, anything that might admit liability."

"You can't be serious."

"I know, that's what I said, but they say you're not dealing with decent people like the Ryans, there's always a load of gangsters waiting to get on the bandwagon if they can. Urging people on to litigation."

"But what litigation? You said you'd pay?"

"Yes I did and I will, but there's a danger that people could take you for all you had if you admit too much, that's all."

"I don't understand you at all. You told me that you had made several attempts to see her. So why are *you* going? Isn't it much more likely that *you* would commit yourself or whatever?"

"No, because I'm a careful man. I guess I was just afraid you might have said something like Patrick will look after everything."

"I didn't say it because I assume she knows it, and so does everyone."

"Let's stop this, Rachel," he said wearily.

"Yes, let's." She was back in her passive role of pleasing him now. She didn't remind him that it was he who had started the conversation and refused to let it go.

He looked old and worried.

* * *

"Wouldn't it be great if Mary Donnelly would smile sometimes?" Fergus said confidentially to Sheila Whelan. "She's not a bad-looking woman, but there's a terrible ferocity about her."

"She puts that on. Underneath she's as nice as anything."

"Well, life is short. You wouldn't have the energy to dig down for it," Fergus said.

"She's doing well enough above in the pub, I think?" Mrs. Whelan's voice was anxious. "She's not putting people off by glowering at them, is she?"

"It would take more than a glower to put a thirsty man off his drink. Not at all, she's part of the furniture there now, and John is delighted with her. He says she's the most efficient person he ever had working in a bar in his life."

"She's grand if she has plenty to do."

"There's plenty in that house all right. How poor Kate ever managed *and* did my work as well I'll never know."

"You speak of her as if she were dead, Fergus. She'll be home in a matter of weeks."

"She might as well be dead for all her life can give her now."

"Lord Almighty, I hope you don't go saying that to her."

"I haven't been allowed near her to say anything." He sounded bitter.

"Well, she just wanted the family for a while."

"Oh, but I think I'll be allowed to go next week. After all, O'Neill's tart has been in so that should open the floodgates."

"That is not only unlike you, it's disgusting."

Fergus said nothing.

"We're all upset by what happened, you're not the only one to feel it. You'd be a very unwise man to talk like that. I mean it."

He had never known her so sharp.

He nodded. "Right."

"If you know how much I mean it. We need people like you of good sense, people who are right about things and know what to do. Half the people have gone mad in Mountfern since Patrick O'Neill came, and Kate's accident is only one of the big changes we'll have to see here. Fergus, let you not change too, I beg you."

"It was a cheap, vulgar thing to say. I'm glad I have a good friend like you to put me right from time to time."

"That's the only time I ever tried to put you right in my life," Sheila said simply. She patted his hand. They were indeed friends.

* * *

The traction was over. They were moving her into a chair. Everyone spoke about it as if it were a huge breakthrough, as if she were going to be able to fly.

Kate felt leaden. She'd had a low feeling since she woke but she tried to take part in all the enthusiasm around her. After all it would be ungracious and mulish not to show pleasure at a step forward.

It didn't hurt, the moving, they were able to lift her and anticipate what would give a stab of pain and what would be fine, and really there was a lot of her that didn't ache at all.

There was a little team around her, the nice young nurse Geraldine and the staff nurse, there was Sister Winston, and two of the hospital porters who seemed to be on call for everything that involved movement, from ambulance stretchers to windows that were stuck with paint. The great Mr. Brown the surgeon was there, and so were two physiotherapists.

She got her first shock when she saw the chair. It was a wheelchair. "I didn't think . . ." Her hand was at her throat.

Sister Winston was quick. She must have been used to this reaction. "Why be in a chair that can just face one way when you can face any way in this?"

"But an ordinary chair would do . . ."

"It would *do*, certainly, but you wouldn't be able to go to the window and back to your bed or to the handbasin."

"I don't *want* to go to any of those places, I just want to sit in a chair like an ordinary person."

"This one's been prepared for you; tomorrow we can discuss an ordinary chair."

There were so many people looking and hoping for her to be well and upright in the chair, Kate could say no more.

"Of course," she said in a small voice. "I'm sorry."

The lifting was surprisingly easy, just a gradual movement. After those weeks of lying down and thinking it was normal to wake looking at the ceiling and that people always talked bending over you slightly, it was going to be hard to readjust to sitting up again.

They had eased her into the chair, her legs wrapped well in a rug. The family would be so pleased to see her sitting up, the nurses said. The porters who had brought the chair smiled their pleasure. Mr. Brown said she was making great progress, the two physiotherapists moved here and there to settle her. And that was it. She sat and tried to smile back at all the good humor around. But the smile wouldn't come.

She felt faint, and a roaring in her ears.

They saw it at once, and her head was pushed down. A glass of water, medication was discussed and waved away. It often happened. Sister Winston had seen it all before. That's why she never let the friends and relatives in until much later.

Kate Ryan's mouth was in an O of horror, her hands gripped the sides of the chair.

"I can't feel . . ." she cried. "I can't feel it."

"What can't you feel?" Geraldine was on her knees beside the chair, holding Kate's hand. "Shush now, you're grand altogether, everyone's delighted with you . . ."

"I can't feel my bottom, I have no bottom, no legs, nothing. There's only emptiness where I'm sitting in the chair."

Mr. Brown was gentle. "You've known always . . . you've known about the paralysis. The realization comes and goes. You've adapted so well in traction, now it's just a new adapting."

"It's like air, it's not real. I can't be going to live like this till I die, can I?" Kate looked around piteously at the semi-circle.

"No, no," said Geraldine soothingly.

"I couldn't stand years of this, I couldn't stand it. There's nothing *there*," Kate cried.

The silence of sympathy broken by clucks of encouragement frightened her even more. Perhaps there weren't going to *be* years ahead. Perhaps her life might be nearly over already.

They put the family off. It seemed the wisest thing. They said there was no cause for alarm, but she needed sedation and it would be tiring for Mrs. Ryan rather than comforting to have to cope with visitors.

They didn't tell John that his wife sat for her first day in a wheelchair staring ahead of her and thinking of a life of dependency on others. Thinking of the fears she would have . . . or they all would have if she got any infection and she might not have the strength to fight it.

She thought about the children having to push an old mother around in a wheelchair; because she would be an old mother, she might as well be their grandmother for all the say she was going to have in things, for all the fun and companionship she could give them.

She thought about the bar and what would happen if Patrick's hotel took away all their business from them as she had been afraid it would. They couldn't go on living on his charity as they already were, a private room, a car at John's beck and call, and anything she said she'd like she knew he would give her.

It wasn't his fault that she had walked past those notices saying danger, and men at work. It wasn't Patrick's fault that she had walked across the line of a man with a digger who had not expected there to be another human on that part of the site.

But Kate wept as she had never wept lying flat on her bed. This was the best she could hope for. This terrible dependent sitting posture worse altogether than lying down, which everyone knew was only temporary.

And when she had learned how to propel the bloody thing with her weak arms and learned how to lift her wasted legs out of it and onto some hideous-looking lavatory bowl, they would say she was cured and send her home. Cured! Cured to go home a cripple and watch this Mary Donnelly, whoever she was, taking Kate's place.

Mary Donnelly didn't want to speak to the men from the brewery or the men from the distillery who called to the pub.

"I've had quite enough huggermugger with men since I came to this establishment," she said to John. "And in any event you are the man of the house, whatever that expression means. You should talk to them yourself."

John sighed. Every day he realized more how much of the running of the household Kate had done. Had he been properly grateful? No of course he had not. He had taken it for granted. Now there was no time to go and write his poems, there was no time to take a walk to clear his head after the smoke and noise in the bar. The days fell into a pattern.

As August became September and Mary got the children ready to go back to school, John began to think he had known no other life than the one where he was picked up at two o'clock in the afternoon and driven in to see his invalid wife in a hospital bed. Like any life, some days were better than others. Sometimes Kate was tired and impatient after long sessions trying to use the wheelchair and maneuver herself from bed to chair, with failure all the way. Some days she was elated. There were times when he was tired and depressed and picked a row, there were good afternoons where he sat and talked to her easily without either of them thinking how the situation had changed and would still be changed when he got her home.

He was glad that she seemed friendly with Rachel. He couldn't quite see what they had to talk about and giggle at, but it was undoubtedly good for her.

She didn't want too many visitors, she said, it tired her, so it was rationed to one a day apart from the family and Rachel. John was pleased that she now saw Fergus Slattery, the poor fellow seemed to be most upset about her and very black about apportioning blame and responsibility. He even kept trying to make appointments with John to talk about the case and the compensation.

"What case?" John had wanted to know. "There's no case, surely. It was a terrible accident."

Fergus had become more impatient than ever about it. And finally Kate said that John should agree to talk about it. Just to calm Fergus down.

"You don't know the way he is, John. I worked for him, remember? He's up to his eyes in the letter of the law, not what things people are really involved in. You should see the small prints, and the clauses about this and about that, and the whereases. It's a different world. Just do me a favor and go to see him in his office, tell him how good Patrick has been, tell him we're not the kind of people who sue over things, it would be flying in the face of God."

"The office? But that would be like as if I'd gone in order to take him on."

"You're not going to get much talked about in the pub, are you? The door opening every time you're getting somewhere?"

He agreed. Unwillingly. And went to Fergus on a bright September morning.

Miss Purcell had told him of a novena that was being done for Kate, and a bouquet of masses which would be offered on the first Tuesday of the month. She wondered when would poor Mrs. Ryan be able to travel to Lourdes, the fund had been generously subscribed. Eventually John got away from her and sat down in the room where his wife used to work every morning.

"Haven't you got anyone yet?" he asked kindly, knowing that Fergus Slattery had put off getting any permanent help out of loyalty to Kate and to the belief that she might work again.

"Your wife told me off about that too. I'll have to, I will. Soon."

"Right." John didn't nag him, he knew how irritating it was to be told to do something if you didn't want to. Jack Coyne was always urging him to get a new roof or a light-up sign over the pub. Things that sounded sensible, things that he might do one day, but not immediately.

"I'll speak as simply and quickly as I can, John. I know you don't want to be here in case it looks as if you're going to take Patrick O'Neill to court, so I'll try to put you in the picture as best I can."

"I know you will, Fergus." John nodded politely like an obedient child.

Fergus felt his collar a bit tight around his neck and loosened it with his finger. He seemed almost reluctant to begin now that he had the undivided attention of the man who was usually moving away to pull pints or to greet those who came in the door.

"Well, it's a matter of just spelling it out," he said.

John looked at him and waited.

"And if there's anything you don't agree with you'll say . . . of course."

"Of course," John agreed.

"Well, obviously it *wasn't* the time before, with everything being so upset and on top of us, but now we have to think in terms of practicalities. Like what happens when Kate comes home."

John was silent. He was looking around the room thoughtfully as if imagining Kate working here, moving quickly from typewriter to cupboard, from big scales where she would have weighed the long narrow envelopes of documents before they were taken to Sheila Whelan's to mail.

"John," Fergus said.

"Yes, I know, practicalities. Well, those are being thought of in most ways. Judy Byrne will come in three times a week at first to keep Kate doing the exercises. And Patrick's getting his builders to even out the floor levels so that she can come into the pub on the chair without anyone having to lift it. He's been very generous, Patrick has, generous and thoughtful." John's glance went around the lawyer's office again, slowly and deliberately.

Fergus could barely conceal his irritation.

"I don't doubt that. *No*, look at me, John, I know you've heard me giving out about the man, I don't doubt that he has been generosity itself, but can I beg you to listen? Now two years ago there was this act passed, the Civil Liability Act of 1961, and up to this there were just three kinds of person who were deemed to exist on your land: an invitee, a licensee and a trespasser. There were no other people. So if anyone got injured the decision was, which kind of person were they? If they were an invitee they got one kind of compensation, a licensee got another—a licensee would be somebody, say, who had permission to be there in some category or other—and the trespasser got another."

He saw John fidgeting.

"Please listen John, I'm making it very short and you'll see why it is important in a minute. There used to be lots of innocent trespassers, people who weren't intending trespass . . ."

"But Kate wasn't . . ."

"*Listen,* will you, like children or like Kate, say, who was a neighbor and friend. So the law was changed making the landowner more liable than he used to be in the old days. So Patrick or his insurance company has a legal liability to pay compensation . . ."

"But he has, I tell you, we don't want to be blackmailing him . . ."

"The law; God Almighty, the law of the land we live in says he has to pay it, he knows he has to pay it, he doesn't live in some cloud-bloody-cuckoo-land like you do."

"Why are you shouting at me, Fergus?"

"I don't know. I don't know. I think it's because I'm being so long winded and you won't wait till I get to the point."

"All right."

"So the system is you have to sue Patrick. Kate has to sue him. That's the machinery, that's the way it's done. His insurance company won't pay, can't pay until there's a case set up, until the proper requirements of the law are complied with."

"We don't want to sue him."

"He knows that, you know that, I know that, his lawyers know that. Even his insurance company knows that. Jesus, Mary and Joseph, people are suing each other day in and day out who are the best of friends."

"I don't believe you!"

"But it's the way, it's the system. You know Marian Johnson up at the Grange. When she was about eighteen she drove her father home from someplace out the country and they had an accident, he was badly injured, he sued her. The insurance company gave him compensation. He didn't sue her because he was her enemy, he sued her because that's how it's done. That's the way you unlock the money."

"It seems very hypocritical and devious to me."

Fergus was weary. "It's not really, John, it's sensible, it's the only way to keep control, otherwise insurance companies would have to be paying out huge awards and they couldn't afford it and the premiums would be enormous. This way at least they know it's a genuine case when the parties are prepared to go to court about it. It gives them a sort of authenticity, if you see what I mean."

"You're very good at explaining the law, and you obviously understand it too, which is more than a lot of lawyers . . . but Fergus, do you have any understanding at all about what it is to be a neighbor? I mean, you're here in this house in the middle of the street, nothing changes for you no matter who comes to live here. You don't depend on good will and rubbing elbows with people like we do in a pub. It doesn't make sense to go into a court of law and say things about a neighbor, things that cannot be unsaid." John was calm but he seemed very resolute.

Fergus tried again.

"There'll be very little said, and you and Patrick won't have to do any of the saying. The question is, would you like a different solicitor?"

"Not you?"

"I'm very close to you, to all of you. Perhaps it might be easier with someone from the town. It often is."

"If we want to have anyone, Fergus, then Kate and I would want to have you."

"Right."

"Do we need to do anything immediately?"

"No, not for a while, leave it with me."

"Oh and Fergus, could you explain to Patrick O'Neill about it all being friendly when it starts? You know, tell him about Marian Johnson in the Grange and her father and all. It would make it a bit less formal."

"I don't need to tell him that, he's a businessman, John, he knows."

"I'd like you to tell him all the same."

"If it comes up easily I will," Fergus said.

Chapter XIV

Patrick was pleased to get a message from Rachel that Kate would like to see him on Friday afternoon.

"She must be getting better." He said.

"She says she is," Rachel said doubtfully. "I think she looked a bit feverish, excited. Still, it's better than that terribly depressed way she was last week."

"What would she like? She has a radio, you say?"

"Yes, she hardly listens to it. She might like a game—Scrabble, say. She could play it with the little guys when they go in."

"That's a great idea, Rachel," he beamed. "Where in the world will I get Scrabble? I may have to go to Dublin for it, or Shannon."

"Don't be silly. I'll get it for you."

She had already got a set, and many other things. She wanted Kate to think that Patrick was thoughtful and concerned.

John sat on the edge of the bed and told Kate everything.

"He seems dead set that there's going to be a case," she said, biting at her lower lip.

"I'm just reporting everything that he said, and trying to give you the sort of tone he said it in."

"You're doing very well." She grinned ruefully. "I can practically hear him speaking."

"He's so out for our good, he wants the best for you."

"The best for me is not to have to lock horns with Patrick O'Neill in public. The best would be not having to lie here worrying myself sick what he'll think, what he'll do when we turn on him like an ungrateful dog. That's what it's going to be like, John, no matter how many fine words Fergus says about the law . . ."

She was distressed, her eyes full of tears and her face red with exertion.

John took her hand. "You're not going to spend any time lying here worrying, not even five minutes. I'll tell you what we'll do . . . and you're the one who can do it."

Soothing and shushing down her protests he explained to her that she could sort everything out if she happened by accident to arrange that Patrick O'Neill and Fergus Slattery should both turn up at the same time in her hospital bedroom.

Then it could all be said out in the open.

Fergus was told by the hospital that Friday would be a good day to come in and see Mrs. Ryan. He drove glumly to the hospital. She had been so low the last time, it had been an effort to keep up any kind of conversation at all.

He had brought the application forms of the four young women who had applied for jobs as his secretary. He knew two of them, daughters of local farmers who had done secretarial courses. He thought they would be very unlikely candidates, he wanted Kate's advice badly. Wouldn't it be great if she was in good sparkling form? Dr. White said that some days she was the old Kate, laughing and joking, and you would think she was just lying down for a rest. Other times she had been awake all night, convinced she had not very much longer to live, and was railing at the injustice of it.

Please may it be a good day. For all their sakes.

She was as flushed as a girl, he hoped it was a good sign. She was delighted that he had brought the confidential files and urged strongly in favor of Deirdre Dunne, a girl who lived about three miles away.

"Look, she's given you all kinds of detail, like how it will be no trouble to get a lift in and out. That's sensible. And I know Deirdre, her father comes into Ryan's. A tighter-mouthed man you never met.

He wouldn't tell you what day it was let alone anyone else's business."

She was indeed like the old Kate, teasing him, sending him up, full of plans. Rachel Fine had said that her room should be moved downstairs; soon builders would go in and flatten out all the steps in the downstairs so she could come into the pub and the kitchen. The parlor was going to be made into a big bed-sitting room for her, with a special bathroom beside it. There would be a rail all around it, and garden doors—you know, those French windows with glass in them down to the floor—out to the side yard, which would be made posh, and she could wheel herself out there.

Fergus took off his glasses and wiped them because they had misted up with delight that she was able to think of a life after this white hospital room, and with pity that it would be limited by wheelchairs and rails around walls.

John Ryan came in then, told him to sit where he was, no need to go, he'd been in and out a dozen times during the afternoon and would be again. Just then there was a tap, and Patrick stood there.

He looked shy in his country tweeds and his crisp shirt, and his curly hair combed just outside the door. In his arms he held a big gift-wrapped parcel and a glass bowl with fruit in it. Nothing very dramatic, just healthy-looking apples and thick-skinned oranges and two yellow pears.

Fergus wished he had brought something like that instead of the box of sweets which lay on the cabinet beside the bed.

"They tell me that I'd find you better today than any day." Patrick was lit up with pleasure. You could see it.

Kate stretched out her arms in greeting from the bed.

"Thank you for all you've done. I can never thank you enough. The room, the car for everyone to come in and out. You've been too good."

"I couldn't do enough, Kate, to tell you how sorry I am that it had to happen. And if it did have to happen why did it have to be on my land, with bulldozers working for me?"

There was no mistaking his sincerity.

"Don't I know that. I've every proof of it," Kate said.

Patrick seemed to notice for the first time that John and Fergus were in the room. He went to John first and shook him by the hand.

"My, doesn't she look well, after all she's been through."

It was just the right touch, Fergus thought miserably. He in no way minimized her agonies, yet he concentrated on the hopeful side. Then it was Fergus's turn.

"Slattery, you must be as pleased as all of us. It's a good time to meet."

"Yup." Fergus got this urge to behave like a taciturn cowboy every time he met Patrick O'Neill nowadays. The fact that he was somehow ungracious made him even more annoyed with himself.

"And I'm very glad you both happen to be here at the same time," Kate said, looking at them eagerly from her bed, her cheeks pink, her hair tied with a yellow ribbon matching the ribbon in her lacy bedjacket, both given to her by Rachel Fine.

"Why is that?" Fergus was suspicious: Kate was too bright, John was looking at the floor.

Patrick knew nothing about it, whatever it was. He smiled to know what Kate was going to say.

"Because I am determined to get out of here and live a proper life again, and I'm tired of people coming to my bed and talking about formalities. All I want to know now, and it will help me to get better, is that there will never be any animosity between us no matter what formalities there are."

"How could there be animosity?" Patrick cried.

"Kate, why don't you leave this until later? Until you're better," Fergus said levelly.

"One of the things stopping me getting better is this," she said. "Honestly it is, I swear it, at night I wake up and think my life is over, it's so unfair; and other nights I wake up and think of the things people tell me down in physiotherapy—that I should claim this and I should claim that, and it would make life more bearable, and it's all from faceless insurance companies anyway so nobody gets hurt. Then I think of Patrick living beside us and what it's going to be like, and of Grace and Kerry and the twins and how I'd hate a fight more than anything . . . So that's why I'm asking you, my friends, will it be done without animosity?"

Fergus opened his mouth and closed it again like a fish.

John said nothing, but laid his hand supportively on Kate's arm.

Patrick O'Neill smiled more broadly than ever as if he could have heard no better news than this current subject Kate wanted to discuss. "But of course we'll talk about it, from now until you feel too tired. Kate, John, I assure you I was only waiting until you felt *able* to talk about it. And obviously since you have Mr. Slattery here too I feel he would be glad it was brought up as soon as . . ."

"I assure you, Mr. O'Neill," Fergus began a trifle pompously.

"No, I know it just happened to come up, but let me say something, straight out. For weeks now I've been wanting to say to someone of you three and never finding the right moment. I *know* the law, I am so well insured it would make your head swim. The courts will decide a compensation and they will pay it.

"Kate, you can never get your spine back, but you can get *some* comforts, goddamn it. I'll see to it that you do."

"But we don't want to go to court against *you*, Patrick," John said, avoiding Fergus's eye.

"Nobody wants to go to court and maybe we mightn't even have to go inside the door," said Patrick. "It could all be settled at the last moment. That's what always happens. But that's the machinery, that's the formula . . . the same way as there's a process for getting a license for a pub or permission to hold a raffle . . . That's right, isn't it, Attorney?"

Fergus nodded, not trusting himself to speak. The man was making himself clear in a way that Fergus hadn't been able to do. John and Kate hadn't trusted him. He felt his mouth full of acid. "That's right," he said.

"So, let's get the insurance guys, hey? God, if you know how much they get me for every year. It will be a pleasure to get them to give you as much as we can squeeze from them. All I say, though, is that it's a tremendous shame that it has to be over something like this."

He was so full of generosity, no mention of the no-claim bonus he would lose, no mention of the pressure that giant insurance companies who handled his business both here and in America would put on him. Fergus felt moved by the man's warmth. But in his heart he felt sure that Patrick was right. Some settlement would be reached on the steps of a courthouse, and at this moment Patrick knew exactly how much it was.

Fergus felt an urge so strong that it was almost overpowering to take him on and fight him in every court of the land, refusing offers, settlements and recommendations until he got for Kate Ryan something that would even in a paltry way compensate for the life that Patrick O'Neill and his mechanical bulldozers had taken away from her.

Later he remembered, with his mouth in a thin line, that the cute fox O'Neill had said nothing about the private room in the hospital being a gift from Patrick to Kate or the use of a car for the Ryan family being a gift from Patrick to Kate. Oh, no. These would be included in the settlement when the time came.

He remembered how pleased Kate had been with the game of Scrabble. He wished he had thought of it, with a pain that almost tore him in two.

He felt that there was great truth in Mrs. Whelan's words that everyone had gone a little mad since O'Neill came to Mountfern. He hoped he hadn't gone madder than most. Fergus knew that he must do something practical rather than sit and rage against what had been done and couldn't be undone.

He decided to teach John Ryan to drive and get them a second-hand car somewhere so that O'Neill couldn't claim months more of transport when the day of reckoning arrived.

It was so strange going back to school without their mother to harass them and organize the huge hunt for satchels, text books and clean shirts, and shoes being taken to the mender's. This is what the end of the summer holidays meant before.

Mary Donnelly had it all in order. The Ryans' house had never worked in such a streamlined way before. There was no fuss about going back to school. All the clothes were ready mended and ironed anyway. The children had almost forgotten a time when they didn't strip and air their beds every day, and when there wasn't a weekly examination of shoes and clothes, so that the one could be brought to old Mr. Foley's odd wordless brother who stitched away silently at the soles of Mountfern in the back of Foley's bar. Clothes were all darned or mended at that weekly session too.

Kate Ryan in her hospital bed looked in amazement at neat patches and false hems to be told that Dara and Eddie were a dab hand at any kind of dressmaking now. Michael and Declan had resisted it and were responsible for shoe polishing instead.

A cupboard had been cleared in the dining room and all schoolbooks and bags were stored there. The four children had a shelf each. The summer exercises had continued, and even Eddie was able to approach an exercise book now without scribbling all over it. Mary had always shown such surprise and horror at any doodling it was easier to leave the book clean.

And when school did begin Mary seemed to regard it with a reverence that the children found disconcerting. She almost spoke of school in hushed tones. She managed to inquire about their progress and particularly about what homework they had to do with an air of such interest that they did not realize how much they were giving themselves away and putting their lives into her hands.

"Now, Dara, let me help you clear away, you've got all those geography questions to do tonight, you said. And Michael has that big long poem to learn. Eddie, you aren't too badly off—only ten sums, was it?"

They would look at each other glumly. Why had they been so specific? Now there was no escape.

The breakfast room became a study both before and after tea. There was always a dictionary, an atlas, rulers, pencils and spare paper. The wireless was turned down respectfully. Callers were discouraged and if their father ever came looking for them for anything, the children heard Mary speaking to him in low urgent tones explaining that they were doing their homework. It was said in the voice that someone might have used about the College of Cardinals being in conclave to elect a pope. And after a few false starts it worked. The homework did get finished, and almost in silence. It was easier to learn the poem, Michael would decide, rather than have Mary offer to hear it to him at breakfast and expose his ignorance. Dara would find that Mary, when approached about homework that had been completed, was always cooperative and helped to get her better marks, but Mary would not even discuss work that had been left undone.

Eddie felt life was too short to have to put up with Mary mentioning that she must ask Brother Keane why the children in Eddie's class got no homework. It really was simpler to admit to the homework and do it. Then at least he would be free.

Declan at seven didn't have very much homework, but he liked the scene around the table. Mary had drawn him a map of Ireland and he spent each evening coloring in the different counties and labeling them. He had asked Mary was this the kind of thing a person could do in a circus as a trick. Mary had said that to be truthful it hadn't been done much, but there was no reason why there couldn't be a first time. And she could say hand on heart that to know the thirty-two counties of Ireland, how to spell them and where they all were would be something that would advance you in *any* career. So Declan sat happily mastering difficult spellings like Monaghan and Laoghais.

Sometimes John looked in at the industry and gave a deep sigh of relief.

By the time he got Kate home, some kind of order would reign in the house, and all the time Kate's new domain was being built. With huge financial help from Patrick O'Neill, and great advice and care from Patrick's lady friend Rachel Fine. Even Leopold was better behaved these days, John noticed, and slept outside Mary's door on a sack which he dragged out to the yard each evening. It was as if he lay there protecting her from the world.

"What does Kerry do all the time? He's never around and his school doesn't open for another week." Dara and Grace were sitting in Dara's room. Sometimes Grace came to do her homework too; Mary Donnelly looked in and out casually to make sure that the time was not being wasted around the table, but the little O'Neill girl seemed industrious enough.

"Kerry never says. I think he studies quite a bit. This is his last year, he wants to get a good Leaving Certificate."

"And will he?" Dara loved to hear news of the handsome Kerry. "Will he get a lot of Honors do you think?"

"He thinks he'll get four. Or so he says, I don't know." Grace seemed doubtful.

"Why don't you know?"

Grace wondered whether to speak and then decided she would.

"Well, I just said I think he studies a lot, I'm not sure. You see, he goes to these extra lessons."

"The Latin, with Mr. Williams?"

"No, as well as those. He goes into the town twice a week, there's a schoolmaster there and Kerry's meant to be going for math."

"Maths," corrected Dara automatically.

"Yes, well, whichever, he's not going to it. He takes the money from Father and he gets a lift with Paudie Doyle or Brian or someone, but the teacher called last week to say he was sorry that Kerry hadn't showed up for the lessons." Grace shook her head.

"Where was he?"

"That's it, I have no idea; and as it happened, I answered the telephone. Not Miss Hayes, and not Father. So I just said that I'd pass on the message and the man said he just wanted to clear things up because Father had sent him some kind of letter thanking him for his time."

"Oh dear," Dara said.

"So it looks as if Kerry wasn't going at all. But saying that he was." The girls sat in silence to contemplate the enormity of this.

"What *could* he have been doing instead?" Dara hoped he didn't have a girlfriend or anything awful like that.

"I asked him, but he just laughed, said it was great I had headed the guy off at the pass, that was the way he said it. And you know Kerry, Dara, he didn't say any more and he will not say any more."

"Does your father know?"

"No, he doesn't know."

"And Miss Hayes, she wouldn't . . ."

"No, I have a feeling that even if she did know she wouldn't . . ."

"Well then, it's all right." Dara was always optimistic.

"I suppose so." Grace was less sure.

Tommy Leonard told Michael that the Lourdes fund for Mrs. Ryan was getting huge now. There was going to be enough for someone else to go with her. People were wondering who it would be. Would it be Mr. Ryan? Or would one of the children get to go? Imagine Lourdes, in France. Imagine being there.

"Do you really think Our Lady came there? She did, didn't she?" Michael was very anxious to have it confirmed. If Our Lady hadn't, if it had all been some kind of misunderstanding, then there would be no chance for Mam.

"I suppose she must have," Tommy said. "I mean, it would be the kind of place you'd go, France."

Michael agreed.

Tommy said that Maggie Daly was often afraid that Our Lady might come to Mountfern, like she came to Fatima. Maggie didn't look up into trees in case she saw her.

"Why doesn't she want to see her?" Michael was interested. "I mean, if she came here you'd want to *see* her."

"Maggie thinks that you'd be martyred if you saw her, it's what always happens," Tommy said.

"Poor Maggie, she's always worrying," said Michael sympathetically.

"Not like Kitty. Kitty was off on the back of a motorbike with Kerry O'Neill." Tommy loved a bit of excitement.

"Kerry's not old enough to have a motorbike, is he?"

"Oh, Kerry's old enough for anything, he took it out of Jack Coyne's yard and brought it back secretly, and he and Kitty went off miles on it."

"How do you know?"

"Maggie told me. Did she not tell you?"

"No. I wonder why," Michael said.

* * *

"Why didn't you tell me all about Kerry and the motorbike and everything?" Dara was furious with Maggie.

"I—I don't know. It was a secret," Maggie stammered.

"If it was a secret, Maggie Daly, why did you tell Tommy Leonard?"

"I don't know."

"Oh, you don't know, you don't know," Dara blazed. "You're so boring, Maggie. You don't know anything, you have nothing to say."

"I know," Maggie said wretchedly.

There were Halloween games in Ryan's kitchen. Snap apple with everyone's hands tied behind their backs and the apple hanging from a string in the middle of the room. And bobbing for apples in the sink of water, and trying to pick up the sixpence in your teeth from the floor.

Carrie loved the fun of it, and John Ryan came in from the pub occasionally.

Rachel Fine looked on; she had been seeing to Kate's new room and was in and out of the house a lot. The Whites were there, bitterly disputing whose turn it was to play, and Tommy Leonard was there.

"Where's Maggie?" Tommy asked at one point.

"I didn't ask her," said Dara. "I forgot. Like she forgets sometimes."

Dara's face was set and cross. She was very annoyed that Maggie had not told her about her sister's carrying on. And she was even more annoyed to hear about Kerry O'Neill off gallivanting on a borrowed motorbike.

"I'll run down for her," Michael said. "She'd be upset. I'll just go to Daly's now."

"I'll come with you," Grace offered.

Dara felt that she had been too mean. She would go herself for Maggie. But it was too late. Michael and Grace had run off.

They came back later without her.

"Her mother said she had a cold, she was in bed."

"Oh well then, it wouldn't have mattered anyway," Dara said airily. But in her heart she felt ashamed of herself. And she felt that Maggie didn't really have a cold.

* * *

Grace was very nice to Maggie. She insisted too that Maggie come with them on the day that Patrick O'Neill drove some of the children in on what he called an official visit to Mrs. Ryan in the hospital.

The twins were delighted to show their mother off to Liam, Jacinta, Tommy and Maggie, and Kate was touched to see the small crowd around the bed.

"There's a small fortune in the Lourdes fund, Mrs. Ryan, you'll be able to take the whole family with you," Tommy said enthusiastically.

"My goodness, isn't that generous? But if anyone's going it should be other invalids, don't you think?" Kate said.

"Mrs. Williams has a broken arm," Jacinta suggested.

"You don't go to Lourdes with a broken arm, eejit, you have to have much worse." Liam looked half fearfully at Kate.

"Oh, I think you can go with anything, really," Kate said, trying to make light of it.

"Now." Jacinta was triumphant. "And Mrs. Williams is always very nice, giving us things out of her garden. She should be one of the first to go."

"She is a Protestant of course," Tommy said doubtfully.

"Not to mention a vicar's wife," Kate said, trying to keep her face straight.

"It might convert her to the real faith, though, if she was taken there," Maggie suggested.

"Particularly if her arm was cured." Patrick O'Neill laughed.

He shooed the children out of the hospital room and told them there would be lemonade and biscuits.

"You're marvelous to bring them all in to see me," Kate said. She felt easy and relaxed talking to the big American.

"I love playing the big guy," he mocked himself.

"No, you don't, not at all. You're very fatherly to them all. My twins tell me how kind you've been up at the lodge, teaching them chess and Scrabble and spending the time playing with them, a busy man like you."

She smiled at him warmly.

"They're very easy to like, your children," he sighed.

"Well, aren't yours also?" She was genuinely surprised.

"Grace is."

"Fathers and sons always have friction. It's a known thing."

"John doesn't."

"You should hear him with Eddie."

"Kate, I know you'll forgive my saying this, but most of the Western world has some kind of friction with Eddie at some time or another. No, my case is a bit different."

He looked very strained somehow.

"Would it help to tell me about it?"

"Someday, maybe. Yes, it might help a lot. But not just now. I have a gang of people who were promised refreshments, I can't go back on that. And you'll be back home to us soon, isn't that great?"

He seemed genuinely delighted.

"In a couple of weeks," Kate said. "Then it will be as before."

His eyes rested on her for a moment. "It will not be as before, Kate. But please God it will be a good life." He had so much concern in his voice that it quivered a little.

Kate swallowed and gave him a smile.

They didn't say any more because there wasn't any need.

Dara got a postcard from Kerry O'Neill from the town near his school.

"We are here for a half day, they took us to see a castle on a river. The river is brown and muddy, I think it's nothing compared to the Fern. Glad to hear your mother is coming home soon. Hope to see you all in Mountfern during the Christmas holidays. Kind wishes to all, Kerry."

Dara hugged it to her and knew every word, not only every word but how every letter of each word was formed.

"Just tell me straight out, Maggie, no dithering, did Kitty get a card from Kerry O'Neill too? Just a yes or a no would do."

"No. There was no card from Kerry for Kitty. I can tell you that."

Maggie spoke firmly. Because what she said was true. There had been no postcard for her sister. But Kitty had been looking very cheerful, and there were letters from time to time, which were not discussed. And they did have a postmark of the county where Kerry's school was. But it would be foolish to enter into that kind of speculation. Maggie never wanted to draw things on them. And she had been asked specifically about postcards, nothing else.

Maggie was glad when Dara took her arm. It would have been stupid to upset Dara over something that might not even be true. Kitty could have been getting letters from anyone.

"I hope Mrs. Ryan will like the way I run things," Mary Donnelly said doubtfully.

"Why wouldn't she?" John was unused to Mary in an insecure role.

"She's the mistress of this house, it will be hard for her coming back after five months and seeing another woman in her place."

"But hasn't she told you over and over how delighted she is with you, and all you've done for us?" John was bewildered. Mary had been a visitor several times to Kate in the hospital. They had gotten on very well.

"But her coming home, and to that grand room, it will be hard for her not being in total charge again. If you'd like me to go I'd quite understand."

"Mary, we'd die if you went." John was alarmed. "You couldn't go, not now that she's coming back at last. Please don't think of leaving. Is it that you think she'd be giving you orders? Because Kate's not like that. She'll be only too glad for things to go on the way they are. You'll be happy here. Please don't go."

"I'm very happy here, Mr. Ryan. It's very nice, it's the first place I ever thought of as home, and it's a place where people don't make your life a torture for you."

"But who would make your life a torture for you. Ever?"

"My mother did, my colleagues at the school. The other women around where I lived."

John was at a loss for words.

"Well," he said eventually, aware that it wasn't enough.

"So what I say is that Mrs. Kate Ryan, if she had to be married and evidently she had, could have done far worse for herself with the husband and three sons that she found."

John knew he would never hear such praise again.

"Thank you," he said very seriously. "I hope we will always be able to have your trust, my sons and I."

Fergus had found Mary a surprising ally when he was trying to teach John to drive. She had urged the two of them to go out as often as possible, saying that she could well keep an eye on the bar. It never occurred to her that Fergus might have any work to do himself, so she was always putting forward unlikely hours like 11 a.m. as good for a quick lesson.

As it happened the little girl Deirdre he had gotten for the office was every bit as reliable as Kate said she would be. She was always able to tell a caller that Mr. Slattery had gone out on urgent business with a client, and she would take all the details. Somehow, like her father, she gave off a look of utter secrecy. You felt that she would survive well under torture, rather than reveal the most trivial of business.

And she wasn't telling lies, she explained to Fergus. After all, Mr. Ryan was a client, and teaching him to drive was important business.

It took twenty lessons, and then John felt confident enough to drive all on his own into the hospital. This, too, was a secret and a surprise for Kate. Several times he nearly blurted it out, and Rachel Fine nearly let it slip as well.

Then together Fergus and John went to Jack Coyne and put it to him squarely: he was to supply the soundest second-hand car in the world. Not just the country, but the world.

It was to be ready and roadworthy and shining clean on the morning of Friday November 23, for that was the day it would be driven into the town by John Ryan, and he was going to pick up his wife and bring her home to Mountfern.

They all wanted to go, all the children. John said there would be no room in the car. But they wanted to see her face when she saw him driving, that was part of the fun.

Very well, they went with Paudie Doyle as usual, they drove in convoy. Fergus first with Sheila Whelan, then John in the Vauxhall, and then the four Ryan children speechless with excitement in Paudie Doyle's Austin.

There were a lot of tears in the hospital, and Geraldine the nurse said she would miss Kate more than any other patient.

People in wheelchairs came out to say goodbye, and in her own wheelchair she went to say a word to people who weren't even able to move.

She said she'd be in and out of the hospital for treatment.

All the time she thought she was going to be in Paudie Doyle's Austin.

"Where will all the children fit?" she asked Rachel.

"Hush, wait, wait."

Kate knew something was up but she could never have believed anything as splendid as the sight of her husband drawing up in the big black Vauxhall.

Both her hands went up to her mouth as she saw him at the wheel. "Glory be to God, he'll kill himself," she said, and then they all cheered.

John Ryan got out with a flourish. "Here's your coach, Katy Ryan,

and your coachman come to take you home and anywhere in the
world you want to go."

In a blur she saw the children's faces in front of her. The twins
were struggling with what looked like a banner and Kate saw it had a
welcome-home message on it. Eddie and Declan looked faintly mutinous as if they had wanted to share in the banner but had not been
allowed to have any part of it.

John had learned to drive, this was their car, he kept saying it. In
the confusion it was hard to take in, they had a family car now. The
children were racing around it in excitement, Rachel Fine was trying
to line them up so that she could take a picture.

John had learned how to drive a car! They could maybe go off for a
day without having to ask Jack Coyne or Fergus or Paudie Doyle.
How had he learned to do that? Were there any more surprises and
could she cope with them?

"I'm only crying because I'm so happy," she said into Declan's
tousled head. He had run to throw his arms around her when he saw
the tears.

"*I* wanted to have a welcome home," he snuffled.

"But you have a welcome home for me," she protested. "Isn't all
this lovely? It's the best welcome I could have."

"I wanted to put *my* name," he said, fists digging into his eyes still.
"They wouldn't let me"—a hate-filled glance at the twins.

"But you can do your own when we get back, when we're back in
Mountfern. Tell me, Declan, Eddie, am I really going back or is it a
dream?"

Eddie took it on himself to explain the realities of the situation.
"It's real enough," he said grudgingly, pleased to have been singled
out to define things.

Kate put her hands out to the twins and their banner. "Let you
both hold it high up there so that Rachel can get it into the picture,"
she said.

Her eyes told the twins that the banner was something that had
touched her so much she hardly dared speak. She sat with her hands
holding theirs tightly as the picture was taken.

And then they moved her to the car. She was near to hysteria as
they lifted her into the front seat.

"Don't tell me you can really drive this, John Ryan," she gasped.
And then out the window to the nurses: "Listen, don't give my room
away, I'll be back with more injuries in half an hour."

But the pride as she sat beside her husband in their own car was shining out like a beacon.

The entourage would follow them, Fergus with Sheila as his passenger, Rachel in her own car, and the Ryan children traveling for the last time in Paudie Doyle's car.

A rug had been placed over Kate's knees, and she sat straight and proud like a queen in the front of the second-hand Vauxhall that Jack Coyne had found as the bargain of the century.

When Rachel turned aside so that nobody would see her brushing away the tears, she saw that the nice nurse and the lawyer were doing the very same thing, wiping their eyes at the sight of so much delight.

Mountfern never forgot the day that Kate Ryan came home from the hospital. Years later they could remember every detail of that evening.

It had been arranged that the bar remain open as usual, with Mary Donnelly serving. Sheila Whelan was brought in as well, in case there would be extra people there pretending to be having a drink but in reality waiting to see the return of the invalid.

There was a great cry that they were coming when the car was reported to have come in view of the Rosemarie hair salon, and Rita Walsh was out waving from the salon doorstep. Loretto Quinn ran up from her shop, and Brian Doyle ran over the bridge to be there too.

The procession went through the bar, where old men got off stools and shook hands, unable to say the words. They were relieved she was back, and stricken to see her still so pale and sitting awkwardly in a wheelchair.

Carrie was excited, in a new navy dress with a white collar, and she ran in and out of the kitchen a dozen times asking Mary when would she serve the tea. A dozen times Mary replied that she should ask Mrs. Ryan.

But Kate was beyond listening to any subtleties like this. There was so much to admire.

Why had nobody told her that the whole place had been repainted? And the steps, all those steps—one down here and one up there—had gone. That must have been huge work, leveling everything.

It *was* a big undertaking, John Ryan agreed, as if he had done it himself. All they had done was stand back and use the back doors while Patrick's men were withdrawn from work on the hotel to do a job on it.

Then there was the room. Kate couldn't believe it. Walls of light green, huge glass doors framed by green flowery curtains. The big bed was white, with a green and white cover. All around the room there was a broad white shelf like a counter, almost. The wheelchair would fit under it, and there were magazines, sewing things, books, files laid out at intervals to suggest activities for Kate. One section of the shelf was a dressing table. It had a mirror and lights around it like a film star would have in a dressing room.

The bathroom was huge. Rachel called it the dressing room. It had huge presses for Kate's clothes, on rails that could be lowered so that she could reach them and choose what to wear. There were drawers that moved in and out silently, effortlessly. Not like the drawers that stuck and had to be pushed and pulled. The bath had a seat, and a shower, the lavatory had rails. But it wasn't like the hospital bathroom, all white and clinical. It was soft green colors, with big fluffy green towels and bath salts in a big green glass jar.

In her life Kate had never seen anything so elegant. And it was hers. It wasn't something she was looking idly at in a magazine.

They crowded around, Fergus and Brian Doyle, Rachel and Loretto, John in the middle and the children on the edges pushing in and out to see her face.

And that's how they all remembered it because that was when the news came in from the bar where the wireless was on. The news that President Kennedy had been shot in Dallas.

They all went slowly toward the bar to wait for more news. The phone kept ringing, people wanted to tell other people. There was television up in the Grange and some of those with cars said they would drive there and see if they could find out any more. Anything was better than not knowing what had happened to him—the president who had waved at them all in Dublin only five months ago.

"It'd be better for him if he died, poor bastard," Brian Doyle said in the middle of a silence. "Young man like that stuck in a wheelchair for the rest of his life. He couldn't take it, he'd go off his head."

It was a long minute before anyone realized what he had said. They were all thinking of John F. Kennedy, not about Mrs. Ryan, a younger woman stuck in a wheelchair for the rest of her life.

Then Brian Doyle noticed a couple of faces crumpling up and remembered.

"But of course they can do great things now," he said desperately. Nobody helped him out.

"Great things altogether," said Brian, wishing he were dead and six feet under the clay.

Chapter XV

The spring of 1964 was a wet one in Mountfern. The river flooded its banks twice, and there were even photographers sent from Dublin to take a picture of the Fern in flood. The trees hung heavy over River Road and let loose what felt like waterfalls when anyone shook them.

The children's raft broke loose from its moorings and bobbed down to the big bridge in the town, where it remained battering itself against the side.

The schools smelled of wet clothes and everyone had colds.

People still managed to go out for a drink, however, and often the wet weather meant that there was more custom than ever in Ryan's bar.

In her light room with its soft green colors Kate Ryan sat and spent the first spring in a wheelchair.

She would have gone mad, she realized, if she had not got the side garden to look out on through the big glass doors. She was the first to know when snowdrops came, when crocuses started to open and when the primroses and cowslips began in a yellow corner that she had never noticed before.

Jaffa the big orange cat looked out longingly, waiting for the days to come when the sun would shine and she could sit and sleep on the old stone walls. Sitting still in her chair, Kate Ryan scratched the cat's ears and told Jaffa that for her the day would come. She sighed a lot and wondered had it rained like this always but because she had been so busy she had never noticed it?

Little by little the people of Mountfern came to accept that this would be Kate Ryan's life. They ceased to shake their heads over the sudden accident, the one quick blow that would leave her forever paralyzed. Once people had seen the bright attractive room and the handsome dark woman in her chair, laughing and cheerful for their visit . . . then that was how she remained in their minds. They didn't tell each other any more about how swift she had been, and how light running up and down the steps of Mr. Slattery's office. They talked no longer of the way she ran down River Road like a young girl.

Rachel had found a great roll of green rush matting. She said they should cut it off in lengths and spread it out to make a path over Kate's new carpet. Otherwise people would be afraid to visit her in the room for fear of bringing in mud with them.

Rachel came every day; she had become adept at helping to lift the two white, wasted-looking legs out of the bed and on to the wheelchair. Then she would bend while Kate pulled herself out of bed by putting her arms around Rachel's neck.

She wasn't able to do it with Carrie; the girl was too nervous and might move away. She didn't want to ask Mary Donnelly to help her. It would place too much of an emotional burden on Dara. And she didn't want John to see her like that *every* day. On the mornings when he came in and found her dressed and sitting at some part of the giant desk that went three sides of the room, he could almost believe that things were normal.

The two women had tea and a chat, as if they had been neighbors for many years, as if they had been young married women together and shared all the years of childbirth and watching toddlers. Neither of them ever felt it was odd that they had only met on one day before they were in the roles of hospital patient and visitor. It was as if they had always known the easy companionship and the undemanding shorthand of friendship.

Kate could tell of her unreasonable dislike of Mary Donnelly, Rachel of her irritation with Marian Johnson.

"He has no interest in Marian Johnson," Kate assured her friend. "She's much more suitable for this life . . . the life he wants."

"Oh, but no, you mustn't think that. Can you imagine him loving

her? Even loving her a little bit?" Kate shook her head at the idea of
it.

"He can't love *me* much, either. One day I'll accept that I'm not
part of his plan. Then I'll be free."

"But you'd be very lonely," Kate said.

Rachel smiled, relieved. This was the counsel she had wanted to
hear.

"Will Mrs. Fine be here for long?" Dara asked.

She had gotten into the habit of sitting with her mother as soon as
she came back from school, and the others agreed without ever saying it that this was Dara's time.

"I don't know, my love, I don't ask her. Do you mind if we ask her
for meals now and then? It's terrible for her up in that awful hotel all
the time."

Dara agreed immediately. "Oh we must ask her as much as possible, she'd start talking to herself if she had to stay in the Slieve
Sunset all the time."

Kate laughed. Dara had become so grown up, she was able to talk
to her much more freely than before. The months must have made a
huge difference to the girl, living here in the pub without her mother,
unsure of what was going to happen and if Kate would ever come
home. It was a very noticeable change. Before the accident Dara had
been a tomboy, dying to get away from the house, to escape any kind
of involvement or conversation, sighing at grown-up conversation,
and flinching away from any confidences. And now, that was all gone.
She seemed older than Michael too, while once she had waited for
his every move before she decided what to do herself. She was techni-
cally a woman, and Dara already felt the stirrings of . . . well if not
love . . . at least hero worship. Kate had noticed how her face
changed when she spoke of Kerry. That little crush must have developed since the previous summer.

Kate felt she could tell Dara things that sometimes might seem a
bit petty when she told them to John. Maybe it was a conspiracy kind
of thing between women . . . she hoped she didn't overdo it. Dara
seemed to approve of Rachel coming to the house. Her connection
with Patrick O'Neill was never mentioned; Kate was far too loyal to
bring up the matter herself, but she felt that Dara instinctively had
some understanding of it.

* * *

"Will Mary Donnelly be here for much longer?"

Kate tried to look concerned and kind. "I've no idea, she must suit herself." A sharp note had come into her voice.

"Why don't you like her, Mam? She's very helpful."

"I know, I know. What do you mean I don't like her? Don't be silly, Dara."

"But you don't. Why? It's not as if she's after Dad or anything. She hates men, she even hates them when they're only Michael's age."

"She's so childish to be going on with all that kind of rambling out of her," Kate snapped.

"Is that why you don't like her, because she's against men?"

"No, I'll tell you the truth, I don't like her because she's doing what I should be doing, she's standing there serving people in the bar and not talking to them when I would be talking to them pleasantly, she's going down to Loretto Quinn and beating her down over the price of this and that instead of paying her. She has the kitchen clean and tidy, better maybe than I'd keep it. She has Leopold changed beyond recognition. But she has Carrie terrified of her, and crying if she breaks a saucer. She has the sheets clean on the beds but she has a smell of boiling in the house from Monday to Saturday."

Dara looked at her mother open-mouthed.

"And mostly I don't like her because she has two good legs that start at the top and go down to her feet and she can put one of them in front of the other and walk. If she's in a hurry she can put one in front of the other quickly and she can run. She doesn't have to drag herself by her arms and strain and stretch and pull and at the end of it be just a few inches toward the edge of the bed. I suppose *that's* why I don't like her."

Dara still couldn't speak.

"Because I'm a mean old pig," Kate added as an explanation.

Dara flew into her arms, literally hurled herself at Kate.

"You're *not* a mean old pig, it's the unfairest thing in the world that you should be like this. I told Sister Laura that God must have a very cruel streak in him to let you be just in the path of that machine."

Dara sobbed into her mother's shoulder as Kate patted the dark hair and the heaving slender body.

"What did Sister Laura say about God's mean streak?" she asked gently.

Dara drew away from her for a moment and looked at her with a tear-stained face.

"She said that Almighty God had a purpose in everything, and that we couldn't see it now. In years to come we'll see it. Do you think we will?"

Kate held the hands of her daughter and spoke slowly. "I don't know. That's the truth. I don't know. If it was something that might be cured, *then* perhaps all these months and even a couple of years in a wheelchair might have a purpose."

"But . . ." Dara waited anxiously.

"But because it's *not* going to be cured, and I will never walk again, I find it hard to believe that God has a purpose. God *can't* believe that I'm a better citizen, a better Christian to him stuck in this chair. Maybe it's just that he knew I might be a desperate sinner if I was out of the chair so he keeps me in it. That could be his purpose, I suppose." She half smiled.

"But you wouldn't have any sins would you, Mam, in or out of the wheelchair?" Dara could never imagine that grown-ups committed sin anyway, they were allowed to do everything just because they were grown up, it seemed impossible to know what was left except murder and worshipping idols which Mam wouldn't be likely to be at.

"I suppose the biggest sin I have is not accepting what God has sent me. That *is* a sin, you know, Dara. I'm going to have to confess it to Father Hogan when he comes today, and I'm going to tell him also that I don't want to go to Lourdes. That's going to be even harder."

Dara's eyes were filled with tears again. "You *must* go to Lourdes, Mam, you must, it's the only hope. That's what Michael and I say all the time. There have been miracles and you could be one of them."

"No, darling Dara, I'm not going, there's no miracle for me there. If Our Lady wants to cure my spine she can do it in Mountfern, I am not going to spend all those people's money going there, and have all their hopes disappointed. That's it. I didn't mean to tell you so suddenly, I was going to put it gently, maybe even differently. But you're such a joy to me and such a comfort, I treat you like a grown-up daughter instead of a child."

The tears had dried and Dara was as pleased as anything. "Well, I'm going to have to look after you properly if I'm a grown-up. If you get your way about Lourdes can we have your word that you'll be sensible about Mary Donnelly and be civil to her in case she packs her bags and leaves?"

Kate burst into peals of laughter. Dara's voice was such a good imitation of her own when she was being bossy. Even her face had the same look.

"I'll be so civil, it will frighten you," she laughed.

"There's no need to over-do it, Mam," Dara said disapprovingly.

John was taking a stroll with his daughter along the river bank.

"I'm glad that Rachel is here," he said. "Your mam likes her a lot. It will take her mind off things."

"Do you think her mind's on things a lot?" Dara wanted to know.

"It's so hard to know. She says she's almost forgotten her life before the wheelchair. She doesn't even dream of herself as being able to walk anymore." He sounded sad.

"Don't get all depressed, Daddy, she hates that more than anything."

"I wouldn't be depressed in front of her, Dara. But Lord, on my own or with you, can't I let the mask drop a bit?"

They walked on companionably past the people fishing, careful not to disturb them by idle chatter. They were both remembering some of the scenes when a red-faced and furious Kate would shout and cry that she wanted no sympathy, no sad faces around her. She had even thrown a jug of milk and had broken plates and saucers, flinging them at John when he was in what he considered a gentle and concerned mood. Kate had taken it as defeatist and said it made her worse.

"I can't even bloody walk, you can all do everything, so for Christ's sake stop moaning and saying, 'Poor Mam, Poor Kate'. What is the point of that? I'd prefer to be dead. Dead, dead and buried long ago than to be poor Kate, poor Mam."

She had frightened them so much they had rung for Dr. White. He came to see her, and the family waiting outside got little consolation from him as he came out.

"Nothing wrong with Mrs. Ryan except that she is paralyzed," he said bluntly. "And that she is surrounded by people who don't give her any reason or point in living. They call the doctor if she shows any bit of fire and life, and their way of supporting her is to offer her pity. Good evening."

They never forgot it. Even Declan and Eddie knew that the mood was to be optimistic. Mam wanted to believe that things were getting better all the time. That's what gave her the energy to drag herself from bed to chair, from chair to lavatory or bath stool, and to push herself to the garden or the kitchen or the pub. If she didn't believe that things were getting better all the time, she wouldn't even sit up in the mornings.

Dara linked her father as they turned to come back along the road. "What do you think *really*, Dad, about the hotel? Is it going to take away all our business? Mary Donnelly says it could be the ruination of us."

"Mary, for all that we are blessed to have her, is wrong about almost everything."

Dara looked at her father affectionately. "It would be a terrible thing to hate men, not to see them as friends."

"I think it would be a pity all right," John agreed. "I think you'd lose out on it in the long run. And on the same subject, what's a beautiful girl like you doing on a summer evening walking the river bank with her old father? Why aren't the Tommy Leonards and the Liam Whites and the others of Mountfern beating me out of the way? Tell me that."

"Because they're all eejits, Daddy, and you're not."

"That's nice to hear. But isn't there anybody who isn't an eejit? Anybody at all?"

"Not a one." Dara was airy about it. It was just a fact. "I might be hard to please, like Mary Donnelly, or just a bit slow in seeing my chances. I keep dreaming of course, that something marvelous would happen, like that beautiful Kerry O'Neill would notice me."

"Would you like that?"

"I'd *love* it, but I'd have to fight the whole town for him. Grace says he and his father don't get on."

"Nobody gets on with their father," said John, patting Dara's arm.

"Stop fishing, Daddy," she said.

"I think Declan's turning into a proper hooligan," John said to Kate.

"God, he must be really bad if you say a word against him." Kate was surprised to hear such criticism. "What has he done now?"

"He hasn't *done* anything, it's just that he has the instincts of a gangster. He goes around punching things for no reason."

"What kind of things?" Kate was alarmed.

"I don't know, the hen house for one thing, he nearly knocked it down."

"I could knock that down myself even in this thing." Kate gave a disgusted wave at her wheelchair.

"You could knock the house down in that chair, you look so terrifying when you head for us," John laughed. "No, he just seems to tear things apart automatically without even knowing he's doing it."

"He's upset."

"We're all upset," her husband said.

"No we're not, we're fine. He's just a baby. Send him in to me when he gets back. I'll play with him for a bit."

"He'll probably have you on the floor."

"It's just being the youngest . . . poor little fellow."

"I was the youngest, I'll have you remember, and look at how well I turned out."

"You did, too." She looked at him admiringly. John Ryan had lost some of his beer belly, he stood more erect and, despite new lines on his face, he looked a younger man than he had been at the beginning of the summer.

Kate found herself turning to him for a lot more than just physical assistance. He had been able to manage in some kind of fashion without her for almost half a year. There were a lot of areas where she had to look to him now for advice.

"Do you think it's going to affect them all?" She spoke in a small voice. "You know, will it change their lives altogether . . . all this?" Again she waved in exasperation at her legs and the chair.

"No, I think they'll be less affected by it than we expect. You know how adaptable children are, they get used to any old thing after a while." He spoke gently and lovingly to take the possible hint of indifference out of his words. "I think that now you're home they'll all get on with their lives. Normally—almost embarrassingly normally."

"I hope so." She closed her eyes.

"Kate, we've been through all this before. What makes you start worrying now?"

"I expect hearing that Declan's going around kicking things, and I think maybe I treat Dara as too much of a grown-up. I've taken her childhood away from her."

"No, no." He was soothing. "She's flattered that you talk to her as an equal. No, don't worry about that."

"And Eddie?"

"He's with a gang of toughies, he hasn't time to think about anything except walls to be climbed, orchards to be robbed, jam jars to be discovered in far places so that he'll collect enough to go to the pictures."

"So that leaves Michael. He's too quiet these days, isn't he?"

"He is, and I was going to say that if you don't think it's the act of a madman I was going to ask him to go off fishing for a day with me. We keep telling people the Fern is full of pike. Why don't we go and see is it true?"

She reached over and touched his hand. "Do, of course, and tell Michael I love him."

"I won't tell him anything of the sort, he'd knock me into the river."

"No, I mean say it without saying it."

"He knows, but I'll say it without saying it anyway."

"Will you come out fishing with me on Saturday?"

"*Fishing!* In this weather? We'd be frozen, and what would we catch?"

"We spend our time telling people that the Fern is alive with pike all year round. Shouldn't we see are we right?"

"God, Dad, it'd be miserable out there. Why would you never ask me a thing like that in the summer, I'd love it in the summer."

"I'd love it in the summer, too, son, but the pub wouldn't be half empty like it is this weather."

"But why, why now?"

"I wanted us to have a day out—a chat even."

"What have I done?"

"Oh Jesus God, you haven't done anything. It's great when your son thinks the only reason you're going to ask him out for a treat is to attack him, punish him."

"But you never ask me out," Michael complained with what John had to admit was some justification.

"And I don't seem to make too good a fist of it when I do. All right, if it's not fishing what would you like to do on Saturday after lunch?"

"I suppose the pictures are out?"

"You suppose correctly."

"Could we do the book?" His eyes lit up.

John genuinely didn't know what he meant.

"The book, Dad, Mr. O'Neill's book, you haven't done it for ages. I mean, take out the boxes of papers and things . . ." His voice trailed away. John was just standing there with a blank expression. "I mean, you *are* going to do it . . . to finish it?"

"What? Oh yes. Yes."

Michael looked relieved. "Well then, could we look at some of the research and I could help you like I did before?"

"Yes. Certainly."

"Is anything wrong, would you prefer to go fishing? I suppose if we wrapped up . . ."

"No. No, you're a very good fellow . . . no."

"So have you been thinking about doing the book . . . or maybe after everything . . . you sort of didn't want to?"

"I think you're a genius, that's the very thing we'll do on Saturday. We'll take the boxes upstairs out of everyone's way and you can indeed help me. What with everything that happened I never found a moment to get down to it again, and it's been there at the back of my mind . . ."

He beamed at Michael, but the boy had the feeling that there was some sort of struggle taking place. His father had been deciding there in front of him whether to go on writing the story of Fernscourt for Grace's father.

"It's not as if it would make Mam any better by not doing it," he said suddenly, and his father gripped him on the shoulder.

"That's the truth, Michael. We must never forget that."

"Well, how much purgatory did he give you?" Rachel asked when Father Hogan had left and she was allowed to come in to see Kate.

"It's not purgatory he gives me, you heathen, it's penance, it's to keep me out of purgatory."

"It's all nonsense, you're a saint already. Did you tell him about Lourdes?"

"Yes, he hated it, poor man, but he's going to help me. He said to put it a different way, say that I'd like it to go to a parish fund to send others there, get even more money, and not to dwell too much on the fact that I'm not going to take it up myself. It might hurt people or offend them."

Rachel nodded.

"You look restless. Is anything wrong?"

"Hard to hide anything from you, Kate. I've been thinking, I should go back. Back to the States."

"You don't call it home, you don't say back home."

"It doesn't feel like home, not this year."

"Maybe because you are in the middle of moving . . . all these plans about the hotel, and what it will look like and what will be here. No wonder the office in New York doesn't seem real. But your flat— think of that. It's going to be like paradise compared to the Slieve Sunset."

"Yes."

"You don't have to go, you could stay here with us."

"No, I have to go. I'm only inventing work here . . . and . . ."

"But isn't he glad that you like the place so much, feel so at home here in Mountfern? I'd have thought he'd have been delighted with you."

"I thought that too."

"Whyever not? What did he say?"

"He just wondered why I was spending so long here. I stupidly said something about getting the feel of the place. He was extremely curt with me."

Kate reached for Rachel's hand. It was hardly credible that this elegant woman with the wine suit trimmed with suede, with a silk blouse which must have cost a fortune—a cream silk with a floppy bow —should be as awkward as a child when it came to the great Patrick O'Neill. No sixteen-year-old could have been more distraught.

"You'll come back here again, it's not just a job." Kate soothed her as she had soothed her daughter earlier in the day.

"But the message is loud and clear. It will never be my home."

Rachel had never been so careless of her make-up, her silk blouse or the fine wool rug that lay on Kate's lap. She cried as she had cried in Yiddish to her mother years and years ago when the children on the block had called her a little Jew girl.

Each time Kate got a letter from Rachel she wrote back that very day. That way their letters stayed in order. They weren't crossing in the mail; they could ask and reply.

Rachel must have written just as quickly.

They learned to depend on each other in a way they would never have believed possible. Rachel wrote about working for O'Neill Enterprises in New York, though finding that the heart had gone from the business since Patrick O'Neill was many miles away in an Irish village.

Kate found it a great ease to be able to tell someone how boringly well Mary Donnelly ran the house, and how irritating it was to be told a dozen times a day, perfectly accurately, that they were blessed to have found her. It was true, which made it worse! Kate said it was a sneaky relief to be able to tell Rachel that if she heard one more Mountfern person say that Mary Donnelly was a genius she would go berserk and race around the pub in her wheelchair knocking over tables and pouring drinks onto the floor.

Rachel wrote that she had to put up with the insults and veiled triumph of Gerry Power, who had said in one hundred different ways that he was sorry it didn't work out for Rachel in Ireland. In one hundred different ways she had deliberately misunderstood him and said with a broad smile that it had all worked out magnificently and he *must* go over someday himself and see the wonderful place that Patrick had bought for himself.

Kate could admit that her new-found all-girls-together relationship with Dara was becoming very rocky, and Rachel could admit that sometimes weeks went by without Patrick telephoning her, even though she stayed in to wait for his calls.

Week after week the two women wrote of their lives, month after month they told of the changes that were happening. Neither really noticed things changing, it was only by looking back over the old letters that each realized how the other's life was moving from one direction to another.

Kate wrote of John more and more as the man who made the decisions, not as the man who was trying to cope. She never said it in so many words but Rachel could read it like a thread in the letters. There was the tale about John and the rough crowd of tinkers who came into the pub. Everyone had feared a fight if he were to throw them out, and a worse one if he were to let them stay. But there had been no fight in Ryan's, the tinkers were served as pleasantly as they could have wished. It was just the number of times that John said how heartbroken he was from Sergeant Sheehan dropping in that sent the band on their way. John had leaned conspiratorially over the counter and said that a man wasn't free to breathe in this day and age without that sergeant coming and poking his nose into what people had in the boots of their cars or on the crossbars of their bicycles. The tinkers, who were practically festooned with pheasants they had taken illegally from Coyne's wood, were on their way, with grateful glances at John and vaguely dispiriting promises that they would return.

Rachel read how John Ryan now had poems published by two newspapers, to a total of seven published works, and there was the distinct possibility of an anthology. The history of Fernscourt and its surroundings was proving long and complicated, but there were no pleas to hasten it from the man who had commissioned it, so it was taking its time.

There was the story of John and the man trying to sell him an insurance policy: John had refused it and the man had turned ugly. He had said that John must be expecting to come into a big windfall from the Fernscourt insurance people. John had been icy in his dismissal, but the man had retorted that he was only saying what half of Mountfern was saying behind his back. Kate had been upset but John had shrugged and said that a village had to have something to talk about, and since they hadn't had a two-headed calf born recently, nor a cure at the may bush, nor even a visit from a politician, they had to fill in the long winter evenings somehow.

Kate read about art galleries that Rachel had visited, and a course of ten lectures that she had been attending. She heard of trips taken by train to cities in the United States which were further apart than the whole width of Ireland.

She knew that Rachel had seen a lot of movies and heard too little from Patrick, and that she was now considered a world authority on Ireland by the people in her circle.

Without Rachel having to write it, Kate knew there were a lot of empty nights.

Without Kate having to put it down on paper, Rachel knew that Kate sometimes found the imprisonment in her chair almost more than she could bear. The frustration seeped across the Atlantic in spite of herself. The days when it seemed to rain and rain and her lovely side garden with all the plants that she was meant to admire from her green room had turned into a mire of mud.

There were the times when it was obvious that Kate Ryan might in fact explode if she hadn't this safety valve, this marvelous friend she could write to and explain everything as it was.

Like how irritating Dara could be, how downright maddening her own lovely daughter had become.

Dara had lost her unruly look, Kate said in these letters, she had become graceful in a way that was very hard to describe. She had also become almost impossible again. Everything was a shrug, a sulk and a sigh.

The record player that had been a gift from Grace played high and loud in her room, then the sounds of that dreadful Radio Luxembourg and its awful music replaced the record player.

Kate wrote in a matter-of-fact way about Patrick. She told how he was working night and day, and had little time for socializing. She knew this would please Rachel on the other side of the Atlantic Ocean. It was also totally true.

Judy Byrne, who came twice a week to do the exercises that were meant to strengthen Kate's arms, and improve the muscles that would pull her from chair to bed to bath and back, often let slip how she had invited Mr. O'Neill to this concert, or that exhibit, but never had he been able to accept. Judy shook her head sadly as she pummeled Kate, and made her repeat again and again the tiresome and stressful movements, saying that there hardly seemed to be any point in having all that money and power if you were never able to enjoy yourself.

Marian Johnson had said more or less the same thing: How sad it was that Patrick O'Neill didn't get more cooperation from everyone so that he would have some leisure time, poor man. Marian would tinkle in that *unwise* little-girl laugh and say that he had been simply desolate not to have been able to go to the hunt ball, or the charity dinner or whatever social ruse she had tried yet again in vain.

Life went on as before in the lodge, Kate wrote, or so she thought. Grace was utterly charming, and the more loathsome Dara became the more sweet and endearing did Grace appear to be. She would sit for any length of time talking to Kate, asking her advice, begging to hear stories about Kate's own teenage years. Dara couldn't bear to be in the same room as her mother these days.

Kate had heard some disturbing things about Kerry. That he had been in a game of poker up in Foley's bar, that he had been playing for high stakes with men who should have known better than to play cards with the son of the man who was going to change the face of the town and make their fortunes for them. She didn't tell that to Rachel, since it was only a rumor, no point in worrying her over something that might not be at all likely.

Several times she apologized for the trivia and small-town gossip, and she said she was sure Rachel thought of her as a poor country cousin who was to be pitied for the narrowness of her life.

But as the months went on Kate apologized less. She realized that Rachel did indeed love to hear of the small town where she had felt so much at home. Rachel wrote about how she had glorified Mountfern in her memory now. She had forgotten that there was any rain, any mud or any bad temper. She had begun to think of the terrible Slieve Sunset as a place of worth. As she spent Christmas in the

Catskills the notion of her ever sitting down at a table and having turkey with the Ryans seemed so remote that she wondered how she could ever have considered it as part of her lifestyle.

John realized that without the trade from the site they would be in a poor way. The foremen, the surveyors, the visiting experts of one sort or another came for drinks at all hours of the day. They didn't necessarily drink a great deal but they sat and discussed plans . . . opened out big grey bits of paper, argued over lists of supplies.

It was all much more comfortable for them than the prefab site offices that Brian Doyle had put beside the actual Fernscourt, which was rising very slowly from its foundations. It was Mary who noticed that they bought packets of chips and this was often their only lunch.

"Do you think there'd be a future in sandwiches at all?" she asked Kate.

Kate was annoyed she hadn't thought of it first. Grudgingly she agreed that there might be a small profit in providing something to eat. She arranged to make a dozen sandwiches a day—ham and salad, cheese and home-made chutney. Anything that wasn't eaten would be devoured by the family in the evening.

John was against them at first. Turning the place into some kind of café, he sniffed, not what ordinary men wanted. But when he saw Brian Doyle and the two engineers eating two rounds each the very second day, he changed his tune.

Kate and Mary smiled their first genuine smile of friendship. And Kate said that they might even think of serving soup later on if there seemed to be any demand for it.

Mary nodded her head approvingly. "You're absolutely right," she said. "I think you should get the soup going as soon as possible. Better do something before the Yank takes all the business off you with a smile."

"That's what's going to happen, isn't it?" Kate said.

"Unless we try to fight back," said Mary gruffly. "And we'll have to fight the way he does. Like a man, of all things. Like a dirty, rotten man."

In fact there seemed to be delay after delay in building the hotel. Patrick O'Neill said that if he were a superstitious man he would think that he wasn't really *meant* to build it.

First there was an earth subsidence, not too serious, but serious enough to mean a rethink. And then, expensively, a redoing of a whole wall.

There was the time that all the cattle had gotten in through a hole in a fence and done unimaginable damage to wood that had been stored in an open shed. The hole in the fence was never explained, but was said to be the work of a crowd of kids after school one day. Patrick tried to find out if it had been malicious but Brian Doyle told him that children were the devil incarnate. There was no use looking for malice or virtue in them, they were just bestial by nature.

There was the time that no vehicle seemed able to start or move on the site, and it was discovered that those which didn't have bags of sugar poured into them had water mixed with the petrol. Jack Coyne couldn't be blamed because he was away at Shannon Airport on the day it was all discovered. But there were definitely tales that he had been telling youngsters how to immobilize cars should they ever need to know, and further tales that he had said it would be a real laugh if none of the cars up on the site could move. Nothing could be proved. Those who were most protective of Patrick were those who most wanted to ensure that he stayed. They would never confirm any of his suspicions that there was vandalism and that much of it was directed at him.

Then there was a problem about a farmer who had said he would sell his acre of land and it turned out when the title was investigated that he didn't own the land at all, it had been signed over to his son years ago. The son being a cunning man realized there was capital to be gained and the deliberations delayed the work that should have been underway long back in that particular area.

Patrick wondered whether the bad-tempered attorney Fergus Slattery had anything to do with it, but was reliably informed by Sheila Whelan that the reverse was true. Fergus had refused to act for the mean-minded son on the ground that opportunism was something best left to wily Americans, and that since a fair price had been offered, the normal man should accept a fair price.

Each time Patrick visited Kate Ryan he felt better in his heart. The frailty, the wan look seemed to be less. Or maybe he was only telling himself this.

He liked to sit in her airy green room and talk. Here he was far from the problems that seemed to beset him everywhere else. It was a peaceful room even though it was only yards from a noisy bar. It reminded him of Rachel's apartment, an oasis of calm right in the middle of the mad Manhattan noise. Then he remembered suddenly that it was the same woman who had created both places. He never discussed Rachel although he knew how friendly the two women had become; he spoke no words of his increasing despair over ever finishing his project, his life's dream. Nor of the anonymous letters he had gotten telling him that Irish businessmen could well have developed that site, or even more upsettingly that he was responsible before God and man for Mrs. Ryan being in a wheelchair.

He smiled as he talked. The crinkly lines were still there around his eyes, but Kate thought they had etched a little deeper and there were other lines too. His voice was still cheery and his laugh hearty but some of the evenings they sat and talked she wondered was he forcing his humor and begging his laugh to echo a little more.

Kate suspected that he was a man who had a lot of doubts about the way his life had taken him. She never brought the subject up.

He had accepted her paralysis when she was in the hospital. But it seemed totally out of place in Ryan's pub. He kept looking up expecting her to swing in as she used to behind the counter. It seemed to come as a repeated shock each time he heard the high slow whine the wheelchair made on its approach.

Sometimes she did serve there, if there were friends in. A ramp had been made to a corner wing of the bar where Kate could position herself.

But usually it was that appalling virago Mary Donnelly who looked at him as if he were the devil made into flesh each time he appeared. He had been told that she felt some similar distaste for all men, but he felt singled out for her particular dislike.

Leopold had a new collar. Mary had been at a carnival where they made dog collars with names on them. In a fit of generosity she had bought one with the words Leopold Ryan. The dog had been suitably grateful and seemed pleased with it. He would approach people and arch his neck pathetically, looking like a whipped hound showing off his wounds, but in fact wanting his collar admired.

"We have to have you looking well for Princess Grace," Mary whispered to him.

Dara heard her. "Why don't you like Grace?" she had asked straight out.

"I couldn't like the seed or breed of anyone who would do such harm to your poor mother."

"But it wasn't their fault . . . the accident," Dara cried.

"I don't just mean the accident. I mean the living, taking the living away from her."

"But Mam has a very good life," Dara said, not understanding. "She always says that she hates us not to think of it as a real way of living."

Mary had opened her mouth and closed it again. "That's a fact," she said unexpectedly. "She's a great deal happier than most."

In the hope that it might soothe some of Dara's outbursts Kate suggested that she invite Grace to spend the night with them. They might enjoy chatting together and it would save Grace the long journey back to the Grange.

"Oh, so I *am* allowed to have her to stay now. There was a time when it wasn't suitable."

"I never said that," Kate said.

"No, but Daddy did when you went to the hospital first. It wasn't suitable, he said, because of . . . oh, I don't know why."

Kate sighed. "That was a long time ago, Dara, all those kinds of worries are long behind us now."

"I don't think she'd really want to stay here anyway."

"Whyever not? She always seems happy when she comes to visit."

"Oh, that's just being polite." Dara was lofty.

"The offer is there, if she'd like to come." Kate kept her temper with difficulty.

"She might come, of course," Dara said as if it were all a favor to her mother.

Rachel had written that although she didn't know from personal experience, every other mother of every other thirteen- and fourteen-year-old girl in the entire world told her the same story. And the story had a happy ending. They grew out of it. Kate hoped with all of her heart that Rachel was right.

It's hard to change the habits of a lifetime, and when Deirdre Dunne came across the two young Ryan boys as part of a gang that wrote silly things on the walls of Fernscourt, she said nothing. She just walked past with her eyes ahead of her as if she were slightly wandering in her mind.

The kids, who had hidden when they saw her, breathed with relief and told each other that Deirdre Dunne was as mad as Papers Flynn and Miss Barry and would be no threat to them. Happily they carved out "Yank Go Home" and "This is Ireland not America" with big nails, scratching away.

Deirdre Dunne had grown up on a small farm where the great philosophy had been to say nothing. She had been warned not to say anything since she was a child, and even when the neighboring farmer was known to come back drunk from a market and beat his wife senseless, the same rules had held.

It would sort itself out, she was told, and indeed it had. One day the farmer fell into a ditch on the way home. It was a cold night and he had a weak chest anyway. Deirdre had seen his wife pass the ditch where he lay, and throw more brambles and briars over it in order to make sure that there was even greater delay in finding the body.

Or had she pieced together afterward that this is what the woman had been doing. But like a true Dunne, and the daughter of her taciturn father, she said nothing.

She was almost designed to work in the office of a law firm which dealt in the human everyday business of the community. Sometimes she wondered whether she stood too far back. People like Mr. Slattery and Mrs. Whelan did get involved when they saw things as a matter of right or wrong. Perhaps it was more honorable.

Fergus Slattery was very pleased with Deirdre. A pale girl with sandy hair, she was quiet as a mouse and efficient as one of those huge new computers people were always talking about. She was as discreet as he could have hoped and when a rich farmer left a totally untoward sum to Mrs. Rita Walsh of the Rosemarie hair salon you would never have known from Deirdre's impassive face that it was anything except the norm.

She had high praise for Kate's filing system and was just as adamant that he kept in touch with how it worked. It had fallen into great chaos in the months after Kate's accident and it was a measure of Deirdre's intelligence that she had brought a notebook to the hospital to Kate to ask for confirmation of new decisions she had made.

One of the files that Deirdre had to open was called Katherine Mary Ryan versus O'Neill Enterprises and the International Insurance Society.

PART FOUR

Chapter XVI

The twins were to have a fifteenth birthday party in September. The excitement was intense, there weren't many parties in Mountfern. To be honest none of them had been to a party since they were children. But Kate Ryan had insisted. By letter she and Rachel had decided that something which would concentrate and channel all Dara's energies would be a good idea. Kate didn't suggest the party herself, of course, that way Dara would reject it as some plot. The wish had to come from the twins themselves.

So Kate spoke of the party to everyone else in a sort of sighing voice, saying she supposed now that Dara and Michael were so grown up they would want a party when they were fifteen.

It didn't take long. Carrie wanted to know what they would do at the party, would there be dancing? Loretto Quinn said she'd love to be fifteen again and she thought it was the best age of all.

Grace was asked by Miss Hayes what she was going to wear to the twins' fifteenth birthday party. And Tommy Leonard's father told him that he would have thought that poor John and Kate Ryan would have had more sense than to lash out money entertaining hulking young folk who wouldn't give them a word of thanks for it.

And so Michael and Dara realized that a party was a possibility.

"Where could we be?" Dara wailed. "We can't be in the pub, or in Mam's room, and the kitchen is a mess and the breakfast room is tiny."

"There's no point in asking for a party unless there was somewhere to have it," Michael agreed.

But Kate had that planned too. The big outhouse attached to the pub looked fine from the outside. It was whitewashed and as its only entrance was from the side garden nobody knew what a mess it was inside.

If it were to be cleaned out . . .

They could always use it for something . . .

And it would be ideal for the party.

So John suggested that as a way of earning more pocket money they should all work on it. Even involve their friends if they wanted to. It involved a few days of dragging rubbish off to the dump. There were broken beds, old bits of wood with nails sticking out of them. There was a box of jam jars with spiders in them, and a load of things that had been taken from the other outhouse in the other yard to make room for Mary Donnelly.

On the afternoon that the boys had whitewashed the big room, Jacinta looked around it in admiration.

"It's fabulous looking, it's good enough to have a party in."

And that was it.

They wheedled and begged and cajoled. And pretending an unwillingness, Kate and John gave in. The music was not to be too loud. Everyone was to be well gone home by midnight, the children had to organize the food themselves. There was to be no trick-acting, overexcitement nor people jumping into the river. They agreed to everything and began the preparations.

Kate wrote to Rachel saying that she felt as guilty as anything pulling all these strings but it did seem to be working like a dream. Dara had even hugged her in excitement one day.

She wrote that the invitation list had been assembled and discarded and readjusted more often than anyone could believe; there had never been such a magnificent way of keeping them all totally content.

Grace had all the Beatles records, and Gerry and the Pacemakers and Freddie and the Dreamers, so she would bring those.

Tommy Leonard wondered about the lighting, they would need some kind of power brought out into the place.

John Ryan said he wasn't made of money, installing electrical lighting into a place that would be used once. But he would be able to get them one extension lead which meant they could plug in one lamp, and the record player as well if they had an adapter.

Maggie said you could make marvelous lights with old turnips and pumpkins like people did at Halloween.

There was endless scooping and hollowing, and Loretto Quinn provided a box of night lights that would be put inside.

Kitty Daly said it all sounded terrific, which alarmed Maggie greatly. She had hoped that Kitty would think it was childish and beneath her and not want to come. Maggie knew that Dara had set her heart on Kerry O'Neill being on his own and maybe taking an interest in Dara herself. It would be very complicated if Kitty was there too. But before Maggie had to discuss it with anyone a letter arrived in Daly's with the good news that Kitty had been accepted for nursing in Dublin. It was a good hospital and the Dalys were pleased; their elder girls had gone to Wales where there was a shortage of any kind of nurses, so Dublin seemed like a step up to the Dalys.

Dara asked Rita Walsh was there anything in the world that made hair look shiny like all these advertisements, or was it all a cod? Mrs. Walsh told her that it was all a cod really, but gave her some sample bottles of conditioner and said to comb it through and leave it on for as long as possible.

Carrie said that if Dara was really badly stuck she could use the new hair lacquer she had bought, but to go sparingly on it.

Eddie said that Dara was trying on lipstick in the bathroom and rubbing it off on bits of toilet paper. They all said that Eddie was a boring sneak to have announced this for no reason except getting Dara into trouble because Mam said she looked like a tart with that white-colored lipstick on. Eddie said he didn't care what people thought of him because he'd be grown up soon and out of this place and he would never write to anyone not even at Christmas. And when he got rich he'd send a telegram saying "Yah Boo" and Mrs. Whelan would have to take it down and have it delivered.

Eddie's mother said that he was going to end on the gallows, and that if she had her legs she would get up and catch him and paste him into the wall.

Eddie's father took him aside and said that life was all about rubbing elbows with other people and not making fights out of nothing.

"But if I do *anything*, I'm murdered," Eddie complained. "Dara can do anything she likes and people think it's grand."

"To be fair," said John, "you do things like daubing the walls of

Fernscourt with white paint. Dara only puts white paint on her own mouth in the privacy of the bathroom."

That startled Eddie, who didn't know that his father was up to date on the last little activity.

"Yes, well. Yes," he said, at a loss.

"And another thing, Eddie. You don't really want the O'Neills to clear out, do you?"

"Well, you know. It's not right him coming in here and changing everything." He was a small parrot of Jack Coyne's whining tone.

"So no more of it. If you're going to write on walls and get caught for it, then for God's sake get yourself caught for writing something you mean, not something a fellow with a grudge told you to write."

"A fellow. What fellow?" Eddie was too innocent.

"Do you know why Jack Coyne does all this? He doesn't give a damn about Mountfern and whether it's changing or not. He doesn't give a damn about your mother having the accident there, for all that he claims he does."

"He says it was all that man's fault."

"That's balls, Eddie, and if you think about it you'll realize it is. Patrick O'Neill doesn't send any business to Jack Coyne because he was cheated by Jack years back, and he knows what a gangster he is. Jack can't bear that, and it makes him look a fool."

Eddie's eyes were round.

"I'm telling you this _not_ so that you'll tell all those other beauties you hang around with, but just so that you'll know. When you're sent to a reformatory or whatever you should know _why_ you're going."

"I wouldn't be sent to a reformatory?"

This was much more frightening than his mother's belief he would end on the gallows. What made him sure that he was in real danger of a reformatory was this plain speaking. His father was treating him as a grown-up and telling him that Mr. Coyne was a cheat. And he had said "balls." As far as Eddie was concerned that clinched it. Things must be in a bad state if his own father would use words like that to him instead of belting the ear of anyone else who might be heard to say it.

Eddie was allowed to help at the party, he was told, but under no circumstances was he to join in. And when asked to leave he must leave at once with no arguments. It seemed a poor sort of deal. But it was the only way he would be let near the place at all.

"Will I empty ashtrays?" Eddie asked helpfully.

Dara and Michael looked at each other in despair. Wouldn't you know that Eddie would manage to bring up the subject of smoking somehow.

"There will be no need for that, thank you," Dara said in a glacial voice.

"Just be generally helpful," Michael said.

"Doing what?" Eddie asked.

It was unanswerable.

He couldn't take their coats; they wouldn't have any. He couldn't pass around the bottles of orange and lemon because they would all be on a table. He wouldn't be allowed near the record player and it was probably better to keep him well away from the food too. The thought of Eddie presenting a plate of sausages or serving a trifle was not one that gave any pleasure.

"Maybe you needn't help at all," Dara said after some thought. "Maybe you would like an early night."

Michael was more sensitive; he knew that an early night was something Eddie Ryan would never like, now or anytime in the future.

Eddie's face was bitterly disappointed. "I can't go to bed on the night of the *party*," he said, hurt disbelief all over his round freckled face.

Even in her wish to have him one hundred miles away from the scene Dara saw that this would be too harsh.

"Perhaps you could control the animals," she said.

"What animals?"

"Our animals—curb them, sort of."

"Do you mean Leopold and Jaffa?" Eddie was totally bewildered.

"Well yes, and Maurice."

"God, Dara, what could a cat and a tortoise do at the party?" Eddie asked.

"Aha, you put your finger on it. Not much, but Leopold might break the place up. Perhaps you could be in charge of Leopold."

"Like how? Not take him on a walk now, that wouldn't be fair." Eddie was cunning.

"No, but . . . um . . . put him on a lead and sort of patrol with him. They do that at parties in America, I saw it at the pictures, somebody patrols the grounds with a dog. You know, you must have seen them, they wear sunglasses and uniforms."

Dara was thinking of a security guard she had seen in a film.

It worked like a dream.

"All right, I'll borrow some sunglasses and get Leopold's lead and patrol a bit." Eddie sounded pleased with this role.

"Not inside, of course," Michael said hastily.

"Of course not." Eddie was superior. "Leopold mightn't know it was all posh now, he might think it was the old shed still and squat down."

"Yes, that's what we don't need," Dara said, feeling faint.

They spent ages on the invitations. Nothing in the Leonards' shop was right for them. Either they were teddy bears holding balloons asking people to come to a jolly party or they were heavy silver lettering saying "You are invited." One was too babyish, one was too formal.

In the end they bought plain white cards and wrote them out individually. They knew that these invitations would be kept for a long time in the different homes of Mountfern. Written invitations didn't often arrive in the mail.

There had been long debates about the food. Dara had wanted food on a plate, like a real supper. Michael said that sausages and rolls would be better, food on a plate would be messy, people might let bits of gravy fall off.

Carrie was looking out big dishes that could cook lots of sausages at the same time. Mary got one of the beer companies to give them brightly colored trays which they could use for serving the rolls. There would be sandwiches too on the ground that everyone loved tomato sandwiches at moments of high excitement, and there would be tons of chips and nuts.

The pudding was a trifle which Kate would make herself. She loved putting on the hundreds and thousands, she said, and she explained to Grace that it was because she never had jelly and cream or trifle herself when she was young that she got so excited over party food. Her parents had not been festive people, birthdays were low priority.

Grace told Mrs. Ryan that her own mother had often been too ill for any real birthday, but she did remember years back when Kerry was twelve and Grace was nine, Mother had put on paper hats and they had all had a birthday tea in the garden. The three of them.

Father had been out at work. Like he always was.

Kate patted the golden curls and wished that Dara would be eager and confiding like this.

Still, it had to be said that since the party was planned Dara was a much easier soul to live with. Kate was forgiving, it was hard being fifteen whether you had a family that loved you or not. Dara did, Kate hadn't, but at fifteen nobody was too clear about that sort of thing.

The cake was to have thirty candles, and it was a surprise. Kate had asked Marian Johnson, who knew all kinds of people, to recommend a firm that would deliver a cake already iced.

Marian had been very cooperative and even got something off the price because she knew the people who owned the firm.

Kate thought it was sad to see Marian boasting of all the connections she had and the people she knew socially. It was not at all the way to make Patrick O'Neill think more warmly of her. Patrick needed someone like Rachel. How blind and stupid he was not to realize it. How insensitive he was to write her a note every three months or so just at the exact moment when she was making a resolve to forget him and get on with her own life.

Rachel had sent the twins magnificent shirts for their birthday. Michael's was black and red, Dara's was silver and white.

Kate had encouraged Dara to buy a white pleated skirt. But not directly. She had just left a magazine about, and let enough hints fall without saying she thought it was nice. Grace as usual did the persuading. She said she thought the skirt looked fabulous and when Dara got her birthday money in advance of the day she went into the big town and bought it.

They were dressed and nervous, ages before people came. Michael was handsome in the unusual colors, Dara dazzling, Kate thought, in the shimmering silver and white. Her eyes were huge and dark, her hair shone like satin. Kate looked at them proudly.

"I hope it will be a night you'll always remember," she said, trying to keep the choking emotion out of her voice.

"I wish you were able . . ." Michael began.

"To be able to run in and out a bit," Dara finished.

Kate brushed the tear away quickly and decided to be very unsentimental. "Not at all, that's the last thing you'd wish. If I had to come in and upset the proceedings you'd hear this old chair a mile away. It will be great altogether, the place outside looks like a palace. Your father will go in from time to time to make sure you have enough of everything."

The twins nodded. That was understood. Their father would be calling in to make sure there wasn't too much of everything, that's what was really meant.

* * *

It was awkward in the beginning, because these were people they saw every day. The girls were at school together in the convent, the boys in the brothers, they knew each other from Fernscourt in the old days, some of them from the bridge, and some from the raft, Coyne's wood or just around the town. They saw each other a dozen times a week, in the cinema, on their bicycles. They were suddenly ill at ease in their finery in a room hung with hollowed-out shells holding lights.

The conversations began and died.

Apart from Grace O'Neill: she seemed not to notice any little silences any shyness, her laughter pealed, she begged for chips, and more fizzy orange. She praised the room over and over, she admired the girls' dresses, and said that she was just dying to dance. Could they get some music started? And arm in arm with Maggie, who looked nervous in a pink dress with a thousand polka dots on it, she rummaged through the records, exclaiming over them even though they were her own. In no time the party had started.

Eddie, patrolling, would stop wistfully and lift his sunglasses to watch the dancing inside what used to be the old shed. It was full of mystery and enchantment tonight, but Eddie could never pause too long. Leopold would look up thoughtfully at the sky and Eddie knew that an unmerciful baying was about to begin, so the dog had to be hastened away to the river bank until the wish to howl at the stars had passed.

Tommy Leonard told Dara that she looked beautiful.

"That's the only word for it," he said, anxious that there should be no misunderstandings. "It's not just pretty, or nice, it's beautiful."

"Thank you Tommy, you look great yourself," Dara said, pleased.

"No, it's not just a question of looking well or not looking well. This is a description of what you *are*. Beautiful."

Poor Tommy was bursting with eagerness to make it clear that this was no ordinary exchange of pleasantries. But Dara wasn't really listening. She was looking at the door.

Kerry O'Neill had sent a note saying that if he was able to make it he would very much like to attend the party.

The note had been addressed to both of them.

Grace had said that Kerry was very unpredictable. He had left school, had gotten six Honors in his Leaving Certificate, and he was about to start work in a hotel in Donegal. Father had thought the best way for Kerry to learn the business of running a hotel was to start in someone else's. Nobody knew when he would be off.

Grace hoped it wouldn't be before the party, but with Kerry she said you never knew.

Dara hadn't wanted to keep asking. It looked so babyish.

Maggie wondered if her dress clashed with her hair. Pink and polka dots would not have been her choice but this was a dress which had never fitted Kitty properly and was therefore pronounced almost new in the Daly family. Maggie had brought it to Miss Hayes over in the lodge and Miss Hayes had trimmed it with a red ribbon and assured Maggie that all girls with red in their hair wore this color now.

Maggie danced with Liam White a lot at the party. Liam said that Maggie was easier to dance with than the others because she was smaller than normal girls and there wasn't the same danger of being knocked down by her doing rock and roll. Maggie thought this was a mixed compliment, but at least it did mean she was being asked out into the center of the floor a lot.

Jacinta White asked Tommy Leonard did he intend to dance with the hostess all night, because there was a good variety of other partners around.

Michael realized that as host he must dance with everyone, but his head turned from time to time to watch Grace as she whirled with her golden curls tied in a huge black velvet bow, and her head thrown back laughing. Grace was so alive and so beautiful. He would love to have danced with her all night, but he knew he couldn't. He went over to Maggie Daly, who looked very nice. Maggie was talking to Liam by the record player.

"Will you dance?" he asked her.

"Who, me? Are you sure?" Maggie looked startled.

Michael was annoyed. He was only asking her to dance, for heaven's sake, why did she have to look as if it were some huge thing and she wasn't worthy of it?

John looked in on the pretense that they might need more mineral water from the bar. He sneaked back and reported to Kate that all seemed to be under control.

"Nobody smoking, no one with a bottle of brandy under the table, and they all have their clothes on," he said.

"My God what a terribly dull party!" Kate exclaimed jokingly, and the two of them smiled at each other in the bar. He touched her face suddenly and she held his hand to her cheek.

Brian Doyle at the counter saw it and wondered if all that sort of thing had gone by the board for the Ryans. He presumed it had. You couldn't get up on an unfortunate woman who had all those injuries, could you. It was a terrible thing to happen to them. But still, Brian brightened, they were in their forties after all, they'd probably given all that sort of thing up long ago. Brian was thirty-four with a girl-friend in the town who was going to pack her bags and move off to another town if he didn't make a move one way or another. He put the idea out of his mind and ordered another pint.

Carrie wanted to know should she serve the sausages and Mary said give them a bit more time yet.

Mary kept a weather eye out for Leopold and Eddie. She could see why the twins had resisted having their brother around, but she wanted to make sure that Eddie didn't tie Leopold to some far-off tree and forget him. The animal wasn't used to being taken on such heavy walks with the lead.

When Mary saw them pass again, she made signs and invited Eddie to join her in the kitchen.

"What's it about?" Eddie was suspicious.

"I thought you and Leopold and I might have a sausage or two ourselves before the rush starts, what do you think?"

Eddie thought it was great. Carrie served them all and brought a big bottle of tomato ketchup as well, which was more than the people outside at the party would have.

Jimbo joined them for a few moments and gave Carrie's ear a nuzzle.

"Enough of that, Jimbo," Mary said firmly.

"It's only a bit of affection," Jimbo said.

"It's roguery and trickery and what's more it's unhygienic in a place where food's being prepared," Mary said.

"All right." Jimbo was good-natured.

Eddie was given another sausage to reward him for his hard work patrolling.

"What are you patrolling?" Jimbo asked.

Eddie was at a loss. He didn't rightly know.

"What is it exactly?" he asked Mary.

"Anyone knows you have to patrol at a function," Mary said.

"Will there be patrolling across the river when the hotel starts?" Jimbo asked.

"Bound to be," said Mary.

"Maybe I should get in quick and apply for it."

Eddie smiled to himself. It *was* a real job, he had been afraid it might have been Dara and Michael making something up to keep him out of the way.

Kerry was the last to arrive. Dara was the first to see him; she tried to stop herself running to the door, but she got there very speedily all the same.

Kerry looked wonderful. He wore a pale blue shirt with dark blue stitching all over it, it was like the kind of thing a cowboy might wear. He carried two packages, one he left by the record player, one he gave straight to Dara.

"Happy birthday, Princess," he said.

"Why do you call me that?" It was what Mary Donnelly called Grace when she was speaking disparagingly.

"All beautiful girls are princesses on their birthdays, and you more than most." He smiled at her warmly.

Dara got that breathless feeling as if she had been running.

"May I open it?"

"If you like."

She was almost afraid to lose him by struggling with the wrapping paper too long, and yet it would be terrible to rip it off.

She managed to open it, and he was still standing there. It was a beautiful hair clip with a big red rose attached. If you wore it, it would look as if there was a rose in your hair. Dara looked at it in delight.

"I must put it on, I'll go to a mirror and see what I'm doing."

"Don't run away. Here, I'll put it on for you." He lifted the thick dark hair and slid the grip with its big silk rose into place. He had drawn the hair right back from her face on that one side; it gave her a faintly gypsyish look.

"Is it nice?" Dara asked eagerly.

"It's quite lovely," Kerry said.

At that moment the record player began to play a slower number, "Michelle." Without asking her or breaking the mood, Kerry's arms went straight around Dara and they were dancing.

Dara looked around her and sighed with pure pleasure. The lights from the lanterns were twinkling on the white walls, the paper garlands hung artistically around, the tables looked festive with all the bottles of fizz and plates of snacks. Outside the night air was warm and the flowers in Mammy's side garden looked romantic and like something in a calendar picture. She and Michael were fifteen, almost grown up, all their friends were here. But mainly Kerry O'Neill, who was eighteen and the most handsome man in Ireland, had come in the door, given her a magnificent rose for her hair, told her she looked beautiful, and was holding her in his arms as they danced to Paul McCartney. Dara hadn't known it was possible to be so happy.

Maggie Daly said to Michael that she thought this party was like something you'd dream about.

Michael didn't really listen, he was wondering if as host he could reasonably change the music. He wanted to put on something more lively, like the Rolling Stones. And it was particularly silly to have Grace dancing with that good-looking but basically thick fellow John Joe Conway. Grace was so nice to everyone, she shouldn't be so polite to stupid John Joe Conway, letting him hold her close like that.

The sausages were passed around, the trifle was eaten, every bit of it. The parents and a few people from the pub, plus Declan and Eddie in his dark glasses clutching Leopold for dear life, gathered for the birthday cake. Mary Donnelly, Carrie, Jimbo, and by chance Papers Flynn who was passing by, all gathered at the door for the blowing out of the candles. There were no speeches but a lot of clapping and cheering which made Leopold over-excited and Eddie had to clench his mouth closed for fear of rousing the neighborhood.

Then the grown-ups, relieved that the party was going so well, retired, and someone had taken out the bulb of the only real light so now the place was lit entirely by the lanterns on the walls.

It smelled of the end of the summer, of Nivea Cream and Blue Grass perfume, of cheese and onion potato chips, of sausages and of the September flowers in the garden.

The music was almost all slow now. It was as if the energy for jumping around to the noisier tunes before supper was no longer there.

Michael didn't mind if there were girls he hadn't danced with yet; they probably didn't want to dance with him, they all seemed happy. He stood and talked to Grace or they moved out to dance. All the time she laughed and listened to him and told him things, and many times she said, "Michael, you are wonderful," and he knew she meant it.

Liam White danced a lot with Maggie.

Tommy Leonard looked wistfully for an opportunity to dance with Dara again, but he never got one because Dara had never left Kerry O'Neill's arms from the moment he had come into the room and given her the beautiful rose for her hair.

"It's a quarter to twelve. I suppose we should start making some noises," Kate said.

"You don't know the whole principle of drinking-up time," John said.

"Jesus, Mary and Joseph, you scared me to death. Tell me they have no drink in there."

"No, I was speaking figuratively," John said.

"Don't," said Kate.

"I meant we told them twelve, so just after twelve we go in making noises, that's the way things are done."

"How right you are," Kate said. She felt a yearning to hold John close to her tonight. And she knew he felt the same.

She had always thought that people in wheelchairs didn't feel like that anymore, that the feeling just sort of disappeared when so much else had gone.

There were so many things she hadn't known.

"I hope this isn't all very babyish for you," Dara said to Kerry.

"How do you mean? It's lovely!" He looked at her fondly.

"No, this party, lemonade, no real drink, no band, it must be a bit . . ."

"I don't want real drink, we'd never get a band as good as the Beatles to come to Mountfern so we have their records instead . . . What are you worried about?"

"Nothing," she said.

"That's good," said Kerry, "because you're very beautiful when you are not worried. I don't want to see you frown again. Is that a deal?"

"It's a deal."

Tommy Leonard asked Jacinta White to dance.

Jacinta was pleased.

"It's been very successful, I suppose," Tommy said.

"Yes, it's terrific." Jacinta liked Tommy a lot.

"But the O'Neills took over a bit, didn't they?"

"Did they?" Jacinta was genuinely surprised.

"Maybe they didn't." Tommy struggled to be fair. "I just thought they did, for a bit. Like as if they were the only ones that mattered."

John Ryan came in and collected the empty bottles rather noisily.

"It can't be time yet, Daddy," Michael hissed at him.

"No, not at all, only about ten past twelve. I was just clearing a few of these away." John was pleasant.

He noted that the light bulb was laid neatly beside the record player. He put it back in its socket and the place became suddenly very bright. John continued collecting the bottles as if he were unaware how the appearance of the place had changed.

In ten minutes, without his having to call out any message or threat, the party ended.

The youngsters of Mountfern walked home by River Road or up toward the main road or in some cases with their bicycles they headed off to the small farms around Mountfern.

The river rippled and rustled in the dark, the moorhens and ducks clucked gently in their resting places as children's feet swished by. The moonlight shone on the nearly completed buildings in Fernscourt, where a new Georgian mansion had risen from the ruins, and where the two great bedroom blocks swept away behind it looking like half-folded wings. For most of them it had been the first night like that they had ever known, and they were filled with thoughts of a future where there would be many more.

The twins sat on the window seat and talked for ages about the party. They talked about how funny Liam was and rude without meaning to be, and how pretty Maggie had looked, and what a clown that big John Joe Conway was, and wasn't Eddie a scream with the dark glasses, and how nice Carrie had been and wasn't it great that Declan had been shy and hung back, and how Mam hadn't come near them and how funny Dad was at the end.

Dara didn't tell Michael about the end of the party.

Michael didn't tell Dara about how much he loved Grace. Yes, love. That wasn't too strong a word for it.

Dara ran her tongue across her lips again and tried to remember Kerry's kiss. It had been so soft.

His mouth had pressed on hers gently at first, and then a little more firmly. That was the first time, that was when they were in the darkest corner of the room, where nobody would see.

She had closed her eyes. She didn't know why but it seemed to come naturally, and he had said again that she was beautiful, so it must have been a normal thing to do.

Then when the party was over and they were all going through the side yard and filing out, he had pulled her back suddenly and behind that archway with the climbing rose, he had held her face between both his hands and kissed her again for a long long time.

"Happy birthday lovely Dara," he had said.

During all the goodbyes, he had said he would see her soon. She stopped herself from asking when.

The next day and the day after she stopped herself asking Grace had he gone away to Donegal. She knew he wouldn't go without saying goodbye. Not after that kissing.

Dara hugged herself and wanted to cry out to the night skies about it all. But she didn't; she told nobody. Not Michael. Not Grace. Not Maggie.

And certainly not Tommy Leonard, who had said he loved the party himself personally of course, but he would have thought that Dara might have found it a bit dull, what with only dancing with the same person all night.

"No," Dara had said airily. "Funny that. I didn't find it dull at all."

Rachel was responsible for the entire design and decor of Ferns-court. She knew she would come to Ireland again, since this could not be done at long distance. For a while she had hoped she could cut Patrick and his hotel from her life totally. Then she would hand over her meticulous files to her successor, or to whatever firm of interior decorators Patrick could employ.

But this was not to be.

Too much of her life had been spent too deeply enmeshed. She was not going to leave before she saw his dream castle built and built right.

Patrick would not allow himself to be convinced by the unscrupulous in any other field, but when it came to the design of this hotel he had several very blank spots. He had been going to build a phony castle with turrets and Disneyland looks because someone had suggested that this would be suitable for a conquering O'Neill. Rachel had been the one to insist that the original house be built again and the bedroom wings tucked away at an angle.

He would have had it filled with shamrocks, shillelaghs and leprechauns if her watchful eye had not been through every stage with him. Now that the building was complete, and the decorating about to start, it was time for Rachel to return.

She was stronger now, and harder. She was a more lonely woman than the Rachel who had left here eighteen months ago hoping every moment that he would beg her to stay. Now when she came back it would be with fewer illusions.

And with fewer millstones around her neck.

Like she knew she would not set foot in the Slieve Sunset.

She asked Kate to put her mind to thinking about this, and within hours of getting the letter Kate was on the phone.

"I've found you the perfect place," she said, overjoyed that her great friend was coming back to Mountfern and coming to be beside her. It had taken a little persuasion. But she had found exactly the right place for Rachel to stay.

Loretto Quinn was appalled.

"A smart American woman with all those grand clothes like Mrs. Fine. No Kate, honestly, I couldn't cope with that. I only agreed to do all this because you said there'd be a few shillings in it once the hotel was built. No, I don't want the fright and the worry of trying to please people that are way beyond me like that."

"Shush, Loretto, listen. This is the best thing you could have. Rachel will be coming back and forward all the time, she will want her own place, she might even take them permanently."

"Won't she be staying in the hotel yonder when it's finished?"

"It won't be finished for ages and the Grange is too far away. Your place would be just ideal. I only thought of it this morning when she was on the phone. I am a sort of genius so I am."

"You might be and all, Kate, but you scared me to death. There's only beds and chairs in those rooms, there's no proper furniture, only the plainest of white curtains on them that you'd see in a lunatic asylum . . ."

"Leave it just as it is, I beg you. That's Rachel's job; that's what she gets paid a fortune for, knowing what to put on this and what not to put. You and I couldn't see it in a million years. She'll give you great advice altogether. I mean it. Look at what she did for me. She'll have your bedrooms the talk of the town. Marian Johnson will be green with envy; she'll be climbing the drainpipes to get a peep at them."

The thought of Marian Johnson being envious of poor little

Loretto Quinn was such a happy one that the women laughed imagining it.

"What'll she put her clothes on till it's all done up though?" Loretto was practical.

"I know, we'll get one of those coat rails they have in shops, a big long one. Jimbo could get you one from one of the bigger shops away in the town. I'll ring a few places for you."

"It wouldn't be too bare?"

"Nothing can be too bare, apparently. That's what having style is all about."

Rachel brought them all gifts. For Dara a red dress with white tassels, bright and showy and ready to transform her into the colorful girl that Kate always knew she could be. For Michael a huge book about fish and fishing all over the world, for Eddie a bicycle lamp that looked like something from outer space, for Declan a box of horrible joke items including a cushion that made a sound like a fart when you sat on it.

Rachel had remembered that John had lost weight—there was clearly nothing she had forgotten from Kate's letters—so she had brought him two smart linen jackets: one in navy, one in a daring gold-tan color. He looked bashful trying it on but delighted with the inspection in the mirror.

Kate was right, John Ryan had slimmed down and looked somehow taller. He was so pleased with the tan jacket he planned an entire outfit based on the color and said Rachel would have to come to the big town with him one day to advise him.

For Kate there were magnificent green, blue, and gold silk scarves, each one more elegant than the next. Rachel had magic in her fingers when it came to draping them and arranging them. Everyone gasped as Kate spun her wheelchair around for admiration in the blue and silver scarf. Leopold, who had been watching through the glass door, set up a howl of approval and chased his tail happily.

It was lovely to be back in this place, and better to be back on her own terms. Rachel didn't have to worry about Patrick, about what mood he would be in, or what time he got back from Dublin. She didn't have to feel alarmed when Marian Johnson put her ludicrous oar in trying to drag up remembered incidents and share jokes. No indeed, she didn't miss Patrick here, and as Kate had said, it *did* make her feel more independent. More her own woman.

She was touched at how welcome they made her and especially by the nervousness of Loretto Quinn, who was up at Ryan's apologizing for the bedrooms before Rachel had even seen them. She hastened to inspect them and put the nervous woman at her ease.

"This is magnificent, Loretto," Rachel had said. "And if you wouldn't take it amiss I'll have plenty of spare samples of fabrics and little extras and if you like we could do these rooms up for next to nothing while I'm here."

Loretto thought that she was in heaven. In days beautiful lilac-colored curtains had arrived—and by an extraordinary coincidence they were just the right size—together with the heather carpet and the cream fabric with lilac flowers for bedspread and cushions. In front of her eyes and with no fuss Loretto saw her rooms transformed. She would walk upstairs and look at her tasteful guest rooms and clasp her hands with pleasure.

There had also been some extra material in big heavy red for a bedspread for Loretto's own room, and red and white curtains. Rachel for all her glamor was as nice as anything; she had even found a very bright colorful extra piece of linoleum that was just the right size for Loretto's shop, and since it looked so smart in that nice green and red, why not paint the counter red and the shelves green? Those young lads of Kate Ryan's would only be delighted to help out. People began to praise Loretto in terms that they never had before. Wasn't she the smart little thing now to brighten up her huckster's shop in readiness for all the visitors? Who would ever have thought that she had so much sense?

When Patrick called on Loretto Quinn he couldn't believe the transformation. Her pathetic little place looked smart and cheerful. Even the woman herself looked as if she had been made over by some women's magazine for a before and after feature.

"Mrs. Fine about, is she?" he said casually.

Loretto had been given her instructions very clearly.

"She's away on business, Mr. O'Neill."

"What business?"

"Mrs. Fine didn't tell me, sir."

"When's she coming back?"

"She didn't say that either, Mr. O'Neill."

"She's being mighty secretive about her movements, I must say."

"Oh no, nothing like that, she's full of chat, Mrs. Fine, such a nice person. I was nervous of her coming here in the first place, but now I can't think why. She couldn't have been more help to me."

Patrick had suspected he saw Rachel's hand in the transformed shop.

"Yes, I'm sure that's true, Mrs. Quinn, it's just that I expected her here to give me a report on everything."

"Did she know you were coming here, Mr. O'Neill? She couldn't have surely?"

"No, well it was a last-minute thing."

"There you are." Loretto was triumphant that her new friend Mrs. Fine hadn't been at fault.

"I'll take a look at her rooms while I'm here," Patrick said grumpily.

Loretto looked embarrassed. "I don't think . . . I mean . . ."

"Oh, Mrs. Fine wouldn't mind, Rachel would like me to see that she had a nice place to stay."

"It's just that . . . you see. If I let rooms to one person I can't be responsible to let other people in. You do see that, Mr. O'Neill. I can't be letting people traipse through."

"I'm not other people, I'm not traipsing through . . ." Patrick was very annoyed now.

"But you do see. Perhaps when Mrs. Fine gets back, if *she* would like to show you her rooms, it would be different."

Patrick banged out of the shop.

The woman was right, of course, but for God's sake the last time he had been here she was like a bag lady shoveling potatoes out of dirty old bags. Now she was all dressed up, the potatoes were in big clean containers, Loretto was taking attitudes and striking poses about showing the rooms upstairs. It was too much.

Patrick didn't risk going into Ryan's Licensed Premises. He had managed to fight with everyone he met since getting back, so he decided to put off the possibility of taking John by the lapels or entering into a screaming match with Kate in her wheelchair. He parked his car out of sight of them, and walked across the footbridge. The mansion gave him scant pleasure this morning. All he could see were the faults—the ugly angle of the drive for one thing. How much better it would have been to have come straight down in one long tree-lined sweep to the river. But how could he have suggested that when, the very day he was going to propose buying their property, Kate was crippled for life on his own building site? Then he didn't like the huge forecourt, either. It was too bare, too like a parking lot. Which was what it was. Rachel had urged him to leave three trees there but he had thought they would hide the house too much and they would be just further objects to negotiate for buses and cars. He had been wrong and Rachel had been right.

Where *was* she for God's sake?

Brian Doyle was glad to see him anyway. That made a nice change, Patrick thought grimly. He took off his jacket and sat down in Brian's site office.

"Tell me why you're glad to see me, Brian, is it because I am such a good kind employer responsible for the livelihood of at least two hundred people give or take, responsible for your own inflated life-style and yet another new car which I see parked outside? Is that why my presence makes you glad? Or is it because I'm the first peasant within five hundred miles who bought the Big House and made it live the way we want it to live? Or is it because of my curly brown hair and twinkling blue eyes?"

Brian looked at Patrick in alarm. He supposed the man must have been drinking, it could be the only explanation.

"Would you like a cup of coffee?" he began.

"This may come as a shock to you, Brian, but I would not like a cup of coffee. I have never, since all this began, liked any cup of coffee I have had here. It has become an interesting guessing game to know whether it *is* coffee, or tea or Postum or the water that all these things have been washed up in."

"Oh well then, forget it." Brian wasn't at all offended at the insult to the coffee made on site, he took it that Mr. O'Neill was beyond coffee, and wanted a drink fast.

"Will we go down to Ryan's and talk then?" he said agreeably.

"We will *not* go down to Ryan's, we will talk here. It may have escaped your notice that it is ten-fifty in the morning, not a time for adjourning to a pub even by your standards."

"Jesus Christ, nothing would please you today."

"You may be right. Why were you glad to see me?"

"There's been a lot of messages for one thing, people wanting to get in touch with you. The phone's not stopped all morning."

"Right," Patrick grunted. "Where's Rachel?"

"Who?"

"Rachel Fine. Has it escaped your notice that she has been working with me since 1963 in the design and interior decoration of this hotel which has made you a millionaire ten times over?"

You couldn't insult Brian Doyle, which was one of his great strengths.

"Oh, Mrs. Fine? I've no idea where she is, she's been in and out, but you know what she's like, a very helpful lady—never gets in the way, does her work, leaves a note about it and is gone."

"Yes, well what note did she leave?"

"It was measurements, someone here gave her the wrong figures for the dining room, they'd got it all wrong, the shop was going to send twice too much material. Mrs. Fine headed them off. She's saving you a packet that lady, I tell you. A packet."

"I'm glad somebody's saving me a packet, with the way that other people throw it around."

"Maybe when you feel more yourself," said Brian in the tone that you'd use to talk to a drunk about to fall off a bar stool.

"I *am* myself, you idiot," said Patrick. "I just want you to *ring* these guys as you call it. *Ring* them on that phone, as you call it, and tell them I'm not here."

"Everyone calls it *ring*, it's not a word I made up," cried Brian, stung at last to some kind of response. "And you told me yourself that you always grasped the nettle, Mr. O'Neill, you always took the bull by the horns, you said that was the one sure road to success. I've been following your example, I've been doing it myself, and it does seem to work. I've been doing much better."

"You've been doing much better because I handed you the job of a lifetime on a plate and you are taking a lifetime to complete it!" Patrick was aware that his bad temper was doing him no good but he wasn't ready to stop yet.

"Now Brian, listen to me. You do what I say, and do it now. I'm getting the hell out of here before I have a heart attack and the litigation about the hotel becomes legal history and with any luck you'd never get paid the last bit."

"And when do I say you're going to be here?"

"You don't know. You haven't a goddamn clue."

Patrick grabbed his jacket and got up to head for the footbridge.

"But Mr. O'Neill, can't I show you what we've done . . ."

"I see what you've done, the front is like a tarmac in an airport."

"Shit, Mr. O'Neill, everything was in the plans . . ."

"Don't you say shit to me . . ."

"But don't you want a tour of the site as usual?"

"How can I if I'm not here?"

Patrick was half way down to the footbridge when he saw Dara Ryan running toward him excitedly.

"Hallo, Mr. O'Neill," she called, pleased to see him.

"Well Dara, good to see you." He noticed that she was becoming a striking-looking girl, tall, dark, in a white tee shirt, jeans and a red flower tucked behind her ear—or maybe it was a bit of jewelry.

"When did you get back?" she asked.

"A little while ago. Everyone I've met has fought with me so far. You're not going to have a fight are you?"

"Lord, no." She seemed eager to talk. "Did you have a good time?"

"In Dublin. No, not really, not at all in fact. Nothing but meetings and more meetings and nothing much at the end of it. Despite what you may think I actually don't enjoy fighting."

"I never thought you enjoyed fighting," Dara said. She was anxious to ask him something. He wondered what it was.

"Well, you're right." He smiled warmly at her. It was true, he didn't enjoy a fight. He had not enjoyed the scenes some weeks back after a demarcation dispute between two sets of workers. In front of fifty men he had told Brian Doyle that they had three hours in which to decide which men did what work. If it were not agreed then every single man would be paid off that afternoon. There had been something in his face that sorted out the dispute in far less than the three hours he had given them.

It was a victory but he hadn't enjoyed it.

"And what are you doing here on the footbridge? Were you lying in wait for me?" he asked.

"Not really, I was wondering when you'd be back, there's a folk concert up in the grounds of the ruined abbey, lots of quite well-known singers, and I was wondering . . ."

"I think I'm a bit old for it, Dara," he teased.

"No, I meant if Kerry was interested in going. I wasn't sure when you were both coming back so I kept an eye out."

He looked at her and sighed. "Kerry won't be back for the concert," he said.

"He's not with you?"

"No, he wasn't in Dublin, he went straight to Donegal, did he not tell you?"

"I must have gotten it wrong," said Dara Ryan. The light had gone out of her big dark eyes.

"Can we go out for a walk?" Rachel said. It was a very sunny afternoon but with a nice breeze.

"Sure, hold on a moment until I get some gum and stick my spine together, then I'll leap up and come with you," Kate said without rancor.

"I meant me going for a walk, you going for a push."

"It's boring," Kate said. "You have to shout over my shoulder, I have to crane my neck. I wish I had a pram, people can talk *to* babies, not over their heads."

"We can talk when we get there," Rachel said.

"Get where?"

"Mystery tour."

"Why not? Let me drape one of your scarves elegantly around me so that I'll knock the eyes out of anyone we meet."

They went first to Loretto Quinn's. Kate couldn't believe the changes that had been made. Normally Loretto was so indecisive she couldn't decide whether to wrap your potatoes in newspaper, put them into a paper bag or feed them straight into your shopping bag. Now it appeared that in under two weeks her entire shop had been refurbished. There was even a man redoing the sign over the door.

Two men in the shop lifted Kate's wheelchair inside so that she could see. She propelled herself around touching this and stroking that. There was so much room here now. The place looked an entirely different *class* of a shop. Much more upper-class or something. Yet her prices were the same. Kate was full of praise.

"But it's all Mrs. Fine, Kate, she's a walking saint—a bit like yourself. I don't know why she did all this for me, I really don't. I'd never in a month of Sundays have been able to think of it all myself, or if I thought of it, I'd never have been able to do it."

Loretto looked taller, Kate thought, suddenly, which was nonsense. But maybe she was standing up more straight now, and she had tidied herself up. It wouldn't do to be the old wishy-washy Loretto with pale hair falling into her eyes and a grubby pink overall. She wore a smart brown shopcoat, with a white blouse underneath. Her hair was clipped back with a smart red barrette, undoubtedly a gift from Rachel.

Kate sighed. "You're a sort of magician, you know, you've changed Loretto's life," she said to Rachel as they went back along River Road.

"It's easy to change other people's lives, it's your own that's the problem," Rachel laughed.

"Hey, is the tour over? That was very short as a mystery tour—up to Loretto's and back."

"No, no, it hasn't begun. I thought we'd go across the footbridge and look at the hotel."

It was said lightly, but they both knew it wasn't light. Kate hadn't been across the Fern for more than two years. Not since the day she had walked across the footbridge herself and been carried out of the site unconscious in an ambulance.

"Oh I don't think so, Rachel."

They were at the footbridge. Rachel came around to the front of the wheelchair and squatted down in front of Kate. Her perfectly arranged hair in its short natural looking curls that took her thirty minutes to arrange every morning hadn't been disturbed. Her make-up made her look like a young girl. Her big dark eyes were troubled and fixed on Kate.

She spoke very seriously.

"I'm not some kind of psychologist trying to get you over the shock of where you had your accident. Lord, Kate, why would I want to do that? You could live for the rest of your life without going back to the spot where your back was broken. What good on earth would it do you to see the place? Not that you *will* be able to see the place now anyway."

"So why do you want me to go over there?"

"I want to talk to you."

"Can't we talk here or go back to my green room and talk?"

Kate sounded upset but Rachel pretended not to notice.

"Please, Kate, I want to talk to you about the hotel. We might as well talk about it in Brooklyn if you don't come with me and see what I mean."

"I know what it's like, I've heard."

"Please."

"You're the one with the legs, I might as well give in graciously."

"This is giving in graciously?" Rachel laughed.

The little path that Rachel hadn't been able to walk on that summer day because of her high heels and flimsy shoes was now a tarmacadamed all-weather pathway. With little seats placed here and there, often set into rocks or under trees. It wasn't neat and orderly like a public park, it was more as if someone had decided here would be a good place to sit and talk. The ground had been turned and dug and planted, with evergreen bushes here and lawns there. The steep slopes were planted in terraces.

"I had no idea there was so much work done here," Kate breathed as they paused to look at shrubs and rock gardens.

"It cost a fine penny I can tell you, fleets of gardeners still working on it, but it's destined not to need too much maintenance once it's finished."

On and up they went toward the house.

Although she had seen it many times from her own home across the river, Kate was unprepared for the sheer size of it. This was a huge place. She looked at the big sweep up to the front door. A dozen tour buses could come in and turn here, and perhaps fifty cars park as well, but this wasn't the real car park, that was around the side. The three-story house faced across the river. It was a reproduction of a classic Georgian house, with its high windows, its fanlight over the door. Plain and clean-lined and already, Kate noticed, at least twenty well-watered plants of virginia creeper. In five years the place would look as if it had always stood there. Patrick had been given very good advice.

Kate noticed the broken urns that she had heard about, the expensive ornaments that had been dashed to the ground one night. There had been talk about it in the pub, children some said.

There had been much more than the usual run of vandalism and hooliganism around the place. Sergeant Sheehan had confided that it looked as if it were orchestrated, which seemed hard to believe. After all, who would have a grudge against Patrick O'Neill setting up a business that would bring prosperity to everyone, the Sergeant had asked.

Kate looked up at the house in wonder. It was so like those old pictures that John had unearthed in journals and lithographs of the time. It was like the sepia pictures that he had also shown her. A big house with its two bedroom wings folded away neatly behind, not spoiling the impression of the main house. She could hardly wait to see inside.

There was a ramp into the hotel at one side, where Rachel pushed the wheelchair easily.

"What made you think of this?" Kate asked in self-mockery. "Was it so as I could come to call?"

Inside there were men working still, putting in light fitments. Others were working on the huge staircase going up from the hall. Some of the men knew Kate to see and came over to welcome her. Others remembered her from the day of the accident. Everyone knew Mrs. Fine and everyone could have given their view on her relationship with the big man Mr. O'Neill, if pressed.

"The elevators are installed but they haven't been passed as safe yet, so all things considered I don't think we will . . ."

"Too right," Kate agreed enthusiastically. "To be carried unconscious from here a second time would be overdoing it."

Brian Doyle, who was surprised to see her there in the first place, scratched his head in wonder.

Kate decided she had been very stupid. Rachel had taken her on a tour of the Thatch Bar, a huge place with seating for two hundred and a stage for the entertainment. Four thatchers had been working on it for months and the roof looked like velvet. Not at all like the real thatch around here, often neglected and full of weeds, but perfect and what was more the perfect American idea of a dream Irish cottage.

They had been around the back and seen the terrace where little stone tables had been installed. The plan was to serve drinks out here in the summer.

Then inside the house one of the paneled rooms was called the Study Bar. Here, from a bar surrounded by old books in glass cases, further drinks would be served. Of course there would be a cocktail lounge too, just before going into the dining room.

Slowly it sank in.

"I see why you took me on the mystery tour, Rachel, dear Rachel," Kate said.

"Can you wheel me to one of those nice stone seats we passed, somewhere where no machinery can fall on us? And we can have our little talk."

In silence Rachel found them a quiet place. Looking downhill and over the footbridge they could see Ryan's Licensed Premises nestling where it always had nestled.

"I didn't realize. I really didn't realize," Kate said simply. "Nothing was hidden from me, no lies were told, but I just couldn't see."

"That's why I wanted you to come here," Rachel said.

"We might as well close down now, rather than wait until the opening."

"No, that's not what I was trying to tell you," said Rachel.

"Well what then?"

"I'm not sure yet, something different."

"What's different than closing down when you've no business?"

"No, I mean could you do something different, could you change things a bit?"

"Dancing girls maybe?" Kate was bitter-sounding now. "That's about the only thing he hasn't thought of . . . a big neon sign, Ryan's Raunchy Roadhouse . . . see the ladies in corsets flinging their legs around. Maybe Canon Moran could come and take the money at the door."

"What would make them come down a path, cross a bridge to go somewhere else?"

"Somewhere much duller."

"What would make them?"

"If I knew that, would my heart be pounding inside me?"

"Think, Kate, think what visitors want, what do you want when you go somewhere?"

"I don't ever go anywhere. I go to Mass, and what do I want then, I want it to be Father Hogan because he's quicker, I want there not to be two collections, I want not to be parked in a draft."

"Kate. I'm trying to help you."

"I *know* you are, but why ask me what do I want when I go somewhere? I swear I don't go anywhere. I've only been on three holidays in my life, the first one down here when I met John, the second our honeymoon in Killarney and the third when we went to Dublin to see President Kennedy. How do I know what I'd want or what anyone would want?"

Rachel gave up trying to draw things out of her. She leaned over. She counted on the well-manicured fingers of her hands.

"Listen, one, they might want fishing gear, you could specialize in bait and hooks."

"*Bait?*" screamed Kate. "*Bait* in a public house where people are supposed to be drinking, a nice smelly jar of worms and a glass of Guinness!"

"No, I meant around the side. Two, they might want stationery to write home, postcards. You could sell those."

"How could I tell Jack Leonard I was going to sell writing pads and envelopes? Have sense, Rachel, you've been here long enough to know that we wouldn't *do* that sort of thing to each other."

"What else do people need?" Rachel went on remorselessly. "Three, they'll need their hair fixed, and I can tell you that Rita Walsh is getting ready for that in the Rosemarie hair salon. She has offered me a free permanent in return for a little advice about how to make the place right."

"And did you help her?"

"Sure I did, I got her a bit of this and that, suggested she rent a few new dryers—hers would frighten you just to look at them. Then I told her the truth, that Patrick had been planning a beauty salon in the hotel itself and I had said give the Rosemarie a year to see if it can cater for the guests. Rita has no time for her other activities these nights, she's too busy getting the place right before the grand opening."

Kate was impressed. "That's Rita and Loretto fixed up, and I suppose Jack Coyne might get a bit of business now. Is the feud over?"

"Not really, but Patrick must see that it is handier to have someone across the road in case the guests want to rent a car. He'll have to watch him like a hawk, and all accounts direct to the hotel, not to the client."

"So that only leaves the poor Ryans, and we won't sell bait or stationery. What had you planned for us?"

Rachel took Kate's hand. "Please, Kate, don't be like that with me."

"It's unforgivable, you're quite right. Here, lean over and give me a kiss, I'm afraid to lean over at you in case I upset the wheelchair and roll down into the river."

They held on to each other for a long minute.

"Right. Seriously, I've gotten over it now, that rotten spiteful temper of mine. Please help me, Rachel."

"I was wondering would you consider doing traditional Irish teas, and selling souvenirs. Potato cakes maybe, toasted brack, Irish soda bread."

"We couldn't. Not in a pub. Rachel, you don't understand pubs and drinking people. They would go stark staring mad if there was a hint of a leprechaun for sale or a cup of tea being served."

"Not in the pub. Beside it."

"Where we had the twins' party?" Kate asked in disbelief.

"It wouldn't be a big job," Rachel was saying thoughtfully.

"It would be way beyond us even if we'd consider it, which we would not in a million years."

"No, it wouldn't be expensive, a couple of the men could come from here, they're paid by the week anyway and sometimes there just isn't any work *for* them, and Patrick is never anxious to pay people to stand about, he prefers to have something for them to do—"

"And I know," Kate broke in, "there's going to be a few extra pieces of linoleum and carpet and end rolls of tablecloths and starts of rolls for curtains, and you'll furnish the whole place for us and we'll think we did it ourselves. And one day when Dara is dressed as an

Irish colleen and the boys are all doing step dancing between tables of soda bread, we'll say to each other, '*Whatever* was it like in the old days?' "

Rachel looked at her and saw the tears were pouring down Kate's face. "I'm so sorry, Kate. Oh God, I'm sorry."

Kate sat alone in her room for a long time. She told herself that she hadn't learned much since her accident, she was still impatient and quick to judge what was right and what was wrong. But at least she had learned something about thinking before you speak. She wouldn't burden John with all she had discovered today, no more blurting out everything. She would definitely think before she spoke. In the old days she used to say it was the hallmark of a knave and a con man, someone who would have weighed up the pros and cons before venturing an opinion. But that was the old days.

She tried out some of her notions.

You need to test market ideas, she had read somewhere.

"Dara do you think we should run a guest house? You know, have people to stay and charge them. For staying like?"

"I know what a guest house is, Mammy," Dara said.

"Well, should we?"

"Here? There's hardly room enough for us in this house, let alone other people. Where would they sleep?"

"I suppose we could build rooms for them?"

"But why? Why on earth would we do that?"

"I don't know. I just thought we might. Everyone else seems to be —Loretto, and I believe Rita Walsh is thinking of it too."

"What would we want to get into it for with all that competition?"

"We have a license, they don't. We could have a bar trade. Maybe keep commercial travelers."

"Are you feeling all right, Mammy?"

"Perfectly. Why do you ask?"

"Only a very unwell person would think up such an idea. And *now* of all times, where's all this business going to come from suddenly? Nobs across the river by the busload, ordinary people on this side, and now you want a guest house full of drunks."

"I didn't say that."

"Yes you did, you said there'd be a whole lot of commercial travelers who'd want to get blind drunk at night and stay in rooms that we'd have to build on for them."

"I never heard of anything so mad," Kate said, exasperated.

"That's what I thought, Mam, that's why I asked you were you feeling all right. If there were all these drunken commercial travelers roaming the land looking for places to stay we'd have heard of them surely?"

"Loretto, where do you buy your eggs?"

"From about four farmers' wives, I spread it around a bit to give them all a turn, and then I have four families who come and deal with me as a result."

"Are they very dear?"

Loretto was puzzled. "No of course they're not, they're whatever the cost, you know."

Kate felt that Loretto should really be able to explain things a bit more clearly. "I meant it must be hard on you having to depend on farmers' wives."

"It's not a bit hard, aren't they dying to sell the eggs and make a few shillings? What made you think of that?"

"I was thinking of how much handier it would be if you had someone near you with a lot of hens, someone you could rely on."

"Oh, I'd hate that," Loretto said airily. "I'd have to pay them whatever they said, it wouldn't be the same at all. I like the women coming in and chatting. Everyone likes that, that's the way they buy eggs above in Bridge Street too."

"I see." So there was no point in thinking of a small poultry farm.

Loretto's face suddenly took on a new expression.

"Oh, Kate, I'm very thoughtless, I forgot you had a few hens. Did *you* want to sell me the odd half-dozen or anything?"

"No, we've only five hens and we eat all they produce and more. No, I was just thinking about the economy, that's all. I do sometimes, but it's always a mistake."

"Sheila, did you ever wonder why nobody ever started a launderette in this place?"

Mrs. Whelan said the thought had never crossed her mind.

"It has to be something that nobody thought of, that's all. You can rent the machines, you know, you don't have to have any great outlay. Then all you do is watch the people coming and filling them up with coins."

"It wouldn't ever take off here, of course," Mrs. Whelan said simply.

"I don't know, the place is getting bigger, what with the hotel and everything, it's going to be a much bigger place than we thought."

"It is and it isn't, Kate. But the hotel will have its own laundry, you won't see the guests taking a pillow case of dirty washing down to Bridge Street . . ."

"Or . . ."

"Or to wherever someone would put it." Mrs. Whelan seemed anxious for Kate to divulge no mad little hopes.

"A laundermat or whatever they're called would need a place where there'd be young people living on their own, there isn't even a bank here employing a dozen youngsters. No, nobody would be seen going to a laundermat. Can you see Miss Purcell taking Fergus Slattery's smalls to a public washing place? The humiliation of it!"

"You don't think it would work?"

"No, Kate, I think it would be foolish."

"I see."

"Times will get better."

"Times are fine now. It's later I worry about."

"You'll manage, you always have."

"I don't know, I really don't."

"Fergus, it's Kate Ryan."

"Well now." The warmth and delight in his voice were obvious.

"I wanted to talk to you about a worry. Would you be able to come out here at lunchtime?"

"I'll come right away." He took a file from the cabinet. Deirdre paused in her work to notice that it was Kate Ryan's compensation file.

"Is she going to talk about it?" she asked.

"I think so," Fergus said.

Mary Donnelly looked at him suspiciously.

"She's been a bit flushed and feverish. You won't upset her?"

"I never upset any woman, Mary," said Fergus. "That has been my weakness and sorrow in life."

"Don't make a mock out of something very serious." Mary banged into the kitchen but she was back in twenty seconds.

"I forgot, Mrs. Ryan, you said you'd look after the bar for an hour . . ."

"I forgot too," Kate said agreeably. "Still, I can do it. No one comes in this early, we'll have the place to ourselves. You go on about your business, Mary."

Fergus marveled at the easy graceful way Kate maneuvered the wheelchair into the bar. Up the ramp behind the counter.

He went to his accustomed place on a high stool.

"Would you like a drink since you're in the right place for it?" She smiled.

"No, even mad country solicitors don't start this early." He looked at her. Mary was right, her eyes were very bright, her color high.

"What is it?" He was gentle.

"I hate saying this to you of all people, because I always shut you up about it, but I'm worried. I think that we're going to be in big trouble when Fernscourt opens."

"You're in big trouble already." He looked at the wheelchair.

"No, we are not going to go over that again. I can't fight a man on the grounds that I went in despite all those notices and got hurt. I'm talking about something else, about the trade. I think he and the hotel are going to take all our trade."

Fergus was silent.

"So I just wanted your advice. I was thinking of all kinds of things we might do. I mean I could do anything. *Anything.*"

"Oh Kate."

"Don't 'Oh Kate' me . . . I can and will do anything to keep this place in the black, I really will. It's just that I got a bit frightened. I seem to be the last person in Mountfern to realize how changed everything is going to be."

"But I tell you."

"No, don't go on about how terrible he is and how he should have stayed in America, that's useless. It's practical advice I want. Look at everyone else: Loretto is all smartened up, and have you seen Rita Walsh's place, it's like something in Grafton Street."

Fergus smiled bitterly. "I've looked at everyone all right. Oh, they were all able to jump at the smell of money. Simple country town, how are you? This lot have their eye to the main chance, they'd be a fair match for the shysters on Broadway or the Bowery or the Bronx, wherever it was your man made his money."

"Don't make people out to be grasping, they're not, they're just . . ."

"No, not all of them are, I give you that. There are a few who have their loyalty. Not a lot, but a few."

"But what loyalty?" Kate was puzzled. "Who are they being loyal to if they don't want to make a bit of money out of all the changes?"

"To you for one," Fergus said simply.

"Oh, don't be ridiculous." She was really annoyed now. "What has it to do with me? I don't want to be the cause of any fighting. I was talking about the changes and how we should all be ready for them. Yes, us too. I've been thinking about nothing else. How it's going to change our lives. How everything's going to be different."

"It will be different all right." Fergus was grim. "You were up there yourself, Jimbo told me that Rachel brought you up for a gander at the place. How many bars did you see? Not counting the ones they'll have in the function rooms whenever there's a do on. I counted them. I counted four, didn't you? That's a fair amount of drinks for a guy to get through before dinner, if he wants a hightail or a screwball."

"Highball, screwdriver," she corrected him automatically, as she would Michael.

"I know, I wondered if *you* did."

Her eyes flashed at him angrily. "All right, Mr. Know-it-all, if you know so much can you tell me what to do?"

"Yes, certainly I can." He took the file from its big brown envelope and laid it on the bar.

She flinched away from it. "*No*, that is *not* what I want. I don't want his charity, I don't want it all to be in court. That's not what I want at all, a future based on money I got from him by a trick of law. I want to earn a living, be his equal that way." She was both troubled and annoyed.

So was Fergus. "Stop being a Christian martyr, Kate, it's too late for all that."

"I will *not* have this place divided over my accident, I will not have them taking sides, I don't want the whole of Mountfern getting upset about this and fighting over it . . ."

"If I have to tell you this once more I will lose what marbles I have left, and I assure you they are not many. It is *not* his charity it is his insurance, and the whole of Mountfern is not fighting about you. Can you get that into your thick skull?"

"Fergus!"

"I mean it. I really have lost patience with you. You pay insurance here, if a man falls off this stool and breaks his head, it's your insurance that pays for it, Einstein, not you and John. That's why you pay the bloody thing."

She laughed and relented. "I suppose you're right. I'll talk to John about it tonight. We must stop behaving like ostriches."

He looked a little mollified.

She reached across and took both his hands in hers. "You are a good true friend to us, I mean that."

As they sat holding hands the pub door opened silently and in the way nuns have of moving without appearing to take steps Sister Laura rolled silently into the bar.

Kate cursed the greater freedoms that allowed nuns to enter public houses instead of denouncing them.

Fergus wondered was there a law of timing like a law of gravity. Something that almost made people arrive in places at the wrong time.

"I hope I haven't come at a wrong time, Mrs. Ryan."

Sister Laura had a great devotion to St. Francis of Assisi which was unfortunate because Leopold sensed an animal lover and opened his great jaws, closed his sad eyes and gave a treble wail drowning any possible explanation that Mrs. Ryan and Mr. Slattery might have been about to make about their untoward conduct.

"There's no doubt about it, Sister, but your lot are everywhere now," Fergus said admiringly. "I'll be off."

"Well, if you're sure you've finished." Sister Laura's eyes were innocent.

"It's very hard ever to be finished in a pub, Sister, but of course your lifestyle hasn't as yet led you to explore that side of the human condition."

He waved from the door. "Kate, I'll come up with some ideas and when you've talked to John I'll come and discuss them."

"Thanks." Kate waved back.

"Very nice young man," Sister Laura said, sitting down as if she had been used to going into pubs all her life. "Does the most marvelous work for the community for minimal cost. Of course it's really time he got married and settled down. Bachelors don't seem to fit into today's world like they did in previous generations. Steady him down, don't you think?"

"Well yes . . ." Kate was at a great disadvantage now. Anything she said would be bound to be taken the wrong way.

"I won't stay long, Mrs. Ryan, it would turn away trade seeing a nun in here. What I wanted to say was that we've had a letter from a convent in France and there are a lot of families there who are very anxious to make contact with Irish Catholic families and have Irish Catholic girls come out there."

Kate sighed. "You know, that was something I had really hoped for Dara, to do an exchange with a French girl, but we didn't have the money this year when I was working it out. The cost of having a girl here would not be great, I know, but we'd have to entertain her, take her places. That would cost money."

"No, this is au pair. You know, doing a little light domestic duties and speaking English to the children."

"When would that be, Sister?" Kate was interested.

"It was summer they were really thinking about. Two families in particular. We have the highest references. It's in the Loire country where the châteaux are. It would be a great opportunity."

"I'll have to talk to Dara's father, Sister Laura. There are a lot of things to take into account. The fare, and that. And if she'll go! She's very thick with the Americans, she may not want to go off to France in the middle of her summer."

"She'll learn no French and very little else from an American girl." Sister Laura had fairly trenchant views about everything. "I'll be off anyway and if you do decide, let me know."

"I will indeed, Sister. Thank you for your interest."

"She's a nice bright girl that Dara," Sister Laura said. "She's a very bright girl. She lost a lot of ground the year you had your accident, poor child, she was grieving for you a lot."

"I don't know how she managed at all," Kate said.

"Of course she's probably like a lighting devil nowadays, they all *are* at home." Sister Laura spoke in a matter-of-fact way that made Kate giggle.

"I don't seem to be able to do much right, that's true," she admitted.

"I think you'd find her a lot more appreciative after a spell in France, they learn to be grateful for home comforts."

The nun had bright laughing eyes. Kate wondered what life would have been like for Sister Laura if she hadn't entered the convent. Would she have been an all-wise all-knowing mother of a fifteen-year-old? Very possibly.

"John?"

"Hold on a minute, I'll come in to you." He came in and perched on the edge of the long table that went around the walls. He looked at the pages of notes and files strewn around Kate but didn't ask her what they were.

"Wasn't that a great idea, that long table? In a million years I'd never have thought of anything so useful." He patted the furniture admiringly.

"Is there nobody in the bar?" Kate didn't want business neglected.

"Divil a one." He was hamming at her. It annoyed her suddenly, there would be enough call for all that stage Irishry later.

"Well listen, if you have a minute I want to tell you . . . well to ask you really. To discuss . . ." She shuffled all the papers with her writing on them together.

"Yes?" He was mild and encouraging. Could he really be so blind to his surroundings, and to the fact that his business was going to the wall?

"We'll have to change a lot, I was thinking."

"I know. I know."

She didn't want to hear a soothing voice, she wanted some fire, she wanted him to take the initiative.

"I think we've been fools sitting here believing that it's all going to be sunshine and laughter when the place beyond opens . . ." She paused for a moment, half expecting him to say something in defense of Patrick, but he said nothing.

"I think we'll have to start up something else, it would be mad to think they'll leave all the bars they have over in that place to drink in ours."

"Particularly on a bad day," John agreed. "And our own crowd will want to be where there's all the activity. So we'd better offer them something else apart from drink."

Kate looked at him surprised. "What would you think about a café, you know, traditional sort of teas? I know it's not what you're used to, what you expected things would be like."

John didn't look at all taken aback by the idea, she realized. He must have come to the same conclusion himself.

"Nothing's what we were used to," he said, touching the wheelchair. "Nothing was what we expected things to be like. But we've survived, and we'll go on surviving."

Chapter XVII

Fergus Slattery told Kate that the case was on the court agenda for next September. That it would now have to be heard, no further delays would be tolerated. Fergus hoped that the case would coincide with the hotel opening. He would love the thought of the great O'Neill missing his party because he was in court hearing a huge award for compensation being given against him. The thought of it made Fergus almost dizzy with delight. He felt his life had become grey and tired; only the thought of Kate's compensation gave it any fire at all.

Sometimes Deirdre saw Fergus finger the slim pile of documents as he took out a letter or added one to the pile. It was moving very slowly, and even when Counsel had been briefed and it should have gone much further ahead, all kinds of things intervened. There was the delay caused by the courthouse in the big town being declared unfit for use, and so cases were adjourned. Then there was a backlog occasioned by that delay. Then the insurance company changed by merging with another insurance company and all the documents had to be reissued.

Fergus had never failed to refer briskly and efficiently to the delays and adjournments, he was always up to date on the last letter that had been sent backward and forward and you would believe that he had no other case on his files.

Patrick was invariably polite and equally informed; he made it his business to be equally up to date in case he might be accused of not caring what happened.

He had offered on more than one occasion to pay some money on account. It had always been coldly refused. Barely within the bounds of civility, Fergus would hint that by paying any sum now Patrick would be getting himself in well as a philanthropist with the courts later when the assessment came.

"Any sum I paid now would be without prejudice and would be to alleviate hardship."

"They don't live in hardship, they don't need handouts and American food parcels to alleviate poverty," Fergus had snapped.

"Do you dislike all Americans, or is it only me?" Patrick had asked one day, exasperated.

"I'm interested to note you describe yourself as American, O'Neill. Anytime I've heard you speak you always call yourself an Irishman . . ."

It was never announced that the Ryan compensation case had been listed for hearing, but still everybody knew. Kate and John realized to their alarm that people had begun to take sides. There were those who wished the Ryans to take O'Neill and all belonging to him for as much as they could win in the Irish Sweepstakes. There were, it seemed, as many who said that the whole thing was flying in the face of all the generosity that Patrick O'Neill had shown to this parish. That they hoped the compensation would be insignificant and that somehow by this he would know that nobody in Mountfern or anywhere in the environs wished him anything but good.

"We'll have to pretend we don't know what they're saying, after all they never say it in front of us," John said.

"But that's very hard, why don't we tell people that we have no fight with him, and try to explain all that business about insurance companies and how it's all a formula?"

"We can't start explaining our business like that, you'd be the last to want us to air it all."

"But it's so unfair," wailed Kate. "Why should we spend our lives pretending that things are fine."

"A lot of people do," John said mildly.

"Not the *whole* time," she stormed.

"A fair bit of the time." He spoke so quietly she stopped in her tracks. She picked up his hand and laid it to her face.

Perhaps John was pretending things were fine for a fair bit of the time. And she had never noticed.

Michael couldn't see any difficulty ahead about the court case. Several times Jack Coyne had said that the twins shouldn't be too friendly with Grace O'Neill since one day they were all going to have to face each other across the bar of the court. But that was nonsense. Everyone knew that it was all a matter of what insurance the companies would pay, nothing to do with Mr. O'Neill himself who had been so good to them all.

When Michael talked to Grace they never felt there was any problem between their families. That's what made it so galling to hear the fellows at school talking about the big battle ahead. And even more infuriating to have those two eejits of younger brothers joining in all the silly antics and writing "Go home O'Neill" on the walls.

In the summery feeling of his first love Michael Ryan was able to brush all these annoyances aside. It was only Grace he thought of.

The lodge was three miles away. He could cycle two and a half miles and she could cycle half a mile and they could meet in that nice clump of trees on the hill which looked down on Mountfern. But it took so long, and then there were the explanations of where he had been. And Grace had to explain.

And all he wanted was to lie with her and stroke her and read her the poems he made up about her, about her eyes and her feet and her soft skin. And recently her beautiful breasts. Oh God, how he yearned for it to be like it had been just after the party, but there was *nowhere* they could see each other now without causing the most immense fuss.

Perhaps Mam understood more than he thought because occasionally she would ruffle his hair and say that it wouldn't be long now before the hotel was open and Grace would be living across the river from them all. But Mam said it with a shiver too, as if it were going to be somehow very frightening when the hotel opened. Michael was counting every day until his Grace could move from the lodge, which seemed a million miles away.

She had told him she loved him, she told him she had never dreamed it could be so lovely lying beside him as he stroked her from head to toe, and she trusted him and let him linger where he wanted to, she said she liked it too, and she knew he would never force her to do anything she didn't want to. Which of course he wouldn't. Never in a million years.

Kerry was learning a lot about the hotel business in Donegal; old Mr. Hill who had been running a family hotel for years there was a good teacher. He was getting a sizable fee to have O'Neill's son in his place for a type of apprenticeship, and he was determined to earn it.

The boy would learn the business from every angle. He would work in the kitchens and at the reception desk, he would groom the ponies for the day's trekking, he would stand by the trolley as the beef was being carved. Dennis Hill said that he could give a better training than the Shannon Hotel School if he was asked to.

"Why don't you?" Kerry asked him one day. "You could easily set up a sort of training course here."

"And build up a whole breed of rivals to myself?" Mr. Hill shook his head.

"Well what about us, aren't we rivals?"

"Not at all, boy, aren't you down in the midlands there where no one in their right mind would want to spend a holiday, a big turf bog of a place miles from the sea. You're no rivals to anyone there."

His eyes were laughing. Dennis Hill was no fool, he knew that O'Neill's Fernscourt would be no threat to him as it was so far away; he also knew that if he did a good job on this handsome troublesome playboy then O'Neill would send business his way for a long time.

Hills of Donegal was a famous hotel already, its name easily remembered, its clientele faithful, its food vastly superior to almost anything Ireland offered. Dennis Hill had a large family; he kept his hotel open at a loss all winter so that they could practice for the very busy summer season.

He had never taken a foolish step.

Sometimes he looked at Kerry O'Neill's striking face and cold eyes and wondered what would become of the boy. At the first sign of any trouble here Kerry would be packed off from the Hills of Donegal household back to his father, who seemed a grand fellow all set to make an outstanding success of his venture if reports could be believed.

Dara got postcards from Kerry, but they were inside envelopes so that anyone and everyone couldn't read what he wrote. There were things you wouldn't want anyone to read, like how he wanted to kiss her lovely lips again, and he wanted to smell her beautiful hair and hold her in his arms. And there were things you would want everyone to read, like how much he missed Mountfern and was looking forward to being back.

She wished he realized that he didn't *have* to write on a postcard, he could have gotten a notepad and written pages and pages to her. Dara wrote pages and pages back.

Tommy Leonard said when she bought the notepad that she must be going to get like St. Paul and write epistles that nobody read.

"What do you mean, that nobody reads, aren't we demented with St. Paul?" Dara said.

"Yes we are, but the Corinthians and the Ephesians and whoever didn't take a blind bit of notice of him."

"They did too. He converted the lot of them."

"No he did not. Most of them went on their own way."

Tommy's father came over and asked through gritted teeth would it be possible for his son and young Miss Ryan to continue this interesting screaming match about the New Testament outside working hours.

Kitty Daly came home from Dublin for a weekend. She looked very much more grown up, they all thought. Her skirt was very short and she had a lot of make-up. Instead of taming her wild frizzy hair she let it all hang in a long curtain down her back. They nudged each other at mass when she went up to holy communion.

"I'd say she's up to no good in Dublin," whispered Dara, who always feared that Kitty had her eye on Kerry O'Neill.

"She can't be up to that much if she's going to communion," said Michael, which settled it.

Mrs. Meagher told Kate Ryan in great confidence that her bold strap of a daughter Teresa was pregnant at last. It had only been a matter of time. Mrs. Meagher wept. It was bound to happen. What in the name of the Lord was she to do? Kate soothed her, sent for more tea and spoke in low tones. Teresa could stay in Dublin, that was one thing, or she could have the child and they could bring it up in Mountfern together, that would be another. It would be a nine-day wonder and then Mountfern would let them settle down, mother and daughter living together, and then a new life to look after. It might be the making of them. Mrs. Meagher didn't think so.

There was no question, apparently, of the father being forced to marry Teresa; the girl was vague to the point of confusion about who the father might be. Mrs. Meagher wept again.

Kate said that they were living in 1966, not the dark ages, surely she wouldn't want to *force* some child to marry another child over this?

Mrs. Meagher said if there was any chance of it that is exactly what she would like.

"Wait for a little while," Kate begged. "Don't go around telling everyone, just wait, something will turn up to make it seem clear to you."

She was so calm, so confident sitting there in her chair, unruffled, and unshocked. Mrs. Meagher really *did* feel better and was glad she had come to see her.

She would have been interested to know that five minutes after she left Kate Ryan had reached out of the wheelchair, and caught Carrie's arm in a hard grip.

"Listen to me, Carrie, listen to me good. Get some kind of organization into your life with Jimbo, do you hear? Fix a day whenever you like, and don't get yourself thrown aside."

"What do you mean?" Carrie was frightened.

"I don't care if you have a baby, I'd like a baby for God's sake, I'd love to be playing with it, looking after it. I'm never going to have any more of my own, but it's going to be no good to *you.* It may well be 1966 but as far as Mountfern is concerned it's centuries ago and you'd be an outcast."

"B-but there'd be no question of that . . ." Carrie began to stammer.

"Of course there would, Carrie. I'm not a fool. And you do like him, don't you? So put it to him straight. Say you'd like to get married. Give yourself some kind of a chance."

"But he wouldn't think I'm good enough. You know he's doing great as a singer, he'd want someone with a bit more class."

"Then for Christ's sake develop a bit more class."

"Why are you shouting at me, Mrs. Ryan?"

"I don't know, Carrie, I really don't."

"Will Kerry be home for a weekend soon?" Dara asked Grace.

She got the usual reply. "Oh, you know Kerry."

It was a very unsatisfactory reply indeed. Because she didn't really know Kerry. She would love to get to know him much, much better.

She wished he would say in these cards if he was ever coming back home.

Brother Keane said that the boys were to write a letter to Mr. O'Neill that would try to put into words how grateful they were for the new playing field. It would have taken years and years to have gotten what they now had through the generosity of this good man. Their own sons would have barely been playing on a good field like this if it hadn't been for Mr. O'Neill.

Tommy Leonard was the best at English; he was chosen to write the letter. Every boy in the school was to sign it. It would then be framed in carpentry class and presented to Mr. O'Neill at a public ceremony.

Tommy's first three efforts were refused. Brother Keane said to him in a voice like thunder that it was hard to believe Tommy could be so insensitive as to begin by saying "Despite the fact that you did not think this school good enough for your own son . . ." Really and truly, Brother Keane thought, all this jazz and the like had young boys half cracked these days.

Brian Doyle liked Rachel Fine. She had a very good way with people, he noticed, she spoke in a very low voice so that they strained to hear rather than shouting over them. Sometimes he felt she wanted to criticize something here and there but never did. Once or twice he actually asked her did she like something or if she could suggest an alternative. Very reluctantly she would give her views. Like the dock. Brian was going to paint it brightly. Rachel wondered would it be better in natural woods. It looked much better without the garish paint, but Rachel never claimed any of the credit, she joined in the general admiration and praise of Brian Doyle.

He wondered why O'Neill hadn't married her yet.

"Kerry's coming back this weekend," Michael said.

"Never!" Dara felt something like a lump of coal in her throat.

"Yes, he called last night, he's got a couple of days off. Grace's father was very surprised."

"When does he arrive?"

"I think he's going by Dublin so it won't be till Saturday."

"He never said."

"Does he write much to you?"

"The odd card." Dara was deliberately casual.

"It may have been a last-minute thing." Michael was reassuring. "He probably didn't tell any of the other girls either."

"What other girls?"

"Oh, can't you be sure that Kerry would have girls everywhere?"

Michael looked at Dara's face and was sorry that he had said that.

Maggie Daly's mother had sent her in to inspect Loretto Quinn's and see was it true that the place had smartened up beyond all recognition since the Jewish lady had gone to live upstairs. The Dalys had heard disturbing rumors that it would nearly be a rival for their own place. Loretto of all people! God help her, she used to look like a poor tinker.

Loretto was kind to Maggie and spent ages helping her choose between one kind of sweet and another while poor Maggie did her best to spy on the lay of the land.

"Wouldn't you have these sweets for nothing in your own place?" Loretto asked innocently.

"Yes, but I'm not meant to be eating too many of them." Maggie knew she was hopeless at this kind of subterfuge.

Mrs. Fine came down the stairs just then; she had armfuls of materials with her.

"Heavens, haven't you the most beautiful auburn hair!" she said, standing in admiration.

"Who me?" Maggie looked around in case someone else had come into the shop.

"It's gorgeous, isn't it Loretto?"

Privately Loretto thought all the Dalys had terrible heads of frizz, but maybe Mrs. Fine was just being kind.

"Lovely altogether," she agreed.

"It's Maggie, isn't that right?"

Maggie was delighted. "That's it, Mrs. Fine."

"Listen Maggie, I have something here that will look lovely with that hair." She put down her materials and found a length of ribbon. It was in a copper satin.

"Shall I fix it in your hair for you, would you like that?"

Maggie was thrilled. This woman looked like something out of a magazine herself. She was very old of course, but her style was the talk of the place and here she was playing with ribbons in Maggie's hair.

"I'd love it," she said.

Rachel took a strand of the hair and half plaited it in with the ribbon. She swept back some of the rest of the hair. Then she took a compact out of her handbag and showed Maggie the mirror.

"Look, aren't you lovely!" she said.

It was true. Maggie *did* look much nicer. Her face split into a huge smile.

"You must keep it, you're like a little Pre-Raphaelite," Mrs. Fine said.

Neither Loretto nor Maggie knew what it meant but it sounded good. Loretto's eyes held genuine admiration and Maggie could see it. She went home to abuse from her mother because she couldn't remember how or in what ways Loretto's shop had improved.

Liam White told her she wasn't looking as scraggy as usual, and Michael Ryan stopped on his bicycle for a chat.

"You look a bit different today," he said in approval.

Mary Donnelly said that if they were going to make any kind of a fist of this café they were going to run in the hopes of getting a bit of custom, they should have a plan.

"We'll have to get into the minds of Americans, that's a hard thing to do," Kate said.

"Aren't you best friends with an American woman, for heaven's sake?" Mary said as if she expected Rachel to help them every bit of the way.

And in many ways Rachel did. She told them of places that sold cheap but very authentically Irish pottery and even ordered it for them so that she could get a proper discount for them. She told them that American visitors would love to feel they were somewhere that was *really* Irish.

"Do you mean leprechauns and begorras?"

"No," said Rachel, but she didn't say it with a great deal of conviction.

"Do you mean a hint of leprechauns and begorras?" Kate suggested again.

"That's exactly what I mean, a hint of it."

"Jesus, Mary and Joseph," Kate said. "It's worse than I thought."

Eddie had another breakage. This time it was the side mirror of Judy Byrne's car. It had been parked outside Ryan's while Judy was inside doing the exercises with Kate. Eddie had been seeing how far it would turn around. Not as pliable as he had thought.

It was there in his hand when Judy came out.

"I'll fix it."

"You won't," said Judy. "You'll pay for it."

Mary suggested a source of money to him. "Your mam will pay you piece work for hemming the green napkins for the café."

"Me hem table napkins? You must be mad," Eddie stormed.

"Look at it this way: there aren't many jobs open to you, and you've done the Protestant graveyard already, so what else is there? You've a fine hand with a needle, I'm always telling you that."

"Just as long as you don't tell anyone else . . ." Eddie warned.

"Do a dozen a night, up in your room if you don't want anyone to see you, or you can come out to my house if you like, and sit there with Leopold and the wireless."

It wasn't the life Eddie Ryan had planned for himself. Sitting in a converted outhouse hemming green linen serviettes with a mad dog and Radio Eireann for company. Mary's wireless didn't seem to get Radio Luxembourg.

Still, it paid for Miss Byrne's old mirror, and Mam was very nice to him and sometimes said that he was an old dote despite everything.

Dara and Michael waited for Grace to collect them on Saturday to go to the pictures. They met Tommy and the Whites just outside—it was going to be very crowded. Declan Morrissey rubbed his hands happily. If he had his way he'd show musicals all the year round. This was the third or fourth time he had *Seven Brides for Seven Brothers* and it was always the same, you got the old and the young alike to come to it.

Michael was pleased to see the queue, it meant that they might all get separated. Then he and Grace could go to the back somewhere. There couldn't be any touching Grace if the others were all there.

Maggie was late. "Sorry," she apologized, even though it didn't matter, they were still in the line waiting to get in.

"Sorry, Kitty called from Dublin, she wanted me to think up some story about why she's not coming home for the weekend."

"She picked a poor one to invent a story for her," Tommy Leonard said affectionately.

"I know, I get so flustered," Maggie said.

"Why can't she tell them herself?" Dara said.

"She didn't want to talk to Mam, because Mam would worm it out of her, so she called when Mam was at benediction."

"Worm what?" Dara said.

"She's meeting Kerry in Dublin, that's why she's not coming

home," said Maggie excitedly, and looked around at the faces of her friends.

Kerry arrived on Sunday evening. He called into Ryan's at a slack time. Kate was behind the counter in her wheelchair.

"What can I serve you?" Her smile was pleasant.

"I don't drink alcohol at all, Mrs. Ryan."

"Very sensible of you, but then that's a little hypocritical of me. If everyone was to feel like you do where would our business be, I wonder?"

"Your business is going okay, isn't it?" He looked pointedly around the almost empty pub.

"Usually a little more lively than this." Kate felt annoyed somehow that this young fellow hadn't come in when they were doing a really good business. She wondered why she was trying to impress him.

"I just came to find out if I could take your lovely daughter for a walk by the river on this beautiful evening," he asked.

"My lovely daughter has homework to do." Kate smiled.

"I'm sure she'll be able to do it later." Kerry smiled.

"At just fifteen she's a little young to let walks with young men get between her and her studies." Kate was still smiling a smile she didn't feel.

"Oh now, Mrs. Ryan, she's not *just* fifteen. I had the pleasure of being at her fifteenth birthday, a long long time ago. Way back last September, if I remember rightly."

"You remember rightly, Kerry."

"So you are saying she can't come out with me. Is this what I hear?"

"No it is not what you hear, you must go and ask her herself."

"Oh well, that's all right then. May I go into the house?"

"No, I'll call her."

Dara had seen him coming from the window seat. She had combed her hair and rubbed a little lipstick on and off again.

"Hi," she said.

"Lovely to see you again," he said warmly. "I was trying to persuade your mother here to let us go for a walk."

Dora looked at him levelly. "I'd love to, Kerry, but I have all this homework to do," she said.

He was surprised. "Can't you leave it till later?" He was sure he would convince her.

"No, at this stage there's so much to be done. I wish I'd worked harder earlier in the year but you know how it is, I'm afraid I've left it all to the end."

"You're not graduating this year." There was an edge to his voice.

"You've obviously never met Sister Laura, she thinks this is the most important year in our lives. We have exams nearly every week."

Kerry was furious. "Another time then," he said, and walked out.

Kate looked at her stricken daughter.

Round One to Dara, she thought with a mixture of pride and anxiety.

Miss Hayes had never known a prayer to St. Anthony to fail, but this time it had. Nowhere could she find the two silver salvers that had stood on the sideboard.

Marian had admired them often and said that they were magnificent silver. She had been startled to discover that Mrs. Fine had bought them for Patrick at an auction, at his request.

Mrs. Fine often bought old Irish silverware, and had said that the O'Neills should have the pleasure of looking at it before it went to the hotel eventually.

Every two weeks Olive Hayes cleaned the little collection. Mrs. Fine had visited once and praised her highly for the wonderful way it had been cared for. Now Miss Hayes was worried—what could have happened to them? It was unlikely that they had been robbed. There had been no break-in, and anyway there was always someone in the house.

Marian Johnson did drop in from time to time but she would never . . . of course not. And those little Ryan twins and Maggie Daly from the dairy. No, it was out of the question.

She would have to think again—was it possible that she had placed them somewhere else? Or perhaps Mr. O'Neill had already taken them to the hotel, or to have them valued.

Olive Hayes was very troubled.

Americans would want entertainment. Kate knew that.

But what kind? It couldn't be amateurish in their café when it was professional and well organized across the river.

What would they expect in an Irish café? If it was to be truly authentic then of course there wouldn't be singing and dancing, nobody would be doing anything except getting stuck into their tea and scones. But this plan was for something that wasn't quite authentic but looked as if it might be.

What a pity that none of them played the harp, and that they didn't have a big tuneful harp handy in one of their outhouses.

Carrie asked Jimbo would they get married sometime.
"Sure, we'll get married sometime," Jimbo said.
Carrie felt vaguely dissatisfied with this reply.

Jack Coyne asked Loretto did the great O'Neill spend the night above in the rooms with your woman.
Loretto said certainly he did not.
Jack said Loretto was right to keep her mouth shut. He would do the same in her place. Loretto was annoyed about that, since she was not being diplomatic. It was the truth. Patrick O'Neill came to call sometimes but he never stayed the night.

Dennis Hill telephoned to know whether Kerry's father had recovered from his illness.
Olive Hayes told him that there had been no illness.
"There has to have been an illness, why else did he go home?" Mr. Hill wanted to know.
Miss Hayes decided to rescue the situation. "There was a bit of trouble all right, it wasn't exactly an illness," she said.
Mr. Hill never pried. He had just been calling out of courtesy, he said. When would they expect Kerry back?
"I'll ask him to call you himself," said Miss Hayes.
She told Kerry that he should call Donegal. She told him that Mr. Hill was now under the impression that what he had thought was an illness was in fact a little trouble.
Kerry smiled a great charming smile at her. "You are a great ally, Miss Hayes," he said.
"I wouldn't rely on it, Kerry," she said.
"I get the picture," Kerry said.

Dara and Maggie were on the footbridge, when Kerry came along.
"Maggie, could you do something for me? Please." His eyes were a piercing blue. They looked straight at little Maggie.
"Sure," she said good-naturedly.
"Could you go up to the hotel and see if my father is around? I want to go up and talk to Brian Doyle about something, but my father thinks I've gone back to Donegal so I want to make sure he isn't there. Can you look and see if his car is there? Do you mind?"

"Not at all, but am I the right one . . . ? I often get things wrong."

"No, you're perfect, you look so innocent no one would know you were my spy."

Maggie scampered up the path by the laurel bushes.

"Well," Kerry said to Dara.

"Well what?"

"Well what was all this drama, you had homework to do? I came straight out and put myself on the line and asked your mother . . . and you turn me down. What was all that about?" He looked very angry. Dara's heart began to pound. It had been a very risky thing. She had wondered afterwards had she been mad.

"No reason," she said, shrugging.

"Don't do that, it's so silly, it makes you so cheap, so common. I came to see you. I thought you liked me. Why are you playing silly games?" His handsome face looked hurt.

"Well . . ." She didn't know what to say.

"Because if you don't want to see me, that's fine, just say it straight out. But if you do, let's go up to Coyne's wood."

"When?"

"What's wrong with now?"

"You can't mean now. You've just sent Maggie on a message."

"That was so that I could talk to you. My father's in Shannon today."

"You told her a lie . . . !"

"It was so that I could ask you what was wrong."

"And you met Kitty in Dublin too!"

"Silly little Maggie, getting everything wrong. I *saw* Kitty in Dublin and she clung and clung. Kitty the clam I call her."

"We can't go off and leave Maggie to come back and find us not here."

"Yes we can if you want to."

It was the longest moment of Dara's life.

"No, I'll wait for Maggie. You sent her on a fool's errand," she said.

If Kate Ryan had been watching she would have said, "Round Two, Dara."

"John, will you read me some poetry?"

"Aren't you too tired, love?"

Kate sat in her green room, her eyes too bright, her face drawn.

"No, I have that feeling I'm not going to sleep."

"Let me get you into bed first then I'll go and find something you might like. I haven't written anything for so long."

"How could you?" She touched his hand in sympathy. "But tonight I want you to read me other people's poetry, not just your own, and no, I won't go to bed yet."

"Other people's poetry?" He was disappointed.

She was deliberately light and joky. "Yes, isn't it very presumptuous of them, but other people did write poetry, like Yeats, or Oscar Wilde or James Clarence Mangan."

"Will I read you the *Lays of Ancient Rome?* I love that . . ."

"No, something Irish."

"Or *Hiawatha* . . . I've never read the whole of *Hiawatha* aloud. *That* will send you off to sleep all right."

"No." She gripped the sides of the wheelchair in impatience.

"All right, all right . . ." He went to the bookshelves and ran his finger along the backs of books for what seemed a long time. Eventually he took out a book and began:

> "Oh my dark Rosaleen
> "Do not sigh do not weep . . ."

"Stand up over there so that I can see you," Kate said. "Now start again."

He read the poem with gestures, putting a lot of emphasis into it and giving the repetition a fine sonorous sound.

"That was very good," Kate said approvingly.

John's face was empty. "That wasn't me reading poetry to you, that was an audition, wasn't it?"

"Yes," Kate said in a small voice.

"Well?"

"It was very good. Could you bear it?"

"Of course, if we *have* to."

"We have to."

Rachel was adamant about not letting him stay the night. If Patrick wanted to preserve the fiction that he and Rachel were just good friends, then preserve it. She did not even countenance making love in her rooms. She was a respectable woman staying in Loretto's, she didn't want any reputation, thank you very much. And Patrick always had to leave early.

Once or twice they had managed it in Coyne's wood, and in the back of the car and in a far distant corner of the river bank on a rug. It had been exciting and uncomfortable at the same time.

"I may have to go back to New York for a week, come with me," Patrick said suddenly one May evening, in Loretto's.

"What for?"

"Well, we could make love properly for one thing without risk of half the town discovering us or getting curvature of the spine." He was grinning at her in the way she loved and hadn't seen a lot recently.

"No, I have a lot to do here."

"You've nothing to do here, stop fooling yourself."

A flash of anger. "Shall I list the things I have to do here . . ."

"No, don't be tedious, Rachel, we both know why you're here, we both think it's a great idea, so what? Just quit pretending it's a real career and you can't be taken from it to come to New York for a week."

Never had she been so angry. Never.

They both knew why she was here, it was so obvious was it?

She knew she must keep calm. Nothing must be thrown away for the very unimportant luxury of losing her temper.

"What had you in mind for us in New York?" she asked levelly.

"I don't know." He put on a teasing smile. "Maybe we could get ourselves to a justice of the peace and get hitched, that way I wouldn't have to be thrown out of here like a college boy at ten o'clock at night."

"Would you like to get married?" Her voice was calm.

"No, what man *likes* to get married? Hell, of course I don't want to get married, Rachel, I'm too old, you're too old, we're fine as we are. Hey?"

No response.

"Hey? Rachel, you're not sulking now, are you? We're fine as we are. Why complicate it? Why think I love you more if you tie me down by some bit of paper?"

She looked at him levelly.

"Well, say something, woman, for God's sake, have I done the one unforgivable sin saying this? You did ask me would I *like* the idea of being married. I'm telling you. Straight up."

"Sure," she said.

"What does that mean?"

"Not much, I guess."

"So what did I say that was so terrible?"

"I suppose what was terrible was that you thought a piece of paper would only tie *you* down, you never thought that it might also tie down whoever you married. It's a bargain you know, marriage, not just one person being lassooed by another. It's a sharing thing."

"You didn't do very well during your attempt at it," he lashed out.

"You weren't exactly faithful during *your* attempt at it," she said straight back.

He was silent.

Rachel sat still in her chair. Her cream linen suit and her little sprig of purple heather worn at the lapel matched the room perfectly. She didn't look at Patrick, she looked across at the sun setting over Fernscourt. Her face was not sad, she was calm and entirely in command. She was thinking that this was the end of the road. She had traveled so far, so many years and so many thousands of miles and it would end now, in recriminations like so many relationships.

"It's got nothing to do with you. With you as a person," Patrick began.

Rachel said nothing, she didn't even listen, it was as if she had always known it was coming, this conversation, the goodbye.

"In fact I want your company and to be with you more than anybody. You know that."

She looked across and saw men still working in the fading light. They were getting overtime now to finish the job in time.

"Shit Rachel, why did you have to go and suggest we get married? Why couldn't you let things go on the way they were?"

Almost reluctantly Rachel lifted her eyes from the men who were finishing the stone wall around the forecourt, and brought her glance to Patrick.

"I did not bring up marriage, Patrick, *you* did. You said we would find a justice of the peace in New York and get hitched. Please be fair."

He was wrongfooted over this. "Yeah sure, but you said . . ."

"Forget what I said. Don't let it end in a war of words--you said, I said. What does it matter? And as you said it has nothing to do with me as a person."

She stood up, straightening her skirt. "I'll show you out now."

"Well . . ."

"Good night, Patrick. I'll be going to Connemara in the next day or two, probably tomorrow. We'll consider we said goodbye now. Right?"

He put his hands on her shoulders. "Listen . . ."

"Yes?" Her eyes were large and dark, they looked into his very directly, they didn't dart about anxiously trying to read his face.

"Listen Rachel, I'm not worth it."

She smiled patiently as she might have smiled at a child.

He was struggling for words.

"Even if I were, if I could . . . even if I did feel . . . there would be so many complications, there'd be all hell to pay. You have no idea how much trouble and everything . . ."

He looked at her, pleading, begging her to understand that their marriage would be opposed by Church and society even if he could bring himself to propose.

Rachel Fine had some dignity left. She chose not to understand what he was saying.

"Patrick, you've a lot of work to do tomorrow and so have I." She kissed his cheek.

"But . . ."

She had closed the door behind him.

She leaned against the door as she had seen so many heroines do in movies. But no heroine had ever behaved as stupidly, she thought, no woman who ever leaned against a door like that had been such a downright idiot as Rachel Fine letting her man go like that.

Possibly to the arms of Marian Johnson. And even, when the hotel was built and he was lonely, possibly he might marry Marian Johnson. Church and society wouldn't oppose that, they'd be delighted with it, and the divorced Jewess could be moved from the scene. She didn't cry, she felt too empty to cry. She didn't go to the window to see him driving off.

She just stood motionless for a long time.

John Ryan sighed. Sometimes he wished he could discuss things with someone. Mary Donnelly was out, she hated Patrick O'Neill with a passion. He couldn't speak to Fergus because young Slattery seemed to hold the O'Neills personally responsible for Kate's accident and could only think of the day when the huge compensation would be paid over.

Dr. White was not a good ally. He seemed to think that John was a bit of an old misery. On more than one occasion the doctor had told him straight out that Kate's condition could be made much more bearable if her immediate family surrounded her with hope and optimism.

No point in talking to his son, the boy was like a moonstruck calf pining over the little American girl.

He felt unwilling to bring his worries to Dara. She was still a child and it made him seem weak to tell his own daughter that he couldn't communicate with her mother.

As he went ahead with the preparations for Ryan's Café, John's heart was heavy.

One afternoon when Mary was minding the bar, when Kate was busy hemming green table napkins for the café, when the children were at school and the menagerie reasonably peaceful—Leopold snoring in the garden, the cat purring like an engine on the windowsill—John sat down to write a poem.

This time he didn't write about the land or the people who had once walked this land. This time he wrote about the cage he found himself in; the cage which he couldn't escape from because he himself had built the bars. They were bars of concern and love and good manners. They were rules he had made so that he would not hurt anyone else. He wrote how by forcing yourself to take one course of action and adopt one set of attitudes you can also be untrue to yourself and deny your real worth.

It was the cry of a strong man who found himself trapped and couldn't see an escape. He looked into Kate's room—she had fallen asleep over her sewing. Gently he took the needle and green linen from her hands and arranged the cushion behind her back in the chair. He left the poem beside her and went for a long walk. He walked up to Coyne's wood and beat at the undergrowth with a stick for a while. Then he found himself climbing that big mossy hill toward the Grange.

He went in and asked for a pint of beer.

Marian's place was slipping, he noticed, the bar was not clean and it was late afternoon, there were still ashtrays full and glasses uncollected. The stocks hadn't been checked, you could see some bottles had nearly run out and others had marks of liquid down their sides.

It had been years since he had come here and it used to be much smarter in the old days.

The youth serving had neither manner nor charm. He gave the wrong change and didn't apologize when it was pointed out.

Who would stay in the Grange when there was a luxury place like Fernscourt opening three miles away? John gave a little shiver. He had heard too of the way that Patrick had interviewed the staff, how he had told them that American guests liked to be made much of, to

have their names remembered. They liked people to say "You're welcome" when they said "Thank you." Patrick had searched Ireland for
the right manager and, not being satisfied with any of the applicants,
had gone to another hotel and offered Jim Costello twice his salary to
leave at once and come to manage Fernscourt. Costello, an attractive
go-getting young man, had given the matter five minutes' thought,
which had raised his salary even higher, and then left the hotel after
serving three weeks' notice and finding a successor for himself. Costello was the right man for Patrick O'Neill. A man who would not
burn his bridges, he had left his old employers on good terms and he
could always go back if Patrick and he had a falling out; on the other
hand he had impressed his new boss with his quick thinking and
decision. He was a man of great charm; he had drunk many a pint in
Ryan's and delighted everyone with his easy ways.

Patrick O'Neill and Jim Costello wouldn't have employed a surly
youth like this boy behind Marian Johnson's bar. John pondered on
just how much the old order was changing.

He left, thanking the boy and getting no response, and walked
down the hill. There was a scurry at one stage when he passed the big
clump of trees, as if he had disturbed a courting couple. He smiled to
himself, thinking how stony and uncomfortable the ground must be.

For half a moment he wondered whether it was Michael and
Grace he saw disappearing into the bushes. But he dismissed the
notion. For heaven's sake, it was the middle of the afternoon.

What would they be doing up here? And anyway they were *far* too
young for that sort of thing.

Mary Donnelly was glaring at an inoffensive couple of farmers who
took no notice of her whatsoever.

"This is a great pub, Mary," John said as he came in.

The farmers looked up, amused.

"If you can't say it who can?" one of them laughed.

"Have you been drinking?" Mary asked suspiciously.

"You're right, Mary. God, it would need to be a sharp man to fox
you. I was up having a pint in the Grange, as it happens."

"And it wasn't to your liking?"

"It was not. There was no warm service with a smile like you get
when you come in this door. Oh boy no. There was only glares and
surly shrugs. What human would want a pint in a place like that?
People want to be made welcome in a place, that's what running a

pub or a hotel is about, it's not just about pouring alcohol down their throats."

The farmers looked at each other and grinned conspiratorially.

Mary flushed a dark red. "If you're saying that I . . ."

"I'm saying that it's lovely to be back in a friendly atmosphere," he said firmly. "That's all, and if we're going to keep any custom from going over to O'Neill's Thatch Bar we'll have to let them know that they're welcome here, and really welcome too."

He banged out of the bar and into the house.

Mary was open-mouthed. That was the first time John had ever admitted publicly that there was a threat from O'Neill, and imagine admitting it in front of two customers. He must be really upset.

Kate was sitting by the open french window, wearing her gardening gloves and tidying up one of those high urns that Rachel Fine had cleverly positioned, one on each side of the door. These were Kate's alone, she grew herbs and heathers in them, they were easy to reach and made her feel she was really gardening.

"I've been thinking," John said.

He pulled off her gloves and held her hands.

"So have I. When I read your poem and realized what it's like for you, not wanting to upset me, and not knowing how to talk to me, I felt I could have put the power into my body and run after you. I woke up and read it and I could feel such energy surging through me, I was sure I'd have the strength to stand."

Her eyes were wild with trying to explain, she was like a child straining to have more movement than she had.

"Gently, Kate. Gently," he soothed her.

She would not be calmed. She thought as she had so often thought about that summer's day when he had wanted to make love and she said no, it was ridiculous in the middle of the afternoon, and that she had felt restless. Restless indeed! If she had stayed with him as he had wanted she would never have wandered into Fernscourt and into this life in a chair.

"You *do* have great strength," he told her. "Aren't you the strongest woman in this county? I mean it."

"But tell me that you *know* I'd be nothing without you. The children will grow up and go away, and the pub may win or lose but the only thing I want is for us to be together. Insofar as we can ever be together because of this bloody chair." She hit the arms of the wheelchair in frustration.

"But you're only saying what I know. I know you love me." He was smiling a huge smile of pleasure.

"I can give you nothing. Nothing a wife can give."

"Stop, stop."

"I've been so selfish, I never sort of helped you or anything."

She was talking about some of her earlier attempts to give John pleasure. They had both been embarrassed and Kate had cried at not being able to do it properly. John had been embarrassed at something so obviously selfish that could not be shared. They had attempted it less and less.

"I'm all right, look at what you have to bear, for God's sake. It doesn't seem all that important to me that we can't make love as we used to."

"But I was thinking we could." Kate's eyes were definitely excited, her color was high.

"How do you mean?"

"Draw the curtains," she said.

He closed the glass doors and pulled the soft green and white curtains.

"Come here," she whispered.

"Wait till I lock the door. It would be the one time we'd have Leopold, Mary, Carrie, the children and half the bar arriving in on top of us."

She laughed like a teenager.

"Get me out of this bloody chair, John Ryan, and love me."

He lifted her onto the bed. Her dress opened easily; she had all her clothes made front-fastening so that she could dress herself with the minimum of fuss.

"But we c-can't . . ." he stammered.

"Why not? It's my body. It won't hurt, I won't feel much but I can feel above the belt, if you know what I mean. That's nice."

"But can I . . . inside you . . . wouldn't that be bad for you?"

"Why would it? It's just paralyzed, it isn't out of bounds." She was high with excitement and was stroking him encouragingly.

"Kate, I don't want to do anything that might damage you . . ."

"It won't. I checked."

"You checked? When did you check?"

"This afternoon. I called Dr. White."

"My God! What did he say?"

"He said fire ahead, and that he was delighted, he thought we'd never get around to it."

* * *

Fergus Slattery called and was told that Mr. and Mrs. Ryan were in Mrs. Ryan's room and weren't to be disturbed.

"Nothing wrong?" Fergus inquired.

"John is like a lighting devil today, perhaps they're having a row," Mary Donnelly said. "There isn't a man in this house that will speak straight to you, I'm afraid."

She was still smarting from Michael's cross-questioning. He had been highly alarmed to find that his mother and father were closeted together, and felt sure that the only reason could be that Dad had actually seen him with Grace. The thought was too mortifying even to entertain for a moment.

What could Dad be telling Mam, and how soon would he be called in and *what* would he say? And why couldn't that awful Mary stop snarling at him and tell him what *kind* of a peculiar humor had his father been in when he came home?

Michael, white with anxiety, had gone to throw stones from the footbridge, and pray. If God arranged it so that Dad hadn't seen, then he would . . . what would he do? He couldn't offer to give up being with Grace because that was what he wanted most in the world. Suppose he offered God a rosary. Not enough. God was known to be particularly against Immodest Touches, and whatever he and Grace were up to it would certainly come into that category. Perhaps if he gave God a promise that he would go to confession soon, and fixed a firm date. Perhaps that might do.

"Was it important, your message?" Mary remembered belatedly John's startling instructions that she was to be high on charm.

"You could always write it down, Mr. Slattery, and I'd see that they got it."

"No, I'll phone them later," he said.

"They've taken the phone off the hook," Mary explained.

"God, it must be a terrible row altogether," Fergus said.

Rachel looked into the window of Meagher's. As always she was looking out for the kind of thing that Kate might be able to display in a glass cabinet when they got the café going.

Meagher's window was not the most inspiring of places, and the woman who ran it seemed to know little or nothing about the odd selection of stock she carried. People had told Rachel that it was the late Mr. Frank Meagher who was the one who knew something about the business. The window held the usual collection of musical boxes, travel clocks and some really appalling candlesticks, and there in a box with tissue paper were the two silver salvers that Rachel had bought for Fernscourt. Salvers that had been on Patrick's sideboard on the only occasion when Rachel had visited the lodge. She had been there once when she knew both children would be far away.

Rachel stared unbelievingly at the two pieces of silver. They were worth everything else in the window three times over. Patrick surely could not have sold them. Surely, surely not. Rachel went in and bought a brooch shaped like an L which she would give to Loretto. She spoke to Mrs. Meagher, a sad-faced, worried-looking woman about the silver salvers, and with shaking hand managed to pay for the brooch. She needed to be in the open air quickly.

In the Lodge Olive Hayes had come to a decision. She was going to mention the salvers to Mr. O'Neill.

The only question was the matter of approach. Should she ask whether he had in fact taken them elsewhere for safekeeping? Or should she say that she had not been able to find them?

There was nobody she could discuss it with. If only her sister Bernadette were not at the other end of the earth.

She could have talked about it with Sheila Whelan of course. Even if it had been Marian, Sheila would not have told the whole town.

She could even have approached Mrs. Ryan in the pub. She would never have thought of it as a slight on her own twins.

Sergeant Sheehan was the kind of man she could speak to quietly, but it wouldn't have been fair. Once she spoke to him it would have to be official.

No, it would have to be Mr. O'Neill himself, without the luxury of asking advice from others.

Patrick came in, his face weary.

She decided to give him a while to settle down.

But he had read her face. "What is it, Miss Hayes?"

"How did you know there was anything, sir?"

"I haven't worked with people since I was fourteen years of age without learning something. What is it?"

"It's the silver salvers, sir, for the hotel, that used to be on the sideboard."

"It's all right, Miss Hayes." He looked very weary.

"I only noticed today they aren't there."

"It was a misunderstanding. They'll be back."

"Oh, that's all right then." She moved away, about to go back to her kitchen.

Patrick realized that she was not going to launch into a line of questions or explanations.

"Miss Hayes."

"Sir?"

"I value you more than you'll ever know."

Her face became brick red with pleasure. "Thank you very much indeed, Mr. O'Neill. It's a pleasure working here. You are all very appreciative people."

"I meant what I said about coming to the hotel with us. I think we'll need you."

"Oh, we'll discuss that nearer the time, Mr. O'Neill."

"How sensible you are. I'm afraid those nuns in your sister's place will snap you into the convent and you'll never be heard of again."

She went away smiling. But she looked back at him before she got to the kitchen and saw that the smile had fallen away and under the genial affable face that he presented to the world Patrick O'Neill was angrier than she had ever seen anyone in her life.

Brian Doyle had handed him a note. It was all sealed with sticky paper.

"Mrs. Fine said you were to open this on your own over a desk or something. It's got something very fine in it that might fall out." Brian was uncaring, but keen to deliver the message exactly as Rachel had instructed.

"All right."

He had opened it in his car. Alone.

Patrick,

I am writing this because there is no way you and I could discuss it usefully.

In Meagher's the jewelry store on Bridge Street you will find the two silver salvers. Mrs. Meagher bought them from Kerry three days ago for a fraction of their worth. Mrs. Meagher is not to be blamed for trying to cheat him, she is also selling them at an equally impossible price.

I have no idea, nor do I want to know what happened. For all I know you may be party to this, but I think not and I wanted to forewarn you. Naturally I said nothing at all to Mrs. Meagher that would indicate I knew anything about the pieces.

For your own information Mrs. Meagher is a gossipy, unstable person who is unhappy here in Mountfern and has been considering leaving. Her problem is that she has little capital and even less get up and go.

I leave it with you. Obviously I will be happy to do anything to help but I feel this is something you will want to handle on your own.

I told Brian Doyle a rigmarole about this letter needing to be opened carefully, I thought that way you would be sure to read it on your own. I feared if I said it was very urgent and private he would have had every kettle on the building site at work on it. But perhaps I misjudge him.

Love always,
Rachel

"Mrs. Meagher, how are you this fine day?"

"Dragging the divil by the tail as usual, Mr. O'Neill. How is it that you are always so cheerful?"

"It's in my nature, I expect." Patrick smiled broadly.

He pulled up the small rickety chair close to the counter. "About those salvers that my son brought in, the ones that are in the window."

"He said he had full authority . . ."

"Oh yes, no problem like that at all . . ."

"And if you want them back, Mr. O'Neill . . . I did think that maybe it wasn't a good enough price but your lad seemed very pleased . . ."

"Not at all, nothing like that . . . no no." Patrick's voice was soothing.

"So I hope I didn't do anything out of turn . . ."

"You know the way children are, Mrs. Meagher, you do your best and then you wonder *what* was the right thing to do . . ."

Mrs. Meagher sat down on the other side of the counter and leaned across to Patrick.

"Mr. O'Neill, you don't know the truth you're saying . . ."

Patrick O'Neill drove himself slowly back to the lodge to wait for his son. In his briefcase he carried the two silver salvers.

"I'll give them a little polish, will I?" Olive Hayes had suggested.

"That would be lovely, Miss Hayes."

The evening shadows lengthened, he sat alone looking in front of him. He had telephoned Loretto Quinn's. No, there was no sign of Rachel and she had not said where she would be.

He had telephoned Ryan's and she was not there. The ridiculous harridan who looked after the bar for them said that Mrs. Ryan was not to be disturbed.

There was no sign of his daughter either.

The key turned in the lock.

Kerry came in.

He was surprised to find his father sitting alone and with no work in front of him.

Surprised but not alarmed.

"This is all very peaceful," Kerry said slightly mockingly.

"I'd like to go out, Kerry." Patrick's voice was very calm.

Kerry decided to be flip. "Well then you *must* go out, Father, don't let me stop you," he said.

"We'll go right away."

Something in his tone made Kerry follow his father's look, and on the sideboard he saw the two gleaming silver salvers.

His face did not change. "I see," he said.

"Good." Patrick looked dangerously quiet.

They left the house without words.

Miss Hayes watched them from the kitchen window. They walked toward the woods.

"Why did you do it?" Patrick asked his son.

"I needed the money."

"You are a fool as well as a thief. Do you have any idea how much they were worth?"

"A great deal more than that woman gave me, but that wasn't the point."

"What was the point?"

"The point was that I needed that amount and she could give it to me, so it couldn't matter less what the real value of those trays was. They only represented to me a way to get what I needed."

"So if you are going to steal from my house and make us a public exhibition in my town, my place, it doesn't even matter that you get a fraction of what these items were worth."

"No. Their worth is not important."

Patrick's hand went into a fist without his having any control over it.

Kerry saw. "Don't forget all you spent on that orthodontal work,

Father. I mean, if you're talking about value for money, why smash it all up? It cost you a fortune to get me all this bridge work."

The spasm of white anger passed; it was replaced with something much deeper. Something, Patrick felt, that was going to be with him for a long time.

"Do you hate me, Kerry?"

"Of course I don't, Father."

"Then why?"

"I told you, I needed money. Why do you have to be so Italian about everything? Love, hate—life isn't like that."

"What is it like then? Tell me, I'd love to know what life *is* like."

Kerry leaned against a tree. He looked impossibly beautiful in the evening light. He looked like a painting of a young hero, not a cheat and liar who had stolen from his own father and showed not an ounce of remorse.

"Life is about excitement, Father, it's not about the past and the old days and the old order and righting wrongs that were done centuries ago—if they were done at all."

"Excitement?" Patrick said.

"Yes, that's about the best I can do to explain." Kerry seemed bored.

"Is there not sufficient *excitement*, as you call it, in Donegal? Why did you have to come to that center of excitement—Mountfern—and humiliate me in my own place?"

"You are not humiliated, Father, I'm sure you got out of it."

"You're goddamn right I did. I bought Meagher's shop."

"Hey," Kerry laughed. He gave a natural, amused little laugh. The boy was not even remotely touched by what he had done.

"I told Mrs. Meagher that there had been a misunderstanding, she told me that children were all the same. I listened to her woes, one of them being that she couldn't find a buyer. We need a place in Bridge Street. She's leaving almost at once. She will say nothing about your misunderstanding. I will say nothing about some of her circumstances."

"Like her daughter being a teeny bit pregnant." He laughed again.

"We don't have you to thank for that, do we?"

"Teresa Meagher, Father. Please. You must think I'm hard up!"

"Why did you need the money?"

"My business, Father."

"No, Kerry. My business now."

"Are you going to beat me again?"

"No, of course not."

"There's no of course about it, you want to."

"No, I want you to tell me. Tell me why."

"You're such a man of the world, you have this sixth sense, you tell me, Father. You always say you have a feel for things."

"Cards?" Patrick said.

Kerry paused. "Yes," he said.

"Was that it at school all that time ago?"

"Sort of. Betting, big talk."

"Aren't you a fool."

"No, sometimes I win."

"I'm sure you do. At the start of every game in the sucker's build-up."

Now it was Kerry's turn to look scornful. "How would you know, Father? You're much too cagey, too cautious to play a hand of cards."

"I did once. For long enough to know I hadn't the time to invest in it."

"Very praiseworthy," Kerry mocked.

"No. Very practical. That's what it was. If I wanted to play cards I'd have learned how to do it, not get taken by every half-assed two-bit man around, like what seems to be happening to you."

"I was unlucky one night, that's all."

"Unlucky? Do you even know the odds?"

"It all depends, Father."

"It does not depend. There are odds on filling a straight, there are odds, you fool, on getting a house if you have two pairs. Actual odds —you don't know them and you expect to steal my silver to pay for your idiocy."

"Yes, I can see that from where you stand, it's hard."

"No it's not hard. It's easy."

"How do you mean?"

"You get taught, taught to play properly. If that's what you want."

"It's not like that. You can't enroll in night classes."

"You can if you want to."

"How on earth?"

"Brian Doyle's brother is a card player, deals in a club somewhere out the Galway Road. One of the best, they tell me."

"He can't be great if he's dealing cards in a club near Galway."

"He liked the liquor as well. That's what slowed him down. Go to him next time you're home, bring him a bottle of Powers, say you'd like to learn a few fancy deals, waterfalls, that kind of thing. He'll straighten you out."

Kerry's mouth was open.

"He doesn't deal from the bottom, he doesn't have marked cards. He'd be the first to tell you of people who have no fingers to play with if they do that sort of thing."

"This is Ireland, Father, not Chicago in Prohibition."

"This is card playing all over the world, Kerry."

"Do you mean that I should go to this guy? You'll set it up?"

"I won't set it up, you set it up. You heard of him, turn up there. Meanwhile get your ass back to Dennis Hill. I suppose you told him some lie."

"I had to. They were pushing me a bit for the money, these guys."

"Are they in the hotel?"

"God no, the hotel's as dead as a dodo. They're over the border, in Derry."

"That should be excitement enough for you."

"They're good people, it's just that someone else was pushing them."

Kerry got a feeling that his father wasn't interested.

"How did you find out, Father? About Meagher's?"

"My business."

"And you don't seem to have . . . well, too many hard feelings."

"I don't have any feelings. That's what is so strange. I have no feelings at all. Maybe you always felt that toward me so you know what it's like. But it's new to me. When I got up this morning I suppose if anyone asked me how I felt about you, I'd have said I loved you. When I saw those salvers in Meagher's and had to negotiate with that stupid woman, and saw you leaning against the tree there . . . I might have said I hated you. But now. Nothing. Nothing at all." Patrick seemed mildly regretful.

Kerry knew that his father was speaking from the heart.

"What happens to me now, Father?"

"As I said, you go back to Dennis. After the opening you and I talk again, it could be you want to go to the Shannon school. You could go abroad to a hotel in France, Germany, Switzerland. We'll have visitors from there too, and that seems to be the way of the future.

"Of course you might want to go to university. I don't know, Kerry, let's not look too far into the future."

"And this . . . this business?"

"It's over now, isn't it? I mean there's nothing else gone in the house, I won't go into the church and see our candlesticks on the altar?"

"No, Father."

"Well that's it. Twice. Anyone's allowed two mistakes. The third time is it."

"How do you mean, it's it?"

"It's goodbye, it's notice in the paper time, I am not responsible for the debts of . . . That sort of thing."

Kerry was silent.

Patrick rattled his car keys. "I don't expect you to stop playing cards—that would be childish of me—and anyway if you're going to talk to Francis Doyle, you may get quite good and make a nice living. I don't expect you to stay clear of debt. If you do get into debt again come to me, come back and we'll discuss it. Within reason, and in return for work or whatever, I will try to help you, and you must come home here for the holidays and stand by my side at the opening and all of that. But if you steal from me or from anyone else, then it's over, it's as if you were never my son."

No emotion in his voice. No pleas no hate. No wishing for love.

For the first time in his life Kerry felt a chill of fear.

Rachel and Patrick missed each other by minutes. She went to walk along the towpath in the evening light. He went into Ryan's for a drink. There was always company there, he thought, always a welcome.

It was odd that the only people who should make him feel really welcome were the very people whose business would suffer most by his coming to Mountfern in the first place. He looked at John and Kate Ryan and how they seemed to sparkle so well at each other. As if they were still very much in love. After all these years. After that terrible accident.

He wished that Rachel were at home. He had seen that there were no lights, and there was no car outside Loretto's.

He would have liked more than anything else to talk to her tonight and to have slept with her, to have laid his head on her breast while she stroked his hair and soothed away his worries. She knew him so well, and he had hurt her so badly.

Rachel walked alone on the towpath past bushes and brambles and briars. She couldn't understand why they hadn't been cut back to give the guests a better walk to the town. But there had been some story about a fairy ring which it would have been bad luck to cut down.

She met Maggie Daly walking along.

"All on your own?" she asked. A foolish question, she thought, just as she said it.

"Just like you, Mrs. Fine," the child said with no hint of insolence. She was only stating a fact.

"Where's everyone?" Rachel persisted.

"I think Grace went for a cycle ride with Michael, and Tommy's been playing football with John Joe Conway and Liam White, and Jacinta's gone to get a new coat, and Dara's . . . I don't know where Dara is. So I came for a walk on my own."

"I don't know whether it's a great idea or not. I do that sometimes."

"What else is there to do?" Maggie asked simply.

"What would you like to do? Now, this minute."

"I think I'd like a gorgeous new dress in just the right color that would make everyone notice me and people say, 'Would you look at Maggie Daly?' That's what I'd like."

"Well come on home with me and we'll look through some books and magazines and we'll see what might suit you."

Maggie hesitated for a moment. Her mother had been a bit disparaging about Mrs. Fine, something to do with her not being baptized, and leading an immoral life. But her mother didn't know where she was, and wouldn't it be lovely to have Mrs. Fine give her ideas like she had with that beautiful ribbon that everyone had admired?

"I'd love that," she said, and they went across the footbridge, away from the sound of Ryan's and up to Rachel's rooms.

Mary Donnelly was glad the row had blown over. In fact it must have ended in some kind of reconciliation. They kept smiling at each other that evening in the bar. At one stage she even saw them holding hands.

It was probably about that business of John going to be reciting poetry in the bar. He had been dead against it at the time, but tonight he had books of old Irish poems out on the table and was busy marking some of them as if he were a boy back at school. And talking about boys back at school, Michael had recovered his good temper and even apologized to her for being short with her earlier. A misunderstanding, he had said humbly.

She saw John take his wife's hand and bring it to his lips when he thought nobody was looking. The way they smiled at each other gave her a lump in her throat. For the first time for a long while she thought of the man who had let her down and wondered what it would have been like to have him take her hand like that. Then she put the thought out of her mind and concentrated on being charming, which frightened the farmers more than anything she had done so far.

Chapter XVIII

"Wasn't it odd that the Meaghers left so quickly?" Loretto said.

"Oh I don't know, they got a chance of a place in Dublin, a small lock-up shop, and Patrick paid them a good price for the shop in Bridge Street. It was all for the best to go quickly. She's never been the same since poor Frank died."

Kate had congratulated herself several times on the amazing foresight she had had in telling Mrs. Meagher to hang on for a bit, something was bound to happen. And hadn't she been right! Imagine Patrick O'Neill wanting a small place in the center of town. It had solved the Meaghers' problems at a stroke.

Loretto was still musing. "She'll have the divil of trouble with that strap of Teresa in Dublin. If she was able to run wild in Mountfern, imagine what she'll get up to in Dublin."

Kate didn't agree. "She may have done all her running wild, she could be about to settle down for a bit now, have a quiet period for a change."

Loretto looked at her in wonder. "Isn't that extraordinary, Kate. Her mother said almost the very same thing to me herself."

"Would Dara be insulted if I offered her some material to have a dress made?" Rachel asked Kate.

"Insulted? She'd grab it out of your hands. But you can't be giving them things. You're too generous as it is."

"No truly, I have lovely bits of material, really nice pieces of fabric. They're samples, some of them are for drapes or wall hangings—furnishing fabrics. But they're quite elegant enough for a skirt or a dress."

"Well wouldn't she love it!"

Kate was never without something in her hands these days—if it wasn't the table napkins it was tray cloths. They were sitting companionably in the green room. The summer was almost with them, and the weather was warm enough for the two glass doors to be left wide open.

Carrie served tea on a trolley, another gift from Rachel; she said she had ordered some for the hotel. Kate hoped she was telling the truth; sometimes she thought that Rachel disguised her generosity by pretending it was some cast-off from the hotel.

"Am I imagining it or is Carrie thickening around the waist?" Kate whispered.

"You *are* imagining it." Rachel pealed with laughter. "My goodness, what a suspicious mind you have. Perhaps Carrie and Jimbo just sit and talk when they're out together."

"Not very likely," Kate said dismissively. "But you're right, I mustn't start fancying things."

"Is anything worrying you? Anything apart from Carrie?"

"No." It was not very convincing.

"I don't mean to pry," said Rachel.

"I'd tell you if it was sensible." Kate sounded as if she were ashamed of herself.

"Worries are rarely sensible." Rachel smiled.

"I'll tell you. I worry a bit about Dara and Kerry. I get this feeling that Kerry is a bit . . . well, a bit dangerous."

"I worry about Kerry too," Rachel said unexpectedly. "And I think Kerry is very dangerous."

The two women sat, heads close together, sewing forgotten, and sighed over the impossible situation. The more that Dara was warned against him the more attractive he would be to her. And if Kate were to put difficulties in his way about meeting her daughter, he would enjoy the challenge and come home more often still from his Donegal posting to move heaven and earth in pursuit of Dara.

* * *

Jacinta White told Dara that Mrs. Fine was the mistress of Mr.
O'Neill. They had been lovers for years in America. Jacinta knew this
on the highest authority. She said that Liam didn't believe it because
he didn't really understand mistresses and lovers. But it was true.

Dara, who thought it was indeed true from the days when Grace
had told her of their fears that Mrs. Fine might become their step-
mother, denied it utterly.

"You're full of drama, Jacinta," she said, defending her own friend
Grace from having a wicked father and defending her mother from
having a wicked friend.

"And you're full of airs, Dara, and you haven't a hope with Kerry
O'Neill."

Jacinta flounced off in a bad humor.

"What's wrong with Jacinta, why won't she come with us anymore?" Grace's eyes were big and innocent.

"Oh, Jacinta's an eejit, she's always taking notions over one thing
or another." Dara gave no explanations.

"She's very jealous of you, of course," Grace said.

"Of me?" Dara sounded like Maggie now.

"Yes, she likes Tommy and Tommy has time for nobody but you."

"Oh that's not true. Is it?" Dara was pleased.

"Michael tells me that Tommy writes your name all the time on
his notebooks at school. Michael says he writes mine, but he says
Dara is interleaved with all those celtic letters—you know, on the
front of notebooks."

"Heavens." Dara wasn't quite sure what to say. It was nice to be
someone fêted on the cover of exercise books, as Grace herself was.
But it was not Tommy Leonard that she wanted writing her name.

"I wish I was really really beautiful like you are, Grace," Dara said
suddenly.

Grace stared at her in amazement. "But you are *much* more beautiful than I am." She seemed to be burningly sincere. "I've only got a
round chocolate-box face, I look like that silly boy blowing bubbles in
the picture up in the Grange. I have no looks, you are the one with
the gorgeous face . . . Dara you *must* know that. Kerry was saying . . ."

"What was he saying?" Dara was eager.

"He was saying that," Grace said.

"How did he say it, I mean what was it exactly . . . ?"

"Just that." Grace couldn't see any need to dawdle on what Kerry, who was only her brother, said. "And you look terrific when you have a suntan, Dara, you look great. I look as if I have a skin disease if I stay out in the sun."

There was going to be no more about what Kerry had said and when he had said it. Dara hadn't much pride, but she had too much pride to ask again.

He was home the next weekend.

"Fair and square. Permission and everything." He grinned at his father, and to Grace's pleasure Father smiled back.

Things were definitely better these days.

"How do we spend Saturday?" Kerry asked his sister when Father had gone off to the hotel. Patrick O'Neill didn't work office hours, he worked a great deal too many hours for Brian Doyle's taste.

"Oh good, are you going to be around?"

"Well yes. I think so."

"Michael and I are going fishing. I've gotten rather good at it lately." Grace giggled a bit. "We cycle off for miles and find really quiet places." She looked down and up again and caught Kerry's eye.

He wasn't smiling.

"You *are* sensible aren't you, Grace?"

She pretended not to understand.

"Oh very. Anyway the places we go, the river isn't dangerous. It's narrow and shallow, usually."

"That's not what I mean."

"Oh."

"Father's not going to look after you, as long as he has his folly . . ."

"Why do you call it that? You used to love Fernscourt."

"Someone has to. You're very young, Grace, it would be terrible if you made a silly mistake."

"No, Kerry, I wouldn't."

"But it's different for boys. Does Michael respect you, or does he take advantage of you?"

"We just kiss a bit. That's all." Grace looked down again.

"That had better be all, and don't go to far-away places to kiss. Listen to me, Grace, I know what I'm talking about. Michael's only a kid but he could make you do something . . . something foolish."

"No, it's not like that . . ." She wished the conversation would end.

Just then there was a ring at the door. Miss Hayes didn't go immediately so Grace seized the opportunity.

It was Rachel Fine.

Kerry looked annoyed.

"I'm sorry, but Father has gone up to Fernscourt," he said, barely politely, when Grace had ushered Mrs. Fine into the room.

"I'm very sure he has." Rachel smiled pleasantly. "He was always an early worker, and all days of the week. No, I didn't come to see your father, Kerry. I came to visit with Miss Hayes."

Kerry smiled at her as if this were the way things should be. Rachel Fine was welcome in the lodge if she had only come to talk to the help.

Olive Hayes had spoken once or twice before to Mrs. Fine—a very pleasant woman, she had always thought. A Jewess they said, and a lady friend of Mr. O'Neill, but there had never been any impropriety in this house and not in Loretto Quinn's either. She was surprised to see her come into the kitchen.

"Patrick has told me how well you run this household for him, Miss Hayes, and perhaps I am speaking out of turn when I ask you if you have enough free time to make a few simple summer dresses."

"For you, Mrs. Fine? I'd not be able to make anything good enough for you."

Rachel smiled easily. "No, I won't ask you to take on my complicated figure, Miss Hayes, you would have nightmares trying to get anything to hang straight on me. I meant for some of the girls, for Dara Ryan, Maggie Daly . . ."

"Make dresses for them . . ."

"Yes, I've been told that you're the dressmaking genius of Mountfern . . ."

Rachel took out two lengths of silky material—one copper-colored, one in a clear aquamarine. They were beautiful fabrics.

Miss Hayes ran her hand lovingly under the folds. "Oh, these are too good altogether for children, Mrs. Fine."

"Suppliers send me samples, Miss Hayes. There's two and a half yards there in each of them, they're no use to me and I was thinking that if you could make a dress each for the girls—"

She broke off. Grace was standing at the kitchen door.

"Aren't they *gorgeous*," she said in admiration.

Rachel was pleasant. "I have all these pieces, Grace, and I was asking Miss Hayes if I could persuade her to make dresses for Dara and Maggie. Miss Hayes is very gifted. She made a wedding dress last year that was the talk of the town, Loretto told me."

Olive Hayes looked very pleased.

"I didn't know that." Grace was interested.

"Oh, I do a bit now and then in the afternoons." Miss Hayes was as pleased as punch.

"So if you and I could come to an agreement about a fee, do you think . . ."

"It would be a pleasure, Mrs. Fine."

Grace fingered the copper silk weave. "Who's this for?"

"It's for Maggie, it's the exact color of her hair."

"Is it?"

"Yes, it will look quite lovely on her. This is for Dara."

"Do they know, or is it a surprise?" Grace had heard nothing about it.

"They know that I was coming to see Miss Hayes, and they've seen the fabric."

"Heavens," Grace said.

"I've plenty more, Grace, if you . . ."

"I didn't mean to ask."

"No, and I'm sure Miss Hayes . . ."

"I'd love to make something for Grace, but she has such expensive clothes already, I didn't like to . . ."

None of them were finishing their sentences but there was already an easy friendship between the three.

Kerry could see this when he came out to see what was happening. And his handsome face frowned slightly.

Sister Laura didn't know that there was such an interest in clothes, but she did realize that there wasn't sufficient interest in work. And she was disappointed that she couldn't drum up any greater enthusiasm about these exchanges with little French girls. All the families would have to find was the fare, and Lord knew they were well able to find money for other things like drink and television sets.

Sister Laura wished that she'd had such opportunities when she was young. Nobody ever went anywhere then. She had always wanted to see the great cathedral of Notre Dame in Paris, and go to Chartres. Girls had so many chances today. And an easy life too! No school on Saturdays now. Sister Laura's lips were pursed about that. It was better far when they had lessons right up to lunchtime, and this new way made the weekend far too long, they got up to all kinds of mischief.

Dr. White had urged Sister Laura to take more exercise and get more fresh air. Dutifully she took a Saturday constitutional through Coyne's wood, down to River Road, along up Bridge Street and back to the convent by the Protestant church and graveyard.

In Coyne's wood she found Dara Ryan sitting on a stile watching eagerly to see who came through the trees. The child seemed disappointed—even dismayed—to see her teacher.

Down by the river bank she saw Grace O'Neill—holding hands, no less—with Dara's twin brother. They were much too young to be at that class of thing. Sister Laura barked a greeting at them that made them drop hands hastily.

When she called into Daly's for a cream cake—which Dr. White had told her should form no further part of her diet—Sister Laura was met by a saga of complaints about little Maggie who, according to her mother, had taken up with the foreign woman and was spending all her waking hours admiring herself in the mirror. Across the road from Daly's was Dr. White's. Sister Laura quickened her step and lowered her eyes in case she might catch the doctor's observant eye and he would read the cream cake written in her guilty face. Instead she saw Jacinta swinging on the gate and for once anxious for a chat.

Jacinta said that it was great to see nuns being normal now, and eating cream buns. Everything had gotten much better since the Vatican Council.

Sister Laura realized she had a mustache of cream on her face and pounded up Bridge Street in a very bad temper, thinking that fifteen-year-old girls in 1966 were a severe cross to have to bear.

She was glad she had not been called to the Married State. It was quite enough to have to deal with them in the classroom.

Kerry came through the wood and smiled easily.

"Well this *is* a lovely thing to discover in the woods on a summer day."

"Hello Kerry."

"Is that all you have to say to me?" He slid his arms around her but she wriggled out of them.

"What is it? Don't you like me?"

"I like you well enough."

"So what's with all the hard-to-get nonsense, then?"

"I'm not being hard to get, it's just that I haven't seen you for a while, I thought it would be nice to talk, you know, rather than . . . straight away."

"Sure, let's talk." He sat down on the ground and stroked her foot. "Could we talk about your ankles, for one thing? They're very beautiful . . ."

"Oh, please." Dara was at a total loss.

"Why don't you like me to admire you?" He looked genuinely bewildered.

"Because . . . because it's like as if you're not admiring me as a person, it's only an ankle or a mouth or whatever." She looked troubled.

"Oh Dara, that's not so, if you must know I like you as a person. You are totally special. I've told you that so many times."

"No you haven't, we haven't talked much at all, you and I."

"You're right!" he said, grinning broadly. "We haven't talked nearly enough. I think about you so much, that's what makes me think we did talk much more than we have. Will you come and walk with me, we'll walk through here and down to the river, and honestly"—he held both his hands up in the air— "no touching, promise."

Dara felt very silly, but it did look like a sort of a victory.

"That would be nice," she said and leaped from the stile.

Kerry got up lithely from his sitting position without putting his hands on the ground.

"That was clever," Dara admired.

"Oh come on, anyone can do that," Kerry challenged.

"Maybe, but you had your legs crossed."

"Go on, try it."

Dara sat down on the mossy ground and crossed her legs. "Let me see, what did you do?" She automatically kept trying to put her hands on the ground.

Kerry stood looking at her, laughing.

"It's not nearly as easy as you make it look." Dara was cross.

"Here, I'll sit down beside you and show you."

But when Kerry sat down beside her they were very close.

He looked at her flushed face.

He bent a little closer to her.

Dara bit her lip with indecision.

"It's very easy," Kerry said. He put his head slightly to one side and smiled at her.

"I don't think I'm going to be able to do it . . ." Dara said.

"Oh, I think you are," Kerry said. His face was closer still but he made no move to hold her.

She moved toward him. Their lips brushed lightly.

Kerry pulled back slightly. "No hands," he said triumphantly, showing both hands as he had done before.

But it didn't matter now. Their lips were together and nobody was working out technical details like that.

Kate was impatient that evening.

"Dara, where on earth were you? You look as if you rolled around on the ground, you're so full of leaves and dirt."

It was so precisely what Dara had been doing that she got a shock, but she realized her mother was on a different track.

"Really and truly you twins are like tinkers. When you see how neat and clean Grace looks, and even Maggie has smartened herself up a lot. I don't know what we're all working our fingers to the bone earning money to dress you pair for, we might as well buy the clothes and just rub them in the ground."

"I'm sorry," Dara said automatically.

"No, you're not. Where were you anyway?"

This was the question she had been trying to avoid.

"Oh, Michael will explain, I'd better go and have a wash," she said, and ran off.

Minutes later Michael burst into her room. "That was beautiful," he said furiously. "Why did you have to do that?"

Dara giggled. "I'm sorry, I couldn't think of anything else. What did you say?"

"I said we were down playing on the towpath. Where all the brambles were. You should have warned me."

Dara was sitting on her bed hugging her knees.

"I think that if we're going to spend this summer with the O'Neill family in different parts of the forest we should think up a story and stick to it," she said.

"Were you with Kerry?" he asked.

"Of course." She looked triumphant.

"Gosh, Dara. What were you doing?"

"Never mind!"

"You'd better be careful. Kerry's very old, and experienced."

"I know."

"You're awfully silly when you put on that face. You think you sound grown-up and clever, but in fact you sound silly. Like Jacinta when she's having one of her awful moods."

"You should hear what *you* sound like sometimes—Grace says, Grace thinks, Grace always believes, Grace was wondering . . . Like a record stuck and going on over and over."

"I don't," Michael said. "Do I?" he asked anxiously after a minute.

"A bit. Listen, let's not have a fight about it. Mam's on the warpath. The main thing is to keep the peace."

"Sure." Michael was distracted. "Does everyone else notice, about my mentioning Grace I mean?"

"No."

"Grace always says that I believe people too easily, I get taken in," Michael said.

Miss Purcell had a problem. Old Mr. Slattery had once said there was no problem that could not be solved by walking along by the river. Canon Moran said that God often spoke to the heart in peaceful riverside surroundings more clearly than he spoke in the midst of rush and bustle.

Miss Purcell took a riverside walk to try to work out her worry. Should she leave Fergus Slattery and go to work at the presbytery? To leave your post was an act of desertion. That was true. To work for the priests of God was a high calling. That too was true.

To forget the Slattery family who had been good to her for many years would be base ingratitude. To replace Miss Barry would mean that Miss Barry would definitely have to go for treatment to the county home. Would that be a good or a bad thing?

Miss Purcell walked on long and purposefully, hoping to hear some voice that would make things seem clear.

What she did hear among the reeds and rushes was some giggling and laughing. She craned her neck to see what was going on and stepped up to her ankles in water.

She saw two fleeing figures, children she thought. One of them was almost definitely that little O'Neill girl, she couldn't identify the boy. When she came back bad-tempered, with soaking feet and no decision made, she met Fergus in the hall.

"Really, Miss Purcell, if you go paddling the point is to take off your shoes and stockings," he said in a mock-reproving voice.

Miss Purcell was in no mood for light hearted banter. "I don't know what this place is coming to," she said. "I saw that young

O'Neill girl and she's only a child, up to no good at all, keeping company up in the reeds. She can only be fourteen or fifteen. It's disgraceful." Two red spots burned in Miss Purcell's face.

"Oh a chip off the old block, her father's the greatest whoremaster for a hundred miles," Fergus said casually.

"Mr. *Slattery*, please." Miss Purcell had never listened to this kind of conversation before and she didn't intend to now. Unwittingly Fergus had made the decision that no voice had made for her on the river bank. Miss Purcell would spend the autumn of her life with the Clergy. Where she wouldn't hear words or sentiments like that.

Kerry had a long weekend, he didn't have to go back until Monday night he told Dara. He would be able to see her on Sunday *and* on Monday.

"Don't come to the pub . . . I'll go out and meet you," Dara said.

"I'm trying to be respectable," Kerry said. "Do the right thing, ask your parents' permission and everything. Is that not the way to go?"

"Of course it's not," Dara said. "They'd never give their permission for what we do."

Kerry smiled. "They wouldn't know."

"They'd guess. I'll say I'm going up to the lodge."

"Whatever you say."

"And where will I meet you?"

"I'll come and find you in the wood."

He did. But only late in the evening. Dara had been waiting, she was upset and annoyed.

"We didn't make a time," Kerry said. "We didn't fix a date and a place, you wouldn't let me come and pick you up. So what's all the drama?"

"There's no drama," Dara said.

"Good, I hate girls that make a fuss over nothing," Kerry said.

Dara heard two warnings in that.

One warning. There had been and probably still were plenty of other girls. And also the warning that fussy girls mightn't last long in the picture.

Dara gave a watery smile.

"Sure, anyway it was nice here. I love this wood, I always have."

"It's beautiful in the evening," Kerry said. "I think it's one of the loveliest places ever. Imagine Jack Coyne having a wood called after him. I wish we had an O'Neill's wood."

"It's not really Jack's wood, there have always been Coynes in this part." Dara didn't want to give the ferret-faced man from the motor works any part of the mossy, flower-filled place.

Kerry seemed restless. Edgy almost.

"What did you do today?"

He looked at her in surprise. Dara swallowed. It hadn't been such a terrible question, had it?

"I beg your pardon?" he asked.

"I was just wondering what kind of things you did." She bit her lip and wished she had let the silence be. It was so hard to talk to him today; yesterday he had been like an angel.

"If you must know I went to a bar way out on the Galway road."

"A bar. But you don't drink?"

"No, Miss Curiosity 1966, you are right. I do not drink. But I do play cards and that's what they were doing there."

"Cards in a pub on a Sunday?"

"In a back room. Brian Doyle's brother works there—well, sort of deals cards there. It was great."

"Did you play for money?"

He paused. As if he were debating something.

"No. Not this time."

"Will you another time?"

"Yes, no point in it otherwise."

"Why didn't you put money on the cards today then?"

"Francis said not to, just to watch, watch him dealing. It was great."

"Could I come with you next time?"

"No way. I'm even a bit young for this place, they'd think you were a baby in a cradle."

"I'm pretty grown up."

"You are very pretty, and very grown up," Kerry said, slipping an arm around Dara. "So I won't let them set eyes on you."

Dara smiled happily. She wriggled out of his arm for a moment as Sheila Whelan walked past, greeting them both briefly.

"I hope she won't tell," Dara said.

"What can she tell?" Kerry sounded bored.

She changed the subject. "Did you have woods like this back in America?"

"Not like this. We had trees of course on our property . . . but it was different from this."

"Did you walk under the trees?"

"Yes. With my mother, when she was well."

Even Grace hardly talked about their mother. Dara held her breath a little.

"What was it like?" she asked tentatively.

"It was good. We used to walk in the evenings, and watch the fireflies. You don't have them here?"

"Fireflies?" asked Dara.

"I've never seen any. I wonder why that is."

"What are they like?"

"Like little points of light, like a million tiny stars."

"They must be lovely," Dara breathed.

"It was lovely then, but it all changed. Anyway, it's silly wanting fireflies when we have so much else here."

"What have we here?"

"We have some very beautiful girls for one thing."

"Oh, lots of them is it?" Dara pretended a sense of outrage and started to run off down the slope.

"Yes thousands, but you're the most beautiful. By far." He ran after her and caught her easily.

Because Dara wasn't running very fast.

Dara Ryan is too young for Kerry O'Neill, Sheila Whelan thought to herself. Far too young. She shouldn't be up in Coyne's wood alone with him at this time of the evening.

But Sheila had never told anyone anything about anyone else's business. And even though it was a fifteen-year-old girl, she felt this sense that she must not interfere.

She wondered, if she had a daughter of her own, what would she like a good friend to do? It was impossible to know.

Fergus Slattery had a distressing case to cope with. The parents of a fifteen-year-old boy came to him saying that their son had been named as the father of a girl's baby. It was a matter of a paternity order.

They were stern unblinking people who did not believe such a thing to be possible.

"It couldn't be done, a child of fifteen to father another child," the farmer said in bewilderment.

"It could be done all right," Fergus said. Even though he was twice the boy's age and had fathered nobody he knew it could indeed be done.

"The girl's a dirty tramp who lay with half the country," said the farmer's wife.

Fergus had already spoken to the terrified schoolboy.

"We'll get nowhere talking like that. Your son is too young to marry, it's a simple case of finance. We have to work out what can be fairly paid."

"You're not saying that our child is responsible for this girl's bastard?"

"I'm saying that we'll save ourselves a heap of trouble if we try to bring it down to pounds, shillings and pence, and keep all the recriminations for your own kitchen around the fire, or even better not have them at all."

"God knows what you can be thinking about Mr. Slattery, you mustn't be of this world at all."

"I'm probably not of this world," Fergus agreed. His face was grim, what he had been thinking of was Michael Ryan. Suppose by some horrendous ill chance Michael were to father a child of Grace O'Neill's. What in God's earth would happen then?

He wondered should he warn Kate Ryan or was it the action of a mad maiden aunt?

Dr. White called to see Kate as a matter of course and courtesy rather than because he could do anything for her.

He never referred again to her inquiry about whether sexual intercourse would be wise or indeed possible. He was a dour man without great charm but Kate liked him. She trusted him because he never gave her false hopes, and he had always been able to interpret the more flowery pronouncements of consultant doctors at the hospitals, and the specialists she had seen.

"Nothing wrong with you these days except a broken back," Martin White said in a manner that some would have found offensively direct.

"No, not a thing. That and being the mother of teenagers. It's a hard old station, isn't it?"

"Ah, don't talk to me. We have Jacinta around the house day and night now, a fit of the sulks. Some awful slight or row or something, she has us demented."

"Oh dear. Who with?" Kate hadn't heard any of this.

"Your lot I think, and that little one of the Dalys' and Tommy Leonard. Never mind, it'll pass, that's what we keep telling ourselves. The only thing is will *we* survive it?"

"Oh, I hope Dara and Michael weren't out of turn with her . . ."

"You wouldn't know what it was all about. Jealousy I think, mainly. Jacinta complains that Dara and Michael have fallen in love with the O'Neill children and are wandering around starry-eyed hand in hand, and the old gang as they knew it isn't the same. Fat lot of time we had for that sort of thing or indeed talking about it, at their age."

"I thought they all played together still." Kate's voice was tinny.

"God, Kate, they may well do. Jacinta would remind you of one of those circular saws when she gets started, I don't listen half the time."

Kate allowed him to change the subject.

At supper the children's father spoke sternly.

"There's going to be an end to all this rambling off on your own from now on, you're all to be where we can keep an eye on you."

"That would mean being in the bar," Eddie was quick to protest.

"Shut up, Eddie, not you for once."

"Why not?" Eddie was outraged.

"I meant not only you, I meant all of you. Dara, Michael, are you listening to me?"

They exchanged glances.

"Where *do* you go anyway?" their father persisted.

"Here and there," Michael said.

"Mainly the lodge," Dara lied.

"That's odd, your mother had a message from Miss Hayes above in the lodge asking if you could favor her with your presence for a fitting for this dress she's making you. She hasn't seen hair nor hide of you up there all weekend, apparently."

"She must have been in a different part," Dara mumbled.

"Yes, it's a huge place all right, four rooms I believe, you'd easily lose a battalion up there."

John's face was not amused. He hadn't liked what Kate had reported to him. The thought of anyone making free with Dara made him feel bile rise in his throat. The fact that Dara was so obviously lying made it quite sure that Dr. White's information had been correct.

"Where do you want us to be?"

"Where I can call you, by the footbridge, or down by the real bridge at the end of the town."

"We're not old enough for the bridge," Eddie said.

"Get on with your tea, Eddie," John Ryan said wearily.

"Why's nobody interested where *I'm* going to be?" Eddie wanted to know.

"Do you think he suspected?" Michael asked Grace that evening. They stood on the footbridge while Michael explained the new edict.

"No of course not."

"I want to be with you, on your own. We're not doing anything *really* wrong."

"We can still be together," Grace was soothing.

"It's not together with awful people about."

"They're not awful people, they're our friends."

"People like John Joe Conway." Michael was mutinous.

"Don't be ridiculous, Michael, you're always imagining that he has some interest in me."

"Everyone's interested in you, Grace, we know that, it's just that John Joe is so coarse, I couldn't bear him looking at you, touching you . . ."

"He doesn't touch me."

"Looking at you even."

"That's crazy to talk like that."

"I am crazy about you." He put out his hand toward her.

"Watch it," Grace said, "we're in full view of the pub."

"This is going to be great for the rest of the summer," said Michael.

Olive Hayes asked Mrs. Fine to be present for the fittings.

The dresses were all at the same stage—the aquamarine for Dara, a soft rosy pink for Grace and the unusual burnished copper for Maggie.

"Don't you have another friend, isn't it Dr. White's daughter who goes about with you? I could get her some material too," Rachel offered.

"Jacinta. Oh, she'd love that," Maggie said.

"She doesn't deserve it," Dara said sternly, remembering Jacinta's view of Mrs. Fine as a mistress.

"Come on, Dara. Don't be mean. We're all having a dress, why not Jacinta?" Grace was always generous.

Rachel looked at the beautiful blonde daughter of frail Kathleen O'Neill and Patrick. She had always felt the child was withdrawn and hostile toward her until recently. Now Grace was looking at her delightedly as if she were her closest friend.

"Could *you* suggest it to her, Mrs. Fine? We had a sort of falling out with Jacinta. Could you tell her about the dresses? It would mend things again."

"Oh *please*, Mrs. Fine," Maggie asked.

"What do *you* think, Dara? I'd need to have everyone's point of view."

"I think Jacinta's being silly. But Grace is right, and if *you* said it she couldn't snarl and take offense."

"All right." Rachel was pleasant about it. "I'll stop by the house, I have an excuse anyway." It was true. Rachel wanted to ask Dr. White if it would be too tiring for Kate to go on a shopping trip to Dublin with her. She felt her friend needed a break away from the pub and the worry about the new café.

"This needs to be lifted a little here, do you think, Mrs. Fine?"

Miss Hayes didn't want to take any initiatives. She held the fabric in place where she was going to put the little dart that would shape it.

The others looked at Maggie Daly's small thin shoulders and her little pointed breasts seen to their best advantage.

"You look great, Maggie," Dara said spontaneously. "You look totally different to usual."

Maggie saw only the compliment, she didn't want to believe it. "You're only saying that," she said.

"Why would I say it? Doesn't she?"

Grace was looking at her wordlessly. "Honestly Maggie, it's extraordinary, you look like a painting."

Maggie clasped her hands together and pulled them apart in delighted embarrassment. It was as if she were clapping.

"I'll never be able to thank you enough, Mrs. Fine, imagine there being this bit of curtain just the right color."

"I know, isn't it extraordinary!" Rachel marveled, thinking of the hours she had spent in the material departments of Brown Thomas and Switzer's looking for the exact shade.

"You're terrific, Mrs. Fine," Grace said, delighted that Maggie was getting the Cinderella treatment.

Rachel looked at the beautiful daughter of the man she loved and knew she must not say anything that would threaten this new friendship.

"It makes a very nice change for me to see three good-looking girls

getting dressed up than to see yards and yards of wall coverings, and
to work out why half the bedroom carpets are one shade and half are
different when they were all meant to have come from the same
batch. This is the fun part here, I assure you."

She mustn't give them any hint about how it was the only part.
This and her conversations with Kate Ryan.

Why else was she in this town? She felt that she and Patrick were
miles apart. Further than they had ever been, even when they were
on different sides of the ocean.

Jacinta White didn't want a dress.

"I don't have to follow everyone else, be a copycat," she said.

"I think you're right. Anyway you look good in those pants."

Jacinta looked down at her jeans and boots in surprise. "What?"
she said suspiciously.

"I was never able to wear anything like that—slacks, trousers,
pants, whatever you call it. My bottom was too big. I always wanted
to, though."

Jacinta would not be won so easily.

"Oh, I haven't much time for clothes," she said loftily.

"Sensible of you. Anyway, it's always there if you want it."

"Thank you, but I haven't time for fittings and choosing and all
that sort of stuff."

Rachel saw the aching loneliness of a fifteen-year-old who had
fallen out of the pack. She knew that any more persuasion would
result in further refusals.

"Maggie and Grace were saying that they wanted you to have a
dress too. But don't be dragged in if you don't want to." Rachel
prepared to leave.

"I bet Dara didn't want me to have a dress. Dara's a pain in the
neck, she thinks Tommy Leonard is her little slave. It would sicken
you."

"I think Dara did want you to share in all these remnants, actually,
and I definitely heard that she fancied Kerry O'Neill rather than
Tommy Leonard."

"Well, she's out of her mind fancying Kerry O'Neill, he's far too
old for her, and he has girlfriends all over the place. You don't have
any material that would make jeans, do you?"

It was very ungracious.

"No, but what I do have that might be nice is a bit of leather
fringe. We could put some on your shirt and some on your boots."

"On the boots?"

"Yes, isn't there a man up in Foley's who does shoe repairs? If we asked him nicely he could stitch some of this fringe onto the top of the boots."

"And you would give it to me, would you?"

"With pleasure," Rachel smiled.

Fringes on her shirts and her boots, that would make Tommy Leonard sit up and wipe the smile out of Dara's eye, Jacinta thought.

"I'll come along with you now and get it," she said in case Mrs. Fine might change her mind.

Patrick was in Meagher's with Brian Doyle organizing the changes. The place was going to be a small office and travel agency.

He would employ just one person, who would arrange tours for the guests and do any other business that Mountfern might need.

He saw Rachel coming down Bridge Street with that sulky child Jacinta, the daughter of the gloomy doctor fellow.

Patrick was about to go over to them but he stopped himself.

In front of this child they would have to behave as near-strangers. They would have to play a role.

Was it worth it? There were so many of these non-conversations all day. What was the point of another? He stopped just on the door way of the shop and turned back in again. Rachel saw him, and her heart felt cold. He had actually gotten to the stage of avoiding her now.

"Kerry?"

"Yes Mr. Hill?"

"A word if I may?"

"Of course."

"My own sons don't listen to my advice, you probably don't listen to your father. That's the way things are, always have been possibly."

Kerry held his head politely on one side, waiting for the old man to come to the point. He was working in the bar this week, and liking it. The summer business was beginning to build up and Kerry was an easy conversationalist, people got on well with him.

Dennis Hill looked at him without speaking for a few seconds.

"That crowd who were in last night, McCann, Burns, those . . ."

"Yes Mr. Hill?"

"They're not the class for this hotel. Too rough. They don't fit."

"Are they barred?"

"Of course they're not barred. They were never here before, they came to see you. They're from Derry."

Kerry's eyes narrowed slightly. The old man noticed more than he thought.

"Yes, I did meet them outside the hotel, I thought it was good to ask them to come in and swell the crowd. But if you think they're not the right kind of guests, I won't encourage them to come back here. Is that what you'd like me to do?" The insolence was well hidden, you'd have to dig deep to find it. But it was there.

"No, I don't mind if they come in or not, we're well able to move people on if they're difficult, don't worry about that. It's you I'm thinking about."

"Me?"

"You. They're a rough crowd. I don't mean their accents or the way they dress. I mean what they do."

"What do they do?"

"A good question. A very good question. Nothing you could describe too well, or put down in the space on your passport where it wants to know your occupation."

"I think they're in business."

"Yes, that's what I think too. Mainly criminal business."

"Oh Mr. Hill . . ."

"Some of it's just on the right side of things, but only some of it and only just."

"So?"

"So. I'm warning you about them. You need take no notice, you might appreciate having your card marked. You might just wish that I'd clear off and shut up."

"No, Mr. Hill, I appreciate your advice."

"Which means to hell with your advice. All right Kerry, I've done my duty. Now about your holidays. Would you like to take off now before we get really busy in July and August?"

Kerry got the feeling that the old man was sending him away from his new friends. He was about to make an excuse and then he thought of Mountfern in the sunshine, and the sparkling river and the beautiful little Dara waiting like a fruit to be plucked.

"That's very nice of you, Mr. Hill, and I'll think about what you said."

"I'm sure you will Kerry," Dennis Hill sighed.

Kerry went out with Tony McCann and Charlie Burns that night to play cards. He was luckier than he had been before. Or was the advice of Francis Doyle, Brian's pisspot brother, really working? Anyway he would be going back to Mountfern with a billfold full of pound notes and fivers.

Patrick told John and Kate that young people's lives were like a holiday camp nowadays. There was his Kerry being offered three weeks' holiday from Hill's hotel. Kerry was buying a car no less, imagine it. Not nineteen years of age, and he had everything he wanted.

"Isn't that why you killed yourself working, so that your children *could* have everything they wanted?" Kate asked him.

"I suppose so." Patrick was doubtful.

"Well it certainly was," John said. "What else would any of us do anything for, if we didn't have the next lot coming after us to provide for?"

"What would you do if you hadn't a family and children?" Patrick asked with interest.

"I think I'd put a pack on my back and wander off around the world talking to people about this and that, as it took my fancy."

"Like Papers Flynn," Kate scoffed.

"I'd go further afield than Papers, but that's what I'd do." John was adamant.

"You would not!" Kate flashed. "Even if he had none of us trailing out of him, he'd still stand here looking at his river."

She wanted to find out Kerry's plans for his holiday at home. She didn't like the sound of the car, she felt it might be used to spirit Dara to places well beyond the jurisdiction.

"Won't Kerry find it very quiet for him here? Playing with youngsters?" Her eyes were innocent. But she swore that Patrick saw what she was getting at.

"I'll keep an eye on him as much as I can," he promised.

"Perhaps he'll go off to other parts of the country. Specially if he gets a car?" Kate was hopeful.

"No, I've a feeling that he sees a lot of attraction here. Still, as I said, we'll make sure that he doesn't get too carried away."

He had said nothing, and he had said everything.

Kate gave a little shiver of fear.

"I wish there could be another party," Maggie said.

"Why don't you ask your family if you could have one? There's plenty of room in your house," Dara said.

Maggie rolled her eyes. "Us have a party! It's on our knees saying the thirty days prayer tacked on to the rosary and ending up with a trip to devotions. That's my mother's idea of a good evening."

The others giggled. Maggie seemed to have much more confidence these days. She apologized less, she was even joining in the swimming from the bridge. Maggie used to be shy to be seen down in the middle of town in her bathing suit; nowadays she would sit and laugh with the others, not self-conscious anymore.

The old raft they had made way back, which had floated down to the bridge, became their center of activities. They used it to dive from. Sometimes they piled boxes up on it to make a higher diving platform. Tommy Leonard could dive from the bridge itself. He was like a swallow, Dara said admiringly, he just seemed to swoop down. The rest of them bent their legs or belly flopped.

Only Tommy, John Joe Conway and Jacinta were any good diving from the bridge, they were the undoubted champions.

Gradually Jacinta had come back into things. She couldn't stay away anymore, the fun had moved to the bridge at the end of the street where she lived. This was the summer they were old enough for the bridge, there was no way Jacinta would stay out of things.

And being so athletic was an advantage. It was no use when you were at the pictures or being watched parading up and down Bridge Street, but it was marvelous when you were the only girl who could dive from the wall of the bridge and when Tommy Leonard admired you.

"Do you mind if I buy a car from Jack Coyne? I know you and he don't get on," Kerry said.

"How have you enough money to buy a car?"

"We said there would be no discussion about money, ever again."

"No, we said there would be no discussion about stealing unless it happened again."

"Well it hasn't."

There was a silence.

"I won it up north."

Patrick nodded. "Very well. Now about Coyne, he's a mean, dishonest little shit, but Rachel warned me against alienating locals, however unlikable. Go ahead. Watch out that it's a real car, mind. Make sure he doesn't sell you a lemon."

"No, he'll be so anxious to get into your good books he'll give me a fantastic bargain." Kerry grinned.

Patrick smiled too. This was good thinking. That is exactly what Jack Coyne would do. How sensible his son was to capitalize on it.

"You might find that the pattern has changed a bit this summer," he said.

"Changed in what way?"

"Not so much wandering off on your own, it looks like, everyone swimming by the bridge."

"Well, I'll have a car, that should change the pattern a bit more."

"You might find a bit of resistance along the way. Dara Ryan's mother for one." Patrick spoke lightly.

Kerry was sunny. "That's no problem, there are plenty of other girls to take for drives. And anyway I like swimming too."

He smiled at his father as if there weren't a problem in the world.

Loretto Quinn told Rachel that Jack Coyne was like the cat that got the cream. The young O'Neill boy had said he would like to buy a second-hand car from him. Jack Coyne had sped off to the town in high excitement. He said he was going to find a little honey of a little car for the boy. Loretto hadn't known him as pleased for years.

"He calls in here a lot. Is he an admirer do you think?" Rachel asked.

Loretto pealed with laughter. "Jack Coyne an admirer? Lord, all that man ever admired was a roll of fivers. But it's very flattering of you to think I might have a caller, Mrs. Fine."

"You're a fine woman, Loretto. Why wouldn't you have callers and admirers?"

"Ah, Mrs. Fine, you've improved me but not that much. Not in a place like this. Anyway I wouldn't want them, I'm happy as I am. Much happier since you came."

Rachel was pleased. Even if she had to resign herself that her coming to Mountfern had not achieved its aim, at least she could console herself that she had done a lot to help the women and girls of the place. Rachel was reading about the women's liberation that seemed to be sweeping the States at the moment. Not much of it had found its way to Mountfern. But she was definitely helping to improve the quality of life for a few of the female citizens of the place anyway.

Maggie Daly hung up her new dress all by itself on the back of her door. She didn't want to put it in the wardrobe in case it got crushed. And anyway she couldn't see it in the wardrobe.

She wondered what Kitty would say about it. Kitty was coming home for a weekend.

Kerry's car was red and had an open roof. It wasn't quite a sports car but it was almost.

He took Grace for a lap of honor up and down Bridge Street, turning neatly in front of the Classic Cinema, which nearly gave Declan Morrissey a heart attack as he thought the boy was through the cinema doors. Grace's hair, blown by the wind, stood like a halo around her head. Michael fixed a smile on his face and wished with such intensity that it hurt him physically that he was old enough to drive, that he had the money to buy a *white* sports car and that he and Grace could drive around Mountfern like that.

Dara fixed a smile on her face as she sat beside Maggie on the wall of the bridge.

She wished with an intensity that hurt her that she could be sitting where Grace was and that Kerry and she would do one more tour of the town and then drive off for miles in the beautiful car. She wished that her hair curled under and that she had her ears pierced. Then she would be truly happy.

Father Hogan and Canon Moran were taking a walk when they saw the red car. They were about to cluck at each other and say that Mr. O'Neill really spoiled his children and gave a bad example when the car stopped.

"Do you want to test it out? I only have it an hour." Kerry sounded excited.

"Test it out?"

"I'll take you for a test ride."

The priests looked at each other in amazement. Nobody had ever offered them anything so racy.

"Us?" Canon Moran croaked in disbelief.

"Yes Canon, one at a time, it only seats two."

"It's very nice of you, Kerry . . . but my old bones."

There was naked longing on Father Hogan's face.

"What about you, Father, you'll risk it won't you?"

"Aren't you very good to be bothering with the clergy . . ."
Grace had gotten out and was holding the door open, Father Hogan had gathered up the skirts of his soutane and settled himself in.

"But of course I bother with the clergy, Father Hogan, aren't they the most important people in town?" Kerry smiled and slipped through the gears to roar off with Father Hogan in the passenger seat.

It was a warm evening, warm enough to come back to the bridge and swim again after tea.

At seven o'clock they gathered there again.

Jacinta did some spectacular dives. This was the first time Kerry had seen them, he was full of praise. Jacinta was gruff and red with delight. She looked at Tommy Leonard to see whether he had noticed. But Tommy's eyes were wide. Maggie was approaching in her new dress. She looked quite different to the Maggie they all knew.

"I didn't know we were going to wear them now, I thought we'd wait till there was something special," Dara grumbled.

"What will there be special?" Maggie asked.

"You look like a picture," Michael said.

"That's exactly what I told her," Grace said eagerly.

"Hey, you're even more dazzling than your big sister," Kerry said.

Dara felt plain and foolish.

Mam had been watching her like a hawk—where are you going, what are you doing, will you be with Michael? It was maddening. Just as she was coming out Mam had told her not to be dressing up like as if she was going to a ball, so she wore her striped tee shirt and the plain blue skirt.

She felt like a deck chair in the outfit, canvas and stripes. Who would look at her? And here was Maggie with her hair all brushed and shimmering and reminding Kerry of Kitty up in Dublin.

The light went out of the evening for Dara. Hands in the pockets of her dull plain skirt, she turned away. The others were so busy admiring Maggie they hardly noticed.

Dara began to walk toward River Road. There was nothing here for her, every moment she stayed just pointed out how dull she was. She couldn't do dives like Jacinta, she wasn't lovely like Grace was or Maggie was turning out to be. She was boring old wooden Dara.

She had turned into River Road and was nearly at Jack Coyne's when she realized Maggie was running after her.

"Why won't you stay?"

"What do you care?"

"We were having fun, weren't we?" Maggie asked anxiously.

"Oh Maggie, can't you ever make up your mind about anything?" Dara snapped.

Maggie looked at her, dismayed.

"You're so weak. You don't even know whether we were having fun or not. You ask me were we? I don't know about you. I wasn't, so I came home. But at least I know. You never know."

"What don't I know?"

"See!" Dara was triumphant. "You don't know if you'd like an ice cream, you don't know if you'd like a trip in Kerry's car, you don't know if you want to swim or to wear a bathing cap. You don't know *anything.*"

"What did I do, Dara?" wailed poor Maggie after Dara's back.

Dara didn't even turn around, she just shouted over her shoulder. "You did nothing. You never do anything. That's just the point."

Maggie stood stricken on the river bank, Dara stormed home and threw herself on her bed to cry.

Mary came up and knocked on the door. "Your mother would like you to go to her room and talk to her."

"Tell her I'm in bed."

"Dara. Please. Your mother sent me up specially."

"I'm in bed, I'm not going down."

"She can't come up."

There was a silence.

"So please, Dara, will you come down?"

The door opened and Dara's tear-stained face appeared. "That's the most cruel blackmail I ever heard. Reminding me that Mam can't ever get up the stairs. How mean and unfair." She stormed past Mary and nearly took the hinges off the door of her mother's green room.

Mary sighed. It went against her principles to say that boys were easier around the house than girls at this age. But maybe it was because women were so much more sensitive.

"Yes?" Dara stood inside the door she had just banged.

"I was wondering if you could help me."

"Do what?"

"To think of a name for our café. We will have to get it painted for one thing and then if we call it something we can start painting that on trays and perhaps even embroidering it on aprons."

Dara looked at Kate as if her mother had gone mad.

"I don't care *what* you call it," she said.

"You'll be looking at it for a long time."

"Not necessarily," Dara said.

"Well, even if you're going to leave home, you might want to have a say in what the café is called."

"No, Mam, honestly I don't. I'm not being rude, I don't mind what name you choose." She made as if to go.

"Ryan's Ridiculous Café, maybe?" Kate tried. "Ryan's Rubbishy Café, Ryan's Wreck of a Café. Ryan's Roadhouse." She pretended to be considering each of them. Dara couldn't raise a smile even.

"Could you sit down do you think?"

"No Mam, if you don't mind . . . I'd prefer to go to bed."

"It's not eight o'clock, you're the one who told me not two hours ago that it was inhuman to ask people to be home by ten o'clock. Do you remember?"

"Yes."

"Is there anything I can do? Anything at all."

"No. No there isn't, really. Thanks all the same."

"Dara?"

"Yes."

"I asked you to come down because I love you, no other reason, I love you with all my heart and I don't want you to be unhappy. I know it's not much use just to have *me* loving you, but it might be a help sometime, so just remember it will you?" Kate smiled at her and continued, "No, of course you don't need to sit here anymore. I got lonely too sitting by myself and I thought it might work if you came and sat with me, we might get less lonely. But it didn't work. Off you go to bed. Good night now, love."

"You'll think of a name."

"Yes I will, or you will or someone will."

"Why does it have to have a name at all?"

"I'm not sure," Kate said. "Rachel thinks it would stick in people's minds more. You know the way they like things to be defined— Emerald Isle, Land of Shamrocks. I suppose we're the same with other places, we think of Spain and we think of castanets."

"You *could* call it Shamrock Café," Dara said.

"Ryan's Shamrock Café," Kate said slowly. "That might do."

"Good night Mam."

"Good night my love."

Dara longed to rush back and throw herself into her mother's arms, but it would have meant too many tears and trying to explain what she was crying about. So she resisted it and went back upstairs to the window seat, where she sat and watched the sun set over the

River Fern, and saw Michael walk disconsolately home at five minutes to ten.

Grace flashed by in Kerry's little red car.

"Were you swimming and all till now?" Dara asked Michael.

"Jacinta said you went off in a sulk. Did you?" he asked.

"Of course not," Dara lied. "What did everyone do?"

"If you'd stayed you'd have found out," he said and went into the boys' room and closed the door.

Dara felt more alone than she had ever felt.

She thought about Mam saying that she loved her. It was a nice thing to say but Mam was right, it wasn't much use at the moment.

The next evening they had all made separate resolutions.

Dara was not going to sulk. She wore a red shirt over her black bathing suit, and the silk rose that Kerry had given her on her fifteenth birthday all those months ago behind her ear. She smiled at everyone.

Maggie had decided not to wear her good new dress. It had been overdoing it, they had all gotten annoyed with her somehow. She wore an old Viyella dress that used to belong to Kitty once, it was faded and shrunk now. It made Maggie look about ten.

Jacinta's father had told her that he was prescribing himself headache remedies because of the continuous whine tone in her voice, so she had resolved to speak more cheerfully.

Michael had decided that it was not the end of the world if John Joe Conway said "Fine girl you are" every time he looked at Grace. And that it only made *him* look the stupid one if he reacted all the time.

Tommy Leonard had decided that Dara *did* like him, she wasn't sighing at him, she was sighing at everything around her.

Liam White thought that he might ask Maggie Daly to the pictures. She was so small he could even get her in for half price as an under twelve.

Grace made a vow to be much nicer to Michael. It was awful for him, his parents had turned into policemen and insisted that they all move in packs. Someone must have seen them. She shuddered to think what her own father would say if anything was reported to him. But then he was so busy and out so much he wouldn't notice.

They sat swinging their legs on the bridge, the four girls, Dara, Maggie, Grace and Jacinta. The boys perched on their bikes and chatted to them.

Half a dozen others came and went, John Joe Conway with his loutish laugh saying there was nothing to look at since the girls were all covered up.

There was no sign of Kerry.

Then they saw him walking down Bridge Street, the evening sun hitting his golden hair. He looked like a young god as he walked, in his open-necked blue shirt the exact color of his eyes, and his white trousers gleaming. He looked like a cowboy in a Western, the good guy who had come in to save the town. Tonight he did not have the red car—he had left his bike slung casually against the railing of Slattery's house.

He was coming to join the gang on the bridge. The evening could begin.

They had never seen Kerry swim in this part of the river. Up beyond the footbridge yes, long ago. But here was more public somehow. Up in the old place with the raft it had never mattered whether you could swim or not, it was wallowing and flapping about in the water from the bank to the raft and back.

But here it was altogether more showy.

They watched as Kerry kicked off his canvas shoes and slipped off his trousers. He was wearing his swimming trunks underneath. He stood in the golden rays of the evening sun, blinking. Then he threw off his blue shirt, and laughed at them.

"It only gets worse thinking about it," he said as if he were totally unaware that all their eyes were on him. Lean and tanned, golden and confident, he stood on the parapet of the bridge and did one long clean dive into the River Fern.

Tommy Leonard thought gloomily that that was that. There went his only chance of being good at something. Kerry O'Neill turned out to be much better at diving than Tommy. Wouldn't you know?

Dara looked at Kerry in wonder. He was perched on the raft, the drops of water clinging to his tanned shoulders and arms making him look shimmering. He was so very very handsome and he was smiling straight up at her.

"Come on, Dara, let's see you do it."

Without thinking, Dara peeled off her red shirt, took the silk rose carefully from her hair and scrambled up on the wall of the bridge.

"Careful, Dara," Michael said.

"Move more to the middle," Tommy Leonard warned.

Dara dived in. She seemed surprised at herself when she surfaced, shaking the water from her face.

"Great stuff," Kerry said, moving over on the raft to make room for her.

"Very good, keep your legs straight though," Jacinta called.

"Is it very high?" Grace shouted.

"Not bad, don't stop and consider it." Dara laughed.

In her smart stripy bathing suit Grace turned to Michael for advice. "What do you think?"

"Why don't we go down the side? We can dive from the raft," he said.

But Grace wanted to do the high dive.

Once up there it looked very far.

"Stop thinking about it!" Dara called.

This was good advice. In a splash Grace was beside them in the water. She looked back up at the bridge.

"I never thought I could dive that far," she said in wonder.

And so it was that they all managed it. It was the only summer when they were all able to jump or dive from the bridge itself. They all remembered summers years ago when some people went from the high bridge, but there was never a summer surely where everyone was able to do it.

Little Maggie Daly realized that. It looked like a million miles.

"Try a jump first," Liam White encouraged. "Once you've done the jump it's easy to do the dive."

"Is it deep enough?" Maggie asked fearfully.

"It's over twenty feet," Liam laughed. "That's enough water for you, Maggie."

Quivering with determination that she would not be left out, Maggie clambered up onto the wall.

"Hey Maggie, it's too high for you," Kerry called.

"Come down the side," Grace shouted.

Maggie took no notice. She leaped out as far as she could and appeared from the huge splash she had made still quivering. She climbed onto the raft beside Dara and Kerry.

"It's not that cold," Kerry said soothingly.

Maggie was shivering not from cold but from fright.

Now they had all done it, even Maggie, and in the evening light, pleased with themselves, they climbed back up again. Dara straightened her legs, Tommy Leonard did a back flip which Kerry said was terrific and insisted on getting Tommy to teach him.

Suddenly Tommy felt important again.

Grace told Michael that she thought he dived better than either Tommy or Kerry because he had more style and less showing off.

Jacinta said they could get a much better angle if only they could have a proper springboard attached to the bridge.

Maggie climbed up again. This time she was going to try a dive. Just as she was poised to go her foot slipped.

Maggie Daly fell at an awkward angle, not into the deep water that flowed under the bridge. But to the side where her head hit the corner of the raft with a sickening crack.

For years afterward they remembered that sound. It was so sharp. It was like the crack of a rifle shot, or of a big twig snapping on the mossy earth up in Coyne's wood.

And they looked unbelievingly as Maggie lay splayed half in the water and half over the raft.

At a very awkward angle indeed.

It wasn't the blood coming from the corner of her eye that was so frightening. It was the way Maggie lay.

As if her neck was broken.

They didn't have to go for Jacinta and Liam's father. Dr. White heard the screams himself.

He was coming out of the presbytery where he had been talking seriously about Miss Barry's limited life expectancy if she were allowed to continue in her present ways.

His heart lurched when the sound of panic and crisis reached him. He started to run. As he ran he knew the thought that was going through his head like a refrain was unworthy. Please God let it not be Liam or Jacinta, Please God not Liam or Jacinta. Please God.

Charlie who worked in Daly's was coming out of Conway's pub when he heard the commotion.

Charlie was a man who frightened easily. He ran back into Conway's and ordered himself a brandy.

"That's not like you, Charlie," Mr. Conway said.

"There's been an accident on the bridge," Charlie said.

Mr. Conway lifted the flap and ran out from behind the bar.

"Mother of God may it not be John Joe," he cried, and ran down Bridge Street to see if he could find his big bostoon of a son John Joe, whom he had given three blows in the ear earlier on.

He saw John Joe running up toward him and his face flooded with relief.

John Joe was crying, fighting for words.

"It's Maggie Daly," he cried. "They think she's dead. She can't be dead, can she?"

Mr. Daly was given a sedative. Dr. White was able to get him on to a bed and to roll up his sleeve while it was injected into his arm.

Mrs. Daly was different. Her face was white and still. But she was calm to the point of being unnatural.

"It was the will of Our Lord," she said in a matter-of-fact way. "He wanted Maggie this evening. Tonight she is with our Blessed Lord and his Holy Mother. She is in a better place by far than Mountfern."

Martin White looked at her angrily. How could a mother be so philosophical? What kind of God would want Maggie by dashing her to her death from a bridge at fifteen years of age with the complete understanding and acquiescence of her mother? A vein started to throb in his forehead.

"It's all right, Martin." Sheila Whelan was gentle at his side. "Everyone has to mourn in their own way."

"This is grotesque," he whispered.

"No, isn't it great that she has this kind of faith?"

"It's not faith, it's hysteria. Her child is dead, she hasn't shed a tear."

"You're always very good to people here in this place, don't start making judgments on them. Not now."

It was a timely warning. Martin White looked gratefully at Sheila Whelan. He spoke now in his normal voice.

"I'll leave you with Mrs. Daly, Sheila, and I'll try to sort out the children. They're almost all in shock."

He left the Daly's house, walking through the little knot of people who had already gathered around the door to sympathize.

The children were in Fergus Slattery's house.

Miss Purcell had made cups of tea and opened a tin of biscuits.

Dr. White had told them to get out of their wet things and put on their clothes.

He had asked Fergus and Miss Purcell to get them rugs and blankets. Fergus had turned on two electric fires. One at each end of the room.

He had been coming out of his house when he heard the screams.

He was at the bridge in moments, at the same time as the doctor. His eyes had met Martin White's, and the doctor had shaken his head.

"Get them into your house, Fergus, and let someone tell Seamus Sheehan to come down."

Fergus shepherded the children into his house and sent them off to various rooms to change.

Then he went to telephone the Ryans. John wasn't there. Kate said it was his only social engagement in the year, a meeting of the county Historical Association. As a published poet and a man finishing a book about Fernscourt, he was now highly regarded there.

Fergus cut across her pleasantries. "I have your twins here in the house with me. They're fine, they're both here."

She caught the tension in his voice at once. And knew something terrible had happened.

"What is it? Tell me immediately," she said.

He did. Without frills. She would hear within minutes. He wanted her to know that what could be done was being done, and that he would look after Dara and Michael.

"God, why does it have to be the night that John is out, the one night in the whole year? Will I come up there? Eddie could push me."

"No, there are too many people up at the bridge. There's nothing you can do. The children are all right here. I know it's hard, but stay where you are."

She saw the reason in this.

"I'll call Patrick," she said firmly. "Otherwise he's bound to get a garbled version too, above in the lodge. Are his two there?"

"They're here," Fergus said grimly.

He looked at Grace and Michael clinging to each other wrapped in a blanket, Grace unable to stop shivering and refusing to be parted from Michael even to the point where she could remove her wet bathing suit under her dress.

Kerry was sitting on a chair, his handsome face drawn with shock. Tucked into his side, almost under his arm, was Dara Ryan, white and still disbelieving what had happened. Kerry absently stroked Dara's dark hair, which had a curiously inappropriate artificial rose stuck in the side.

Fergus didn't like to see the young Ryans so firmly enmeshed with the O'Neills. But this wasn't a time for such thoughts. He tried to put the haunting little face of Maggie Daly—those huge worried eyes and all that massive hair—way out of his mind. What could have possessed a frail nervy little thing like that to jump from a high bridge? And why didn't some of the others stop her? Looking around the stricken group in his house Fergus realized that this is what they must all be thinking too.

The night seemed to go on forever.

John Joe Conway's father excused himself from the bar and went into his workshop at the back. There would be need of a small coffin.

John Joe followed him out and railed at him. Why did his father always have to think of business, and making money, when someone was dead, for God's sake? John Joe kept saying the word over and over because he couldn't believe it.

His father was short on explanations and excuses.

"What would you like us to do with Maggie? Leave her lying there looking at the sky? The only thing we *can* do for the dead is to give them a decent burial. If this is ever going to be your place John Joe, you'll have to learn that."

"I don't want to run a business, I don't want to be grown up," John Joe said.

His father gave him a long look. "I know son, it's not the greatest thing in the world being grown up and being in business. But look at the alternative."

For the first time in their lives John Joe Conway and his father looked at each other with something like understanding.

Rachel was in her room reading when she heard the commotion from the bridge. At first she thought it was just horseplay and high spirits. Then she became worried. She closed her book and came downstairs. Loretto was standing fearfully on the doorstep, her hand at her mouth.

"There's been an accident," she said to Rachel. "Jack Coyne's just run up to see what happened. I couldn't go myself."

"Of course not." Rachel knew the story of how Barney Quinn had been taken from the river in his new truck that he was so proud of. She put her arm around Loretto's shoulder.

"Come back in. Can you make us a cup of tea? Jack will come and tell us soon. We can't help by peering out here."

Gratefully Loretto went back into the kitchen.

They were barely sitting at the table when Jack Coyne rushed in. He had tears in his eyes, something the women had never expected to see.

"Poor stupid little girl," he said over and over before he could even manage to give them her name.

"Poor stupid little thing, she hadn't begun to live and now she's lying under the bridge with a broken neck."

Even though Jacinta and Liam's mother had come down to collect them, they wanted to stay with the others. They wanted to stay in the unreal world of Mr. Slattery's, where there were cups of tea and people pressed biscuits on them, where the night began to fall outside and the electric bars of the two fires began to glow red in the room where nobody turned on the light.

Fergus was in and out, reassuring without fussing them. Comforting them by the very fact that he didn't say it was all right, he said it was terrible.

Marian Johnson arrived to know whether she could take the O'Neill children back to the lodge. Fergus looked into the room and raised his eyebrows in a question. The children had heard her voice in the hall. Kerry shook his head. Grace said nothing, just huddled closer to Michael.

"I'm sorry, Marian, they think they should stay here for the moment. I'll get them home later, or their father will."

Marian was disappointed not to be able to participate.

"One feels so helpless," she said to Fergus. "I just wish there was something I could do to help."

He felt a wave of affection for Marian. She was ridiculous and snobby at times of course, but she was lonely, and what was so vile about regarding Patrick O'Neill as possible husband material? Marian was a decent honorable person for all her nonsenses. Fergus added to his list of things he disliked about Patrick O'Neill the way he made a fool of this woman. Leading her on to believe there was some interest, when everyone knew he had installed his mistress in rooms above Loretto Quinn's huckster's shop.

Sergeant Sheehan had seen a few sad things in the course of his work. And many accidents that were the result of thoughtlessness. He had no daughters, only sons, he would always have liked a little girl. He thought fondly that a daughter would have hung on his every word in a way that his wife did not. A daughter would not have been ambitious for him and wanted his promotion and preferment, and even for him to meet people of importance and be recognized by them. He knew it was a sentimental notion. People with daughters had just as many problems with them as he had with his sons.

Look at poor Mrs. Meagher and that Teresa for example. And Dr. White's little girl could be a bit of a madam, they said.

But poor Maggie Daly. Nobody had ever anything to say against her. Even her own disagreeable mother could only complain that the child was not constantly in the church at prayer.

Seamus Sheehan's hands were gentle as he lifted the broken body off the raft and laid it on the stretcher.

He and Martin White had been up to their waists in water pulling the raft toward them. The doctor had pronounced life extinct.

Seamus Sheehan had closed Maggie Daly's huge frightened eyes tenderly and arranged her thin body with the arms straight by her sides. He was watched by a crowd of about fifty people.

The child looked incongruous and unsuitable for death in her skimpy blue bathing suit. Young Grace O'Neill had lifted a shabby print dress in a faded color and given it to him.

"That's what she was wearing."

"You're meant to be back up in Mr. Slattery's house."

"I couldn't bear her to be without her clothes. You know Maggie," the child said.

Then Michael Ryan had come running to take Grace away.

Sergeant Sheehan thought the shabby dress was even less suitable. But he laid it over her, before they drew the sheet over her head.

Quietly and with great dignity in front of the shocked and silent crowd Dr. White and Sergeant Sheehan carried Maggie Daly back up to the stretcher. The ambulance had come from the town very quickly. But now that there would be no need to speed back the men stood waiting while Maggie's own people lifted her body from the river. She would be taken to the hospital; the post-mortem formalities would have to go ahead. The date for the inquest would be fixed and then the body would be released to come home to Mountfern, to lie surrounded by candles in her own house, and then the church and then the graveyard.

A great sense of heaviness came over Sergeant Sheehan. He wished he could stand in the water and cry all alone.

The sun was becoming a red ball of fire, and mocking them with its beauty and its sense of peace in the light it shed over the small town.

* * *

Fergus realized that when the O'Neills went home everyone else would.

Patrick's big car drew up outside his door and he came in with his quick light step.

Grace had somehow managed to disentangle herself from Michael, and was in her father's arms.

Then Fergus saw him put a hand on Kerry's shoulder.

"I've come to take you home," he said firmly. "None of us are going to help Maggie by sitting here in the dark. Maggie is at peace now."

It was a good thing to say somehow. Fergus wished he had said something like that himself. It seemed to break the stranglehold.

The children began to move normally, not like puppets. They even got ready to go back to their homes.

Tommy Leonard said he'd walk up River Road with the Ryans.

Liam pulled Jacinta and said to come on, their mother would be annoyed and would come looking for them again.

"I can't believe it," Dara said. "It's not something you can believe, I keep looking around for Maggie, I feel she should be here, coming with us. She should be running to the door ahead of us."

Dara had put into words what they all felt.

Their group was never together without Maggie, and running to the door is exactly what she would have been doing, hurrying people up, apologizing to Mr. Slattery for having stayed so long, asking anxiously where they were going to meet next morning in case there was some change, and they were all going to meet without her.

There was a charged silence when Dara spoke. It was almost too true in its realizing the way they were all thinking.

Suddenly something in Jacinta snapped. "Well, if it hadn't been for you, Dara, she'd never have done it," she said. Taking no heed of the horrified looks she went on. "Stop being all upset now that it's too late. You were horrible to her yesterday and had her crying and running after you, and even today you were just showing off and didn't throw a word to her.

"Maggie would never have done a dive like that unless she was trying to show that she was as good as the rest of us. Show Dara, please Dara. That's all Maggie ever wanted to do. It wasn't much, and now she's dead, she is dead from trying to please Dara . . ."

Jacinta began a laugh which veered from tears to laughing, and the sound got higher and higher.

Patrick O'Neill let go his daughter and strode over to Jacinta. The one quick crack across the face was all it took. Jacinta was silent.

"I want to go home," she said eventually.

"Take her home, Liam. I suppose your father will dislike me more than ever now but try to tell him it had to be done, will you?"

Patrick took his children out of the door, down the stone steps and into the car. Fergus saw him lift Kerry's bicycle and fling it into the boot as lightly as if it had been a toy.

Tommy Leonard and Michael took one of Dara's arms each.

"She was hysterical," Fergus said. "It takes people different ways. She didn't mean a word of it. None of it is true."

The little procession went silently to the door.

"It was a terrible accident, that's what it was. An accident," he called after them into the night. And it stirred something in his mind, something about people telling *him* it was a terrible accident three years ago when Kate Ryan had gone into the town in an ambulance.

As expected the hospital released Maggie Daly's body within twenty-four hours.

Mr. Conway had been in there to see to things.

Mrs. Daly wanted her laid out in the house.

Dr. White protested. This was a child, it would be too distressing for everyone. A child didn't have the tradition that a lot of the older people might know and want. Better to close the coffin and leave it overnight in the church.

Mrs. Daly had said with that ominous calm that she thanked the doctor for all his services so far, but his words were useless. Friends and neighbors would come to pray for Maggie's soul by her body in the way it had been done for centuries.

Martin White went in a rage to the presbytery.

"Canon Moran, you have a duty, a duty I tell you to stop that madwoman talking about sins on Maggie Daly's soul. There are no sins, for God's sake. What kind of a mockery is this, getting people into a hysteria, coming and droning prayers for nonexistent sins?"

"Calm yourself, Dr. White, I beg you." The old canon's faded eyes looked at him kindly. "You're not going to tell me that prayers to God and his Blessed Mother could ever be wasted, could ever go unheard?"

"Oh, forget it, Canon," Dr. White said and banged the presbytery door behind him.

"He's under great strain, poor man," the canon said forgivingly to young Father Hogan, who was making a poor attempt at scrambling some eggs for the two of them.

Martin White had to admit that the American had done the right thing to his daughter. He had heard an account of the scene both from Fergus Slattery and from young Liam.

Jacinta was unwilling to speak about the incident.

Her father came and sat by her bed.

"We all lose our tempers, you know," he began.

Nothing.

"I lost mine with the canon now, it's an easy thing to do. You must have inherited it from me."

Silence.

"The only thing to do is to apologize for it as soon as possible. That neutralizes it a bit, like an acid and an alkali. You know?"

"*You* never apologize," Jacinta said. It was true. He rarely did.

"Say something to Dara. She's very upset."

"We're all upset," Jacinta said.

"What *is* all this?" Dr. White looked old and tired suddenly.

Jacinta bit her lip as she looked at him. "You wouldn't understand, Daddy," she began.

"I might," he sighed. "I just might if you told me."

"It's just I got cross with Dara, she's got everything, she's gorgeous-looking and they're all mad about her, Kerry and Grace, and her brother Michael's lovely to her not like Liam, and Maggie sort of worshiped her, and Tommy Leonard can't stop talking about her." Jacinta's face was red and her shoulders were heaving.

"Of course I shouldn't have said it but it's not all that terrible, people often say things in a hurry and don't mean the half of it."

She looked at him to see if he had any glimmer of understanding. To her surprise he was patting her hand.

"I know," he said. "It's very hard."

"Oh Daddy, I'm sorry," she wept.

He held her while she cried and he patted her as if she were a baby.

Then when the storm had died down he said gently, "I'll go and bring the car around, you get up out of this bed now and get dressed. I'll take you over to Ryan's, and you can tell Dara you didn't mean it. That it's not true."

"Do I have to?"

"Yes, you have to.

"Dara has been sitting there all day, apparently, and not taking in what's going on all around her. She's in a very bad way."

"It's not due to me surely . . ."

"No, it's not all due to you. This time yesterday your little friend died. Died, Jacinta, that's a terrible thing to have seen. No wonder you are all upset. What we have to do is try to make it a bit easier on everyone, not harder."

"Very well." Jacinta swung her feet out of bed.

She stood in her pajamas choosing which garments to wear. She looked for a moment at the shirt with the leather tassels on it. But she rejected it, it was too festive for these times.

Kate was surprised to see Dr. White and Jacinta. She had heard various versions of the incident. But in view of everything else that had happened it seemed almost minor. Surely Dara would understand when the shock lessened that Jacinta had only been grumbling and complaining the way she always did.

"I'm afraid Dara's up in her room," she said.

Dara had come down for meals and said nothing. She had eaten nothing either. She said that the food literally would not go down.

Kate had decided to leave her for one day.

John had been up to see her several times, maddened with his grief not to have been in Mountfern when it happened. Shocked still at the news that was waiting when he came back happily from his meeting and the beer and sandwiches that had followed it.

But Dara hadn't talked to him. He told Kate that she sat there white-faced, twisting this false rose on a wire stem and a clip back and forth in her hands. Sometimes tears came down her face. Strange tears without any sobs, they looked as if they were painted on.

"Can Jacinta go up and see her?" Dr. White asked tentatively.

"She doesn't seem to want to talk to anyone. It's terrible times for all of them, all of you." Kate gave Jacinta a slight pat on her arm as some kind of token that she wasn't siding against her.

Jacinta understood. "I said something a bit stupid yesterday. I wanted to tell her I didn't mean it."

"Well then, why don't you go up and tell her? I'm sure she'll be relieved," Kate said.

She poured a whiskey for Martin White without asking him whether he wanted one or not, and he took it without asking himself

the same question. They sat and waited for their daughters to make
their peace.

"Dara?"

"Yes."

"Can I come in?"

Jacinta stood at the door.

Dara looked up listlessly.

"I'm sorry for what I said."

"What?"

"It had nothing to do with you. She just fell. She would have fallen
anyway."

"I know."

"But I'm sorry I said it."

"That's all right."

Jacinta and Dara had never had the arm-in-arm friendship of any
of the other girls. There would be no embracing, no tears, no emotional reconciliation.

"It's like a nightmare, isn't it?" Jacinta said.

"I wonder did she know," Dara said.

"Did she know what?"

"That she was going to die."

"She couldn't have. It was so quick."

"But they say people do . . ."

"No, Dara, she couldn't have, it was too short. Try to think of a
jump or a dive, it's over in a second, it would have been for her too."

"Yes."

"Will you . . . will you be all right?"

"Who, me?" Dara sounded like Maggie without realizing it. "Yes,
I'll be all right."

Jacinta came back into the bar.

"That didn't take long," Dr. White said.

"She doesn't feel like talking. She said it was all right."

"I'm sure it's all forgotten now," Kate said. She didn't really feel
that at all, but she had to say something to try to console this
wretched child in front of her.

"She looks very lonely there, as if she could do with some company," Jacinta said.

"I know. But what company? Even if I could get up the stairs I'm not what she wants. And she can't talk to her father, or even Michael." Kate looked anxious.

Dr. White stood up. "Come on, Jacinta, we've done what we came to do, no point in wearing everyone out."

"Will they have her in an open coffin?"

"Apparently." Martin White was grim.

"The children shouldn't go."

"Of course they shouldn't, it's not the goddamn middle ages, but that madwoman will probably go out to the highways and byways finding children to terrify them."

"I wouldn't be afraid of seeing Maggie lying in a coffin," Jacinta said suddenly. "In fact I'd prefer to. Anything would be better than seeing her all broken on the raft."

Martin White and Kate Ryan exchanged surprised glances. They hadn't thought of it like that.

They brought Maggie's body back that evening. Twenty-six hours after she had died Barry Conway's hearse drove down Bridge Street and parked almost opposite his own premises.

The front parlor in Daly's had been made ready. Candlesticks burned and holy water fonts hung on the wall.

Her father looked a broken man, her sisters from Wales looked unfamiliar and startled. Kitty, who had been going to come home from Dublin for the weekend, sat white-faced in a corner. Charlie brought more and more chairs into the parlor.

They were not going to sit there all night, it was not a wake in the old sense of the word. But between nine o'clock and midnight almost every single man and woman in Mountfern would call to tell the family how sorry they were about what had happened.

They would look at the face, and say a prayer. Then they would leave their mass card, a silver or black-edged card stating that the holy sacrifice of the mass had been offered for the repose of the soul of Maggie Daly. Most of them wrote Margaret Daly. Maggie seemed the wrong kind of name for a dead person.

"I'm not going to go," Kate stormed to John.

"Of course you're not to go," he soothed.

"No, I mean even if I had my own two good legs I wouldn't go."

"Easy, Kate, easy."

"The children? Do you think Jacinta was right? Would it be better for them to see her . . . ?"

"I think it might." He was quiet but firm. "Don't forget they have already seen her dead. This has to be better."

"Will you tell Dara?"

"Yes." His heart was heavy. "I'll go up now."

"If you like, Dara, I'll walk along to Daly's with you. Is that what you want to do, or would you prefer to remember her the way she was, laughing and running around?"

"Will her eyes be open, Daddy?"

"No, pet, they'll be closed."

"I couldn't bear to see her eyes, but I would like to say goodbye to Maggie in some way."

"You tell me when you want to go, I'll come with you."

"Michael?" It was the first time she had mentioned him all day.

"He says he would like to say goodbye to her also. You always say the same you two, it never changes." His smile was gentle.

"It must be the only thing that doesn't. Everything else has changed. For the worse."

"Call me when you want to go, Dara."

"Is Michael ready now?"

"Yes, he is, love."

"Can we go right away?"

They walked in complete silence by the river.

They didn't even look into Loretto Quinn's. They might have seen Rachel sitting by her window. And Loretto sitting downstairs with all the memories of the night that Barney died clear in her mind. They didn't look into Coyne's Motor Works. They might have seen Jack Coyne doing something he hadn't done for a long time. He was sitting at his table with his mug of tea in front of him as usual.

But Jack Coyne was not reading the newspaper, which is what he usually did at night, hunting bargains through the small ads. Jack was reading aloud to himself a verse of poetry.

He had been trying to remember it all day and in desperation had gone up to the brothers. Brother Keane had lent him an anthology. And he had found it under Yeats.

Come away, O human child!
To the waters and the wild.
With a faery, hand in hand,
For the world's more full of weeping than you can understand.

He didn't read any more of the poem. He didn't even know what it was about, but it seemed to sum up what had happened in Mountfern.

Tommy Leonard stood at the door.

He knew that sooner or later Dara would come to Daly's.

He moved over to join the three Ryans. "I wanted to wait so that we could go together."

"Thank you," Dara said simply.

John Ryan almost felt he should let them go in on their own.

Just as they got to the door of Daly's Dairy, Dara paused. The others stopped, thinking she didn't want to go in.

"We should ask Jacinta and Liam to come as well," she said.

Michael ran up to Whites'; in minutes he was back with the two White children behind him.

"Grace's father didn't want her to come," Dara explained. "He doesn't understand that this is the best thing we can do."

Just then a car drew up. Grace got out and she walked slowly, almost hesitantly over to the others.

"Father didn't want me to come, but Mrs. Fine saw you all walking down the road so she called him, and he drove me here at once."

Nobody asked where Kerry was. It was as if they had forgotten him.

Unaware of the sympathetic looks they were getting from the adults, the six children walked into the house. They went to the front room where the candles flickered and they heard the rise and fall of prayers.

Maggie looked like a wax doll. Her face was a clear almost transparent white. Because she had been injured so badly by the fall her hair was arranged to cover the sides of her face. The great cut over her eye wasn't visible.

She was dressed in a white gown with long sleeves, and had a rosary threaded through her hands.

She didn't look what they thought of as dead, she looked odd. Too still, and as if she were acting a part.

Mrs. Daly sat by the coffin. "Thank you for coming to pray for Maggie," she said.

The children knelt down. They hadn't intended to, but that was what Mrs. Daly seemed to expect.

They said a decade of the rosary together, then they stood and looked again, a last look.

It was as if they had forgotten the presence of her family and the other adults in the room. They talked to each other in low voices.

"It doesn't look *too* frightening," Tommy said.

"She doesn't have that worried look she sometimes has," Grace said.

"She won't have to worry about things anymore," said Michael.

"It can't be possible that she won't get up," Jacinta said.

"She was very nice, you know, very, very nice," said Liam White.

"I'm terribly terribly sorry, Maggie," said Dara.

Eddie Ryan arrived at the door of Daly's.

Sheila Whelan exchanged glances with Martin White and Judy Byrne who were standing in the corridor.

She was about to discourage him.

"It's all right," said Eddie. "I know nobody would want me here."

"It's not that . . ." Sheila began.

"I'm too young to see anyone dead. But I brought some flowers."

Sheila looked at the wilting collection in his hands. Some of them were wallflowers taken from Judy Byrne's windowboxes, some were the purple wild valerian that grew in the cracks of walls. There was a selection of cowslips and some dandelions.

There was little life or bloom in any of them since they had been squeezed in a hot hand.

They were almost entirely weeds. To Eddie Ryan they were flowers.

Sheila took them gently from the boy's hand. "Thank you very much, Eddie. I'll see that these are put in a special place. Mrs. Daly will be very grateful that you had such a kind thought."

"They might need a bit of water if they're to go on the coffin," Eddie said anxiously.

And Mrs. Whelan said she'd see to it, never fear.

Everyone said that it would break your heart next day to see the children at mass. They sat so still near the front of the church. The nuns were all there from the convent, and all the brothers too. The men had come from the building site; many of them knew the Dalys in one way or another.

Rachel asked Kate if it would be out of place for her to attend the service. She didn't want to do anything that would be out of place.

"You'll be expected to be there," Kate assured her. "Weren't you one of her great friends?"

The small coffin covered in summer flowers stood at the steps of the altar. Father Hogan had asked Sister Laura if she could assemble some of the better singers in the school to act as a choir.

She found a dozen of the older girls whom she hoped would not cry. Girls who were two classes ahead of Maggie. She arranged they should sing "Ave Maria" and "Panis Angelicus," and at the end of the mass they would have "The Lord's My Shepherd."

There was no time for a rehearsal, Sister Laura said to them, it had to be right first time. She put all her sorrow and loss into conducting the hastily formed choir. It meant that she didn't have to think of why the Lord saw fit to take Maggie Daly so soon in such a strange way.

Rachel had been to one Catholic service in her life. A big Italian-American wedding where the church had been filled with mink coats and expensively decorated by a florist. She had particularly remembered the incense, it was a heady thing and went up your nose, making you slightly light-headed.

She got the same feeling in the church in Mountfern. Tommy Leonard and Michael Ryan were serving the mass; this meant they were attending the priests as assistants of some sort, Rachel noticed. They wore choirboy surplices, both of them were pale and they swung the thurible with the incense around the coffin that held the body of their friend. Rachel didn't see Patrick in the church, though she knew he was somewhere there. She hadn't told him she was coming nor asked his advice. This was nothing to do with Patrick or her wish to fit into his community. This was all to do with the death of Maggie Daly, her friend.

As the pure high voices of the girls from Mountfern Convent sang the words of the Twenty-third Psalm, the tears came down Rachel's face. It seemed curiously inappropriate to hear the children singing the words about "He leadeth me the quiet waters by." It was odd to be able to think of quiet waters as a kind of heaven when the child had ended her life in the water not two hundred yards from this church.

Rachel remembered the excitement on Maggie's face over the dress. The look of disbelief when she saw herself in the mirror that day up at the lodge, the way she had clapped her hands with pleasure.

Rachel thought about Maggie's anxious look and her unsureness: "Are you sure I'm not staying too long, Mrs. Fine?"

"Is it really all right if I keep this ribbon all for myself?"

"I used to want all my hair to fall off and start again until I met you, Mrs. Fine, now I think it's grand, I'm delighted with it."

"Tell me what it was like for you growing up, was it all Jews and Jewesses where you lived or were there ordinary people there too?"

And on that last day: "I did wear the dress once, Mrs. Fine, but it wasn't really the right time to wear it. You know me, I'd get it wrong. But next time I'll make sure that it gets a proper showing."

Rachel heard that Sheila Whelan had suggested Maggie should be buried in her new dress, it had meant so much to her.

Mrs. Daly had not even considered it. The child would not go to Eternal Life in the trappings and vanities of this life. She would wear a white shroud.

The dress still hung on the back of Maggie's door.

Rachel felt an overwhelming urge to ask for it back, but she knew it would be misunderstood.

She couldn't bear to think of Kitty Daly wearing it someday. Or it being given away and worn by some other girl in some other town who had no idea how much it had meant in the short frightened life of a girl who was being buried before her sixteenth birthday.

Uncaring of the careful make-up and the streaks that must be all over her face, Rachel let the tears fall. She looked across the church and saw Kate Ryan, still in her wheelchair. There were tears falling on her face also.

They followed the small coffin to the grave. In the background the river sounds went on, familiar and almost unheard now by everyone who lived by its side. The June sunshine came down on the graveyard and marble headstones shimmered and shone as if they were lovely exciting things instead of the record of death.

The children stood almost huddled together for comfort. Kerry was a few paces behind.

As the last holy water was shaken and the last prayers said, the grave diggers began to fill the great dark hole in the ground, a space that looked far too big for Maggie.

The children waited motionless until the very last sod was in place. They gathered up the flowers and wreaths and laid them on top. Only then would they leave.

As they walked through the other headstones—the celtic crosses, the plain iron cross shapes, the marble slabs—they remembered all the times they had spent examining the words on the tombstones in the churchyard. Fingering the inscription to William James Fern who died young at Majuba Hill in the Transvaal. He had been young all right but not as young as Maggie. And the tombstone of James Edward Gray which had been so neglected and they had tried to smarten it up for him. They decided that they would go again and do something to James Edward Gray's resting place.

Maggie would have liked that.

"I suppose you think it's barbaric that people will come in here to spend hours drinking on account of the funeral," Kate said to Rachel.

"No, I think it's very comforting somehow," Rachel said. "I'm becoming more and more assimilated you know. Not looking from the outside in anymore."

"I've always said they gave your mother the wrong baby in that hospital, you're more Irish than we are." Kate said it as a high compliment.

"It was the last thing I expected when I came here," Rachel said. "I used to hope that he would find it a disappointment, and decide to go back, back home to New York. I never thought for one moment that I would feel it was home myself."

Kate looked at her in concern. Despite her praise for Mountfern there was a very lonely note in Rachel's voice. As if she had been abandoned.

"You do know how much you mean to everybody here."

Rachel smiled. "Yes, I feel very much at home, very peaceful here. More so than Patrick does in ways. He expected so much, and I expected so little. That must be it."

"What kind of things do you expect now?" Kate spoke gently.

"I've no long-term plans anymore, no strategies, hardly any hope. I just go along one day at a time."

Dara walked up to Coyne's wood with Leopold.

Mary Donnelly said you should never underestimate Leopold. There were times when no human being could give you the company and solidarity you needed and Leopold often rose to those times.

More to please her than from any great hopes of companionship Dara took Leopold to the wood.

To her surprise he was very well behaved, pausing considerately to inquire her intentions at every turn rather than racing off wildly on one direction or sitting down whimpering and refusing to follow.

Dara thought that secretly Mary must have been training Leopold. He actually *looked* much better too, as if somebody had been brushing him. Dara had never thought you could make any impression on that coat but in fact it looked quite shiny and his eyes were bright rather than alternately dulled with despair or rolling in a madness.

She sat on a tree trunk and Leopold went sniffing and snuffling but keeping a courteous eye on Dara in case she decided to move. She didn't move. She sat there with a long daisy, and threaded the heads of other daisies on its stem to make a flowery bracelet.

She hadn't wanted to spend any more time with the others. Tommy Leonard had been nice, he said it was bad at a time like this to go off on your own, you needed others around you whether you felt like it or not. Michael said he was going to go up the river and fish on his own. He hoped Dara didn't think that was rude. She squeezed his arm. She understood completely, as people always said they seemed to feel the same about everything.

She didn't expect Kerry. This was a part of the wood she had never been with him. It was a place off the main path, a big bank of fuchsia hedge surrounded it. Kerry came in softly through the trees.

"If you like to be on your own I'll go away," he said.

He was still in the dark grey suit he had worn at the funeral. He had opened the collar of his shirt and his black tie was loose around his neck. She had never seen him more handsome.

"No, no I'm glad to see you." She spoke simply.

She sat playing with the daisies, her hair falling over her face as she bent in concentration. She wore a plain white tee shirt and a denim skirt, changed from the good navy dress with the white collar she had worn at the funeral. She looked very young and lost.

Kerry squatted down beside her. He picked a daisy and started to make a collection of daisy heads on one stem too. For a while they said nothing.

Leopold realized that this was somehow important. He stopped his burrowing and sniffing. He sat politely with his head on one side as if waiting for the conversation to begin.

"I wish I could do something to help you," Kerry said.

"I'm all right. It's just so terrible for Maggie."

"It's like being asleep," Kerry said.

"And she wouldn't be in purgatory or anything. You know, waiting to get into heaven."

"Oh Dara, of *course* she wouldn't!" Kerry laughed tenderly at the very idea.

"Well why were we all praying that she'd be forgiven her sins and soon see God? She can't be there yet can she?"

"Where?"

"Heaven. She'd not have gone straight to heaven unless she died coming out of confession."

Kerry was confused. "Dara sweetheart, it's like being asleep, I tell you. I saw my mother when she was dead, it was a big sleep. Grace said she saw Maggie's face last night, her eyes were closed. That's all it is."

"And are you sure that she's not in the fires of purgatory?"

He reached out and held her close to him. "I'm very sure. I know definitely."

Dara sobbed into his chest. "Oh, I'm so glad, I couldn't bear Maggie to be all by herself in purgatory, she'd be terrified."

Sister Laura said that there would be a lot of delayed shock about the accident. The girls were taking it too calmly. They went up and tended a grave in the Protestant churchyard, they planted a tree near the footbridge. They had asked Mrs. Daly without success if they could have her copper-colored dress. They didn't know what they wanted to do with it but they wanted it anyway.

Sister Laura couldn't understand why Dara, Grace and Jacinta did not want to come up to the school to join in a special novena for the repose of Maggie Daly's soul.

"It's reposed already," Dara had said, and the others had gone along with it.

Sister Laura was confused. Dara really meant this, as if she had been given a special message that Maggie was sleeping the sleep of the just. And the others all agreed with her.

Grace and Michael went fishing a lot. Or that's what they said they were doing. Michael left early and came back late.

Nobody expected any games or swimming to continue on the bridge. Tommy Leonard had to work in the shop almost all the time, Jacinta and Liam had a horrible cousin from Dublin staying with them and they had to entertain her. They were rightly too embarrassed to bring her anywhere near their friends so it was a matter of cycling energetically to the old ruined abbey by day and going to the pictures at night.

Dara was all alone.

This is what she wanted to be.

She wanted to walk by herself, she wanted to think.

Sometimes Kerry O'Neill came to find her, and when he did they walked, often without saying a word for a half hour or more. Then he might take her face in his hands and kiss her gently. Or he would lay his arm comfortingly around her shoulders as they walked.

"It will pass one day," he said. "One day you'll realize that it's a different sort of memory." He looked very thoughtful.

"Did you feel that about your mother?"

"Yes. One day it didn't hurt as much thinking about her. I didn't believe people when they told me. I thought they were just being nice."

"What did it feel like, after the day you changed?"

"I felt she was at peace and I must leave her there and not keep thinking of her all the time, and regretting, and wishing and getting angry . . ."

"Ah, but you loved your mother, you were good to her. Grace told me you used to sit by her bed and read to her."

"That was hardly much consolation." His face looked bitter.

The silence fell again, easy and companionable.

Dara didn't ask him why he thought his mother needed consolation. He didn't ask Dara why she sounded so guilty about her friend.

"Do you dream about Maggie?" Dara asked Grace.

"No, I haven't." Grace seemed apologetic. "I do think about her but I haven't dreamed of her at all."

She looked at Dara anxiously. Dara's face was very white.

"I do," Dara said simply. "Every night."

"Were you nice to your father?" Dara asked Fergus Slattery unexpectedly.

"No, I expect I was fairly unpleasant to him. I am to most people. Why do you ask?"

"I was wondering do you wish he was back here so that you could explain things to him?"

"No, Dara, he was old. His life was lived. It's different with Maggie, everyone wishes she were back so that they could explain things to her. And anyway you have nothing to explain, you were all very nice to her, she had a load of grand friends even if her mother was a bit of a trial." He was trying to be light without being flippant.

"No, I don't think her friends were good to her," Dara said. "I think she was lonely and frightened all her life, and I didn't know it until now when it's too late."

* * *

"Kerry, why do you like me? Seriously. I'm not joking." Dara's big dark eyes were troubled.

"Because I like to be with you. You are beautiful and loving, you are bright and intelligent, and funny. And that's enough for a start, isn't it?"

"I'm not old enough for you," Dara said.

"What's age got to do with it?"

"I don't know enough, I'm only a schoolgirl when all's said and done. You should have someone much brighter, who knows things."

"You know enough things for me."

"It's very mysterious." Dara shook her head. "If I were rich I'd say you were after my money, and you *know* I'm not going to sleep with you . . . So I can't see why." She spoke in a very matter of fact tone.

"You might sleep with me someday," Kerry said.

"I don't think so."

"We can but hope," he said lightly. "But in the meantime we have to try to take you out of this melancholy. Maggie wouldn't have wanted you to be like this."

"I'm sick of people telling me what she would or wouldn't have wanted," Dara snapped. "Her mother was telling me that Maggie's in heaven looking down on us all and very heartsore about the kind of films that Declan Morrissey is getting in the Classic Cinema."

"Gently, Dara," he said, reaching for her hand.

"I'm not mad or depressed, I just feel very confused," she said.

He held her close and the confusion seemed to go further away. After that, he held her close all the time.

They didn't laugh and race away from each other as they once had. They didn't swim and splash and shout in the river. They lay together on the mossy ground of Coyne's wood and clung to each other.

The sunlight came flickering through the trees above and Kerry O'Neill peeled off the little blue shirt that Dara wore. He opened her simple cotton brassiere and took it gently away from her. He lay his head on her breasts and heard her heart beating.

At no stage did she stop him.

They lay like that and he stroked her so that it felt both exciting and peaceful at the same time.

At no time did she feel it was wrong.

Only when he made a move to take off his own clothes did Dara stir.

"I don't want to," she said.

He sat up coldly. "As you say."

"Don't be cross. Don't change."

"Don't be a tease then, don't promise and then go back on it."

"I didn't mean to," she said piteously.

"But you liked it. You like my holding you."

"I don't know what to say."

"Well, tell me when you do." He had leaped to his feet and was walking angrily through the trees.

"I think Dara spends all her days with Kerry in Coyne's wood," Kate said to John.

"Don't they all go out together? I thought they were never out of each other's sight," John said.

"No. The Whites have this cousin, poor Tommy's stuck in the shop, Grace and Michael are off fishing."

"How do you know all this?"

"When Rachel took me up to Bridge Street today I was in Leonard's. I was talking to Tommy. He looks very badly still."

"Why do you think she's with Kerry?"

"She looks flushed and nervy but she doesn't have the look of a child who sat alone all day in a wood."

"What will we do?" He was anxious.

"I don't know. What *can* we do? I mean even if she is with him, we can't upset her anymore by hounding her," Kate said resignedly.

"I don't suppose he . . ." John didn't finish the sentence.

"And I don't think if he wanted to that she would really . . ." Kate didn't finish the sentence either.

Olive Hayes was sitting at the kitchen table writing to Bernadette. The young Ryan girl knocked at the door.

"I'm afraid Grace has gone off out. I thought she was meeting you and your brother," Miss Hayes said.

"Oh yes, they're all down at the river," Dara said, covering up for Grace and Michael. "I was just passing and I thought I'd call in just in case Kerry was here."

"No, child, he went off in that car of his. Off to a place way out on the Galway road."

"Oh I see." Dara looked disappointed.

"Do you want a drink of milk or tea or anything before you go back down to the others?" Miss Hayes thought the child looked disturbed. It must have been harrowing for them all to have watched a violent death.

"The others?" Dara said vaguely.

"Down on the river. You said they were all on the bank . . ."

"Oh yes, I forgot. The others." Her voice sounded dull.

"Are you all right, Dara?"

"Fine, Miss Hayes. I'll be off now."

Olive looked out of the window. The child didn't take the road down toward the river. She headed out to the main road.

Dara had never hitch-hiked before. She would have to be very careful not to stop anyone she knew.

A big and unfamiliar van came into view. It wasn't anyone from Mountfern so she held out her hand.

It was a traveler looking for a bit of chat, even from a schoolgirl. He had a van of chips and peanuts.

"Do you know this place . . . it's a kind of roadhouse?" Dara told him about the pub where Kerry said he had been playing cards.

The man knew it well, he'd be stopping there himself. A few other places on the way before they got there. Funny sort of a place for a girl to be going on her own.

Dara told him a story about looking for her brother. The commercial traveler thought this was perfectly reasonable. He chattered on, hardly noticing that the grave dark-eyed girl spoke little in return.

He talked about Mountfern.

"That place is going to get a rare shake-up, used to be the sleepiest town in the midlands," he said.

He seemed to expect a reply. "Is that right?" Dara asked.

"Well, seeing as how it's where you came from you'd know better than I would. I bet you're looking forward to the new hotel?"

"Yes, in a way." She was looking out the window.

"It'll bring a fortune to the town, you might get a job in it yourself when you grow a bit older." He was a good-natured man, he would like to think that this attractive girl could stay in her own place rather than be forced to emigrate.

"Of course there's always going to be some who'll lose by it. You're not connected with the Grange there where I picked you up?"

"No, no, I was just visiting someone in the lodge."

"Well the Grange will feel the pinch, I tell you. Who'd stay there when there's the new place? And who'd have a drink in Ryan's, come to think of it?"

"Why not?" She turned to look at him.

"Your man, the American's going to have a real bar, not a fancy lounge with uppity prices, but a normal bar across the bridge there from them, it will take all their trade. Very hard on them. Poor man's wife in a wheelchair already after an accident and now this on top of it all."

Dara turned away and looked out the window.

"Tell me, did you know that unfortunate child who was killed there last week, wasn't it the saddest thing . . . ?"

His voice trailed away as he saw the glint of tears on the girl's face. "Of course you must have known the girl. I'm sorry," he said, mad with himself.

Dara just kept looking out at the road taking them toward Galway.

"Will I wait and see that you meet your brother all right?"

"No thanks, I'm fine now. Really I am."

"You must take no notice of me, Mikey the big mouth, that's what they call me."

"No, you were very kind to give me a lift."

"The little girl who died is in heaven of course."

"Of course," Dara said in an odd flat voice.

There didn't seem to be a back room when she went in first. Just a shabby-looking bar with a loud jukebox. There were cigarette butts on the floor and bits of litter everywhere.

It must be through the door that said toilets on a hand-scrawled sign.

She pushed through the door and saw ahead of her another one, she touched it and it opened a little. Kerry sat at a table with a drunk. Kerry was shuffling cards in a way that they seemed to make an arc. His face was clenched in concentration.

She stood looking at him for what felt like a long time before he looked up and saw her.

His face didn't change, he looked neither annoyed nor surprised.

"Hi," he said and continued with the shuffle.

"Not that way, Kerry, get your thumb in there properly." Francis Doyle's voice was slurred.

Dara sat down and watched. The drunken man helped himself to more whiskey from time to time. Neither of them even acknowledged her being there.

"I felt lonely so I thought I'd come out here," she said eventually.

"Sure." Kerry was pleasant but abstracted.

"To find you," she said.

"And you did," he said.

Francis Doyle took no more notice of her than if she had been a fly that had buzzed into this close, overpowering room. She felt slightly light-headed as if she might faint.

"Are you going to talk to me?" she asked Kerry.

"Not now, no."

"When?"

"When I've learned the waterfall," he said.

Dara's mind went blank as she sat in the airless room. She was unaware of her surroundings or how long she sat there. Then she felt Kerry touching her shoulder.

"I'll drive you home now," he said in a light casual way as if it were the most normal thing in the world to find her in this strange place miles and miles from home.

He held open the door of the little red car. They drove back to Mountfern, fast through the twisty roads. Dara didn't speak. But she felt more at ease. She settled herself low in the car and once or twice she closed her eyes. On a hill a few miles from Mountfern the car stopped. Kerry looked at her.

"What are we going to do with you, Dara?" He said it with a mixture of affection and irritation.

She turned to him. "I don't know. I felt so empty. The only thing that made any sense was to be with you."

"But you don't *want* to be with me. You made that clear in the woods."

"I don't want to sleep with you."

"We were wide awake."

"You know what I mean."

"I know you keep pushing me away. Why should I think you want to be with me?" He looked puzzled.

Dara took Kerry's hand and held it to her lips. "I've never loved anyone before. You see this is the first time and it's very confusing. It's all mixed up with everything else that's happened, and I feel strange and frightened."

She looked terribly young. He took her hand and kissed it gently the way she had his. He said nothing.

"You mightn't even love me at all," she continued. "So I had nothing to lose by going to find you. I'm not playing any sort of game."

"I don't know if I love anyone," Kerry said. "But if I do the nearest I'd come to it would be you. Come here to me."

He took her in his arms and she stretched across the little red car to reach him.

He had ten more days' holiday.

Dara still looked pale and anxious. But she went to sit in the woods each day. Some days he came there, some he did not. She never knew whether he would be there or not.

Each time he held her close to him, he seemed to be more demanding and urgent. Dara felt her resistance changing in degree. What she had fought off a week previously seemed acceptable now.

"When is Kerry going back to Donegal?" Kate asked Rachel.

"Patrick says he still has a few days."

"I wish he'd go now."

"Don't worry so much, Kate."

"I can't help it. She looks totally feverish and her mind is a thousand miles away when she's here, or to be more precise three miles away up at the lodge."

"I asked her to come for a drive with me, but she said no." Rachel had done her best.

"I know you did, you're very good. I suppose we can just hang on until he goes."

"Do you have friends in Donegal?" Dara asked.

"Not really. It's mainly work, you know . . . I play cards sometimes, with a couple of guys I met, Tony McCann, Charlie Burns, they live in Derry across the border."

"Don't they have red buses and red letter boxes there?"

"You've never been to the north?"

"No, how would I go to the north, Kerry?"

"They have red everything, and red, white and blue flags."

"Well it's part of England."

"It's part of the United Kingdom."

"Same thing."

"Don't you care about it not being part of Ireland?"

"Not very much. It will be eventually, I suppose."

"McCann cares, and his friends care. They feel very strongly about it." Kerry's voice sounded as if he were quoting rather than talking.

"That's all big talk because you're an American," Dara said.

"What do you know about it?"

"Nothing," she giggled.

"Will you miss me when I go back?" he asked.

"Very much. Do you have to go back?"

"Maybe I could stay . . . perhaps I could think of an excuse to stay . . ." he said teasingly.

"Really?"

"If I stay will you be nice to me?" He had reached his arms out for her.

"I'm always nice to you. How would you get off work?"

"I can get anything I want," Kerry said.

"When's Kerry going back?" Kate asked with an innocent air.

"I don't think he is," Dara said, eyes dancing.

"That's right, Grace said he was hoping to get some more time," said Michael.

"Doesn't he have to work in Hill's?" Kate's voice was crisp.

"Oh, Kerry could talk his way out of anything," Michael said.

Dara frowned: she didn't want Kerry presented as too much of a playboy. "He'll be able to arrange more time, there's going to be no problem," she said.

She looked excited and eager.

Kate's mouth was a hard narrow line.

"Would you like me to take Dara off on a trip somewhere?" Fergus asked Kate next day.

"Dara?"

"It would keep her out of Kerry O'Neill's clutches. At least you'd know she was safe with me. Everyone's safe with me," Fergus added gloomily.

Kate didn't give the usual good-humored riposte. She said nothing for a moment.

Then she said, "No, I think it's time for Dara to go on a trip much further afield."

"Where do you mean?"

"I don't know. I'll talk to John about it. We have to stop pretending it isn't happening."

"Of course we don't know if anything *is* happening." Fergus began to backtrack.

"We have an educated guess," Kate said grimly.

They sat in the side yard. The whitewashed walls of the big outhouse which had been where the twins had their party now had clematis and honeysuckle growing up and winding around. The front of that building out on River Road looked well too, bright-colored windowboxes getting ready for the day it would open as Ryan's Shamrock Café.

John and Kate often sat for a while in the side yard. After a night in a room that smelled of cigarette smoke and porter it was like a cool waterfall to sit here where the flowers took over. The night-scented stock and the jasmine were everywhere.

"What will we do with Dara?" Kate's voice was heavy and sad.

"I've been thinking," John said slowly.

"I knew you would." She looked at him hopefully.

"Do you remember what Sister Laura wanted us to do in the first place? Why don't we send her to France?"

Chapter XIX

Madame Vartin looked like the Mother of Sorrows. She had a long white face and a thin mouth that trembled as if on the verge of tears constantly. She had pale blue eyes swimming in sadness. Monsieur Vartin was quite different—he was small and round and laughed like a machine gun firing in continuous rattles and blasts. Neither of them spoke a word of English. Mademoiselle Stephanie, who was a cousin of Madame Vartin, spoke enough to explain Dara's duties to her.

She was to prepare breakfast for the three small Vartin children, she was to take them for a walk and teach them five phrases in English each day. Then she was to play with them till their lunch; after that she was free to study. At dinner she was to help serve at table and to clear afterward.

She got pocket money which worked out at about £3 a week and there was nothing to spend it on as they were miles from anywhere in the middle of the country. The children were horrible and Monsieur was inclined to touch her a lot, pressing up against her when he passed by. Madame's eyes brimmed with such sadness Dara felt almost afraid to talk to her at all. If it had not been for Stephanie, Dara felt she would have gone mad. It was hard to know what Stephanie did in the house. She was often to be seen folding linen or gathering flowers. She made curtains for one of the rooms, a job that took her almost all the summer. Sometimes she took the small car and drove off in the afternoons, sometimes she picked fruit. Dara couldn't make it out at all.

"*Avez-vous un vrai* job, Mademoiselle Stephanie?" she asked one day. Stephanie laughed at her and quite unexpectedly gave Dara a kiss on each cheek.

"*Je t'adore, mon petit chou,*" she said, still pealing with laughter.

Dara was confused. Why did Stephanie adore her? Why didn't she say whether she had a job or not? Why did she use the familiar *tu* form? Ever since she had arrived she had known that she must be formal and call everyone except the children *vous*. It was a mystery. For a couple of days Stephanie would keep repeating *un vrai job* and shake her head with laughter each time.

Dara could hardly believe how quickly she had managed to find herself transported to France. She, Dara Ryan, who had never even been to London or Belfast had been through Paris in a car and had seen the Arc de Triomphe and the Eiffel Tower. Then she had been driven by Mademoiselle Stephanie to this far-away falling down house in the French countryside.

Mademoiselle Stephanie, blonde and curvy, said she liked the opportunity to practice her English; one day she would visit Ireland and meet all the great and famous people in Ireland. Dara wondered fearfully if Sister Laura had exaggerated the attractions of Mountfern or the connections of the Ryan household.

But mainly she wondered why she was here. It had been so sudden, the explanations all quite unsatisfactory.

Mam had been no help. She had been all excited and said it was wonderful, that Dad had found the money, and what a great, wonderful chance for Dara. Michael had said it was a pity they didn't take boy au pairs, Grace said it was the most exciting thing she had heard of in her life. Tommy Leonard had said he would write to her every few days in case she was lonely. Mary Donnelly told her that of all men, Frenchmen were known to be the lowest.

Kerry had said nothing.

She had rushed to tell him in Coyne's wood and he had shrugged.

"Well if you *want* to go, that's great."

"I don't want to go and leave you."

"Why don't you do what you want to do, Dara?"

It was a frightening echo of the way she had spoken to Maggie.

She remembered the way she had spoken to Maggie the night before the accident.

"You don't ever know what you want." She had shouted that as an accusation, and Kerry was saying the same thing to her. She looked at him aghast.

He relented a little. "Have a lovely summer," he said, and kissed her on the nose.

"Will you write to me?" she asked.

"I'll send you a card."

"Will you?"

"I said I would." He sounded impatient.

"Will you stay here now that I'm going back or do you think you should go back to Donegal?"

"Who knows, little Dara? Who knows?" He had kissed her again on the nose.

She had gone to the lodge twice in the hope of seeing him. But he had been out both times.

Grace thought he might have gone to some place he liked miles out on the Galway road. Miss Hayes said that she hoped he had not. It was a place with a bad name, full of drunks and layabouts.

"No it's not, it's just shabby and dirty," Dara had said and they looked at her with surprise.

She longed to ask Grace to write and tell her about Kerry. She longed to tell Grace how much she yearned to hear of him. But it would be useless, Grace had no idea how much Dara envied her the easy access, the nearness and the closeness to Kerry.

She nearly asked Michael, but she couldn't do that either.

"I'll miss you a lot," Michael said the night before she left.

"No you won't, you have Grace."

"That's different, I'll still miss you, Dara," he said, surprised. "You're my twin, for heaven's sake."

"So I am," she said emptily.

"Is anything wrong?"

"Everything's all changed."

"We're just getting older."

"Maggie didn't," she said.

And suddenly here she was in the French countryside taking children for walks down strange kinds of country roads that had no character in them at all. The fields didn't have proper walls, they went on for miles and miles without any fences even. The farmhouse was terribly shabby on the outside, but very rich and full of huge furniture on the inside.

There was Maria, an Italian maid who had great tufts of long black hair at her armpits and who seemed almost as miserable as Madame. Only Madame, Maria and Dara went to mass on Sundays, which seemed to make nonsense of the nuns saying they were Catholic families looking for equally good Catholics to come and stay. Monsieur had been to the church five times he told her, for his christening, his first communion, his wedding, and the christening of two of his three children; the third managed without him. At least that's what Dara thought he was saying; he seemed to be counting out the occasions proudly on the fingers of one hand for her. She shuddered to think what Canon Moran, or anyone at school would think if she told them, and for some reason she didn't quite understand, she felt that she wouldn't tell them.

Madame's visit to Lourdes involved a lot of preparation. An open suitcase sat on the landing and there was a lot of folding and refolding of clothes, and placing and replacing of missals and small prayer books. There was never a smile or an eagerness, just a more determined business than ever. Dara wondered what the woman could be going so far to pray for.

"*Desirez-vous un miracle*, Madame Vartin?" she asked boldly on the morning of the departure.

The thin dark woman stopped and looked at her as if she had never seen Dara before.

"*Un miracle!*" she repeated. "*Un miracle. Tiens!*"

And suddenly and totally unexpectedly, she took Dara by the shoulders and kissed her on each cheek. There were tears in her eyes.

Dara felt terrible. Perhaps Madame Vartin was very sick. How stupid to ask her if she was seeking a miracle! Dara wished she could have bitten back the words, but strangely Madame's softness remained, and when she was being waved off by the entire family at the door she had a special pat for Dara. It was impossible to understand the French.

Dara went for her usual walk in the orchard to find apples that would stave off hunger until the impossibly late meal that evening. She decided to write a long letter to her mother and went upstairs to get her writing paper.

There was summer lightning out over the strange unwalled fields of France. She ate the green apples, and she wrote about Madame going to Lourdes and her own tactless remarks. Dara had gotten into the habit of writing to her mother just like she talked. She knew that the letters were not read out at home, but that her mother gave edited extracts.

"I wonder why she's so sad," Dara wrote. "I mean she doesn't have any awful things to put up with like you do, not being able to walk, and getting stuck behind the counter listening to old bores drinking and chattering on for hours. I can't understand why Monsieur married her really, he must have known she would be a misery. She looks like a disaster area even in their wedding picture. But I think you'd need to live here for a lifetime to know what any of them are at."

Next morning she knocked on Mademoiselle Stephanie's door to ask for a stamp. They gave their letters to the mailman when he arrived with the incoming mail.

Mademoiselle Stephanie was still in bed, which was odd. Beside her was Monsieur Vartin, which was so unexpected that the letter fell from Dara's hand.

"I'm terribly sorry . . ." she began.

Mademoiselle Stephanie didn't seem in the slightest put out. She indicated the middle drawer of the desk for the stamps, and asked Dara to remember to give the mailman some other letters which were on the hall table.

Now that Dara had gone to France it was a little more difficult for Michael to meet Grace without calling attention to himself. Eddie and Declan were particularly revolting this summer; they made kissing sounds when he said he was going fishing with Grace. Admittedly Dad and Mam shushed them up, but it was very annoying.

Grace didn't seem to care, which was a relief. She came into the pub as regularly as when Dara had been around. She asked to see Dara's letters but Mam said that letters were only for the people they were sent to. If Grace wrote to Dara then she would get letters back, and so would Michael.

Dara felt tears of homesickness fall down her face. Madame Vartin found her reading her letter, and put her bony thin arm around the girl's shoulder. She said soothing things in French and Dara said cheerful things between noseblows, things like she wasn't really lonely, and she was just being silly.

Then she looked at Madame Vartin's long sad face and she became more weepy than ever.

She had tried to tell Madame Vartin about Maggie. It was so hard to explain, she had looked up words in the dictionary but even then it was too complicated. Sometimes she had to abandon the story in the middle. And anyway she was more sorry for Madame Vartin than she was for herself. It became almost unbearable when she saw Monsieur give Madame a little peck on the cheek as if nothing untoward had ever gone on in her absence.

Dara sighed. Perhaps men were by nature faithless. Sister Laura had more or less implied it, said that it came from nature where a male animal was used to servicing several female animals. Mary Donnelly never said anything else. Dara thought sadly of the world of men. Starting with Kerry.

There had been letters from everyone, even a card from nice Fergus Slattery. Pages from the Whites, and almost daily something from Tommy Leonard. But from Kerry nothing at all.

He couldn't have found somebody else already. He *couldn't* have. Why say all those things, and want to be so close to her if he could forget her so quickly?

But then Dara thought gloomily of Mrs. Whelan's husband who had gone away, of Kerry's father who wouldn't make up his mind between Mrs. Fine, Miss Johnson and quite possibly Miss Byrne the physio-therapist. And Brain Doyle had a girlfriend in the town that he hardly paid any attention to.

And those men who called on Rita Walsh in the Rosemarie hair salon. Dara knew now they hadn't come to fix hair dryers or to see to the hot water. No, now that she was a sophisticated woman who knew about the world. Now she realized only too well why they went there, and why they looked so secretive when they came out and scuttled off home.

Dara thought about all the men she knew and only her father and brother seemed blameless to her. Her father wouldn't look at another woman and Michael had put Grace on such a pedestal that he probably just kissed her chastely. She couldn't imagine Michael doing what Kerry had. She thought about Kerry for a bit and supposed she'd better tell in confession about all that stroking and kissing. Though how to describe it was a mystery.

It would be lovely to know enough French to confess to a French priest. By the looks of things you'd get away with murder here.

"How's Dara getting on minding the children by the Loire?" Fergus asked.

"It's the poor French children I worry about," Kate laughed. "I got a letter from her this morning and she said that she has taught them all to say *pogue mahone*. They think it's Irish for good morning."

Fergus laughed. "Knowing the French I'd say they'd be pleased to think their children were being taught anything as racy as kiss my arse. A very lavatorial sense of humor, I always found."

"Don't be lofty, you always found. When did you always find? On your five-day trip to Paris ten years ago was it?"

"How many days did *you* spend in Paris, brain box?" he asked.

"No days. And now I'll never go."

"Remember we wanted you to go to Lourdes."

"Yes, but it would have been the wrong thing, Fergus. Lourdes doesn't mend broken spines. Nothing does. People would have been so disappointed and I would have felt I would have failed them somehow if they saw me in a wheelchair for the rest of my life."

"I think it's a load of rubbish," said Fergus.

"You can't mean that." Kate was shocked. "Why would Our Lord let people believe it and go there in millions if it wasn't true?"

"Have you ever considered that Our Lord mightn't be there?"

"No I have not, and neither have you. This is being said to shock me, like a schoolboy. Of course you believe in God."

"Well if I do I don't like him much," Fergus said. "He's taken away my housekeeper weeping and wondering where her duty lies. She came to a tearful conclusion, Canon Moran and Father Hogan's need is greater than mine."

"I'm delighted," Kate said. "Best thing for her, for them and for you."

"Why for me?"

"You'll have to live like the real world lives now, instead of having everything done for you, being a peter pan with occasional flashes of bold atheism now and then. It will be the making of you."

"What will I do?" shouted Fergus.

"Find a wife," Kate said.

"No, seriously what will I do now? Miss Purcell's going."

"I'll get you someone to come in and clean the house. That's all you need."

"But the cooking, the washing."

"I'll teach you to cook. I'm teaching Grace O'Neill so I might as well have two pupils, and until you find someone who takes in washing properly you can bring it here."

* * *

Kate wrote to Dara about the lessons. She said they were priceless. She said that Grace hadn't known you could get rashers of bacon cut for you, she thought they started life in plastic wrappings. She said that Michael put half the dough in his hair and on the kitchen walls, and that Fergus was in grave danger of becoming a kitchen bore. He kept saying there was nothing to it, and when were they getting on to something a bit more elaborate?

The entire Vartin family had taken to saying *pogue mahone* as a greeting each day, and Dara wished mightily that she could be around the first time one of them actually said it to anyone who understood Irish.

As an act of solidarity she decided to tell Madame Vartin what it meant. It was the only gift she could give her, a little superior knowledge. Laboriously she translated it: *Va baiser ma fesse.*

Madame's face was quite stunned when she heard it, and Dara wondered had she gone too far? But no. Madame Vartin thought this was a nugget of information and hugged it to herself with glee.

"*Pogue mahone,* Stephanie," she would say to her rival each morning, and she and Dara exchanged winks of delight when nobody was looking.

Rachel told Patrick that he might need to organize activities for the bad weather. She chose a particularly wet and gloomy day to tell him this so that he could see what she meant.

"Fishermen would be out on a day like this, and golfers never let a little rain get between them and their game," Patrick said.

"Their wives?" said Rachel.

"They can get their hair fixed, their nails done."

"Not every day they can't."

"What do you think then?"

"Some activities, maybe cooking classes even. How to make traditional Irish fare."

"Not a bad idea," Patrick said. "Who would we get to do it?"

"Let's think nearer the time. There could even be people around here?"

"Hey," said Patrick suddenly. "Kate Ryan's done well teaching Grace, and Grace says she's very funny and has long stories about the ingredients and everything. Do you think she could do it?"

"I don't know where you get your ideas, Patrick," Rachel said in admiration.

Jim Costello, the young manager, had not yet met Kerry, son of the house. Jim had been away finding staff and interviewing applicants when Kerry had come home.

He had not been in Mountfern for the tragedy. He knew the Dalys, of course, and remembered the little girl with the long hair and big eyes as a friend of Grace O'Neill's. He called to the dairy to sympathize on his return.

He was surprised to see an older girl there. "I don't think we've met," he said and offered his hand.

"Mountfern is really looking up now that I'm off nursing in Dublin," Kitty Daly said, eyeing him up with unconcealed pleasure. "You *and* Kerry O'Neill. I must say it's the place to be."

"I haven't met him yet, I hear he's a matinee idol," Jim said.

"He's all of that. He's like something from another world," Kitty said.

"Ah well, no chance for the rest of us then." Jim was courteous, admiring and yet distant. He had come to offer his sympathies, it would be crass to let it turn into flirting. And anyway Jim Costello was much too cautious a young man to become too involved with anyone in a small town. His career was of much greater importance than any dalliance with a local girl, even one as pretty as this tall willowy girl with the beautiful crinkly hair.

As he left he said again that he was so sorry about her sister.

"It's impossible to believe it happened," Kitty said bleakly. "This is the first time I've been home since, and three times I've gone upstairs to call her. And I keep expecting all those friends of hers to come traipsing in looking for her."

"I didn't mean to upset you."

"No, it's nice to talk a bit. My dad won't talk about her at all and my mam has more conversations with her in heaven than she ever had when poor Maggie was on earth." She smiled gratefully as Jim Costello went out the door.

"Let's write to Dara," Grace said.

"You always say that when you want to wriggle out of my arms," Michael complained.

"Not true. Anyway I'm much better about remembering your poor sister stuck with all those awful screaming children than you are."

"How can she be learning any French if she keeps writing to us and reading our letters?" Michael grumbled, annoyed to be distracted from his long embraces with the lovely Grace.

But Grace was sitting up and had gotten out the notepad. "Come on, Michael. Stop fooling around . . . I'll start. What will I tell her?"

"Don't tell her about Declan Morrissey getting drunk and asking Mary Donnelly why she was never married. I want to tell her that."

"That's not fair, that's the best part. I can remember nearly all the speech."

"No, I thought of it, you say something boring about clothes or something first."

"I don't write about clothes. Hey, I'll tell her Kerry's coming back for a weekend."

"He'll probably have told her that himself."

"I don't imagine Kerry writes, he's bad at letters."

"Well, to Dara he would surely?" Michael thought that it would be very bad of Kerry to be so neglectful.

"Yes, maybe." Grace was doubtful.

"And I'll write about Kitty Daly being back."

"I don't know." Grace was still more doubtful.

"Grace, for heaven's sake, you're the one who said let's write; now you don't want to say anything."

Eddie Ryan went into Leonard's. Tommy looked left and right. His father was busy talking to Mr. Williams. Swiftly Tommy handed Eddie three aniseed balls from a jar.

"Thanks," Eddie said briefly.

"Don't eat them here," Tommy hissed.

Tommy paid Eddie protection money of a sort. He fed him a small amount of sweets that would not be missed from giant jars in order to buy some peace and quiet from Eddie's gang. Eddie swaggered in most days and the arrangement was sweets of Tommy's choice, otherwise they all came in together and Tommy's father got into a temper, ordered them out and told Tommy that the young Ryan boy was an out and out hooligan. Tommy didn't want any guilt to attach to Dara by association.

He wished that she would write. All he had so far was a picture postcard of some château on the Loire with a list of complaints about the food, and the price of ice cream and the price of stamps.

"Any news of Dara?" he asked Eddie.

"You ask me that every time," Eddie said.

"And you usually have a smart answer rather than saying yes or no," Tommy snapped.

"There was a letter this morning, Mam read bits of it at breakfast. What would be in the bits she doesn't read, do you think?"

"Maybe about how great it is to escape from you, Eddie."

"If you're going to be like everyone else then we will drop our deal?" Eddie said with menace.

The thought of Eddie's gang jostling and pushing and creating havoc in the newsagent's shop made Tommy Leonard feel faint.

"We'll go on the way we are," he said.

"I thought that's what you'd like," Eddie Ryan said cheerfully.

Tommy watched him go out of the shop and head for the shop that used to be Meagher's until Mr. O'Neill had bought it. It was a sort of travel agency and tours office. Surely Eddie wasn't going to terrorize them and be paid off in excursions by coach to the Ring of Kerry?

Tommy found the days very long, and on his half day he found the hours very long. Twice he had headed off up the street to look for Maggie to come and talk to him. He didn't dare tell anyone that in case they thought he was going mad or that he hadn't cared about her death.

Tommy woke a lot with his heart beating thinking of Maggie's fall.

Jacinta and Liam had discovered that the cousin wasn't too bad after all. Her name was Amanda, which was a bit rich for Mountfern, and she loved horses. She had been very disappointed that they didn't ride, being in the country and everything. In desperation they asked their father if they could ask Miss Johnson to teach them.

Marian had two tame ponies she said, they were practically geriatric she admitted; nobody could come to any harm on them. She bit her lip when she had said that. The raw grief of the children in Mountfern was still in everyone's minds.

"Why don't they have the ponies and play with them up in the paddock?" she said to Dr. White. "There'll be no fees, no lessons, it will take their minds off things."

"You're a decent woman, Marian," Martin White said, and meant it. He used to think that she was a bit uppity and gave herself airs, but he didn't like her being publicly humiliated by O'Neill either. And it would stop his children from driving him into the asylum on the hill where he had sent so many patients over the years.

* * *

Grace saw the activity in the paddock behind the Grange. "Would we be in the way if we joined in?" she asked.

Liam and Jacinta were delighted to see Grace again, at first they were ashamed of Amanda, but Amanda turned out to get on famously with Grace. Like everyone else.

When Marian saw that Patrick's daughter was interested she brought further and better horses, and a regular little riding school began.

"Come on, Michael. Get a hat, that's all. She insists we wear hard hats."

"Don't be mad, where would I get something like that? It's like asking me to get a top hat or a bowler."

"Please, Michael."

"No. I can borrow yours if I'm going to have a go, which I may not, I haven't decided yet." Michael was very disappointed at the turn things were taking.

He had seen a summer ahead of them where he and Grace would sit and talk and fish and hold each other and kiss. He would wander with her, telling her the secrets of his heart as he was starting to do already. He would tell her his plans and hopes for when they were older, and how he would study hard—at accountancy perhaps, he had heard her father say that a man who was trained as an accountant was trained for everything. He would tell her how they would travel together. But Grace wanted to play childish games and walk round in circles sitting on an aged pony.

"Grace, we don't have all that much time together, why are you wasting it?"

"It's not wasting it, we'll know how to ride horses," she said unanswerably. "Your way we just sit and talk and whatever."

"But remember, before, they sort of split us up, didn't want us going off on our own. Do you remember, that's why we all went to the bridge." He gave a shiver.

"I remember." Grace patted his hand soothingly. "But then isn't this all to the good? If they know we're all together with Jacinta and Liam and Amanda, they'll be pleased. They won't start breaking things up?" She looked at him with her big clear eyes as if it were the most obvious thing in the world and he was the only one not to see it.

"Don't you want to be with me?" he asked nakedly.

"Oh, Michael, of course I do, but we have all the time in the world to be together. Can't you enjoy this? It's new, it's fun."

* * *

Jim Costello took about five minutes to sum up Kerry O'Neill as trouble. And he spent a further five minutes working out how he was going to cope with him. This job at Fernscourt was the prize; it was up to him to make sure that nothing ruined it for him. If he made a success of Fernscourt, then in five to seven years there wasn't a bank in the country that wouldn't advance him money for his own hotel. And in the meantime he would meet exactly the kind of tourists and have just the right way to entertain them as he could have dreamed. His last hotel had been a trifle stuffy, still concentrated on the business-lunch trade which was only a status thing. Jim Costello knew that you made nothing by serving unimaginative and underpriced set luncheons to the local solicitors and bank managers and insurance brokers, but in a small place, that was what kept the image of a hotel high. Here in Fernscourt it was different.

He liked Patrick O'Neill and admired him. But the son. Jim Costello had been in the hotel business all his life. Since he could remember he had been in his father's small hotel, then in the Shannon training school and in France and Switzerland; he was twenty-four and he knew how to spot trouble. The man at the bar who was going to be troublesome, the customer who might not pay his bill. The respectable woman who was using a hotel foyer as a pick-up place. One of Jim's strengths was that he always saw it in time, just *before* the incident happened, and managed to head it off.

With Kerry he spotted it the very first time he met him. When he sauntered into the hotel with Tony McCann from Derry.

There was something about Tony McCann that seemed like a challenge. He greeted Jim as if he expected to be thrown out.

Kerry on the other hand was full of charm. "My father tells me there's nothing you don't know about the hotel business," he began.

"Let's hope he still says that when his hotel is open," Jim laughed back easily.

"Bit of a backwater this—for a hotshot like you," said Tony McCann.

"I don't think so, it's a friendly place and we hope to be so busy that I won't have much time for the bright lights myself."

Tony McCann looked at Jim Costello without much pleasure. "One of these ambitious fellows, all work and up a ladder, I suppose."

"That's me, the fellows at school used to hate me too—study

study, creep, teacher's pet. Are you in the hotel business too, Mr. McCann?"

"No."

"You're in what?"

"This and that."

Kerry stepped in smoothly. "Tony's a friend of mine up in the far north, just brought him in to see the ancestral home rise again."

"Are you pleased with it?" Jim spoke directly to Kerry.

He shrugged. "It's my father's dream, I guess he's really got what he wanted. It's looking good."

"But you'll be coming back . . ."

"Relax, Jim, there's going to be no fatted calf killed for me, not for a long time. No, you're safe here for a few years yet."

Jim flushed with annoyance. He had to decide now how to handle Kerry. Did he remain poker-faced and remote, loyal entirely to his employer? This way he would build a wall of resentment between him and the boy, who was only a few years younger. Or did he make Kerry an ally of sorts? Wouldn't that be easier? He decided to go the friendship way.

"I'd say there's plenty to keep us both occupied if you *do* come back. Your father has some very grand plans."

"Do you think they'll work out?"

"Not all of them by any means, but enough of them will and I'd say he's a man who would learn by mistakes. Am I right?"

Kerry seemed amused to be consulted. "Yes, that's true in most areas. He's extraordinarily practical, but I'm not sure about this one. He wants so much for it to succeed it could blind him."

"As I said, let's hope it will and the problem won't arise." Jim had decided how to play it: friendly but not servile, discreet but not what the Americans called tight-assed. He would always repeat pleasantly to Patrick any conversation he had with the son. With Kerry you'd need to cover your back.

He hoped McCann would clear off out of the place too. He was pleased to see Kerry's car drive off to the big town with McCann and then come back without him. The fellow had obviously gone back north. What on earth had brought him down for such a flying visit? There was something watchful about him as if he hadn't believed Kerry O'Neill came from this kind of set-up and had come down to check.

He reminded Jim of a very tough Guard he had once known who came on Saturdays for a steak and a few whiskies to thank him for being lenient about closing time during the week. That Guard had a swagger when he came in to collect. Tony McCann had the same kind of swagger, as if he had come to Mountfern to collect.

It wasn't easy to find Kate alone. Patrick made three tries. Finally he hit a morning when Mary seemed occupied with deliveries in the yard, when John had driven to the town and the guard seemed to be relaxed.

Kate was sitting by her big french window, studying the typing manual from which she intended to teach Dara. He had tapped lightly on the door, and she hadn't looked up when he came in.

"I'd have thought you knew all about typing," he said.

Kate looked up surprised. "It's you Patrick, sit down won't you? I didn't know you were in the place at all."

She smiled at him encouragingly but she got little response. He sighed deeply.

"Did you come in to draw big heavy breaths at me?" Kate asked.

"No. I'm just low, that's all."

"What has you low?" She was sympathetic but not totally sure that he was serious.

"I *am* low, Kate. I feel everything's gone wrong. So many terrible things have happened. That child, that poor child dead and buried."

"Ah, sure, Patrick, that has us all low. There's neither rhyme nor reason in it."

"It was never meant to be like this. Pointless tragedy, and confusion everywhere."

Kate looked at him. It seemed out of character, this type of talk. She waited to hear what it was about.

"You see, I got everything I wanted—the land, the permission to build—and God knows how, I've actually built the thing."

"So what's wrong?"

He went on with his catalog of what was right first. "The children like the place. That's not saying it as it is, they love it. This is a real bonus, I thought they would be pleading for brighter lights, but no. That's largely due to your children, by the way."

"I know, my twins have formed a welcome-the-O'Neill-family movement, haven't they?" Kate was polite and almost hid her anxiety about just how warmly they were welcoming them.

"No, don't worry about that, Kate. Grace and Michael are a couple of kids still, and you got Dara well away out of Kerry's clutches."

So he had realized! She laughed guiltily.

But he had moved on. "I worry now all the time. About the way it all happened, it's as if it weren't the right thing to do somehow . . ."

"Coming back?"

"Yes, or coming back in this way. Nothing's gone right since . . ."

"That's not like you—not the Patrick we know."

"Shit, Kate, can't you quit acting like someone's li'l old grandmother? Every time I look at you in that bloody chair, I think to myself that if I'd stayed where I was, you'd be on your two feet. When I see all the signs being put up on the road, when I have to meet the people from the tourist board and talk about projections and over views and market share, I wonder what the hell it's all about. Why I'm not out on the freeway in New Jersey buying up a couple more neighborhood bars. What am I *doing* changing every single thing I touch here, getting the priests and the parson to tidy up their graveyards? Christ, that wasn't what I wanted to do. I wanted to be welcomed here, but nobody remembered anyone belonging to me—"

"Oh, stop all this self-pity, for God's sake," Kate interrupted. "You knew that on day one, nobody remembered the O'Neills from a hole in the ground, so stop saying it's come as a surprise to you now. Four long years ago you knew that. You wanted a life here where you came from, and you've got it. Stop bellyaching about changing things and being remembered . . ." Her face was flushed with anger at him.

He reached over and took her hand. "I suppose you don't believe me, but it's looking at you that gives me the worst feeling of regret. Honestly and truthfully if I could turn it all back I'd never have come if it meant doing this to you."

"You *didn't* do it to me, you big loud-mouthed clown. I did it. I walked under the bloody bulldozer. You had signs, I didn't see them. How many times do I have to say to you and to Fergus, to everyone. I'm *not* looking at you every day and saying 'Why oh why didn't he stay in New Jersey, and I'd be able to walk?' "

Her eyes blazed and she had flung his hand away.

"If I say I wish you had stayed in New Jersey—and I do, believe me, I do say it many times a day—it's not because of that . . . not because of my being in this chair . . . oh no."

"Then what . . . ?" Patrick was alarmed.

"I wish you had stayed in your precious America because if you had then there would have been a living for us here, for John who never really wanted it in the first place but who worked so hard at it for us, for his wife and children, and a living for the children them-selves if they want to stay here. It's been in John's family for years, it's not easy to see it go up in smoke because of some Yank looking for his roots."

Patrick's mouth was open.

"I mean it, I knew I shouldn't have started but since I have I won't suddenly clam up like you do, I'm not cunning and watching what I say. *That's* the reason I wish you hadn't come here, not because I had an accident. I have to think of this whole bloody business as an accident otherwise I'd go insane."

Patrick was shocked. "But we've been over this a dozen times, all of us. You're not going to lose business, you're going to gain it. You'll have the customers from the hotel . . . We've been through this."

"Yes, we'll have them buying musical shillelaghs and leprechauns, that's what we'll have. They won't come in to drink here, neither will anyone with an ounce of sense in their head when they can have your Thatch Bar."

"You never said . . ."

"Why *should* I say anything to you? You never say anything real. You always work out where the advantage lies and then you speak. I was damned if I was going to tell you how I felt, specially since we didn't put in any objections in the beginning. Like Fergus said we should."

"Please, please let me assure you, let me promise . . ."

"I don't want any charity, I just want us to be able to make our own way as we always did. Surely you'd understand that."

"I understand that better than anyone would. Jesus Christ, I know about dignity and having your place somewhere. I was raised by a man who was a wino, a bum, we had no place anywhere, I wanted to be called Mr. O'Neill, I wanted to make my own way more than anything in the goddamn world . . ."

"You never said that about your father before . . ."

"Why *should* I tell you, or tell anyone? It's my business, and it's a part of my life I don't boast about."

"Oh no, you wouldn't mention anything unless there was some purpose . . ."

"What do you mean? What are you saying?"

"Nothing much, just showing how bad-tempered I can be, I ex-pect." Kate seemed to have run out of steam suddenly.

"There's enough for us both here, Kate."

"I hope you're right."

"Do I really only say things that are for my own gain?"

"I never said that," Kate insisted. "I said you didn't speak without thinking—like the rest of us do."

"I suppose you're right, but you've got to cover your back in my world," Patrick said. His tone changed.

"I came to say something to you, something quite serious."

"What is it?" There was alarm in her eyes.

"No, serious, as opposed to trivial," he reassured her. "I wanted to warn you about the case."

Her eyes narrowed. "Fergus said it wasn't proper to talk about it at all, that we must remember not to speak of it even to the children because of . . . well, because of Michael and Grace I suppose."

"Yes, my lawyers said the same thing. Talk about covering their backs . . ."

"So?"

"So, I wanted to say this, just between the two of us. You've had a terrible injury, nothing will make you walk again. You must get something, the *only* thing, that can make life a bit better. You must get as much money as you can."

Kate looked at him, startled.

"This is just us. For three days I've been trying to get you alone, and then we nearly messed it up by having a fight. You only have one chance, Kate."

"Why are you telling me this?"

"So that you will get what is fair."

"Still, it's not right of you to talk to me about it. Fergus said that if you did then I was to . . ."

"Fergus said, Fergus said, don't talk to me about Attorney Slattery, he makes me sick, that fellow with his calf's face—"

"You will *not* say that about Fergus." Kate flashed again.

"Sorry, sorry. Peace, peace." Patrick spread out his hands. "Look, I'm just trying so hard and I seem to fall every step of the way . . ."

"But Fergus said that if you came and offered . . ."

"And for once he was right, the attorney Slattery. If I *was* such a bastard as to come and offer you a deal then of course you should not talk to me. But I'm not, Kate, I'm offering you a warning: They will try to make you accept a low offer out of court. If it goes to court they'll try to trip you up, try to make you take less, try to prove to the jury, who are ordinary people without great wealth, that you live a fine life and that since your little pub would never have been a gold mine, and since you're a woman who should be damn grateful to have a roof over your wheelchair, then the least compensation should have you on your poor broken knees with gratitude."

"Why . . . ?" she began.

"Why? Because I know you, I know your pride which is a great strength but also a weakness. The 'I'm fine thank you' air you wear around you like a cape . . . nobody is to dare offer a word of sympathy to Kate Ryan or if they do they'll bear the consequences."

"I cope the way that suits me," Kate said.

"You cope brilliantly, and it's not just to suit *you*, it's to help your husband and your family and everyone. Nobody feels you're a cripple, but in three weeks' time if it goes to court you have to drop it, you have to lose this brave way of going on. You've *got* to tell them what it's really like, otherwise you'll get nothing."

"You mean, lie? Act?"

"I do *not* mean lie and act, you stupid woman, I mean tell them the plans you had for this place and how you can't damn well see them happening now. The life you had with your husband, how you wanted another child and that's over."

"Why do you want me to stand up and spin these self-pitying tales, make a public exhibition of myself, tell a tissue of lies just to get money in the bank? How little you understand anything."

"Jesus Christ, how little *you* understand anything. I didn't break your back, if I did I could pay for it. Sometimes I wish I *had* broken it, gone out with a cleaver and broken it. That way I could have gone to jail." His face was working and he was close to tears.

She looked at him wordlessly.

"What kind of pride is this that means you are denying your family what is rightfully theirs?"

"You sound just like Fergus," she said.

Patrick stood up. He shrugged helplessly.

"I'll leave you, Kate, before we start again." He smiled and his face was transformed as it always was. He looked at her sitting so still in the chair.

"It's no wonder half the town is in love with you," he said. "I could fall in love with you myself."

"Oho, it's a well-known thing that, to say you could fall in love with the unattainable. That's very Irish, Patrick, you've inherited a lot of your forefathers' little ways of going on. That's the kind of thing all those mountainy old bachelors would say."

"I'm a mountainy old bachelor too—by nature, I guess."

"That will certainly disappoint the gossips here."

His eyes were cold. "What do they say, the gossips?"

"That you intend to ask Rachel to marry you someday."

He was startled. For Kate who was Rachel's close confidante to speak like this.

"Well," he said.

"However it's not something Rachel and I talk about," she said.

"You don't, like hell."

"You mustn't flatter yourself too much. We *used* to talk about you certainly, but not nowadays."

There was an unsettling truth in the way she spoke. There was a little silence.

"I don't handle things very well sometimes," he said eventually.

"There are some things that it isn't a matter of handling, or coping with or sorting out like business deals."

"I know."

They sat companionably for a few moments.

Kate was a much more still person than she had been before. There was a time when Kate Ryan could not have allowed a silence of longer than two seconds.

Patrick was not a man much given to sitting and musing either. But here he sat and looked ahead of him into the flower-filled garden where the big orange cat sunned herself and the soft cluck of the hens in the distance was soothing. There was no sign of the terrible dog, perhaps someone had been dispatched to take it on a far-distant walk so that its baying could upset another parish.

"I must go now," he said.

"You were very good to come and see me. Thank you for what you said. No matter what happens I'll remember that and appreciate it."

He leaned over lightly and kissed her on the forehead. He had never done that before.

"And you promise me you'll remember what I said? It doesn't make you weak, it makes you strong."

"I'll remember," she said.

And he left.

Kate sat still for a long while. She could understand why Rachel was so enmeshed with this man. He was alive and aware and reacting all the time.

It must have been a heady thing for Rachel to realize how essential she was to him and how much he needed her.

No wonder she felt bereft now that he most likely didn't need her anymore. Kate's fists beat on her useless legs. The only point in living was to be needed, to be an inspiration, to be the power in something. Nobody understood that, nobody.

Fergus, with all his childish spite against the O'Neills didn't have the glimmerings of an understanding. He didn't know *why* she was a person who needed compensation. It didn't have all that much to do with paralysis. It had to do with having no role.

John Ryan in a million years would not understand. He would say she was being hysterical, and that of course she was important, more than important . . . but essential to all of them.

But Kate Ryan knew she wasn't essential anymore. They didn't need her like they had once needed her. John was stronger and more his own man, he made decisions with certainty, he coped with the pub as she had once wished and prayed that he would. He still found time to write his poems. He was not as gullible as she had once thought him to be. He was firm with the children, he drove a car, their own car, around Mountfern. He was a slimmer, fitter man than the man of three years ago, more confident in every way.

But he didn't lean on Kate as he once had. He didn't need her at every turn of the day.

That was why she needed some goddamn compensation. Not that money was any good, but the reason she should get anything was because her husband didn't depend on her anymore.

And the only man who had the faintest understanding of this was the man who was *meant* to be their great enemy. Patrick O'Neill.

"I can't like that young Costello," Fergus said to Kate.

"You can't like anyone with hand, act or part in Fernscourt."

"Wrong. There's a lot of decent people working for him. Don't make me out to be unreasonable."

"Lord, you're the most reasonable man in the world usually; this is your only blind spot. What has poor Jim Costello done now?"

"I heard him talking to Canon Moran, meant to be a sort of private chat. But I could see what he was getting at."

"You listened to his confession!"

"No, it was in the open air out in the church grounds. You know, beside the garden that O'Neill's workmen built up for them. He was telling the poor doddery old canon how great it would be if the bishop came to the opening."

"Well the bishop *is* coming to the opening, surely?"

"Yes, but Jim wanted him to speak at the blessing bit and he was explaining this awful insincere way to the canon that Mr. O'Neill wouldn't like to suggest it, and Mr. O'Neill wanted it to be the canon who spoke, but wouldn't it be great if the bishop were to say a few words too. You know, a lot of devious bullshit."

"And you're the one always giving out about Patrick's language!"

"The poor old canon thinks he's the one now who thought of asking the bishop, he's back up at the presbytery trying to word the letter."

Kate changed the subject. Fergus was getting moody.

"And how is your Miss Purcell up there with the clergy?"

"As happy as anything."

"Well it leaves you a bit freer, anyway. Whatever you want to do you don't have to take her future into consideration."

"I don't want to do much, Kate. I just want things to stay the same."

To his surprise she leaned across from the wheelchair and patted his hand. "I know. I know just what you mean," she said.

"Are you going to the hotel opening, Mary?" Fergus was civil.

"It's very kind of you to be so interested but the answer is no. Some one person should be here to keep the door open in case in the Republic of Ireland there happens to be one or two souls who are *not* going to the opening and think they might be served a drink in a wayside pub."

Mary's face was flushed with anger and loyalty to her stance about the rightness of everything the Ryans did and the wrongness of the O'Neills.

Fergus blinked wearily. He had brought this attack upon himself and there were many ways that he supported her entirely. But she was a trying woman.

He had only broached the subject of the opening to her on instructions from Sheila Whelan.

"Say the odd kind word to Mary when you're passing," Sheila had asked.

"Have you a suit of chain mail for me to put on when I'm talking to her?"

Fergus had been bitten too often to feel easy about saying anything to Mary Donnelly.

"She's a great woman when you get to know her. She has all the qualities of a good wife—loyalty, determination, everything." Sheila sighed.

"Are you trying to make a match for her by any chance?"

"Oh, I think it would be a brave soul who would attempt to make a match for Mary these days."

"Or for me?" Fergus teased.

"Oh, we're dying to marry *you* off, Fergus," Sheila said.

"Who's we?"

"Kate and myself, we'd love to settle you down. But I'm only giving you a big head. Listen, when you see that cousin of mine, Mary, will you tell her she's to go to the opening of the hotel. It's only a false kind of loyalty to the Ryans saying she is going to boycott. Use your charms."

"My charms haven't much of a track record," Fergus had said gloomily.

And indeed he felt he was right, Mary Donnelly showed no reaction to his charming manner except to reject the notion of going near the new hotel. She sniffed and said that the Ryans were going not to show offense, and because they had a standard of manners much higher and more generous than the O'Neill family.

Fergus sighed again. Talking to Mary was like trying to climb up a waterfall.

"Can I talk to Kate? I have to get her to see Kevin Kennedy, that's the barrister. I want to fix up a proper consultation but Kate's always too busy making potato cakes, or hemming serviettes or some other nonsense. If the woman could only understand that she must give her whole heart and mind to Kevin Kennedy and the court case, then she won't *have* to hem all those table napkins."

"Will you be able to get her a great compensation do you think?" Mary looked eager and excited. "I'd love more than anything for her to take a fortune off that man. I'd really love it."

"That's not the way it's going to be, he'll pay nothing, it's the insurance company. I don't know, I really don't. These cases are like throwing a dice. It could be any figure that comes up."

"There must be some system."

"There is a sort of system, but it depends what way it's presented. It's very practical you know, very matter of fact. What were her earnings, what could be said to have been lost in terms of money? There's something built in for pain and suffering, and then there's a category called mental distress. But it all depends on judges and juries in the end, and they're often cautious men, careful with other people's money even if it's insurance companies. Oh God, I wish I knew."

"You sound very worried." Mary's face looked quite pleasant when she wasn't making some strong point, she had a softness about her that wasn't in her normal style.

"I am worried, Mary, I'm worried that Kate and John are turning down their only chance of getting what they deserve and are owed. They don't seem to grasp that this is the one and only time they'll ever get any stake together for any kind of life."

"And show that bastard what the courts of Ireland think of him."

"Yes, but with respect, Mary, mightn't we do better if we played down that side of it?"

"I know what you mean, I'm as bright as the next man. I'll sing low on the revenge bit—is that what you mean?"

"That's what I mean."

"I'll feel it in my heart though," Mary said.

"So will I," said Fergus.

"Oh bring him along, certainly," Kate said when Fergus suggested a consultation with Kevin Kennedy.

"He's quite important, Kate, you won't just play along and joke and make eejity remarks about it being half your own fault?"

"I never make eejity remarks. Remember when I was your right-hand woman in the office, don't say I make eejity remarks."

"I remember. I remember well," Fergus sighed.

"So, I'll be polite and use long words. But isn't he on our side, is he not our lawyer, why do I have to be impressing him and putting on an act for our own counsel? Isn't it the judge and the jury I have to do the tragic queen act for?"

"It's no act, Kate. You are badly injured in the name of Jesus, will you stop being the bravest girl in the school about this and start thinking of your future and your family's future?"

"You're cross with me."

"I'm furious with you. You think it's not quite nice somehow to let anyone know how much your life was changed that day, how much your chances lessened. One day, one day when it's too late you'll wish you'd listened, you will be very sorry then. In three or four years' time when the pub might need a new roof, or when Dara might wonder why there was no money to send her to university or the kids might want to go on a school trip to Rome or John, God forbid, might get a virus pneumonia and be off work for four months and you'd have to pay someone to come in and run the pub . . . Won't it be a great consolation to yourself to say that way back in 1966 when you had your chance, your one chance to explain your case, you were too refined, too well-brought-up or some kind of bullshit to get the compensation you and your family deserved? Fine warm comfort these high and mighty principles will be to you and your family then."

His eyes blazed with rage on her behalf.

Kate changed immediately. She sat upright in her chair and reached for a notebook.

"You are perfectly right as always," she said without a trace of irony. "Tell me what kind of things will we cover with Mr. Kennedy when he comes."

Kevin Kennedy wore an expensive suit but it was crumpled, and his shoes needed a good shine. Kate looked at him and decided that he was a bachelor whose housekeeper was lazy and indifferent. He had a big mane of greying hair, a rather theatrical bow tie and nicotine-stained fingers which groped restlessly for more cigarettes still. Kate judged him to be about fifty, and realized after a very short time that he was much sharper than he gave the impression of being. He seemed to shamble through explanations and accounts but yet he remembered everything that had been said and came back to points which she had been sure he had forgotten.

He was very good at drawing her out. Kate found herself responding easily to his questions about the limitations to her life caused by the accident. She agreed that their earnings were considerably diminished since she could no longer work for Fergus in the mornings and since they had to pay out a salary to Mary Donnelly. Kate told how her concentration had lessened, she found it very hard to read a book to its end, whereas once she always had her nose in some book from the library.

Fergus was startled to hear this, she had never said it to him. But that was often Kevin's gift, he managed to make people tell things. Very often when he was on the other side of a case cross-examining, his gentle persuasive voice made people tell things they wished to keep secret. But here in Kate's green room Kevin Kennedy was slowly drawing the picture he would need.

Fergus sighed with admiration as Kevin talked to the Ryan couple about how their life had changed, the pain, the huge incapacity, the lack of being able to act as a real mother to the children the way other mothers could, like going up to the school or joining in any outings and activities.

"And of course your normal married life, the life between the two

of you that you would have expected to have?" Kevin Kennedy was
gentle.

Fergus felt a hot flush coming up his neck.

Long ago, long before Kate's accident, he had put the thought of
her sex life with John Ryan far from his mind. He knew it must exist
but he never wanted to think about it, and yet it used to come back
to him, the notion of the two of them entwined. He assumed that
since the accident it had been out of the question. To his embarrassment John was beginning to stammer.

"Well, I wouldn't say that it was exactly over . . . you know, sort
of . . ."

Fergus felt the bile rise in his throat. Surely John could never be so
gross and unfeeling as to expect Kate . . . No, it wasn't possible. He
felt unsteady for a moment.

"I'll slip out and get something from the bar . . ." he said.

"Thanks, Fergus." Kate was cool. "I asked Mary to get a tray
ready, perhaps you could bring it to us . . ."

He went out, loosening his collar.

"Kate said she thought sandwiches and a bottle of the good Jame-
son," Mary suggested. "I have it here ready and all, I didn't want to
go and disturb you."

"That's good of you."

"Are you all right, Fergus?" She looked genuinely concerned.

"Yes, I'm just tired. Give me a large one while I'm waiting."

"What are you waiting for?" Mary obediently poured him a
double and waved away the pound note he offered.

"I don't know really, just giving them a chance to talk, I suppose,"
he said, wondering how long would Kevin Kennedy spend on lack of
conjugal rights, and compensation for same. Wildly he wondered
whether John was saying that really it wasn't fair to blame Patrick
O'Neill in this area because he and Kate were able to have a very
satisfactory coupling despite everything.

Fergus felt his hands shaking and he gripped the glass tightly with
both of them.

"It must be very hard, this kind of thing, when you're a friend of
the family as well." Mary was sympathetic.

"Have a drink, Mary."

"No thanks, Fergus, I don't think . . ."

"Have a bloody drink."

"Very well, keep your hair on. I'll have a vodka and tonic, thank
you very much."

"Not at all. Good luck."

Mary raised her glass solemnly. "Good luck, really and truly good luck. They're relying on you."

"No they're not, they think they're grand, they think it's lovely to be financially ruined and crippled."

"Shush now."

"I won't shush. And anyway nobody would rely on me, it's Kevin they should rely on."

"Oh him?" Mary sniffed. "From Dublin, and a man."

"Yes, I suppose those are points against him. I wonder has it crossed your mind that I too am a man, Mary. Perhaps you should take that into consideration when you and I are having these little social drinks."

"I know you're a man, Fergus," Mary said.

"I'm glad someone does, I've almost forgotten myself."

"But you're not a real man, not like ordinary men." Mary was full of beaming approval. "Here, will you take this tray in that you came out for or they'll think you fell into bad company."

"You're not the worst, Mary," Fergus said, picking up the tray and carrying it back into the room.

They seemed to have exhausted sexual dysfunction or the possibility of suing for removal of conjugal rights. They were on to the topic of what they could expect to be awarded.

The tray was left beside Kate on the big round table which Rachel had found and covered with a floor-length green cloth. Nowhere else in Ryan's pub had the elegance of this room.

They looked like four ordinary people having a drink, Fergus thought as Kate poured generous measures and added a splash of water from their only cut-glass crystal jug. No sign of their business together.

Sheila Whelan came back quietly by bus.

It should only be two hours and three quarters, but the bus visited every townland on the way. It took mountainy routes and it went almost full circles into the countryside to pick up and drop farmers from crossroads that were off the beaten track. There was plenty of time to sit and think.

Think about Joe with his gaunt face and his sad tales clutching her from the hospital bed.

It hadn't turned out as he had hoped, he told her. He wanted to come home to Mountfern. To die.

"There's no question of dying, Joe," she had soothed him, her words automatic, her expression effortlessly kind. Even to the man who had left her all those years ago, hurling abuse to justify himself as he went.

His life had not indeed turned out as he hoped. There were children, four—two sons and two daughters—children that Sheila was not able to bear, and he had scorned the idea of adopting and raising another man's sons.

The woman he had left everything for was a restless woman. The children had been reared wild, left to run wild. None of them would settle in anything, school or work. The eldest boy had gone to England a few hours ahead of the Guards, it turned out.

Joe had got to thinking about Mountfern in recent weeks. He thought of all the people he knew there, Jack Leonard and Tom Daly. He hadn't heard that Tom Daly's little girl had met with such a terrible accident. Sheila told him about Maggie, but his mind wandered away in the middle of the story. She stopped after a while when she saw he wasn't concentrating. It was too sad a tale anyway.

He remembered Jack Coyne and that nice dour Dr. White. Was old man Slattery around? No, well the son was a grand young fellow. And of course the canon. It would be good to wander down River Road to Ryan's like in the old days. He had heard of the new hotel across the river, there was a lot of talk about it in the papers. He hadn't known of Kate Ryan's accident but he was sure that they'd got great compensation.

And since there were no real ties with Dublin, no—for all that he had a home—it was a house really—and she would understand that he wanted to go home at the end. She'd probably be pleased for him. When all was said and done. So could he come back to Mountfern? Could he come home?

Sheila had talked to the nurse who recognized instantly that Sheila Whelan was someone to whom the truth was told. She heard that Joe had weeks and possibly only days to live. She had confirmed what she suspected—that he would never leave his hospital bed.

She told him he could come home.

She begged him not to worry what people would say and what people would think. Nowadays, she said, people were much too busy with their own business to worry about the middle-aged postmistress and her husband. She said that Dr. White would be able to continue any treatment.

Joe's eyes had filled with tears at her goodness. He had never meant to hurt her in the past, he had never wanted to be cruel.

She said she understood. She sat and held his hand until he fell asleep. Three days she was there helping him make his plans, telling him where they would put his bed.

He said it would be good in a way for her to have a man around the house again, and that was the only time she had cried. The tears had come down her face and she wept at the useless lives most people led and how little anyone understood about anyone else.

She asked the nurse to make sure that nobody was kept away because of her visits but the nurse shook her head and said that poor Mr. Whelan's wife wasn't in the best of health and wasn't able to come and see him. Sheila read this to mean that the woman who had borne Joe Whelan's four children suffered from her nerves or drink or both. She discovered that there were neighbors who would supervise the funeral, kind people in the small Dublin street who had known nothing of any previous existence in Mountfern.

When he fell into his coma and she was assured that he would not know anyone around him again, she left as quietly as she had come and took the bus back to Mountfern. She did not feel saintly or unselfish; she felt a weary tiredness. And for the first time in her life she felt something like anger. Anger about people who stood by and let things happen. At herself for wasting all those years thinking that Joe knew what he was doing and that there was some sort of plan. She might have been better not to have been so dignified and discreet. She could have gone after him and fought for him. And got him back.

Or she could have gotten a court order and got maintenance from him if she hadn't valued her good name so highly and been too proud to ask for it. That way she would have strong shoes to wear instead of making do with patched soles and avoiding puddles. She would have had the money to go to Rome when the diocese was making the pilgrimage. She could have given Mary Donnelly something better than she had, some holiday or some outfit to get her over the worst days of the pain, the days when you need some distractions.

Instead she was coming back on the bus to Mountfern where nobody except Kate Ryan would know whether Joe Whelan was alive or dead. She would ask Canon Moran to say a mass for his soul, but she would just say that it was for a friend. It wasn't that the canon would ever tell anyone but she had been so silent and secretive about this, she would keep it that way to the end.

But for the rest of her life she was not going to sit and take a back seat. She was going to take part in things, not just observe them.

Chapter XX

Patrick finished the steak and kidney pie. "That was quite excellent, Miss Hayes."

"It's a pleasure to serve you, Mr. O'Neill."

He sat by himself at the table. Grace was having supper at the Ryans'. It was a night of a cookery lesson, she had explained. He knew it was just another chance to see young Michael but he pretended to take the cookery classes very seriously. Kerry was miles away in Donegal. When Olive Hayes had gone back to her kitchen he sat quite alone. As he sat many an evening.

It would be different when the hotel opened, he told himself. There would not be this stark realization that he found himself reading through his meals, and sitting idly after them, fiddling with the television, if he didn't get out more work. He had discouraged Marian from suggesting outings, and now she had ceased trying to interest him in little trumped-up schemes. He wished he could ask Rachel here.

He stood and stretched . . . the evening seemed to stretch as well.

He had put off so long and so firmly any thought about what would happen to Rachel when the hotel opened that he found himself doing it again automatically. But tonight somehow he felt able to think about it.

She *could* take instruction. And if she did, then there would be no problem about her previous marriage, since it wasn't a Catholic marriage. Hell, it wasn't even a Christian marriage.

And she *could* fit in here, there were ways where she seemed to have adapted better than he had.

Rachel got on so well with Kate Ryan, with Sheila Whelan, with Loretto Quinn. Brian Doyle said that she was the only person connected with the entire enterprise who might be considered sane. Mary Donnelly, that madwoman running a one-woman band for the annihilation of men, said that Rachel was one in a million.

Why did he hesitate to ask her even to something simple like supper in his own house?

He knew why, it was out of guilt.

He still felt that this woman was part of his past. He had gone willingly and excitedly to her arms while the children had stayed in a big white house in New Jersey with their always-ailing mother.

And Rachel wasn't Irish, or part of the great scheme. That's why he kept her at such a long arm's length.

Dara's postcard arrived at Hill's Hotel for Kerry. It sounded very casual with an attempt to be sardonic:

I heard there was a bank strike at home, I didn't know there was a postal strike as well!! But then how does everyone else manage to write to me, I wonder? It's a puzzlement, as they say in *The King and I.*

France is magnifique.

I'll be back in Mountfern on the last Thursday in August.

Love Dara.

Kerry read it and smiled. He would have taken a hotel postcard and written straight back, but he had a lot on his mind. He had lost a great deal on three consecutive nights.

It was time to call Father.

But if he won tonight, it would all be sorted out. No need to tell Father about anything.

Tony McCann was apologetic. If it were up to him there wouldn't be a problem in the world, Kerry knew that, didn't he? If it were only

McCann himself or Charlie it would have been a no-problem area. But *these* fellows . . . McCann's voice trailed away a little. For the first time Kerry began to feel a little afraid.

"Do you not have any idea where he is, Miss Hayes?"

"No, Kerry, he doesn't tell me where he goes. He just said that he would be back late."

"Whatever time he comes in, do you hear me, whatever time, can you get him to call me?"

"I'll leave a note, certainly. I don't want to intrude but is there anything wrong?"

"No no—heavens no." His voice was falsely bright.

"It's just that you sound so urgent somehow. I wouldn't want Mr. O'Neill to be alarmed."

"No no, it's nothing." He sounded impatient.

"I'll leave him a note then in case I'm gone to bed. I'll say you'd like him to ring back but it's not urgent."

Kerry spoke very slowly and deliberately. "Tell him it *is* urgent but there hasn't been an accident or anything. It's very urgent."

"Very well, Kerry, whatever you say."

Patrick came in at eleven-thirty.

He had spent a very pleasant evening with Rachel. He called at Loretto's and asked whether she would like a drive. He wanted to look at the ruined abbey in case it would be a place they could take the guests on the barge that he was going to operate from the new landing stage.

"You're going to have night boat trips?" Rachel was surprised.

"No, but maybe it's not a bad idea. They could go through the trees and along the river, the only light . . . the fireflies in the darkness."

"They don't have them here," Rachel said.

"Fireflies? Of course they do."

"No. Didn't you notice?"

"Anyway, will you come with me in the car and let's see if this abbey is worth our time?"

"It's been around since the fourteenth century, I think it might be worth a glance all right. Let me get sensible shoes."

They had walked easily and companionably like the old days. Three times he was about to tell her that he wanted them to be more open and seen to be close friends. Three times he stopped himself.

After all he wasn't yet ready to offer her anything much, and he would clear it with his children before changing things even slightly. He left things as they were.

Next morning up at the hotel Jim Costello came to Patrick, there was an urgent call from his son in Donegal.

"Would you like a bit of peace and quiet to take it?"

"No thanks, Jim, it won't be long."

Jim had sensed the tetchiness in Kerry O'Neill's voice. He moved away.

"Did she not leave you my message?"

"That's some greeting, Kerry. Yes, Miss Hayes did leave a message but it was late when I got in."

"What time?"

"Eleven-thirty." Patrick took a deep breath. "I went for a walk with Rachel Fine up around the old ruined abbey . . . she thinks that we could . . ."

"I'll hear Mrs. Fine's thoughts another time, Father. I'm in a bit of trouble. Financially."

Patrick's voice was ice cold. "Yes, Kerry?"

"And I would be grateful if you would bail me out."

A silence.

"Are you still there, Father?"

"Yes. I'm still here."

"What did you say?"

"Nothing yet."

"Will you?"

"I don't think so."

"You *said* you would."

"No, I said I would discuss it, we are discussing it. How much?"

"A thousand pounds."

Patrick was shocked. Literally shocked. "You can't be serious."

"I am."

"Well find it then."

"We made a deal."

"We made no deal, I said I'd discuss it. I will not hand out a year's wages to an insolent young punk who calls and demands it as if it were his right."

"Father, this is serious."

"You bet your fucking life it's serious," Patrick said.

"I thought you were going to—"

"I thought my father was going to do a lot of things for me too, like getting me enough to eat and shoes to wear. But it didn't happen. Learn the hard way, Kerry."

"Aren't you going to discuss it?"

"Yes I will discuss it. When you come back." Patrick's anger was ebbing a little.

"I could come back today."

"No you could not. You can stay there and do the work you are meant to be doing. I will discuss it in a few weeks' time, when you're back here for the opening. Meanwhile get out of it the best you can, and if you steal from Hill like you stole from me, I'll see you go to jail."

There was a silence.

"Life isn't easy, Kerry, it's a matter of finding ways around things; and if one thing doesn't work, try something else. You'll discover that."

"Yes, I probably will," Kerry said slowly.

Rachel Fine sat in her sitting room and watched the evening fall on Fernscourt.

She felt very tired. The game was too arduous. She blew cold, he ran after her—she showed some response, he ran away. It was so immature, so unsatisfying. Somehow tonight, for the very first time, Rachel was prepared to stop the struggle, the never-ending spiral of hope, the belief that things were going well.

He was a man who hadn't enough room in his heart for a full-time loving relationship. He never had time for it with his wife Kathleen either. Whether she had been frail or not he would still have wandered, and it was not without importance to note that he had wandered to a business colleague rather than find a sheerly social relationship.

She sighed, thinking of the years behind and the years ahead. The music on her record player was low so as not to disturb Loretto below. Chopin, soothing and familiar. Perhaps even at this late stage of her life she might even take up the piano again. When she was back in New York.

Would she be back in New York?

Yes, sooner or later. Why not make it sooner, go at her own time? See the opening just because she had worked so hard for it. Give him one ultimatum so that he would never say he didn't know, and then go. But she had to be prepared to go, not to give herself nine lives like a cat, otherwise what was the point of giving ultimatums?

There was a soft knock on her door. Loretto would never have let him upstairs, and yet who else could it be?

She walked wearily over to the door and opened it.

There stood Kerry O'Neill, the boy she had always hoped would be her stepson one day.

He leaned against the jamb of the door. "Hi Rachel."

"Hello Kerry."

She made no move to ask him in.

"How are you?"

"Fine, and you?" They still stood there.

"Reasonably fine, I'd be better with a drink, to be very frank."

"Well you know me, Kerry, a non-drinking lady. But I'm sure if you were to go to Ryan's . . ."

"I don't want to go to Ryan's," he said sharply.

She shrugged.

"Surely my father keeps something to drink here."

"Your father lives in the lodge, Kerry. I live here."

"So you never see him?"

"At work."

"I want to talk to you, not him."

"I told you I don't have anything to drink."

"I know. It doesn't matter, I have." He waved a bottle of whiskey. "Now can I come in?"

Mary thought she had seen the blond figure of young Kerry O'Neill slip quietly across the footbridge earlier, but since he hadn't come into the pub and there was nowhere else he could be heading, she must have been mistaken.

Rachel stood back and let Kerry come into her sitting room. He stood looking at it with his cool objective eye.

"Lovely," he said at last.

"Thank you."

"I mean it, you have wonderful ways, Rachel. Anyone else would have ruined this place and filled it with clutter."

He sat in the chair by the window where Patrick always sat and looked across in the darkening evening at Fernscourt.

"I can provide a glass and water," Rachel said.

"Great, this is far too elegant a place for a man to sit drinking from a bottle."

He was so engaging, just like his father. His compliments were not so frequent and lavish that they sounded automatic. Instead, they made people feel very touched and grateful to be praised.

She brought a tray to the little low table—Irish crystal glasses and a jug. A pretty china bowl with ice in it, a tray of cheese biscuits and for herself an orange drink. She sat down opposite him. She had not invited him, but since he was here she would be gracious. Being a hostess was second nature to Rachel Fine, she had waited on Kerry's father for many years in the same elegant way.

"Your health," she said politely, raising her glass of orange.

"And yours." His eyes were bright, he raised the very large goblet of neat Irish whiskey and looked at the patterns of the glass admiringly.

Rachel was very good at not being the first to speak. She had learned that first from her mother, who said that the men in the family were the ones to be considered, and then from many many nights waiting to assess Patrick's mood before she spoke. She knew how to leave a perfectly agreeable silence that would encourage the other person to begin.

Kerry smiled as if he could see into her mind. It was a knowing smile full of confidence.

"And how long are you going to be with us?" he asked genially.

Rachel was shocked by the insolence of his tone. So shocked that it made her speak sharply.

"I was just going to ask *you* the same question. Are you with us for long or do you have to get back to Donegal?"

Kerry smiled even more broadly; he sensed a fight and he welcomed it.

"Oh, *I'm* here for the duration, Rachel, this is my home."

She controlled herself with difficulty. "Well of course, and has your father decided what part you will play in the hotel?" Polite interest, but letting him know that everyone realized it was Patrick who called the shots.

"I'm sure you're much more aware of what my father has decided or has not decided than anyone."

She smiled coldly but made no reply. From years of training herself not to over-react, not to fly off the handle, Rachel had perfected a calm and measured response even to situations that were outside the bounds of any manners or fairness.

"My involvement is always in ideas for design, and sometimes it's an uphill job." She forced a little laugh that she did not feel. "I can tell you the designer is the one who always ends up taking the blame —it's too stark, it's too cold, it's not Irish enough—my, but you need extraordinary patience in this job. Lucky I have it!" Again her tinkle was very false and again she felt that Kerry recognized this.

"Perhaps you've been too patient."

"How do you mean?"

"You know, hanging around too long, hoping that when this is over —when that is over—the world will settle down as *you* would like it, as *you* design it."

She wondered how much more of this she could take, this pretense of deliberately misunderstanding his discourtesy.

"At least the day of the opening is in sight," she said. "We'll see then if it works."

"And what will you do then? Go back to Brooklyn?"

"I live in Manhattan."

"Sure, but you *do* live in New York, will you go directly back there? After the hotel opens?"

His question echoed so much her own bitter thoughts and decisions of earlier that evening that it brought a heavy, weary feeling to Rachel. It was as if she suddenly decided to give up the bright sunny response.

"I don't know," she said simply. "I'm not sure."

"Rachel!" He was teasing. "Not sure? Of course you are, you've every step planned out, haven't you?"

"No. Not every step."

"Most of them then. You've been part of my father's life for a very long time. A lot of people didn't rate your chances very highly."

"I don't know how you could know any of this. You were a child."

"Sure I was a child, I didn't know really, not for certain, not until my mother's last illness. That's when I knew."

Rachel looked at him impassively.

Kerry poured another large goblet of whiskey, his hand trembling slightly.

"Those nights when she was alone in the house, and he was with you—in Manhattan, as you remind me. Out until the early hours of the morning. Sometimes I stood on the landing and watched him come in, go into the bathroom and rinse his mouth, freshen himself up before he came up to her bedroom. She was always awake, always waiting for him to come back from you. From your apartment in Manhattan."

Rachel looked at his white and angry face.

"He sat in a chair drinking whiskey, that's why he used a mouth rinse, it was not to hide traces of me. He sat talking about her illness, about you all. That's what I gave him in those months, just a chair, a whiskey, and an ear for his troubles."

"He had plenty of ears at home if he had come there."

"Sure he had, but you were so young, your mother was so frail, he couldn't . . ."

Kerry's eyes blazed at her suddenly.

"Don't you dare to talk of my mother, don't bring her in casually like that . . . don't speak of her."

"Kerry, this is absurd. *You* mentioned your mother, you mentioned something that has upset you in the past, I was merely telling you what it was really like . . ."

"I don't want your version of what things were really like. If it were a true version it would be fairly sordid."

"You are unfair to your father and to everyone if you persist in believing all this . . ."

"Oh, it was all hand-holding and platonic. Don't be pathetic, Rachel."

"I am *not* pathetic, I am telling you what is true. During the time of Kathleen's last—"

"I told you not to mention her name."

Her eyes filled with sudden unexpected tears. She turned her head away in a vain attempt to hide them.

Kerry put his glass down on the table. "I'm sorry."

She didn't trust herself to speak.

"I mean it. I am sorry. I guess I'm upset. I shouldn't take it out on you."

She stood up wordlessly as if to say that his visit was over. But Kerry decided that it was not over yet.

"Please, I said I spoke out of turn. Please?"

He had such a persuasive way, she noticed almost dispassionately. Kerry believed that if you were charming enough in sufficient doses it would open every door. And he had usually been right.

"I didn't intend to come here and harangue you, I intended—"

"What did you intend?"

"I guess I wanted to know what was happening. Is that so bad? Things are fairly unsettled. Father has me up at the other end of the country, he's so unapproachable, he tells me none of his plans, I hear from this side one set of things, from another side a different . . . It sure is a rumor factory here, isn't it?" He grinned companionably, the shouting put well behind.

"And what do they say on all these different sides?"

"Oh, some say that my father is the object of a hate campaign, vandalism, slogans, mysterious happenings; others say that since the prophet Elijah there hasn't been such a welcome appearance. Then they say that the hotel will be open on time and that it hasn't a chance of opening; that Father's going to marry Marian Johnson and she's going to change her hairstyle and get some new clothes, or that he's going to marry you and you're going to keep all your nice clothes the way they are but change your religion . . . And I hear that he has hundreds of bookings from the States and that he has no bookings . . . So do you see why I came to have a talk in case you could set me straight on some of these issues, anyway?"

She looked at him, and realized that he was making it all up, there was no way that people in Mountfern would confide such things to the son of Patrick O'Neill. But he was right in his summing up of the different viewpoints.

Kerry patted the chair beside him. "Come on, Rachel, sit down and talk to me. I won't get nasty again. Promise."

She sat down, knowing it was a very dangerous thing to do.

"There, that's better. And now have a drink. Come *on* Rachel, if you're going to be an honorary Irish person you'll have to learn to drink."

It was easy and comforting to sit there with him instead of sitting on her own.

He had admitted his temper and his feelings. It was only natural that a boy should love his mother and want to keep his memories of her almost frozen in the viewpoint of the troubled teenager that he was at the time.

Rachel sipped the drink that he mixed for her, a whiskey and dry ginger. It tasted sweet and warming, not like the wine she sometimes sipped at functions, which was bitter and alien. Here in the sunset looking across the river with the handsome boy admitting his petulant temper and smiling at her like a conspirator it was easy to sit and talk and drink the sweet, fizzy, harmless liquor.

Kerry talked of the hotel in Donegal, how lonely he was up there and how the place seemed so remote. He often went to Derry across the border, it was exciting somehow to be in a place that was ruled by another country, to see other flags flying. Most of the people in Derry were basically Irish, he explained to Rachel, and they felt much more at home in the republic. He had met a few guys who were easy to get along with there. Rough guys, not the kind who would be welcomed with open arms in the front doors of Fernscourt, he said scathingly. Still, they were alive all through, which was more than you could say for many of the people you met in this country, north or south. Rachel took this to mean that they were able to play cards with him or point him to some kind of game down town.

And Rachel found herself telling Kerry more than she intended to about some of the problems in getting deliveries in time and how she always tried to shield Patrick from the more troublesome side of things, partly because he had so much to think about he really could not be expected to give time to wondering why some weavers in Connemara had not been able to come up with the consignment they had promised months back. And partly because any complaining or even mild criticism always seemed like a condemnation of his decision to come back to this land and build his dream castle.

Together they sighed amicably about the difficulties of dealing with the great Patrick O'Neill. There was none of the usual fencing between them and no hint of the flash of anger and the instructions not to speak his dead mother's name.

Rachel told of how Maurice, the Ryans' missing tortoise, had been discovered in the hen house where apparently he had been living for months in total contentment. And Kerry told how he had discovered that Jimbo Doyle really was making it big on the ballad-singing circuit; he was even booked for an appearance in Donegal, which had to be the Vegas of Ireland.

The sun sank behind the big house and the trees. The river took on its black rippling look where it seemed like a dark ribbon instead of a living, flowing thing.

Somewhere, possibly from down near the bridge, they heard the sound of a fiddle playing, an air that sounded sad and plaintive, but all Irish airs seemed sad to Rachel and Kerry. The boy reached across and patted her hand. There were tears in Rachel's eyes again but this time she wasn't hiding them, they fell down her face.

"I could have fit in here, I could have stayed and been part of it," she wept.

"But now you think you'll go back?" His voice was soft, like honey.

"I decided today I'll have to go back. He thinks he doesn't need me, he thinks he can manage on his own . . ." She let a sob come through her voice.

"I know, I know."

"You can't know."

"Well I do, he doesn't need me either. He never did."

Rachel looked at him, tear-stained. He was so different tonight, vulnerable, understanding.

"I think he finds it hard to express himself to you . . ." she began, trying as usual to build bridges.

"I'm only his son, his flesh and blood. It shouldn't be so very hard to express himself."

"He does care for you . . . I know."

"And I know how fond of you he is too. I didn't always want to see it, I can tell you, but . . ."

He looked so straightforward. Rachel felt fuzzy and a little confused, but she could see that Kerry was being genuine toward her and she wanted to reassure him that he was important to his father.

And now Kerry was admitting that she, Rachel, was a part of Patrick too. She was certainly a little heady.

She placed her hand on Kerry's knee. He lifted it to admire her rings.

"These are very beautiful," he said softly. "Did you choose these yourself or were they a gift?"

She saw no guile in the words. It was a question. She held her hand away and admired the topaz and the emerald.

"Your father bought me the topaz a long long time ago. The emerald I bought myself. I have a little garnet too, but I don't wear them all at once."

"No, no." He was holding her hand and admiring the way the light caught the stones.

"It means fidelity, a topaz," she said dreamily. "I remember that very well."

"Is it your birthstone?" Kerry asked interestedly.

He was so relaxed and easy to talk to tonight, Rachel wondered why she had ever thought him prickly and difficult.

"No, I'm Gemini—that's the emerald." She turned her hand in his to examine the green stone.

"I got the emerald because of that and also because it means 'success in love.' I guess I wasn't so lucky there."

Kerry said nothing, he fingered the tie tack he always wore these days. Even when he wasn't wearing a formal shirt and tie he seemed to have this pin on his lapel somehow.

"My, that's a topaz also," Rachel realized for the first time.

"Yes. Topaz, that's right." His voice seemed strained.

"And was *that* a gift or did you buy it, like I bought my emerald?" She was being giggly now.

"It was both, in a way. I paid for it to be made into a tie tack, but it was a gift, from my mother. Father gave her a topaz for fidelity also, you see. He never asked where it was when she died, I don't know if he realizes this is where it ended up."

Rachel felt a sudden lurch in her stomach. "I think I'm going to be sick," she said, staggering to her feet.

Loretto Quinn was serving Jack Coyne next morning when Kerry appeared in the shop. He was in his stocking feet, walking lightly, and his clothes were crushed and rumpled.

"Hi Loretto. Well hi Jack, how are things?"

"Things are reasonable." Jack wasn't able to reply as quickly as usual, he was so startled to see O'Neill's son come in casually through the back of the shop, meaning that he must have been upstairs.

Upstairs with O'Neill's woman.

"So they are with me, pretty reasonable. Loretto, can I have some oranges please, perhaps half a dozen . . . Sorry Jack, am I cutting in ahead of you?"

"No, please." Jack could hardly wait to see what else the young Kerry O'Neill was ordering.

Kerry said he'd take eggs, bread, four slices of that really great bacon—how could anyone in America *think* they had tasted bacon until they came to Ireland? And he'd better take a packet of those aspirin tablets too.

He smiled at them both, punched Jack playfully, and said that the little red sports car was a dream on wheels and he thought he'd either have to buy it so that it would be his own or possibly play Jack a game of poker for it.

Then light and cheerful he ran back up the stairs, leaving Loretto and Jack open-mouthed below.

Rachel woke painfully. Her head was pounding and she had a sense of unreality. What *could* have happened to make her feel so ill? Bits of it came back to her. The whiskey, the long chat with Kerry.

Then with such a shock that she sat bolt upright she remembered vomiting.

Her hand flew to her throat and she looked around her wildly. The bed was rumpled. Kerry's jacket was thrown on her chair. His shoes were lying on the floor where they had been kicked off. The other side of the bed had a little table and on the table was Kerry's watch, his cigarette case and his lighter.

With disbelief Rachel tried to take it in. She felt too frail to contemplate what could have happened. She wanted to lie down and pull the sheets and blankets over her poor hurt head. But she couldn't lie down. Not yet. Not until she knew.

As if on cue Kerry came into the room. He was wearing his shirt open, he was smiling.

"Hi there."

"What . . . what?"

"It's orange juice," he said delightedly, misunderstanding her. "I squeezed six oranges so you'll love it. And if you feel strong enough I'm going to do you some eggs."

"Not eggs," Rachel said.

"Oh yes eggs, Rachel, they're known to be good for you. I got some bacon but I wasn't sure. I didn't know . . ."

"No bacon." She struggled with the words.

"Sure sure. Well coffee anyway, after the juice."

He sat on the bed familiarly, too close to her she thought in alarm, and pulled back.

She realized she was in her slip and that her brassiere was open. She realized that Kerry O'Neill was looking at her affectionately. The room seemed to swim and tilt a little.

"Kerry, how did . . . how did . . ."

"I got them in Loretto's," he said sunnily. "Oh, and I got you some aspirin too. Sip the juice first, then I'll fix you some aspirin with the coffee."

"You told Loretto . . . ?"

"She's really improved that little store, hasn't she? Jack Coyne was in there, he's an okay guy, I think. Father always says he's a gangster but these things are relative. To some people Father is something of a gangster. But enough about him, let's talk about you and me . . ."

Rachel gave a jump.

". . . and what we're going to have for breakfast if it's too non kosher to fry a little bacon." He smiled at her warmly and Rachel

Fine with her drawn, lined face, her aching head and upset stomach looked up at him piteously. And knew she was somehow in his power.

It was the last Thursday in August and Dara Ryan had returned to Mountfern.

She felt quite different to the Dara who had left two months earlier. Older, wiser, more a woman of the world, she thought. After all she had lived in a household which had things going on under its roof that Dara would not have believed possible. She was going to look with new eyes on the clientele, male and nocturnal of the Rosemarie hair salon. She hoped she had become more sophisticated-looking. A girl she was talking to on the train told her that she could easily be eighteen, she looked *much* older than almost sixteen.

Dad thought she looked older, which was great. He held her at arm's length when he came to meet her at the station in the town. Grace and Michael had wanted to come too he said, but he had to refuse them, he needed the car for supplies.

Dara looked around and indeed the back of their old black car was filled with boxes. Things for the café, Dad said, every day now there was more stuff being brought in. They were ready to open it for business anytime now.

"And what kind of form is Mam in? She doesn't get depressed too much now, does she?"

Dara kept looking lovingly at her father; she knew that in a changing world he would remain constant. It was hard to imagine Dad in bed with anyone, including Mam before the accident, but Dara knew that he wouldn't ever cheat on Mam like that appalling Monsieur Vartin.

"Your mother is a marvel," he said simply. "I don't know where and how she gets the ideas and the energy. She's an example to us who have the legs. She's so delighted that you're coming home. For ages now she's been saying only eight days more, only six days more . . ."

Dara was pleased. "Isn't that nice, I was just the same, I hope we won't start to fight and ruin it."

"Of course you will." John was philosophic. "But not immediately. We'll have a few days of a honeymoon period first."

They drove down Bridge Street. Liam White was waving, and John slowed to a stop.

"You look different, did you have an illness?" he asked.

"Jesus, Mary and Joseph, Liam, that's lovely," said Dara.

"No, you look foreign. Maybe it's the air, or the food."

"I think she looks great altogether." Dara's father was partisan and proud of his dark, handsome daughter.

"Oh, you look fine," Liam said, as if that had never been in doubt. "The question is, will it last?"

"Where's Jacinta?"

"Off somewhere with Tommy, she's the only one able to get him out of the shop. His father is afraid of Jacinta."

"Aren't we all?" Dara said with some feeling.

Dara looked over at Daly's shop. It still looked the same. People came in to buy cakes and butter and groceries. Life went on. Dara swallowed hard. Everyone else had had two months to get used to Daly's Dairy without Maggie. Dara would too one day. Charlie was cleaning the windows, he waved his wet cleaning rag at her. The shop that used to be Meagher's seemed to have been all done up.

"What does Mountfern need a travel agency for?" she asked.

"Oh, there's amazing needs created in this place nowadays," her father said almost ruefully.

Dara's eyes raked the town for Kerry.

Perhaps he was back. Could he be running the travel agency? Would she ask Dad was he around? No, she was only minutes from home. And she had sent him a card giving the exact date of her return. There was bound to be some message from him when she got there.

The sign was up for Ryan's Shamrock Café. Nobody had told her it would look so big. There was a new door now in the front of the building that used to be the outhouse, the place where they had their party almost a year ago.

The old windows had been repainted and new glass fitted. On each windowsill brightly colored boxes of geraniums stood nodding in the sun.

Dara gasped. "I never knew it was like this . . . like . . ."

"Like nothing on earth," her father finished cheerfully. "Still, it might keep a roof over our heads. Now here's your mother waiting for you."

Kate sat in the door of the new café. She was all dressed up, one of Rachel's scarves draped around her, which was what designated the outfit as for an occasion. She stretched her arms out in welcome as Dara scampered from the car.

Dara's heart gave a little jump.

Mam's smile was wide and warm, but she had big circles under her eyes and she was very pale.

Mam didn't look at all well.

There was huge excitement at Dara's return.

Grace and Michael came rushing in. Grace hugged her and said that she had become very French.

Michael said she had begun to lisp and speak broken English.

"What ees zat you say?" Dara punched him until he admitted it was all jealousy on his part.

Eddie wanted to know why she hadn't tried snails. He'd told all his friends that Dara was eating snails for her breakfast, dinner and tea and now he'd look like an eejit.

Declan asked could *he* go to France next summer, he wouldn't mind looking after children, it would be nice to have something younger than himself that he could boss around and give orders to.

Carrie asked if they ate everything raw—Jimbo told her he had heard that.

Mary Donnelly said she was pleased to hear that Frenchmen were not always making free with their attentions, as had often been reported.

Grace and Michael giggled at this and Kate and Dara exchanged glances. Mary had not been told about the discovery of Monsieur Vartin and Mademoiselle Stephanie.

It was marvelous to be back at home with everyone speaking English and everyone speaking at once.

But it was awful not to be able to ask about Kerry. Nobody had mentioned his name.

After supper Dara linked Grace out into the garden. They were meant to be doing a tour of the café.

"And what news of your big brother?" Dara tried to be light and joky.

"Oh, didn't he write to you? I *told* him you were coming home today. He was on the phone looking for Father."

"How was he?"

"He was mainly sounding off about Miss Hayes. I had to keep the telephone very close to my ear in case she'd hear, he'd called the night before for Father, and a . . . oh, I don't know, she hadn't given the right message. But I did tell him you'd be back today."

"Thanks, Grace." Dara was bleak.

"Was it great, France?" Grace was eager. "Did you go out at all to any parties or dances?"

"No, nothing like that."

"What was the best part?"

"We had a picnic . . . they call it peek neek, honestly. They had huge loaves of French bread and cheese and peaches and wine . . . And we went to this place on a river, not the Loire itself but a smaller river like the Fern, and we went swimming, all of us. Even Madame. And we stayed there till quite late and it got dark, and they all seemed very happy . . ."

Grace looked at her, trying to see why this had been the high spot.

Dara went on. "They seemed so safe, sort of. As if they'd always be together, and I understood all the conversation, which I usually didn't. I think it might have been the wine . . . And suddenly there were all these little pinpoints of light everywhere. Fireflies they were."

"Oh, yes, fireflies are lovely," Grace said.

"I told them we didn't have any here, and Monsieur said I must look again when I got home. That was the best time, I think."

Grace seemed pleased that Dara had a happy if unfathomable memory. She hugged her friend. "It's great to have you home again," she said.

And Dara felt a great ache.

It would have been great to come home if there had been a note from Kerry saying when he'd be back in Mountfern. If Maggie had been running up River Road after supper, hands clasped and eager to hear every detail. If Tommy had come in making jokes about the French.

And if Mam's face hadn't this tired look, and if she'd been able to eat her supper instead of moving the cold chicken and ham from one side of the plate to the other.

Loretto Quinn had to tell someone so she picked Sheila Whelan. "It could be totally innocent," Sheila said.

"It has to be," Loretto said. "Mother of God, you don't think that they'd have been sleeping together as man and wife would you?"

Sheila sighed a "no".

"But what was he doing back in town, let alone above in her

room?" Loretto's open face was puzzled. "Rachel told me herself that he wouldn't be coming back until the opening. And young Dara Ryan said that Mr. O'Neill said he was still above in Donegal."

"It's a mystery all right," Sheila said. She had a feeling that something was very wrong here. If Kerry really had been sneaking into Mountfern and to Rachel for any purpose under the sun, not to mention the interpretation which would be put on it, then why had he advertised it so publicly?

People didn't die without orange juice and eggs. He could have waited until Jack Coyne had left the shop, he would have heard his voice before he came in. Kate Ryan had always been worried about Kerry, she had said there was something very strange about him, he didn't react like ordinary people.

Maybe Kate had been right.

Tommy Leonard was disappointed that he had missed Dara coming back. He had gone out with Jacinta to find good angles where Mountfern could be photographed.

Mr. O'Neill was having a photographer next week who would take glossy pictures of the place and they would be turned into postcards. Some would be sold in the hotel, some in Leonard's. Privately Tommy thought that if the visitors could buy them at the information desk in the hotel they would be most unlikely to want to trek the whole way to Leonard's to buy the same thing. But his father had been very respectful and over-thanked Mr. O'Neill.

Jack Coyne came in to buy a paper. He ignored Tommy and went instead to the older man. Jack lowered his voice so Tommy made an effort to hear. It seemed to be about Kerry O'Neill having breakfast with Loretto Quinn. Or was it Mrs. Fine? In either case hadn't they little to talk about!

Tommy's thoughts went back to Dara. He wished he hadn't gone out with Jacinta, he felt sure no good would come of it. Liam White said that Dara had changed totally, gotten a smaller waist, a bigger chest and a sort of bold flashy look about her as if she had seen it all and done it all. Tommy knew that this couldn't be true, but he did wish that he had been able to see her himself and make these observations about her chest and her waist instead of hearing it all from Liam.

He stood there, legs aching, wishing that his father had not been so infected by Mr. O'Neill's diligence that he now kept the shop open until nine o'clock in the evening.

* * *

Fergus went for a stroll which took him, as his strolls nearly always did, to the door of Ryan's.

"Can I have a look at the Parisienne?" he asked John.

"She's within, chattering to her mother, saying 'oui' instead of yes half the time. The boys are giving her a desperate teasing over it. Take your pint and go in to see them."

"Ah no, I'll let them talk. I'll see her plenty in the next few days." Fergus knew how much Kate had been looking forward to the daughter's return.

"Wasn't it a great chance for her, Fergus?" John was very pleased with the way it had all turned out. "We didn't know what we were sending the child to, really, it was just that . . ." He let the sentence trail away.

"Well, didn't it all work out very well when you consider . . ." Fergus Slattery didn't finish his sentence either.

He thought that this particular conversation was better left untold in this house. He hoped that the handsome young Dara Ryan had her head well turned by Frenchmen and that she would forget O'Neill's dangerous-looking son.

It was so good to have Dara home. Kate wondered how she had survived without her daughter. With Dara there was no need to pretend, with Dara there was a feeling of hope all around her. Kate knew that Dara could hear the true plans and the true worries about the Shamrock Café.

"It's not what we had planned, like, for our lives," Dara had complained.

"A lot of things weren't what we had planned," Kate said, touching the sides of the wheelchair.

Dara had noticed how much Kate hated the chair. Since the very first day she had been in it, it represented the prison bars to her. She could not make herself see it as a liberation, a way of getting about. Instead she regarded the chair as a hated object and put all her anger toward it, as if it were the cause of all her incapacity. She wanted it out of her sight when she was in bed, no matter that she might need it in the night. She disguised it by draping rugs and scarves over it.

Dara seemed to understand. Once she had written a notice on it: "I'm only a chair for God's sake, Mrs. Ryan." Kate had pealed with laughter when she woke and saw it.

They could talk easily now, the trip to France had been an inspired idea.

Dara gave her mind eagerly to the problems of survival when the new regime arrived.

"There's only one thing I don't like, Mam."

"Tell it then."

"I don't like you going up to the hotel to give cookery lessons."

"Aha," Kate said.

"What do you mean, aha?"

"I have a little plan about that, I can't tell you yet, but let's say it's not going to be a problem."

"Tell me, I tell *you* everything."

"I'll only go for a very very short time."

"What's the point in it, then?"

"This is the point, once I've gotten myself established, then Dr. White will tell me, and indeed tell Patrick, that the strain is too much, and I can't do it anymore, so . . . so I'll have to continue the lessons here. Do you understand?"

"Mam!"

Impulsively Kate opened her arms and Dara rushed to her.

"It's so good to have you home, child. I missed you so much. What do people do if they don't have a daughter? Tell me that."

"Oh Mam, it's great to be back. They were nice in their way and they went to endless trouble over things but they'd have you starved half the time and they were riddled with sin."

Kate laughed until she nearly cried; her pale face looked more colorful now.

Dara felt happier but she still resolved to ask Mrs. Fine if Mam had been having any bad turns. She would ask her tomorrow. She half listened to Mam as she wondered whether Kerry might be home for the weekend. Grace was useless for any information. But of course he would come home this weekend. Now that he knew both from her postcard and from Grace on the phone that Dara was back.

Kate looked at Dara's face, lightly tanned from the hot French sunshine. She knew how Rachel would admire her, and indeed make further representations about getting Dara's ears pierced for her and giving her little gold studs.

It was odd that Rachel wasn't here. She hadn't been in all day.

Rachel Fine stayed in her room all day.

She crouched like an animal in the forest that is afraid to move because it doesn't know if it has been too badly injured. She heard the noises of Mountfern on a late summer morning. The carts that went by, the delivery vans, the sounds of hammering from across the river. She heard voices too in and out of Loretto's shop and children calling to each other as they chased along River Road.

Kerry had gone as light-heartedly as she had ever seen him. He had kissed her affectionately on the nose; he had been teasing and flirtatious. As he would have been after a night in bed with any woman.

They hadn't been together in that way. But she had no way of proving it.

A hundred times she told herself that no one would believe she could have opened her body to Kerry O'Neill, who was a boy, who had been a child when she first met and loved his father.

It would have been like an act of incest.

"So I'll head for the hills of Donegal now before anyone knows I've been here. And thanks, Rachel, thanks for everything," he had said.

What was he thanking her for?

"But people do know, they'll think . . . You said you spoke to Loretto, to Jack Coyne . . ." she croaked.

"That's not what I mean. They don't count. I don't want to meet my father, I'm going to have to tell him about some money I owe, sooner or later. No point in getting him steamed up before I ask him."

Rachel looked at Kerry and fought back waves of dizziness and nausea.

And when he was gone she felt a coldness through her bones that made a mockery of the sunny summer day outside.

She didn't answer when Loretto called up to know if she should bring up a parcel of materials that had just been delivered. So Loretto, more confused than ever, just left the parcel on the stairs and shook her head from side to side.

Rachel didn't go to see Dara, newly returned. She didn't call to collect mail at the post office, nor did she touch the parcel on the stairs.

When Brian Doyle sent round to know had some fabrics arrived, because young Costello was behaving like a pregnant cat over them, Loretto said there was no point in trying to get any answer from upstairs.

Brian said that he had always known it would happen, most people in the place had now gone clinically insane and the place for them all was the asylum on the hill.

He had been told that Kerry O'Neill was in Donegal and yet he had nearly been killed by the little bastard reversing his car at top speed this morning.

He had been told that Rachel Fine was waiting night and day for some swatches of material and now they had arrived she had apparently gone to ground like a broody hen.

O'Neill was like a lighting devil, and that leggy young Ryan child from the pub had snapped the head off him when he had addressed a civil word to her.

It was time to ring the asylum and tell them to come down with the straitjackets and take the people of Mountfern away.

As soon as he got to Fernscourt, Patrick was called to the phone in Brian Doyle's hut.

"Dennis Hill here, Patrick. I just rang to know if everything's all right?"

"That's good of you Dennis. It's crawling along, crawling, but we might have hot water to make them a cup of coffee at the opening. You will come, I hope?"

"I meant about your little girl."

"Grace?" Patrick was alarmed.

"Is she recovering?"

"Recovering?"

"The accident. The accident on the bridge."

"Grace didn't have an accident." Patrick's heart was beating very fast. Could something have happened to Grace this morning that he didn't know about? He shouted to Costello. "Was there any accident on the bridge this morning, did anything happen? Answer me!"

Costello was quick. "Nothing at all," he said crisply.

"And Grace, is she all right?"

"I saw her cycling by not five minutes ago with Michael Ryan."

"Thanks, Costello."

Patrick's breathing had changed its pace now.

"Sorry, Dennis. I was away from the phone for a moment. What did you hear?"

Mr. Hill's voice was cold. "I heard what your son told me yesterday, he had a call saying his sister had an accident in a fall from a bridge, she had been playing jumping and diving games with other children. He said that he had to go to Mountfern at once. Naturally I gave him permission."

"There was no accident," Patrick said dully.

"And I am delighted to hear it," Dennis Hill said courteously. There was a pause.

Mr. Hill spoke again: "He's a difficult lad, your son."

"Come to the point. Did he steal anything?"

"No, nothing like that!" Mr. Hill was surprised.

"Well you'd better check before you fire him. You *are* going to fire him, aren't you?"

Another pause.

"Yes, yes I think it's better to send him back to you. There's something there that attracts him."

"Well I'm damned if I know what it is." Patrick's voice was weary.

"Could be a girl. He's a handsome fellow."

"The only one he spends any time with is an under-age schoolgirl. But that would figure. He's never done anything that you'd hope he would."

"They don't, you know, children. I've got sons here in the business, and sons-in-law. They think I'm an old fool, they want me to clear out of it. That's the thanks you get for building up a business and handing it to them on a plate."

"Thanks Dennis."

"What for? I'm letting your boy go, that's not much to thank me for."

"I mean for letting me know about your sons. It's less lonely somehow."

"You'll survive. The girl's good, isn't she?"

"Ah yes, the best."

"I've got one good fellow in my brood, wants nothing to do with the hotel, works out on a headland on a small farm. Best of the lot of them, it's a pleasure to sit and talk to him for hours. You'll find that with the girl."

"When I see Kerry should I tell him to call you?"

"Why prolong it all? Speeches, lies, excuses. Tell him to pick up his things when he wants to."

As Patrick replaced the receiver, he hoped he wouldn't see Kerry for a while. Like a day anyway. He might lose control completely. A boy who could use the circumstances of Maggie Daly's death, graft them on to his own sister. And all as an excuse to go to some gambling game or other. He might very possibly kill him.

* * *

Kerry looked across the Fern. His father's car wasn't outside the hotel. That meant he must be at home. He would set out for the lodge. Easier to talk to him there anyway. He would go by River Road—he would meet too many people on Bridge Street. This way he only had to pass Coyne's, Ryan's and the Rosemarie hair salon. Jack Coyne he had already met; Kerry smiled to think how the story would be reported. Jack would find a dozen excuses to talk to people that he would not normally have any business with.

He wondered if Rachel would offer any version of events. Probably not. He would hear soon.

He turned on the car radio and they were playing "Pretty Flamingo." He turned the volume up high, pulled down the visor to keep the sun out of his eyes, and took a corner very fast.

The car that he pushed off the road was his father's. The sound of Manfred Mann was silenced by the screeching of brakes.

Kerry stopped the car and let out a sigh of relief. It had been close and it had of course been his fault. He ran his hand through his hair as he watched his father climb out of the car that was half in the ditch. His father walked toward him slowly and flung open the door.

"Get out of that fucking car," he said in a voice that Kerry had never heard before. It was as if he were being held back by two strong men. Kerry could almost see them straining to pull him back.

While all the time his father wanted to tear him limb from limb.

He got out. "I'm sorry. I was over too far . . ."

His father said nothing.

"And going a little fast, I guess."

Silence.

"Still, no real harm's done. Can we get it out, do you think, or should we walk back for Jack Coyne?"

"What are you doing here?"

"I was coming to see you. I wanted to talk to you urgently and then I was going to head for Donegal. I said I'd be back at lunchtime."

"You don't have to be back by lunch or at all."

"But I said to Mr. Hill that I'd do my best to get back today, he trusts me, and I think I should—"

"Hill doesn't trust you as far as he can throw you, Kerry, he's just fired you."

"He wouldn't do that."

"He has done that. Just that."

Kerry thought for a moment.

"He suddenly made up his mind and called you to tell you, rather than tell me. That's unlikely."

He was cool still, not blustering or defending himself with excuses and lies.

"You probably find it unlikely because you forget that some people have generous human impulses. Dennis Hill didn't like thinking of a girl falling off a bridge in a terrible accident, and her brother having to hotfoot it to her bedside. He called to learn how she was."

"I see." Kerry's face was impassive.

"No you don't see. You'll never understand that it would turn anyone's stomach, what you did."

"I had to say something. I wanted to get away."

"What a great thing to choose."

"I needed to be out of there, I needed to be here."

"Why?"

"I wanted to sort something out and see you."

"You're looking at me, Kerry. Say what you have to say, and say it quickly."

"Father, the money?"

"The money you called about yesterday, that ridiculous sum . . . You are not getting one penny of that from me."

"I wanted to come and tell you personally the kind of people they are."

"I don't care if they are cousins of the pope, they're still not going to find me coughing up their winnings at poker."

"I'm not saying they're respectable people we don't want to offend. They're the opposite, they're very tough."

"Good, then you've met it at last. People who are not going to give in to your every wish."

"You wouldn't say good, Father, if you knew . . . Tony said that they're getting very annoyed with me."

Patrick looked at his son.

"You are a spoiled selfish brat. It is my fault, it is not your mother's fault. I didn't see what was happening to you, I saw every other goddamn thing but I didn't see you for what you were. I was too busy. God forgive me."

"I'm sure he will forgive you, Father, God always forgives people who talk nicely to him and turn up at mass, no matter what they've been up to."

"Don't give me that."

"And people who put stained-glass windows into churches, and new buildings into Catholic schools, God loves them mightily."

Kerry's eyes were flashing. He would not be stopped.

"You can get away with it, Father, you always have, you can cut corners, you can break promises, you can give every slut in town a topaz, but as long as the Easter donations are generous God turns a blind eye."

Patrick moved at him, his arm up as if to strike.

Kerry went on. "And God understands a bit of battering too, if it's done in the right cause. Go ahead. Go on, I don't care. I don't give a damn."

Patrick withdrew.

"You'll care when you're working in a real job for the first time in your life to pay these punks, you'll care then when three-quarters of your wages will go to pay off a debt that not one of these farmers here could sleep a wink if he owed in a lifetime."

"You don't think for a *moment* that they'll wait to be paid at fifteen pounds a week. That would take more than a year. They want it now. On Monday at the very latest."

"Give up, you'll never get it. If you play for it you'll just end up paying twice as much. Work for a year, two years, regard it as your apprenticeship. They'll wait."

"They can't wait, they're not ordinary people. They're in an . . . organization."

"Cut that shit, they've organized themselves to smell a sucker and to rob a bank or a post office or two. Those fellows have no cause but themselves."

"You don't understand . . ."

"I know that for a fact, Hill warned me about them a while back. There may be some fellows in a movement in Derry since the border campaign ended, but not your gang. They're in it for themselves."

"Hill's an old fool, he knows nothing."

"I said you would stop by Hill's for your things, and he knows you're not to be trusted so there's no point in trying to make up any shortfall by dipping into the till before you leave."

Kerry looked at him sharply. Things had gone very far if his father had warned an outsider against him.

"Can I stay at the lodge when I come back?" he asked.

"Yes."

"Have you told Grace."

"That she is meant to be lying like her friend Maggie under the bridge, but that in her case there's some hope she'll survive? No."

"What *will* you say?"

"As little as possible. To you and about you."

"That will be hard if we're living in the same house."

"I'm moving into the hotel shortly, so is Grace. You can have the lodge until Christmas. We've paid for it until then."

"Miss Hayes?"

"She'll be going to her sister in New Zealand in a couple of weeks."

"And my room in the hotel?"

"Will not exist, Kerry."

"I'm not going to make a speech or plead, Father, this isn't about the future of the hotel or anything. It's about now. Could you give me just this amount? Then I'll never ask you again."

"No."

"Please. I've never said please before, maybe I should have. But I'm begging you."

"No. If I do it now, then next month it will be fifteen hundred pounds. Go to them, tell them they have to wait a year or whatever it takes for you to make it."

Kerry's eyes narrowed.

"It's on your head then, Father. If you won't give it to me I'll have to get it elsewhere."

"That won't be easy, you're running out of credibility."

"I think I know where I can get it," Kerry said and he almost smiled.

He got back into his car and drove away toward the main road. Patrick walked to Jack Coyne's and got three lads to come up and move his car. He didn't tell them how it had ended up in the ditch but he did not like the way Jack Coyne was looking at him.

There was something knowing and triumphant about the way the small ratlike man kept glancing at him.

"Have you been talking to Kerry?" Carrie asked Dara in a conspiratorial whisper.

"No, he's not home yet, but he might be back at the weekend. I keep hoping," Dara said.

"But he *is* here. I saw him."

"You never did!"

"Yes, last night. I said that's funny, Kerry home on a Thursday in the middle of the week. And then again this morning, he drove past here at a hundred miles an hour."

"Had he anyone with him?" Dara was almost afraid to hear the answer.

"No, not at all. Why should he have anyone with him, isn't he your fellow?"

Carrie saw things over-simply, Dara thought.

Dara sat on the window seat looking out at the moonlight. She couldn't believe that Kerry had been in Mountfern without even coming in to say hello.

Grace could never have told her a lie. There could be no awful thing that they were keeping hidden from her, like that he was going out with Kitty Daly. No, Michael would never be a party to that.

Michael came to sit beside her.

"There's nothing you're keeping secret from me, is there?" she asked.

"How did you guess?"

"Oh God." Dara's hand went to her throat.

"You see, Grace will soon be living across there," he began.

"What is it?"

"I was wondering, I was wondering if I could . . . if we could show her the tunnel."

"Is that all?"

"Well, I know it's quite a big thing to ask."

Dara didn't seem to listen.

"Was Kerry home today?" she asked. "Did he stay at the lodge last night? That's all I want to know. It's not very much to ask."

"Of course he wasn't. If he was, he'd have talked to me. He talks to me quite a lot, as it happens."

"He wasn't back then?"

"No. How many times do I have to say it?"

"Carrie must be going mad, that's all," Dara said.

"And what do you say about . . . ?"

Michael let his voice trail away. Dara was sitting happily on the window seat, her leg tucked underneath her, all the anxiety gone from her face. She didn't want to talk about tunnels or to talk about anything, she wanted to think about Kerry O'Neill.

Kerry said his goodbye's briefly in Hill's hotel. The staff were sorry to see him leave; some of the students who had been working as

chambermaids for the summer were particularly sorry. He had been
so sunny, so handsome, like summer lightning around the place.

He told McCann that he could get the money and have it on
Saturday afternoon.

McCann had said he would come with him to get it.

That was not what Kerry wanted.

"Look you've been in Mountfern, you know the set-up, it's a one-
horse place. We're the kings of the castle there, if I say I'll get it I
will, and then I'll get it to you."

"No point in your driving all over the country," McCann said
laconically. "I'll come with you. Then I'll get the bus back."

It was a dispiriting drive. The back of the car was filled with
Kerry's stuff, they couldn't give a lift to any of the girls they saw on
the road even if they had wanted to. Which Kerry didn't.

They listened to music the whole way down. Tony McCann liked
"These Boots Are Made for Walking". He said it was a great song,
and sang it tunelessly with Nancy Sinatra.

Kerry said he liked "Pretty Flamingo", he didn't know why but it
reminded him of Dara Ryan, who was only a kid but very attractive.

"Is she pink and does she stand on one leg?" McCann had wanted
to know with a laugh.

Several times Kerry O'Neill wondered why he found McCann
such good company.

In Mountfern he told McCann there were three pubs he could
drink in, and that he would be an hour at the most. Then he'd come
with the money.

McCann had said that a check would be fine. His friends knew
that Kerry wouldn't be foolish enough to give them a check that
didn't work. That would be more stupid than not giving them anything at all.

Kerry had nodded fervently.

He settled McCann in Foley's, realizing that between taciturn old
Mr. Foley and the silent McCann little chat would be exchanged.

Then he drove down Bridge Street, looking neither right nor left
of him. He realized that when he was back here full time it would be
like living in one of those fish tanks that old Hill had in his hotel
where people could look at the lobsters from every side. He averted
his eyes from Fergus Slattery and turned right into River Road.

Loretto's eyes were like dinner plates as he walked past her and up
the stairs to Rachel Fine.

* * *

Her face was as white as a sheet. She was sitting at a table with papers on it. A coffee cup sat beside her, full but cold.

She looked up in alarm as he came in softly.

"We have to talk, Rachel, you and I," he said.

And he pulled up a chair beside her.

Friday afternoon. Could she really have been home only twenty-four hours? Dara felt she had been back for weeks.

She had gone to look for Jacinta and been told she was at her riding lesson with Marian Johnson.

Some time or other Dara would have to go into Daly's. It had better be now.

Mrs. Daly smiled at her warmly and wanted to know all about France.

"Did you get to Lourdes at all while you were there?"

"No, Mrs. Daly, but the lady I was staying with did. I asked her to say a prayer for Maggie. I wrote the name down for her on the back of a holy picture."

Mrs. Daly was pleased. She patted Dara's hand.

"You're a good child in spite of everything," she said.

Dara repeated this to Tommy Leonard in a cross voice. "In spite of what? What did she mean?" she asked.

Tommy couldn't take his eyes off Dara. She looked utterly lovely, he thought.

"In spite of being good-looking, she means. Mrs. Daly hates good-looking people, she likes them with faces like ironing boards."

Dara giggled. "I don't suppose you can come off with me for a bit?"

"I can't. I used up all my time off going to hunt out sites and vantage points with Jacinta yesterday. You look just great, you know."

"Thanks, Tommy. Well, if you've spent your free time with Jacinta I can but go in search of fun and games elsewhere. Sit out on the street and wait till King Kerry turns up for the weekend."

"Oh, King Kerry as you call him is here already." Tommy was pained to have to acknowledge it but at least it was good that Dara didn't seem to be tied up with him the moment she came back.

"He can't be!"

"Well then, he has a double. I saw him with a fellow from a horror movie going into Foley's, maybe they've taken to drinking in there."

"Kerry doesn't drink," Dara said.

"He could have started," Tommy suggested.

"Today was it?"

"Oh, don't go up looking for them in Foley's, Dara, for heaven's sake."

"I've no intention of going looking for them anywhere," Dara flounced. "Kerry will come and look for me when he's ready."

Dara waited on the footbridge. She knew he would have to come and find her.

She saw the shadows getting a little longer. She leaned over and looked at her reflection in the water. She looked all right, she thought. Not a beauty, but all right.

Where *was* he?

She didn't hear the car stopping and his light step behind her. She felt his arms around her waist and as she looked into the river she saw him reflected there. He kissed her.

"In front of the pub, with them all looking out the window?" she protested.

"Right, let's go somewhere with no windows. Get in." He opened the door of the little red car.

Dara walked toward it slowly. Was she being very cheap, very easy-to-get by going with him right away? He hadn't written. Not once. Not even a card.

He hadn't gotten in touch when he got back. But for seeing her now, he might never have stopped.

He looked up at her from the car. "You're so beautiful, Dara. I hope those Frenchmen didn't get what you wouldn't give me."

He was talking out loud. Anyone could have heard him if they had been near the pub window.

She scrambled into the car at once.

"I'm only getting in to keep you quiet," she said.

"Aren't I clever?" Kerry smiled at her and the car sped off up River Road and toward the stile in Coyne's wood.

In the wood he stood and looked at her.

"I can't take you in, I don't know what it is. In two months you've changed. I missed you," he said, head on one side, smiling to charm her.

"No of course you didn't, you never thought of me at all. You never wrote, not once. You didn't even come to see me when I got back even though I sent you a card to tell you."

"I wanted to but I couldn't, I just wasn't able to," he said.

Dara looked hard at him. He was so handsome. But of course he was making excuses.

"They tied your hands?" she asked.

"No, of course I should have written but I'm hopeless. No, I meant to be there to welcome you, but I had problems. A lot of things to sort out." His face was troubled.

"What were they?"

"Okay, I'll tell you. I was trying to get free from Donegal so that I could be here all the time. Here with you. It took a bit of organizing."

"And have you organized it?" She sounded doubtful. She expected him to say it hadn't worked out.

"Yes," he said surprisingly.

"By good timing, by the most spectacular good timing in the world, I'm free, just as you come back."

"You're leaving Hill's Hotel?"

"Yes, ma'am." He did a mock salute.

"How did you do it?"

"Not easy, a lot of aggravation I assure you. I'm still tidying up loose ends. I've got all my things in the car, see?"

"You mean you've just left *now?*"

"Just now. You're the first person I came to see." He reached out for her.

He looked as if he didn't want to talk about it anymore. Dara moved to what she thought were safer waters.

"I'm very pleased you're going to be around. Even if you *are* faithless and forgetful, I like you."

"Why am I faithless and forgetful? I raced here to find you. Let me hold you."

"Not for a moment."

"Why? What is it?"

"I'm much older now and I understand more. I don't want to hold you and have you . . . um . . . touch me . . . and then for me to say no and you to get all upset."

"Well it's very simple, you don't say no, and nobody gets upset."

Dara looked at him with her big dark eyes. "That's not what I want, and even though I like being with you, and like it a lot, when all is said and done it *is* my body, isn't it? And I can do what I like with it. Or not do what I like with it."

He stood smiling at her, and admiring. "Well, well, well," he said.

"I thought I'd rather say it now. Sort of before anything got started so that you wouldn't storm off."

"Very wise." He nodded his head sagely, making fun of her.

"So, it's a bargain, then. You don't get all upset if I say I don't want to go any further."

"Sure, and you don't get all upset, as you say, if I don't turn up all the time like a little lap dog. I'm going to be living here now and it will have its ups and downs. Give me some time and space to sort it out. Don't go asking a lot of questions all the time."

"It's a deal," she said. "And I promise not to keep asking questions, if you'll tell me one thing. Is it true that you still don't love anyone but if you did love anyone it would probably be me?"

"Where did you hear that?" He smiled.

"You told me once. When we sat in your car. After I had come to look for you in that roadhouse."

"It was true then and it's true now," he said. "If the situation changes in either direction, you will be the first to know."

The weekend would be their last one before term began.

Grace said she hoped that she would be living in the hotel by the time school started.

"Kerry never said." Dara was puzzled.

"Kerry's not coming to the hotel yet. I mean I'm sure he will later." Grace seemed flustered.

"Why on earth isn't he going to the hotel? What happened?" Dara was astounded.

"Nothing, nothing at all."

"I'm your best friend, for heaven's sake. I tell you everything, Grace, why don't you tell me?"

"I haven't even told Michael. I think there was some kind of row, I think Father didn't want him to leave the hotel in Donegal, but he insisted; he said he had to come back to Mountfern."

He had to come back to Mountfern. Dara hugged this to herself with delight. He had indeed gotten into trouble over it but he had braved it all because he wanted to be back in Mountfern. With Dara.

Chapter XXI

By Sunday Kate was concerned about Rachel.

She hadn't called on Thursday to welcome Dara home. She hadn't been in on Friday, nor Saturday.

Sunday morning Loretto called to the pub to buy two bottles of stout.

"Going to have a bit of a spree?" Kate asked as she wrapped them in brown paper.

"No, I'm having Jack Coyne to his Sunday dinner, he was very helpful to me over a lot of heavy lifting and putting up shelves. I thought I'd cook him a meal for once."

"Terrific. Where did Rachel go, by the way?"

"Rachel?" Loretto looked shifty.

"Yes, she must have told me but I've forgotten. She hasn't been in here for days, was it to Connemara this time or Dublin?"

"I don't . . . um . . . know." Loretto wanted to leave. She had no intention of telling Kate what had been going on.

Later that evening Kate looked across the footbridge and saw a figure walking on the other side, along the towpath that led down from the bridge.

It was Rachel Fine, wearing a headscarf and sunglasses.

It wasn't cold enough for a headscarf.

It wasn't bright enough for sunglasses.

It was almost as if she didn't want to be seen.

On Monday morning Dara knew she would see Kerry. He had told her that the weekend would involve a massive reconciliation job with his father, so he wouldn't be around.

Dara did herself up to the nines. She was dying to see him again. She knew too that he didn't want her telling too many people that they met. That suited her very well, she was anxious to keep her own parents as much in the dark as possible.

"You're looking very flash, Dara."

"Sophisticated is the word," Dara said. She was alarmed if Jack Coyne thought she was flash. She must have gone too far with the lipstick.

"Like a dog's dinner, anyway." He was admiring.

"Considering what Leo's dinners look like, that's not much of a compliment."

"Leopold's not a dog, he's a freak," Jack Coyne said. "You should have let me drown him instead of having him there turning away custom."

"Oh, don't be ridiculous. People love him."

"Well, that's debatable. Any sign of Kerry O'Neill, by the way?"

"No, why do you ask *me?*" Dara was suspicious.

"I thought you might have heard from him. Specially seeing you're all dolled up."

"Lord no." She was overly casual. "Kerry O'Neill isn't my type, nor me his, I'm certain."

"Well, they say his tastes run to the maturer lady all right, but you'd never know."

"Maturer?"

"Much maturer. Old even, some would say. Still if you *do* see him tell him I have that poker game in mind. He mentioned one the last time he was here a few days ago."

"Then he *was* here the other night."

"He was certainly here at breakfast time in the morning getting aspirins and orange juice for his lady love upstairs."

"His what?"

"No, I'm saying nothing, but I'm surprised Loretto hasn't passed it on to your mother. Still, what with herself being your mother's friend and everything I suppose it's a bit complicated. Forget I said anything, will you."

He was gone, leaving Dara fuming on River Road. She bent down and pulled up a handful of dried grass from the riverbank to wipe off her lipstick.

Jack Coyne was always a pain and she knew that Mam and Dad didn't like Eddie and Declan hanging around his yard. But surely not even Jack Coyne could make up something like that about Kerry and Mrs. Fine unless he had some reason.

Mrs. Fine. She was older than Mam, surely. It was disgusting.

"Oh, Patrick, this *is* a surprise!" Marian Johnson patted her hair with pleasure.

"Hardly a surprise," Patrick growled. "It is my office."

"No, I heard you were going to Dublin."

"No." Patrick was unforthcoming. "What can I do for you?"

"Nothing really, I just came down to have a look around the place, to see the coach house and stables."

"They're outside, Marian," Patrick said dryly. "They often are in houses like this."

He realized he had been overly sharp.

"Come on, I'll take you on a tour," he said good-naturedly. "Not that there's anything to see of course, we're only playing at ponies and horses here, the guests will all be taken up to the Grange."

"I know." She patted his arm gratefully. "I don't know what we'd do without you. You've changed the whole face of Mountfern."

"That's not what I set out to do," he sighed.

"All for the better, of course. You've improved the place out of all recognition. I mean, look at poor little Loretto's place across the river there . . ." Marian waved a dismissive arm at the bright shop frontage of Quinn's grocery and greengrocery. "That used to be a real huckster's shop, and now it's grand enough for Kerry O'Neill to be seen coming and going at all hours of the day and night." She smiled what she hoped was a mischievous smile.

Patrick looked at her almost pityingly. "I know, Marian. I know. Don't wear yourself out trying to think up ways of telling me what half the town has told me already."

"I don't know *what* you mean." She flushed angrily.

* * *

As Dara passed Loretto Quinn's she saw Mrs. Fine standing at the upper window. She was looking out over the river. She hadn't seen Dara.

For a moment Dara hesitated. Jack Coyne had been very definite. Then she shook herself. It was ludicrous. Mrs. Fine looked a hundred.

On a sudden impulse Dara decided to go up and tell her that Mam was upset. It might do some good and it couldn't do any harm.

Loretto was out the back somewhere, so Dara ran straight upstairs. "Mrs. Fine?" She tapped lightly on the door and went in.

Rachel Fine turned around from the window. However badly she looked from down below she looked worse now. Dara could hardly hide her shock.

"Sorry, Dara I wasn't expecting you. You look very nice."

"Thanks Mrs. Fine . . . um . . . Are you all right and everything?"

"I've had a bit of a cold, I think. Flu perhaps."

"Oh, I see. Mam was wondering where you were."

There was a silence.

"Well, I'll be off then, I suppose," Dara said awkwardly.

"You enjoyed France? It . . . it must have made you grow up a lot."

"Yes, I got lonely a bit of course, I didn't really expect that. I missed everyone here. All the time."

Another silence.

"Mam's very fond of you, Mrs. Fine, she wouldn't be afraid you'd give her an old cold."

To Dara's fright, big tears came into Rachel Fine's eyes.

Rachel went to her bedroom and sat in front of the dressing table mirror. She looked old and tense, she looked lined and pathetic. Methodically she removed her make-up, cleansed her skin, applied a gel that was meant to restore the cells and carefully put on her make-up again.

As she did the feathery strokes around her eyes, Rachel Fine began to wonder was she going mad. First avoiding her friend for days and then making herself up like a call girl to go and see a kind woman in a wheelchair who wouldn't notice if she arrived dressed in a pillow case.

* * *

Kate was a little prickly at first.

"I must say it's nice to see you. Dara will be glad to know you called."

"I've seen Dara. She told me you were wondering why I hadn't been in."

"I didn't send her with that message." Kate's eyes flashed.

"I know," Rachel said wearily.

The first silence they had ever known fell between them. Eventually Rachel spoke.

"It's no use, Kate, I'm empty, drained, there's no me to talk to. I'll go away, you've nothing to say to me, nobody has."

Kate's eyes blazed with anger. "I have nothing to say to you! Don't give me that. Take offense if you bloody want to, sulk, imagine yourself wronged, insulted in some way, but don't give me that about my having nothing to say, I have a million things to say, to ask, to tell, to share. I'm not the one who slides past the door, I'm not the one doing the avoiding. I can't avoid anybody for God's sake. I don't have that little luxury anymore."

"I didn't think you'd be upset."

"No of course not, what right has a vegetable to be upset? Poor old Kate, she's lucky she had anyone come and visit her at all."

"Kate, you know . . ."

"I know nothing. I'm scared sick about this café I've talked them all into doing. I don't want to make John into some kind of clown doing party pieces for Americans, the next thing we'll have his cap on the floor and ask them to throw dimes into it. I don't want the boys to be serving cakes and potato bread in case their friends call them sissies. I don't want Michael to be besotted by Grace with her honey-eyed words and smiles. I don't want that bloody Kerry O'Neill raising his little finger and taking the clothes off my daughter, my beautiful Dara, and then throwing her aside . . . So now tell me about the wonderful trouble-free family life I have."

"What's the worst bit?" Rachel asked suddenly.

"I think it's Kerry. He's playing her like a fish on a line. He'll have her as soon as he wants to, he's the kind that gets everything he wants, and doesn't care about who he hurts on the way."

"You're right."

"I'm so frightened, and I wanted to talk to you, and now you've turned against me too. I'm sorry to be such a fool." Kate groped around ineffectually for her handkerchief and cried salt tears down her newly powdered face.

Rachel's eyes were full of tears. "I couldn't come near you because I didn't want you to know how stupid I've been. I've done something so stupid you wouldn't believe it, I was too ashamed . . ."

"You don't have to tell . . ."

"It's Kerry . . . I've done something so stupid . . . so terribly stupid . . ."

Hand in hand the two women sat in the darkening evening, and Kate patted the beautifully ringed hands of Rachel Fine, who told how she had put herself in Kerry's power.

Tony McCann did not have a bank account. But he had been in and out of this particular branch so often to get change, to cash checks made out to him by other people, that he always regarded it as his bank. He had missed it during the strike.

He handed over the check for a thousand pounds.

"In the money, I see?" the cashier had said to him pleasantly.

"If it were all mine I'd be hundreds of miles from here on a beach sipping rum and Coca Cola," said Tony McCann.

The cashier sighed and thought about it for a moment. "How do you want the money?"

"Ten-pound notes, a hundred of them," McCann said. He looked idly around the bank as she went away to verify the check. How did people work here five days a week for forty years? Surely they must all have been tempted to take a carrier bag of wads of fivers and run. It was remarkable that so few of them did when you came to think of it.

"Mr. McCann?" It was a man now, a senior man in a suit, with a pinched-looking face.

"Yes?"

"There seems to be a problem about the check."

"That's not possible."

"I'm afraid so. It has been cancelled and reported stolen."

"It's me. McCann."

"Yes?" Kerry O'Neill's voice was anxious suddenly.

"The check doesn't work."

"I don't believe you."

"You'd better believe me."

"The bitch. The stupid bitch."

"You'll sort it out then?"

"I'll sort it out."

"Mr. O'Neill?"

Brian Doyle was hesitant. Patrick O'Neill was like a devil these days, even the most mild request was met by a bout of bad temper.

"Doyle?" He was curt.

"Mrs. Fine wants to have a word with you."

Once Brian had called Rachel by her first name, and that had not found favor either with his boss.

"Good, then I'm sure she will," Patrick said.

"On the telephone," Brian explained, as if he were talking to a child.

It had been as much as Patrick could do to stay sane when faced with the Irish telephone system. He had been assured that it was a European thing, not just Irish, but that didn't make it any easier to bear. He said he would make a mental note not to open a chain of hotels on the continent of Europe, and people had smiled at him indulgently. The eager American, hustle bustle. He knew what they said.

But if Rachel was on the telephone for him that meant he had to leave his office and walk across to Brian Doyle's headquarters, that was where the only phone link so far had managed to be installed.

Patrick moved quickly. He would not let Doyle see how annoyed he was to be summoned by Rachel, whom they all knew to be his fancy woman, to walk across the courtyard, through the Thatch Bar and over to those excrescences that Doyle called his headquarters.

"Yes?" He said curtly, watching Brian pretend to busy himself elsewhere in the cramped space.

"Can we talk?"

"Here?" He couldn't believe it.

"No. Anywhere. It's important."

"Why didn't you come up here in the first place instead of having me walk half way around the country to tell me you were coming?"

"I don't want to come there."

"I don't have time to go over to Loretto's."

"No, I don't want you to come here either."

"Is this a game of hide and seek, by any chance?"

"Please."

"Where then?"

"Coyne's wood. At the far end up by the old ruined church on the small back road that leads to the Grange. There's a gate."

"Jesus," Patrick said.

"I'll leave now, I'll wait. You get away when you can."

He held the receiver in his hand for a while and out of the window of Doyle's headquarters, through the clutter of the ledge, he saw across the Fern in the distance a figure come out of the door of Loretto Quinn's shop and get into a small green car.

"Thanks, Brian," he said as he replaced the receiver.

"Lovely day for a bit of a spin out into the country," Brian said.

Patrick gave him a look that told Brian that the wise man addressed no words at all to the great O'Neill these days.

Canon Moran was picking flowers near the stile up in Coyne's wood. That was all Patrick needed.

The old man looked up with pleasure as the American approached. This was a bonus for him, he liked a good chat.

Patrick looked at him thoughtfully. It was a good life being a country priest in Ireland. Canon Moran had all the respect and none of the work in the parish. He had baptized and married and buried people from the place for as long as anyone could remember. There was no way he would be sent away nor his honors stripped from him.

He could wander in a second childhood, collecting summer flowers.

"You know what you were asking me, about marriage to those who had never been baptized?"

Patrick tried to keep the maddened irritation out of his face.

"Yes, Canon Moran. It was just something I wondered about in the abstract. Like I sometimes wonder about the angels. You know, thrones and dominations and seraphim. I wonder why they'd have a VIP system in heaven."

Canon Moran had often wondered about angels too, and particularly about guardian angels. He couldn't ever see on what basis the poor angels were given mortals to look after. Some angels must have had a very easy time and others a desperate job altogether.

Patrick wondered was he going to spend the entire morning debating guardian angels with an almost senile cleric who held an armful of daisies and heathers and some prickly yellow gorse. Still it was better than discussing marriages to infidels. He looked around wildly for any trace of Rachel.

The canon's old eyes may have been sharper than Patrick thought.

"Well, I won't hold you up, you're a busy man, Mr. O'Neill, a busy man, a good man, and a generous man. It's very heartening to know that men like you with all your worldy wealth still keep the laws of God."

Patrick was rarely at a loss. But now he had no idea what to say.

Canon Moran filled the gap for him. "And if ever you should need any further talk—just in the abstract of course—about the marriage of unbaptized persons who convert to the Catholic faith, then I know just the man in Archbishop's House. We were in the seminary together. He didn't end up in a quiet place like Mountfern, he's a big expert in canon law and there's nothing he doesn't understand about previous marriages contracted outside the Church or any other church which would be recognized as solemnizing a Christian marriage according to their own lights . . ."

"Yes, yes."

"They would be entirely null and void and wouldn't need to be taken into consideration," Canon Moran finished triumphantly.

"Well yes, that's good. I'll remember that if I need to think about it," Patrick said.

"It would be good if you needed to think about it, Mr. O'Neill. Life can be lonely at times, and we're all very pleased here that you've come back to the land of your fathers. We wouldn't want you to feel . . . well to feel a bit alone back there in that big place."

For a second time Patrick was without words. He was touched by the old man; he felt a lump in his throat.

Again Canon Moran filled the pause. "So I expect you'll want to be off for a bit to wander down there by the trees with all the climbing roses on them. They look so beautiful at this time of year, someone should make them into a calendar, I always think."

The old man walked back toward the road and Patrick went slowly down to the trees where the roses did indeed wind around the big heavy trunks and the branches, and where Rachel sat on a fallen tree.

"How's Jimbo's singing career these days?" Kate asked Carrie.

"He's doing very well, he's going to cut a record," Carrie said proudly.

"Is that a single or an LP?" Kate was well up in records from hearing the children talk.

"It's going to be an EP, ma'am. You know, the middle kind of one." Carrie's face was shining.

"And does he like all this traveling around? I hear he was as far afield as Donegal."

"Oh he likes it all right, Mrs. Ryan, it's grand for him. But I don't like it all that much, to tell you the truth."

Kate was sympathetic. "And does he not suggest you go along with him?"

"He's always suggesting it, but how can I?"

"It's hard all right."

"Well it is. You see he's never suggesting I go along as Mrs. Jimbo Doyle, if you know what I mean. Just as Carrie." She looked very glum.

"Suppose he got work around here, wouldn't that keep him at home?"

"But that's the point, there's plenty of work around here, with the hotel he could be working seven days a week. But he has his heart set on being a star, you see, so the work is only interfering with it."

"But if he got singing work, I mean. When the hotel opened."

Carrie's face lit up. "Wouldn't that be the makings of us. But Mr. O'Neill thinks of Jimbo as a handyman, he wouldn't employ him as a singer."

"I could have a word, maybe."

"Oh ma'am, and if you were to say it to Mrs. Fine, maybe Mr. O'Neill would listen to her, too."

"We'll see what we can do." Kate promised, and Carrie went out to the kitchen and made a big dinner for Leopold in order to have somebody to celebrate with.

"Wouldn't it be great if poor Jimbo got a chance to do a turn over in Fernscourt when it opens?" Kate said to John.

"Less of the poor Jimbo, there was a bit about him in the papers on Sunday. He's doing fine."

"Well then, it shouldn't be hard to get him taken on now and then in the Thatch Bar."

"I wouldn't say he'd have time for that," John said.

"What do you mean?" Kate couldn't follow the reasoning.

"We'll offer him a job singing in Ryan's Shamrock Café. If he's good then let him sing here, not have him across the river."

Kate got a sudden cold feeling. There was a time when she was the one who would have thought up that plan.

"That's a better idea altogether," she said dully.

"Of course it is." He patted her hand.

* * *

"Dara will you give me a hand with these table napkins?"

"*No*, Mammy, *no, no, no*."

"That's lovely, I must say."

"I'll do anything but that, I hate hemming bloody napkins."

"Do you think I like it?"

"Well, you've got nothing—" She stopped.

"Nothing better to do. How right you are. Sit in a wheelchair, give her some napkins to hem, stop her hands from becoming paralyzed as well as everything else . . ."

"Oh Mam, really . . ."

"What do you mean, really? Really nothing. That's what you were saying, wasn't it?"

"It's not like you to be so sorry for yourself."

"It's not like you to be such a selfish little madam."

A pause. "I'm sorry, and that *wasn't* what I was going to say . . ."

"What were you going to say?"

"I stopped but I'll have to say it now because the way you finished it is worse."

"Well what was it . . ."

"I was going to say you've got nothing more important to do like I have, I want to . . . well, I want to be around a bit . . ."

Kate looked at her blankly.

"Sort of outside, you know, not in here putting hems on squares."

"I'd like to be outside a bit too."

"I know, Mammy, I know, but you've sort of had your life. *Oh God*, I don't mean that. It's so easy to say the wrong thing. I mean, you've had this bit, the bit of hunting and deciding and doing things that matter."

"Yes."

"You don't understand."

"I do. I've had the bit that matters. You haven't. Off you go, find the bit that matters."

"Sometimes there's no pleasing you, Mam, do you know that? You get annoyed if we don't tell you what's going on, you get more annoyed if we do tell you. It's not just that you have all this . . ." Dara waved at the chair. They never used words like cripple or paralyzed or invalid in the house. Sometimes, not often they spoke of the "accident."

Kate looked thoughtful, not annoyed, and not so sad, either.

"I will do a bit of hemming, Mam, but not now, I want to be around, if you could know what I mean at all."

Kate seemed to have recovered her humor.

"No, I do see what you mean. You must be around. But Dara, he may not be back for fun and games this time, he may have other things on his mind."

"Oh, him?" Dara flushed and flounced a bit. "I wasn't thinking of him."

"Of course not, and even if you were why should you listen to me about him? It's just that I think he's here for a purpose this time."

"God, you're very dramatic at times." Dara was gone, mascara and lipstick in the pocket of her white jacket ready to put on when well out of sight of Ryan's Licensed Premises.

Patrick sat down on the fallen tree beside Rachel.

For a moment neither of them said anything. The wood smelled fresh and flowery. Canon Moran had tottered away; there was nothing to disturb them. Butterflies went in and out of the trees, and sometimes a bird rustled in some kind of activity. It was a peaceful place.

"We should have spent more time here," Patrick said.

She smiled at him. Perhaps this might be a bit easier than she had feared. He had sounded so forbidding on the phone.

She twisted her hands together. "It's so difficult to tell you this."

He moved his cuff slightly so that he could see his watch. "But I am going to hear it. Right, Rachel?" he said.

He had the smile she had known for so many years. It was the smile when someone was going to waste his time. But he owed them. So he would listen.

It was to that smile that she would have to tell her tale.

"Give me a large brandy will you, John."

"Things must be bad over there if you're at the large brandies before lunch," John Ryan said mildly, putting the glass in front of Brian Doyle.

"I'll be hiding it in a tea flask, I tell you."

"Any one thing, or things in general?"

"Who knows? Nothing would please him. He went off to meet your one up in Coyne's wood as if they were a pair of kids. That didn't last long, he's back inside there now with a face on him that would stop a clock."

"It can't have gone well, the outing," John agreed. "Did Rachel come back with him or what?"

"Did she come back with him? Indeed she did not. Those two are like the things you see—you know, kind of statues of a man and a woman. When one comes out the other goes in, one means sun, one means rain. I saw them once somewhere. Blackpool I think it was."

John laughed. "Are they as bad as that?"

"Oh, God, John, the older people are the worse it hits them, this love carry-on. I think I'm too old for it myself and I'm years younger than O'Neill."

"You'd better hurry up and marry that girl of yours in the town before someone else does," John advised him.

"I don't want to be tied down. Men are miserable when they're tied down; they're meant to roam free, wild like nature intended."

"It's easy known Mary Donnelly's over in the post office today," John said.

"She is too, I went in to send off some forms for O'Neill that had been lying on his desk for a month and he wouldn't look at, but today he took the face off me about them, and there was the hatchet face standing behind the grille, snapping and barking at poor Fergus Slattery because there was too much sealing wax or something on his parcels. God, wouldn't a man want to be free, not tied to a woman who'd yap the arse off him."

John was mild. "I don't know, look at the people around here who are not tied to women—Jack Coyne, Fergus Slattery, Papers Flynn, O'Neill himself . . . You can't say that makes a flight of free birds, now can you?"

"Go on out of that. You've one of the few happy marriages around, and look at the thanks you got for that. I'll have the other half of that brandy now, if you don't mind."

"It's just as well you weren't laying into the booze like this when the structure was going up," John commented. "Nobody would dare go into the place at all for fear of it coming down on top of them."

"You could do yourself a favor, Eddie," Jack Coyne said.

"What's that, Mr. Coyne?" Eddie was suspicious now. He saw in his mind the shadow of Sergeant Sheehan at every turn.

"You know where they're digging out the road for the new entrance up on the road beyond. Where all the vehicles are parked?"

"Yes, I know it."

"I was just thinking that if someone was to let the brakes off a couple of those vehicles, well there'd be an unholy mess when they started to move them again in the morning, there'd be people skating into each other and falling over . . . It would be great sport altogether."

Eddie looked at Jack Coyne and remembered what his father had said about him. "There's been enough accidents up in that place," he said in a voice more courageous than he felt.

This was unanswerable. Jack was taken aback, but he rallied.

"It wouldn't have anything to do with anything like that, and wouldn't that make you of all people anxious to make sure that O'Neill doesn't get away with everything and ride roughshod over the whole place?"

"I'm out of it now, Mr. Coyne."

Eddie spoke in a cloak and dagger voice.

"You are like hell," Jack said. "Wait till I tell your father, not to mention Sergeant Sheehan, what you've been up to with cans of distemper."

"They'd want to know who gave us the distemper, Mr. Coyne."

"I suppose O'Neill's paying you more than I am. That's what it always is in the end."

"You never paid us anything, Mr. Coyne." Eddie was stung.

"So you're looking for something now, you mean little jerk."

Eddie walked away in what he was sure was exactly the way the good sheriff would turn his back on the bad guys in town.

"Don't turn on the light."

Rachel turned on the light and saw him lounging in her chair.

"Why did you do that?" Kerry asked. "I wanted us to sit and have another nice talk in the dark summer evening. Maybe you could have another drink and become amorous again. Hey, that would be good."

"If you don't leave I will," she said.

"You're not surprised to see me."

"I got your message. I knew you'd be here sooner or later."

"It's sooner because there was some little misunderstanding about that check you gave me."

"I changed my mind. I cancelled it."

"That was a very foolish thing to do."

"Are you going?" she asked him.

"No, and neither are you. This is Mountfern, Rachel; this is not an apartment; it's a couple of rooms over a downtown store. It's where you have to stay because you aren't good enough to stay in the Grange, and because you'll never stay in Fernscourt."

She moved toward the door.

"Wait," he ordered. "Just see how hopeless it is for you, Rachel. Write this check out again, with a note saying that it was all a mistake. *Do it.* Tell them that you apologize for the embarrassment caused to Mr. McCann."

"*Mr.* McCann." Rachel gave a great shout of mirthless laughter. "That guy's never been called Mr. in his life, and never will be. You don't frighten me, Kerry. I'm going for Patrick."

"You're going for my father."

"Of course I am. If his son is behaving like this and harassing me then he will want to be told."

"Rachel, Rachel." Kerry was languid. "You live in a world of romantic movies and women's magazines. You see yourself as the lady who has been slighted and insulted. Grow up. Look at the reality. You're a has-been, you're a passed-over, middle-aged woman . . ."

"You're not hurting me."

"I'm glad, because that's not my intention. I just want you to see how ridiculous you are. Once people can see how absurd they are, they are better off for it."

He walked over to her, a notepad and a pen in his hands. "Write it Rachel. It makes sense."

"Like hell will I write it."

"I'll tell my father what fun and games we had."

"You can, I've already told him."

Kerry's face didn't change. Not a muscle moved.

"He knows nothing happened between us."

"Does he?"

Kerry looked down at the check. He looked back at Rachel.

Something about his smile alarmed her.

"So could *you* explain why you wrote the check in the first place?" he asked.

He knew by her face that he had hit home. That was the one bit of her unsatisfactory conversation with Patrick in Coyne's wood that had been worse than all the rest put together. He had listened impassively from his seat on the fallen tree. The drink, the dizziness, the passing out, the tears, the hangover, the arrogant behavior of Kerry going down to the shop in the morning . . . all those things were capable of some kind of explanation. But why had she given in so readily to the demand for money? Unless she had hoped somehow to pay him off.

It had seemed a long day to Dara since she set out that morning all dressed up and had the upsetting meeting with Jack Coyne.

People were behaving strangely in Mountfern today. Jacinta said that there was some terrible row between Mrs. Fine, who was Mr. O'Neill's mistress and Mr. O'Neill, and he had ordered her back to America because of something unmentionable she had done.

Dara asked what it had been but Jacinta said her lips were sealed.

Liam White said he thought Mrs. Fine had gotten drunk and made a pass at Kerry.

Tommy Leonard said there was some scandal about Kerry, he had had breakfast in the wrong place. But he, Tommy, knew nothing about it and wasn't going to start speculating.

Mary Donnelly admired Dara's dress and said that now that she was so grown up why didn't she find herself some nice new friends instead of just staying all the time in the same little circle.

"It isn't a circle, it's just whoever is here," Dara cried out in confusion.

Nobody had ever talked about circles before in Mountfern.

She came home confused and somehow let down. She sat with her mother for a little. Even Mam looked odd, she thought.

Kate looked with love at her beautiful daughter. Please may something happen that would take this dangerous Kerry O'Neill away from their place.

His deliberate cruelty to Rachel, his blackmail, the cynical way he treated everyone around him made Kate shiver.

"Are you all right, Mam?" Dara had noticed the way her body had trembled suddenly all over.

"I'm fine. Can you pass me that light wool stole . . . the new one Rachel brought me?" Kate settled it around her shoulders.

Dara had a look as if she were going to say something and had thought better of it.

"What is it?"

"Well, I don't suppose it's possible that Mrs. Fine could fancy Kerry. I know it sounds ridiculous, but do you think it could by any chance be true?"

When Dara saw the look of shock and embarrassment followed by anger come to her mother's face, she knew that there must indeed be

something in what awful horrible Jack Coyne had said. She wished
with all her heart that she had never asked.

It was about the most revolting thing she had ever heard in her
life, and the worst thing was that her mother had known about it
already.

"What are you going to wear?" Fergus asked Kate.

"To the hotel opening?"

"No, Kate, to your court case."

"I thought you said it would be settled before we *got* to court."

"I did, and that's what Kevin thinks too, but we have to be prepared to go into court. All of us."

"I didn't think about it."

"Well *do* think about it."

"Do you want me to paint my cheeks white and draw circles under
my eyes?"

"No, but I don't want you dripping in all Rachel Fine's silks and
scarves and jewelry, either."

"Fergus, I'm weary of this. It's a sum. It's a sum no matter what I
wear. It's going to be ten thousand pounds at most and two thousand
pounds at least. Isn't that what we all agreed?"

"That's what you and John and I and Kevin Kennedy and about
three others agreed. It's not what those hotshots across the river and
their big faceless insurance companies agreed. It's not what a jury of
pudding-faced farmers and shopkeepers agreed. Not yet."

"What do you want me to wear? I'll wear it." She sounded tired.

"It will be over soon." Fergus sounded tired too.

Dara's bedroom door was open, she was standing by a picture of
Our Lady Queen of the May.

"What are you thinking about?" Michael asked.

"Should we pray for a lot of money next week or would that be
wrong?" Dara asked.

"I don't know."

"I was just wondering what you thought. You say so little these
days, I thought you might have *some* opinion." Dara was annoyed.

Michael was even more annoyed. "I say very little, I have no
opinions, *you* are the one who says nothing, you've this awful shrug,
this awful way of just putting anyone down."

"Ha ha." Dara was bitter. "I've often heard of people accusing
others of the very fault they have themselves. *You* haven't a word to

throw to a dog these days, yes even Leopold doesn't bother to come and snuffle at you anymore, you might as well snuffle at a block of wood."

"I only have to come into a room for you to leave it," Michael cried. "Look at you now, standing up already, off again. I don't care. I don't care one tuppenny damn, just don't go around saying that it's *me* that's being difficult, you're the one like a bag of weasels."

"I'm standing because I haven't sat down yet, you great clown. I only asked you a civil question, a reasonable question, like should we be saying the thirty days prayer or not. It's the kind of thing we used to talk about once. When you talked, that was."

Dara's lip was trembling a little. Michael saw it.

"I don't think prayers work," he said. "I'm not sure but I don't think they do."

"I'm not sure either, but suppose they did, would it be wrong?" She looked very near tears.

"Why the sudden interest in money?" Michael asked. "We never needed it before."

"I know, I just thought it might help to make things better, stop everyone from being so worried. Stop all the terrible things happening."

Awkwardly he put his arm around her shoulder. "It's not as bad as that."

"Sometimes it is."

"I know, for me too."

"Oh you! Everything's fine for you." She sounded envious.

"Not all the time. I'll tell you sometime."

"We never talk these days," she said.

"Remember when we got into such tempers because we couldn't sleep in the same room anymore!" Michael said.

"I still think you got the better room."

"Yeah, but I got Eddie and Declan."

She smiled at him. This was better, more like old times.

"Let's go out," she said. "It's the last day of freedom. We'll go to the tunnel."

"It's such a sunny day . . ." Michael began.

"Oh come on, it was always a sunny day when we went to the tunnel." She looked eager.

With great misgivings Michael agreed. They walked along River Road past Loretto Quinn's at the very moment that Rachel came out, in her cream linen suit with its cream and brown blouse.

She stopped when she saw them. Uneasily.

Dara stopped too.

Rachel spoke first.

"Can I give you a ride?" she asked.

"No thanks, we're just going for a walk," Michael answered.

Dara said nothing.

"Well, if you're sure . . . ?"

Michael looked at Dara, waiting for her to answer. There were no words so he had to speak again.

"Honestly, thanks. It's our last day of the holidays."

"Yes, the last day of the holidays," Rachel repeated. "You will never forget this holiday . . ." Her eyes went toward the big bridge. "Nobody knew it was going to turn out like this."

She got into her green car and drove away.

"Why were you like that?" Michael asked.

"Like what?"

"You know."

"I can't tell you. Not yet."

"All right." He looked disappointed, Dara noticed. Perhaps she would tell him in the tunnel.

Miss Hayes had gone to Dublin. There were a lot of things she had to do. There was the matter of her passport, and her traveler's checks. There were formalities about her ticket with a travel agency, a meeting with some distant cousins, and she wanted to buy material to make a few nice suitable garments for the journey. Mrs. Fine had been very helpful about the need for pure cotton, and avoiding synthetic fabrics. Mr. O'Neill got her a lift to the town, and she would take the day excursion train from there.

Kerry came to the lodge to see Grace. He looked disheveled and scruffy.

"I wish you wouldn't behave like this, Kerry, like someone on the run. I know you and Father had some big row again, and nobody even told me. Grace isn't supposed to know anything upsetting . . . but he hasn't thrown you out, it's you who are making the big drama out of it."

"It's sort of complicated. I just have to straighten things out and then it will all be fine. I don't want to be at home, not until things are settled."

"Can you tell me about it?"

"No, Gracie. Not yet."

"Kerry, where are you staying?"

"I'll tell you eventually, honestly."

"You're so jumpy, you said you wanted to talk to me about something. What is it?"

"Gracie, you believe that everything's marvelous. Everyone's good and all things are going to end happily ever after."

"I don't believe that, but I only concentrate on things that make me happy. You concentrate on things that make you miserable, like fighting with Father and only seeing the old fussy side of Miss Hayes. She'd be so pleased to do all your clothes for you . . ." Grace shook her head in wonder that Kerry couldn't see the easy route to everything.

"I have to go out, there's someone I have to meet, then I'll come back, and you and I will talk about plans and the future and you can lecture me to your heart's content."

They were barely into the tunnel when Dara felt at peace. She had been happy here with Michael like they had been happy when they played in the ruins of Fernscourt.

"You know, there are plenty of these tunnels, we used to think this was the only one in the world," she said.

"For us it was," Michael said.

They walked along the narrow passage to their special room. Dara chattered away more easily than she had done for a long time.

"It looks different," she said.

"Of course we haven't been here for ages," said Michael.

They lit the candles in the old rusty candelabra they had found on a dump and polished.

The place was full of shadows and shapes, as it always was.

But Dara saw that there were bunches of grasses tied in a way that they never had them before. She saw there were cushions that they used to keep on the floor as seats all piled up on the broken couch. She knew instantly that this was not the way they had left it.

She knew that Michael had brought Grace to the tunnel. Her heart turned over at the betrayal.

She decided not to make an issue out of it. There had been too much drama. But she wouldn't tell him about Mrs. Fine and the terrible story that she knew was true. She couldn't trust him anymore.

So they talked lightly of other things. They talked about school tomorrow. And they talked a little about Mam's case next Thursday.

When they would both be in their classrooms trying to concentrate on their work.

Dara fought down the feeling that her twin brother had been disloyal. She tried not to think of him in this tunnel with Grace. She thought he looked a bit edgy and worried, as if he had seen something that was upsetting him, but since he didn't say what it was, she didn't ask him.

Papers Flynn said to Sergeant Sheehan that it was going to be a cold winter; he had heard that as a fact.

"The winter is months away," Sergeant Sheehan said, wondering what this was leading up to.

"There's a very nice kind of a shed behind the presbytery, a place where no wind would come whistling through at all, if a person was to want a bit of shelter."

"The very thing for a bit of shelter," the sergeant agreed. "Unless of course you'd be lifted out of it by some housekeeper that isn't herself a person of the cloth at all."

"That would be a hard thing if it were to happen. I just mentioned it in case anyone would think of making it their headquarters," Papers explained.

The sergeant nodded sagely.

Papers was getting old. There was a time when he would take his chances in anyone's shed. His main priority in life was to avoid being organized. But now he found battles hard to fight. This was his way of asking Sergeant Sheehan to square it with Miss Purcell and the clergy that he could live there when the cold weather came.

Patrick said that he didn't mind if the rest of the hotel wasn't finished for another decade, he wanted his own suite completed and ready to move into this week.

"That wasn't on the schedule," Brian Doyle was unwise enough to say.

"Your schedule, Doyle, should be published and bound and sold, it would be the comic best-seller of the year."

It was totally impossible to insult Brian. "That might well be right but we'll have to take men off other work to sort it out for you. It's not just getting it ready, it's making it so that we don't have to traipse through it all the time."

"That would be very acceptable," Patrick said with heavy irony.

"Not to have this army of craftsmen you employ traipsing through my quarters. Yes, that would be a great bonus."

"When do you want to sleep here?" Brian was practical.

"Tomorrow night."

He wanted to be resident in the hotel before the compensation case began. He wanted to be well out of his son's way. It was becoming increasingly obvious he should be in his own place. At once.

He walked around the unfinished set of rooms that were to be his new home. Three bedrooms, two bathrooms, a sitting room, a study and a small kitchen.

The main rooms faced the Fern and were on the first floor of the house. He hadn't wanted a kitchen but Rachel had insisted. He wouldn't always want hotel food. There might be times when Grace would want to cook for the family. It was good to have a place where they could close the door and leave the hotel to get on with itself.

His study was the biggest room. Two walls were lined with shelves. Rachel said they could get antique furniture later, visit auctions in big country houses maybe, but for now he should have space for his papers and his books.

Had she ever seen herself with him there, he wondered. There was no hint ever in her suggestions, that she might join him in this life style. No room for her clothes was ever taken into consideration. Instead she had urged him to fit out rooms for both Kerry and Grace from the outset so that they would always consider it their home.

Grace had been busy throughout, deciding where she wanted her closet, her bureau. Kerry's room, though it existed, had not been furnished or discussed, it was now an official dressing room.

Brian accompanied Patrick on his tour of inspection.

"Tomorrow night," he repeated in the tone that he would use to soothe a dangerous drunk or someone who was both soft in the head and violent.

"Good." Patrick deliberately misunderstood the tone, and averted his eyes from the open floorboards, the electric wires and cables still loose from the wall.

The windows were smeared with squiggles to show that there was glass in them, and there were heaps of wood shavings where the carpentry was still in progress. Furniture in crates stood in the corridors.

Patrick smiled at it beatifically.

"As long as I have my own little place here, Doyle, I'll be fine," he said.

"I often think, Mr. O'Neill, God forgive me, that if you'd come home and built yourself a nice bungalow on this site you'd have saved yourself and everyone else a lot of trouble."

"How unselfish you are, Doyle. Imagine thinking that you could have passed over the entirely disproportionate wealth I have made available to you, not to mention all the extra you made on the side."

He clasped Brian warmly by the hand and patted him on the back at the same time.

"Tomorrow around six o'clock I'll move in. Come and have a drink with me here to celebrate."

"I will, Mr. O'Neill, I look forward to that. I was always a great fan of *Alice in Wonderland* myself."

Rachel's choking feeling in her throat returned as soon as she got into her car and drove away from the twins. Dara had been filled with scorn and hate.

And no wonder. A girl of barely sixteen, in love for the first time with a handsome boy who probably filled her head with lies and false assurances. And then the town is saying everywhere in whispers that he has slept with her mother's friend.

No wonder those dark eyes blazed with contempt and hurt.

Rachel remembered those days in June when she had gotten very close to the girls. She had loved the elder-sister role. That was all part of a Celtic mist of fantasy now.

But it wasn't time for self-pity yet; she must get into the hotel, get her business done, and be on the road as soon as possible.

If she were to have any tatters of dignity left over the whole incident, then she must keep calm and workmanlike until she was well out of sight of the cast of interested spectators.

She parked her car and walked purposefully up the hotel steps in search of Jim Costello.

They had run into a problem over some of the Irish-linen panels. It was proving difficult to get exactly the same shade of dye in each batch. Young Jim Costello had understood the matter at once. It was a question of deciding whether to attempt to get them all the same or to have deliberately different toning shades.

Together they had walked the public rooms, climbing ladders and dropping swathes of material.

Jim wanted this hotel opening to stagger his rivals and quite possibly his future employers or backers. Rachel knew that he was as eager and keen as anyone to get it right.

Eventually they agreed that it would be gradings of color. They had to do this in case some wall panels were to fade in the sunlight and could never be replaced exactly.

It would mean another visit to the small linen mills.

The workmen saluted her on her way out to the car. They had respect for her since she never threw her weight around and had a quick smile, but didn't stop to bore them with woman's kind of chat.

Leaning against her small green car was Kerry.

"What are you doing?"

"Waiting for you."

"You've waited in vain. I'm just leaving. Excuse me . . ."

She tried to get past him. He did not move.

She turned around and walked purposefully back up the steps. Kerry ran after her; it was as if he knew that she was heading straight for his father.

"I'm giving you one last chance," he said.

She didn't stop. He was beside her now.

"Look at this house, Rachel, this is your one chance to have it all, it's what you gave your whole damn life for, isn't it? Don't throw it away. Write that check out. This minute. Or I tell him everything."

"Come with me and we'll tell him together." She was heading for the staircase.

"I have to have the money. McCann's people are very angry with you and with me because of you. These guys don't play around."

He stood in front of her barring her way up the stairs.

"*Will* you get out of my way?" She raised her voice so significantly that the workmen all stopped whatever they were doing and nudged each other. A barney between O'Neill's woman and his son in full view of everyone was worth watching.

At that very moment Patrick O'Neill appeared on the landing at the top of the stairway. He took in the scene in a second and saw the gawping faces looking at the unexpected floorshow.

He did the one thing guaranteed to end the excitement and to wound more seriously than any other action he could have taken. He looked at them both dismissively and walked past them without addressing a word to either of them.

Most of the journey to the weavers was on a good straight road, which was just as well. Rachel drove with minimum concentration.

Her eyes blurred over sometimes, and she had to blink hard to clear her vision.

For no reason at all she thought of a little old man who was in the garden of the Hadassah nursing home, a psychiatric home for elderly Jewish clientele. It was the home where Rachel's mother had died. The old man sat in the garden looking almost unbearably sad. Once Rachel felt compelled to ask him what was upsetting him so much.

"I'm not mad, you see," he had said to her resignedly. "I'm as sane as you or any other visitor. My nephew put me in here because he wants to steal all my inventions and pass them over as his own. But it *sounds* like such a mad thing to say, that it only gives everybody further proof that I am indeed mad."

She had been struck at the time by the logic of the old man's argument. But she had only shaken her head sadly and marveled at how sane the very far from sane could sound.

Today, driving across Ireland in the late summer sun, pausing sometimes for a flock of sheep, a herd of cattle, or on one occasion for a great group of young laughing nuns who were going on some kind of outing, Rachel Fine remembered the old man and wished she had been more sympathetic to him.

Grace was startled to see Kerry looking so wild when he came back to the Lodge.

"I've just seen myself reflected in the window and you are quite right, I do look a wreck. Listen, I'm going to clean up. Grace, can you put all these newfound cooking skills to work and fix me some eggs. Then we'll talk."

She heard him singing in the bathroom, and her face brightened as she went happily to the bright sunny kitchen of the lodge.

She would be sorry to leave this little house in the middle of all the trees. She would miss the pleasant company of Miss Hayes, and her bedroom where the small brown rabbits often hopped up on her windowsill and snuffled their noses against the pane.

Still, it would be exciting in the hotel.

Jim Costello had told her that there was nothing as heady as a successful hotel, the place buzzed with activity and you got the feeling that it was alive twenty-four hours a day. She smiled at the memory.

He had added that every hotel needed a really beautiful woman to be at the center of it, and now Fernscourt was going to have that as well as everything else.

Kerry came out, his hair damp, wearing clean white trousers and a white sweater.

"That's more like it," he grinned at her. "Now tell me what you've been doing."

Grace felt that it was he who should do the telling. She had been doing nothing, she said.

"Nothing? Every day, all day, off on a bicycle with young Ryan. Don't tell me you've been doing nothing." His eyes were very bright.

"Well, you know, we've been fishing and talking and just fooling around." She giggled apologetically.

His face looked hard somehow. "What kind of fooling around?"

"Oh heavens, you know. Nothing too serious."

"It had better not be serious, it had damn well better not be."

"What do you mean?" She was frightened.

"Don't make yourself cheap; you're not to throw yourself away on some kid from a pub who's wet behind the ears but who knows like any animal what he wants and will do all he can to take it."

Grace jumped up, eyes blazing. "Michael is *not* an animal. I will not have you speak of him like that."

"I will until I know he has done you no harm, that he hasn't forced you to do anything you shouldn't have done."

"I've done plenty of things I shouldn't have done, like you have as well," Grace cried with spirit. "Anything I do with Michael I do because I want to."

"You must not want to; he must not make you *want* to. You're so young, you're my sister, you shouldn't put out for any country hick."

"It's not like that."

"It had better not be."

"And what about you, you and Dara, why is nobody saying anything to you about all this?"

"That's different." He was dismissive.

"But why is it different?"

"I'm a man; it's different for men."

"Dara isn't a man."

The phone rang sharply into the silence between them.

"That's Michael," Grace said in relief. But it wasn't; it was a man with a Northern Ireland accent to speak to Kerry.

Kate sent Declan away when she heard that the doctor had arrived.

Martin White smiled at the youngest Ryan, who hadn't yet turned into a hooligan like his brother Eddie.

"Will you miss them when they go back tomorrow, or will it be a bit of peace for you?" he asked.

"I suppose I'll feel they can get up to less trouble inside the walls of the convent and the brothers' than roaming wild around this place," Kate sighed.

"I know, my two have gone cracked on this riding nonsense, hard hats and crops and boots, and God knows what else, you're lucky you were spared that. You're pale, any pains and aches?"

"I've an upset stomach, I seem a bit nauseous somehow, but I think that's only tasting all this food we're going to be offering in the café . . . if there's anyone to offer it to."

"Do you need to take this on?"

"It's take this on or go under."

"The compensation maybe?" he suggested tentatively.

"It won't keep a family, Martin. Oh Lord God how I'm dreading Thursday, the palms of my hands start to sweat at the thought."

Dr. White said that he would give Kate a mild tranquilizer on the day of the case.

"Will it make me dopey and stupid-sounding?" Kate wanted to know.

"Nothing could do that." Dr. White was amused.

"Maybe I don't need any tranquilizer. I'm slow enough already." She seemed very down.

"It will take the sharp edge off the anxiety, that's all. It won't affect your powers to say yes or no to a million pounds."

"I'm not the one saying yes or no. It'll be John—John and Fergus."

He looked at her sharply. In the last few weeks she had seemed less alive to him. It was hard to pinpoint exactly what it was.

"I know I don't have a degree in psychiatry, but is there anything wrong, Kate? Anything you want to talk about?"

She gave him a brittle smile. "Anything wrong apart from being paralyzed, in a wheelchair for life, possibly losing all our trade to a bar across the river? No, not much."

Dr. White was often accused of having a poor bedside manner. He was unsparing of his time and energy to help a patient but he was never at hand with the coaxing and condolences that a lot of the parish felt they needed from time to time.

He stood up and prepared to leave. He didn't even acknowledge what Kate had said.

"See you on Thursday," he said briefly and was almost out the door when Kate called out.

"Martin. I'm sorry."

"Why should *you* be sorry?" He had his hand on the door.

"I mean for being a smart aleck. You were being kind. There *is* something wrong. But it's very hard to say it."

Dr. Martin White stood sympathetically waiting for her to find the words. He would have stood there all day and all night if necessary and Kate knew it.

"I'm not in charge anymore. I'm not a person who decides things . . ." She fumbled with a lace-edged handkerchief. The doctor looked at her, trying to get her to say more.

"It's just that there's no *me* nowadays, as if I'd lost my personality or something."

He was blank in his lack of comprehension. "I don't know what to say to you except that you must be half cracked. Aren't you a legend for miles around, and as for being in charge, wouldn't you buy and sell the rest of us? They say it was you that thought up that café idea. Bound to be a gold mine."

Kate knew when there was no more to be gained. She thanked the doctor, said that it must be just an attack of nerves over the court case, and told herself again that it was a strange irony that the only one in the whole place who understood what she felt was Patrick O'Neill. She had a very strange dream about Patrick that kept coming back to her because it was so vivid.

She dreamed that she was in Coyne's wood with him and he had taken out a huge shovel and started to dig a great hole.

It was a grave, he said, like one of the mass famine graves and it was for all the people in Mountfern. They should have died over a hundred years back at the time of the Famine, but they had gone on living by mistake. That was why he had come back, to finish the job properly.

In the dream she asked him if anyone would be saved, and he had said only Kate herself could go free. She wasn't from this place to begin with, and so if she ran now, she could go back to where she came from. She had tried to run and had woken in terror with none of the usual joy that a dreamer would feel waking from a dream like that. Because asleep or awake, Kate Ryan would never run through the wood, and she kept seeing Patrick's face smiling sympathetically at her. He seemed to be across a room as he smiled. A courtroom.

Michael and Dara walked quickly across the bridge.

They told each other they had better hurry to Leonard's to buy exercise books and pencils for tomorrow. They ran past the presbytery and up Bridge Street. They weren't really hurrying to buy their stationery, they wanted to be over the bridge before the thoughts started to come, as they always did.

And because in their different ways they wanted to think about the tunnel.

Dara thought that if Michael had taken Grace there, then she too could have used it. It made her furious to think that this was why she had lost Kerry O'Neill, because she wouldn't trust him, she wouldn't love him properly. And she had wanted to so very much. Why hadn't she told Michael ages ago that she would take Kerry to the tunnel?

There it would all have been safe and it would have been like a home.

Grace and Michael obviously thought so, she told herself bitterly, remembering the sofa piled with cushions.

Michael had thought they would never leave the tunnel. Everywhere he could see signs of Grace and he being there together. It was astonishing that Dara hadn't noticed. But what was alarming him much more was what he had seen. The cushions on the sofa like that —he and Grace hadn't put them there, and there was a rug that didn't belong to them. There were matches and some orange peel.

Somebody else had been in the tunnel.

He could not believe that Grace would have told anyone else. And it wasn't possible to believe that she might have been there with anyone else.

Jim Costello spoke briefly to Brian Doyle.

He said he knew O'Neill's demand to have the rooms ready was ridiculous, but for God's sake let Doyle not forget who was paying their salaries.

"He's more nervous about the bloody court case than he is about sinking his whole fortune in the hotel," Jim said wonderingly.

"Wouldn't you think he'd have more sense?" Brian had little time for finer feelings.

"In a way I can see what he means. The whole place is waiting eagerly to know what will happen. If Kate Ryan doesn't get enough, the mood will turn against him fast. It won't be easy for him to carry on here."

"Ah, that's only a small problem compared to the troubles he has with his family life . . ."

Jim hadn't gotten where he was by being a gossip. "I don't know much about that, I only see the work side of him."

"You do in your arse. You know like the rest of us know that his son had a go at his woman, and if the place doesn't go up in fireworks over that, then it never will."

"At least his daughter is no trouble to him," Jim said primly.

Brian knew everything. "I saw you had your eye peeled in that direction. Sound man," he said approvingly.

"She's only a child, but are we going to see your fiancée Peggy at the opening?"

"Probably," Brian muttered without any great enthusiasm.

"Good, make sure she's on the invitation list, they're posting them next week."

"Isn't it a miracle that it's going to open at last?" Brian looked around him in surprise.

"Take that look off your face, Brian, people will think you're surprised it's staying up. That's not good for business."

Kerry was listening carefully to the voice at the other end of the phone.

The lady had told the bank that after all she had made a mistake, the check had not been stolen.

Kerry let out a great sigh of relief. Rachel must have seen that it was pointless.

He had never felt so relieved in his whole life. But the voice on the phone told Kerry that his problems were far from over. They were only starting. There would be no criminal proceedings since the check was no longer deemed stolen. But it was still stopped. It could not be cashed.

Kerry still had to find his thousand pounds.

"It's impossible," he said in a thin unnatural voice.

There was a silence.

Then he was given a proposition. He could do something for them instead. Repay his debt that way.

His whole body strained and his knuckles were white as he waited to hear what they wanted him to do.

It would involve storing some merchandise out of sight in a very safe place. A place that nobody knew about.

Kerry could feel his muscles relaxing. He knew the exact place.

Michael went to the lodge that evening.

Miss Hayes had come back on the excursion train from Dublin, she was showing her materials to Grace.

"I'd make you a dress for the opening, but you'll want something smarter from the shops," Miss Hayes said.

"Why can't you wait till the opening?"

"The ship sails before."

Michael seemed impatient and not anxious to join in the conversation. Grace eventually seemed to understand and went outside with him.

"Did you tell anybody? About the tunnel—did you tell anyone else?" His eyes looked wild.

"Why? What's wrong?"

"I went there today with Dara. She didn't notice we'd been there, but it's all changed, someone else has been there, maybe even sleeping there."

Suddenly it clicked in Grace's mind. Of course that was where Kerry had been spending the nights.

Michael had made her swear she would tell nobody, but she had told Kerry the last time he was home from Donegal. She hadn't thought it mattered. Not Kerry.

Looking at Michael's face she realized it did matter.

"No," Grace said. "Of course I didn't, you told me not to tell anyone, didn't you?"

Dara walked in Coyne's wood. She didn't expect to see him, and she didn't want to see him.

But he was there, as some part of her knew he would be. Because she didn't feel very surprised.

He looked happy and relaxed, not strained as he had been before.

Dara said nothing. She stood there in her yellow and white candy-striped dress with the big artificial yellow rose pinned to it. Mademoiselle Stephanie had given her that when she was leaving France, that and a wink of complicity.

Tomorrow she would go back to school, and this strange summer would be over. There was no birthday party planned for the twins this year. Their party room was a café now, and the date was almost coinciding with their mother's compensation case.

She looked at him levelly.

He put his head on one side and smiled.

Dara would not smile back.

"What is it? Tell me."

"You know. The whole town knows."

"I don't." He was innocent and bewildered.

"Mrs. Fine."

"She's pathetic," he said with scorn. "She is quite pathetic. You know that she fancied my father for years, he got tired of her and now she made . . . Well, it's too much to talk about really."

"No it isn't."

"Well, she made some silly advances toward me, she got all drunk and slobbery, and crying, and saying she loved it here in Mountfern and these are her type of people and why couldn't she stay . . ."

It sounded familiar and likely from Mrs. Fine's conversations with Dara's mother. From what she had overheard and picked up in the past.

"And then she became silly. Well, it's gross, and I had to untangle myself, and put her to bed. I went back the next morning to see that she hadn't done herself in or anything, and I got her breakfast and because I did these uncharacteristically nice things the whole place says I'm sleeping with her."

Dara looked at him. Willing it to be true.

"I mean, Dara, look at me. Am I the kind of guy who would go for a woman of that age, a little tubby Brooklyn Jewess? It's ludicrous."

He was so handsome, he was not the guy to go for a woman old enough to be his mother.

"Are you going to say anything to me or will you stand there all day just repeating accusations?"

"I don't know."

He looked hurt and bewildered.

Dara spoke. "When I was in France I saw these fireflies. I didn't know what they were, they were like little teeny weeny fires in the evening. I asked Madame what they were called. She said *'mouche á feu.'* They used to make me pronounce words so that I'd get it right. I kept saying it, *'Mouche á feu, voici la mouche á feu.'* Firefly, firefly. And I thought of you. I thought of you every time."

He took her in his arms, and she laid her head against his chest. She could hear his heart beating.

Dara spoke almost dreamily. "I found out why we don't have them in Ireland, I asked, and now I know. They're sort of exotic fireflies, and Ireland is too cold and wet and windy for them. They wouldn't survive here. They wouldn't survive at all."

Grimly and with far less pleasure than he thought that he would feel, Patrick O'Neill moved into his hotel. He decided to do it without ceremony, without any marking of the occasion. He would reserve all the festivity for the grand opening.

He moved his own things in and slept a night in the place he had created. He did not sleep well.

All kinds of unwelcome thoughts came to him, dreams, and half dreams. He got up eventually and walked in the moonlight, as he had walked years and years ago it now seemed, when the place was a ruin.

The moon hadn't changed much nor had the river that it shone down on. But everything else had.

Chapter XXII

Olive Hayes left Mountfern exactly the way she wanted to, in dignity and with style but with no razzamatazz.

For four years she had lived quietly in this family, kept their confidences and made no judgments about them. Now she would no longer be part of their lives.

Kerry barely acknowledged her departure.

She had known this would be the case. She was no longer of any use to him. There had been a time when he had been charming, but charm was a currency, no need to spend any of it on Miss Hayes.

She felt a great sense of peace and achievement, and no last-minute regrets about leaving. It was what she had always planned.

Mr. O'Neill's generosity made it possible to come back if things did not work out. She was letting her little house in the town to a young couple with a baby. They paid a small rent and would continue to put that into Sheila Whelan's post office for her.

When Olive Hayes called quietly and decorously to say goodbye to the people in the pub, she had a quick moment with Kate. Unlike most of the place who would have wished her luck in the compensation case, Miss Hayes had a different wish.

"I spent a lot of time, Mrs. Ryan, wondering what to say about this and perhaps I am just an interfering old busybody, but perhaps, being confined to the house, you mightn't realize that Kerry O'Neill is a very dangerous young man."

"Oh Miss Hayes, don't I know it," Kate sighed. "I know only too well how unstable he is. I did my best by sending her to France, but I can't banish the child from her own town forever."

"With respect, it's not that he's unstable, he is very aware of what he is doing and what he wants. He is totally self-centered. Perhaps with the help of God your daughter will see through him."

"Get out there fast to those nuns and start them praying." Kate smiled wanly.

Olive Hayes took her seriously. "When I heard that he would be living in the lodge on his own, I did ask Bernadette to get some prayers said for a special intention."

Kate held her hand for a long moment before Olive Hayes left Mountfern.

It was, as Michael expected, not nearly as easy to see Grace once she was in the hotel. The excitement of the new life, the attention and the fuss kept her busy all the hours that she had free from school.

They had arranged to wave to each other at certain times at night and make mirror flashes across the river.

Michael had worked out "I love you" in Morse code, but Grace said it was endless, and you'd be exhausted working out all the short-long short-longs of it just for one sentence.

Tommy Leonard seemed to understand. "Wasn't it easier before girls?" he said to Michael.

"Like when there was just Adam in the garden of Eden?" Michael laughed.

"No, you know what I mean."

"But you don't have any problems with Jacinta; she's there all the time, living on the other side of the street and everything." Michael was envious.

"It isn't Jacinta I want, you thick oaf."

Grace told Michael that her father was giving her a new dress for the opening. She was to go to Dublin to buy it. She was going to ask for the day off from school. Could Michael come with her and help her choose?

School had reopened and the notion of giving Michael a day off to go shopping with a girl in Dublin was about as acceptable to the authorities as suggesting a trip on a flying saucer.

"Come on, Mike, think of something."

"But it's not just Brother Keane, he'd have to explain to Mom and to Dad and if I went without saying anything to them, Eddie would hear and tell, or Tommy Leonard would. Lord, Grace, we can't just waltz off to Dublin as if we were adults."

"We are adults—in lots of ways." Grace pouted at him.

"Yes, well." Michael reddened, thinking of their last visit to the tunnel. He felt it was official to go there now, now that Dara had given permission. So he was more adventurous in his approach to Grace as a celebration of this.

"Don't be such a mother's boy," she taunted.

That hurt. Especially since it was really his mother he feared most. He had the feeling that she worried about his friendship with Grace. And that she would be astounded to think he would even suggest the shopping trip.

That morning Kate had spoken for the first time to Dara and Michael about the upcoming court case.

She had said that she wanted them to give her all the support they could. What she needed was to know that they wouldn't go around blabbing or being silly about it. That they would be the model of good behavior for just these few days, since the eyes of Mountfern would be on the whole family for a short time. Some people wished them to get a fortune; some wished them not to get anything significant in case it would prejudice the hotel in any way. But the truth of the matter was that there would be a respectable sum of money which would be placed in a bank for the children's education.

It was all upsetting having to go to court, but what would make it worthwhile was the knowledge that the Ryan children were working hard and would deserve any benefit that might come to them.

She had been quite solemn, and for the first time for a very long while she had sounded sad.

She had said that in many ways her own life was over, and that this was not something to feel bitter about; people's lives ended in different ways. But it would all have a meaning if her children were to be strong and to have a bit of class when faced with the wagging tongues and overexcitement of a small parish.

Michael and Dara had promised that they would not let her down.

Going to Dublin midweek on a train, telling Brother Keane a pack of lies—that would be letting her down.

Michael said he couldn't go and help Grace choose a dress.

Grace said that was all right, then, she might ask Jim Costello was he going to drive to Dublin anytime soon, she could get a ride in his car. Michael wasn't to give it another thought.

The District Court sat every week in the town, and cases that were of a higher jurisdiction or that were appealed were heard when the Circuit Court came four times a year for a period of three weeks each time.

At one stage there was a judge who had been interested in fishing who had driven out to the Fern each evening after the summer sessions and sat on his little stool looking for all the world like an old tramp. He and Fergus Slattery's father had struck up a friendship without either ever knowing the other was involved in the law, so great was their interest in the fish that swam the Fern and the methods of taking them out of the river.

Nowadays, with better roads and better train services, the barristers and judges didn't spend long in the town. They rarely came as far as Mountfern.

Kate and John Ryan were surprised to see Kevin Kennedy come into the pub the night before the case.

"Fergus didn't say you were coming," Kate said, flustered.

She moved the wheelchair in her quick agile way back over the ramp, and they beckoned him into her big green room. How right it had been to make this room into a proper sitting place for her. Seeing that she was going to sit for the rest of her days it made it much more bearable to sit in pleasant surroundings and not to apologize for wherever you were.

John got Mary to take over his place pulling pints. Most of the clientele would know who Kevin Kennedy was anyway and what it was about.

"Good luck and get them a fortune," said one man as Kevin squeezed his way past the counter.

"Luck is exactly what it's about," he said, turning around, "it has not a thing to do with what people deserve, or they would get a king's ransom."

His serious voice startled the drinkers. They had expected some sort of joky answer.

"Fergus doesn't even know I'm here . . ." he began when they were in the room.

"Well, don't you think maybe . . . ." John began.

"No, no, I'm on my way to him, it's just that we've had an offer. A firm offer. Six thousand pounds. A yes or a no. That's what they say."

"Yes," said Kate.

"We must ask Fergus," said John.

"What do *you* think?" Kate asked John.

"I don't know what to think. We could go into court and fight all day and come out with less but the fact they offer it at all twenty-four hours before the case means they think it might go further against them."

Kevin Kennedy looked from one to another.

There weren't many consultations on his cases, usually it was a matter of working straight from the brief, from the case to advice. But when he had met the people involved in their houses, he had often felt his city prejudices against country people were confirmed. They were so often inarticulate, and often grasping. This time it was different. There was a gentle pace of life that he liked in Mountfern; there was a graciousness about this couple and their handsome dark-eyed children whom he had seen briefly.

There was a sense of repressed energy about the crippled Kate Ryan that gave her more life than most women who were able to walk and run. She was quick, opinionated and impatient, and she had had a long hard lesson in having to learn that she must lean on others. He liked the husband too. All very genial and easygoing on the outside, but he had a logical reasoning mind. Fergus Slattery had said the man was a poet too, in a small way.

He felt involved with these people in a way he hadn't felt involved for a long time. He had been through every case reported: the factory worker who only this year had been awarded £3,000. The sum had been based on his earnings, and how much more he could have expected. He had been twenty-eight, he had lost an eye. Everyone had accepted that £3,000 was fair; he had been earning £14 a week.

There was an agricultural laborer in his mid forties. His injuries were terrible even to read about. He got £7,000. His case had included the plea that he would never be able to marry and have a family. The award was considered high. There was that woman who had spent four months in the special hospital in England. Her barristers had proved such mental anguish, the compensation was £7,000.

They were looking at him, as if he should know. And he didn't know. He couldn't tell them either what was fair or what would happen.

"It's very tempting to say that we'll take it," Kate said. "It's so tempting that I have to think it's the wrong decision."

John had his hand on hers as he spoke. "It would be such an easy way to finish it off. To say we'll take it and put it in the bank for the children to go to university maybe, or for rainy days which may well come this way." He nodded his head across in the direction of Fernscourt, and Kevin Kennedy remembered the danger to their small business from the new hotel.

"So you'd like to refuse it . . . ?"

"I think we shouldn't accept it too readily," John said. "I know that sounds like sitting on the fence . . . I'm not a gambling man, and I'm not in the world of doing deals or bargaining, but I have this feeling you shouldn't accept the first offer. Am I right?"

Kevin was about to say there was no need to accept anything now as there would undoubtedly be time to do so tomorrow, but Kate spoke first.

"I'm sure you know how much more than just a mere solicitor Fergus has been to us. It's as if his own spine were broken." She spoke clearly and without any sense of drama. She just wanted to be sure he understood how important the tall gangling country lawyer was in their lives.

"Yes, of course, of course," he murmured.

"So I suppose you will bring him in on this, won't you, and ask him what he thinks we should do. I don't think John and I should really make any decision without Fergus being here."

"Of course. I just wanted to get a gut reaction. Sometimes a surplus of lawyers can confuse people rather than help."

"Did you get a gut reaction?" Kate asked.

"Yes. You'd take anything, Mrs. Ryan, anything not to have to face a court. It's your back, it's your legs, we should listen to you. Your husband is aware of all this, but he's thinking about what you'll both feel years from now, and trying to take that into account. I'm with Mr. Ryan, but then, it didn't happen to me."

Fergus said, as they knew he would say, that it was not enough.

Kevin Kennedy said that it was about what they could hope for from the jury.

Dr. White said that was a lot of money, he had many patients with broken bodies after car accidents and they hadn't got a third of that.

Fergus said that they were dealing with multimillionaires here, big foreign international companies with coffers of money which they guarded like misers and wouldn't give out to the people that were struck down and obviously deserving it.

John said that he knew he was a cautious man but wouldn't six thousand pounds go a very long way, and buy them everything they ever needed? And since no money would buy Kate the chance of walking again, then maybe they should take this now and be done with it. But, then . . .

Kate sat very still as they talked.

They leaned over to make a point; they interrupted each other. Four men all wanting the best for her, and coming at it in their different ways. She felt curiously detached from it. As if up in the air looking down at them, the doctor, the solicitor, the barrister and the publican.

They talked themselves out at around the same time, and they all looked at her.

"It's up to you in the end, Kate. Whatever you say, that's what we'll do."

She looked slowly around the little group.

"Fight," she said. "I think we owe it to the children to do this for them. Let's fight to the finish."

Kevin Kennedy said that he was going to spend the night in Mountfern. He had heard there was a delightful old-world place called the Grange. Everyone exchanged glances. What was wrong with it? He wanted to know. Nothing, it was just that Patrick O'Neill stayed there.

"He's moved," Kate said. "He went into the hotel."

This surprised the others, but then Kate always knew everything ahead of most people.

"That's fine then." Kevin Kennedy was businesslike. "I'll give them a call. If our friend Mr. O'Neill has moved out, that's all right, then."

It was a sunny morning.

"I don't know whether that makes it better or worse," Kate said.

John had slept on the divan bed in her room. Not that either of them slept very much. He had gotten up to make tea twice. He pulled back the curtains over the glass doors to reveal Leopold sitting mournfully outside.

"If that animal lets as much as the smallest yowl out of him, I'll kill him with my own bare hands," Kate said.

Leopold seemed to sense the danger. He raised his front paw hopefully, as if someone might shake hands with him through the closed door.

She looked sleepy and anxious.

John stood beside her bed. "Could you get another hour if I closed off the light again, and left you in peace?"

"No, no. I'm too jumpy."

"So am I. I can neither stand, sit, nor lie."

"What are you going to do?" She saw him pulling on a jumper over the shirt he had worn the previous day. He obviously wasn't going to get washed and ready for the court at this early hour.

"I don't know. I feel trapped in here, somehow."

Something in her face made him realize how trapped Kate must feel all the time.

"Not that I'm going to go out or anything," he said hastily.

"Take me out too."

"It's only halfpast six in the morning."

"Come on, we'll go for a walk."

He dressed her, and she slid into her chair. Quietly they let themselves out the front door of the pub—they didn't go through the backyard for fear of waking Mary Donnelly.

The river was glorious in the September early morning. Leopold trotted with them, delighted with the chance of an early-morning outing but staying at a respectful distance.

Up past the Rosemarie hair salon, its pink curtains drawn firmly.

"Do you think she's still at it?" John asked.

Kate laughed. "Not at all, she's far too busy getting ready for American hairstyles, she even has books on how to do it so that they'd like it."

"Oh, she always knew how to do it so that they'd like it," John said. "They tell me of course, I wouldn't know from any personal experience."

And as they came back again to the footbridge and the day was about to begin for everyone else, they stopped and looked over at Fernscourt.

They could see Patrick O'Neill in his shirt sleeves at one of the windows on the first floor.

"It's a hard day for him too," Kate said.

They looked across the river to the dock, up the path with its rockeries and shrubs leading to the great sweep where the drive came in. They looked at the steps up to the big house, the bedroom wings fanning back on either side, the workmen beginning to arrive in twos and threes.

And they saw Patrick standing still at his window.

He must have seen them too.

But because it was the day that it was, nobody waved at anyone else.

Rachel was coming to get Kate dressed.

They had been such friends for so long that nobody saw anything remotely odd about this merging of both sides of the case.

They had several differences of opinion about what she should wear with the simple gray-and-white dress which had been ironed by Carrie, and then done again by Dara, and finally given a going over by Mary.

Rachel said no lady could be seen without gloves. Kate said only the gentry wore gloves around here.

Rachel said a little eye shadow made Kate look much more attractive. Kate said that a country jury would think eye shadow meant she was the whore of Babylon.

"Stop making people into yokels, Kate, this is the sixties; they all move with the times here like everywhere else."

Kate said she wasn't going to risk it. She had promised Fergus she would look demure.

They were ready far too early.

Rachel tried to distract her with tales that didn't have any bearing on what was about to happen.

That was harder to do than she had imagined. Almost all her conversation was related to Patrick or to his hotel.

"Grace is going to Dublin for the day," she said, thinking this might be a fairly neutral road to go down.

"Don't I know!" Kate exclaimed. "My poor Michael is distraught over it all. I told him that it was very vain of Grace to go miles and miles to buy *another* new dress when she has trunks of them, but that was the wrong thing to say. No criticism of the lady."

"Princess Grace," Rachel said.

"She *is* a bit of a madam, isn't she? But I'm prejudiced. Anyone who could lead Michael Ryan any kind of dance should be in the darkest hob of hell in my view."

"Perhaps she'll not get anywhere with the young hotel manager." Rachel smiled at the wonderful partisan nature of Kate's reactions.

"I'd prefer if she tired of Michael, really, and did it soon, so that both the twins could get over these glittering young O'Neills sooner rather than later."

"Yes, we'd all be better if we had gotten over the O'Neills early in life," Rachel said bitterly.

Rachel looked very sad, and for the first time since Kate had known her she thought that her friend looked old. The life had gone out from her face. And when that vivacity wasn't there for all to see, there were lines instead, lines that looked quite deep.

She took Rachel's hand in hers and stroked it silently for a moment. She hardly trusted herself to speak in case she said the wrong thing or that she started to cry.

"Stop it, quite enough self-pity," Rachel said. "It's your day of woe today, not mine. Do you feel all right?"

"Yes, Dr. White gave me something to calm me down. I feel fine."

"Have you been to the lavatory?"

"Yes, *and* I've hardly had food or drink pass my lips so I should be all right."

They talked to each other through the mirror, each seeing the reflection of the other. It wasn't quite the same as talking face to face. You could be more indiscreet.

"Kate?"

"Yes?"

"He wants you to get a lot, you know that. He was delighted you refused the offer. He says . . ."

"No . . . please, no."

"You're my friend, you'll always be my friend, even when I'm an old lady in a home in Flatbush."

"Of course I will."

"When he's married to somebody with ten saints' names who had the good fortune to come from this one-horse town . . ."

"Rachel . . ."

"What loyalty do I owe him? He says you shouldn't take any less . . ."

The chair spun around. Kate's eyes were blazing.

"No, do you hear me, *no*. You must stop. If there's going to be any dignity, anything saved from this circus and farce that I'm heading off to, then the only way is to do it honestly . . ."

"I wasn't going to . . ."

"Yes you were, you were going to tell me what his side are prepared to go to. I can't know that, don't you see that? I must never know what they're willing to give."

"It's just because you're my friend. I wanted the best for you," Rachel cried, still bewildered by the intensity of it all.

Kate's voice lowered. "I *know* you mean well, but can't you see, if I have any hope at all of living what passes as a normal life with this man as my neighbor across the river, with my son head over heels with his daughter . . . with us depending on him for our custom from his hotel . . . then how would I feel if I had seen his hand?"

"He's on your side, that's all I was saying."

"I know, I know. Now please, can I beg you to say no more than that. Now, Rachel Fine, can you kiss me goodbye and good luck?"

Rachel bent to kiss her in the chair. She put her arms around Kate and laid her cheek against Kate's thin cheek.

"May you always have the best of all possible things and even things that are impossible," she said in a shaky voice.

"Haven't I you as a great good friend? That's worth a lot to me," Kate said as she maneuvered her chair to the door.

John and Dr. White were waiting for her in the pub, Fergus and Kevin Kennedy would be already at the courthouse.

Rachel stood in the green room after Kate had gone. She didn't know if this was praying or not, but she went to the mournful picture of the Madonna, one she had chosen herself because there were a lot of green and blue hues in it and it went with the room.

She stood in front of it and looked into the big sad eyes of the picture.

"Please don't let them cheat her, don't let them talk her into a cheap deal. Go on, please. It's not much to ask. There are thousands of good things and bad things happening all over the place today. Let this be a good one for Kate Ryan. Please."

The morning was hot and heavy. Dara's mind would not stay on parsing.

"Come on, Dara, wake up. Subordinate adverbial clause modifying what?"

"What, Sister?"

"What is it modifying?"

"I'm not sure, Sister Laura."

"You might be a lot surer if you looked at the book instead of outside the window, it isn't written in letters of fire on the Dublin Road. The clause, for your information, reads . . . Come *on* Dara, this is very simple if you just concentrate."

"I know, Sister." The girl's face looked wretched.

Sister Laura knew all about the case that was coming to court today.

"There's no better way of taming the language than this. You'll know forever how sentences are constructed." The nun's round face was eager to help the white-faced child.

"Who else knows . . . ?" Sister Laura decided to take the attention away from Dara Ryan.

"Sister! Sister!" A few of them waved their hands.

Sister Laura looked around the classroom to choose, and her eye fell on the empty seat where Grace O'Neill normally sat. The child had gone to Dublin for the day. Her father had asked permission.

"Grace will say she has to see the doctor. That's not true, she's going to buy a dress. But it's not as frivolous as it seems, Sister Laura. I want her to be out of Mountfern on the day of the compensation case, so I asked the young manager to invent an excuse to take her. It would be more diplomatic. More sensitive."

He had been right, of course. He was a very good man. Not just because he had given them the money for the school hall or all that extra material for curtains that the Jewish lady had delivered. But he really was kind and out for people's good. Sister Laura couldn't bear it when she heard people speaking badly of him. It was only envy, envy of a man who had done so well and come home to spend his money where his father had been nobody. She knew that if the compensation had been up to him, he'd have given the Ryans all they ever needed. But of course it would have been very hard to live with for them, knowing that it was his charity.

Sister Laura's eyes turned to the holy picture which hung in the classroom, Our Lady of the Wayside. She looked into the sad eyes of Our Lady and made a quick prayer that she would ask her Son to give proper compensation to the Ryans. Then she said that she would parse the sentence herself and would like the entire class to give their undivided attention.

Brother Keane had warned them not to trifle with him today; he had a toothache. Nothing that was bad enough to mean he had to leave his charges and go into the town to the dentist, but certainly something that was bad enough to remind him of its existence every waking moment. He felt it was only fair to the boys to apprise them of this fact.

Michael wondered again and again where Grace and Jim Costello would be now. There had been no difficulty in her getting off school and she had said they were going to set out early.

Michael had cycled across the Grange early to wish her a good trip;

she had come down the stairs all dressed up in a yellow flowery dress he had never seen before. She looked as fresh as a daisy.

"You look terrific," he had said. "You don't need a new frock at all. Wouldn't that be lovely for the hotel opening?"

It had been the wrong thing to say. Still, she had been pleased he had cycled all that way to see her. She kissed him without his suggesting it. Just put both her arms around his neck and stood on tiptoe to kiss him, and at that moment Jim Costello's car had pulled up.

"I know we swore we wouldn't talk about the case," she whispered to Michael.

"I know." He swallowed.

"But whatever happens we'll still be as we are. And I hope your Mom gets a lot, I really do."

Something in the way she said it made him feel put out. But perhaps it was the fact of that awful Jim Costello with his sickening smile sitting waiting for her. That must have been what it was.

The classroom was airless. A dying wasp beat uselessly against the window. Even if it got out, it wouldn't last another hour. Michael wondered if he should finish it off now with his ruler.

Brother Keane was looking at him. Did he imagine it or was there some sympathy in the teacher's swollen face?

Today they were doing an exercise which the class hated more than anything. Brother Keane would ask them to speak on any topic for one minute. There were to be no ems or ahs. There was to be no fooling around or imitating the speaker. The brothers hoped it would make the boys more articulate and able to express themselves. The boys hated it, and though never short of a word in the playground, they were struck dumb when asked to speak in front of the class.

"Michael Ryan. Give us the benefit of your knowledge and experience of the pike, a fish which abounds in our River Fern."

There was a snort around the room. Either this was a trick question of Brother Keane's or else he was going soft. The pike was dead easy to talk about; they'd all been fishing for pike since they were old enough to be allowed near the water.

"What would you want to know about it, Brother?" Michael's face was anxious. "There's so many ways to start."

"Well, kindly choose one, and don't hold up the class anymore." Brother Keane's hand was on his face.

"Well, like any fish the pike needs oxygen, not for its lungs because they don't have human lungs or animal lungs even; they don't have any lungs to speak of. Not lungs as we'd know them."

"Could you tell us what they do have instead of what they don't, please. Start again."

"Pike have to take in water through their mouths, and in that water there's a bit of oxygen like there is in the air. And they let it out the gills. But that's what all fish do. So what's different about the pike? The pike has a bad reputation like a wolf has in the animal kingdom. They say he preys on the other fish and lies in wait for them in the reeds on the river bank. But in a way that's all to the good because a pike is carrying out a function; he's making the river bed a cleaner better place. It's his nature to go for what he can. It's only ignorance, really, to condemn the pike; we'd all be pike if we could, and the world might be a better place if there were more pike in it ready to go out and scavenge for themselves."

The boy's face was red and angry. Nobody had said a word against the pike. Not ever, to Brother Keane's knowledge.

Out in the yard earlier, Brother Keane had heard voices raised about the court case which was being decided at this very moment.

The boy was said to be very friendly with the daughter of the house, and it was probably a question of divided loyalties.

Brother Keane liked Michael Ryan. Compared to his younger brother, Eddie, he was like the Archangel Gabriel.

"That's very informative and well explained," he said, to the mystification of the class. "Now Tommy Leonard, may we have your discourse please on the benefits of the Rural Electrification Scheme."

"Ah, God, Brother, that's much harder than pike," said Tommy Leonard, who had been discovering that life was very far from fair.

Mrs. Daly asked Rita Walsh when there would be any news from the court house.

But Marian Johnson answered first, she said that it could be anytime from eleven in the morning on. It might be settled outside without their having to go in. She knew this from the highest authority. A Mr. Kennedy, who was representing the Ryans, had stayed in the Grange last night. A very pleasant man, from Dublin. He was going to spend a second night there no matter what the outcome. He said it was too far to drive back to Dublin, and the Grange was exactly the kind of place he had always wanted to stay in but never come across.

Marian patted her hair reflectively and Rita Walsh sensed another reason to bring Miss Johnson and her thin flyaway hair back on a regular basis to the Rosemarie hair salon.

* * *

Canon Moran and Father Hogan had been asked by several parishioners to pray for a special intention. And indeed to offer Mass for that intention. Nowhere had the intention been defined.

The priests agreed that it must have to do with the court case, and that one side definitely wanted the Ryans to get a great deal of money and the others wanted them to get very little in case it would somehow offend O'Neill.

"It's a poser, isn't it?" Young Father Hogan had said.

"Not at all, we will just pray that justice will be done in the courts today. That covers it all," said Canon Moran, who had lived a very long time and understood almost everything.

"I'd better leave you and stop hiding here in this nice quiet place." Sheila Whelan had drained the teapot.

"It *is* a nice quiet place. You were very good to settle me here." Mary Donnelly spoke gruffly in her gratitude.

"Wasn't it lucky they got you, just when they needed someone? They'd never have survived without you."

Mary hardly remembered that summer and its shock and sadness now. She rarely thought of the man who had let her down so badly. Even when she was condemning men in general, the face of this one did not come easily to mind.

Sergeant Sheehan passed by as the women came out into the sunshine.

"Starting early, Sheila," he said jokily.

"Lord, I've been discovered," she laughed.

She looked thoughtful when he had gone.

"What is it?" Mary noticed her face.

"I don't know, I was tempted to talk to him there about something, but I can see I'm getting as bad as the rest of them."

"What was it?"

"Probably nothing, but I saw a lot of activity over on the towpath. You know, beyond the bridge on the other side of the river. Lights in the middle of the night over there, and banging about."

"What on earth were *you* doing on the towpath in the middle of the night?"

Sheila had been walking because she couldn't sleep.

She had heard that Joe had died. The nurse had let her know quietly, as she had asked.

She would go to no funeral in Dublin, nor would she tell anyone but Kate Ryan of his death.

Still, it had been impossible to close her own eyes, knowing that Joe Whelan was lying in the mortuary of that Dublin hospital where they had all been so kind to him, and where presumably his woman would recover enough to go and pay her respects, and three of his four children would be with her. The fourth mightn't dare come back from England in case he faced charges.

It had been too hard to try to sleep, so she had walked instead.

"Oh, you know me, Mary, I'm as odd as two left shoes."

"Maybe you imagined it," Mary said.

"Maybe I did," said Sheila.

Fergus felt his hands shaking when he started to shave, so he had put down the razor immediately. He didn't need to come to the court spattered with blood. He wondered what would make them steadier. He thought absently of a small brandy and port; his father used to take that concoction sometimes when he had what was called a chill.

But Fergus rejected it. Warming and steadying it might be, but very soon he might need one every day before shaving, even before getting out of bed.

By the time he was ready to leave the house, his hands had calmed down. He'd done a magnificent job on his face, he thought, not a nick anywhere, and he tied a firm knot on his dark gray tie.

He knew that Kevin Kennedy would barely comb his hair, and yet here was he—the poor country solicitor, an unimportant figure—titivating himself like a peacock. Like a medieval champion going to battle wearing his lady's favors.

God, let him be right, urging them to go on. Kevin Kennedy had said to him a dozen times that it was impossible to know with country juries, but then Kevin was a city man who always feared the country and was never at ease when milk didn't come from bottles and when land didn't mean small manicured gardens.

Fergus gave a wan wave across the street to Sheila Whelan before he climbed into his car and drove to the town. He knew she was the one person in Mountfern who would have the tact not to wish him luck as if it was all a bet on the two-thirty.

Please God let them get twelve thousand pounds. A sum that would see them right for the next fifteen years, until the 1980s. Let them get that. Let Kate know no more anxiety and fear.

* * *

Kate sat in the car looking out calmly left and right as they drove the straight road into the town. The September countryside was beautiful this year, it had been a good summer but not too dry. They passed through villages as small as Mountfern, but places with somehow more importance because they were on the main road. Of course, that would all change soon. Already there were new signposts; they wouldn't be a little Midlands outpost for much longer.

"I should come out driving with you more," she said to John, who frowned furiously at the road. "You went to all that trouble to learn to drive for me, and I hardly ever get into the car with you. From now on we're going to have grand drives together, the two of us."

Martin White said gruffly that he hoped they'd be able to afford a better car than this one when the day's work was finished.

"I never thought of getting a new car, did you, John?" Kate was startled at the very idea.

"Lord, not at all, isn't this one fine for us and whatever we want to do in it?"

"Well, what will you do with the money?" Martin White had known them long enough and well enough to ask that question.

"The future, the children . . ."

"Shore the place up a bit . . ."

"Try to keep the business we have . . ."

"And maybe attract a few of the nobs that come to the place across the river."

Suddenly they both laughed.

"We're like the twins," Kate said, wiping her eyes.

They were driving up to the steps of the courthouse.

It was a big ugly building. Neither John nor Kate had ever been in it. Dr. White said he had, a few times, and it was the most disappointing place you ever saw. From outside it was all pillars and steps and looked very imposing. But inside you wouldn't give it the time of day.

The Garda station was attached to one end, and the library to the other, so most people had some kind of knowledge of bits of the building anyway.

It was right slap in the middle of the town, otherwise, they might have been able to pull it down and build something more suitable. Nobody would regret its passing; it was no national monument. It came from a time when justice was administered by the English anyway, so nobody would have any sentimental attachment to it.

But to take down the courthouse would mean dismantling the town. It would also mean losing the only landmark. "I'll meet you on the courthouse steps" was as good a way of making sure you'd find someone in the crowded narrow streets as any other. The bus stop was opposite the courthouse. There were always a few people gathered on its steps, most of them having nothing at all to do with the business of law and justice.

But today they recognized a few people who had to do with their own case.

Mike Coyne, a cousin of Jack who worked on the local newspaper. Two of the hospital staff who would have been called as witnesses. And parked right at the bus stop where he was certain to be moved on was Fergus.

Fergus stood beside his car like a soldier on point duty. He could hardly believe it when John Ryan drove Kate and Dr. White into his sight and all three of them were laughing aloud, as if they hadn't a care or a worry in the world.

People stood around in little clusters. Kate's wheelchair was taken without fuss from the back of the car and moved up to where she was sitting. Gracefully and without making any big production out of it, she slid from one seat to the other. She looked at ease in her chair.

She had been told that there were seventeen steps up to the courthouse door, and there were two choices: either two strong men lifted the chair with her in it—Dr. White and John would do that—or else she could go in a back way through damp long corridors.

She said she preferred the back way. It would be too nerve racking for those carrying and those watching. And she said that somebody should write a letter to the local paper on the lack of facilities for wheelchairs.

They headed toward the back door.

But they didn't get there. Down the steps at a fast pace came two men, the Dublin solicitor and a local man; more men followed—one was in robes, a barrister—and behind him Kevin Kennedy, also in robes.

Fergus felt his heart turn over and realized there had been a last-minute offer.

"Wait for a moment," he called in a strangled voice to the little procession with the wheelchair.

"Is anything wrong?" Kate asked, turning around.

John narrowed his eyes. "It's Mr. Kennedy, he seems to want to talk to us."

"Oh, Jesus, let them not have an adjournment," said Dr. White, who had often made it known that he had little respect for lawyers.

Far far away, it seemed, Patrick O'Neill stood by himself at the other side of the wide steps.

Kate thought it was strange for him to be alone, she had so many people with her. Then who would have come? Grace was at school, Rachel was back in Ryan's pub, and Kerry? Who knew where he would be?

Patrick looked nervous and very much alone. She longed to call out to him. She wished she could send him a message saying his own words back to him, telling him that they would always be friends. It was as he had told her, a formality that was necessary to maintain their friendship.

But she couldn't speak. And anyway they were coming toward her, her side. Kevin Kennedy, and Fergus. Their faces were impassive. Neither of them spoke; they each looked at the other.

"You say it, Fergus," Kevin Kennedy said, standing back a little to give the stage to Fergus Slattery.

"They have made a suggestion." Fergus felt his voice was very thin.

"Yes, Fergus, and what do you think?" John asked.

"What do they say?" Kate was calm.

"They say eight thousand pounds," Fergus said in a voice that came from a million miles away.

"Eight thousand pounds." John said the words.

"Two thousand pounds more than they said yesterday," Kevin Kennedy said, as a further explanation.

"My goodness," said Kate.

There was a silence.

Behind Fergus and Kevin, the other side stood in a little group. Patrick was still at a distance from them. He was not joining in.

Kevin Kennedy spoke then. "As your counsel, I can only give you my opinion, you do not have to take it. You do understand that, Kate?"

He hadn't called her Mrs. Ryan. Nobody noticed.

"Yes indeed, and what do you say?"

"I say that you should have a quiet moment with your husband, and ask each other do you believe that you can live with this as fair and reasonable compensation, and if you can, then I will accept it for you."

There was a pause. Nobody moved.

"And if you think that you will always wonder and worry about what you would have gotten if you fought on, then we will fight on."

Almost imperceptibly Fergus, Kevin, and Martin moved away, and John and Kate were left looking at each other.

John bent down and looked into her eyes. They didn't say anything; neither of them said a word, nor did they nod a head. Then after the long look John stood up.

"We'd like to take it," he said simply, his hand in his wife's cold hand.

Fergus let out his breath like a whistle. "You're doing the right thing, I'm sure of it. I'm sure of it," he said happily.

Kevin Kennedy was smiling too. And Martin White.

The little circle was almost unwilling to break up, but Fergus was the one to do it.

"Come on, Kevin, let's go and tell them," he said like a schoolboy.

Kate held John's hand to her cheek. She didn't need to say anything and neither did he. Dr. White was the only one to speak.

"Look, they're coming over," he said, and there, moving first with halting steps, came Patrick O'Neill. But as he got near them he broke into a run.

In the small dark public house behind the courthouse they went to drink a toast. They drank to insurance companies and to justice being done. Kevin had to go back into court as he was in other cases, cases that had not been settled so amicably on the steps.

He shook their hands and said he hoped to meet them again socially, as he was going to spend the rest of the week in the Grange. In fact, it was so infinitely better than the Grand, the Commerical, or the Central. It was fortunate for him that through this case he had discovered the ideal place to come when he was on circuit. He was delighted that everybody was satisfied. That's what barristers actually wanted, despite their reputation as loving the sound of their own voices.

And Fergus told himself that £8,000 was almost what he had wanted for them, so near that it made no difference. It was worth so much not to have poor Kate go through all that ordeal she had been dreading.

And Dr. White was quite forthcoming for him, and told stories of cases way back where he had been called as an expert witness.

John noted that this pub would not survive if it hadn't been lucky enough to be so well positioned right behind the courts, the library, the county council offices, and the barracks. It had shabby scored tables, and torn dirty linoleum, but it was in the right place. He found his mind straying and hoping that Ryan's Licensed Premises was really in the right place, that it would really get all this extra business that had been promised. He didn't want to worry Kate with it, not now, not for a long time until she had gotten over the trauma of all this.

He looked at her sitting there with them all. Nobody who came in would know she was in a wheelchair; she looked a handsome lively woman, her head thrown back; laughing at some silly tale the doctor was telling. They were all half hysterical with relief that it was over.

Patrick was in high good form too. He resisted the urge to keep buying drinks for everyone and waited instead while the doctor went to the counter or Slattery threw a ten-pound note on the tray of the boy in the dirty apron who was serving them. They were all so happy, so relieved that it was over. He knew he had to go along with the good will and the delight. Because it could do nothing but harm and destruction if he were to let them know that Kate Ryan hadn't gotten half enough for her compensation. The insurance companies were prepared to go to £12,000 outside the court, and even to £14,000 as soon as the case began.

At £8,000 they thought they had gotten away very lightly indeed. But Patrick knew that if this were ever known it would destroy everything he had tried so hard to build.

And of course it wasn't known. It wasn't the kind of thing that the insurance companies would ever reveal. Instead it was reported with excitement in Mountfern. It was quite possibly the exact sum of money that pleased everyone. It was large enough to seem like a sum you look at in the bank and consider yourself a family of substance, which the Ryans would never have been able to do under any other circumstances. But it was not so large it sounded like a punishment. As the news filtered through Mountfern, heads nodded with satisfaction. Even the Dalys, who had always said that anyone could be hit at any time by a bulldozer and that it was a scandal to go suing that good man who was such a benefactor, could find no reason to condemn the settlement. Even Jack Coyne, who said O'Neill should be hounded to the ends of the earth to prove he couldn't go around throwing his weight and machinery into the citizens of this place, had to stop his tirade.

By anyone's standards, including Jack Coyne's, £8,000 was a lot of money.

Sheila Whelan was one of the first to visit Kate.

"You must be so glad it's all over," she said. As always, she had said exactly the right thing and struck the note that Kate wanted to hear. There were no congratulations offered, nor curious questions on how the huge sum of money was going to be spent. Kate was grateful to sit and talk to her.

"There'll be a procession through shortly, I'll leave you alone," Sheila said. "You'll want to talk to everyone else."

"No, I will not. I feel like issuing a bulletin and sticking it up outside over the fuchsias there, saying Mrs. Ryan would like to thank all the inquirers . . ."

"Sit out in the pub, I'd advise, then you won't have to have heart-to-hearts with people, and if anyone you really want to talk to comes, you can come back in here." There was a look of strain around the postmistress's eyes.

"Did anything happen?" Kate asked.

"Not now, I'll tell you all about it again."

"Is it bad?"

"No, it's all over now."

"Oh Sheila." They sat in silence. The sympathy was so great, there were no words for it. A man who walked out and who only wanted to come back when he was on his deathbed. Such things couldn't be mourned in formal ways. They had to remain unsaid.

Sheila had been right; the procession did go on all day. Rita Walsh was in, delighted at the news, overjoyed that it was all over, wondering should they invest it in something that a gentleman friend of hers had told her about. It was like a syndicate and you all put in so much and there was hardly any risk, and people had been known to double their investment in a year. Rita could get the details. Kate told her that she herself would like nothing better but unfortunately John was an old stick-in-the-mud. Rita sympathized over the dullness of husbands in general and said that the offer of advice was always there if Kate needed it. A woman has to look to herself, Rita advised sagely.

Kate couldn't meet John's eye as he pretended not to be listening; she was terrified they would break out laughing.

Canon Moran and Father Hogan came in together. They said they were out taking a little constitutional and good news of the happy outcome had reached them. They wanted to say how very pleased they were that God's justice had been done, and it was a wonderful example of how patience and resignation to the will of the Lord was often rewarded, even on this earth.

At least, Canon Moran did all the speaking. Father Hogan looked in disbelief at the trays of currant bread and scones that he saw on the counter. The rehearsals for the Shamrock Café were well under way. There were tables and chairs already in position, and any day now it would be ready to go. John had decided on no big opening ceremony, just let it creep on people.

Father Hogan's pink round face was alight with excitement. "We'll be able to come by here regularly on our constitutional, Canon," he said, as Kate was murmuring that out of their very generous compensation she and John were most anxious to make a small contribution to the needs of the parish. It had been a highly satisfactory visit for the clergy.

Dara heard on the way out of the convent. Jacinta White told her.

"Eight *thousand* pounds. You'll be the quality now." Jacinta sniffed.

"Don't make jokes like that." Dara could hardly take in the amount.

"It's not really a joke, you'll be as good as anyone already."

"We were always as good as anyone."

Jimbo Doyle rang Carrie to tell her.

"I know already, they're all here celebrating," she said.

"Will I come and bring my guitar?" asked Jimbo.

"I don't think they're celebrating *that* much," Carrie said firmly.

Miss Purcell, who was now happily installed in the presbytery looking after the canon and Father Hogan, dropped a note into her old employer, Fergus Slattery. She said that she was delighted that he had been able to get so much money for Mrs. Ryan and her family, and that his late father would have been proud of him. Miss Purcell added primly that money wasn't everything, but she was sure that the

Ryans would use what they got wisely, and perhaps Fergus could tell them about the damp that was seeping through at the Sacred Heart Altar since good people to whom much had been given were often anxious to give some of it back to God at the earliest opportunity.

Michael and Tommy were walking out of the schoolyard when they heard. Tommy was still complaining about the unfairness of teachers. Brother Keane had now in fact succumbed and been taken to the town to visit the dentist by a delivery man who thought he had been bringing boxes of notebooks, pens and other stationery supplies to the brothers, not taking one of the brothers with a swollen face off to a dentist.

One of the younger lads came running up.

"Your Ma got a fortune," he shouted.

Michael felt his stomach constrict.

"Eight thousand pounds," shouted the young fellow, delighted to be the one who brought the news.

"That's all right," Tommy said. "That's about what they said would be fair—in our house."

Patrick had told the Ryans that he would come in later for a drink, he had a few things to attend to in the hotel first. He had clasped their hands warmly, and any reserve that might have been between them was now gone.

Back in his office, he sat with a curiously empty feeling at his desk. For once there were no interruptions; most times he had never been able to have a full five minutes without some crisis. But today nobody came near him. Brian Doyle had said that he heard it was a fair settlement and Patrick had agreed.

The sour taste in his mouth just wouldn't go. Last night he had wanted to offer £12,000 and had been told very sharply that it wasn't up to him to offer anything.

"Let me add to it, secretly," he had asked.

They wouldn't hear of it. A claim had to be settled and be seen to be settled. It was not fair on other insurers if Patrick was going to play Father Christmas with awards.

If the Ryans were known to have received something way above what they would expect and were about to accept, then would not all other claimants have similar expectations?

There was nothing to stop Patrick O'Neill making any ex gratia payments himself, out of his own funds. But it must not come with the name of the insurance company.

But Patrick knew that if it came from him, it would be charity.

He sat at his desk and wished that his daughter was back from Dublin and that she would walk in the grounds with him talking to him as she once had, before she had become coquettish and head-turning.

He wished that Kerry was different. That was it, just different. Like another person. He could see hardly any way now that he and his son would have any warmth and understanding between them. A gambler, a liar, a callous boy caring nothing for anyone. And quite possibly Kerry had been with Rachel. The thought of his son in an intimate embrace with Rachel was a thought he had tried to keep far from his mind.

Rachel lying back on the bed, confused with unaccustomed drink, laughing maybe, in a silly way. Her thick hair spread out on the pillow, and Kerry, his own son, leaning over her. It was *not* believable. He hit his desk with his fist. He would not believe it.

He had always been able to cope before, or if there was something that he couldn't deal with he had put it out of his mind. He had decided not to think about Kathleen's illness when he was not with her, and so never in his long drives to work or in his business day had he let it come into his mind. After he had beaten and fired his first dishonest manager, he had allowed no thoughts of the man, no regrets to come back to him at any stage. Kerry's expulsion from school, his stealing the silver, these he had managed to banish. But the image of his son and Rachel was too horrifying to get rid of.

Everything was turning out like a nightmare, just a few short weeks before the day he had dreamed about since he was a boy. The day he would open his own huge palace on the spot where the landlords had once driven his grandfather to an emigrant ship.

Fergus Slattery sat alone in his office too. Deirdre Dunne with her usual discreet face, pursed lips and habit of looking left and right before she delivered any utterance had said that it was an excellent result and he must be very satisfied.

Now, as he sat by himself and tried to give time to the other files that were on his desk, Fergus let his mind go back over it all.

He still wished that O'Neill had never come to Mountfern. There was nothing the man could do which made Fergus glad that he had invested the savings of a life's work and investment into changing the face of the village his grandfather left.

Why couldn't he have just come back for holidays, like these people he was hoping to find to fill his hotel? He could have worn a shirt with shamrocks on it, bought a fake shillelagh, had his picture taken beside the tinkers with their donkeys, or at a cottage where he might conceivably have roots.

But O'Neill had to do it his way, no matter who got hurt. And to Fergus's mind a lot of people had. Not just Kate Ryan.

People had changed and become greedy. Everyone seemed to be doing things for the wrong reason. Look at his own poor Miss Purcell, for instance, talking about having to do up the Sacred Heart Altar in the church and get rid of all the damp to smarten the place up for the visitors. If it was important to spend all that money getting rid of damp around the small side altar, and Fergus didn't think it was one of life's essentials, then it should be done for God surely, or for the people who were going to pray in the church, Mountfern people, so they wouldn't have to see weeping walls and fungus around the statue of the Sacred Heart and drips coming down to endanger the altar lamp. The visitors in Fernscourt might not even be Catholics, and if they were they would probably go off to mass at the old abbey fourteen miles away and take in a bit of history as well. And the vicar was busy getting his graveyard weeded and cleared up before the visitors came. This *had* to be the wrong approach too, Fergus thought. If old Protestant graves and tombstones were to be honored, then why wait till some Americans, possibly of Episcopalian stock, came to see them?

But Fergus wasn't going to get anyone to agree with him. Kate had often warned him against becoming an old eccentric before his time. He was thirty-one. Could his time have come now, by any chance?

Loretto Quinn heard the news from Rita Walsh. She was dying to run up and say a few words of congratulation to Kate but she couldn't leave the shop. At that moment Jack Coyne came in.

"Would you mind the place for me, just ten minutes? I'll be back by then."

"God, what am I, a messenger boy?"

The man who owned Coyne's Motor Works and thought of himself as a substantial businessman did not like being thought suitable to fill in behind the counter in what he would always think of as a huckster's shop.

Loretto was struggling out of her shop coat, one of the smart coats that Rachel had gotten her months back. Rachel had said it was always a good idea to have something to wear to show you were working and to take it off when work was over. Loretto had agreed eagerly, and also it happened that everyone said how smart she looked in the shop coats, anyway, so it had been a great suggestion.

Jack Coyne grumbled but agreed to hold the fort for ten minutes. "One minute later now and I'll leave and pull the door after me." Loretto was gone, flying up to Ryan's to add her good wishes.

"Who's minding the shop?" Mary Donnelly wanted to know. Mary was beaming like a sunrise and couldn't do enough for people.

"Jack Coyne said he'd keep an eye on it," Loretto said.

"He has his eye on you," Mary said in a doomed voice.

"Never in a million years. He hasn't said a word." Loretto tossed her head. She *had* wondered why Jack Coyne came so often to call. And perhaps in his narrow mean face there were the traces of interest.

"Oh, certainly he has," Mary said. "Wouldn't it be a nice tidy little business to add to his own?"

"Yes. Well." Loretto seemed a bit put out. And yet again Kate and John Ryan exchanged glances across their pub.

Happy to be on the same wave length and happy that the ordeal was over and their future was secure.

Jim Costello was glad the court case was out of the way because now his boss could give undivided attention to the hotel opening. It had all been full of problems, and there was a pressing need for Patrick to call everything to order. Jim suggested a meeting with an agenda.

Patrick was scornful. This was ninnies' work—agendas, and "it was agreed" and "it was decided"—that was the stuff for nobodies. He hadn't made his fortune by sitting on his butt attending meetings.

"There are areas which have to be sorted out in the presence of other people," Jim said—rather prissily Patrick thought.

"Like what and like which people?"

"Like line authority and what position you want your son to hold in the hotel, and that must be discussed in his presence. That's one thing.

"Like what penalty clauses you have arranged with Brian Doyle about what he calls the last little finishing touches and I regard as work still left undone. Like whether Mrs. Fine is or is not in charge of the decor and the arrangements for the presentation on the opening day."

Patrick felt stopped in his tracks. These were three punches he hadn't expected to be hit with. He took the easiest one first.

"There's never any problem with Rachel," he said. "Give her complete charge. She's had years of knowing how to get along with people, she doesn't get their noses out of joint like I do. What's the fuss anyway? Who's objecting?"

"No, that's not the point. Mrs. Fine says that you don't want her to make the arrangements for the opening. She says that she won't be here for it, and you want the public-relations people from Dublin to make the arrangements. They've been on the phone twice wanting to know. Mrs. Fine just smiles at me and says she won't be here, *you* just say 'Rachel will sort it out.' I'm sorry, Mr. O'Neill, I know it sounds like whining and running to you with every little problem. But can you see how hard it is to decide what is and what is not my responsibility? They're all quite major things and rather sensitive areas."

Patrick looked at him. Costello was unflinching; he didn't sound like a moaner. The man had right on his side.

"I see your point. First tell Doyle that I'll kick his ass from here to Galway tomorrow morning and then from Galway right across to Dublin unless he has all those shithouses, or whatever they are, moved tonight. Do you hear me? Tonight."

"The things he calls offices or store rooms."

"I don't care if he calls them the *Cathedral,* they're shithouses and they are not to be here tomorrow morning. But he is, and eight A.M."

"Yes. Will I arrange . . . ?"

"Just tell him I'll see him here at eight A.M. And Costello?"

"Mr. O'Neill?"

"If you see my son tell him to fuck off. If he wants to show up properly attired on the day of the opening then I shall of course be pleased to see him. Not otherwise."

Jim Costello's eyes flashed. "No, I'm afraid I can't give any message like that for you. That is family business. I will *not* be put in the position of delivering one kind of ultimatum and then delivering back the news of another kind of shrug. I'm sorry, but no."

Patrick looked at him with admiration. "I was right to pick you. Alright, I'll deal with Kerry, but your side of it is clear. He has no position in this hotel."

"And the other . . . ?"

"I'm going to find Rachel myself. Do you have any idea where she might be?"

Jim shook his head and seemed about to say it wasn't any of his business. But Patrick forestalled him with a laugh.

"Hey, relax. If you're not going to do my dirty work for me with my son, then I don't suppose I have any hope of getting you to patch up a lovers' quarrel for me, do I?"

He punched his manager genially on the arm and went out the door of his hotel to stand on his steps and glare at the offending prefab huts that Brian Doyle would be asked to remove the next instant. He noted that Jim Costello had had the good sense not to acknowledge even by a glance that Patrick had just let slip to him that the dispute with Rachel Fine was a lovers' tiff. Jim Costello had been a very good choice indeed.

Where was Rachel?

Kate had expected her at any moment, but she knew now that she need not doubt her friend. Rachel would be here at some time, it didn't matter when. She would be so glad to share the good news, and to know that a whole day and even more did not have to be spent arguing in open court.

She would be delighted too that Patrick was so pleased and thought it was a fair sum.

Kate looked at the door more than once. She was anxious to go back into her cool green room and talk to Rachel alone.

Rachel walked alone along the riverbank. She walked from the dock upriver, on a path that was overgrown still but not as covered with briars and brambles as the stretch from Fernscourt downriver to the bridge.

It was quiet here and she would meet nobody. She walked, a small woman in her flat-heeled stylish brogues. Rachel had hardly walked without high heels since she was seventeen years of age, but in Mountfern she had learned to change so many of her ways that changing her footwear seemed minor. She had her hands in the pockets of her suede jacket, her Hermés scarf tied jauntily around her neck.

To anyone watching, she looked an elegant woman enjoying a stroll by the river. Over the years she had learned to keep her feelings well away from the public view. Her face was in a pleasant half smile.

But her thoughts were very different from the gentle expression on her face.

Patrick O'Neill had said that Kate would get at least £12,000 and the insurance company was quite prepared to pay £14,000 without any great quibble. How had it come out at so little in comparison to that? And why had Patrick said or done nothing to show that he thought it had not been adequate?

From what she had heard, and Rachel had heard plenty of accounts, there had been roistering and celebrating, and banging each other on the back, and everyone was now everyone else's best friend.

She felt sick to the bottom of her stomach that he could be so hypocritical. And even more sick that she had not had the guts and courage to shout down her friend and tell her what the bottom line had been.

If, a few short hours ago, Rachel Fine had been brave enough to resist this girl-guide mentality of having to fight fair that Kate had been babbling about, the Ryan family could have had £14,000 in their bank account. Enough to make them secure forever. No matter what happened to their business as a result of the building of Fernscourt.

Rachel turned and looked back at the hotel. She knew very surely that she would not now wait for the opening, she would go back to New York as soon as she could manage it without upsetting innocent people.

She would go back home.

There were a lot of people in the bar when she came in. She went straight to Kate and kissed her on each cheek.

Kate's eyes were full of tears. "Isn't it wonderful? It's like a dream," she said.

Rachel swallowed.

"Have you been talking to Patrick?" Kate asked.

"No. No, not since."

"He's delighted, he thinks it's fair."

"I'm sure he is." Rachel was pulling away.

"Oh, do you have to go, really? I wanted to talk to you more than anyone."

Rachel had rarely been so moved. She couldn't say anything.

"And Rachel, I wanted to thank you for trying to do what you did. But it wouldn't have been fair, you do see that, don't you? It couldn't have worked. As it is, it all worked out just as we wanted. That's what

he said they were going to give, and that's what we took." Kate's eyes
shone. Her face was tired but her eyes were dancing with light.

"He said that?" There was no incredulity in Rachel's voice, just a
flat tone.

"Well, yes, we asked him, you see, afterward. In the pub."

"Yes of course. Kate, I'll be back, later or tomorrow, and we'll talk
for all the hours that are in the day, but this is something I can't put
off."

"All right, I won't hold you, and thank you again for all the support. I'm going to sleep well tonight, for the first time for a long
while."

Rachel laid her hand against Kate's face in a way she had never
done before. It was as if she were trying to say something through the
palm of her hand that she couldn't say in any other way.

Then she hurried out of Ryan's and walked down River Road. She
didn't cross the footbridge to Fernscourt, nor did she stop at Loretto
Quinn's. Rachel Fine walked the whole way to the bridge and turned
left. Then she walked up the steps and knocked at the door of the
ivy-covered house where Fergus Slattery lived and had his office.

It was short and it was clear.

Rachel found herself giving no complicated explanations, she did
not stop to go into her motives, nor did she twist her hands and her
handkerchief as she had when she was trying to explain to Patrick
that she had gotten drunk with his son but had not made love with
him.

Fergus was a different kind of listener. There was no stony impassive face, he reacted angrily and loudly to every sentence.

She gave him all the details of the various meetings, the strategy,
the decision to offer six but to expect a strenuous refusal, the decision
to go to ten the moment that eight had been refused and to settle at
anything up to fourteen even as the case was about to begin. Then it
was over and they sat in silence for a full minute.

"I suppose you wonder why I'm telling you all this."

"No, it's very natural that you should tell me, you're Kate's friend,
you are hurt on her behalf." He was gentle.

"But I'm also Patrick's friend. You must know that."

"Yes, of course I know that."

"It's not just because it's over, and because Patrick doesn't want
me here anymore . . ." She saw him raise his eyebrows in surprise,

and went on hurriedly. "No, it has nothing to do with that, surprisingly."

"Of course," he said, but she wondered whether he believed her.

"It's because it's not fair. Patrick has always been fair. And recently some madness has entered into him, and he's not being fair at all."

She looked very troubled. He saw what a very beautiful woman she was in this afternoon light, huge dark eyes moving restlessly about her.

"You do know that nothing can be done now?" Fergus said. "We have taken their offer and accepted it willingly. I thought it was enough, and so did Kennedy. But more important than that, Kate and John were perfectly satisfied."

"I know." Rachel's voice was small.

"And everyone in this place thinks it was enough, so they have their pride, and people don't say it was too much, so the Ryans won't become objects of hate and envy."

She looked at the tall gangling young man with the white face and the hair that would never sit in any order or style. Rachel could see that he had always loved Kate Ryan in a hopeless, ineffectual sort of way. His face was stricken to think how poorly he must have represented her on this, the only occasion he had ever had a chance to ride out to battle for her. Perhaps he was trying to justify the small award by saying that it was what the village would tolerate.

"She could have had so much more if she only would have listened to me this morning. I tried to tell her but she wouldn't hear."

"No, that's Kate for you," he sighed.

"But we were friends. It couldn't have been unethical between friends."

"What do you want me to do, Rachel?"

She looked at him, surprised.

"No, I mean it. What should I do now? My own instinct is to put it out of my mind, pretend we never had this conversation. Do you think I should do anything different?"

"Are you mad at me?"

"Most certainly not." He leaned across his desk and took her hand to reassure her on this. "You have always been a great friend to Kate, I have to say that sometimes I thought she spent too much time with you, seeing that you were so close to O'Neill, and that O'Neill is in many ways her adversary."

"He *is* her adversary, even though he doesn't intend to be," Rachel said. "He will close their business, and eight thousand pounds is not enough to compensate them for that." She was agitated and distressed.

Fergus let a little silence fall between them.

"Fergus, would *you* have listened if I had told you, instead of trying to tell Kate?"

Again a little silence, but eventually he spoke.

"Truthfully, yes. I think I would have listened. It would be unethical and if anyone heard me saying this, I would be in danger of being struck off the rolls, but I would have listened."

Rachel warmed to his honesty. "I don't think it's unethical to help a friend."

"The Incorporated Law Society might not see it that way." He smiled ruefully. "They mightn't be so understanding about how fond I am of Kate."

"You sort of love her, don't you?"

"Yes, that's it, sort of." He spoke without embarrassment, but he looked out the window onto Bridge Street not at Rachel as he spoke.

"She has everything, you know, life and common sense, and a quick lively mind which I don't, and . . . oh, a lot of things. But you're right, it's only a sort of love, not real love. I don't want to take her away from John, I don't want to go to bed with her. I suppose in ways I avoid getting involved with people, and this type of feeling I have for Kate does as a substitute. Very silly, really."

"I had to tell you, Fergus. It's up to you what you do now that you know. If you want to go along with this charade that it was the greatest award since Lord knows when, then do. I won't be here. I'm going home."

"Isn't this your home?"

"I thought it was, but it's not."

"We'll miss you. I wish you were not going away."

Eddie Ryan avoided Jack Coyne very deliberately. But Eddie couldn't avoid trouble. He had been so used to playing around Coyne's Motor Works that vehicles of every sort fascinated him now.

Mr. Williams had an old battered station wagon. He left it outside the graveyard where he was busy tending the graves. Eddie couldn't see anyone around. The grass in the graveyard was high. Mr. Williams was bent low.

Eddie looked left and right and slipped into the driving seat. He would drive the car to the end of the road where there was a farmhouse with two gates. He could drive in one and out the other, and back to where the car was now.

He had reckoned without the herd of cows which were coming out one entrance on their way back to the fields after milking. They seemed to be coming in the windows, and his grasp of driving was not as sound as he would like to have thought.

The cows were delighted with a break in the normal milking routine and were prepared to stand chewing the cud and dribbling until the last day dawned. At that moment a tractor came around the corner. Eddie knew the explanations of what he was doing in the vicar's station wagon would be difficult, not to say impossible. He left the car rapidly and slipped past the staring cows. He heard the tractor hit the car, and kept running until he got to Bridge Street.

His face was innocent when the story got to Ryan's pub, the tale of poor Mr. Williams's car, and poor Brigid Kenny's cows, and Brigid Kenny's poor son on the tractor, who was somehow held to blame for it all.

To his shock and outrage he heard Mrs. Whelan from the post office coming in and telling his father and mother that Brigid Kenny had seen young Eddie running away from the farm. Mrs. Whelan, of all people. She had always been so nice.

Eddie's father was furious.

Eddie was asked to come out to the backyard.

That could only mean one thing.

Kate was furious too. The danger, the stupidity, the downright disregard for human life.

"You'd think that in this house of all houses there would be some attention paid to what can happen when people get hit by vehicles," she stormed at him as Eddie had slunk back into the house with his hands, legs and bottom aching from the hiding he had been given in the backyard. He looked miserable and wretched, and a tiny grain of sympathy stirred in her.

"Why are you so awful?" she asked him, interested genuinely. And he could detect the change in her tone.

"I don't feel awful inside," he said, his tears not far away. Tears that had not come during the beating.

"What do you feel inside?"

"I feel it's all very boring," he said truthfully. "I'd love to be somewhere else, somewhere that I'd be important, and that people would talk about me."

"They're talking about you tonight."

She tried not to let her voice sound as if he had been forgiven in any way. Terrible things lay ahead, like the apology to Mr. Williams, like asking Jack Coyne to give an estimate on how much it would cost to repair the damage to the station wagon, like trying to explain to Brigid Kenny (a sour woman at the best of times) and to her son (who was slow by any standards, even among the Kenny family), what exactly Eddie Ryan had been doing on their property running amok.

"I suppose I'd like to be important to someone," Eddie said simply.

Kate looked at him, and to his amazement she had tears in her eyes. "You're very important to me."

"Only to be giving out to and telling people you're sorry about me." He wasn't complaining, that's just the way he saw things.

"Why do you think that?"

"Well, when I asked was I getting anything to wear at the opening, they all laughed. Nobody even thought I'd be *at* that opening. That's not being very important."

He was totally unprepared for her to lean forward from her wheelchair and take him in her arms.

"I know what you mean, Eddie. It's hard not being important enough to go to Dublin to get an outfit. I'd like to go too. I'd love to go in and out of the shops, in Grafton Street, and down Wicklow Street. Not to buy there, it would be too dear. Then I'd go to George's Street, and I'd buy something there, and a bit of other shopping—oh, stuff that would bore you, household things. And maybe into a bookshop, get a present for your dad, and then give myself plenty of time and walk down the quays with all my parcels and get the train home. And your father would meet us in the town and drive us home, and I'd try on whatever I'd gotten, and turn around on my own two good legs and show it off, and you'd all say what you thought, and people would take notice of me, and I'd be important again."

She was still holding him to her as she spoke. When she released him and held him away from her, she saw that the boy was biting his lip.

"I never knew, Mam . . . I never knew," he said.

"It's all right, Eddie," she said. "We'll survive."

"If I had the money, Mam, I'd take you to Dublin for the day," he said.

"I know you would."

She was silent now, so Eddie crept away.

Things were very odd at the moment; there were no two ways about it. Mrs. Whelan shopping him, Dad belting the life out of him, and Mam throwing her arms around him and saying she'd love to have two proper legs again.

And there were more peculiar things happening at every turn. Mr. Coyne, who was a hundred if he was a day, had brought a bunch of flowers to Mrs. Quinn, who was nearly a hundred, and the two of them were carrying on like something out of a musical. And Kerry O'Neill had told him to fuck off when he had asked him what was he doing with a boat going up and down between the bridge and the dock. Marty Leonard, who was Tommy's younger brother, said that Tommy had four pictures of Dara stuck up in his room and he kissed each one good night before he went to bed. And Father Hogan had asked him what were the opening hours going to be in the Shamrock Café and was there any chance that he could buy some of the potato cakes to eat walking along the road.

Eddie thought that everyone in Mountfern was going mad.

Dara found that her mother seemed withdrawn and somehow wistful these days. She sat and looked out into her garden where the summer flowers were coming to an end.

"Will I bring you the trowel and fork?" Dara asked.

"No. Let's leave it for a while. Who sees it?"

"You do, we do."

"That's what I mean."

"Well, we were always the ones who saw it, it hasn't been on Telefis Eireann or anything," Dara replied with some spirit.

"Are you happy with your linen dress for the opening?" Kate asked suddenly.

"Happy isn't the right word, it looks what it is, a boring linen dress that gets a huge balloony bottom in it if you sit down. It's a nice blue color, and Mrs. Fine gave me that necklace. I suppose it's all right, and for all that will be looking at me over there, it's fine. Why?"

"You can have a new dress if you like," Kate said.

"What kind of dress, Mam?"

"Whatever you like."

This had never been said in the history of their lives together. Dara's mouth was open. There had been a long lecture on thinking that they were millionaires because of the compensation. They had been warned against false expectations and a change of lifestyle. Now out of the blue she was being offered any kind of dress she liked.

"Do you mean something from a shop in Dublin?" she said in disbelief.

"Certainly."

"But why, Mam? We're meant to be saving the money for the day we might need to expand the Shamrock Café. And the fees for university."

"It's my money, it's mine, I got it by breaking *my* back. If I say you can have a new dress you can have one. Do you hear me?"

Kate's eyes were full of tears. Dara rushed to her and threw her arms around the woman in the chair.

"Mam, I'm sorry, of course I want a dress, I just didn't want you to be spending all your money on me. That's all."

She could feel Kate's body heaving.

"I'd *love* a dress. I'll go to Dublin on the excursion train on Saturday. I'd *love* it."

"And Michael, he can go and get a jacket. Will you go with him and see he doesn't buy an old rag or anything?"

"I will, Mam."

"You're going to be dressed like the finest in the land. I'll get you both off school mid-week one day. If Princess Grace can go to Dublin for her clothes, so can the Ryans take time off from their studies to do the same thing."

Sergeant Sheehan was tired. It had been a day when nothing that could have been straightforward was straightforward, everything had more turns in it than a corkscrew. Even the relatively simple business of organizing extra guards for the hotel opening had turned out to be a minefield of petty politics. Was there nobody who would talk straight left in the town? His face creased into a smile when he saw Sheila coming out of the church.

"What were you praying for? Let me guess. You were praying not to have to walk into one more person asking you eejity questions like I do."

She looked at him affectionately. She had known Seamus and Mary Sheehan for years, she had been with Mary sometimes to see their unfortunate son in the home over on the hill. Seamus was usually too upset to go with his wife, and it was a long lonely journey for the woman to go on her own.

"No, Seamus, I wasn't praying at all."

"Well, God, you've enough to do. I hope that mad Miss Purcell hasn't roped you in to clean the church and take the damp out of the Sacred Heart Altar."

Sheila laughed. "Oh, I get roped in like everyone, but I was in there for a different purpose entirely, and you were the very man I was hoping to meet as a result of it. In fact, I was going to come over to the barracks."

"Anything wrong?"

"I'm not sure. I think something may be very wrong. Will you come in and I'll tell you about it?"

"What'll you be doing in Dublin?"

"Shut up, Eddie," said Dara. "You know it's meant to be a secret, we don't want half the place to know we're going. Mam's saying it's a special favor and not saying that we're going on the train. Sister Laura and Brother Keane only think we're going into the town with Daddy."

"But what'll you be *doing*, will you be going to George's Street?"

"God, he's heard of George's Street, is there any end to his sophistication?" mocked Dara.

"I just want to know."

"You're not coming with us, you're not." Michael was vehement. "You'd ruin every single minute of the day, not just for us but for everyone on the train, and everyone in Dublin as well."

"I couldn't ruin the day for them *all*," Eddie protested.

"You could, they'd be the worse off for your being there. Go *away*, Eddie." Dara was impatient.

"I just thought maybe you'd take Mam," he said.

"What?" They looked at him in amazement. Eddie had never suggested anything remotely unselfish in his life.

"Yeah, she might like an outing, and get something to wear herself."

"She doesn't need anything to wear. Mrs. Fine gets her things," Dara said.

"She might like to get her own."

"She'd hate all the fuss and the noise and how could she manage in the chair?"

"You could push it down the quays. Down to O'Connell Bridge," Eddie said.

"Is this some trick?" Dara asked.

"What's behind it?" Michael wanted to know.

"I was just being nice," Eddie said.

They didn't believe him, but they did tell their father.

John Ryan thought it was well worth putting to Kate. He came into her room to suggest it.

"How about if the children were to take you with them tomorrow?"

She was flustered and pleased. But no, she couldn't think of it; it would be too much of a drag. It would slow the twins down too much, it would spoil their day.

"Nonsense, I've talked to them, they think it's a terrific idea; they'd love you to go. And if they want to wander off and leave you for a bit, they can, and come back to you, can't they? It'd be just like here or going into town, or the time we went to the abbey on the lake, people came and went from you and you had a grand time."

"I did." She smiled happily. "Thank you for thinking of it, John." Her voice was small and full of emotion.

"Oh, I didn't think of it," he said airily. "Credit where it's due. It was Eddie, apparently, gangster Eddie who thought you'd like the trip."

He grinned at her, expecting her to think it as unlikely and funny as he had. He was surprised to see some of the pleasure go out of her face. Kate had thought that this was all John's idea to give her a treat. But it hadn't been his idea at all.

Fergus had known that he had to face the Ryans fairly soon. He would never tell them about his conversation with Rachel, and he knew that no matter how bitter and resentful on their behalf she might feel, she too would keep her counsel to herself.

But he had to go soon, otherwise, it would grow to become a huge secret and it would get out of all proportion.

He had hated having to go there knowing what he did, but after the first time it was easy. Nobody else knew that O'Neill's side had gotten away so lightly. Fergus believed that O'Neill must accept a great deal of the blame in this regard. It was not, he thought, just his natural and long-standing dislike of the man; it was just the way things had to be.

To try to take some of the fire from Rachel's anger he had pretended to think O'Neill might have been an innocent party. He knew that this is what she had wanted to believe. But in his heart there was nothing that would take away his belief that O'Neill was a villain and would remain one until the end, whatever the end might be.

Fergus was astounded that he had defined his feelings for Kate Ryan so openly to O'Neill's woman. He had hardly defined them to himself before this. But the very act of articulating that he half loved Kate, and that it was not the kind of emotion that would destroy him or make him destroy anyone else, was a liberating thing.

When he sat in Ryan's and joked about the potato cakes for the café, and planned outrageous stage Irish jokes to be played on the visitors to the hotel when they arrived, Fergus felt a kind of freedom. It was as if some burden had been lifted. As if he knew that he could leave this place if he wanted to, he wasn't tied by any cords. He knew he would stay here forever. But now it would be because he wanted to, not because of anything unsettling that would never be said.

Grace was in Fernscourt examining her room without much pleasure. Not long ago it had been great fun here. Mrs. Fine was pointing out where the light was best to put her bureau, Father had taken her in his arms and hugged her on almost every occasion, saying how wonderful it was that the dream was coming true, and Jim Costello had been around smiling and admiring.

It was all very different now. Father was distant and distracted, there was no sign of Mrs. Fine, and Jim had been so prissy. Yes, that was the only word for it.

"Grace, I'm going to have to ask you not to throw yourself at me, the situation is quite impractical."

Impractical. How *dare* he come on like this, using words like impractical, and suggesting that she had thrown herself at him. She had merely told him she was a big girl now and ready for anything.

Jim Costello had told her that she was the most beautiful girl he had ever seen in his whole life. *That* bit, at least, was something. But he had said that it would be playing with dynamite to get involved with her at this stage, under the eyes of her father and brother.

And then he had gone and more or less said this aloud in front of them. Grace hadn't known where to put herself.

She wished she hadn't been so harsh to Michael about the trip to Dublin. It had turned out that Father had wanted her out of Mountfern on the day of the court case, and Father might have been able to arrange for Michael and Dara to have gone too.

Grace sat on her bed and felt that it had all been handled very badly. She was even having second thoughts about the very expensive dress she had bought.

Mrs. Fine would have chosen something better for her.

Dara and Michael sat on the window seat. It was nearly like old times.

"What are you reading?" Michael asked.

"It's a letter from Madame Vartin. It's quite hard to read, she's awfully squiggly writing."

Michael grinned. "And an awful squiggly habit of writing in French."

"Oh, I can read the French easily enough," Dara said loftily, if not very truthfully.

"What's she writing about then? Here, let's see." Michael reached for the letter.

"No, there might be things in it you shouldn't read."

"From Madame Vartin? You said she was a religious maniac."

"Yes, but she might be writing about sex."

"Oh, I know all about sex," Michael said.

"Do you?" Dara was eager and begging. "Do you really know all about it? Is it great?"

"Well not *all*, not . . . well not everything. But it's pretty great as far as it goes."

"I often wondered did you . . ."

"Sort of, not completely . . ."

"How nearly . . . ?"

"Give us the letter."

The confidences were over, Dara realized. She read a paragraph from the letter.

"This is the bit I don't understand, it's got something to do with Monsieur leaving his job—or being sacked I think. I hope. Anyway she says he is too young to make a retreat. What in the name of God would he make a retreat for anyway? He's full of mortal sin all the time and glories in it."

"Where does it say about him going on a retreat?" Michael read the paragraph and began to laugh. "Fine use of money it was sending *you* off to France, even I know that, and we're all desperate up in the brothers'. It's retiring, you eejit, *"Faire sa retraite* means *retire."*

"He'll be jumping on Mademoiselle Stephanie all day," Dara said gloomily, and then brightened up. "Oh, no, he won't, she's getting married, isn't that great?"

"They all sound cracked to me," Michael said.

"There's Grace going down the towpath," Dara said suddenly.

Michael jumped up on the seat to look. True, Grace was walking purposefully along toward the bridge. She wore her blue jeans and those funny little red lace-up shoes she had, and a blue and red stripy shirt, and there were red ribbons in her hair.

She looked as pretty as a picture.

Michael was pale and unhappy. Dara decided she would break their code of not offering advice.

"Do you know what I would do if I were you?"

"No," said Michael gruffly.

"I'd ask Grace straight out. I'd say, 'Is anything wrong, things seem to have changed?' At least that way you'd know."

"She'll just smile and say nothing's changed," Michael grumbled.

"She might actually tell you if there is something wrong."

"I don't want to hear it if there is," Michael said. He feared that Grace was greatly smitten by the handsome young hotel manager, and because Jim Costello had the sense to play hard to get Grace fancied him all the more.

"Do girls like being asked direct questions like that?" he asked doubtfully.

"I do," Dara said. "If anyone asked me a direct question like that, I'd respect them, and that's the truth."

"Dara, I was just passing," Tommy Leonard said.

"Oh Tommy, how could you be just passing? The brothers' is at the other side of the town to the convent."

"I know, I heard they built them that way on purpose, so that we couldn't all get at each other."

Dara giggled. "Not at all, it never crossed their minds."

"Listen, I hear you're one of the few people in the world who likes direct questions rather than beating around the bush . . ."

In her head Dara heard a warning bell. She didn't want to lose Tommy Leonard as a friend.

"I used to be like that, it's true, but I've gone off it again," she said hastily. "I hate direct questions now, and I snap the head off anyone who would ask me one."

"Phew, I'm glad we sorted that one out," said Tommy Leonard in a mixture of disappointment and relief.

* * *

Grace told Michael that she couldn't imagine what he was talking about. Of *course* she loved being with him. But there was so much school work to do, and she had a little table fixed up for herself in one of the residents' lounges where she could work in the evenings. And she couldn't be going out all the time. And sometimes when she did get through with homework there were things about the hotel she had to learn. After all, she would be living there and working there always.

"But not immediately," Michael cried. "We're going to go to the university, aren't we? And get degrees and travel, before we come back to work in Mountfern."

"Oh, yes, of *course* we are," Grace said.

But she didn't sound convinced.

"Then why are you learning about the reception desk now from Jim Costello?" Poor Michael let it all slip out.

Grace gave him a long look.

"I'm sure you wouldn't want me to be discourteous to anyone on my father's staff," she said, and Michael heard a ring of the boss's daughter in her voice that he had never heard before.

Since the day Kerry had told her about Mrs. Fine and the awful scenes, Dara felt as if a huge boulder had been lifted out of her rib cage. She had known always, of course, that Kerry couldn't possibly . . . not of his own free choice . . . but people had been so definite.

And of course, that was the interpretation that would be put to it. As Kerry had said, he had been uncharacteristically nice, and look at the thanks he had gotten for it. If he had fled, which is what you'd expect him to do from a drunk boring woman who was telling him her life story and looking for consolation of every sort . . . then things would have been better by far.

She didn't get to see him often. He had told her that because of this very bad row with his father he was doing a very ordinary menial kind of a job, he was keeping quiet about it, and in a few weeks it would all be over and they could see each other as much as they liked. He had made her promise to cut school one day and he would drive her to Galway. They would walk along the beach in Salthill in the autumn sunshine, they would buy bag after bag of lovely crisp chips, they would eat those ice-cream cones with big bars of milk chocolate stuck in the middle of them. And best, they could wander around hand in hand and kiss each other in the main streets of Galway if they wanted to.

"I know a place we could go, Kerry," she said suddenly. "It's a tunnel. It used to be a secret place for Michael and me when we were younger but nobody uses it now." She looked at him eagerly.

To her shock his face changed completely.

"No," he said sharply. "No tunnel, that's out of the question."

He stood up. It reminded her of that time he had walked away before when she had refused his embraces. The sense of loss was sharp in her memory. She looked at him longingly.

"Will you promise without any whys. Just for me?"

"Yes, I promise," Dara said, feeling slightly ashamed of herself as she did so.

Martin White wasn't surprised to hear that Kate Ryan wanted him to call. She said it was for a check-up before she committed herself to the big journey to Dublin.

"It's about more than that isn't it?" the doctor said.

"How did you know?"

"I thought it was possible one day there not long ago."

"I couldn't be . . ." Kate looked horrified.

"Why couldn't you? You know the way it's done, and I'm delighted you're able to do it." Martin beamed uncharacteristically.

"But not with me like this."

"Of course it could, and will."

She leaned forward and clutched his hand. "I'm very strong, you'll admit that, and a lot of my strength came from you giving me things straight. Be straight now. Will it be dangerous?"

Martin took her thin hand in both of his. "Not only will it not be dangerous, it will be wonderful. I couldn't be more pleased for you."

"Do you think you'll go to jail?" Declan asked Eddie when they were both in bed.

"No. Not this time."

"Will you next time?"

"I might. Why?"

"Then I could have your bed."

"You'd be just as bad as I am if you were brave enough."

"I am brave."

"No you're not, you think there's a ghost in the press."

"I don't really think there is, I think there might be."

"There is, a big one, but *I'm* not afraid of it. Good night."

Eddie turned over and went to sleep knowing that Declan would be awake for hours looking at the door of the big cupboard in the corner of the bedroom, fearful over what might come out of it.

The river had never looked so lovely as that night. There was a flutter of birds in the trees, and they heard the cry of a fox in the still night. For two city people to recognize a fox at a distance wasn't bad. Rachel was wearing her flat shoes as if she had known they were going to walk, and he helped her over the fallen branch of a tree or through the complicated little gates that the local people called stiles.

They had driven there separately. Rachel insisted. They had parked both cars on the river bank. Behind them Coyne's wood rose dark and mysterious and further over were the hills around the Grange.

The sound of their footsteps was soft and rustling in the leaves. They came to an old wall, a good vantage point to look up at Fernscourt. Until now they had talked not at all, yet there was no air of expectancy. No tension or waiting for one of them to bring up the subject.

It came up very naturally. Patrick laid his hand over hers.

"I wish it had been different," he said.

"Oh, so do I," she sighed. But not with accusation; more like people sighed when it was no longer spring or when the heat went out of the day.

"It isn't anything to do with the not being Irish bit . . . believe me."

"I do believe you. You see, you've always had a different feeling about being an American than the other people I've met in my life. They all loved being American, *and* being whatever else they were, but to you being American meant losing being Irish, so you had to come back and recapture it."

She walked apparently contentedly beside him, and they came to the footbridge opposite Ryan's.

She led the way across into Fernscourt. He had been hesitant in case on this, her last night, she might not want to go into the place that had taken all his money, his time and his heart. They walked to a seat which she had arranged a long time ago when the garden plans were being discussed.

They sat and looked across the Fern at the lights in Ryan's pub where there were still a dozen or so in the bar. And at Loretto

Quinn's where the rooms were being held in case Rachel might
change her mind. In the soft dark night dogs were barking, they
could hear an owl hooting far away, and the moths flew around them
gently. There was the permanent sound of the river, but they had
grown so used to it, they didn't hear it anymore.

"I'll be very lonely here."

"No, no, you'll have far too much to do," she said. "Your days will
be filled from morning to night. I'll think of you sometimes at this
time, and I'm sure you will be in your office there or with Jim Costello as the host. You won't be sitting idly here watching the stars
over Mountfern."

"And what will you do in New York?" He was gentle too, and
wistful.

"I don't know yet. I'll work hard, I can come to anyone with great
references now . . ." She waved her hand at the hotel behind them.
"I've kept a portfolio of all my work. I must have known I'd need it."

"Do you think we will be friends, you and I?"

"Sometime, not for a while."

"Nobody has shared as much of me as you have. I'm not good at
giving bits of myself." He looked at the ground.

She wanted to shout at him and say she was the most betrayed
woman in the land. She had worked ceaselessly for his dream and to
keep his relationship with his family good. She had bought presents
for his children's birthdays for as long as she could remember; she
had advised and cajoled and succeeded in keeping some kind of family love alive between them all. What was her reward? She was assumed to have slept with the son and then to have paid him to keep
quiet about it.

"And because we *are* being so civilized, can I say just one thing
. . . and you won't get up and walk away?" she said.

"Certainly." He was ultra formal.

"And you won't put on that formal mask with me."

"Very well, say it, Rachel." He smiled at her, that familiar smile
with the starry lines going out from the sides of his eyes.

There was a catch in her voice which she hadn't intended. She had
forgotten how much she loved his smile.

"About that night that Kerry came to my rooms."

"Yes." He sighed as if he had known it would be this.

"He came for a purpose, a very specific purpose."

"Yes, so he said," Patrick agreed.

"Don't be absurd, Patrick, don't be utterly ridiculous. There is really something lacking in you if you could believe that he could have wanted to . . . to be with me in that way."

Her voice sounded confident and dismissive. This was not the woman who had wrung her hands in Coyne's wood and explained and contradicted and apologized. Rachel was firm and decisive now, she was dismissive of Kerry and all his tales.

"For what purpose?"

"He came to warn me off, to send me home. And he has achieved that purpose."

Her eyes were angry but her voice was calm.

"What was he saying . . . ?"

"He was mainly saying that if I had any hopes of replacing his mother, I should forget them, that I was not worthy to mention her name, that our affair was sordid and disgusting and that her memory would never be . . . sullied, I think, by the insult of your marrying me. It was very bitter. Very violent."

"I think this is all very exaggerated. Kerry has no feelings for me . . . Whether I marry or not, it hardly concerns him."

"You may be right in that he has no feelings for you, but he has very strong feelings about his mother."

"He doesn't give any sign of them to me."

"How would he, to you? To you of all people. He doesn't tell you that he had Kathleen's topaz made into a tie tack, that he has her picture in a watch chain, in his billfold, and in a plastic folder just loose in his pocket."

Patrick started to speak, but Rachel went on. "And I don't say this just because he told you a pack of lies about me; in itself, that's not the worst thing."

"What *is* the worst thing?"

"The worst thing is that you believed him. That he was able to make you believe him. That Kerry—with his record of deceit, gambling, theft, lies, and utter selfishness—was able to make you, an intelligent loving sensitive man, believe him rather than me . . . the woman who has loved you, worked with you, and for you all these years. That's the worst thing, how he was able to convince you so easily . . ."

"And is that the reason you're going?"

"That and one or two other things. I think you've changed. I think the effort of making this place changed you a lot."

"How has it changed me?"

"You were always so honest. Back in New York when there was a fight you fought fair. If another guy won the contract, you shook his hand, you said it was only money, only work, you wished him well. If a guy lost, you shook his hand too. You were honest."

"I haven't cheated anyone here." Patrick was bewildered.

"You cheated Kate Ryan."

"I had to, Rachel. What else could I say? 'You were robbed, madam, but please accept my personal check for the balance'?"

"You celebrated with them that justice was done. Justice was *not* done."

"Do you really believe I am at fault over this?"

"Yes," Rachel said simply.

He picked up her hand and stroked it. "We have grown apart, you and I. There was a time when we could have talked it out all night and you would have agreed that I did the only possible thing in giving them their dignity if I couldn't give them an adequate settlement."

"Even if we had been able to talk it out all night, if we still had that kind of life, I don't think I would have agreed."

"But you would have understood why I did what I did," he sighed.

"Yes, I'd have understood."

Together they sat and looked across at Ryan's, where the lights had gone out finally and stragglers walked or bicycled home along River Road.

"Won't you stay for the opening? Please, Rachel."

"No, no, you can call me when it's all over and tell me how it went."

"It will be good to talk to you on the telephone, anyway. There are so many day-to-day things I'll want to tell you about."

"No, Patrick. No calls. Only on the day of the opening."

"No calls?"

"If we're going to live our own lives, it's childish to keep calling each other."

"But as friends, even?" He was begging her.

"No, we're not friends yet. We will be some time."

There was a long silence.

"I feel very empty. I let you down, didn't I?"

"Let's be the only couple in the history of the world who said good-bye without any recriminations," she said, standing up to go.

She bent down and kissed him on the forehead.

He put his arms around her waist and held her to him.

Gently she released herself and walked away. Down the path to the footbridge and across the Fern.

Patrick sat in the grounds of his hotel and watched Rachel walk without turning back all along the river bank, past the old wall and the funny stiles.

He heard her car start and drive away toward the town.

Chapter XXIII

The weather forecast had said sunny with scattered showers.

"I hope they'll be scattered over the rest of Ireland and not all concentrated in this direction," Miss Purcell said sternly.

The canon had a chest cold that would not go away. Dr. White had said that a man the canon's age was to expect chest colds and not to stay in a draft.

Miss Purcell would have liked more concern and a preciser prescription. The canon would have to be in a considerable draft during the blessing ceremony. She had been very insistent about woolen underwear, and the wearing of a scarf while not actually involved in the religious offices.

Father Hogan was reassuring. Most of the time Canon Moran would stay well away from drafts. The huge marquee built by the dock was meant to be utterly windproof. And then there would be plenty of activities inside the house proper. Miss Purcell was to have no further worries.

Father Hogan also described at great length what he heard was going to be served to eat. There was an amount of salmon being delivered to the hotel that would frighten you, and there would be plates of it all afternoon if people wanted it; they could come back for helping after helping. There would be potato salad, and all other kinds of salads, and buttered brown scones.

Father Hogan said that there had been considerable discussion about whether or not to have a hot lunch, but the salmon faction had prevailed. There would be soup first, of course, served in cups so that it would be easy for people to manage it. There were two huge tureens of soup on their own little heaters, and you could come back for second cups or even a third cup here too.

By the time Father Hogan had begun to weigh up the merits of the fresh fruit salad and lashing of cream as opposed to the hot apple tart with ice cream, Miss Purcell began to wonder if the young priest could possibly be becoming *too* interested in food. She had let out his soutane once already, and it needed a further easing at the seams.

But she dismissed the thought as unworthy. And almost blasphemous. What was better than to see a healthy young priest enjoy his food? She thought back on the days that Fergus Slattery wouldn't notice what she served, so long as there was a bottle of tomato ketchup on the table.

Papers Flynn stirred in the outhouse where he had slept well all night. There was something happening today. What was it? He remembered that it was the hotel opening.

A barge had been brought from a Dublin canal, and painted in bright colors. There were going to be tours up and down the river to the old abbey near the lake. It would be great sport to watch it. Papers would find himself a good vantage point on the bank to see the comings and goings.

He was pleased to think of a day filled with such activity. He had all the details from Carrie. Papers had called there about his usual business and Mrs. Ryan had invited him into the kitchen for a plate of dinner.

Mrs. Ryan was a lady he liked a lot. She never asked him to clean himself up. She wouldn't give him any old guff about finding himself a roof over his head. Mrs. Ryan knew that Papers didn't want to be tied down. She gave him useful things like a pair of big burlap bags with strong handles on them: she thought they might come in handy for transporting his belongings, and they were the very thing.

Mrs. Ryan had taken Papers aside and said that he may have heard that recently they had been given a very substantial sum of money as compensation for her accident. Papers had heard it, certainly. Up in Matt Foley's at the top of the town they had said that the Ryans were going to spend it all on a carpeted lounge bar with music playing in the background. In Conway's pub they had said that the lot had gone into a building society and there wasn't going to be a penny of it spent ever. It was to be their nest egg, their insurance policy for years to come. He had traveled on further to Paddy Dunne's pub, where the story was that the money had been set aside to send Mrs. Ryan to a hospital outside Boston where they were able to do miracles with what other places had said were incurables. It cost five thousand pounds before they would look at you, and there would be the fare and everything, but she'd be walking again by the springtime. Paddy Dunne had read an article about the place in a Sunday paper.

Papers would never dream of asking Mrs. Ryan which, if any, of these stories were true. He was surprised when she suddenly volunteered the information.

"We've been very lucky, Papers, and I was wondering if you'd join us in celebrating our good fortune."

"Well, now, ma'am." Papers was cautious.

"I mean, I wouldn't normally dream of *offering* anyone money, but seeing as how we got so much ourselves. It's mainly in a savings account and it's going to be used for the children's education, in case any of them are bright enough to be able to use it. But we kept a few pounds aside for ourselves, and for people we know."

She handed him three pound notes folded over.

"It's not a great deal but I don't know whether you'd like a cap, I was going to get you a cap, but John said that a man should choose his own cap for himself."

"He's right there," Papers agreed sagely.

"Or it might not be a cap at all that you'd like, so will you get yourself something, and regard it as sharing part of our good fortune?"

Papers had been very pleased indeed to have had his wishes considered and discussed so carefully without anyone making mention of the county home, which usually came up when people had his welfare at heart.

In an uncharacteristic burst of speech he had told Mrs. Ryan that he might buy himself a little spirit stove that he had seen in a shop. He had been debating if it was worth the investment, but it would give him more freedom, he'd be able to go farther afield if he had his own way of being able to make a cup of tea.

He had thanked Mrs. Ryan very formally and assured her that he would report progress on the spirit stove. If he bought it, he promised that he would be very careful with it. And ended his speech by saying that she was a great woman to be celebrating good fortune when there were many in the land who would say that it was no good fortune to have the two legs struck from under you, but was glad that Mrs. Ryan was able to rise above that.

He had been surprised to see tears in her eyes. And she had said that oddly she didn't worry about her legs being useless, she had gotten over that part of it, she just felt that she herself had lost her personality and was useless as a person. Papers hadn't understood that and he told her it was a bit deep for him. She cheered up then and agreed and told him to have a good plate of stew before he left, and to come and watch any of the activities on the day of the opening from Ryan's bar.

"You know you're invited like everyone else in the place to the Thatch Bar in the evening, he wants the whole of Mountfern to come."

"Well . . ." Papers was doubtful.

"He's not issuing personal invitations, just wants everyone to turn up for a drink and to wish the place luck. Of course, there are some who would prefer to inspect it at their own time rather than being herded together. Some people of the more independent kind, private people will take up his invitation at a later date."

Papers had been relieved to hear that, he thought at first that he might be expected to go, but Mrs. Ryan had set his mind at rest on that point. Papers could join the private sort of people, the people of independent mind who didn't want to go as part of the herd.

Rita Walsh woke with a start. Why had she set her alarm clock for seven o'clock? Then she remembered.

It was the day of the opening. She had two young girls from the convent coming at eight o'clock to start shampooing. The schools had the day off and Rita had picked two of the more reliable Sixth Years to help her. She had trained them in the art of washing hair without drowning the client.

All the towels and capes were clean and ready in little heaps in the salon.

She would get milk and biscuits from Loretto; she had tea and coffee there already, and in honor of the occasion she had bought a dozen nice blue-and-white teacups.

There would be a steady procession all morning. And since everyone would want to be finished and out by twelve-thirty, she had decided to open very early and accommodate everyone.

It was only regulars today. Mrs. Daly, Miss Johnson, Miss Bryne the physiotherapist, Dr. White's wife. Loretto Quinn was coming in to have her hair combed out, she had the set yesterday. She also had the ring. She told Rita Walsh that in your life you found one Barney. It would be too good to be true to imagine you'd find another. But Jack Coyne was a man often very much misunderstood, and he had told Loretto that it was lonely to be in business in a big way and have no company in the evening when he came in after a long day's work. Loretto had understood this too.

Rita had been very pleased for Loretto and agreed that it was often easy to get the wrong end of the stick with Jack until you knew him. She had done Loretto's hair free as a celebration and said she must come in for a lot of back-combing and lacquer since this was a special day, the day that people would hear about their engagement. Loretto must look her best.

Jack Coyne was going to the opening under sufferance. One of the terms of their very unromantic and highly practical contract had been that Jack would end his vendetta with Mr. O'Neill and that Loretto would smarten herself up and learn to drive. The new Mrs. Jack Coyne must be not only a successful shopkeeper in her right but a well-turned-out woman driver.

John Ryan woke at seven. He had slept badly. Twice during the night he had gotten up to get a drink of water, his throat felt dry and he couldn't seem to get comfortable in the bed.

If Kate had been lying beside him in the old days, she would have woken too, and gone to make them a cup of tea. They might have sat during the dark night and talked about the hotel that was finally going to open, and all the fears that they shared, as well as the totally different fears that one had and the other had not. It would have looked less shadowy, that big house across the river, and less full of terror.

But Kate had not been in the room for over three years. Sometimes John slept on the divan in her green room below. He was always aware of how much she hated it when she needed to use the lavatory, whether she dragged herself into the chair and wheeled herself to the bathroom, or used the bedpan. Either way it distressed her so much that he often felt he was more of a hindrance to her than a companion. It was more sensible for him to sleep upstairs, though it was lonely.

And sometimes he felt it was selfish, particularly after they had made love. But then, making love itself was a selfish activity these days. There was no trace of the pleasure and excitement for Kate that had delighted him before.

John looked across at Fernscourt as the morning light fell on the great marquee. Normally he never let his mind go down this particular train of thought, but today he didn't pull himself up. He stood holding the bedroom curtain in his hand and looked at the dock, the brightly painted barge, and the first signs of activity in the big cultivated grounds, and wondered what things would have been like if Patrick O'Neill's grandfather had been thrown out of a cottage in Cork or Galway or Clare, instead of in this small bend on the road in the midlands.

How different everything would have been then.

Grace O'Neill woke with a jump because there was a noise in her bedroom. But it was only her new dress and its heavy coat hanger falling from the door of her closet where she had hung it last night. She wanted to see it first thing so that she could make an instant judgment. Now it was in a crumbled ball on the floor.

She leaped out of bed to rescue it and held it up against the light. It *was* beautiful. She had been silly to think it was baby-dollish; it would look classy and striking.

Grace hoped that Michael would be cheerful today. She hated to see that hangdog look about him, as if someone had taken away his favorite toy.

She went to the window and leaned out. The huge marquee blocked the view across the river. She could not see Ryan's pub properly.

She felt sorry for Michael having to share a room with that terrible Eddie. Declan was harmless enough, but Eddie was too much.

Michael had explained that there was a partition. He had begged for one, and Jimbo had been instructed to build a plywood wall dividing the room.

She compared it to Jim Costello's room. Well, it was more a suite really. He had a study, a bathroom and kitchenette, with a big bedroom that faced the river. She had seen it when he was taking her on a grand tour.

Jim had explained that the big sofa turned into a bed at night. By day the room looked expensive and impersonal. As if it were a genuine hotel bedroom, and Jim was just passing through. There were no photographs or personal things around his room.

Grace liked to think of the frank admiring looks he gave her, and the promise that when the day was over and there was time to think, he would be able to sit down and talk to her properly.

Loretto Quinn woke and examined her hair to see how much of the set remained. Rita was going to brush it up for her and lacquer it like a board later in the morning.

There were several things she wanted to do before she opened the shop. She wanted to finish her letter to Mrs. Fine, telling her that there had been a dozen requests to rent the rooms, and that Loretto was going to give them to a young chef who said that he never lived on the premises, it always led to a hassle, and he had wanted something nearby. He had been very impressed with the little kitchen and said that the cooker was a very good make and one of the most expensive on the market.

Loretto wanted to thank Rachel for that as well; she had never appreciated it at the time. She wanted Rachel's advice on what she should wear for her wedding next spring. Would a lemon-colored suit be nice, or would it take the color from her?

Loretto also wanted to leave a note in to Fergus Slattery. Jack Coyne had said to her that the country had never been the same since the Married Women's Property Act. It was a joke, but she was going to ask Fergus just to make it clear to her in words she would understand that if she and Jack had a bust-up in the years to come, that Jack couldn't take her little shop from her. And Loretto had to iron her dress, and once she had sorted through the potatoes and shaken the earth off them, she would paint her nails pink, as people would be admiring the ring.

And she had to decide about the picture of Barney that hung over the mantelpiece in her kitchen.

She took it down and looked at his face. It wasn't a very big picture, nor a very good one. His hair was sticking out in a spiky way that wasn't really like the way Barney was. The years in between made it hard to remember exactly the way he was.

As she looked at the picture, Loretto noticed that the big old frame was coming apart; it was old and cracked. It would be dangerous to leave it hanging in that position in case it fell on anyone.

Loretto's decision was made for her. She couldn't put the picture up again the way it was.

She took out the photograph of Barney Quinn and put it in a smaller frame, a stand-up type which you could put on a shelf. In front of the potted plant. But in time it could be moved over beside the plant or toward the back of the shelf.

Eddie Ryan woke and looked out the window.

He had promised his mother that he would do nothing today that would bring any disgrace on the family.

"It's an important day, and I'm in a bit of a fuss and bother about it already, so it would be the living end, Eddie, if you were to be a worry to me, if I had to be looking around asking people where is that boy and what's he up to now."

"Maybe I'd better stay in bed all day," Eddie had said quite seriously. It seemed to be the only way he could guarantee being no trouble at all.

"No, I'd be afraid you'd fall out of the window or hang yourself or something. I wouldn't be able to take my eyes off the house while we're over there," Kate had grumbled.

Mam had bought him a great jacket that day in Dublin; it was full of pockets and zippers and wasn't at all the kind of thing he thought Mam would buy. He'd been sure it would be something like a blazer or a suit jacket when he was unwrapping it.

"How did you know this is what I'd want?" His eyes were shining.

"I guessed," Mam had said.

She told him it was in the nature of a bribe, a promise of peace on the day of the opening.

Declan stirred and rubbed his eyes. "Is it morning?" he asked. Declan sometimes behaved as if he were retarded.

"No," said Eddie. "It's the middle of the night, and all those ghosts you're so afraid of have been at it again. They've bitten the head off Jaffa. Oh, God, it's lying on the ground all covered with dried blood."

Declan let out a screech that could be heard on the Dublin road, and leaped out to see if this was true.

Carrie, who had been getting sick in the bathroom for the fourth morning running and was beginning to work out that there might be a very unsettling reason for this, got such a fright at Declan's screams that she knocked over the entire contents of a tray that was perched dangerously on a white chest of drawers. The tray held—or had held

—talcum powder, Dettol, dried-up calamine lotion, milk of magnesia, a glass eyedropper, and a bottle shaped like a crinoline lady full of blue bath salts.

The recriminations were lengthy. The court of inquiry into why all those particular things were on a tray was endless. Kate said that it was a great thing for a woman in a wheelchair to be told that the bathroom she could never go up the stairs to see had now turned into some kind of boxroom or rubbish dump, filled with old chests of drawers and trays and the Lord knew what else.

Dara was accused of having weighted it down too much with the crinoline lady. Dara, woken from sleep with what she considered monstrously unfair charges, said that the crinoline lady was, if anyone would care to remember, a gift from Marian Johnson to say thank you when Dara had gone to help in the Grange at a function. Dara had thought she was being paid, which was the only reason she had gone, and had been outraged by the blue crinoline.

Mam had said then to put it up in the bathroom somewhere out of people's sight, and now she, Dara, was being blamed for it.

Eddie said he would stick a compass in Declan's heart if he told anyone why he had cried out, and that this was no joking matter.

Poor Declan tried to say that he had been having a nightmare; he had dreamed that a ghost had bitten off the head of the cat, and that the side yard was awash with blood.

John said that it was too much for a human to bear. One of his sons was a hardened criminal, the other a certifiable lunatic.

Jack Coyne woke with a feeling of wellbeing that surprised him. What was he feeling so good about?

He remembered that despite all the trials and tribulations, a few of them aided and abetted by Jack himself, Fernscourt was going to open today.

Well, he was going to the festivities of course, no point in making any lone point over something that was happening, anyway, and passing up a free dinner.

Anyway, there would be lots of fellows there from the Tourist Board and from Aer Lingus and the American airlines. And there would be journalists and local councillors, two bishops no less, a rake of priests, four TDs at the last count, not to mention the high and the mighty for miles around. If he couldn't get a bit of business out of today he'd be in a poor way.

Then he remembered Loretto and how she had agreed to everything. It had been well worth getting her those flowers back a bit, and saying that he would be happy to go dancing of a weekend. Women really and truly liked those kinds of things. It was the way they were. And Loretto had been very practical, too, and agreeable to some of his suggestions. She had been adamant about maintaining her own little shop rather than considering its possible sale as a site for some other business once the hotel got going. She had been equally firm about not learning anything whatsoever about maintenance work. She didn't want to spend her life in greasy overalls lying under some lorry. She had agreed to learn how to drive, however, which would be very useful for car delivery or collection or going for spare parts.

She had a nice smile, Loretto had. He had never noticed her at all until recently, thought she was a streelish little one in a shabby boxeen of a shop.

It was extraordinary how she had livened up when O'Neill's foreign woman came to live there. And would anyone be able to explain what had happened to send *her* packing so suddenly?

Fergus Slattery heard the telephone ring at seven-fifteen. That had to be some crisis.

He dragged himself unwillingly from a dream where he was advising the Rolling Stones about their grammar, and telling them that the song "I Can't Get No Satisfaction" actually and literally meant that they *could* get satisfaction, which was fine if this is what they wanted to say.

The Rolling Stones had been delighted with Fergus and had asked him to get on the payroll. He wouldn't have to leave Mountfern but could advise by phone or letter on anything that needed revision. They promised to come and see him when next they were passing that way, and Fergus had told them they'd get a great bed and breakfast in Ryan's. Dara had been so grateful to him and had apologized for ever thinking he should be put down like an old horse.

Loath to leave such entertainment, he went in his bare feet to the phone.

"It's Rosemary."

"*Who?*"

"I know we haven't seen each other a great deal over the past while, Fergus, but I *am* your only sister."

"My God, Rosemary, is anything wrong? It's the middle of the night. Did something happen?"

"Of course something happened. I'm hardly ringing you for a chat out of the blue."

"What is it? The boys . . . was there an accident . . . ?"

"The boys are fine wherever they are. They don't bother to let me know."

He waited.

"It's James. He had me out of the house, changed the locks. He can't do this to me. He can't throw me out of my own home." She was near to tears.

"When did this happen?"

"The locks were changed last night, I stayed in a guest house. I was waiting until I could ring you to know what to do."

A wave of pity came over him for this tall shruggy woman, with no warmth and no charm. He remembered her visit at the time of their father's funeral, her lack of any kindness, her cruel taunting remarks.

And now, at this ungodly hour of the morning, she had finally been locked out of the family home in Manchester.

"Wait until nine-thirty, Rosemary," he said.

"What will you do then?"

"I will do nothing, but you'll go to a solicitor—a solicitor in Manchester, mind, not in Mountfern. And you'll tell him what happened, and the circumstances leading up to it, and he will tell you what to do."

"I don't know any solicitors in Manchester, for heaven's sake. If I did have any legal contacts, do you think I'd be ringing you?"

"No, I know that. I know that very clearly."

"So what's the point in saying find a solicitor, find a solicitor? I could have looked one up in a phone book myself."

"I think that's probably the best thing to do." He kept his tone even.

"Are you serious?"

"Yes, Rosemary. It sounds distant and may even sound harsh, but I can't give you any advice whatsoever. You must see that."

There was a silence.

"I'm sorry about it all. Do you think it can be sorted out, the difficulties with James?"

"Difficulties." She gave a snort of laughter and said the word again, mimicking his accent. "Difficulties! No, I don't think they can be sorted out, as you say." Her tone was scornful.

"Well, then, the best I can wish you is that you are able to work out adequate provisions and a settlement, and that it is done with as little hurt and animosity as possible."

"Jesus, but you're a pompous bore, Fergus."

He had been going to say that if she wanted a holiday she could come to the house where she had grown up in Mountfern. He would not say this now.

He thought of the night that he had been going to give her the old Victorian sewing table belonging to his mother, and had changed his mind over some insult that she had slung at him. Perhaps her whole life was a series of such non-happenings.

"I hope I'm not as bad as you make me out, but I'm sure, like all of us, I must have my faults." He put on a mad simper as he said this. He tried to look at himself in the hall mirror, but the light was bad and he could only see his tousled hair and his crumpled pajamas.

He did a little dance while holding the phone and leering at his reflection. It pleased him to know that Rosemary could have no idea of his manner.

There was no more to say now, so Rosemary had rung off. Fergus was well into his capering dance now so he continued it, round and round the hall, pretending to hold up a ball gown and curtsying at himself every time he came to the mirror.

As he passed the hall door in a spectacular twirl, he saw two eyes looking at him through the letter box.

Fergus stopped in his tracks. "Who's that?" he asked fearfully.

"I'm sorry, Fergus." A thin voice came apologetically through the slit in the door.

He threw open the hall door, and there was Loretto Quinn, a letter in her hand.

"I was just about to put this through the door, but I heard these swishing sounds so I looked in, in case something was wrong."

Loretto had never looked so alarmed in all the years he had known her.

"But you were pleased to see that everything was as normal." Fergus beamed at Loretto as he took the letter. "I always have a little dance like this to start the day. They advised us years ago in the Four Courts, they said there was nothing like it for settling the mind into a good legal way of thinking."

Loretto's mouth was still open as Fergus bowed to her theatrically and closed the door.

* * *

Jim Costello woke with a toothache.

He gave himself five minutes to decide whether he could bear it for the day or whether it would incapacitate him for the day. He decided it would render him speechless.

He rang Dr. White and asked the name of the dentist in the town. Then he rang the dentist.

The dentist was sorry, but he had limited surgery hours today; he was actually going to the official celebrations at the opening of a big new hotel.

"I'm the manager of that bloody hotel, and there won't *be* an opening unless you do something with my tooth," Jim said, maddened with pain and the man's slow obstinate voice at the other end of the phone.

"Well well well."

"Can you do it, or can you not?" As he spoke, Jim Costello realized how like Patrick O'Neill he was becoming in his speech. It sat better on a middle-aged American tycoon than on a young Irish hotelier.

He changed his approach.

"As you can see, I am utterly relying on you. Just a temporary dressing, anything. You've been highly recommended in these parts."

"I don't really . . ."

Jim played his final card. "And if you knew the whole story about the problems we've been having and all the celebrities who are expected today . . . Well, you'll meet them yourself. If it ever gets going at all."

That did it. The man said Jim was to get into a car and drive like the clappers, he'd open his office early for him. A chance to hear the inside story about Fernscourt was too much to pass by.

Mary Donnelly woke and spoke to Leopold, who had been waiting patiently for her to stir.

Leopold was a more intelligent dog than many people gave him credit for. He knew the way to stay in Mary's good books was by not waking her or snuffling around for anything interesting and certainly not by offering any of his paws in the form of a handshake. Mary was of the opinion that there was far too much insincerity and over-greeting going on in the world. She liked silent ruminative thoughtful encounters. Leopold had adapted to her ways.

He was surprised that she seemed to be making a speech to him; it was not her usual way of greeting the day. He held his head on one side and tried to understand what she was telling him.

It had nothing to do with a walk. But there was no abuse in it, either. He couldn't fathom it at all.

"Leopold, this is a black day for this house. But apparently none of us are allowed to mention it. The new way of going on is to pretend a problem doesn't exist. That way we can all go on drinking and slapping each other on the back.

"Listen to me well, Leopold. This is the beginning of the end. You and I could be walking the roads of Ireland with packs on our backs. There's going to be nothing in the profits of this establishment to put a dinner on the table for either of us once this hotel gets going. But to be fair, Leopold, they never put your dinner on the table. More the floor."

The dog looked at her trustingly.

"Don't mind me, Leopold," she said, scratching his ear. "I am totally mad. Not a little mad. Totally and completely mad."

Brian Doyle woke with a thick head. They had been celebrating until a late hour. O'Neill had said that as far as could be seen to the naked eye, the structure seemed sound, and more or less approximated to the plans that had been given to Brian Doyle. He had bought Brian several drinks on the strength of this. Then, back in the town, Brian had decided to finalize the arrangements for taking Peggy, his girlfriend of many years, to the opening. He would call for her at noon, his brother Paudie would drive them so that they need not worry if there were a few drinks taken during the day.

He had been neglectful of Peggy, particularly during these last weeks. He had wanted to explain to her that this was all over. He had not been prepared to meet her mother, a battle axe if ever there was one. The mother had said that Peggy would be going to no opening or closing of any hotel whether built by Brian Doyle or built by the Emperor of China.

Peggy had, according to her mother, belatedly come to her senses over Brian Doyle, she realized that having her name up with him for so many years had brought her nothing but heartbreak and humiliation and, what was more distressing still, had cut her off from any other avenue and future. So that was all in the past now, thanks to the good Lord who had opened her eyes, and she had instructed her mother to pass the burden of the message on to Brian if he ever made an appearance in the next year or so.

This was the heavy artillery.

Brian sat in Peggy's mother's kitchen letting the words wash over him and trying to work out where Peggy might be.

"Don't start it all up again," said the woman in front of him, who had not ceased to speak since he entered the house. "You're a bachelor, Brian, stay one. For God's sake, will you go back out to that hotel and pat it and stroke it and be with it morning noon and night? That's what you want."

"I can't go to bed with the hotel," Brian said eventually.

"And as sure as your name is Brian Doyle, you can't go to bed with my daughter either. Sweet talk or no sweet talk. Ring or no ring."

It hadn't crossed Brian's mind that a ring should form part of the proceedings. There was plenty of time for that.

He had left the house disconsolately and on the street run into Seamus Sheehan, the sergeant from Mountfern.

Since Seamus was off duty they went to a pub and Brian explained that he was not a knave or a philanderer at heart, it was just that he was too young to settle down.

Sergeant Sheehan said that basically all men were too young to settle down, his long life in the Guards had taught him that. He cross-questioned Brian about the tunnel behind the bedroom wing, and whether there was any entrance in it under the brambles and briars.

Brian said that he couldn't bear to think of any more entrances or exits to that hotel than there were already. There had been an unmerciful carry-on about where the drive was going to be at the start; most people thought that it was never going to get off the ground at all.

But Sergeant Sheehan went on and on. Any entrances to old shafts or tunnels or anything they had come across?

Brian Doyle had said that when it was a question of a fairy fort, some of the men he had working for him were as superstitious as old shawlies who would go and tie things to a May tree. They had just avoided going anywhere near it and in the end the best thing had been to build a trellis and drape these creepers over it. Made a kind of wall of sorts.

No, he had no idea if there was anything in it. He didn't give much thought to the fairy world himself, there was too much happening in the so-called real world. If they were there, which seemed highly unlikely, then leave them to get on with it; that was Brian's philosophy. Oh, the sergeant meant non-fairies? No, he could not imagine that anyone with a marble left in their head would want to be burrowing around under all those blackberries and old thorns. But then Brian was always the last to be told anything. The whole Pioneer Total Abstinence Association could be having their annual general meeting in those bushes before anyone would think of telling the poor builder.

But wasn't it a bloody miracle that the place was finished and none of them were in jail or up in the asylum on the hill?

Too late Brian Doyle remembered the youngest Sheehan boy was in that very asylum. He looked glumly into his pint. There were some things you could never backtrack your way out of, and it was wiser not to try.

Sergeant Seamus Sheehan woke and made his wife a cup of tea.

"This is your big day," she said sleepily. "Is the weather good for it?"

He opened the curtains a little and peered out.

"It's bright," he said. "It'll be sunny with scattered showers, they said."

"Ah, well, that's grand, and they'll have a tent set up so you won't notice the showers."

She was pleased that her husband would be on show and a man of importance today. There were very senior men from Phoenix Park, the Garda headquarters, coming to the reception, and there were local guards from around coming in to help with the traffic and because there would be VIPs coming to the reception. Seamus would have more responsibility than he ever had before.

Seamus Sheehan was glad he hadn't told his wife about the plan to close in on the tunnel that morning. He had been in the town last night setting it all up with the force there.

He had been praised for the excellent surveillance he had kept, and the superintendent said that he was a model of what an efficient rural sergeant could do by knowing the people of his place and being able to spot anything untoward.

McCann, Byrne and Red Molloy were no mean prize to get in one net.

The plan was to take them early *and* have it wrapped up before the guests started arriving.

Whatever they were up to, that crowd, it must have something to do with the opening. A possible kidnapping.

Guaranteed, of course, to get the worst publicity for Ireland if it took place when a load of American journalists were actually on the spot feeding their faces with salmon and brown bread. They would get them into different cars and take them by different routes to the Garda station in the big town.

Charlie Byrne was the thicko, he'd certainly tell them what was going on.

Sergeant Sheehan was glad that it would all be over well before his wife had put on the new suit that was hanging up outside the wardrobe so that it wouldn't get crushed, together with the frilly white blouse and a handbag so new that it was still in the paper bag from the shop and had tissue paper inside it to make it keep its shape.

Kate felt that the day had started poorly. All that shouting and the upset in the bathroom.

But these were as nothing compared to the fact that Carrie was now almost certainly pregnant. That was the first thing to be coped with.

She called the girl into her room and asked her to close the door.

"Have a plain marietta biscuit, Carrie, take one there from the tin on the windowsill."

Carrie's eyes were huge. "I was just going to have a drink of bitter lemon or something, ma'am . . ."

"No, the biscuit is best. I remember myself."

Carrie's eyes were full of tears. "It must be definite, ma'am," she said. "I'm very sorry."

"Why are you saying you're sorry to *me*?"

"Well, you've been very nice to me. I don't want to go bringing disgrace on you. That's the last thing I'd want."

"You won't do that. It's all a matter of what way we look at it."

"What do you mean?"

"Mrs. Fine used to say to me that life was all about how you looked at things. If you saw the sunny side, then things were sunny . . . You know, the Americans have some book about it."

Carrie looked at her, bewildered.

"So what I mean is this, there's going to be no tears, no apologies, no shame. No saying to Jimbo that you're sorry. It's not *your* fault, any more than it is his."

"But he could say I'd been with anyone. Jimbo's going to be a known singer. There's going to be people here today who will have heard of him." Carrie was full of awe.

"Yes, but he's your Jimbo. He's not going to walk out on you?"

"If I gave in to him, let him have his way, what's to stop him thinking I let other fellows have their way?"

Kate's face was very impatient.

"Loretto Quinn and Jack Coyne are going to announce their engagement today. I wouldn't be surprised if Brian Doyle might even stir himself to propose to that long-suffering Peggy. What more natural than you and Jimbo too?"

"But ma'am, he mightn't want to . . ."

Kate wasn't listening. "Yes, a big occasion like this, a very good place, we could even get a bit in the newspapers about it: Singer to wed, it's a good time of year to think of an Easter wedding."

"*Easter?*"

"Yes, well that's for Loretto and Jack. But you and Jimbo might find that to fit in with his career you might suddenly get married straight away, before Christmas."

"Oh, ma'am, wouldn't it be great if he'd agree?"

"Of course he'll agree. He'll be delighted," said Kate with much more confidence than she felt.

Sheila Whelan woke with a heavy heart.

Patrick O'Neill had been in last night, anxious to talk.

"You're about the only one I can really sit down and talk to." He looked tired and lonely.

"Haven't you half the country to talk to?" She smiled.

"Not really." He gave a heavy sigh.

"You'll miss Rachel tomorrow?" Sheila was one of the few people who could speak like this without causing him offense.

"I'll miss her, that's for sure. She put so goddamn much into it, I wanted her to see the opening, even if afterward . . . well . . ." His voice trailed away.

"Probably better for her to go at once if she was going to go at all," Sheila said.

"Yes, women see it that way. I'm going to call her tomorrow night. At midnight our time it will only be early evening in New York. She agreed that we would talk on the telephone tomorrow."

He looked boyish and eager. Not the great O'Neill opening the most talked-of hotel in Ireland, who kept his lady friend in doubt about his intentions all the time she was here. Sheila Whelan thought that men were impossible to understand and that perhaps the less time and effort spent trying to understand them the better.

"What are you doing tonight? Getting a good sleep for tomorrow, I hope. You'll have a long day."

"I can't sleep at all these nights. I walk the grounds a lot. I had a few drinks with Doyle. I don't know which of us is more surprised that he hasn't ended up in one jail for fraud and I haven't ended up in another for attempted murder!"

"Go on, you'd be lost without Brian to give out about. You'll miss him, I promise you."

"Sheila, you're very discreet—" Patrick began.

"Not any longer," she interrupted him.

"What on earth do you mean?"

"Just that. I'm *not* discreet anymore. If I see something I don't like, then these days I say it. It's hard to get used to. I keep hoping I'm doing the right thing."

She had told him no more despite his concern.

Sheila knew that if anyone was going to be hurt by what she had done it would be Patrick. She had discovered that Kerry O'Neill was taking boxes and packages into a disused tunnel which led to Fernscourt.

He was involved with a gang of hoodlums, probably thought they were freedom fighters instead of bank robbers, which was what they were. Sheila knew that on the morning of the hotel opening the tunnel would be closed off, the gang taken into custody, and as a courtesy to Patrick O'Neill and to all the employment he was bringing to the area, his son would not be questioned until the following day.

There was a belief that Kerry O'Neill, though most certainly some kind of an accomplice, was not involved in the criminal side of things. Or not yet. Sergeant Sheehan said that it was all being done to pay his gambling debts.

She thought of Seamus Sheehan's son in the home, of Patrick's son running with bank robbers, of her own husband's son, who couldn't come back from England for his father's funeral.

Many times Sheila had wished that she had given birth to a boy. A child of her own who would grow up under her eyes. This morning as she dressed for the day and all it would bring, Sheila felt glad that she had no son. She was better off today only worrying about herself.

Dara's hopes of a long leisurely time to get ready had been dashed. First there was all the work clearing up the bathroom, then Mam wanted to be helped.

Mam looked very pale and even unwell. There was a light sweat on her forehead and she had that distraught look she sometimes got.

"It's going to be fine," Dara said soothingly.

"What is?"

"The opening. The day!"

"Oh, yes. Yes, of course."

Dara looked at her, concerned. Mam hadn't been at all well of late. Look at the way she had felt after the trip to Dublin. Don't say it was going to be the same now. Dara held up the navy-and-white outfit. It had been chosen by Rachel Fine, of course. Hadn't everything? It was smart, but Dara would have dressed Mam in something less severe. It had a lot of small buttons down the back which would need to be fastened.

Mam smelled of good soap and talcum powder. More gifts from Mrs. Fine. Perhaps as the years went by Mrs. Fine's gifts would wear out, and her influence would die away. Mam had said very firmly and very briefly that she would not be coming back again to Mountfern.

Dara sat by the dressing-table part of the green room. She looked long at Mam's face to see any signs of illness.

"Would you tell me if there was anything wrong, if you felt badly?" she asked her mother.

"Yes and no. Yes, if we could do anything about it."

"Then there *is* something wrong!"

"No, I feel jittery today, that's all, a bit like going to the compensation case. You know the feeling."

Dara knew the feeling; she *had* the feeling. She wasn't at all sure that Kerry would like her dress. She had spent such hours choosing it in Dublin, and spent so much money on it. It looked a simple red silk. In the hand it looked only like a crumpled scarf, but when Dara put it on, she looked great! Or she hoped she did. But you'd know with Kerry.

She had fastened the tiny buttons, and Mam looked very well, smart and stylish. The dress had a full skirt. Mam never wore clothes that let you see her legs properly, even though they looked perfectly all right.

Dara felt the overpowering sympathy that she sometimes did for her mother, who could not stand up and who knew that she would never be able to stand again.

"Dara, one little thing about today."

Dara sighed. It was going to be about not smearing on too much make-up, not disappearing with Kerry, about being understanding to

Michael, or keeping an eye on Declan, or trying to stop Eddie from
alienating the whole parish.

"Yes, Mam," she said dutifully.

"If I were your age, and I were as lovely as you . . . I would not
want to listen to someone saying what I'm going to say now, but it's
only very short, and then we don't have to talk about it again today.
All right?"

Dara nodded. What alternative had she?

Kate took her hand. "I just want you to know how sad I am that
Rachel isn't here today. She worked on every stone of this place as
much as any of Brian Doyle's men, as much as Patrick ever did. And
at this moment she's in New York City, probably crying her eyes out
and thinking of it all."

Dara had taken her hand away and was moving restively.

"And the reason that she's not here is Kerry. She did nothing
wrong, nothing bad, nothing that she couldn't stand up in the pulpit
and talk about. She got a little drunk, and she's not used to drink,
that's all."

"Mam, please . . ."

"I said it's short. Kerry drove her out, Dara, for these reasons: he
didn't want her to marry his father. He has always been much more
fond of his mother than of Patrick; he thought that Rachel should
not replace her.

"Then he got into great debt at a card game and he asked Rachel
for money . . . It's very complicated, but he didn't get it finally, so
he let everyone think that he and Rachel were together. You've heard
that, I know. I just wanted to set it straight in your mind."

"Oh, Mam, I heard the real story from Kerry," Dara said.

"You heard a story from Kerry. I doubt if it was the real one."

Kate's eyes were far away. "You're a grown girl, Dara, you are
sixteen—although I think that's young, I'll still think you're young
when you're twenty-six . . . I am not poisoning you, I'm warning
you. That's all. Of course you'll be with Kerry today, and he will be
charming and lovely and make you feel good. But I felt you had to
know that he is dangerous."

Michael wondered for the fiftieth time was his jacket a bit sissyish.
It had looked fine in Dublin. But hadn't everything? Tommy had said
it was great; you'd expect Michael to break into a waltz as soon as he
put it on. Grace had been noncommittal. She had been slightly an-

noyed that he had found the time and possibility of going to Dublin with Dara when he hadn't gone with her.

For no reason Michael kept remembering Maggie talking about the hotel opening. She said there would be television personalities coming to it and that maybe they would all be introduced to them on account of knowing the O'Neills so well. They had laughed at Maggie for her enthusiasm. And she was dead for over three months when the hotel did open.

Something had gone out of their summer, something more than Maggie. They stopped being a group somehow. They hardly saw Jacinta and Liam now, and as he had feared Grace was a million miles further away now that she was just across the river.

Tommy Leonard wished that he had a new jacket like Michael's. He wished that he didn't have skin that looked as if it had been treated with Harpic lavatory cleaner and he wished that he had smooth blond hair that looked good whatever way it fell, instead of spiky awful hair not unlike Eddie Ryan's.

He had heard there was going to be dancing in the Thatch Bar. His mind went back a year to when the Ryans had that great party in the outhouse that was now the café. He remembered not being quick enough or interesting enough to keep Dara's attention when Kerry came into the room. He wondered could anyone ever be quick or interesting enough. It wasn't *only* looks. Dara wasn't so shallow that she would go for appearances only. But Kerry was so sharp and clever. He knew when to say nothing and when to smile. He seemed to know what people were thinking, and say it first.

Suppose Kerry was to get a job somewhere else. Would that make everything all right? Or would the whole place still be watching out for him, looking up the road, almost waiting for him to come back?

Whatever Tommy wore, Kerry would wear the opposite, and he was sure Kerry would look just right today. If Tommy wore his best suit, you could be sure that Kerry would be in some pale blue sweater and jeans, and if Tommy wore his corduroys and Aran sweater, Kerry would be in a formal suit and tie. Wouldn't it be wonderful to see what he was picking out to wear?

Kerry was up very early.

Everything had been neatly stored in the tunnel. They knew to keep well away, today of all days.

It all had been simple. Just provide a depot, they said, the tunnel was a fine idea. Better than a warehouse, a lock-up shed.

The boxes had been stacked. There were crates of drink, and big boxes with cartons of cigarettes.

Kerry understood about the weapons. He wasn't so clear about the drink and cigarettes. McCann had been laconic. These things are sold, they make money, money is needed for supplies.

From time to time he wondered what kind of movement they were in. At times he even suspected basely that they might well be in no movement except a gang of their own. But it didn't concern him now. He had stored their goods; he had wiped out his debt.

The day was starting. He felt that tingle of excitement he knew when something new was about to start. Kerry felt good. There was nothing he couldn't do. Look at what he had done already.

He had shipped Rachel Fine back where she belonged.

He had paid his poker debt.

He would sort out the situation with his father. Father wanted a son around here, for Christ's sake. He wouldn't make a lot of waves.

There would be speeches, and no doubt Father would say something about how sad it was that his wife Kathleen hadn't lived to see this day.

Kerry knew his mother would not have wanted to live here in this town. But if she were to see what was happening, she would be proud of him. That her son had not forgotten her. He fingered his tie tack. That he had not let anyone else take her place.

Papers Flynn liked Kerry O'Neill.

He never understood that Kerry could be laughing at him. Kerry often complimented him on his clothes and said that he thought it was a great idea to tie so much string around the waist—it could be the in thing if the fashion writers got a hold of it.

Papers didn't rightly know what Kerry was saying half the time. But the boy always seemed to be smiling, which was good. And of course Kerry sometimes slept rough too. Papers knew that he slept in that tunnel.

He had been in to investigate it for himself a few times. In theory it should have been a great place to stay, but Papers thought it was a bit closed in, he preferred somewhere less restricting.

Papers never asked himself why someone with Kerry O'Neill's wealth slept out. There didn't have to be a reason. He would greet him nowadays as a fellow knight of the road.

On the morning of the opening he was pleased to see Kerry on the river bank.

"All spruced up and ready for the great occasion, I see," Kerry said to him.

Papers grinned, pleased. "It's going to be a nice day for it," he said, looking at the sky.

"Well, Papers, just so long as it won't interfere with your enjoyment of the salmon." Kerry laughed.

Papers felt he was being invited to more than a drink in the Thatch Bar. He didn't know how to cope. He decided to change the subject and trade information instead.

"If you've still got your place in the tunnel, you'd want to keep an eye on it," he said confidingly. "I saw Sergeant Sheehan and Mrs. Whelan looking at it last night, and the sergeant was there again this morning."

Kerry's heart turned into a lump of lead. It was one thing losing a thousand pounds at a poker game. It was another thing altogether losing the contents of those boxes in the tunnel.

If they were discovered and seized Kerry's chances with the crowd he had been dealing with were very poor indeed.

He left Papers abruptly and walked to a point between Loretto Quinn's and Jack Coyne's establishments, where he could see the towpath properly. Sergeant Sheehan was walking back toward the bridge.

The staff could hardly believe that Mr. Costello was not there to direct everything in his quick light voice that brooked no argument. Instead there was a series of conflicting orders. Nobody could say whose job it was to set out the glasses and whether they should get their final polish before they left the hotel for the marquee or when they were in place on the tables.

The drink which had been kept in cold rooms . . . should it be moved out early or left to the last minute? The temporary staff hired for the day, who was in charge of their arrangements?

Please God let it be true that it was only a quick visit to the dentist, they told each other. Otherwise there was going to be the most appalling confusion and nobody liked to think of Mr. O'Neill's face, and the humiliation in front of all the people who were going to be arriving.

If Jim Costello were here the staff wouldn't be making ten trips back and forth when two would do. Jim would have a timetable, a schedule, and a calm manner that would snuff out any crisis before it had time to develop.

If Jim Costello had been here he would have seen the red, sweating face of Kerry O'Neill as the boy plowed back and forth through all those brambles and briars around the fairy fort. As he got the last lot through, there was a groan and the sound of falling earth. The pit posts had collapsed, barring the way behind him.

Kerry laughed aloud with relief. His laugh could be free while he was underground. When he came to the surface he controlled it. From now it was simple.

Kerry was in his shirt sleeves, struggling with boxes and crates. To the staff who had been hired for the day he was just one more worker bringing just one more load to join the general store of food and drink.

To the regular staff he was O'Neill's troublesome son who had decided to do a bit of work for a change because Mr. Costello had been struck with the toothache.

Nobody found it the slightest bit odd to see boxes being stored in the huge glass conservatory at the back of the main house. After all, this was a gala, there were probably going to be drinks in every room, not only the official bars, the marquee and the Thatch Bar.

There were more boxes than Kerry would have believed possible. His heart pounded with the fear of discovery, and his arms and back ached with having to carry the weight of so many loads.

The conservatory had been an inspired idea. It was one of the few rooms that would not be in use, and the chance of them being accidentally investigated by an eager barman would be unlikely.

It had been decided that there was too much glass in this room, too many panes, and too many plants to make it a suitable place for a party. Jim Costello had been at enough functions to know that it was not wise to mix euphoria, free liquor, and plates of glass.

Kerry's carefully stacked boxes would be safe here. Until they could be collected tomorrow. One phone call saying what he had done. And then he was clear.

"I can either take the tooth out now, which will guarantee you have no pain, or I can give you a temporary filling and we'll try to save the tooth later."

Jim Costello did not need a moment's thought. "Give me a mirror," he asked.

He looked. The missing tooth would show—only a little, but it would be seen.

"I'll have the filling, if you will," he said. He lay back in the chair.

He knew there was nothing to be gained by fussing and looking at his watch; the man was going to take his own time doing the job no matter how agitated the patient was. Better relax and realize that the world can, if necessary, go on without you.

Grace was surprised to see Kerry.

"You look terrible," she said.

"Can I use your bathroom?"

"Yes, but what happened?"

"I want to clean up. I have to go back to the lodge and get changed, and I don't want anyone to see me like this and ask questions. God, how I hate questions."

"Sorry," Grace said sulkily.

In a few minutes he looked more presentable. Now no one would comment.

"Well, are you looking forward to the day?" he asked.

"Yes and no. Michael is still very down. I hate people not to be good-tempered."

"What's wrong with him?"

"Oh, he's being silly, he'll get over it. When can we go back into the tunnel?"

Kerry laughed suddenly. "Anytime you like," he said, then he stopped. "Hey wait, don't go back there; there's been a subsidence. It's dangerous now, some of those old posts have given way."

"They couldn't have—"

"They have," he said curtly. "And anyway, no fooling around, you hear. You're not to be just anyone's. You're Grace O'Neill, you're very important."

She hugged him. "Oh, Kerry, it's nice that you're all cheerful again. Maybe today . . . maybe Father . . ."

"Yes, it could happen. Why not?" Kerry left her room and ran lightly down the stairs, through the hall filled with sprays and blooms and people from the florist's. As he was going down the steps of the hotel to his car, he saw Jim Costello coming up.

"Your big day," Kerry said pleasantly.

"Yes, great beginning with a butcher in a dentist's chair," Jim said ruefully.

"I heard. Is it okay?"

"Look at it this way. I don't think he loosened too many of the others, and I've wiped away most of the blood."

Kerry laughed. He used to think Costello an arrogant little guy. But he did have a sense of humor. And a great sense of command. Kerry stood and watched while he managed to restore order to the huge hall in moments.

Jim Costello looked back at Kerry too. The fellow seemed high or excited. He laughed too readily, like people do when they are in the middle of something dangerous.

Kate had sought the moment to tell John their news. She had not been able to find it.

She had thought that last night when the bar closed, they might sit in the garden and she would tell him then.

But the bar just wouldn't close. The sense of excitement about the opening was everywhere.

Mary Donnelly had worked like an automaton. She said it might be the last good night's business they ever had. Keep serving, keep pouring, keep clanging the till.

There was no danger of a raid. Sergeant Sheehan wouldn't be so discourteous. And even if some of his superiors would be here for the official opening of Fernscourt, none of them would arrive the night before, so a little after-hours drinking would not be anything to come down on too heavily.

There was no time last night. They were both too tired. She had been going to tell him this morning, until all the drama in the bathroom and Carrie's predicament had intervened. It almost seemed like a surfeit of pregnancy to tell John about hers!

Perhaps this evening, in the peace and quiet. Perhaps that would be a good time.

She settled herself in her finery, and waited for him to come and wheel her across the footbridge and to the party.

The music was marvelous. *Tales from the Vienna Woods*, a selection from *The Gondoliers* and some rousing Sousa marches. Jim Costello had known the right band to hire, and the right repertoire for it to play.

On all sides of Mountfern they smiled when it struck up. The gala opening was under way.

* * *

For ages Dara sat on the window seat looking at the crowds gathering.

She could see cars coming down the big drive that led from the main road to Fernscourt. Local people walked up River Road and were crossing by the footbridge.

She saw Dad wheel the chair across, and a little lump came in her throat. Mam would so much have liked to have walked. Poor Mam, missing Mrs. Fine in spite of everything.

Dara had not been upset by her mother's remarks. That was what Mrs. Fine *would* have said, after all. All that about Kerry being dangerous.

She stood up and smoothed the red dress. It did look very, very good. And nobody had said anything about the make-up, which meant that she didn't have quite enough on. She would put on more lipstick and go across. Kerry would be waiting for her.

Mary Sheehan couldn't understand it. Her husband had said that he had to do one simple job, which would put him in great standing with the lads and the superiors today. He had brought guards in early from the big town, saying that there was a cache of stolen goods in some hole or tunnel over on the towpath.

The guards arrived early in order to have it all cleared by the time any festivities began. They had gone in and found nothing but children's playing things.

Seamus Sheehan had looked in disbelief at the clay and the splintered wood. This hadn't been heaped like that last night. The tunnel had stretched farther. Surely it had?

But then he hadn't followed it. He hadn't needed to. The boxes and crates had been here in this room. This room now with nothing but children's tables, chairs, and a broken sofa.

Sergeant Sheehan stared in front of him as he sat stupefied in his chair. It was no use that Sheila Whelan backed him up. What did people from the big town make of Sheila except to think she was the local postmistress? They weren't to know that she was the soundest person in the place.

He had been a fool not to have gone in straight after McCann had left last night. He had thought it would be better to do the thing by the light of the day.

He had been wrong.

* * *

One of the men from the tourist board stood near Patrick and told him who the people were. This was the Protestant bishop arriving now, a very big gesture; people would talk of this for a long time. There were TDs from all political parties and one cabinet minister. There were other hoteliers there, and the man from the tourist board said that their faces were forty shades of green. They muttered from one vista to the next about the size of the grant O'Neill must have gotten, the money he must have sunk in it, the hopelessness of trying to compete with anything like this, the folly of believing that there could ever be a return on such expenditure.

Patrick loved it. Every moment of it.

And he loved it when Mr. Williams, the vicar, introduced him to the Walters and the Harrises. People of substance, who had estates near Mountfern. Mr. Walters said his father used to come here a lot in the old days, and Colonel Harris said that he had old pictures of the place in its previous existence. It was wonderful to see it rise again.

They spoke as if a mere half century of being a ruin had been a slight inconvenience and that it had been no trouble for Patrick to get the place started again.

Patrick gave several grateful looks at Jim Costello. The man was a wonder. He managed to be everywhere and yet unobtrusive. Small, handsome, and efficient, courteous and determined. What he would give to have had a son like that!

His own son was behaving well for once. His face looked flushed and excited. He was the center of attention as he moved easily among the crowd.

But while Costello moved about seeing that people were all right, that no one was alone or feeling outside things, Kerry moved like a glorious light that has no purpose except to be looked at and admired.

The twins crossed the footbridge together, as they had done so many times.

In the days when their lives were full of fantasy and imagination they could not have dreamed up anything as splendid as this.

"You look terrific, Dara."

"Thanks, Michael. So do you. Very very smart."

Dara wanted to hold his hand for some reason, to reassure him. They walked up through the laurels. The marquee for lunch was by the dock and the barge. But the drinks and welcoming party were around the steps and the main hall.

They came into the crowded forecourt and Dara saw him. There stood Kerry in his new white jacket that he had told her about, his pink-and-white shirt. He looked like a hero, not a man. She saw him laughing and bending a little to listen, then he threw back his head and laughed again.

He was with Kitty Daly, who looked stunning. Her long hair hung loose like a huge halo around her, almost like a cape over her magnificent dress.

Kitty was wearing the copper-colored dress that had been made for Maggie. On Maggie it had been a big flowing dress. On Kitty, who was tall and leggy, the copper dress was a mini-dress.

She looked at Kerry O'Neill with all the confidence of a beauty who doesn't need to wonder if other people are looking at her.

She would expect them to be looking. And liking what they saw.

"Are you all right?" Jim Costello spoke to Dara Ryan, who was holding on to one of the huge urns near the steps.

"Yes. Yes, why?"

"I thought you looked dizzy for a moment."

"No. No, I'm fine. Thank you very much."

Jim looked at her appreciatively. "You look very well, I must say, Dara, really very smart."

"Thanks, Mr. Costello."

He wondered why her voice was so dead. She really did look well in that red silk. Unlike Grace, who looked like a meringue in all that pink linen and broderie anglaise.

But Dara Ryan had no life in her eyes; she had hardly heard the compliment.

Michael came back with two glasses of orange. They had sugar around the edge and a slice of real orange cut so that it was fixed to the glass.

"Have this," he said.

Dara took it silently.

"She can't know; she wasn't here for the dress and everything."

"I know, I remembered that."

"She must have just found it at home." He was trying to take the pain out of Dara's eyes.

"Yes. Yes, that must have been it."

"And I'm sure he doesn't like her *really*, it's only with all that hair and everything . . ." His voice trailed away.

Papers Flynn and Mary Donnelly raised their glasses to each other as they sat in the warm autumn sunshine outside Ryan's pub.

Mary produced soda bread and slices of ham.

"Much better fare here than we'd get across there," she said.

"It's that, all right." Papers ate happily.

"I never go for salmon all that much," Mary said.

"Full of bones, it would have your throat in ribbons," said Papers, who had never tasted salmon in his life.

Eddie saw Leopold crossing the footbridge.

He remembered his mother's advice: do nothing, nothing at all, without careful thought. He stood there and tried to think carefully. What would a normal person do? Would they ignore Leopold? Or would they take him home? Would they offer him a plate of salmon? The more he thought, the more Eddie realized that careful thinking helped him not at all.

He watched the dog go around the hotel and out toward the back.

The action moved down toward the marquee. Luncheon was being served. The band had started to play lunchtime numbers like songs from *The Student Prince* and *The Merry Widow*.

Dara watched as Kerry's arm guided Kitty toward the huge lunch tent. He had never even looked for her.

She stood high on the steps of Fernscourt and watched them. Why had he not looked for her? Why had he said he loved her only short days ago; why did he hold her and say she was precious and beautiful beyond all imagining, if he was going to be with Kitty Daly? Did he know all the time that Kitty was coming, that she had turned out to be so beautiful?

Dara didn't believe that he could have held her in his arms and thought of Kitty. It was impossible. Kerry was so good, so true, and he wanted the best for her. For everyone.

Suddenly it made sense to her. He did want the best. And up to now she had been the best in Mountfern. She had been young and not bad-looking, and she had loved him. But now there was a better best. There was Kitty, and he had to have her. The way he had to have that jacket which had cost a fortune. And he had to have the car. And money for gambling.

With a shock she realized that he might have had to get Rachel Fine out of Mountfern. He hadn't liked her and she might have married his father and become a person of importance. She shook her head. All this and seeing Maggie's dress. It made her feel dizzy, as if she were going to fall.

She sat down on the steps, and to her astonishment Leopold came and laid his head on her lap.

"What in the name of God are you doing here, Leopold?" she asked him, and he looked up at her from an awkward angle, trying to explain that he thought there might have been a bit of fun and he had come because everyone else was there.

Eddie appeared at that moment, looking anxiously around from behind an urn.

"Can I take it that you'll be responsible for him now, could we say that I handed him over to you?" Eddie said.

"Wouldn't you know that you'd have to let us down by bringing Leopold?" Dara said.

"I didn't, he came across all by himself."

"Yeah, carrying his invitation in his teeth."

"What'll we do, Dara?"

"We'll take him home. Come on," she said.

"But it's not over. There's lots more to go." He was disappointed.

"Wouldn't it be safer to go, Eddie, before you do anything dreadful that'll be remembered for years, like the confession box?"

Eddie was philosophical. "I suppose it would be best," he said.

They made a funny little threesome, Eddie with his spiky hair, Dara in her magnificent red silk dress, and Leopold, happy now that he had seen all there was to see.

Kerry O'Neill was coming out to look for Dara, and he saw them reach the footbridge. She had probably been sent to take that awful brother and awful dog home. She would be back later. He would see her then.

Michael found Grace with Tommy and Jacinta and Liam.

"She didn't know," he said. "That it was a special dress for Maggie."

They agreed. Grudgingly. Kitty couldn't have known.

"It looks quite different on her, anyway," Grace said. Grace was very disappointed with her own outfit. She wished that Mrs. Fine was still here; she was great at advising people. Mrs. Fine had been so nice to them that time, that short time at the beginning of the summer.

Marian Johnson could look wonderful, Mrs. Fine had said, if she wore tailored clothes. She needed well-cut almost mannish garments, not the soft fly-away things she usually wore.

Today Marian looked very smart in a dark blue and white suit and a blouse with a cameo brooch like Mrs. Whelan wore. She was with a very shabby big untidy man that people said was a barrister. Grace heard them say that he was Marian's escort. Imagine having escorts at that age.

She went over to her father who was standing momentarily alone. "Do you miss Mrs. Fine, Father?" she asked unexpectedly.

Patrick put his arm around his daughter. "It's funny you should say that. I was thinking of her this very moment. She's going to call tonight. Or I'm to call her. Anyway, when it's over, we'll talk."

"So you're still good friends with her?" Grace looked pleased.

"No, sadly not. But tonight is special; she and I will talk tonight and then not again for a long while."

Jim Costello toured ceaselessly. He found smears on some glasses. They were dealt with effortlessly, not by any shouts and roars but by a quick quiet word with someone and the use of the phrase "this minute, please" on almost every occasion.

He ensured that the rooms where valuable antiques were kept had people watching them, and he checked that the revelers had not got into the conservatory. He frowned slightly at the boxes which had been stored there. He looked at the top one. Whiskey.

It was probably some fail-safe idea of O'Neill's. He was determined that nobody in the county would go dry. He must have ordered a few more crates put in this morning.

At least they were out of the way; nobody would think they were meant to come and carouse in here.

"Where's Dara?" Grace asked Michael.

"I don't know. I've been looking for her."

Michael was afraid that Dara might be crying somewhere.

"Do you think she's upset about Kitty being with Kerry?" Grace asked.

"I don't know. Do you think he really likes Kitty, or what?"

"I expect he just wants to have fun with everybody," Grace said. "Isn't that what everyone wants?"

Michael saw Grace look around as Jim Costello passed by. A feeling of sadness came over him. Having fun with everybody. Yes, that probably was what everybody wanted. It was what the O'Neills wanted anyway.

Everyone was in the marquee now listening to the speeches. The band was silent and respectful as the dignitaries spoke. All of them praised the courage and foresight of Patrick O'Neill, to come back to this spot and build his monument. They said that faith like his was needed more and more. They looked forward to the day when Americans who came to stay in his hotel would themselves come to build in Ireland and put stone on stone in friendship as their ancestors had done. There was hardly anyone in the main house to see the curtains move in the breeze that came in the open window. And there was nobody there to see when the curtains flapped against the ashtray and knocked it over. The cigarette smoldered on the carpet for a long time before the breeze fanned it into a flame and the flame caught the curtains. The long blue drapes that Rachel Fine had worked on so long to get the right texture, the right shade, and the right look for Fernscourt.

The kitchen staff were far away from it, Jim Costello was hearing himself praised in the marquee, the staff who would serve in the Thatch Bar were busy setting up the place for the onslaught they would have descending on them as soon as the speeches were finished. There wasn't a man in Mountfern who wouldn't prefer a pint to the glasses of champagne which were on offer in the big tent.

There was nobody to see the way the singeing became a flame and the way a breeze carried the flame to the top of the curtains. The residents' lounge burned discreetly and thoroughly behind the closed doors.

By the time the door burned down, the blaze was out of control.

"Did you see Dara?" Kerry asked Tommy Leonard. "I've been looking for her all day."

"Yeah, I can see you have." Tommy's eyes were fixed pointedly on Kitty Daly's arm, which Kerry still held.

"Well, if you see her tell her I've been trying to find her."

"Certainly," Tommy said. "I'll tell her your sight was taken from your eyes and you're going around with a white stick bumping into things, desperate to find her."

* * *

Sergeant Sheehan saw the fire first.

In years to come he would always remember that. The disappointments of the morning, the shame and the laughter were as nothing when compared to being the hero who discovered the fire and arranged the fire-fighting force.

He wasted no time, when he saw the smoke. He yanked Jim Costello from the marquee and together they ran toward it

Then to the kitchen with shouts about telephoning for further help. By this stage the carefully placed fire extinguishers would be useless. A hose was in place within minutes, and the sergeant got Jimbo Doyle, who had the loudest voice in the county, to give the alarm through the main house in case there was anyone in any of the bathrooms or in any other part of the building

The Thatch Bar was emptied of its staff, who were marshaled into a line of water carriers

Chauffeurs of cars, three bus drivers, and five taxi men from the big town were roped in.

A serious fire-fighting effort had begun before they saw any need to alert the people in the marquee There was no danger to life, and even if the fire could not be contained, there was very easy emergency escape for everyone across the footbridge and over the River Fern.

Sergeant Sheehan had been the first to see the fire. The first in Fernscourt, that is.

Papers Flynn had seen the smoke much earlier

A lifetime of never getting involved leaves its mark Papers never brought up any subject first; he was a person who responded rather than initiated. You only got into trouble by paying attention to anyone else's business.

He sat in the sun outside Ryan's and saw the smoke coming out of a side window. Papers looked at it silently for a long time.

Mary Donnelly had gone into the house with Mrs. Ryan's daughter That boy who was always in trouble had come back, too, and the nice dog. Papers had always admired Leopold and thought him a fine animal.

He wondered should he say anything about the smoke, but the habits of a lifetime held him back.

Eddie came out and joined him on the seat

"I could go back if I wanted to," Eddie said

"Oh, you could, right enough."

"I wasn't sent away or anything."

"No, no, you wouldn't be."

"Well, I usually would be, but not this time."

Papers nodded in agreement.

"I'll have to make that clear to Mam. I came back of my own free will. I wouldn't want Mam sitting in the chair there thinking maybe I'd been ordered to leave."

The mention of Mrs. Ryan in her wheelchair galvanized Papers. Suppose there was a fire and Mrs. Ryan wasn't able to get out?

"Would you think that's smoke over there?" he said to Eddie.

Eddie squinted at it. "It is, it is all right."

He ran back into the pub. Mary and Dara were just coming out.

"I'm going back, Eddie, it's up to you, but maybe you'd prefer to stay here," Dara said. She looked very serious but not as if she were fighting or giving out to him.

"There's smoke," Eddie shouted.

Dara took no notice of him.

"Mary has pointed out rightly that Mam and Dad paid a fortune for this dress, and I must go back and get value out of it for them. Even if I don't feel like it."

It was as if she were talking to herself.

"I think the hotel's on fire," Eddie said.

This time he managed to get their attention.

And by now the figures of Sergeant Sheehan and Jim Costello could be seen, running as fast as they could. Eddie was right; the hotel was very definitely on fire.

Patrick's speech was almost over. He had thanked everybody who should have been thanked, but it wasn't tedious. The officials who had helped him all felt included in his generous tribute to the authorities, and the people of Mountfern felt individually acknowledged as he looked around the crowd and his eyes seemed to rest on them. Each and every person knew how much they meant to him, he said. He explained that a homecoming would be nothing if it weren't for the people. Buildings were symbols but the people were the heart of it all.

He said his family meant a great deal to him, but in a sense he had found a greater and wider family of friends.

He was about to end by wishing that this new family of friends should join him in the Thatch Bar when the cry went up. It was a terrible sound, the cry that told them that Fernscourt was on fire and it was going to burn to the ground unless something was done quickly.

They started to move the people from the marquee.

"Over the bridge" was the cry but nobody wanted to go. They stood in groups watching with horrified fascination, as the flames leaped from the windows of the residents' lounge and appeared, too, in the narrow windows of the piano bar. The line of people passing the buckets was slow. The hose seemed a trickle.

Men ran up, throwing off their coats, to join the firefighting. Orders were given and countermanded. The guards arranged for buckets to come from the river; everyone told everyone else that the fire brigade was coming.

"Ring them again, someone, and tell them to send everything they've got," Martin White said.

Then he moved over to Kate Ryan's side. "Back home with you now. That's an order."

"The children," she said.

"They'll follow. Come on, Kate. I'm taking you home." John had moved the chair on and wheeled it rapidly toward the bridge.

Mrs. Daly blocked their way. "We should get people to pray," she said. "That's what we have to do now. It's about time we realized it."

"You've realized it for years, Mrs. Daly," John said. "Now, could I get past you there? I'm a bit anxious to move Kate across so that I can go back and fight the fire."

She stood aside, hands still clasped.

"God, she's worse than I thought," John muttered as he wheeled Kate swiftly across the bridge.

"She might be right," Kate said grimly as they came to the pub.

Dara thought they looked very formal somehow, like a picture. A man standing, a woman sitting, both staring at something. Something impossible to believe.

Kate put her hand up on her shoulder to cover John's hand which was resting there.

"How in the name of God did it start?" Kate asked.

"It'll be all right," he soothed. "Look, it's less than before, it's much less. They've got it under control."

Dara came to stand beside them.

"Where's Eddie?" Kate asked.

"He's here, and there's Declan coming across the bridge now."

Eddie came up to his mother. "I was over here when it happened, talking to Dara and Mary and Papers. I had nothing to do with it, Mam," he began.

Kate drew him close to her. "Of course you didn't Eddie, darling Eddie," she said into his hair.

Eddie pulled away and looked at her. Nobody had ever called him darling Eddie in his life.

"In fact I was the first to spot it," he said.

"Of course you were." She held his hand very tight and her eyes were full of tears.

Michael caught up with Declan on the bridge.

"Come on, Mam will want to make sure we're all safe," he said.

"Now we're all here, I'm going back across," John said.

"You're going in that door behind the counter," said Mary.

"I can't sell a drink while the place is burning down across the way, I have to help."

"Aren't there plenty of big strong men huffing and puffing and playing fire engines over there? People want to buy drinks to calm their nerves. You're a publican, it's your duty to sell them."

The Ryan family smiled, all together. The same smile. John went back into his pub.

Patrick O'Neill had been quick to organize as well.

No standing dumbstruck at the awful and unexpected happening. Like Jim Costello, he was quick to see the frail and the feeble and get them organized.

"Colonel Harris, I wonder if I can ask you to help the canon out that way. That's very good of you. Liam, it would be a great help if you could get a chair for Mrs. Daly; she wants to do a bit of praying but I think she should do it sitting down. Jimbo, get the drivers to get back into their cars and move them way down the drive."

And all the time, with his dream burning before his very eyes, he kept assuring people it was under control, and that the brigades were coming, and there would be order restored in no time.

Carrie stood with a tear-stained face in a straw hat which had gotten very crushed by people trampling on it, but she had put it back on for some kind of comfort.

"Don't worry now, Carrie," he said. "We'll all be in the Thatch Bar this evening laughing over this."

It was then he saw that part of the roof on the Thatch Bar had caught.

* * *

Kerry worked with the rest on the fire line. Beside him Tommy
Leonard and Jack Coyne passed buckets.

The hose was taken to deal with the straw roof on the bar. So they
were relying on the human chain to keep the first fire under control.

"Well at least it's only a hotel," Jack Coyne said, panting. "Think
what it would be like if it was an army barracks or something, with all
those guns and explosives in it. Everyone here would be blown sky
high."

"Jesus Christ," said Kerry, dropping his bucket.

"Kerry?" The people near him looked at him in alarm.

"Oh my God!" Kerry shouted. "Get back. Costello, get them
back, get everyone away from it, get them away from it. Get back."

They thought he was hysterical. They pushed him out of the way
in their efforts to fight the fire.

They would pause to wipe their foreheads and look to the main
road, hoping for the comforting sound of many fire engines.

But it was a long way from the town.

Jim Costello didn't like Kerry's manner.

"Will somebody get O'Neill's son away from here?" he called in
his cool voice, the voice that was used to being obeyed.

But Kerry had run onto the steps.

"There's guns," he shouted, "guns and gelignite! The whole place
is going to blow up."

"Don't mind him."

"It's under control, we're winning, we've beaten it."

All around him were the soothing sounds of people who thought it
was a brainstorm.

"I beg you, Costello." Kerry was grabbing wildly at Jim's coat.
"They're in the conservatory."

Jim remembered the boxes. The boxes and crates.

"They're whiskey, you madman," he said.

"The top ones are. The others are ammunition."

At the pub they couldn't understand it. Why everyone had started
to run down to the river.

At first people protested, what was it about, they were winning,
the fire was beaten. When they heard what it was about they ran too,
helping others, and looking over their shoulders in the panic of disbelief.

* * *

Grace had been looking for Michael when the cry went up that everyone was to abandon the firefighting. There was something in the hotel that was about to explode.

She looked around wildly for Michael but there was no sign of him.

"Get Grace back over the river," Patrick shouted to Jim Costello as he rounded others toward the footbridge.

"Come on, Grace." Jim ran with her for a few yards, then he left her at the laurels. "Go *on!*" he shouted as she paused.

"I don't want to be on my own . . ."

"You're not on your own, stupid. Look, there are all your friends up by the pub."

"Did Michael go without me?" Grace's lip trembled.

"Go on, please, Grace. That's my job, to get you over the river. Please, just go."

"And you?"

"I'll see you later on. I'll come and look for you."

"Promise?"

"I promise," he shouted over his shoulder and ran back to the crowd trying to hold Kerry O'Neill back from the flames.

The boy's face was wild.

"I put it there, I have to take it out."

Jim Costello felt Patrick O'Neill standing beside him.

"What's in it, Kerry?" Patrick asked.

"I don't know. Guns, ammunition of some kind."

"Of what kind?"

"I don't know, I tell you."

"Was it set to explode?" Jim looked at Patrick with new respect.

"No, Father, it wasn't meant to be here, it was McCann's friends."

"What were they trying to do with it?"

"I was storing it for them in the tunnel until they collected it."

Seamus Sheehan was beside them, and Dr. White.

The sergeant spoke. "Is it gelignite?"

"I don't *know,* I tell you. How do I know what gelignite looks like?"

"Were there detonators with it?" The sergeant was quiet.

No tempers, no lack of control, and here they were, five men standing beside a possible inferno.

"What do they look like?" Kerry was piteous now.

"Were there separate containers, boxes?"

"Yes. Yes, I think so."

"And you've put them all together. In there?" The sergeant indicated the burning building.

"Yes, I didn't look, I didn't have the time."

"We'd better not risk it," said Sergeant Sheehan, and they turned to leave.

"I'll go down the driveway to tell the fire brigade." Jim Costello was a quick thinker.

"Get any drivers, anyone in the buses far away down the drive," Patrick called.

He looked at neither his son nor the doctor, neither his hotel manager nor the local sergeant as he began to walk away toward the footbridge.

"Father . . . Father, they're in the conservatory, the fire hasn't gotten there yet, we could get them out," Kerry cried.

Seamus Sheehan shook his head. "It's too hot, they could go any minute, flames or no flames."

Kerry broke away and ran toward the house.

The sergeant made a move to run after him. Jim Costello was already half way down the drive toward the main garages of the hotel.

"Don't die saving him, Sheehan," called Martin White. "Let him go, he put the stuff there, let him go up with it."

They heard the sound of the fire engines about five seconds before the explosion.

It wasn't as huge as they had thought it would be. But it was huge enough to blow the back out of Fernscourt, and the fire now raged so that they knew it would never stop even if the fire engines dared come near it.

Nobody knew if there would be another explosion. To go anywhere nearer than they were would be suicide. And as it was they weren't sure what had happened to Kerry.

It seemed like slow motion as they watched it from the bridge. Hands to their mouths, stifling cries, and the sound of Mrs. Daly's prayers as a low drone in the background.

Then they saw the figure of Patrick O'Neill walk slowly up the steps of Fernscourt.

It could only have been seconds, but time stood still before he came out dragging Kerry with him.

Kerry was walking, his face was in his hands.

The crowd saw Martin White take off his jacket and put it around Kerry's shoulders. They couldn't see what had happened when the doctor took Kerry's hands away from his face but they did see Patrick and Sergeant Sheehan turn away in pain from Kerry O'Neill's burns.

They had to let some of it burn itself out. It looked stark and terrifying, the Thatch Bar naked apart from a scattering of scratchy burned straw.

Patrick had been handed a brandy of a size that nobody had ever drunk and survived. He stood in the very spot where the entrance to his hotel might have been.

If things had been different.

If Kate Ryan had not had her accident that day.

If things had all been quite different.

The son who had been sharp enough to see where the entrance to their hotel should be had not been sharp enough for anything else. He was heading into the hospital in the big town in the back of an ambulance.

All around him Patrick heard the consolations and the encouragements. It would rise again.

The insurance would pay for everything, wasn't it a miracle that nobody had gotten killed or seriously injured?

They clutched at his arm, he even felt himself being hugged by people too full of emotion to trust themselves to speak.

All around him, he saw people finding each other, exclaiming they thought the other was lost.

He saw Jimbo wiping big tears out of Carrie's eyes with a green table napkin that said "Ryan's Shamrock Café."

He saw the lawyer Slattery who had always hated him and the O'Neills taking off his coat to put it around the shivering Grace. The coat looked enormous on her and it hid her silly pink and white dress.

Slattery had gotten her a cup of coffee and was speaking to her soothingly.

Sheila Whelan was of course beside Patrick. Knowing that he wanted to say something rather than platitudes.

"My God, Sheila, look at the misery I brought to people," he said. "Look at the sheer waste and misery."

"You didn't bring it, Patrick. It came all on its own."

"Jesus, who brought it if I didn't bring it?"

"You could say I did. I told Seamus Sheehan about the tunnel."

"What in the name of God took him in with that gang?" Patrick asked.

"Seamus heard it was because he owed them money." Sheila spoke gently.

"Yes. I wouldn't give it to him." Patrick's heart lurched and he looked at his ruined hotel. "I expect he had to get it somewhere. My God, if I had known the price we'd have to pay."

"You'd have had to call a halt somewhere," she consoled him. "You couldn't have gone on paying for everything all his life, that would have been worse than your father paying for nothing all of his."

"Oh God, how am I going to tell Rachel?"

The sun shone down as mockery on the smoldering ruins of Ireland's finest hotel. Its light played on the remains of what had been described as the dream of international cooperation come true.

In groups they stood and ran it over in their minds, the causes and the possible outcomes.

As usual, because it was Mountfern there were as many theories as there were people speaking.

The electricity was faulty, the chimneys had never been right. It was a cigarette, it was an attempt to assassinate some of the VIPs. It was a bottled-gas cooker, it was a bonfire to get rid of the rubbish.

They said that he would rebuild it right away, it would open in the spring. That he would take over the Grange and put his guests there, that he would walk out tonight and never come back. And then the roof went in.

It went with a series of cracks and groans as the timber fell and knocked down further stonework, and the shower of slates fell on top.

There was something very final about the way it fell.

The people of Mountfern raised a great roar as it went in. It was a startling sound. A roar went up from all the throats at the same time.

It was neither a shout of triumph nor a great wail of regret.

It was just a roar.

Patrick's eyes suddenly filled with tears. He didn't understand these people at all.

He saw Jack Leonard and Tom Daly, who had cheered when they had burned this house down in 1922; they had cheered as the ruins fell, Brian Doyle had told him. Today they cheered again.

How had he thought that this was his place and these were his
people? He didn't even begin to understand why they had made that
sound.

The twins stood together. Very close.
They weren't exactly touching but you could hardly have put a
piece of paper between them. Tommy Leonard envied them their
closeness. He had nobody like that. Nobody who would always be
there no matter what.
For as long as he could remember they had been like that. Not so
much this summer perhaps, but way way back. When they were both
his best friends. Before he started to love Dara. He was right beside
them but he couldn't think of anything to say that wouldn't sound
appalling. He really was getting more and more like Eddie Ryan, he
thought to himself grimly. It was an awful fate.
If he had been Kerry O'Neill he would have known the right thing
to say. The word or the gesture that would have been what they
needed.
He said, "At least we have each other. Everything else has changed
and gone, but we'll always be together in one way or another, won't
we?"
Dara's eyes filled with tears.
"I don't mean love or anything, but as great friends. Won't we?"
Tommy looked from one to the other, anxious that there should be
no misunderstanding. Anxious that he wasn't being seen to presume.
Dara laid her hand against his face. She didn't even try to wipe
away her tears.
"I don't know what I'd do without you, Tommy Leonard," she
said.
Although he could hardly believe it, Tommy knew, when he went
over it again in his mind, that Dara meant it.

Mary served, and Sheila had gone behind the bar to help her.
Carrie, face aglow with Jimbo's delight and pride, ran back and
forth with sandwiches and soda bread that they would never be serving now to American visitors.
Brian Doyle said he was glad that Peggy had gotten on her high
horse and not come to the opening in the end, because a) she was
highly strung and b) she might get very put out by all these weddings
in the air—Jimbo Doyle's and Jack Coyne's, two of nature's bachelors.

Brian said that it would be like a sacrilege to discuss who'd get the job of building the place up again, but he wanted it known that it was a heartbreak and an agony from day one and he wouldn't wish it on his worst enemy.

Kate sat with John in the side yard.
There were no words between them.
She had told him the news in the most natural way.
John had sat with his head in his hands, bemoaning all that had happened.
"I'm weary, Kate, weary and sad. There has been nothing but destruction and death since that place was begun. There's never any hope, no beginnings."
"I'll tell you something about new life and new hope, that you'll hardly believe," Kate said.
They sat together in the yard that was filled with flowers. He held her very close, he pressed her to him.
He would take such care of her, he would make sure that it would all be all right.
A new life. Another person. Another Ryan.

They called Patrick to the phone. Again. He had taken so many calls that Jim Costello had eventually monitored them, standing in Kate's green room and dealing with whoever called.
But this time he called Patrick. It was long distance. From New York.
"Rachel, Rachel." His voice choked and he couldn't speak.
But at last he found the words. The words to tell her about the end of the dream. Then he put down the receiver and walked through the glass doors into the yard filled with flowers where Kate and John Ryan sat in a world of their own.
They looked up at him as he stood there, a big man always filling their place, dominating their lives.
"I came to tell you. I'll be going home," he said.